THE EXPLORER

Books by Frances Parkinson Keyes

THE EXPLORER

By Frances Parkinson Keyes

McGRAW-HILL BOOK COMPANY
New York   Toronto   London

Quotations from "The Explorer" and
"L'Envoi" are from the book *Rudyard
Kipling's Verse,* definitive edition,
by Rudyard Kipling. Courtesy of
Doubleday & Company, Inc.
Reprinted with permission.

With love
to
Maggie Conroy
who for more than thirty years
has personified to me
all that is best in and of
Peru

Contents

Author's Note

(For readers only. Reviewers please skip.)

Every time a book of mine is published, I receive press clippings featuring reviews which criticize more often than they praise and list the Author's Note as one of their major reasons for criticism. Occasionally, cowed by this condemnation, I reduce the Author's Note to a mere mention of the persons to whom I am indebted for help and trust that will ease the situation at publication time. Not at all. The fan mail, which comes direct to me instead of via the publishers (for I have never subscribed to a press clipping service), is full of bitter complaints. "Why didn't you tell us when, where and how this book was written?" these people wail. "What gave you the idea for it in the first place? What steps did you take to give form to the idea? Who helped you most? Is there some special significance to the finished form? Since you didn't tell us any of this in your Author's Note, won't you please write us a personal letter by return mail?"

As it is literally impossible to write dozens of such letters, either by return mail or in the intervening months before another book comes out, I am, perforce, reverting to the simpler method of answering these questions, as well as I can, in an Author's Note.

The circumstances which give me the idea in the first place vary considerably from book to book. Several started with nothing but a title, inspired by something I had seen or done; for instance, *Queen Anne's Lace, The River Road, Blue Camellia, Letters from a Senator's Wife*. Several developed over long sojourns or extended travel; for example, *Silver Seas and Golden Cities, Capital Kaleidoscope, All This Is Louisiana, The Land of Stones and Saints*. The key to *Dinner at Antoine's* was an ambiguous letter, already in the public domain; the key to *A Station Wagon in Spain,* the famous fraud known as the Spanish Prisoner Letter; and so on and so on.

The Explorer is the only book of mine which was inspired by a dream and, by this, I do not mean "a vision voluntarily engaged in while awake," but "a succession of images or ideas present in the mind during sleep." Virtually the whole first chapter of *The Explorer* was embodied in a dream. It was so vivid that, as soon as I waked, I rose and wrote it all down. It was as real to me as if I had actually been present at the wedding where my hero and heroine met, and so were their characteristics and backgrounds.

But, though I knew my hero was an explorer, the dream did not tell me where and when he had explored or with what results. I was still turning this over in my mind and considering Persepolis, whose excavated ruins are to me personally the most impressive I have ever seen, when I happened to find Mrs. Hiram Bingham, the widow of the great explorer, among my fellow guests at a Washington dinner party. I had known her pleasantly, though not intimately, for a long while; I had known her late husband when he was in the Senate and I had been to the site of his greatest discovery, Machu Picchu, the first time I went to Peru, almost thirty years earlier. The last time I had seen them together had been at another Washington dinner party, given by the Duchess of Windsor's famous "Aunt Bessie," Mrs. Buchanan Merryman; and Dr. Bingham, who had then retired from the Senate, and I had talked at some length about the part exploration had played in his life. I finally resolved to write Mrs. Bingham and ask her whether or not the notable career, which culminated at Machu Picchu and had since been terminated by death, had ever been used fictionally, as the inspiration for later discoveries by one of his many ardent admirers and faithful disciples; if it had not, I wondered whether she would be willing to have me do so.

By this time, I had returned to New Orleans and I was surprised and delighted to receive a long distance telephone call from Mrs. Bingham within twenty-four hours after I had written my hesitant letter: she was about to visit a married daughter in Texas, she told me; couldn't she combine that trip with one to New Orleans and spend a week end with me? She was more pleased with my suggestions than she could tell. We would talk it over.

I look back on that week end as one of the most rewarding and one of the most agreeable I have ever spent at Beauregard House. It is a bitter disappointment and a source of very real grief to me that Mrs. Bingham did not live to see the finished product which her glad consent made possible. But, before her death, she had discussed my project with her daughters and other relatives as well as friends, all of whom had given it their hearty approval. Her daughter, Mrs. Phillips Clarke of Woodlawn Plantation, King George County, Virginia, has been especially helpful in supplying me with material which her mother would have wished me to have.

Although my uncertainty as to where I wished to place my explorer's activities ended after that happy week end to which I have just referred, I was hampered for a long time by a missing link in what I conceived to be the best way to handle material generally known in the trade as "conflict." I needed not only one leading male character, but two and, for some time, I did not visualize the second one. Then— ten years after the first illuminating dream—I had another. It seems to me even far more extraordinary that I should have twice been guided in this way than that it should have happened once. The conflict was developed, as outlined in Chapter 46, by a meeting in the street. Then it remained to fill in the intervening part of the story and that was still a big problem.

I solved it, in part, by returning to Peru, where I had been four times already, and spending four months of intensive work there. In this I was constantly helped and guided by Malcolm Burke, with whom my readers are already acquainted, as an invaluable collaborator of mine, if they have read *The Rose and The Lily*. A native of Connecticut, a Yale graduate and an ex-Naval officer, Mr. Burke first went to Peru nearly twenty years ago, on a one-year contract with the State Department, to direct the *Instituto Cultural Peruano-Americano*. The country proved to have such a lasting attraction for him that, except for occasional visits to the United States and to Spain, he has remained there ever since, using it as the base for various types of writing, including articles for *The Reader's Digest* and staff work for *Vision*. He has had two books published, one in Spanish and one in English, and is a tireless and consecrated researcher; the debt I owed him, in preparing my biography of Santa Rosa de Lima, was as great as the one I now owe him in preparing the Peruvian part of *The Explorer*. He has become recognized as an authority on both the natural and the academic history of Peru, has traveled to every known part of it and to not a few that reach the borderline of the unknown; and he has regularly recorded these travels, illustrated by his own photographs, in *The Peruvian Times*, an outstanding weekly periodical. To all the places where I could not accompany him in the literal sense (though as far as possible I did that, too), I accompanied him through the media of maps, scripts, books, articles and endless conferences, as we worked together day after day and week after week in my sitting room at the Hotel Bolívar in Lima.

Other persons who live in Peru and to whom I am indebted for help with the Peruvian part of the story include Luis Gomez Llaguno of the Grace Line; C. N. Griffis, publisher of *The Peruvian Times*, who permitted me to quote at length from the article, "Urubamba; Expedition Finds Ruins After Arduous Journey Into The Urubamba Country," by Guild Walker, published in the July 23, 1954 issue; also, *Don* Pedro Beltrán, formerly Peruvian Ambassador to the United States and Prime Minister of Peru, now the publisher and director of *La Prensa*, the largest daily in Peru, and his charming American-born wife, Miriam Kropp de Beltrán, herself an author of distinction, whose

Cuzco: Window On Peru is a definitive history, as well as a definitive guidebook. Also, the well-known cartographer and painter, Luis Ugarte, who drew the maps used in this book.* Also, my old friends, Dr. Albert A. Giesecke of the American Embassy in Lima and Miss Maggie Conroy, who, as I said in my dedication to her, has for more than thirty years personified to me all that is best in and of Peru.

Others who have helped me and to whom Peru is familiar territory, though they live elsewhere, are: Captain Vincent R. Ritts and Captain William E. Ault, United States Army IAGS, Guayaquil; Warren Holtz, formerly agent for Hiller Helicopters in Lima and now also stationed in Guayaquil. (All three of these men have flown over every known part of Peru and, like Malcolm Burke, penetrated close to those areas marked RELIEF DATA INCOMPLETE.) Mr. Anthony Chapell, Cultural Attaché now connected with the American Consulate General in Guayaquil; Mr. Frederick Shaffer, formerly Cultural Attaché in Quito and now American Consul in Guayaquil; Mr. Jerry James, Director of the Cultural Education Program for all Latin America in the Department of State; Miss Muna Lee, Chief of the North and West Coast Section of the Public Affairs Staff of the Bureau of Inter-American Affairs in the Department of State; Dr. Christopher E. Barthel, Jr., Chief Scientist and Dr. James N. Jordan, Geophysicist of the U. S. Department of Commerce, Coast and Geodetic Survey; Dr. Dean S. Carder, Chief Seismologist, U. S. Department of Commerce; Lieutenant Commander Robert Clare Bornmann, MC USN, U. S. Naval School, Deep Sea Divers, U. S. Naval Station, Washington, D. C.; and the Reverend Karl Maring, S.J., Chief Seismologist, Loyola University, New Orleans.

On the general subject of exploring, I am indebted to Mrs. William Mann (Lucile Quarry Mann), widow of the late Director General of the National Zoological Park, and Mrs. Matthew W. Stirling (Marion I. Stirling), the former President of the Society of Woman Geographers. Both of these remarkable women have accompanied their husbands on the latters' exploratory ventures and have written and lectured about these; and both are prominent members of the Anteaters Association, of which Mr. L. G. Leech is one of the guiding spirits, as far as the famous luncheons are concerned.

For general editorial help with the whole book, I am greatly indebted to Eleanor Carroll Brunner, whom I have always considered one of the ablest editors of my acquaintance ever since she was my boss when I wrote for the old *Delineator*. Since then, she has distinguished herself as Associate Dean and, for a time, as Acting Dean of the School

---

* At the time the large map was drawn, I did not know that Quince Mil would need to figure so prominently in the story. This omission and consequent correlative ones have been rectified by Barbara Long, one of our own leading cartographers.

of Journalism at Columbia University. During the last six years, she has spent much of her time in South America, because of her husband's position as Hospital Administration Advisor with the Aid for International Development, first in Paraguay and later in Bolivia, with frequent trips to Peru, so there has been an additional facet to her helpfulness.

Miss Leone Cassidy. Department One, Aeronautical Chart and Information Service, Washington, D. C. gave me valuable help by completing the file of official maps on the region in which I was interested. I am also indebted to Dr. Franklin K. Paddock of the Berkshire Medical Group in Pittsfield, Massachusetts for copies of his maps made during an archeological expedition in the Paucartambo region during June and July of 1959. This expedition took place more than four years after the one I am presenting as having been made by my hero and his staff and Dr. Paddock's maps are therefore more detailed than I am justified in presenting as typical of the ground Nicolas Hale covered. However, it is interesting to note that, though the members of the Paddock expedition did not touch Noche Triste on their route, they do show it on their maps and that they actually went beyond it on trails which are now verified.

In Washington, four old friends have been extremely helpful: Dr. and Mrs. Stanley Hornbeck changed my casual acquaintance with the Cosmos Club into one of delightful comradeship. Mrs. Robert B. Armstrong, Jr. (Bess Furman Armstrong) of the Department of Health, Education and Welfare checked all details connected with the White House, on whose procedures she is a recognized authority, and whose consultation with Mr. James J. Rowley, Chief of the U. S. Secret Service, resulted in authenticating details connected with the Hale-Porterfield wedding; and Elisabeth Shirley Enochs, who is also connected with this department, though frequently on loan to the State Department, checked all references to a typical ancestral estate in Northern Virginia, either through correspondence or in the course of delightful visits at her own beautiful home, Mount Air. Those referring to horticulture were further checked by Eleanor Carroll Brunner, who adds authority on this subject to the editorial talents already mentioned. Mrs. Enochs' factual story of the great-grandfather's swords was skilfully embroidered by Charles L. Dufour, an outstanding authority on the Civil War; and her descriptions of other weapons, including the famous dueling pistols—whose story I myself embroidered a little—have been checked by my son, John Parkinson Keyes, the hunter and historian of my family, who backed up his statements by reference material found in *The Fireside Book of Guns,* by Larry Koller, a Ridge Press Book.

A few additional references to a typical ancestral estate in Virginia were gleaned from a book which is an old favorite of mine: *Miss Delicia Allen* by the late Mary Johnston. These were used with the kind permission of Brandt and Brandt, the agents for her estate. References to the Alexandria Association Forum and the dinner prepared for it by the Ann Mason Guild of Pohick Church were based on an article entitled, "Colonial America Knew What Was Cooking," by Clementine Paddleford and are made with the kind permission of Miss Paddleford and William I. Nichols, Editor and Publisher of *This Week*.

Miss Katherine R. Andrews, Staff Assistant to the Honorable Norris Cotton, United States Senator from New Hampshire, has been very helpful, as always, in checking with the Library of Congress for data unavailable elsewhere. In this case, they referred to American press notices of the Tennant-Snow Expedition. The same service was performed for me in connection with British press notices by Charles Friend of Eyre & Spottiswoode and, in connection with Peruvian press notices—other than those in *The Peruvian Times*—by Father Antonine Tibesar, of the Academy of American Franciscan History at Washington, who was also in Lima last winter. Julian Tennant's own book, *Quest For Paititi*, published in England by Max Parrish and in the United States by Clark, Irwin, has also been a great help, as have Hiram Bingham's *Lost City of the Incas*, published by Duell, Sloan and Pearce, and *The Silent World* by Captain Jacques-Yves Cousteau, published by Harper & Row. Also, in Spanish, the invaluable *Comentarios Reales de los Incas,* a book written in the sixteenth century by Inca Garcilaso de la Vega, recalled to my attention by Dr. Alfonso Espinosa y Palacios, Counselor of the Peruvian Embassy in Washington; and the *Tradiciones Peruanas* by Ricardo Palma, recalled to my attention by the Marques de Merry del Val, formerly Ambassador of Spain to Peru and now, happily for us, Ambassador of Spain to the United States.

Legal details affecting legacies have been checked for Vermont by Henry W. Keyes and for Virginia by Armistead L. Boothe; those affecting medical requirements for marriage licenses have been checked by Dr. Darrell C. Crain. Reference to the fatal but swift and painless effects of certain poisons have been checked by Dr. Nicholas Chetta, Chief Coroner for the City of New Orleans.

As a girl, I was the proud possessor of two horses of which I was very fond and rode horseback every day when I was in the country. It is so long since I have had either of these happy privileges that I was not certain how the beloved pony of a five year old child should be treated in an emergency, and gladly accepted the suggestion of my personal physician, Dr. Darrell C. Crain, that I should consult Dr. Harold E. Schaden of Frederick, Maryland. This meant motoring a hundred miles and devoting an entire day to the trip and the consultation, but I felt it more than worth while. Dr. Schaden presides over a beautiful hospital, designed and built in accordance with the most up-to-date requirements for the enlightened and humane treatment of animals; and I was much impressed with the thoroughness of Dr. Schaden's questions and answers. For a few minutes the interview had a serio-comic aspect: he did not understand that I was talking about an imaginary pony and was horrified to think there had not been twenty-four hour service, seven days in the week, at his hospital! He had actually started to ask anxious questions of his assistant and his receptionist before I succeeded in calming him. Then we both laughed as he admitted that, ten years ago, it was all too probable that a regular veterinarian would not have been available during a few crucial hours on a Sunday afternoon.

Very few liberties have been taken with facts, where they are represented as such. However, for the sake of complete accuracy, the following should be admitted: there is no penthouse on the top floor of the Hotel Plaza in New York except the one occupied by *Gourmet,* where my friend Earle MacAusland so efficiently and graciously presides as Editor. The famous Anteaters' luncheons never take place in the Zoo restaurant on Sunday, as it is always open to the public on that day. Relief data are still incomplete for the region where Moonstone Lake and Golden Lake have been fictionally placed; but unnamed lakes do show on maps of that locality and gold has, indeed, been found in Quince Mil and the neighboring territory, and gold and silver gardens were actually characteristic of the most splendid era of the Incas. Vivid descriptions of these are found in Garcilaso de la Vega's *Comentarios.* Moreover, the golden bell, alleged to be at the bottom of the Urcos lagoon, has been called to my attention by two of my most trusted authorities: Malcolm Burke and Alfonso Espinosa. Further, both have suggested a cave behind a waterfall as another hiding place of treasure trove. Let us not be captious and label these as legends rather than discoveries.

The persons to whom I am actually most indebted are the faithful and efficient members of my staff, both secretarial and domestic. This book would not have been finished on schedule—in fact, I am not sure it would have been finished at all—had it not been for the invaluable help of Deanie Bullock, Marjorie Lillibridge, Leona Pfister and Carroll Fuller.

F.P.K.

I ❧ MARGARET

"Something hidden. Go and find it. Go and look behind the Ranges—
"Something lost behind the Ranges. Lost and waiting
for you. Go!"

—From Rudyard Kipling, *The Explorer*

Scene of action: New York, Washington and nearby Virginia

Time: Autumn, 1953

(An asterisk before a name denotes a real person.)

Principal characters:

Nicolas Hale, an explorer

Mr. and Mrs. Waldo Hale of Woodstock, Vermont, his parents

Clarissa and Narcissa Hale, his twin sisters

* Hiram Bingham, his ideal as an explorer

Lester Wendell, his secretary

Sam Steinmetz and Esther Schaeffer, New York friends of Nicolas Hale and Margaret Porterfield

---

Margaret Porterfield of Hills' End Plantation, Virginia, who becomes the wife of Nicolas Hale

Cassie, Annabelle and Rufus, colored servants at Hills' End

Dr. Virginius Page, Margaret's uncle

Dr. Leonidas Bates, Rector of Pohick Church which Margaret attends

Dr. George Loomis, Margaret's physician

Perdita, Margaret's dog

The President of the United States, Robert Maynard and his wife, Agnes

The Vice President of the United States, Kenneth Bruce and his wife, Imelda

Assistant Secretary of State for Latin American Affairs, Allan Lambert and his wife, Milagrita

His Excellency, Alfredo Román, Peruvian Ambassador to the United States and his wife, Martina

Director of the National Zoological Park, Charles Madison and his wife, Louisa

President of the National Geographic Society, Jerome LaGuarde and his wife, Miriam

Tom Herbert, Science columnist for the *Washington Star* and his wife, Sally

* Betty Beale, Society columnist for the *Washington Star*

1 ತ

"Elevator number one for the Steinmetz-Schaeffer wedding . . . please take elevator number one . . . elevators number two and three do not go to the eighteenth floor . . . elevator number one full, kindly wait . . . you cannot go direct to the Steinmetz-Schaeffer wedding except in elevator number one . . . yes, sir . . . no, madam . . . elevator number one—"

The starter continued his patient singsong with only indifferent success. He was saying exactly what he had been told to say. There was no time to explain that, since elevators two and three went only as far as the seventeenth floor, the wedding guests would be obliged to climb a long steep flight of steel steps, in order to reach the penthouse which had been rented for the occasion, if they disregarded his instructions. But, either because they were constitutionally averse to being ordered about, however courteously, or because they did not bother to listen, or were unable to hear what anyone else was saying, because they themselves were engaged in such animated conversation, many of them plunged ahead in the wrong direction and were later outraged to find themselves deposited in a fancily carpeted corridor lined with closely shut mahogany doors, where another liveried employe was rather grimly indicating the steel stairway, in a manner that suggested he was enjoying their discomfiture.

"I thought all the space on the eighteenth floor of the Plaza was occupied by *Gourmet Magazine,*" one of the guests who had obediently waited for the return of the right elevator remarked to no one in particular. But, as he spoke, two persons in the same group answered, almost simultaneously, in authoritative tones, "No, there's a second penthouse, very seldom available, but of course Schaeffer could get it." At the same moment, a slim, black clad woman who had been standing a little apart, and whose dress and bearing both seemed somehow alien to the place and the occasion, glanced at the first speaker and, after looking at him attentively though briefly, drew a little closer.

"Isn't this Mr. Hale?" she asked hesitantly. "Or should I say Dr. Hale? Dr. Nicolas Hale?"

"Yes, I'm Nicolas Hale," the man responded pleasantly. "But, as a

3

matter of fact, I prefer the mister. I've never got used to the doctor part. I still feel that belongs to the good old family physician and not to a Ph.D in Geophysics. And you're—why, Miss Porterfield! I haven't seen you in years! It *is* Margaret Porterfield, isn't it? What are you doing so far from those ancestral acres in Virginia to which you insisted on retreating?"

"I might counter by asking what you are doing so far from those remote regions in Peru that you insist on frequenting!"

They both laughed as they shook hands. "To tell the truth, I'm just back from Peru," the man identified as Nicolas Hale replied. "And, as you might guess, for a very short stay. I'm no more contented away from there than you're contented away from Hills' End. And weddings aren't much in my line, either. But Sam Steinmetz is an old friend— classmate at Taft and Yale and his father financed my first expedition. So, as I was in New York anyhow, I felt I had to make an exception to my rule of never attending functions like this."

"I felt the same way. That is, I wasn't in New York anyhow, but Esther Schaeffer is one of *my* best friends. Perhaps you remember she and I were classmates at Holton Arms when her father was Assistant Secretary of Commerce. So I thought I ought to make an exception to my rule of not going *anywhere*."

"Is it actually a rule? Not just about weddings, but about everything?"

"Oh, of course, it isn't actually a rule! But, even at the beginning of Mother's illness, I couldn't leave her long enough to keep running into Washington all the time. And, later, she couldn't bear to have me leave her even long enough to go to Alexandria. So I lost the habit and since she died—"

"Oh, I'm so sorry! I hadn't heard."

"Car number one for the Steinmetz wedding . . . cars number two and three do not go to the eighteenth floor . . . watch your step, please . . . no, sir . . . yes, madam—"

Car number one, emptied of the load which had crammed it five minutes earlier, came to a slightly teetering stop and waited with its door invitingly open. Again a group lunged forward, and Margaret heard a woman near by murmur to her companion, "Do you realize who that is? I mean the tall distinguished looking man—the lean dark one—talking to the pale girl in the queer black clothes. It's Hale, Nicolas Hale, the noted explorer. I've forgotten just what he discovered, but something in Egypt." . . . "No, no, Flossie, it wasn't Egypt, it was Mesopotamia." Margaret could feel herself flushing; she was already beginning to regret the impetuosity of the action that had prompted her to recall herself to the famous man. At the same time, she longed to put these silly women straight, to tell them it was in Peru he had made his discoveries. She had seen a good deal of him when she first came out, for they had moved in much the same Washington circles then; but that was before he had achieved renown and she had become a recluse. However, she had to admit to herself that, if he shared her regret, he was very adroit at concealing the feeling. With every appearance of pleasure and without apparent effort, Nicolas Hale guided her through the crowd to a seat at the rear of the car and, disregarding the admonition to face the front, stood smiling down at her protectively, completely ignoring the hum of conversation around them. He went on, "I'm alone and apparently you are, too. Can't we join forces?"

"I was hoping you'd suggest that when I got up courage to speak to you. Now I'm afraid it was an imposition."

"It wasn't anything of the sort. It was a kindly thing to do—what I'd expect of an old friend. Besides, what's so frightening about me?"

"Well, you're famous, for one thing. Nonentities are always afraid of celebrities—even nonentities who haven't lived in seclusion as long as I have. And then—well, haven't you rather a reputation as a woman hater?"

"If I have, I don't deserve it. Just because I've never married?"

"No. Because, unless I'm very much mistaken, the general impression is that you never wanted to get married."

"And I don't. What would I do with a wife, while I'm poking around those hidden cities in Peru, trying to find one or two more that no one's succeeded in finding yet? I couldn't take her with me. It's a rugged life."

"Yes, I suppose so. But if you had a wife, you could install her in some comfortable place and she could wait there until you had found your city and returned."

Nicolas Hale laughed. "Somehow, I can't picture the sort of wife who'd be satisfied to do that. And, anyway—"

The elevator had arrived at its destination and people were piling out in the direction of a hospitably wide double door, while the operator continued to caution them about watching their step. They were greeted by sounds of orchestral music, raised voices, hearty laughter and clattering tableware. The air was heavy with the scent of too many fragrant flowers in rooms that were too hot and too crowded. The wedding reception was obviously in full swing. As they waited for the elevator to empty and moved slowly forward, Margaret Porterfield turned inquiringly toward her new-found escort.

"You didn't quite finish that last sentence, did you?"

"No, I didn't. Perhaps I shouldn't."

"I wish you would."

"Well, to be quite candid, though I'm not actually a woman hater, it's true that I've never really wanted a wife, even if I could have found one who'd have been willing to sit around waiting for me in some comfortable place while I was off hunting for lost cities. I can't think of but one reason why a wife would add anything to my life and I can't very well ask a girl to marry me for that reason—unless there were a lot of other reasons too, which there aren't so far—but I'd like very much to have a son and, if I had one, of course I'd want him to have a right to my name."

Before she could answer, he was hailed by a long lost friend, and before they reached the receiving line they were stopped a dozen times. It seemed to Margaret that Nicolas Hale had countless acquaintances while she had none, and she could not rid herself of the impression that all these rich, self-important looking persons would have greatly preferred to keep the celebrity of the occasion to themselves, unencumbered by this dowdy little nobody who had somehow attached herself to him. The greeting from the bride and groom, to be sure, was quite as hearty and affectionate to her as it was to Nicolas; but there was something overpowering about the magnificence of Esther Schaeffer, now Mrs. Sam Steinmetz. Her glistening white satin dress was so superbly cut, her splendid lace veil so becomingly arranged, that Margaret's suit and hat seemed doubly drab and dowdy beside them; and Esther herself was so vital and blooming, with her dimpled rosy cheeks and her sparkling dark eyes and her flashing smile, that she did not need the diamonds that glittered in her tiara and her necklace to give her brilliance. There was nothing about her appearance or her manner to remind an old schoolmate of the way she had looked when they both wore middy blouses and munched apples at recess and helped each other with French verbs and exchanged secrets. Now with Sam Steinmetz and Nicolas Hale it was entirely different. Of course, Sam was handsome, in a prosperous showy way, and his clothes obviously had come from the best of tailors and all that; but he could not hold a candle to Nicolas Hale, who was far and away the most striking looking man at the reception and who didn't need expensive clothes to set off the narrow red ribbon in his buttonhole which proclaimed him a Chevalier of the Legion of Honor, or the more conspicuous *Orden del Sol* of Peru.

"Sam, you and I seem to be holding up the receiving line. I mustn't forget how many other people want to shake your hand on this glad occasion. See you later, when you cut the cake." Nicolas was breaking away from the groom's effusive expressions of pleasure because his famous friend had come to the wedding. The fact that Nicolas Hale so seldom went out socially served to make his rare appearances all the more outstanding, all the more complimentary; whereas, in Margaret's case, the fact that she had lost touch was all too evident. Nicolas Hale, who remembered her as quite a pretty girl, wondered vaguely why her nondescript clothes and shy, diffident manner should so effectively distract attention from her honest gray eyes, delicate features, clear skin and fine fair hair. He had not failed to note all these, as well as the grace of her slender figure, with pleasure; the cultured tone of her voice had been a relief after the strident speech with which they were surrounded. Moreover, he regarded her presence as a protection; so long as he devoted himself to her, it would be harder for some over-dressed, much bejeweled woman, who shrieked her enthusiasm at meeting him, to make him her prey.

"There must be some place we can sit down," he said, steering Margaret away from the receiving line and the crowd around it with the same effortless speed he had shown when he steered her to the rear of the elevator. "After we find it, I'll get you a glass of champagne. What would you like with it? There seems to be about everything available."

"I'm really not hungry or thirsty, either. But I would be glad to sit down. And it's—it's very noisy, isn't it? Or is that just my imagination?"

"No, it's not your imagination. Let's keep going. This penthouse must have been used to live in once, not just to rent out for parties. If it was, there'll be some kind of a room that was called a den, at the period this hotel was built, and the chances are there won't be anyone else there, because a den bears a faint resemblance to a library, and if there's anything a crowd like this shuns, it's a place where there might be books, instead of liquor. Ah! I thought so! Now, if you'll just sit down quietly for a few minutes, I'll see what I can find in the way of civilized food. You may not be hungry, but I am."

He was not gone long. During his brief absence, two or three people poked their heads through the half-closed door of the den, saw Margaret sitting there alone and retired without a word. She sat very still, as grateful for the tranquility as she would have been for a harbor after a storm, happily anticipating the return of Nicolas Hale, but not impatient for it. When he came, he was accompanied by a beaming waiter, bearing a tray on which stood a bottle of champagne in a silver cooler and frosted glasses. Hale himself was carrying the plates well laden with food. He set these down on a table, handed the waiter a bill neatly folded into a small square and said they would wait on themselves. Then he opened the champagne and sat down beside Margaret.

"You look a little tired to me," he said. "Why don't you drink that and start on the lobster before you try to talk? Then I'd like very much to hear what you are doing with yourself these days, now that you don't go out at all."

"Why—I keep house," she said after the pause he had recommended and which she found had made her feel much better. "It's a big house and I have only one maid, a colored woman named Cassie who's been with me a long time. She's very faithful and she's a good cook, but she never was one of those marvels you read about. My mother used to say you can't get clean corners and light biscuits out of the same darkie and I reckon she was right—Cassie makes light biscuits, so I clean the corners. And I do a little gardening—flowers and vegetables both. I read a lot, too. The days don't drag."

"There's no one with you on the place except this faithful retainer?"

"No, but I'm used to living that way now. I don't mind it at all."

"Well, I suppose your horses and dogs are good company."

"I don't keep them any more. Mother never really liked having dogs in the house and when she became an invalid they annoyed her, so I had to see that they stayed outdoors as much as possible and when they died I didn't get new ones. We'd given up the horses long before that. Father and I used to ride together a lot, but Mother wasn't much of a horsewoman, even in her most active days and, of course, stables are a luxury item now. Our nearest neighbors, the Huntingtons, have a very fine one, but they're the exception in the immediate vicinity. Nobody *needs* horses any more now that everybody has a car. I've a small one that I drive myself. I use it to do errands and go to church and things like that."

"How about the land? I seem to remember there was a lot of it."

"Yes, there is. But it isn't under cultivation any more. One old barn is stacked with the hay that was left there the summer Father died, and it's still soft and sweet smelling, though I don't suppose it's any good as fodder any more. Now the hay's sold standing and there aren't any other crops."

He checked the impulse to ask if this were not poor economy and asked instead if she were finding the Huntingtons pleasant neighbors. He did not seem to remember them.

"No, you wouldn't. As a matter of fact, I don't think you ever met them. They're newcomers, enormously rich. But they're hardly ever in residence at East Lawn—they have another stock farm, in Normandy, and I don't know how many town houses. I think they just like to feel they own property in Virginia—that it's nice to talk about, but not much fun in itself. Of course, I called, when they first moved to East Lawn and, eventually, Mrs. Huntington returned the call. Then I invited her to tea, but she didn't come and she never asked me to anything after that."

"But you and your other neighbors visit back and forth, don't you?"

"Not much. Some of my old friends have moved away and those who live anywhere near me are all married now. Their interests are with their own families. I'm the only old maid in what used to be my set, except for a few who've become absorbed in politics. Several of them hold very good government positions, but those never appealed to me, either."

"If it isn't impertinent to ask, just how old are you?"

"Twenty-six. I seem older than that, don't you think?"

He looked at her thoughtfully before answering. She had referred to herself as an old maid and he now realized it was true. There *was* something rather spinsterish about her. A few years earlier, the virginal shyness might well have been appealing; but she had passed the stage where the attributes of unawakened maidenhood were a physical asset and she was not the type who could have next assumed the self-assurance, the breeziness, the sophistication or the daring of the career girl, single from choice and economically independent. No doubt all this was what accounted, at least in part, for her lack of allure. But he decided that the emptiness and aimlessness of her life were also responsible for this; inevitably, these affected her outlook and almost as inevitably her expression and her manner.

"No," he said, after a pause which he was afraid might have hurt her feelings; she must have been conscious both of his hesitation and of his scrutiny. "I don't think you seem older than that. In some ways, you seem younger. I mean, if you'll permit me to say so, you seem—well, rather inexperienced for twenty-six. As if you'd lost a great many opportunities for development in those years you dedicated to your mother and as if you hadn't taken advantage of any since. Of course, your devotion to her was a wonderful thing; something you'll never regret and everyone who knows you admires you for it. But now that she's gone. . . . You live within thirty miles of Washington, the nerve center of the world; you can get there in an hour, but you seem as far removed from it, mentally, as if you were on the other side of the globe, in the middle of a desert or on the top of a mountain. Why, I'm much nearer to it in the heart of Peru than you are! And it isn't as if you hadn't ever been part of the life there. It was your center, even more than the plantation, when I first knew you."

"Yes, you're right. But Washington has changed. It's so much bigger, so much less friendly than it used to be."

"You mean *you've* changed. Couldn't you seek out your old friends again? Invite them to informal parties and go to parties at their houses? You might find you have more in common than you think, after all. Or, if the Washington scene has completely lost its appeal for you, what about local interests besides church? I seem to have heard about garden clubs and things like that in Virginia and you say you like gardening. Horses and dogs would be company for you, too. I believe you need company, whether you think so or not. Why don't you try having a dog again, one dog to begin with, and one horse? If you didn't like them, you could always get rid of them."

"Perhaps you're right. I could try having one dog. I don't know about the horse. But of course I could rejoin the Alexandria Garden Club. I used to belong to it but I resigned when Mother did. You see, we always went to meetings together and when she wasn't well enough to go any more, it didn't seem the same—it never has since."

"I see. Well, couldn't you travel?"

"Yes, I could travel—a little. Not much, I'm afraid. You see, it would break my heart to lose Hills' End. And with taxes and everything, it costs a good deal to keep it up, even without animals. I can't afford to do that and travel too. . . . Perhaps I didn't say, but I don't have a great deal of money."

"No, you didn't say it, but I guessed it."

"So I believe it's really better for me to go on the way I am. You see that, too, don't you?"

"I'm afraid I don't. I'd like to argue with you about it. But I suppose we ought to go back into that scene of bedlam. It must be almost cake cutting time. Come on, let's drink up this champagne."

He refilled her glass again. She sipped her drink very slowly and, as she did so, color came into her pale cheeks and she began to look more like the girl he remembered. When she spoke the next time, she sounded not only more like the girl he remembered, but more like the woman he thought she might become if she would only shake off her lethargy and rise above her depression.

"You've given me a wonderful afternoon," she said. "I'm almost glad there isn't time to argue. I wouldn't want to spoil it by a dispute. You'll never know how much meeting you again has meant to me. You've been a hero to me for a long while. Of course, women are always telling famous men that, just to flatter them, but in your case and mine, it's true. And if you want a son, I think you ought to have one— a son not only to carry on your name, but your fame. I don't see why you shouldn't ask some woman to marry you, for that one reason. I don't see why you're so sure no one would want you on those terms."

2 ❧

The brilliant sunshine of early October had been succeeded by a long stretch of drab wet weather. Never, in Margaret's memory, had "the melancholy days, the saddest of the year" come so early in the autumn. Bronzed leaves still clung, stiffly and tenaciously, to the oak trees, despite buffeting winds; but the golden glory of the maples was already gone. The lawns remained green, but they had taken on a shaggy and sodden look, due partly to inept and infrequent mowing and partly to their soaked condition; Margaret found she had to put on rubbers, as well as a warm sweater, whenever she stepped outside the house; and, except for gathering the zinnias and chrysanthemums and harvesting the squashes and cabbages that still survived in the garden, which was otherwise almost stripped of both flowers and vegetables, there was not much she needed to do there or much temptation to linger in the open; even the late roses, usually a source of special pride to her, were shedding their drenched petals and the stalks of the tall growing chrysanthemums were bent or broken. However, since small tasks about the place at least made a change from dreary duties in the house, she was apt to prolong them, rather than to shirk them and the chilly weather was not really a drawback. It was too early in the season to start the furnace, if she were to conserve her meager supply of coal through the winter and, in any case, shoveling was hard work. She seldom used the dining room; when she did, by leaving the door open between that and the kitchen, the old-fashioned range gave adequate warmth for both. Aside from this, she could make do with open fires and intermittent use of small electric heaters for another month or so.

Margaret's mood was as somber as the weather. She was inclined to feel that her trip to New York for the Schaeffer-Steinmetz wedding had been a mistake. In the first place, though she had spent only one night away from home, had ridden in a coach both going and coming, and had put up at a hotel that was inexpensive, according to New York standards, she had spent much more than she could well afford. In the second place, she realized that she and Esther Schaeffer no longer had anything in common and that it was futile to pretend they might have. She had always come swiftly to her friend's defense when Washington "cave-dwellers" spoke with disparagement about Esther's family and said that, of course, if it had not been for Mr. Schaeffer's temporary position as Assistant Secretary of Commerce, his daughter would never have been admitted to the Holton Arms School; the President was really very careless when it came to considering social qualifications for the Little Cabinet. Margaret had been genuinely fond of the Schaeffers, who were warm hearted and hospitable. Their temperament, as well as their enormous wealth, had made it easy for them to keep open house and they did not confine their entertaining to official groups; all kinds of good causes were set in motion under their roof, and the more parties their children gave, the better they liked it. Affection, as well as loyalty, was involved in Margaret's support of her schoolmate. But, as the cave-dwellers had pointed out, Mr. Schaeffer's position as Assistant Secretary of Commerce had been only a temporary one, enjoyed in recognition of valuable campaign contributions; and with a change of administration, the Schaeffers returned, without undue regret, to New York, where the head of the family was a highly successful member of the Stock Exchange. Margaret had twice been invited to stay with them and these visits had been a revelation to her: a house on upper Fifth Avenue with a conservatory, a picture gallery and a ballroom; a box at the Metropolitan, a purring welcome at luxurious restaurants and dazzling shops, where everything from caviar and champagne to jewelry and fur coats was charged as a matter of course. After the second visit, the Schaeffers had asked Margaret to spend a summer abroad with them; it appeared that, besides the house in New York, they had a chateau in France and a shooting-box in Scotland. But Margaret's father had died suddenly just as she was beginning her preparations for a voyage on the *Queen Mary* and a motor trip through France and England; and afterward, there was no question of leaving her mother.

That was six years ago. For a long time, she had grieved over the separation; now she did not care in the least whether or not she ever saw her former schoolmate again.

She could economize on something else to catch up on expenses—food, probably, because she did not have a hearty appetite and neither did Cassie, the old colored servant; and as it was so long since Esther had really been a factor in her life, the tardy realization that the break with her was final did not constitute too much of a blow. So, even if the recent trip had been a mistake, there was no sound reason why she should brood over it. But she could not seem to dismiss the wedding from her mind. Over and over again, as she sat in the library, she found herself laying down her book, not only to mend the meager fire, but to dwell on the details of the showy function: the elaborate setting, the lavish floral decorations, the blatant music, the rich food, the inexhaustible drinks, the costly apparel of her fellow guests. And when she had reviewed all these, whether individually or in sequence, she found she invariably came back to the same point: her meeting with Nicolas Hale and the hour they had spent together in the erstwhile den.

At first, she did not admit to herself that he had disturbed her. She knew that he would not wilfully or even consciously have said anything that sounded critical, that could hurt her feelings; but when he summed up his impression of her by saying that she seemed inexperienced for twenty-six, apparently because she had missed opportunities which were available to her, she knew that she had not measured up to the estimate she would have liked him to make of her.

There was really no reason why she should care whether she did or not. He was no more a part of her world, any more, than Esther, and he had never been a vital part of it—only a pleasant part. And yet, she found that she did care, that she considered his good opinion worth having and that his case and Esther's were not alike, after all, because she, Margaret, rather wished that he *were* part of her world, instead of being quite ready to dismiss him from it. Besides, that was not the worst of it: she was restless, she was dissatisfied. Until he talked to her about neglected opportunities, she had not been uncomfortably conscious of any; she had been busy and content with her house and her books and her garden, her conscientious church work, her inconsequential errands. And now they did not fill her days or her needs any more. Nicolas Hale had meant to be kind and, instead, he had been cruel, by insisting that the pattern of her life was all wrong—well, perhaps not all wrong, but certainly futile. And, suddenly, she was finding it so. She had applied for reinstatement in the membership of the Alexandria Garden Club and had been assured that she would be welcomed; but she could not help feeling that her resignation had been resented, for she was also told the board would not be meeting for several weeks and, until it acted on her application, she could have no official standing in the group. Besides, this was the slack season, when no one was interested, as yet, in devising original Christmas decorations and decorations for harvest festivals were already planned or finished. Defeated in this direction, she had made inquiries about a dog, but there seemed to be none available that she wanted, at a price she could afford. And when she invited a few Washington friends to come out for tea, she found they were already tied up, weeks in advance, with cocktail parties and official dinners. She had forgotten that nobody went out to tea any more, that tea parties had ceased to be social legal tender.

There was still another cause for her dissatisfaction: she thought she had been very silly, talking to Nicolas Hale the way she had. Not after they were sipping champagne in the erstwhile den; that part of her conversation had been all right, except that it had led to those comments about inexperience and lost opportunities; but at least it had been dignified and restrained. But to ask, in that arch way, if he weren't a woman hater! . . . Well, of course she had not meant to sound arch, but she was very much afraid she had, instead of merely friendly, as she had intended. It was the sort of remark women made when they were trying to act playful and which did not go over very well once they were past their first youth; the sort of remark most men —certainly men like Nicolas Hale—found very distasteful. And she had made it in a public elevator, of all places! That was enough to prove she had better stay quietly in the country, that she no longer fitted into any social scene. Yet, what was she to do with herself all the time in the country, now that it did not satisfy her any more?

She had asked herself that question a dozen times and, each time, she seemed further from a pleasing answer than she had previously been. The weather was getting worse and worse, which added to her depression; if she could have taken long walks, in crisp sunny autumnal air, and come home physically exhausted, she could have gone early to bed, slept soundly and wakened refreshed. As it was, she was more and more housebound and she was tired of feeding the fires and listening to the rain. Also, she was more and more annoyed with herself every time she laid down her book and started thinking again what a fool she had made of herself when she met Nicolas Hale.

She had reached the point where she had decided she was going to take that long walk anyway, even if she got drenched to the skin, when she thought she heard a car turning into the driveway and rose to look out of the window. The early twilight of autumn had already enveloped the landscape and the rain, which had been a gentle fall in the morning, had now become a steady downpour. It was impossible to see anything clearly beyond the clumps of boxwood which framed the house and, for a moment, she thought she must have been mistaken. Then she saw a dim glow and realized it must come from the head-lights of a car and that this had stopped either because mud made the road practically impassable or because the driver was a stranger and was uncertain whether or not he had taken the right turn. She was still wondering if she should obey the impulse to put on boots and a raincoat and slosh out to the car, offering what help she could, when it started again, came inching toward the house and drew up under the porte-cochere. As she stepped out of the house, the door of the car slammed shut, the man who had been driving it came up the steps and she found herself face to face with Nicolas Hale.

"Hello!" he said heartily, taking her hand as naturally as if he thought she would be rather expecting his visit. "Nice day, isn't it? I've covered most of the state of Virginia looking for this place. How do you manage to keep so well hidden, only a few miles off the beaten track? The buried cities of Peru have nothing on the outlying districts of

Alexandria. Since I was home last, the nice old country roads have been changed to superhighways and, if you take the wrong turn, you have to go all the way back to Washington and start over again. I took several. One landed me at the place those Huntingtons have bought—East Lawn, is that its name?—and Lord, what they've done to it! It's a good thing they're not here much—they might have corrupted the whole countryside; their taste seems to be a mixture of early Hollywood and late Miami. However, it doesn't matter, I'm here now, to something that belongs in Virginia."

"But Mr. Hale, why didn't you let me know you were coming? I'd have told you exactly how to get here. It really isn't complicated at all. But, of course, I had no idea—"

"Well, I did try to look you up in the Washington telephone book, but apparently you're listed under some obscure suburban exchange and I couldn't find you. I'm very stupid about telephones anyway, perhaps because I hate them. Of course, I could have asked an operator, but by the time I'd thought of that, I'd decided it was better just to come anyway. I was afraid if you knew about my call beforehand, you'd start making all sorts of elaborate preparations—little fancy sandwiches and things like that. And I hate those, too. You might even have opened up the drawing room, which is closed because it's cold, and dusted off your harp, so that you could play for me, when I'd much rather sit by the fire in the library and talk. Besides, I didn't want you to go to any trouble. You told me you do a good deal of your own housework. Remember?"

"Yes, I remember. And you're partly right. I would have made sandwiches and things like that and I would have opened up the parlor. But I wouldn't have offered to play the harp. It's still here, in the same corner it always was, but it belonged to Mother, not to me. You've got your generations mixed, it's so long since you've been here. But you're right about a fire in the library. Come in and get warm. It's almost as cold here in the hall as it is outdoors. I don't know why we stand here talking."

"Neither do I. But I thought it was your place, not mine, to suggest that we go where it's warmer."

He grinned, engagingly, and she managed to smile, too, her first startled embarrassment lessening in the face of his complete ease and her very real pleasure in seeing him. He laid his overcoat and driving gloves on a chair and ran his fingers through his thick dark hair. Margaret could see that it was wet; doubtless it was in character for him to go bareheaded, in any sort of weather, even if he knew he would be getting out of the car to ask for directions. She must see to it not only that he got warm, but that he got dry. She went so quickly from the cold hall to the firelit library that, if he had not hurried to keep up with her, she would have drawn a second chair close to the hearth and thrown on another log before he could forestall her in doing both. Then, as he waited for her to sit down, she asked a hesitant question.

"I'm afraid I haven't any whisky. What about tea? Do you put that in the same category as little fancy sandwiches?"

"Not at all. As a matter of fact, I prefer tea to whisky or anything else at this hour of the day. Coffee is fine for breakfast and dinner and whisky with soda is all right for a nightcap, though it never really reaches perfection except in a julep, but *this* is tea time. It isn't really late—it only seems that way because it gets dark so early in November —an abominable month is this latitude, even when there's a little feeble sunshine. And when it rains, the way it has today. . . ." He left the sentence unfinished, shrugging his shoulders and running his fingers through his hair again.

"I suppose the weather's beautiful in Peru now," Margaret ventured. She felt his remark called for some sort of a reply, before she went to make the tea, and this seemed as good as any. "That is, the seasons are reversed there, aren't they?"

"Yes, spring's just beginning. I find I enjoy that more and more every year."

"And you're leaving almost immediately?"

"Well, in about ten days."

"Then I won't see you again!"

There, she should not have said it. It was all wrong, like those arch remarks she had made at the wedding—not wrong in the same way, but no less mistaken. However, Nicolas Hale did not seem to be taking offense, any more than he had then. He smiled again and, coming closer to her, put his hand under her elbow and gave it a reassuring squeeze.

"That depends on you," he said. "I didn't come here just to make a call. I have a suggestion to make—an utterly fantastic suggestion, but I believe there's just a chance you might consider it. I've been giving a good deal of thought to our conversation at the wedding and—"

"Oh, so have I. I've been very troubled about it. I don't see how I could have been so silly as to say I understood you were a woman hater and—and things like that. I'm sure it must have been very offensive to you."

"If it had, do you think I'd be here today? Planning to make a suggestion which might lead to other visits?"

"Why no, I—I suppose not." She was conscious of a strange fluttering in her heart, a sensation wholly unlike any she had ever experienced before, so startling as to be almost painful and yet shot through with pleasure. "I'll go and make our tea," she said quickly.

"Before you do that, would you mind bringing in a saucer of milk?"

"A saucer of *milk!*" she repeated. "No, of course, I don't mind. But what are you going to do with a saucer of milk?"

"I may as well confess that I brought another visitor with me. I left her in the car because I didn't want to give you too much of a shock, all at once. But she must be getting cold and hungry, too, out there in the car all by herself."

Without further explanation, he left the library and Margaret heard the front door opening and shutting again and then an appealing whimper. When Nicolas Hale came back into the room, he was carrying a small honey-colored cocker spaniel, which looked up at Margaret with large trustful brown eyes.

"This is Perdita," Nicolas Hale said gravely. "I named her myself —for my lost city, you know. But of course, you can change her name if you don't like it. She isn't registered yet. You remember I told you I thought you ought to try having one dog anyway and I was afraid you wouldn't, unless I got it for you. I was right, wasn't I? It's very clear to me that you need a certain amount of direction."

3 ❧

Margaret brought the milk and Perdita lapped it up, stopping, every now and then, to look gratefully at her hostess, who watched her entranced and, after a rapt silence, inquired if it were all right to pet her.

"Of course. That's what she expects you to do."

The rapport between the girl and the dog was as immediate as it was mutually satisfying. Nicolas looked down with pleased amusement as Margaret caressed her new pet and Perdita, having emptied the saucer, curled herself into a compact little ball and went to sleep. Margaret continue to hover over her.

"About our tea?" Nicolas inquired.

"Oh, I'm sorry! I'll get it right away. I was so fascinated with that adorable puppy that I forgot all about tea. And I haven't even thanked you properly!"

"Yes you have—without knowing it. But now it's my turn for nourishment. May I come with you and carry the tray?"

"No, please stay where you are. It won't be heavy—I haven't much to put on it. None of those fancy sandwiches, you know!"

She was afraid she was being arch again, or dangerously near it, and with only one backward glance at Perdita, she left the room hurriedly, so that she would not make any more mistakes. As a matter of fact, the tray was well laden. After she put the kettle on to boil, she went to the corner cupboard where she kept her best china and reached for the Lowestoft tea set that was stowed away on the highest shelf and taken down only on great occasions. It was dusty from disuse, so she hastily washed it, filled the sugar bowl and cream pitcher, and then thankfully remembered that she had a lemon in the house, as it was quite probable the cream would be only for effect. She also remembered there was a small flask of brandy reserved for emergencies, so she ran upstairs and extracted it from the medicine closet. Next, she dashed down to the cellar; in the storeroom there was jam which she had made herself from the fruit of trees on the place—damson and quince. She hoped Nicolas Hale would not put homemade jam in the same category as fancy sandwiches and, somehow, she did not think he would. There was also a loaf of homemade bread in the safe, and she remembered hearing that, in England, it was customary to butter bread as it was cut, in lovely thin slices; she would take the loaf in whole and she and her guest would butter it the way people did in England and eat it cold, or they could toast it over the fire. There was a long handled fork, meant to use for that, among the fire irons. And, of course, she had fruit cake. It was old, but she had kept it moistened with the emergency brandy and some sherry she had bought on purpose. She had blamed herself afterward for such an extravagance, but now she was glad she had been guilty of it. Old fruit cake, properly moistened, was even better than new.

When everything was ready, Margaret realized that she had more than she could carry after all and she started to call Cassie, who, as usual, had gone to her room for a long afternoon nap. Then she decided to let Nicolas Hale have his way and help with it. It would mean that he would have to go through the gun room and the dining room, neither of which was warm or in order, since she had taken to eating most of her frugal meals in the library. But, with only one light turned on, he might not notice that the rooms were dusty, and he would go through them so quickly that he would not mind the cold. It was true that he did not mind it, though it surprised him—surely Margaret Porterfield was not so poor that she could not heat her house properly, and the hall had been glacial, too! Then he surprised *her* by stopping, tray in hand, when he reached the gun room, long enough to look around it in appreciation.

"This was always my favorite, in the old days," he said. "I liked it even better than the library—lots of old Virginia houses have good libraries, but very few have a gun room that can compare to this. Wasn't it here that you used to have your Christmas eggnog parties?

And where the Negroes on the place used to come and sing their spirituals? There was always lots of holly and laurel that you'd gathered yourself and made into wreaths and garlands and a decorated tree in one corner and, of course, the yule log on the hearth. Those were wonderful parties. You never should have stopped having them."

"I explained to you why."

"Yes, and I tried to explain why I thought you should start giving them again."

"If you were going to be here for Christmas, I might."

"I shan't be here, but I'd like to think you were having one just the same. You could write me about it."

"Would you really like to get a letter from me?"

"I certainly would! Now let's get on with our tea before it freezes in the pot."

The tea was a great success. They ate part of the homemade bread cold, as they sliced it from the loaf, and the rest they toasted over the fire, using the long handled fork, just as Margaret had thought they might. And quite definitely, Nicolas Hale did not put homemade jam in the same category that he did fancy sandwiches. She spread both his cold buttered bread and his toast so liberally with it that they were dripping, and he licked the surplus from his fingers. The cream *was* just for ornament. He drank his first two cups of tea clear—it was a sacrilege to put anything in China tea as good as this, he said; he wanted Margaret to tell him the brand. But he squeezed lemon and put sugar and brandy into the third cup, which he drank with the fruit cake. Then he carried the tray back to the kitchen and turned it over to Cassie, who had waked up by this time and who hailed him with delight; she was sure proud to see him again, after all these years, she told him, and he lingered to chat with her a little. When he returned to the library, he lighted a pipe and smoked quietly for a few minutes. Perdita was still asleep, curled in the tight little ball she had made of herself, and Margaret sat down on the floor beside her and stroked her. It was very still in the room, for the fire had ceased to crackle and gave off only a steady glow. Margaret had never known that a silence could be so companionable.

At last Nicolas knocked the ashes out of his pipe and put it in his pocket. "About that suggestion I spoke of," he said. "I think this is probably as good a time as any to make it." Then, as Margaret looked up at him encouragingly, though without answering, he went on, "You've been worrying, quite needlessly, because you thought something you said to me in the elevator was silly. I haven't worried because something I said to you shortly thereafter was pretty crude. But I would have, if it hadn't been for what you said to me next. That's what I've been thinking over. What I said was crude, but it also happened to be true: the only reason I'd consider the possibility of marriage is because I want a son. You were right. I do want one. So does every normal man. But the desire for the holy state of matrimony, so-called, isn't so universal. At least, that's my impression. . . . Shall I go on?"

She did not answer immediately, but finally she said, in a low voice, "Yes, please do."

"I was also quite sincere when I said that I had no use for a wife, that I couldn't take her with me on my expeditions and that I haven't the least idea of giving up my expeditions until I've found the lost city I'm still searching for. Probably I shan't, even then. There's an incurable fever connected with exploration; the only way to keep it within reasonable bounds is to go on and on. Can you understand that?"

"I'm not sure. But I think so."

"Well, if you can't understand, you must just take my word for it, because it's so. And what I'm coming to is this: after I told you that I couldn't ask a girl to marry me, considering how I feel, both about matrimony and about exploring, you told me you thought I was making a mistake; that it was quite possible a girl might be willing to marry me on my terms. Did you mean that? Were you telling the truth?"

"Yes, I meant it. I was telling the truth—at least, what I believe was the truth. I'm sure any number of girls would be very proud to marry you, on almost any terms."

"I'm not interested in any number of girls. But I am interested in one. Haven't you guessed by this time, Margaret, that I'm leading up to a proposal?"

She gave a little startled cry and he realized, with amazement, that he really had taken her completely by surprise, that she had never dreamed he might ask her to marry him. When she said, in all honesty, that she thought any number of girls would be proud to do so, she had not thought of herself among them. Apparently she had accepted her role as a dull, undesirable old maid with the same finality that she had accepted his as a dashing figure of adventure, irresistible to women. He leaned over and took her hand, but he made no effort to draw her up beside him.

"Listen," he said, "I'm not going to mask this in any pretty phrases. I'm going right on telling you the truth. I don't want you as a companion—at least, not as a permanent inescapable one. But I think I'd find you a very pleasant one, if I could see you just from time to time and I'd like very much to do that. What's more, the idea of making love to you rather appeals to me. Am I correct in assuming no one else has the right of way?"

"Do you mean—has someone else proposed to me?"

"I take it for granted that several persons must have proposed to you, somewhere along the line, but that you turned the earlier proposals down, or you wouldn't still be single. What I meant to ask was whether or not there was any present engagement or understanding."

"You're taking too much for granted. No one ever proposed to me until you did just now—if that really was a proposal."

"Of course it was a proposal. And I can't believe—"

"Perhaps you can't, but it's true. I wasn't exactly a wallflower when I came out—if I had been, you'd remember that; you saw me often enough at parties in those days. But I wasn't particularly popular, either. There's no reason why I should have been. I was never at ease with men, I've never had any idea how to make myself attractive to them. And then there were those years with my mother when I never saw any, except an elderly uncle who lives in Charlottesville. You're not only the first man who's ever proposed to me, you're the first one who ever told me he thought I might be a pleasant companion, if my companionship wasn't actually forced on him, the first who ever said the idea of making love to me was rather appealing."

He looked at her thoughtfully. Rather to his surprise, he found the admission she had just made rendered her more, rather than less, desirable in his eyes. She had not passed the stage where the attributes of unawakened maidenhood were attractive after all. This shy virginity was still alluring; there might be elements of unforeseen excitement in overcoming it.

"Then I'd say that a lot of people besides yourself have been missing opportunities, which is all to the good, as far as I'm concerned," he said emphatically. "Don't misunderstand me. I haven't fallen suddenly and madly in love with you. In one sense, exploring is my only great passion—it has been, ever since I first heard Hiram Bingham lecture on his discovery of Machu Picchu. There was a question and answer period afterward and I had a chance to talk with him. He captured my imagination to such a degree that, as soon as I could, I transferred from Middlebury to Yale and I've kept in touch with him ever since. At that time, I was majoring in history and I expanded my field to include the South American scene and shifted from French to Spanish as a modern language. Naturally, since then, I've studied Quechua. Later, for my master's degree, I switched to geology. I'd done some mountain climbing as a teen-ager—Monadnock, Ascutney, Chocoroa, the Presidential Range—and it seemed instinctive, after I met Bingham, to go further afield. As far as possible, I've followed his trail through Venezuela and Colombia, as well as Peru. And I've struck out on my own, too, with the Schaeffer-Steinmetz financial backing as long as I needed it. As far as Peru is concerned, I was lucky enough to have for a classmate a gilded youth of the polo-playing variety who came from Lima. His name is Ildefonso Parra, convivially nicknamed The Peruvian Peril, but he was anything but a peril to me. He and I lived in the same entry and we got to be great friends. It was through the good offices of his family that I had a chance to join the Wenner-Gren expedition in 1940, when the ruins of Huiñay Huaiña were discovered a little south of Machu Picchu, and I was given credit for a considerable contribution to its success: when all the tools and paraphernalia were packed for the return to Cuzco, I stumbled on a ravine that gave me a clue to the site. . . . Well, if I could have carried right on from there, of course, I'd have been famous in no time; but, as you may recall, there was a war on. It interrupted my career as an explorer, just as World War I had interrupted Bingham's. I probably don't need to tell you the Navy had a notion that anyone with a university degree could qualify as a gentleman and be hammered into an officer—a ninety-day wonder, to revert to wartime nomenclature. And that's all I was. But, during some dull shore duty, I volunteered for deep diving and learned how to grope around in several fathoms of salt water. If I'd gone into all that later, I'd have been officially labeled a frogman. Anyway, what I did learn about underwater procedure has stood me in good stead since. First, it made possible the discovery of golden vessels in the deep pool of a cave behind a waterfall and, incidentally, turned me into an author and a lecturer. Of course, the second single-handed find of mine helped even more—the much publicized discovery of the golden bell, hitherto thought to be merely legendary, in the lagoon of Urcos. Now, if three proves to be my lucky number, if I can make the next objective I have in mind, I'll be on top of the world in more ways than one. What's more, there'll be a road named for me, leading to the place I've discovered, just as there's a road named for Bingham leading to Machu Picchu and I'll be the hero of the country just as he is."

Nicolas paused, gazing straight ahead of him, and Margaret had the impression that he was already visualizing the road named for him because of a great discovery, that he was enacting the role of a popular hero and that he had completely forgotten he was in the midst of a proposal of marriage. She was right about the vision, but not about the forgetfulness. Presently Nicolas laughed and turned toward her with a smile she found irresistibly attractive.

"Did you think I was sidetracked?" he asked. "Not really. It didn't seem quite enough, just to say exploring was my only great passion, without a single word of explanation. Now I believe you have enough of one, at least for the present and I can go back to the main line, which is a reference to minor passions. I'm not lacking in what is generally called virility. Do you understand what I'm talking about?"

"I—I think so."

"I don't like to insult your intelligence by asking you that too often. And I don't want to say anything that will be offensive to you, if I can help it. On the other hand, I don't want anything to come as a shock to you later on. It's really not strictly accurate to say I'm a woman-hater —it's marriage, rather than women, that I've avoided. If I've lived more continently than most men, it isn't because I wouldn't have preferred to live otherwise. It's partly because I have an inherent objection to sex combined with commercialism, though I've great respect for each, kept separate. It's also partly because affairs with social equals, which attract me because of their presumably temporary aspects, have a great disadvantage, as far as I'm concerned: I've had one or two—well, two or three—and they've been quite intense while they lasted, but they were over rather quickly by mutual consent, which was all to the good. I'd have hated to have them drag on, once the first fever was over; I'd have hated having a woman cling to me once I was tired of her, and I'd have hated wanting her and not having her. So, in a way, everything was satisfactory. But you have to be careful there aren't any visible results of an affair and, of course, what I'm after *is* a visible result. Therefore, marriage seems to be the only answer to getting a legal heir and, as I've already admitted, you were right, I do want one, I have for a long time. But it wasn't until you said what you did. . . . All right, let's cut this short. I want you for the mother of my son. You'd make just the sort of mother he ought to have. You're a gentlewoman, born and bred. You've had a good education, at least good of its kind and enough of one for all practical purposes. Besides, you're naturally intelligent—what you don't know, but need to know, you'll find out sooner or later. You're kind and conscientious—the way you treated your mother proves that. In fact, you've an almost exaggerated sense of duty and loyalty, but those are good faults. And last, but by no means least, you're very lovely to look at. That is, you could be if—"

He stopped abruptly. It had been on the tip of his tongue to say, "if you'd get rid of those shapeless old black clothes and put on something that brings out your coloring and shows off your figure. If you'd let yourself go and stop worrying for fear something you've said is silly. If you'd lead a normal life for a woman your age." But this would have had the effect of detracting from the tribute of his earlier remarks and would have risked hurting her needlessly. Besides, if she followed his utterly fantastic suggestion—and he found himself hoping more and more that she would—all these things would take care of themselves.

"So I want you to marry me," he went on. "But that isn't saying I want you for my wife, with all that usually implies. I can't think of anything worse than permanent cohabitation if either partner wants to be free and I know I would. It isn't beyond the realm of possibility that you might. I'd like to marry you with the understanding that the marriage isn't to last any longer than I want it to—or, for that matter, any longer than you want it to—after it's fulfilled its primary purpose. But if you married me, you'd have to remember what that is and act accordingly. Am I making myself perfectly clear? Please look me straight in the eye, Margaret, and say yes or no."

"Yes," she said, looking him straight in the eye.

"All right, so far, so good. I'm leaving for Peru in less than a fortnight. My equipment's already on its way by ship, in charge of my assistant—a good fellow, name of Pete Hart. We've been friends ever since we were boys, but he's gone even further from Vermont than I have, metaphorically speaking. I'm flying—my reservation's made. It's too late to make any changes in my schedule now—the whole setup is too complicated. There are also climatic conditions to consider—these are more of a problem in Peru than in most other places. I believe there's a law in Virginia that requires a doctor's recent certificate of physical fitness for marriage, but that ought not to involve much red tape. I'm sure you're still blessed with one of those old-fashioned family physicians, the kind that ushers you into the world and out of it and stands by, in all emergencies between times. The breed's getting rare, but I can't believe it's extinct in Virginia. If it's not, your vet will fix us up in no time. I don't know whether or not it's also necessary to give five days' notice of intention to marry, as it is in some states, but you'd need that long anyway, wouldn't you, to get ready? I know you'd want to have a wedding, I don't mean a big flashy show like the Schaeffer-Steinmetz affair, but a religious ceremony, some kind of a breakfast afterward. As a matter of fact, I'd want it, too. There are several good reasons why everything ought to be done decently and in order, if it's done at all. Once that's decided, we can take up the details. But first, you've got to be more explicit than you've been so far. You've told me you understand the terms on which I'd like to marry you, but you haven't told me whether or not you'd be willing to marry me on those terms—and on five days' notice. You'll have to look me straight in the eye again, Margaret. Is it yes or no this time?"

"It's yes."

He gazed at her fixedly for a moment, his face still set and stern, as it had been all the time he was talking. Then his expression relaxed into something that was almost, though not quite, a smile and very, very attractive. He held out his other hand and drew her to her feet.

"You're quite a girl, after all," he said. "I really didn't think you had it in you to take it this way. You've given me a somewhat staggering, but very pleasant surprise. I'd like to begin my authorized courtship by telling you that I admire you very much. I know that the next step ought to take the form of gradual and gentle approaches to a display of ardor—a chaste salute on the brow, a light pressure of the waist, that sort of thing. To borrow one of your local expressions, I know it's usually a mistake to rush your fences, but considering how little time we've got, I think it might be better if I started serious love-making right here and now. Otherwise, you won't have any sort of preparation for unconditional surrender in less than a week."

4♡

For a long time after Nicolas had gone, Margaret sat motionless beside the dying fire which she made no effort to revive. Indeed, she was quite incapable of movement or effort. Everything that had happened in the last few hours seemed so incredible that its actuality had a shattering quality. When she tardily realized that she was shivering, she thought it was because she was frightened; it took her several moments to recognize the fact that she was also chilled through and through. And even this recognition brought with it no impulse toward action.

A gentle whimper from Perdita finally did this. The puppy, which had lain curled up in her tight little ball, apparently asleep, as long as her new mistress continued to stroke her, had started up, when Nicolas pulled Margaret to her feet. During the interval that followed, Perdita had stood wagging her diminutive tail, looking up at the couple that stood so closely embraced with a friendly, if slightly puzzled expression. Then, after the front door slammed behind Nicolas and Margaret sat down on the sofa, Perdita stood on her hind legs and put her front paws on the sofa cushions. Her expression was one of such unmistakable appeal, in making her needs known, that Margaret, despite her emotional upheaval, could not disregard it. She lifted the little dog up, took her out to the porte-cochere, and set her down on the ground.

The rain had stopped and the stars were shining brightly; a young moon was rocking to rest above the oaks and their bronzed leaves were silvered by its splendor. It would have been hard to imagine a more beautiful night, but Margaret was hardly conscious of its radiance. Still in a daze, she stood and watched the puppy as Perdita nosed her way around the box-bordered lawn looking around for a place that pleased her. After a few minutes she came bounding back and, as soon as the front door closed again, went straight to the foot of the stairs and stood there expectantly. It was evident that she thought it was bedtime and that she did not wish to be left downstairs alone. The steps were steep and it was a struggle for her to get from one to another. She made two or three unsuccessful attempts and Margaret wondered whether or not she ought to help her, only to decide against it. She was not at all sure that she wanted the puppy upstairs and, if Perdita could not manage by herself, that would settle the question. But presently she wriggled her way to triumph and, when she reached the landing, turned to look back and waited to be praised. Margaret did not have the heart to take her down again. Since she had settled herself so comfortably beside the hearth in the living room, probably she would be equally contented on the corresponding rug in the bedroom. Margaret led her toward this, spoke to her encouragingly and, eventually, persuaded her to lie down. She did not seem to be as happy as she had been earlier, but perhaps this was because upstairs there was no fire; or perhaps she found it harder to adjust herself to strange surroundings now that Nicolas Hale was not there to introduce her to them.

Nicolas Hale! As Margaret lay tossing and turning in the huge ancestral four-poster which dominated her bedroom, she tried to stop thinking about him—only to find she could think of no one and nothing else. She had been surprised and pleased at his unexpected arrival, touched by his present of the puppy, gratified by his enjoyment of his tea and—yes, she might as well confess it to herself—spellbound by his fantastic suggestion. It was only when he pulled her to her feet with his ominous remark about unconditional surrender and began what he called preparations for this that she grasped an appalling fact: her failure to voice any offense at his crude approach and her ready acceptance of his bizarre proposal had led to outrageous behavior on his part. And by this time she could not even protest against it, much less defend herself, because his mouth had come down so hard on hers that she was silenced and he had locked her in an embrace so rigid that she could not move. And when he finally raised his head, but was still holding her fast, he had looked down at her with an expression she had never seen on a man's face before and therefore could not clearly identify, but which, because of its intensity, seemed to presage further violence. Then, quite abruptly, he had released her, saying, "No, I'm afraid that'd better be it for tonight, after all," and had gone so rapidly out of the house that she did not have a chance to answer.

Well, of course, by this time he had also realized that her acceptance of his proposal had been insane and his subsequent behavior inexcusable. He would send her a note in the morning and tell her so. He would say that, naturally, he had only been jesting and he knew that she had been, too. He would apologize because the jest had been in rather poor taste and what had happened afterward still more so. She had almost succeeded in persuading herself that this was the way things would be, when she remembered she herself had told Nicolas Hale at that New York wedding, to which she should never have gone, that she was sure any number of girls would be glad to marry him on his own terms. But when she said this, she had not meant they would be glad to marry him on five days' notice, when they hardly knew him at all; nor had she thought it necessary to add, she meant they would be glad to marry him after a suitable courtship, with exactly that gradual approach to love-making which he had described so graphically and then announced he had no intention of following. She had only meant a reasonable wife would not expect an explorer to take her along on his expeditions or resent being left in some comfortable place while he was gone. After all, the wives of naval officers were left for long periods—often two or three years at a time—when their husbands had sea duty. Explorers' wives could logically take it for granted their husbands' absences would be much briefer, especially in countries where the climate rendered exploration impracticable for months every year; why shouldn't they be able to manage quite contentedly? As far as Nicolas Hale's desire for a son was concerned, that was perfectly natural; he had not even needed to point out that most normal men wanted sons. And married women expected to have children, sooner or later. That was perfectly natural, too. But certainly Margaret had not meant to imply that any nice, refined girl would willingly be a mere means to an end, that she would consent to such an arrangement as Nicolas had outlined or even listen to it seriously. Besides, she had been talking in generalities. She had not been talking about *herself*.

Unfortunately, these reflections did not bring her as much comfort as she hoped. She had a queer feeling in the pit of her stomach that Nicolas Hale might be going by what she had *said* at the wedding, after drinking champagne, and not by what she now told herself she had *meant*. The queer feeling was increased by doubts as to whether or not a man of his caliber would be likely to jest over matters as important as marriage and further doubts as to whether or not he was apt to apologize for anything he said or did, even a failure to talk and act like a gentleman. Moreover, though she lacked experience with anything of the kind, she was reasonably sure a man did not embrace a woman the way Nicolas Hale had embraced her as part of a jest; it was unquestionably the sort of an embrace that went with love-making which was undertaken in earnest—in this case, with so-called honorable intentions. Nicolas Hale was not satisfied with affairs, obviously less because he had moral scruples about them—since he shamelessly admitted to several—than because you had to be careful that they did not have "visible results" and these were what he wanted. Therefore, his purpose was marriage. And he had thought there was actually a possibility that she, Margaret Porterfield, might marry him under almost unimaginable conditions, because she had never had a proposal before and might never have one again. And she had played straight into his hand and he had felt free to begin his violent love-making then and there, in preparation for unconditional surrender the next week. *Next week!* His last words, before he went out of the door, had been, "I'm afraid that'd better be it for tonight, after all." What did he mean to do the next day?

"Miss Marg'ret—Miss Marg'ret—wheah you at?"

Cassie was calling her. She had completely forgotten about Cassie, and now the old woman was lumbering up the stairs, looking for her. Perdita leaped up, barking.

"Lawssake, w'at you got in heah wid you?" Cassie inquired, as she opened the door. "Why, hit a dog, a mighty cute li'l dog. Ah ben thinkin' dis lon' while you oughtta have you a dog. Ah bet dat nice man brung hit to you fo' a present. Didn' you ask him would he like to stay to suppah? Ain' you got no mannahs no mo'? Don' you want no suppah yo'self? W'at you doin' lyin' heah in de dark?"

"No, I don't want any supper," Margaret answered truthfully. She had forgotten about supper. Then she realized that she was not answering questions in their proper order. "Yes, it's a dog," she said, quite superfluously, since Cassie had not only discovered this and commented on it, but was already stroking the puppy with a fond hand. "And Mr. Hale did bring her to me. Her name's Perdita. No, I didn't ask him to stay to supper. But I don't believe he wanted to, anyway."

"How you know w'at he want, iffen you don' give him no chance to tell you?"

That's not his trouble, Margaret said to herself; he tells what he wants in no uncertain terms. Aloud, she said defensively, "I gave him a good tea. That was enough."

"Shucks, 'co'se hit weren't 'nuff. Mens wants more'n tea." (Well, that was true enough, too, Margaret thought, still communing with herself.) "Nex' time he come, you give him chicken an' all de fixin's, you heah? Mebbe iffen you feed him real good, hit would put de idee in his head he might come co'tin'. Time somebody did, Miss Marg'ret. Time you got yo'self a man. I done had ten head o' chillen when I wuz yo' age, six o' dem wid de same pappy."

"I don't believe Mr. Hale's likely to return. I hope not. I don't want anyone to come courting."

"Miss Marg'ret, mebbe you thinks you doesn't, but you's wrong. Hits nature fo' young ladies to like young gennelmun to come co'tin'. You fin' dat out some day an' I hope hit won't be too late fo' you. 'Pears to me de gennelmun wuz heah dis afternoon might just fill de bill. . . . W'at you say you wants for yo' suppah?"

"I said I didn't want anything for supper."

"Mebbe you ti'ed, mebbe dat gennelmun wo' you down, cuz you ain' used to gennelmun's ways. But you lissen heah, you bettah get

used to dem befo' you an outen-out ol' maid. I don' want to say
nuthin' to hurt yo' feelin's, but you headed dat way, honey, sure's
shootin'. Nex' time dat gennelmun come callin', you keep him to
suppah. Ah'd be proud to see a co'tin couple in dis ol' house again. An'
a baby in dat cradle you keeps in de hall, full o' ol' magazines. 'Pears
like you don' rightly know w'at a cradle's fo'.''

The chicken broth, thick with rice, the hot biscuits dripping with
butter and spread with ham, the tipsy pudding decorated with candied
cherries were all so appetizing that, when Cassie brought the tray,
Margaret ate some supper after all. Perdita had not been forgotten,
either. There was a bone for her, not a chicken bone, Cassie knew better
than that; a beef bone salvaged from the soup kettle. When she came
back to remove the tray and the oiled paper with which she had
protected the hearth, both the recipients of her bounty were drowsy
and soon they were sound asleep.

Margaret did not wake again until the jangling of the telephone at
her bedside roused her to unwilling consciousness. She would not have
felt justified in spending the money for an extension, but prudence had
prevailed to the point of having the one instrument in the house where
she could reach it during the night. Now she stretched out her hand
toward it only after insistent ringing had convinced her that whoever
was at the other end of the line intended to stay there until she
answered.

"Hello, yourself," a voice said cheerfully and briskly in response to
her half-hearted greeting. "Have I roused you too early? You don't
sound very wide-awake. But I thought perhaps I'd better remind you
to call that uncle of yours in Charlottesville. I could have saved you the
trouble if I'd known whether he was a Porterfield uncle or a Page uncle
and, anyway, I thought he ought to get the news from you first. I was
afraid you might forget this is Friday and that he can't get the announcement in the Sunday papers unless the society editors have it
before noon."

"The announcement! What announcement?"

"Why, the announcement of our engagement! If he's the nearest
relative you have left, of course he's the proper person to give out the
statement, 'Dr. Homer Porterfield, or whatever his name is, announces
the engagement and forthcoming marriage of his niece, Miss Margaret
Porterfield, to Dr. Nicolas Hale and so forth and so forth.' I suppose we
have to use the doctor this time, in view of the different degrees that
will be mentioned in the etcetera. I take it for granted that this uncle
will also be the one to give you away, so perhaps you'd better ask him if
Wednesday's all right for him and if he prefers morning to afternoon
or vice versa. If he's all tied up on Wednesday, we might make it Tues-

day or Thursday instead. Call me back at the Cosmos Club, will you, as soon as you've heard from him? I thought I'd go to City Hall in Alexandria on my way out to Hills' End and find out about the license —then we could go to see your family physician and your padre this afternoon. In that way, we'd get all those details out of the way before night. I'm sorry I can't spend the evening with you, but I accepted an invitation to a State Dinner at the White House three weeks ago. I'm tied up tomorrow evening, too—the Peruvian Embassy. But now that my equipment's on the way, I've got quite a little time to myself during the day and I thought maybe you'd invite me to lunch. I'll bring a nice thick juicy steak with me and any fresh vegetables I happen to see in the market where I buy that. Cassie can manage all right for the rest of the trimmings, can't she?"

There had not been a single moment at which it was possible to interrupt and now that he had paused and was waiting for an answer, Margaret was as speechless from shock as she had been the night before. It did not seem to have occurred to Nicolas Hale that this was what had happened. He spoke again, still cheerfully and briskly.

"What's the matter? Has the line suddenly gone dead or something? It seemed to be all right."

"There's nothing the matter with the line. But Dr. Hale—"

"I told you in New York I never used the doctor if I could help it. I've just admitted that the announcement of the engagement is one time I can't and I suppose the wedding announcements will have to be engraved with it. By the way, I'll bring out a list so we can work on that together. Of course, we'll just have to telephone the people we ask to the wedding. But to get back to this name business: don't you really think, after what happened last night, and what's going to happen next week, you'd better start calling me Nicolas?"

"I think we'd better have another talk together before I start doing anything else."

"Not before you telephone your uncle? I've reminded you that—"

"Yes, I know. But I'm not sure I want to telephone my uncle."

This time, the pause was at the other end, but it was brief and when Nicolas Hale spoke again, his voice was no longer cheery and brisk. It was hard.

"You're not trying to tell me you're a quitter, are you, Margaret?"

"Oh, Nicolas, I can't explain over the telephone, but—"

"At least you've got as far as calling me by my Christian name again. That's something. Just the same, it sounds to me as if you were trying to welsh. I never would have believed any Porterfield would do that and I'm not going to let you do it. You'd better get up, and fast, because I'm coming right out. And I know the way, this time."

"Oh, Nicolas," she said again. But he had already hung up. After a search, she found the number of the Cosmos Club, went through as many exchanges as if Washington were as far away as San Francisco, finally got the Club and was told Dr. Hale's line was busy. She waited five minutes, called him again and was informed by the switchboard operator that Dr. Hale had gone to Virginia and was not expected back until seven that evening. His secretary was out, too, but she, the operator, would be glad to take a message. Margaret said there was none, wondering why her voice sounded so unnatural.

If she had dared, she would have called Cassie and told her that Dr. Hale—Mr. Hale—was coming again after all, but that she did not want to see him; Cassie was to stay by the front door and tell him that and she herself would stay in her bedroom. But she did not dare. In the first place, she did not trust Cassie to follow instructions, after what the old servant had said the night before. It would be just like her to yield to a little wheedling and, though she was essentially honest, she was probably not altogether immune to subtle bribery. Besides, even if Cassie proved trustworthy, Nicolas Hale might not. He might brush by her and, failing to find Margaret anywhere downstairs, come straight up to her bedroom. Somehow, she would not put that past him.

It was just as well she did not. She skipped a real bath, merely "washing off" and mingling a little cologne with the water in the basin. Then she wound up her long hair in the quickest way, which left it still somewhat disheveled, though less unattractively so than she imagined. But a strap broke on her slip and she had so much trouble with a zipper that it seemed as if even inanimate things were conspiring against her, and there was a little puddle on the hearth which she had to wipe up, feeling, as she did so, less enthusiastic about the gift of a puppy than she had the night before, though she recognized that the puddle was partly her fault—she should have taken Perdita out the first thing in the morning. She had barely got into her clothes when she heard a car coming up the driveway, with no hesitation this time; as he said, Nicolas Hale knew the way now, but even so Margaret would never have believed that anyone could get to Hills' End as fast as he had. She had only just started down the stairs, with Perdita again barking joyfully at her heels, when the front door, which she had forgotten to lock the night before, was opened and shut with unnecessary force. By the time she neared the ground floor, Nicolas was already standing beside the newel post and, when she stopped, blushing and looking down at him without speaking, he put one foot on the lowest stair.

"Good morning again," he said in the same hard voice that had marked his final observations over the telephone. "You seem to be a little doubtful as to how you should greet me."

"I am."

"Well, I'm not—not in the least. You come all the way down and then you kiss me of your own accord. That's standard practice for a newly betrothed maiden, the morning after she's promised to marry the man of her choice. And then he kisses her. That's standard practice, too."

"But you see, I think I ought to tell you—"

"You ought not to do anything of the sort. If you mean you're getting ready to tell me that you're not going to marry me after all, I think I ought to tell *you* that I've overcome my aversion to telephones to the extent of calling your uncle. The Charlottesville Information was most helpful. I asked her if there wasn't a Dr. Homer Porterfield at the University and she said no, but there was a Dr. Virginius Page whose sister had married a Porterfield. I got him right away and he couldn't possibly have been more cordial to me—in fact, he seemed to be very much pleased at my news and not in the least disturbed because I was doing the telephoning for you when I explained that your line was out of order. It seems that I met him, several years ago, on the occasion of a lecture that I gave at the Alderman Memorial Library and that I made a favorable impression on him then. He said he'd get in touch with all the papers right away—New York, Washington, Richmond; I believe some others besides and, of course, Charlottesville. Also, he said Wednesday was perfectly convenient for him, at any time of day, so I thought the Town Clerk's office could wait until afternoon I didn't want to lose any more time than was necessary, getting here. And now that I am here, I don't want to lose any more time, standing in this cold hall, waiting for you to kiss me."

"I'm not going to kiss you. I'm going straight upstairs to telephone my uncle and say that it's all a terrible mistake, that I—"

"You won't be able to get him on the telephone. He's using the line to call up those newspapers. Besides, it isn't all a terrible mistake, only part of it, and you're the one that's making that." There was anger in his voice now, as well as hardness. "I wish you'd stop standing on that stair trying to act like a spitfire. It isn't in character and it doesn't become you. I also wish you'd come and give me a kiss of your own accord. Of course, I can't make you. But if you don't, I'll reverse the proper order of things for the morning after and kiss you first, the way I did last night. Only I won't promise that, this time, I'll stop quite so soon. I didn't want to then. I'll want to still less if, besides my natural pleasure at holding a very attractive girl in my arms, my equally natural instinct for getting even with a girl who's tried to cheat has been aroused."

"Oh, Nicolas—please, please don't talk to me like that. I can't stand it!"

He considered her gravely. There was no doubt that her distress was real, for she was very close to tears. When he next spoke, to her great relief, the hardness and the anger were gone from his voice. But she would have been happier if the tone of admiration which had so thrilled her the night before had not been gone, too.

"I see you can't," he said eventually. "Well, I'm sorry. To borrow one of your own regional expressions again, I can see it doesn't do any good to rush my fences. I honestly thought I could—that it would be the best way for both of us, in the end. But come on down, Margaret, and talk things over with me. You're willing to do that, anyhow, aren't you, if we skip the kisses? I want to be sure I'm getting this straight. This time I want to be sure that *I* understand."

5 ❧

Two hours later, he repeated the final words that he had spoken in the cold hall. Meanwhile, he had not touched Margaret, except to hold out his hand as she came the rest of the way down the stairs, and the gesture was so obviously one of mere helpfulness and reassurance, that she was able to accept it as such after only a momentary hesitation. When she reached the bottom, Nicolas asked her if she had had any breakfast; and when she said she had not, he insisted on going out to the kitchen with her and telling Cassie he did not know what she would do to him, getting the Boss Lady up to see company so early that she hadn't even had a cup of coffee, and couldn't they have hot cakes and sirup and sausage, as well as coffee now, to make up for his bad behavior? It was so long since he had had his own breakfast that he was all ready for another; in fact, he was practically starved. He'd meant to bring some steak with him, but he'd been in such a hurry that he'd clean forgot. However, he'd be going to Alexandria by-and-by and he'd get it then. . . .

When he left the kitchen Cassie was beaming with delight as she rattled her pots and pans preparatory to getting a breakfast fit for a king and, presently, she began to sing, "Bend de hills an' come down, Lawd." Nicolas next insisted on going down to the cellar to shake the furnace and stoke it; clearly, it needed attention. When he came upstairs again, he brought a big armful of wood for the library fire, which needed attention, too. Perdita was the next object of his ministrations. She must have a real run right after breakfast and it would do Margaret and himself good to walk around the place at the same time, for it was a beautiful day. But meanwhile, he would take the puppy out on the lawn, while Margaret set the table in the gun room, where he lighted a second fire. She'd like to go back upstairs and really do her hair, she told him, and he said he wished she wouldn't; she had such beautiful hair, and he'd been thinking how lovely it looked, the way it was. But, of course, if she'd feel more comfortable with all those charming little tendrils tucked into a net or something, go ahead, he'd look after Perdita. So when they sat down in front of the gun room fire she was as neat as a pin and managed to make a show of eating a fairly good breakfast, while he ate a huge one. Then he said Perdita didn't need to go out again just yet because he *had* given her a real run while Margaret was fancying up and they could put off their walk until afternoon. But the fire in the library looked wonderful now and couldn't they go and sit beside it and have their talk. And it was then he repeated he wasn't sure he understood, that he wanted to get things straight.

"You did tell me you thought I'd be justified in asking a girl to marry me, didn't you?"

"Yes, I did, but—"

"You said if she could have a comfortable place to stay while I was gone, she shouldn't mind being left behind when I went on an expedition, didn't you?"

"Yes, I did, but—"

"And you do think this is a comfortable place, don't you? In fact, isn't it a place you love very much?"

"Yes, I do. Yes, it is. But—"

"And you did say it was natural for me to want a son? Right? And you *didn't* say that you thought it was unnatural for me to dislike the idea of a conventional marriage. If you thought so, why didn't you say so right away?"

"Because I didn't think so. But all that time I thought we were talking in generalities. I didn't think we were discussing any specific case."

"Not at first. But afterward, you knew we were. You knew I wanted to marry you. You knew I wanted you to be the mother of my son. I told you so very plainly. I told you all the reasons. And they were reasons that ought to make you pleased and proud. I thought you were pleased and proud."

"Yes, I was. I—I am, but—"

"I wish you'd stop saying but. You didn't even balk when I talked about five days. You led me to believe that wasn't an insuperable obstacle. And I admired you very much for the way you took that—the way you took everything. And now it seems that, as soon as I left you—".

"No, that wasn't when it began."

"When *what* began?"

"When the five days began to seem such an awfully short time for a courtship. That began when you said you thought you'd better start your serious love-making then and there because, otherwise—"

"Otherwise, you wouldn't be prepared, within a week, for complete surrender."

"Yes, that's exactly what you said. And you left me without saying *anything* more, except that perhaps, after all, that'd better be it for now—as if you'd thought of something else."

"I had thought of something else. Not that you minded being kissed. That hadn't occurred to me. But since I'd enjoyed doing it so much more than I expected, I thought I'd get even more enjoyment if I went beyond kissing. It would have been the easiest thing in the world. I know that I'd have shocked you, to say the least, if I'd put you down on the sofa and gone on from there. Perhaps it would have been better that way. At least, it would have saved a lot of needless talk."

She looked at him in speechless horror, instinctively drawing away from him as far as she could. He was so angry by that time that he neither noticed nor cared.

"However, second thought, even though it wasn't very sober second thought at the moment, convinced me I wouldn't get any lasting satisfaction out of it. I'd have been tormented afterward by the realization that I'd hurt you terribly, in every sense of the word. And whether you believe it or not, that's the last thing I want to do. I really want to make your complete surrender as easy for you as I can. I don't see why it should be too hard—with preparation. You're a normal woman, even if you're a repressed woman, you can learn to respond to passion, if you have a chance. You haven't had one before. I'm trying to give you one."

"You mean by doing what you did last night?" Somehow, she had managed to speak at last, though she did so in a trembling voice.

"Yes, that's exactly what I mean. I don't deny that I got a lot of satisfaction out of it myself—rather too much, as I've admitted. But I wasn't deliberately offensive. I'm sorry you seem to think I was. If you can't stand having me act like a lover, I don't see how you're going to stand having me act like a husband. And we're getting married five days from now. Unless you go back on your word. Is that what you're trying to do? Have you discovered that I'm not a hero after all, just a man with a beast in him? Doesn't it mean anything to you that, after all these years when I've refused to marry, I want very much to marry you?"

"Oh, Nicolas, I don't know how to explain! Of course, you're a hero to me, you always have been, you always will be. It means—it means everything to me that you want to marry me. I suppose all men have beasts in them, don't they? Perhaps the trouble really is that you *are* rushing your fences. Everything is so new and strange to me. You say such dreadful things. If you could stop talking so crudely, if you could give me a little more time—"

"I can try to stop talking so crudely. I'm making a genuine effort to be straightforward and sometimes it's hard to be straightforward and sound refined simultaneously. And I'm sorry, but there isn't any more time. I've explained all that to you before. I'm not going through it again. You'll have to marry me next Wednesday or never. And if you marry me, you'll have to expect me to act like a husband. Don't let's have any mistake about that."

"No," she said, still speaking in a voice that was not quite steady. "My mother didn't talk to me much about such things. But she did tell me that women had to submit to their husbands. She didn't explain. She made it seem mysterious and menacing. But if I marry you, I won't try to prevent you from acting like a husband."

She heard Nicolas say something under his breath that sounded as if he were still angry, but his next words were partially reassuring; at least, his anger did not seem to be directed at her any more.

"And I suppose she also told you that a virtuous girl didn't permit any liberties before marriage," he said explosively.

"Yes, of course," she said again.

For the first time that morning he laughed and, with his laugh, the tension between them suddenly slackened. "If you'll permit me to say so, I don't think much of your mother's technique, but mine may not have been much of an improvement. Let's try again along different lines. I'd like to make a bargain with you. When you stop saying, 'If I marry you next Wednesday,' and start saying, 'Of course, I'm going to marry you next Wednesday and I expect you to act like a husband,' I'll promise not to take any liberties until then. Those seem to be the main problems right now and we'll meet the others as they arise. Meanwhile, I'll just kiss you in a brotherly sort of way on arrival and departure, say, and stop if you ask me to—I won't hold you so tight you can't get away if you want to. And I'd like you to kiss me in a sisterly sort of way, as I thought you would when I arrived. I was really very disappointed because you didn't. So suppose you do it now, instead, after you've made me that promise. Then I'll take over from there and I don't think we'll have any more trouble."

There was no more trouble. She did not answer immediately, but Nicolas waited for her to do so, without any visible sign of impatience and, after a minute or two, she said, now speaking steadily, "I'll marry you next Wednesday and I'll expect you to act like a husband." Then she leaned over and kissed him on the cheek. She had not realized how that would feel, because before she had been conscious only of his mouth, and she was agreeably surprised at the firm, cool texture of his skin, even at the slight roughness that resisted a close shave and at the impression that everything about him was very clean and healthy. When she withdrew her lips, he smiled at her and said, "That was very nice. But perhaps next time you could make it last a little longer." Next he kissed *her* cheek and told her it was very soft, but that he would like to see a little more color in it. And when the color came, very quickly, he laughed and said, "There, you see how easy I am to please! Come on, let's not wait until afternoon to go and see your padre. Let's do it just as soon as we've consulted the family physician and found out about the license and bought the steak. Then we can have the whole afternoon to talk over those details I mentioned before. Except for the one about where we're going to be married. I suppose we have to decide that before we go to see a padre."

"Well, if we only had more time—" Margaret began.

"We *haven't* any more time. I can't seem to impress that on you. What difference does it make, as far as the church is concerned?"

"It really makes a good deal," she said with some spirit. "If we were going to have a big wedding, with lots of guests and several brides-maids, I'd want to be married at Christ Church in Alexandria. I have a great deal of sentiment about it and, besides, the most beautiful wedding I ever went to was performed there, by candlelight. But it would seem bare and empty with just a handful of people. So I think Pohick would be better."

"I shouldn't be surprised if we had more than a handful of people, even on such short notice. But let's make it Pohick by all means if you think that would be better. We could have candlelight there, too, couldn't we? And it was Washington's church just as much as the other, if that's what you mean by sentiment. Though I suppose Sally Cary went in Alexandria."

"You don't believe that slanderous story, do you, Nicolas?"

"Of course, I believe it. I've seen the original of the letter Washington wrote her just before he died—'The happiest hours of my life are those I have spent with you'—or words to that effect. Personally, I'm very glad to know that he was human, that he didn't just marry rich Widow Custis for her money and make do with that for romance all his life. But don't let's get started on another argument. Let's be on our way. I assume you can direct me to Dr. Loomis' office and City Hall, and afterward to a good market."

He chatted pleasantly, of inconsequential things, until they reached Alexandria. Dr. Loomis, the family physician, who bore an almost uncanny likeness to the mental picture Nicolas had formed of him, received them with paternal kindness, made light work of the tests and said he would have the results ready for Dr. Hale to take to City Hall the next day; there was really no need for him to go there in the meantime, as Virginia did not require a waiting period after the license was issued before the wedding could take place. He was delighted to know the ceremony would be performed at Pohick. He hoped he and Mrs. Loomis would be privileged to attend. As for a market, he would recommend Chauncey's.

Mr. Bates, the rector of Pohick Church, greeted them with equal cordiality. Of course, he would be delighted to officiate. He was rather tied up the earlier part of the day on Wednesday, but five or any time after that. . . .

Nicolas looked at Margaret inquiringly. "You spoke about candlelight. You'd want it as late as that anyway, wouldn't you? And it would give you that much more time to get ready."

"Yes, I did. Yes, it would. But *you* spoke about a wedding breakfast. Would you be disappointed if we made it a wedding supper instead? Perhaps we could have it in the gun room, like those parties you said you used to enjoy so much."

"I think that's a grand idea! Eight o'clock then, Wednesday, Mr. Bates, for the ceremony? Rehearsal the night before—or don't we need one? We're keeping this all very simple."

"I understand. But I think it's always better, and no matter how simple you try to keep it, this is bound to be a very important occasion. You'll want everything to go like clockwork and so will I. Please let me tell you, Dr. Hale, that I feel very much honored because my church has been chosen for this wedding. We don't often have such a celebrity as yourself there—of course there aren't many such celebrities. And I've known Margaret all her life—in fact, I christened her. And she's been one of my best workers for years. I don't know what I'll do without her —she's one of the mainstays of our Ann Mason Guild."

"But you won't have to do without her—she's staying on at Hills' End and I expect you to keep a kindly clerical eye on her while I'm in Peru." Then, noticing the clergyman's bewildered expression, Nicolas went on easily, "We suddenly decided to be married before I leave, instead of after my return, just as so many members of the armed forces and their fiancées decided during the war. In a way, the situation's somewhat the same: my assistant and my equipment are already on their way and my leave from my own theater of operations is almost up. I'm required by my sponsors to work on a pretty tight schedule."

"Yes, yes, I understand," the clergyman said, almost as if he were apologizing because he really did not. "The penalties of success and fame. Well, Margaret will miss you very much, of course, but she'll be busy, as usual, with her good works. She's really a pillar of my church, one of the strongest. I don't know what we'd have done without her when the Guild gave its supper for one hundred guests of the Alexandria Association Forum."

"What in hell is the Alexandria Association Forum?" Nicolas inquired as he and Margaret left the rectory after promising to get in touch with the clergyman about decorations and other final details.

"It's a group devoted to cultural eighteenth-century life along the Potomac," Margaret said proudly. "The dishes for that dinner were taken from Caroline Marsur's *Virginia Hostess*; Ann Mason, the mistress of Gunston Hall, might have chosen the very same menu; punch for chambermaids, nun's beads, beef olives, chocolate wine, and all the rest of it."

"Sounds ghastly to me," Nicolas said irreverently. "Anyway, I hope you'll be busy with much more important things than Guild suppers pretty soon. But I didn't want to hurt the old boy's feelings by saying so. He's a good sort . . . We've done all the necessary errands now, haven't we? Of course, we did have a big breakfast and a late one, but I'm beginning to think tenderly of that steak we bought and which I hope is as tender as my thoughts of it."

"Are you really very hungry?"

"Well, healthily so, but if there is something else you think we ought to do before lunch—"

"It isn't actually a case of ought, but I thought perhaps you would like to see the church. I mean, if you know beforehand what to expect, instead of just walking into it for the first time, the night of rehearsal, it might help to simplify arrangements, to be sure they please you. It's open all the time, so we can be sure of getting in and it won't take us much out of our way to go there."

"Even if it did, you're absolutely right, we should go. It would simplify things later on; and, incidentally, I'm very touched that you want me to be pleased with arrangements. I believe most brides consider that their prerogative. I'm becoming more convinced every minute that I chose the right girl. Do we go straight down the road from here or what?"

"Straight back up the road for about two minutes and we'll come to a brick wall on our right. We passed it coming down, but perhaps you didn't notice it then. It has a big wrought-iron gate that we go through," and, as Nicolas followed directions, looking about him with obvious appreciation of the attractive landscaping and the simple four-square building of mellow brick, flanked with flourishing boxwood and framed with tall trees, she went on, shyly, "I don't know how familiar you are with the early churches in Virginia. This is typical of the way most of them were planned and built—plain and solid outside, but quite beautiful inside. At least, I think so."

"I believe I shall, too."

If she had needed further reassurance on that score, she would have had it from the expression on his face. They paused on the threshold of a side door which stood open, revealing a high canopied pulpit with a baptismal font of rough-hewn stone in the foreground. Nicolas gave a spontaneous expression of admiration even before his quick roving glance had taken in the box pews, the altarpiece done in wainscoting and the general effect of symmetry and gleaming whiteness.

"I'll say it's beautiful! It's more than beautiful!" he agreed enthusiastically. "At least, there *ought* to be some stronger word to describe it, even if there isn't. And I'd have said it was unique if you hadn't used the word typical. We'll have to take a trip sometime and have a look at all the others—if this is a reliable sample, they'd be worth a special expedition!"

"I'd love to take a trip like that with you," she said. There was no shyness in her voice now, only a great gladness that he had understood, that beauty could be revealed to them by the same means. Then, a little more hesitantly, she went on, "Do you know what I've always thought? That the people who built these churches hated the biblical expression of a 'whited sepulchre' and wanted to reveal the exact opposite in their houses of worship: not outer magnificence and inner corruption, but tabernacles that seemed almost severely plain when you first looked at them, but were 'all glorious within.' "

"I believe you're right about that, too. I was actually dazzled at first, but now I'm beginning to recover and I'd like to walk around and take in these various glories one at a time. We should begin at the altar, shouldn't we? I'm not even a very good Christian, much less a good Episcopalian, but I seem to have a feeling that's the proper place."

"It is the proper place to start. Besides, you're a historian, aren't you? You wouldn't be an explorer if you weren't. So you might be interested in knowing that the display of the Creed, the Lord's Prayer and the Ten Commandments was required by an Article in the standard prayer book of the colonial period. And George Washington was requested to import a cushion for the pulpit and cloths for the communion table and the desks, made of crimson velvet with gold fringe, and folio prayer books bound in red leather and stamped in gold with the name of the parish."

"And did he actually do it?"

"Of course. He was tremendously interested in the church from the beginning. He drew the plans for it and was a vestryman for more than twenty years. That was his pew over there—Number 28. Wouldn't you like to go and sit down in it for a few minutes?"

"Yes, if you would; but I have to confess that I'm more impressed with the 'glories' of this church than with its statistics. I'm not as much of a historian as you imagine . . . no, I'll take that back—what's this name on pew 21? As I live and breathe, Honorable George William Fairfax of Belvoir! So I suppose he was a vestryman, too! And that the incomparable Sally did come here to worship and be worshiped—quite as often as in Alexandria!"

"Oh, Nicolas, please, please don't spoil everything by bringing up that scandalous story again."

The gladness was all gone from her voice and her lips were actually trembling again. Nicolas looked at her gravely.

"I didn't mean to," he said quite sincerely. "I see we still don't understand each other as well as we should—and I was just flattering myself that we'd made quite a lot of progress this morning. Keep your image of a plaster saint instead of a real man if you want to—I mean when you're thinking about Washington. But don't make a similar mistake about me. Come on, we'd better get back to Hills' End and eat that steak."

6

She turned without answering and walked so fast toward the door that he did not overtake her until she had reached the threshold. Then he grasped her arm and pulled her back—not roughly, but with sufficient firmness to keep her from escaping.

"Look here, we're acting like a couple of spoiled children, instead of two reasonably intelligent adults. The real reason we came here this morning, unless I'm mistaken, wasn't to teach or learn history and quarrel over it or even to admire a place that is, as you said, 'all glorious within.' It was to map out a plan of action for our wedding—where you'd enter with your bridesmaids, which aisle you'd come up with them, where I'd enter with my best man to wait for you, which aisle you and I would go down together—that sort of thing. Wasn't it? Come on, let's go back and settle all that. I saw as we came in that there's a very nice Vestry House—that should represent a great convenience for an occasion like this. Hadn't we better go over there, too?"

Again she did not answer and when she turned, it was obvious that she did so reluctantly. But she did not refuse. As Nicolas chatted on, making practical suggestions with no trace of remaining anger in his voice or manner, she gradually unbent. By the time they had completed their rounds, she had begun to make suggestions too, and her voice and manner were almost as natural as his. After helping her into the car, he nonchalantly changed the subject.

"Incidentally, I like your idea of a wedding supper, instead of a wedding breakfast, very much, not only because it will recall many other pleasant parties in the same setting, but because that seems singularly appropriate for this one. After all, it is a shotgun wedding, isn't it, with the usual order of things in reverse! But won't that arrangement make us pretty late in getting away?"

"Getting away?"

"Is this something else that's got to be spelled out in words of one syllable? Starting-on-our-wedding-trip."

"Oh, I'd honestly forgotten about a wedding trip. Do we have to take one? Couldn't we just stay at Hills' End?"

He looked at her curiously. "We could, of course. It just hadn't occurred to me. I've always understood wedding trips loomed very large in a girl's mind. But it isn't such a bad idea at that. Is it what you'd rather do?"

"Yes, I'd much rather. I've always thought it would be embarrassing, going to a strange hotel and feeling that people were looking at you strangely and then—"

"And getting very self-conscious as the bellboy arranged the baggage in a stiff impersonal room and fearing he realized, when he went out, that you'd never been left alone at night with a man before?"

The color which made her look so lovely flooded her face.

"Yes," she admitted shyly. "I wouldn't have said it, but that is what I meant."

"Blushing is very becoming to you, Margaret. I think perhaps I'd better keep on saying the things you won't, even if I did promise to watch my language. . . . Well then, let's stay at Hills' End by all means. It isn't as if we had more time. You'll be busy with preparations all of Wednesday, so that doesn't really count as a day—just as a night. That leaves us only Thursday, Friday, Saturday, Sunday and Monday for day and night. My plane leaves at noon Tuesday, so I have to go over to New York some time the day before. But why don't you come over with me? The Plaza ought not to seem like a really strange hotel to you—after all, you were there only a few weeks ago and a mighty good thing you were, too."

"Why, Nicolas, I didn't *stay* at the Plaza! I only went there for the wedding. I stayed at a little hotel you probably never heard of. I couldn't possibly afford to stay at the Plaza."

"You mean you couldn't then. But you can now. Which reminds me, we haven't discussed finances at all. Is that another thing you haven't thought of—whether or not I can afford to support you properly?"

"No—I mean, yes—which is it? I do mean I hadn't thought of it at all."

"Perhaps you need lessons in practical economics, as well as love-making—never mind—suppose we discuss finances, for a change, now that we're on our way back to Hills' End. We can afford to stay at the Plaza, if not indefinitely—that might be something of a strain—at least for one night. We can even afford to have a suite, which impresses bellboys and therefore improves their attitude—but there are a few other items, involving expense, that I'd like to discuss. For instance, you ought to have your heating system changed. I don't like to think of having you shovel coal all winter."

"I don't mind. I've done it a good many winters."

"Too many, I'd say. I don't want you to do it any more. In fact, I won't let you do it any more. Heaving coal isn't the best form of exercise for ladies in what I suppose you'd like me to call a delicate condition—that is, if I'm indelicate enough to refer to it at all, which I am. And when you get your new oil furnace, you'll get a thermostat with it. I want you to keep it turned up high enough, so that the whole house will be warm—not just the library in front of an open fire. My teeth start chattering every time I have to stay in that cold hall for more than a couple of minutes."

"But, Nicolas, coal is so expensive that I—"

"There won't be any coal in use much longer and I'll be paying for the oil—among other things. I'll get in touch with a good plumber right away. I don't suppose there's time to make the installation before the wedding and, of course, we don't want anyone tearing things up while we're on our honeymoon. But I'll arrange to have the work done week after next. You'd better stay over in New York for a few days after I leave—see Esther again, go to some good plays, do a little shopping. That's another thing I've meant to talk to you about. Isn't it time you got out of mourning? I thought tomorrow, instead of staying out in Virginia all day, I might take you in town. We could have lunch at the Cosmos Club and then we could walk over to Connecticut Avenue together and look in the windows. If you saw anything you liked, you could go inside and buy it. I could go in with you, or I could stroll along trying to make a few discoveries myself, just as you preferred. I never could understand why American men didn't adopt the Continental custom of helping the ladies who belong to them choose their clothes. Very good results can be secured that way. On the other hand, if it would bother you to have me around while you're making selections, I'd enjoy doing some exploring on my own. Considering my profession, it ought to be even more in character for me than it was for Calvin Coolidge, oughtn't it? And that's what he used to do."

"But, Nicolas, I couldn't possibly let you pay for my clothes! I don't —belong to you yet."

"You will, when you get to New York. You can do most of your shopping there. Esther can take you to all the right places. But you've got to have something to wear in the meantime. Surely, you don't expect to be married in what you have on—or something similar?"

"No, I don't and I'd thought of that already. The brides in my family have always kept their wedding dresses and I wore one of them in a Pageant of Brides we gave in Alexandria a few years ago. It was my great-great-grandmother's. She was married just before the War Between the States and there was plenty of money in the family then for the most expensive brocades and laces. And the fashions were very flattering."

"Hoops and tight bodices, but bare shoulders? That was the period for those, wasn't it? Yes, I should think those might be very becoming to you and quite in keeping with your candlelighted church and the wedding supper in the gun room. Could we have a dress rehearsal?"

"It's supposed to be bad luck, Nicolas, for a groom to see his bride in her wedding dress, beforehand. So perhaps I ought to tell you that wedding dresses were nearly always highnecked—my great-great-grandmother's was, though everything else in the trousseau was off the shoulders. But it has the hoops and the tight bodice and the materials are beautiful."

"Well, I'll take your word for it that your great-great-grandmother's wedding dress is the right thing for you. But if you're going to New York with me—"

"Yes, and if I'm going to lunch with you at the Cosmos Club . . . I realize what I have on is all wrong, but I don't want you to buy anything for me—yet. I have a little money put by that I was saving for coal. I can use that to buy what I need straight away. I promise you I'll look all right. I really do know about clothes. It's just that I lost interest because it didn't matter to anyone how I looked any more."

He gazed at her thoughtfully. "And now you realize it does matter to someone. Well, that's another step in the right direction—if that's what you want to do, I'll let you have your own way on that point. Now let's get on to a few others. You'll need extra help in the house for the wedding and you really ought to have more of a staff right along than one old colored woman. Cassie must have any number of children and grandchildren and nephews and nieces. Let's tell her, as soon as we get back to the house, that we're going to be married and ask her if there isn't some nice young colored couple we could press into service right away, on a permanent basis, besides all the additional kinfolk that would probably be tickled to death to come on Wednesday."

"Oh, we'll have the kinfolk for the wedding! But I don't need anyone on a permanent basis—at least, not a couple. Perhaps a young girl I could teach about 'clean corners' and a few other things—if you're very sure you can afford it."

"I'm very sure I can afford a *couple*. You need at least one man on the place right along, more later on. You can't do much with the land until spring, but that'll be here soon. 'If winter comes, etcetera.' Meanwhile, from what you told me in New York, there must be a lot of clearing up to be done, I can tell better just how much after we've had our walk. I shan't buy you a horse right away, because of course I don't want you riding this winter. But next year you'll need a mount again, and then we'll have to begin looking around for a pony. You'll be riding all over the place with our son, just the way you used to ride with your father."

They were turning in at the driveway as he said this, and suddenly she seemed to see two riders cantering forward to meet them, a slim little girl with quantities of fine hair blowing around her face, who waved her crop in welcome, and a tall bearded man who sat very straight in his saddle and did not relax his hold on his reins. The vision was so vivid that she caught her breath and sat staring straight ahead of her until Nicolas brought the car to a stop and took her hand.

"I'll continue my discussion of finances this afternoon," he said. "Just one more thing right now, before I forget it. Let me measure your finger. I want to be sure the ring I bring when I come out tomorrow morning is going to fit you."

7

As they entered the house, they could hear the telephone ringing, and Margaret dashed up the stairs to answer it. Then she came dashing down again.

"That was Betty Beale, the Society Columnist of the *Washington Star*," she said breathlessly. "It seems that paper has a rule that news of an engagement must be confirmed in writing by the girl herself or a member of her family, so I've told her I'd send her a note today."

"Good!" Nicolas looked up from the small notebook in which he was scribbling a memorandum. "This is just to remind me to get in touch with the telephone company and ask them to install an extension in the library, right away. I imagine the telephone will keep on ringing, pretty steadily, the next few days, and you'll get all tired out, racing over the stairs. Besides, some of the calls may very well be for me and I suppose you'd rather I took them here than in your bedroom."

"But, Nicolas, it'll be days—perhaps weeks—before you can get an extension put in!"

"Want to bet on it? May I go up to your room, this one time—before Wednesday?"

"Certainly. I'll go with you and show you which it is. It connects with another smaller room that used to be Mother's boudoir and that I thought you might like for yours."

"Thanks very much. But I don't expect to have much use for a boudoir."

"Of course, you won't. I didn't mean for a *boudoir*. I meant for a—a dressing room."

"Well, I'll have a look at it and give you my verdict, as soon as I have this matter of the telephone straightened out."

She listened with admiration mixed with awe as he talked to the unseen functionary at the telephone office: this is Dr. Nicolas Hale of Yale University speaking. Yes, the explorer. Really? Well, it was always a pleasure to hear that the lectures of the National Geographic gave so much satisfaction. No, not this winter. He was soon to start on his third Peruvian expedition, so there wouldn't be time for any more lectures. In the meanwhile, he would be spending much of his time at Hills' End, the old Porterfield plantation, in connection with his preparations. He had been astonished to find there was only one telephone in the Big House and that was in Miss Porterfield's bedroom. Naturally, it would not be feasible for him, Dr. Hale, to use this telephone. . . . Yes, he had been quite sure that everyone at the office would understand. The library would be the best place for him to take calls, but he thought there should also be a second extension in the kitchen, because there would be messages when he was out and Miss Porterfield's elderly cook was getting feeble . . . before closing time that afternoon? Yes, that would be quite satisfactory. Thank you, thank you very much.

He restored the instrument to its cradle, turned to Margaret with a smile and then, still smiling, glanced first at the great four-poster and then permitted his approving gaze to wander around the room. "Very, very nice," he said, "and eminently suitable for the purposes we have in mind. Now could I have a look at the erstwhile boudoir and make suggestions for its adaptation to more masculine needs if I think any are indicated? Next, I think we ought to break the good news to Cassie, so that she can be lining up her progeny and, after that, we really ought to be sinking our teeth in that steak or, what with the telephone ringing a lot more and this and that besides, it'll be dark before we get started on our walk. And we've still got that announcement list to tackle before I hurry back to town to get into white tie and tails."

Cassie was volubly thrilled at their news and was sure her niece Annabelle and Annabelle's husband Rufus would be proud to come and work at Hills' End; they lived just a short piece down the road with Annabelle's kinfolk and Cassie would go there instead of taking a nap, as soon as she cleared up after lunch. My, my that was a handsome steak!

The lunch was a great success in every respect and, as the telephone was temporarily out of commission while the new extension was being installed, Nicolas and Margaret were able to make considerable progress on the announcement list before starting on their walk, which was also a great success. They went first to the orchard where ripe apples still lay on the ground and the trees were in sore need of pruning; those fine Winesaps must be gathered tomorrow, Nicolas said, making a note for Rufus and, in the spring, all the trees must have the needed attention. Then, as they tramped over the fields, Nicolas made suggestions for replanting, pasturage and haying. There should be corn here, oats there, alfalfa in the next lot.

By the time the strollers reached the denuded flower garden, Margaret had begun to plan for its restoration; the border of dames' violets, which had once been her special pride, had been allowed to get thin and scraggly; by March, given a reasonably mild spring, she would be able to begin drastic improvements in it; and she had always had good luck with mimosa, though that was considered something of a risk as far north as Virginia. Under the circumstances, shouldn't she also try to do more with traveller's joy? She had neglected its possibilities shamefully, which was a pity in any case, as there was no question *it* would flourish! And now it seemed so appropriate that she should make a special feature of it, in view of Nicolas' voyaging.

"Why, of course you should! What a charming idea! But I don't even know what traveller's joy is—yours, I mean. Tell me."

"It's a type of clematis. In olden times, it was trailed over English hedges and wayfarers on the highways and byways regarded it as their own special shrub. That's how it got the name. Now it's mostly used on trellises. It has delicate white flowers that bloom all summer and there may be a few blossoms still left on the vines, though usually the fluff of the seeds, with their long stringy attachments, is its greatest beauty at this time of year. Shall we go and see what we find? I meant to take you to the arbor, anyway, to show you the swing made of grapevines which my father helped me to weave, and the secret place where the guineas laid their small brown eggs—eggs I loved to gather when I was a child. Cassie taught me I must do it with a long-handled wooden spoon, for, if the nest were touched by human hands, it never would be used again. The arbor used to have a very special place in my heart."

"And it doesn't any more?"

"Well—you'll see."

The swing was still there, waving rather forlornly back and forth in the wind, and the straggly growth of traveller's joy bespoke long neglect. Nicolas asked a question.

"This place could be really beautiful. And it doesn't look like the garden, as if it just hadn't had quite enough care. It looks as if it had purposely been neglected. Has it?"

"Cassie's already picked the grapes for jelly—that's why those vines are stripped. But yes. . . . I've told you I used to hunt eggs here, as a child, and then I came here a lot with my father, when he made me the swing. One day he said an arbor like this was sometimes called a Virgin's Bower, because this was one of the names of the clematis that grows over it. He said that some day I'd come here with my sweetheart —and then I never had a sweetheart. I've never wanted to come here since my father died."

"But now you do have a sweetheart! You must start calling this arbor the Virgin's Bower right away. Of course! Sir Walter Scott wrote about that in *The Lady of the Lake*:

'The clematis, the favour'd flower,

Which boasts the name of virgin's-bower.'

You're *my* Lady of the Lake—the lagoon of Urcos."

"But, Nicolas, this is the same clematis as the one called traveller's joy. Some people think it was named for the Virgin Queen Elizabeth and some think in honor of the Virgin Mary."

"Of course!" Nicolas said again.

" 'When Mary left us here below,

The virgin's-bower began to blow.'

It's in the height of its bloom, isn't it, around Assumption—August fifteenth?"

"Yes—and it has still other names. The prettiest is 'snow in harvest.' Then there are 'hedge feathers' and 'shepherd's delight' and—"

"Hold on! I'm not all that much of a botanist. We'll call it by both the first two names—traveller's joy and virgin's-bower. They're equally suitable, as far as we're concerned. Come on, let's get to work on this arbor together right now and make it worthy of its names! You're head gardener and I'm the hired man."

As if to compensate for the stormy way in which the day had begun, it ended in pleasantly shared activity, on a note of complete harmony; and, as they bade each other good night, in conformity with the suggestions made by Nicolas, he said he would not risk waking Margaret a second time, but would wait for her to call him.

The greater part of the next morning passed with no message, and he had begun to think there had been some misunderstanding or that she was having fresh scruples, when she telephoned to say she had decided to come into town and start her shopping by herself. Now she had bought everything she needed for the moment and was just leaving Garfinckel's; she would meet him at the Cosmos Club in fifteen minutes.

She very nearly made it; but she was fascinated by the full-length portrait of Dolley Madison, clad in dazzling white satin, that confronted her as she stepped from the west vestibule to the first room in the women's suite, and could not resist the temptation of pausing to look at it; so there was a slight delay before she went on to the adjoining apartment, appropriately known as The Gold Room because of its yellow damask walls, where Nicolas had told her he would be waiting. There, the shyness and sense of strangeness, which were the inevitable result of her new clothes and splendid surroundings, were almost instantly submerged in the realization that her appearance was immensely pleasing to him. She had experienced no difficulty in finding a ready-made suit that was a perfect fit and had chosen one of charcoal gray, in fine English cloth, beautifully tailored. Its narrow collar and cuffs were made of black velvet, and a small black velvet hat, black handbag and sleek black pumps accented these. A frilly white blouse and immaculate white gloves completed an ensemble that had taken every cent of the coal money; but she knew, past any shadow of a doubt, that it had been wisely expended otherwise.

"Why, my dear girl, I hardly knew you!" Nicolas exclaimed. "What do you mean, springing a surprise like that on me, and without even a hint of what you were up to? Here I've been imagining all sorts of disasters as responsible for the delay in getting a message from you! And all the time you were at the marts of trade spending money like a drunken sailor and without my guiding hand! However, I'll say you didn't need it. Turn around, will you, so I can see if the back view is as good as the front? Well, of course, I miss your face, but otherwise . . . and I think maybe we should add a fur—this is a nice day, but getting colder by the minute. Why, of course, I can give you a fur for a present! That isn't buying clothes! Come along, let's go into the Old Club Room and have a drink. That's my pet place; I feel as if I were really sitting in Lafayette Square when I look around at the murals, and it's a feeling I enjoy, but I had more affection for the club when it was housed in Dolley Madison's erstwhile residence. So let's take time out for my nostalgic memories and a dry martini before we go along for lunch. By the way, just as a suggestion, the popovers and the roast beef here are tops."

The popovers and the roast beef were indeed excellent and so was everything that went with them. But Nicolas had reserved a table at the north end of the Garden Room, where a Byzantine colonnade led to a fountain of variegated marble, which emptied into a semicircular pool; and the exotic setting, much more than the typically American menu, added to Margaret's pleasurable sense of strangeness. Several guests who were eating at other tables bowed as Nicolas and Margaret sat down at theirs; and her shyness returned with the consciousness that her appearance with such a famous man was raising questions in the minds of his acquaintances who were not hers as well. Her slight malaise increased when some of these strangers did not content themselves with bowing, but came to greet Nicolas and await introductions to her. These were made with the greatest nonchalance. "Of course, you know Margaret Porterfield? You remember those suppers in the gun room Mrs. Porterfield used to have at Hills' End? I'm sure you'll be delighted to hear they're about to be resumed. You and Peggy will be getting invitations. . . . Yes, that was a good party last night, wasn't it? The present incumbents at the White House certainly have it all over their predecessors when it comes to dispensing hospitality . . . Dr. Thornton—Miss Porterfield. I have such a stupid way of assuming that all my best friends are each other's best friends, too."

"Wasn't that gentleman expecting you to ask him to join us?" Margaret inquired, as one of the table-hoppers took a lingering farewell after a pause that he seemed quite willing to prolong.

"No doubt. But I haven't the slightest intention of making this tête-à-tête a triangle."

As he spoke, he looked around as if to challenge further intrusion. Then suddenly his expression changed and he leaped up to greet a tall elderly man, still strikingly handsome, whose fine head was crowned with heavy white hair and whose keen eyes shone with cordiality.

"Dr. Bingham! What wonderful luck! Are you alone? Would you do Margaret Porterfield and me the honor of joining us?"

"My wife's with me. We've been lunching with the LaGuardes, but they had to leave early, so we lingered on for a little. Suzanne caught sight of you and this lovely young lady before I did and sent me over to ask if we couldn't have coffee with you."

"You know there's nothing that could possibly give us more pleasure. I've been telling Margaret that exploring is my only great passion and that you're responsible for it. Now that she's had a chance to meet you, she'll understand why."

"I think it's more likely, now that I've had a chance to meet Miss Porterfield, that I'll understand if you change your mind," Hiram

Bingham said smilingly. "Somehow I have a feeling that romance has caught up with you at last, Nick."

"May I tell him, Margaret? Of course I may! I'm going to marry this lovely young lady, as you so rightly call her, next Wednesday evening. Will you and Mrs. Bingham come to the wedding?"

"We will indeed. Let's hurry over and tell her the good news."

The four went back to the Gold Room together and for the next half hour Margaret found herself torn between her longing to eavesdrop on the animated interchange of scientific data between Nicolas and his hero and her sense of social obligation to the charming dark-eyed woman, much younger than her husband, whose bracelets jingled in time to her pleasant small talk. At last she glanced at a jeweled wrist watch and reminded her husband that they were late for another appointment; they would, however, greatly look forward to the following Wednesday. Nicolas went to the door with them and came back, beaming with satisfaction.

"Didn't you feel, right off, you were in the presence of greatness? Not just in one direction, but in so many it is hard to count them—literature, statesmanship, military aeronautics, all in addition to supreme achievements in discovery. And, besides everything else, that magnetic personality. . . . By the way, Bingham reminded me about a party that the Director of the National Zoological Park and Mrs. Madison are giving tomorrow. The Binghams can't attend because they're going to Mrs. Merryman's—you know, the famous Aunt Bessie; but I've already accepted an invitation and I hope you will. I'm sure that, when they see our announcement in the morning's papers, Mrs. Madison will call and invite you."

"An evening party?" Margaret inquired anxiously, as she thought of the squandered coal money.

"No, it's a luncheon for a change—you can wear exactly what you've got on now, if that's what you're thinking of, with the addition of that fur we're going out to buy right away. As a matter of fact, it's one of the regular luncheons of the Anteaters Association. It just happens the Madisons are the hosts tomorrow. It might easily have been the Aspinwalls instead. He's the Secretary of the Smithsonian, you know."

"I didn't know—how should I? And what on earth is the *Anteaters Association*?"

"Oh, just a group of congenial spirits who go in for rather exotic menus—elk, iguana, that sort of thing. I don't know for sure what they'll have tomorrow—hippopotamus, maybe."

"Where are these luncheons held?" Margaret asked, with visibly increasing uneasiness.

"Well, sometimes the Madisons entertain in the Reptile House. I know they did once when the Secretary of the Interior and his wife were the ranking guests." Then, as Margaret stifled a slight scream, he laughed and added, "Don't worry, I understand that tomorrow's big shots are the Vice President and Mrs. Bruce and Imelda Bruce doesn't like snakes, either. The party's going to be in the main room of the Zoo Restaurant—nice big fireplace, delightful murals—all the animals going into the ark. Charlie Madison chose the subject himself—said the ark was symbolic of what he wanted his zoo to be—big enough for all the animals there are. Honestly, Margaret, you've nothing to worry about. Come on, let's go and buy that fur; and when we get back to Hills' End I'll show you what I went out and bought this morning, good and early, so that I wouldn't risk not being able to answer when you telephoned. Of course, I didn't realize you were going to pull a fast one on me and never get in touch with me until the middle of the day."

The fur that Nicolas insisted on buying was a blue mink stole, and he declined to be satisfied until he found exactly the right shade to blend with the charcoal gray suit. The respect of the saleslady who waited on them grew with his insistence; and when Margaret walked out of the store, the stole over her shoulders, and involuntarily glanced back, she saw the clerk in conference with a buyer who had been called in for consultation.

Nicolas laughed. "Are you worrying now that they're taking you for a kept woman?" he asked teasingly. "You needn't. Even if you don't look quite so painfully prim and proper as you did before you embarked on your shopping spree, no one will ever mistake you for anything but an incorrigibly respectable young lady."

"You mean you're beginning to fear your efforts to change me are hopeless?"

"It isn't exactly a fear. But you do present a good deal of a challenge and one that I'm finding more and more intriguing all the time—especially now that you're willing to joke a little about the situation instead of agonizing over it."

Their return to Hills' End was greeted with joy by both Perdita and Cassie. The latter reported that Rufus and Annabelle were already on the place; Rufus had first looked after the furnace, so that the house would be good and warm; then he had gone straight out to the stable. Annabelle was fixing to bring in the tea; then, come evening, Miss Margaret and Mr. Nicolas could have a talk with the both of them and see if they would suit. The foam had rang and rang; Cassie thanked the good Lord that she had not needed to keep going over the stairs to answer it and she was sure proud to have one in the kitchen; she had wrote down the messages as well as she knew how. Nicolas remarked, after one glance at the result of her efforts, that he would like to put in a long distance call on his own initiative while Margaret deciphered the messages; he had not yet informed his family that he was about to be married. This would be a good time to do it, while his fiancée was right in the room with him and could respond to good wishes.

"Your family! I didn't know you had a family."

"The opportune moment to break it hadn't seemed to come before. I have a very acceptable family—a father and mother and twin sisters named Clarissa and Narcissa, much younger than I am, who probably would be overwhelmed with delight if you asked them to act as your bridesmaids. They all live in Woodstock, Vermont. It's a pleasant place, but rather on the quiet side. They'll be tremendously excited at the prospect of a wedding next Wednesday."

"Nicolas, you might have told me! I never thought of you as coming from a place like Woodstock, Vermont—I've always associated you with Washington and Peru. Why, your people will be *horrified*—that is, New Englanders are even more conservative than Virginians, aren't they? Here it is Saturday. . . ."

He shook his head to indicate that he was already too involved with the long distance circuits to enter into further explanations and presently he was speaking in the apparently effortless way that seemed to bring about such good results. "Hello, Ma! Why, fine! Yes, it was a grand party. Hope your local paper gave it the right play—hometown boy dinner guest of President, all that sort of thing. No? Well, you can tell me just how they did word the piece when you and Dad and the girls get down here next week. What's that I'm talking about? Well, I'm going to be married on Wednesday and I kind of thought you might like to be here. I've got rooms engaged for you at the Sulgrave Club beginning Monday and reservations on the morning flight, Northeast Airlines, Lebanon to Washington. No, it isn't sudden at all, that is, I've known the girl for years, Margaret Porterfield, you've heard me speak of her dozens of times. But you know how girls are. Sometimes it takes them a long while to make up their minds and after this one finally accepted me, I didn't want her to change hers again while I was gone, so I've persuaded her . . . yes, of course, I want to talk to Dad, too. I need him for my best man. No, there isn't anyone else I'd rather have. Hello, Dad, how's the bank? I'll want to arrange for some sort of a monthly deposit and a trust fund for my prospective wife, so I hope it's sound. I'll give you all the details when you get here. Now I'm sure you want to speak to Margaret and of course she wants to speak to you; she's a little surprised that you've forgotten I told you about her but I think I can smooth that over . . ."

"Nicolas, that was absolutely outrageous!" Margaret said helplessly, when the telephone was finally back in its place, after a call that must have run into more money than she could visualize. "Why, you gave them the idea that you'd been in love with me for years and that I—"

"Well, isn't that a perfectly harmless deception? After all, I'm dangerously close to being in love with you now, and, as you reminded me, New Englanders are apt to be slightly conservative, so I'm sure this version of the story will be more satisfactory than one that's a shade more accurate. Incidentally, it might be a good version to use for everybody, create less of a shock, do away with all that talk of a woman hater and—"

"But you were telling a downright lie, two downright lies! You're not in love with me now! You're only marrying me because—"

"Just a minute. I'll admit—between you and me—to one slight prevarication which will do a good deal to ease what otherwise might have been a slightly startling situation. But I'm not admitting to one downright lie, much less two. What makes you so sure I'm not in love with you? I wasn't, two days ago. But since then I've developed some rather alarming symptoms—alarming to me, I mean. I didn't intend to have anything like this happen. But I've already told you that I enjoyed kissing you a lot more than I expected. When you decide that I wouldn't be taking liberties if I kissed you again, I presume that will be doubly exciting. Meanwhile, I find you very pleasant to talk to and very pleasant to look at. And I've changed my mind about thinking it doesn't become you to act like a spitfire. You're mad through and through right now and you're so alluring that it's all I can do to keep my hands off you. Which reminds me—"

He reached in his pocket and took from it a small box covered in dark blue velvet. "Never mind those telephone messages," he said. "If they're important enough, the people who left them will call again. If they're not important, what's the use of worrying about them?"

"But you told the telephone company—"

"Never mind about the telephone company. It was tickled to death to get the nice fat order—two extensions and the prospect of an indefinite number of long distance calls between Virginia and Peru. Now come over here beside me, like a good girl. This thing's been burning a hole in my pocket. Do you want me to open the box or do you want to do it yourself?"

"I—I reckon I want you to do it."

"All right. Shut your eyes and hold out your hand—your left hand. There's only one way to tell whether or not a ring fits."

She was separated from him only by the small space between the chair where she was sitting, beside the telephone, and the sofa where Nicolas and Perdita were comfortably ensconced. But it required a conscious effort to do what he asked. The call to his parents, with its misleading statements and its disclosure of financial arrangements for her benefit, and the abrupt announcement that he was "dangerously close" to being in love with her, had completely destroyed the composure which she had striven so hard to achieve and maintain. But she was literally afraid to refuse his summons. The easy, jesting manner, the colloquialisms and persiflage might obscure a degree of will power that was appalling to her, but they did not blind her to it or to its possible consequences if it were thwarted. She rose slowly, took two or three steps and sat down beside him, closing her eyes as she did so. Then she felt him take her left hand, as gently as if it had been a child's, and slide a ring over the third finger. It slipped easily into place, as if it belonged there.

"Now open your eyes and look first at the ring and then at me," Nicolas commanded.

Obediently, she looked down at her hand, where a large sapphire gleamed between two sparkling diamonds. Then, still obediently, she tried to look up at him only to find that, although she raised her head, she could not see him because her sight was blurred with tears, and she was thankful that he went on talking, because she was quite incapable of speech.

"I've got a magnificent emerald stowed away," Nicolas was saying. "As I told you, I did a little desultory exploring in Colombia, following Bingham's trail over Bolívar's route, before I began to concentrate on Peru and emeralds used to be as easy to pick up in Colombia as the common cold. I'm sorry to say it's harder now, but anyway I've got this one. However, it's still unset and of course you had to have your engagement ring right away. So I'll keep the emerald to give you when our son is born."

8 ꝏ

Margaret's sense of haste, like her sense of unreality, increased hour by hour.

The telephone rang incessantly. The Director of the National Zoological Park and Mrs. Madison called to invite her, as Nicolas had predicted they would, to the luncheon of the Anteaters Association, and Mrs. Madison thoughtfully added that she would send a list of the other prospective guests so that Margaret could familiarize herself beforehand with their names and occupations. Esther telephoned from New York to say she had never been so thrilled in her life; she was going to take the first plane she could get to Washington on Monday after she had done some necessary shopping, and she wondered if

Margaret wouldn't let her be matron of honor? Sam was going to take a couple of days off and join Esther that same evening, so they'd both be on hand for the rehearsal and everything; and, unless someone else had already asked to do it, they wanted to give the dinner before the rehearsal. They had reservations at the Mayflower. Uncle Virginius telephoned from Charlottesville; he was also planning to come on Monday; his reservations were at the Metropolitan Club. When Nicolas arrived to take Margaret to church, a little before eleven, she was still in her slip; there had been no time to finish dressing, because she had been so steadily at the telephone. And now, she could not take time to tell him about the calls, except hurriedly, after they were already in the car, because, if she did, they'd be late to Morning Prayer, and their entrance at Pohick Church would be even more conspicuous and embarrassing to her than it was bound to be anyway. After they reached the church, she would not have been able to make any of the proper responses, or join in the singing, if Nicolas had not held her prayer book and hymnal for her. She did not hear a word of the sermon and she did not believe many, if any, of Mr. Bates' other parishioners did, either; she was sure their attention was riveted on Nicolas and herself; and this impression was confirmed when the service was over and everyone gathered around to extend good wishes and congratulations. Then, instead of going straight from church to the luncheon, as she had expected they would, Nicolas suggested that they should return to Hills' End so that she could pick up some calling cards, write a couple of notes, and show him the list he understood Mrs. Madison had sent her by special messenger.

"Yes, the list is there, though I haven't had a minute to look at it; and I suppose I have calling cards tucked away some place, but they must be yellow with age and I wouldn't know where to find them. Do you really want me to try?"

"I really do. I've been getting telephone messages too. The White House and the Peruvian Embassy both called me this morning to offer congratulations and express regrets that you hadn't been invited to dinner with me. I gather the President and his wife and the Ambassador and Ambassadress would all come to the wedding, if we asked them, and in those two instances the invitations would have to be in writing. So, after the luncheon, I think we'd better leave cards and notes at both places."

"But, Nicolas, I can't possibly—"

"There you go again! Of course you can. There aren't any buts. We have to go full speed ahead from now on. I'm glad Esther's coming. She's a good organizer, she'll do a lot to relieve you of details—decorations, food, drinks, and so forth. I think you'll find my mother and my kid sisters helpful too, in a quieter way. But we'd better make the most of today, as far as getting better acquainted with each other is concerned. Can we have another long walk after we've been to the luncheon and left the notes and cards? And may I stay to supper with you? There are a couple of cocktail parties and a buffet supper in my book for tonight, but I can skip those. In fact, I shall unless you'll go to them with me. One's a cocktail party to celebrate the birthday of a minor monarch, one's to mark the second anniversary of a minor republic's independence and the buffet is a free-for-all fight at the garish residence of a minor social leader."

"You don't make them sound very inviting; if I don't have to, I'd much rather not go."

"No, you don't have to. I'll keep on telling you about the things you do have to do. The next thing on the agenda is hunting up those cards."

It took Margaret some time to find the cards, which were tucked into the rear of a drawer in a disused desk. They were yellow with age and outmoded in style, and she apologized for them as she showed them to Nicolas. He reminded her cheerfully that they would be needed just this once, so it didn't really matter, and made a note to order new cards for Mrs. Nicolas Hale at the same time he ordered the wedding announcements. When Margaret nervously rewrote the notes a third time, because her first two attempts were satisfactory neither to him nor to her, he drafted a model for her and said he would take Perdita out for a turn while Margaret copied it; perhaps she would do better if he were not breathing down her neck. When he returned, he smilingly pronounced her final efforts a complete success. But by this time it was too late for them to sit quietly by the fire for a few minutes and go over Mrs. Madison's list. Margaret would have to read aloud to him as they sped along over the Shirley Highway.

There was a little breeze and the paper fluttered in her hand as she consulted the list, adding to her sense of nervousness. Nicolas closed the car windows, except for the wing on his side, and prompted her.

"It begins with the Vice President and Mrs. Bruce, doesn't it?" he asked encouragingly. "You remember I told you yesterday, Imelda doesn't like snakes any better than you seem to. Incidentally, she scored a great hit in South America, when she and the VP took one of those so-called good will tours, which usually end up in student riots if nothing worse. She was born and brought up in New Mexico and her Spanish is excellent. What's more, her smile is captivating. She rather overshadows her husband. The Románs dote on her—I mean the Peruvian Ambassador and his wife. But our real Spanish scholar is Allan Lambert—born in Málaga, where his father was American Consul; taught Spanish for years in some small New England college, meanwhile almost starving to death on his salary; suddenly inherited a great fortune from some miserly old uncle and blew in the first of it on a return trip to Spain, where he married a beautiful young *marquesa* whose father is the proud possessor of a fabulous library. In fact, the whole story is rather fabulous. All Allan's qualifications, but especially the fortune, which had been used quite liberally for the benefit of the party during the campaign, attracted the attention of our vigilant President. So, friend Allan is now Assistant Secretary of State for Latin American Affairs. I believe he and the *marquesa*, whose name is Milagrita, are also on the list."

"Yes, and then come the Secretary of the Interior and Mrs. Arthur Ashe."

"A little on the pompous, heavy side. Don't let them wear you down with their self-importance."

"I'll try not to. . . . What about the Secretary of the Smithsonian and Mrs. Howard Aspinwall? They sound rather overpowering too."

"Oh, they're not in the least pompous or heavy! They have that lean and hungry look that Cassius warned Caesar about—or was it the other way around?—which comes from thinking too much. But they're very, very distinguished and they mean to be kind."

"What do *you* mean—'they mean to be kind'? Aren't they?"

"Yes, they are, really. But it may take you a little time to discover this, because they don't seem outgoing with strangers. I think it's partly due to a genuine desire *not* to be overpowering, with all their achievements and degrees and so on. Mrs. Aspinwall has as many as her husband. She's a past president of the Woman Geographers. Is there also a Manuela Reeves on the list?"

"Yes, and evidently she's President of the Woman Geographers now."

"That's right. Her mother was a Panamanian, her grandfather was President of Panama, though he came originally from one of its most remote provinces. She's very good in a jungle."

"Is everyone who's coming good at something that I don't know anything at all about?"

"Well, let me have another look at the list. Perhaps if we take the rest of these people collectively, instead of one or two at a time, they won't sound quite so overpowering, as you put it: Jerome LaGuarde, President of the National Geographic, married to the former Miriam Powers, whose father is Chairman of the Senate Foreign Relations Committee; both extremely good looking, get their clothes from London and Paris, very Social Register but not offensively so, not alarmingly scientific either. Mr. and Mrs. Tom Herbert; he's the science columnist for the *Star* and syndicated in some other papers too; very hail fellow well met and so is his wife. They give nice parties themselves, they'll be asking you to some and I think you'll enjoy

going. Mr. and Mrs. Oliver Gilchrist, archeologists; have six children
and take them everywhere they go, exploring; the last I heard, it had
something to do with a new discovery at Persepolis. He's Chief of the
Bureau of Ethnology, but he's much more apt to talk to you about the
cute sayings of his little darlings than the folkways of the Persians. That
seems to be it, except for Gordon Holmes, a marine biologist, whose
speciality is crinoids. He's a bachelor."

"I should think he would be. I don't see how any woman could co-
exist with something that sounds as horrible as crinoids."

"There's another name for them—sea lilies. I should have called
them that in the first place. And you may feel more kindly toward him
when I tell you that right now he isn't making any deep sea soundings.
He's chasing butterflies all over Virginia."

"Chasing butterflies!"

"Yes, county by county. He's on vacation and that's his favorite
pastime. How are you fixed for butterflies in Fairfax?"

"I haven't the least idea."

"Well, maybe Gordon Holmes can help you to find out. I shouldn't
be in the least surprised if he were put beside you at table."

She did not answer and Nicolas handed the paper back to her
without speaking either. It was obvious that she was appalled, not only
at the prospect of meeting a dozen or so complete strangers, but because
these strangers, without any exception, were worldly wise and widely
traveled, and, with very few exceptions, distinguished for their
intellectual and scientific attainments. Mrs. Madison's purpose in
sending her a list of her fellow guests and their occupations had been
kindly; the prospective hostess had believed the mental preparation
this would permit would make for easy identification and facilitate an
exchange of ideas and experiences. But Nicolas could see only too
plainly that its effect, to use Margaret's own words, was overpowering.
He took one hand off the wheel and put it over hers.

"You're not looking at this the right way, Margaret," he said. "Instead of thinking that you won't know what to say to these people, try
to believe that they won't have the least difficulty in knowing what to
say to you and that they'll do it very agreeably—very urbanely. They'll
be genuinely pleased to meet you, genuinely interested in our engagement. Many of them have been my friends for a long while; they'll
want to be your friends too. And I believe, if you'll let yourself go,
you'll respond to that feeling. I know responsiveness isn't your strong
suit, but try."

"Oh, I'll try, Nicolas, truly I will! But it's just as you said—responsiveness isn't my strong suit. And it's just as *I've* kept saying—if we only
had a little more time! It's only three days since you suddenly burst in
on me and dazzled me so that I agreed to marry you within a week.

And since then, I've had to try to reorganize my entire design for living to conform to yours. It wouldn't have been so hard if mine had been complicated and yours had been simple. But since it's the other way around—"

"Since it's the other way around, you'll do it. You'll do it beautifully. The fact that you're having to do it fast only makes it more of a challenge and the result more of a triumph."

"I haven't triumphed yet, Nicolas."

"No, but you're marching forward—in beautiful clothes, with my ring on your finger. And when you went out this morning, you left a nice warm, well-staffed house, full of lovely flowers and friendly messages. You also left a delightful little puppy, who already knows she's your dog. When you reach home this afternoon, she'll greet you with sounds of joy. And I'll be with you. We'll have supper together by the fire, after we've taken another long walk. By bedtime you'll be so full of fresh air and good food and a sense of happy companionship that you'll sleep like a top. You may even begin to realize, before I say good night, that this happy companionship is only a prelude to something that's better. But even if you can't, I think you'll admit that's quite a lot of progress for three days."

"I do admit it—I admit it freely. And I think if we could not only have more time, but more time to ourselves—"

"If we had more time to ourselves, I couldn't help acting like a lover instead of a pleasant companion. And you don't want me to do that. So it's better this way. Isn't it?"

"I—I suppose so."

"Are you actually beginning to have doubts? If you are, that's further triumph on the march forward. I'll reappraise the situation before I leave you this evening. Meanwhile, I'm afraid I'll have to let go your hand. We're moving into heavy traffic."

They crossed the Memorial Bridge, circled the Lincoln Memorial, and threaded their way up Seventeenth Street to Connecticut Avenue. As they passed through the great iron gates leading into the Zoological Park, Margaret, whose uneasiness with everything connected with the luncheon had been assuaged but not entirely stilled, asked an anxious question.

"We don't go anywhere near the Reptile House, do we?"

"No, and you won't even see many animals at this time of year. It's too chilly—just elk, buffalo, mountain goats and so on, who thrive in cold weather. It isn't feeding time for any of them and besides, it's too late for me to drive slowly, so you won't get more than a glimpse of those."

The "glimpse" had indeed been only a blurred impression of huge horned creatures when Nicolas stopped the car in front of a low stone building bearing a large sign on the front door which read

"CAFETERIA
CLOSED
TODAY ONLY
FULL OF ANTEATERS"

And, as they entered the building, their host and hostess came forward to meet them and lead them to the space near a big open fireplace where a congenial looking group was already assembled. Everyone was wearing a large shiny orange-colored button, rather like a campaign button, labeled in black "I'M AN ANTEATER"; and Margaret was right in believing that she was the only guest who was not already acquainted with all the others. But Nicolas had also been right when he predicted she could not fail to realize that the welcome given her was sincere and hearty. He had been right about the easy conversation too; no one made requirements of her which she was unable to meet; and she so quickly succumbed to the spell of Imelda Bruce's dazzling smile and the Latin grace of both Románs, that the pompousness of the Arthur Ashes did not weight her down. Moreover, Gordon Holmes, who had indeed been placed beside her, launched into the subject of Virginia butterflies so enthusiastically and with so much discerning praise for her native state that her heart warmed toward him and the fantastic menu which had been placed before her ceased to puzzle and trouble her. Presently she was laughing with him over some of the items, "Crocodile tears, cream of scorpion soup, beaver eyeballs on the half shell," she read aloud.

"Yes, those are jokes, of course, but go on."

"Well, next come roast young hippopotamus, bush style, potatoes Mombasa, and carrots Nairobi. Are those jokes too?"

"No, those are real. And I think you will find the roast young hippopotamus quite tasty—rather like tender but overdone beef."

"I like my beef tender and overdone. . . . Nicolas made fun of the items on the menu that the Ann Mason Guild of Pohick Church provided for the Alexandria Association Forum. Things like chambermaid's punch and chocolate wine—which, of course, isn't a wine at all, but a sauce."

"Yes, and a mighty good one!"

"Oh, you know about it and you like it! I'm so pleased! But what I started to say was, now I can make fun of some of the items on *this* menu and get even with him."

"Yes you can—and you should."

Margaret was finding Gordon Holmes so congenial that she was actually reluctant to break the thread of their conversation by turning to Tom Herbert, the columnist, who proved to be the man on her other side. But, as she conscientiously did so, he cordially took the initiative, relieving her of all responsibility.

"This is the first time you've been here, isn't it?" he asked. "So you won't mind if I point out some of my favorite features in the murals. See Noah's wife peering out of the ark's dormer window? And the monkeys taking it easy by getting a ride on the back of an elephant? After lunch, remind me to show you the cockroach."

"The cockroach!"

"Yes, over there in that dark corner next to the rest room. The artist drew only one, but Charlie Madison said in this case that it would be all right—there'd be more tomorrow. . . . Perhaps Nick told you Sally and I usually have a cocktail buffet on Sundays. Very informal, but lots of fun—that is, we think so, and our guests are kind enough to say that they do, too. We're skipping today, because so many of the Anteaters belong to the same crowd that comes to us in Georgetown. But I hope that next Sunday—or will you and Nick be on your way to Peru by then? I understand his equipment's already gone and that he feels he has to go himself as soon as he can after the wedding."

"Yes, he does. He's leaving a week from Tuesday."

"*He's* leaving? What about you?"

"I'm not going—that is, not just yet," Margaret added hastily, when she saw the ill-concealed astonishment on the columnist's face and felt suddenly fearful of what he might do with this tidbit of news. "You see—"

Her halting explanation was suddenly cut short as, like everyone else at the table, she turned instinctively toward a couple who had thrown open the closed door which led to the room reserved for the Anteaters and, despite protests from the headwaitress, advanced firmly toward the host's end of the Madisons' table. "I tell you, Charlie Madison always wants me at his parties," the man, who was tall and pale, with a singularly somber countenance and a heavy head of long dark hair, was saying insistently. "And this is my new girl friend I've got with me," he added, hastily indicating a platinum blonde in spangled scarlet whom he was propelling forward. "Charlie'd expect me to bring a girl friend, if I had one, wouldn't he? Hi there, Charlie! Hi there, Louisa! Meet Angie Melbourne, new this year, does the best web stunt you'd ever want to see!"

"My God! Fritz Hausman with a replacement for Number Three!" Tom Herbert muttered. "This is going to be good."

"Who's Fritz Hausman?" Margaret whispered excitedly.

"The lead clown in the Great East and West Circus," Tom

whispered back. "What's more, he and the Madisons have been cronies for years. And just watch them handle this."

Margaret did so with mounting admiration for both her host and hostess. Mrs. Madison, as well as her husband, had risen and gone forward to meet the newcomers with expressions of welcome in which there was no ring of insincerity or even of astonishment. The guests who were already seated were quickly enjoined to move a little closer together in order to make room for Miss Melbourne and Mr. Hausman, and the flabbergasted headwaitress was told to lay two more places. Then, without hesitation, the seating arrangement was shifted in such a way as to make the inclusion of another couple seem simple and natural; and, after general introductions, Hausman was urged to tell everyone to what the Anteaters owed their good fortune in having him and his fiancée among their congenial spirits.

"Just closed down in Florida, after a bang-up season," Mr. Hausman informed them. "All the way to the West Coast and back again. Now I'm on my way to New York to look for a winter job—circus won't be on the road again before April. But I can always find me a spot in a night club. Leastways, I always have been able to so far and this year I thought I might get Angie in on the act with me. If that doesn't work out, I can go around to the different tables and kid the people who are sitting at them and offer to draw their pictures."

"He's a superb cartoonist," Tom confided to Margaret in another whisper. Then, in his normal tone of voice, he called across the table, "How about practicing on this group, Mr. Hausman? We'd all be tickled to death to have a sketch by you on our souvenir menus. Or is such a suggestion out of order?"

"*Niemals, niemals,* Mr. Herbert," the clown responded heartily. "Just so long as you don't transfer one I draw on your menu to the head of your column and pretend it was you that drew it. I'll get to you in due time after I've finished with the big brass. Now let's see . . . I start out with the VP, don't I? Barging into a bull fight at Lima? I understand that was the only way he could distract attention from his beautiful wife."

"All too true, Fritz, all too true. But you don't start off with me today. You start off with Nicolas Hale, who's off to Lima himself."

"What, to make more discoveries? How do you expect me to draw something that hasn't even been found yet?"

In the general laugh that followed there was also general murmuring and Hausman, nodding his head, called gaily across the table in his turn.

"What's this I hear? That you found a girl at last who would have you, same as I did, even if you didn't make that great discovery you've been talking about ever since I can remember? Well, as far as I'm concerned, I'd rather have a live girl than a dead city any day. And now that you've finally got a chance to make the comparison, I bet you'll agree with me. If you don't, you're not the smart man I always thought you were."

9 ☙

The luncheon continued on a note of increasing hilarity as Hausman made his wisecracks and drew his pictures. After a flurry of jokes and congratulations, it came to a belated end on a more serious note: the presentation by Oliver Gilchrist of the Explorers Club flag to Nicolas Hale. Because of the importance of the latter's mission, this emblem, with its diagonal stripes of red, white and blue, carrying the insignia and initials of the Explorers in red on a white ground, would be his to carry with him to Peru and to bring back, presumably in triumph, after it had been given added significance. Margaret had long ceased to feel overpowered by grandeur and learning, but the jesting, good-natured as it was, had been so alien to her natural reserve that it had taxed this, and the flag ceremony, simple as it was, had carried with it undertones of deep emotion. She was very tired when she and Nicolas returned to Hills' End, so tired that she hoped Nicolas would not insist on the long walk after all, and, to her immense relief, he did not. It had not required very acute observation to notice the dark circles under her eyes and the increasing strain in her smile, as she went on and on, courteously responding to Hausman's badinage and the good wishes of all her fellow guests at the luncheon. As they finally turned in at her driveway, Nicolas made a counter suggestion to the walk.

"Instead of getting into tramping clothes, how about a negligee—or do you call it a wrapper? You must have some sort of a warm service-able garment that covers you completely and isn't in the least seduc-tive."

"Yes, of course I have. I call it a robe."

"Well, why not go up to your room and remove all traces of your elegance and put on this robe? Then come downstairs and stretch out on the sofa beside the fire and let me read aloud to you. No scientific data. I think poetry would be just the thing, not the intense or baffling kind, the soothing variety. You can tell Annabelle and Cassie that you can't take telephone calls for a while and relax until suppertime. Would that appeal to you?"

"Very much. I don't want to disappoint you, Nicolas, but—"

He held up a warning hand and shook his head. "You're not disappointing me, except by your predilection for that one word. Well, look what we have here! A conservatory seems to have been added since we left the premises!"

Annabelle was at the door, receiving an enormous pink flower box, bearing a White House label, and back of her was an array of other boxes, besides baskets and vases filled with flowers which had already come: red roses, pink roses, yellow roses, white roses; purple orchids, white orchids, yellow orchids, green orchids; bronze chrysanthemums, purple chrysanthemums, golden chrysanthemums; snowy lilies, brilliant paradise flowers, modest violets. It took Margaret the better part of an hour, even with Annabelle's help, to arrange the flowers that were there already and list the cards that had come with them, and more floral offerings kept arriving all the time. Nicolas was finally pressed into service, also; and, just as they were beginning to visualize a lull, an enormous Cadillac drew up to the door and a woman of uncertain age and exaggerated elegance brushed past Annabelle and enfolded Margaret in a fervent embrace.

"My *dear!* I simply couldn't resist the temptation of rushing over to pay you a neighborly visit and to meet your distinguished fiancé. . . . Dr. Hale, you must forgive me for barging in on you like this, when I'm sure you're dying to be alone with this dear sweet girl. I'll only stay a few minutes, just long enough to give Margaret a sweet kiss and congratulate you and ask if you won't give us the pleasure of your company at dinner tomorrow night."

"Nicolas, may I present you to Mrs. Huntington?" Margaret asked rather coolly, as she extricated herself from the unwelcome clutches of her impetuous visitor. "The new chatelaine of East Lawn."

"I rather thought it must be," Nicolas said, bowing to acknowledge the introduction and speaking far more coolly than Margaret. His manner was faultless, but she felt that if he had spoken to her in that tone of voice she would have been chilled through and through. "Are you actually in residence now, Mrs. Huntington?"

"Indeed I am, indeed I am," the visitor replied, glancing around for the seat she had not been invited to take and installing herself comfortably in the only chair near at hand. "And such a pleasure! It's a source of great regret to my husband and myself that we haven't been free to really rusticate long before this; but now we're hoping and expecting to be in this wonderful countryside of yours a great deal, dear Miss Porterfield, and we're counting on you to help us feel as much at home here as we do in Normandy. Of course, East Lawn was terribly run down when we bought it, but now that we've succeeded in making it more or less livable at last—"

"I noticed the changes, when I stopped in there last Thursday," Nicolas observed, still speaking in the voice that Margaret found so chilling, but to which Mrs. Huntington responded with a beaming smile. "In fact, I never should have recognized the place."

"Oh Dr. Hale, I'm so sorry I didn't know you had called! Jenkins never told me! He really is too, too stupid! But you know how it is—the awful, awful servant problem! I can't imagine how Miss Porterfield manages to surmount it."

"I think just by following old Virginia customs. Those are still a little new to you, aren't they, Mrs. Huntington? You mustn't blame Jenkins. I didn't come to make a social call, merely to ask for directions. I'd lost my way coming out from Washington in the rain over all these new highways. But fortunately, when I finally reached Hills' End, I found it blessedly unchanged."

He smiled at Margaret, who was so tired that she had sunk down on the lowest stairstep; and again she was conscious of a strange fluttering in her heart, stronger than it had been the first time, but once more compounded of both pain and pleasure. She gathered, quite correctly, that Nicolas was even more irked by Mrs. Huntington's visit than she was; she also gathered that, under the circumstances, it was not necessary to suggest going into the library, much less having tea; nevertheless, she thought she must make some acknowledgment of the invitation to dinner, which Mrs. Huntington was now gushingly repeating.

"It's very kind of you. But Nicolas is expecting his family to arrive from Vermont tomorrow, and some New York friends and my uncle are coming too."

"But you could all come to dinner! Mr. Huntington and I would be simply delighted."

"With that awful, awful servant problem! Nine extra persons and hardly a word of warning! I'm sure we shouldn't subject Jenkins to such a shock, even if we were free, which, as Margaret has just said, we really aren't. And I wonder if you wouldn't excuse her now, Mrs. Huntington? She's had quite a tiring day and she has a rather full week ahead of her. She was just on the point of going upstairs for a little rest after fixing the flowers, when you were kind enough to call. Yes, I was sure you'd understand. . . ."

He opened the front door, still smiling pleasantly and chatting amiably and, after closing it behind the visitor, made room for himself beside Margaret on the stairs and, unrebuked, put his arm around her and kissed her cheek.

"You weren't very polite to her, were you, Nicolas?" Margaret asked anxiously, but without drawing away.

"I was a lot, lot politer to her than she deserved. According to your own story she never came near you when you were sad and lonely and would have welcomed a neighborly visit—that is, from the right sort of a neighbor. But now, when you're about to marry an alleged celebrity, she wants to make up for lost time, like the social climber she is. Don't you dare weaken and ask her to the wedding! If you do, you'll be saddled with her all winter. She's done enough harm already. You were tired before she forced her way in here and now you're exhausted, so we're about to change our plans again. What you want to do and what you need to do is to go to bed right now and have a cup of Ovaltine and a good long sleep. Moreover, it's what I want you to do. I'm off to those cocktail parties. I think I ought to put in an appearance, after all. So we'll also have to postpone getting better acquainted."

Margaret would not have believed that she could fall asleep, quickly and quietly. As Cassie would say, she had been so "upstirred" she was sure that Sunday night, like the previous Thursday night, would find her a prey to restlessness and worry. But permeating her welcome drowsiness was the happy realization of why tonight was different: she had gone through a succession of startling new experiences, impressions and revelations, but none of these offended or frightened her any more. She was about to marry a celebrity, who was on first name terms with presidents and ambassadors and outstanding scientists; no one seemed to feel she was an intruder, as far as their charmed circles were concerned, which was what she had expected; they were eager to welcome her into their midst. The same was true of her fiancé's family; his parents were hastening to accept her as their daughter. And as for the celebrity himself, he was again her hero. Nothing he had said, nothing he had done, throughout the day had made her think again of a man with a beast in him. And his final gesture, in telling her to go to bed and get a good sleep, when he had expected her to take a long walk and have supper and get better acquainted with him, showed not only consideration, but kindness. Perhaps she had misjudged him; if she had, she must make it up to him.

When she waked, the sun was streaming into the room and the tall clock in the hall was striking an unbelievable number of times. She counted, more and more amazed. *Twelve!* The morning, as well as the evening before, engulfed in sleep! There was an old-fashioned bellpull by her bed, a relic of the days when ladies living on plantations rang for their servants whenever they felt like it; and, though Margaret had not used it in so long that she doubted if it were still in good working order, she tugged at it now. Instantly she heard its reassuring, though unmusical, clang, loud enough to sound throughout the house; and a minute later, Cassie, laden with boxes, came lumbering into the room, Perdita at her heels.

"How *could* I have slept this late?" Margaret demanded. "I can't understand why the telephone didn't wake me, or Perdita, asking to go out."

"Mebbe you ain' noticed befo', honey, but de foam don' ring in yo' room no mo'—jus' in de kitchen an' de lib'ry. Mistuh Nic'las done give his ordahs when dem new foams wuz put in. He said he didn' want you should be disturbed. Likewise, he give me ordahs 'bout de pup—said she was to sleep in mah room till aftah he gwine away. You want all dese parcels on yo' bed?"

"Yes, of course I do. I'll open them while I wait for you to bring up my breakfast."

"From now on, hit's Annabelle brings up yo' trays," Cassie announced with importance. "Dat's ordahs, too. Ah'm gwine res' my po' old feet. Nobody else give dem a thought, but he did. 'Stead of openin' presents, when you got a-plenny already, 'pears like you might call dat fine gennelmun dat's co'tin' you. Likely by dis time, he thinks you done died, 'stead o' a weddin', he gwine have a fun'ral on his hands. De Lord Jesus knows you got plenny flowahs fo' one."

No, he did not think she had died, Nicolas said cheerfully, as he responded to her call. She wouldn't play such a mean trick on him as that. But he would remind her this was the second morning in succession that he had waited for hours, hoping to hear from her, before she got around to telephoning him. And now he must hurry off to an appointment with Allan Lambert, the Assistant Secretary of State for Latin American Affairs, whom Margaret had met the day before. It seemed his father-in-law, the Duke of San Ricardo, was a great friend of Don Juan Labrador, the Rector of San Marcos University, and Allan wanted to send the latter a rather important message. If he did so through Nicolas, verbally, of course it would be wholly unofficial and still it might be the stitch in time that saves nine, if there's some sort of trouble brewing with communistic students. Nicolas had hoped to make this the last appointment of its kind; but from the Department of State he would have to go on to the Peruvian Embassy, as he had received a cable from his assistant, Pete Hart, who had just landed at Callao, to the effect that there had been a hitch at the customs about releasing some items of their equipment. This had never happened to them before, and Nicolas was confident he could quickly get the matter straightened out with Román, who was the soul of courtesy and good will. For all that, Nicolas wasn't going to take any chances; the time to deal with red tape was when it first began to tangle. . . . Well, after he had dealt with these details, he would have to meet his family at the airport and see them comfortably settled at the Sulgrave Club. Later, could they all plan to come out to supper? He supposed Margaret would be busy with Esther anyhow, in the meantime, wouldn't she? Everything would work out very well. More flowers? Good Lord, they would have to build a conservatory. And that *hadn't* entered into his calculations! Silver, too? That was certainly carrying coals to Newcastle, wasn't it? He was afraid she'd have to resign herself to writing twenty or thirty notes, thanking people for cake plates and bonbon dishes. But he thought Esther would have more sense about what she brought. . . .

Esther arrived at midafternoon in one of her own limousines, which she had started off from New York early in the morning, so that it would be waiting for her at the airport when she landed and available for her use and Margaret's all the time she was in Washington. Happily untroubled by concern over the expense of excess baggage in planes, she was laden with the tangible results of her morning shopping. But before she began to discuss and reveal these, she devoted some minutes to rhapsodies about her friend's romance.

"My dear, everyone in Washington may have been surprised, but not Sam and I or anyone who was at our wedding! Why, it was as clear as crystal to everybody who saw you and Nick together that he was simply crazy about you! He just didn't have eyes for another woman and of course he took you off to that funny little room on purpose to beg you to change your mind and marry him at last. It must be all of eight years since you came out and he was in Washington that whole winter, without going to Peru at all, so that must have been when he fell in love with you. To think of his being faithful to you all that time! It's the most thrilling thing I ever heard of in my life."

"Esther, you're letting your imagination run away with you. Nicolas Hale hasn't been hopelessly in love with me for eight years. He—"

"Oh, I suppose he's found some slight consolation along the way! How could an attractive man like that escape it, with women falling over each other to offer it to him all the time? But it's evident he never forgot you and that he never gave up trying to get you. And now that he's finally succeeded—well, as I just said, I think it's the most thrilling thing I ever heard in my life. Sam's crazy about me, that is, as crazy as most men are about the girls they marry. I haven't any cause for complaint, goodness knows. But if I'd tried to keep him dangling, the way you've kept Nick, I'd have lost him practically between dates."

Margaret tried again to interrupt and contradict, but, to her distress, found her attempts in both directions hopeless. Then, remembering Nicolas' version of the same story, when he had broken the news over the telephone to his family, and his insistence that this was the version he wanted used, she gave a little sigh of relief. She could disclaim all responsibility for what her father had always designated as a lavender lie and, at the same time, it would be generally accepted. She was automatically overruled again and it gradually caused her fewer and fewer twinges of conscience.

"Now let's get started on these boxes," Esther went on ecstatically as she glanced around the drawing room, where packages of every size and description, which the library had not proved large enough to accommodate, had been piled high among the floral offerings. "Send for your maid, will you? She can help us and a lot of this stuff can be carted right out to the kitchen. I guess I'd better have Fletcher—that's my chauffeur—come in and help, too." She went to the front door and called and, as if accustomed to such summons, the liveried driver appeared promptly and began to cut strings and remove wrappings. "Sam's telephoned Magruder's to send out six cases of champagne and a lot of other things," Esther rattled along. "They promised delivery today, but I wanted to be sure we had something to start with. So I brought along a case myself and caviar and pâté de foie gras and things like that for canapés. Now, if you'll just tell me the names of the caterer and florist you generally go to, I'll get busy on the telephone right away and arrange for the decorations in the church and at the house both, including whatever you need for the wedding breakfast."

"It isn't going to be a breakfast. It's going to be a supper, a very simple supper. I don't need a caterer—my own people will manage all right. I don't have a regular caterer or a regular florist either—I never did. I wouldn't know whom to suggest."

"Well, you've got a lot of flowers. You must have noticed the names on some of the boxes." And, as the doorbell rang to announce the arrival of another delivery, Esther seized the basket from Annabelle, glanced at the tag with which it was labeled, and rushed to the telephone. Five minutes later, everything had been settled down to the last candle and blossom, and Esther was parting the sheets of tissue paper that concealed the contents of the various containers she had brought with her, while the dazzled Annabelle helped Fletcher to lift covers.

"This is what I thought you could wear to my dinner," Esther said, shaking a creation of pale blue velvet free from its wrappings. "I knew it mustn't be too low or too dressy, since you'd have to go straight from the hotel to the church . . . but here's something that I think is really elegant," she continued, as a long slim sheath of gold brocade came into view, "you can wear that for the big party in New York the night before Nick sails. This little ermine jacket will look all right with both those dresses. You said you were going to wear an ancestral wedding dress, so I didn't do anything about that, but I think I remembered everything else you'll need. Of course, all this is on approval, you can send back whatever you don't like. But, my dear, if you send *these* back, I'll never forgive you!"

She held up a nightgown that was a wisp of white chiffon and lace and a matching negligee, designed to drape the wearer's person somewhat more adequately, but obviously not to conceal it overmuch. "Aren't they *divine?*" she murmured. "I honestly think they're the prettiest ones I ever saw . . . Margaret, what makes you *blush* so? You don't mean to say you didn't expect to wear something like this? I've got you six other sets, pastel colors, but of course the first one had to be as white as your veil."

"There could be a little more to it, couldn't there?"

"Certainly not. If anything, you'll find there's too much to this—or Nick will. Well, we won't talk about it now if it embarrasses you so; you can tell me afterward if I wasn't right, when you're more used to the general idea. Of course, these are all presents, nonsense, you're just being silly. I have to do something with my money and I had an even better time buying these things for you than I did buying my own trousseau. It was such a challenge to do everything in one morning. I thought of dashing into Tiffany's too, but there really wasn't time. Besides, I knew Nick would want the fun of giving you jewelry, that I mustn't start selecting brooches and necklaces until I'd found out what he'd chosen. And what was the use of buying you silver? I realized you'd have more than you knew what to do with, in a house like this."

"Nicolas said you'd feel that way about it. He told me you'd have sense enough not to give me silver." Margaret spoke in a dazed way, thinking not about the silver that Esther had been sensible enough not to buy, but of the jewelry she seemed to take it for granted Nicolas would buy. Something *beside* the rings? The ring she was already wearing and the gorgeous emerald that had been promised her? A brooch? A necklace? "Everything is beautiful, Esther," she went on with an effort. "So beautiful I don't know how to tell you how I feel, except to say—"

"I don't want you to say anything. I just want you to start wearing these clothes. For heaven's sake, take off that hideous thing you've got on, and get into one of these smart little knitted numbers, which is just right until it's time to change for the evening. If we're going to have supper here, that rose-colored crepe would be just right then. Oh, Margaret, this is such fun! I never had such fun in all my life. Did you?"

"No," said Margaret gravely. "I never did—never in my life."

10 ❧

The sincerity with which she spoke was tinged with more than relief and surprise; it was tinged with thankfulness. The sensation of unreality and haste had been succeeded by such pleasurable excitement that all other sensations, except intermittent exhaustion, had been temporarily engulfed in it; and the exhaustion had meant simply breathing spells between further experiences so stimulating that she was nearly always able to suppress the still small voice of dread which, every now and then, persisted in making itself heard; dread of the moment when she would no longer be surrounded by crowds whose mood was one of conviviality; of the moment when the exotic flowers and costly presents were missing; of the moment when there was no more festive planning to be done because everything was in readiness; of the moment when the irrevocable vows were behind her, when the lights were dim and the house was hushed, and when she was alone with Nicolas, who was no longer her suitor but her husband and determined to act like one. . . .

While Esther continued to prattle, while there were more boxes to open and more people to see, more directions to give, more decisions to make, she continued to dismiss the thought of this moment from her mind, more or less successfully; and when Nicolas arrived with his family, later that same afternoon, there was a new set of impressions, all agreeable and absorbing ones, with which to deal, and more reasons for thankfulness. No prospective parents-in-law could have been more reassuring than Mr. and Mrs. Hale; their sterling qualities were as obvious as their stalwart build and their pleasant intelligent faces; they were elderly but robust, conservatively but appropriately dressed, endowed with the kind of good looks that come from right living and right thinking, beaming with friendliness. They could not be more delighted, they said, that Nicolas had at last persuaded a wonderful girl to marry him. They were greatly impressed with her home—of course, there were fine houses in Vermont, too, as she would see for herself, very soon they hoped; but this was different, it had more elegance and more spaciousness, they wanted to know its history, the extent of the land's productiveness, Margaret's methods for running the place. They had not been quite sure what to bring her for a present and, of course, with such short notice and so little place in their grips, they had been hampered; but they had decided on some old wedding-band china, left them by a great-aunt who had doted on Nick. Naturally, they could not bring the whole set, there were dozens and dozens of pieces; but, from a neat package, carefully wrapped with an eye to possible breakage, they extracted one teacup, one coffee cup, one soup plate, one dinner plate and one dessert plate as samples. The teapot and the cream pitcher, like the soup tureen and the platters, had been too bulky to include, but the sugar bowl was there to show the general shape and style; they thought Margaret would be able to picture what the other dishes looked like.

Margaret was delighted, both with the china itself and with the thought that had been given to providing just the right present; she wanted to set it out right away, to show it to best advantage with the other gifts that had come in. The boxes full of dresses and lingerie were hurried up to her bedroom, and a definite design began to take place, with flowers interspersed between the silverware and china. When Nicolas suggested withdrawing from the scene, on the plea that this was woman's work, his father said it was no such thing, the ladies would get all tired out unless they had plenty of help, especially as he thought the twins were shirking. It was true that their excitement had taken the form of joyous screams and rapt fingering rather than constructive effort; but, under their father's guidance, they began to do better. Margaret was so intrigued with them that she would have been perfectly satisfied if they had not lifted a finger; they were pretty as pictures, merry as larks, but somehow she could not visualize them as belonging either to their parents or to Nicolas. They seemed to belong only to each other, to live illusively in an enchanted realm of their own —not, however, for any lack of enthusiasm in their attitude toward her. They fell upon her with hugs and kisses, both when they arrived and at frequent intervals thereafter. They rattled off questions and, without waiting for her to answer, asked new ones or burst into exclamations of surprise and gladness. They fingered the harp, they played with Perdita, they darted into the kitchen and up the stairs.

"How old are they, anyway?" Margaret managed to ask, as they scampered off over the lawn, shouting as they went.

"Nearly seventeen. They seem younger, don't they—almost like young colts! But, believe it or not, they've done very well at school. They're going to college—Vassar—in the fall. Their arrival was a great surprise—we hadn't expected to have any more children. And then to have *twins!*" But Mrs. Hale laughed as she said it; obviously the surprise had been an agreeable one.

"Nicolas was an only child until then?" Margaret asked hesitantly.

"Yes. We'd have been glad of more, naturally, but it's better not to have had them than to have had them and lost them—that would have been a source of grief! And we've had so few sorrows, my husband and

I! It wouldn't be possible for me to wish you and Nick any greater happiness, my dear, than Waldo and I have had together. Even if we hadn't had *any* children, we mean so much to each other that we really wouldn't have minded too much. I hope and believe you and Nick will feel the same way." She paused, vaguely aware of something slightly disturbing in Margaret's expression. "Nick's been a good son, a great credit to us, though we haven't seen as much of him as we would have liked these last few years," she went on, after a moment, "and good sons generally make good husbands, just as good daughters make good wives. Nick's been telling me about your devotion to your mother and I knew, from the moment I looked at you, that you were going to make a good wife."

Mrs. Hale kissed Margaret again and Margaret cordially returned the caress. Nevertheless, her growing appreciation of her new relatives was tinged with a quality of uneasiness over Mrs. Hale's happy assumption that children would not be of paramount importance to Nicolas and her and there was also an element of puzzlement mingled with this uneasiness. New Englanders were really extraordinary, she reflected, by no means for the first time; they always seemed to manage to send their children to the best educational institutions, however much they might skimp in other ways; and even when they lived in small provincial towns like Woodstock, Vermont, they seemed to keep very much abreast of the times. The Hales had thought nothing of taking a plane trip, on a few hours' notice, preparatory to meeting any number of strangers, including the President of the United States, at their only son's wedding! Mentally, they could go far afield as easily as their son and there seemed to be no doubt that the twins also had a venturesome spirit. There had never been any question of college, as far as she herself was concerned; it would have been both a break with tradition and an unwarrantable extravagance. Her father had, of course, gone to "the University," but his horizon, though not as limited as her mother's, had not extended very far beyond his own acres, his own kinfolk, and his immediate social circle. He would have been astonished at the suggestion that it might profitably be enlarged. Her first impression had been that neither Nicolas nor the twins was the sort of offspring she would have expected the Hales to produce; now she was not so sure—no wonder she was baffled.

"I'm going to try very hard," she said rather tardily. "I mean to live up to all Nicolas' expectations." And there it was again, the unwelcome consciousness of Nicolas' expectations, which at the moment she was not trying so hard to live up to as to forget, and of which Mrs. Hale seemed quite unconscious. "And I do want all of you to enjoy yourselves while you're here," she went on earnestly. "Especially the twins. The rest of us can just sit around the fire and talk after supper; I imagine we'll all be so tired that we'll be glad to. But won't Narcissa and Clarissa want to go dancing? I don't know any boys the right age, but I'm sure Nicolas must. We could invite them to supper and then afterward—"

"Why, Margaret, how thoughtful of you! Of course, they'd be tickled to death! But I wouldn't want you should go to any extra trouble, with all you have on your hands."

"It won't be any trouble, it'll be a pleasure. I'll ask Nicolas right away."

Nicolas had at last succeeded in retreating from the scene of confusion in the drawing room and library and was engaged in earnest conversation with his father. They were seated at a small table at the further end of the gun room, and several sheets of paper, covered with neat jottings and still neater figures, were spread out between them. As Margaret approached, Nicolas shook his head and held up a warning hand, to indicate that he did not wish to be interrupted at that moment and she waited patiently till he glanced toward her with a smile.

"Sorry, darling," he said, "high finance isn't my forte and I was afraid I'd lose the thread if I stopped right then. Father and I have been trying to figure out what you'd need to run this house on while I'm gone and how much you ought to have for an emergency fund besides. Of course, I've already taken out life insurance, but that doesn't seem to be the answer for everything."

"I'd have liked a little more time to work this out," Mr. Hale said quickly. "Nick didn't make it clear to me, over the phone, that you were going to stay here, Margaret. I took it for granted you'd be going to Peru with him. If I'd understood. . . ." For the first time there was a troubled note in his hearty voice. "Of course, he's explained to me that you didn't make up your mind soon enough for him to change his plans," Nick's father went on. "And like as not, he won't need to be gone so long this time as he was the last, or that he can arrange to have you join him later on. I hope so—one or the other, I mean. Right now, it would help if you could tell me just what wages and heat and light and so on would be likely to come to. And food. And taxes. I don't know whether or not the cost of living is about the same in Virginia as it is in Vermont."

"I don't know much about the cost of living in Virginia either," Margaret answered. "The kind of living Nicolas is talking about. I've been paying only one servant until day before yesterday and she and I haven't needed much food. I've kept the heating bills down by closing most of the house and I've used very little electricity, and no work has been done on the grounds or in the stables. Now Nicolas wants to change all that. Of course, I'm very, very grateful to him. But could you give me time to make up a budget—after there isn't quite so much else to do? I wasn't prepared for this, either, so you must know how I feel."

"You take all the time you've a mind to," Mr. Hale said reassuringly. "We'll set down six hundred dollars a month as our first figure, and then we'll change it if we need to. Meanwhile, the emergency fund'll take care of extra things, if you run short."

"I shan't run short," Margaret answered firmly. "But thank you very much, Mr. Hale."

"Couldn't you begin right now calling me Father Hale, Margaret? I'd take it very kindly if you could."

He had risen and put his arm around her shoulder. Now he patted this gently. He knows there's something strange about the marriage, Margaret said to herself. Nicolas may fool everyone else, but he isn't fooling his father. His father's a shrewd man, along with being a very kind one. "Of course I can," she said aloud, looking gratefully at her prospective father-in-law. "I'd love to. . . . And now, if it's all right, may I say what I came to say when you threw me off by talking about all this money? I thought perhaps the twins would like to go dancing tonight, only I don't know any escorts to suggest for them. And I thought Nicolas might."

Nicolas had not risen at the same time with his father. He had appeared to be still wholly absorbed in figures and his expression had been inscrutable. Now, belatedly, he looked up.

"Why, that was very thoughtful of you, darling, with everything else you have on your mind. I confess it hadn't occurred to me to worry about the twins. Well, there's my secretary, Lester Wendell; he's a good boy and he must have a friend he could get hold of. Of course, I could suggest any number of young attachés at the Peruvian Embassy or aides at the White House, but I imagine the twins would consider them too elderly—they must be pushing thirty or at least in their later twenties."

"I should think your secretary and a friend of his would be just right. Why not telephone and invite them to have supper with us? And perhaps they'd be satisfied to dance here too. We've got to clear this room anyway, to make room for the guests at the wedding reception, and it might be a good plan to do it today instead of tomorrow, there'll be so many other things to do then. I have some old records—Mother used to enjoy them—and we could get some more; the phonograph isn't in bad condition. Besides, Rufus is a very sprightly fiddler and one of his cousins—I think it's Lafe—plays a banjo. I don't know about the talents of the other kinfolk, but there are sure to be some amateur musicians among them, and they'd love to call the numbers and that sort of thing. The twins might actually think a dance like that was more fun than one at the Shoreham and anyway, they can go to a hotel Wednesday night, after the wedding."

"I'll say you'd had a real brainstorm, if you'll forget about the phonograph and concentrate on the kinfolk. Let me get to that telephone quick. Then we'll start moving furniture."

"Just a minute, Nick. While you're on the phone, I want Margaret should tell me something about these guns of hers. I've been interested in picking up a few here and there, my dear," he said, turning to her, "to add to some that came down the line from the Green Mountain Boys. But my collection can't hold a candle to yours."

"Why I hadn't thought of this as a collection!" she said quite honestly. But she was pleased at his appraisal of her ancestral possessions, and again the feeling that he was aware of some disquieting factor in his son's suit and was all the more determined that his own attitude should be one of kindliness and reassurance had exactly the effect she believed he intended.

"This old flint musket over the fireplace was in use on the place before the Revolution," she told him. "I really don't know which of my forebears used that. I don't know whether or not you're interested in swords, too, but this is the one my great-grandfather, Major Lovell Porterfield, wore at Seven Pines and throughout the rest of the war. He was on General Joe Johnston's staff and the general himself gave it to him. While acting as a courier at the Battle of Williamsburg, my great-grandfather had his horse shot from under him and a shell fragment, which barely grazed him, cut away his scabbard and sword. When he returned to headquarters without his sword, General Johnston gave him this one. It had been a gift, the general said, from some friends in New Orleans after the Battle of Manassas."

"Of course, I'm interested in swords. But what about this pair of pistols? I don't know as I ever saw any just like those."

"They're old French dueling pistols. That's all I ever heard about them. I've often wondered if there were a story connected with them, too."

"They were doubtless the property of some jealous husband, who used them to rid himself of an inconvenient rival," Nicolas remarked, as he returned to announce the success of his telephoning.

"Well now, if that's the case, I wonder how he happened to have a chance to get jealous, Nick," Mr. Hale said thoughtfully. "Could be he didn't watch over his wife carefully and tenderly all the time, like he ought."

"If she were the kind that needed all that watching, he should have had sense enough not to marry her in the first place," Nicolas said rather brusquely. "I've had sense enough to choose a girl I could trust. . . . Well, let's not waste any more time in idle suppositions. Here are Sam and Uncle Virginius just in time to help with the furniture."

By the time the gun room was cleared for dancing, Lester Wendell and his friend, whose name proved to be Burt Lassiter, had also appeared on the scene and Annabelle and Rufus had begun to serve cocktails and canapés. Meanwhile, more and more members of the dusky clan were reinforcing Cassie in the kitchen. On this occasion there were no reproaches to Margaret for having omitted chicken with all the fixin's and there had been many toothsome additions to the main dish, including a huge ham and a great platter overflowing with fried oysters, as mound after mound of hot biscuits, carefully wrapped in snowy napkins and dripping with butter, were passed in quick succession.

"I've always prided myself I set a good table, Margaret, but it's nothing to yours," Mrs. Hale said, as she pushed her plate gently aside and gave a contented sigh of repletion. Then, with a startled glance at Annabelle, who was beginning to clear the table, she added, "Don't tell me there's more coming!"

"Why, just dessert! You have dessert in Woodstock, Vermont, don't you, Mother Hale? And this is very light—just floating island and wine jelly and the Great Cake made from Martha Washington's own recipe. That isn't rich like a regular fruit cake. I think you'll like it."

"No one will be able to dance a step, Margaret, after all this food. It'll be as much as I can do to get up from my chair and waddle out of the dining room."

"Oh, Mummy, how can you say such a thing? We're dying to begin right away. And Rufus is ready for us—he's tuning his fiddle."

"Narcissa, where are your manners, jumping up like that? You haven't even asked Margaret if you could be excused."

"But you will excuse us, won't you, Margaret? Because Lester has asked me for the first dance and Burt has asked Clarissa and if we don't get started pretty soon the night will be practically *gone!*"

So Margaret laughed and said, of course, the twins and Lester and Burt were to go ahead and dance in the gun room and the rest of them would be along as soon as they had finished their coffee in the dining room. And presently they were all dancing, Mrs. Hale with Nick and Margaret with Waldo and Sam and Esther together. Then Sam and Nick changed partners and next there was a general shuffle and finally Nick and Margaret were together and she was almost stifled with that strange sensation that was half pain and half joy, only this time, instead of shooting quickly through her and then subsiding, it was stabbing her again and again.

"You know, this is tremendous; in fact, it's perfect," Nicolas was saying, as the tune came to an end and he half released her from his arms. "I mean everything. The way you've handled everything. The way the family's fallen for you. The way you're dancing. I meant to go over some more details with you tonight, about ushers and so on. I've invited Sam, but he doesn't know by sight most of the people who'll be coming. Lester does, but he can't manage without some expert help. Perhaps your uncle can suggest a few highly suitable Virginians. We'll take care of that in the morning—unless you'd like to slip away with me for a few minutes to that boudoir of mine. We can't do much of anything constructive about ushers in the midst of all this racket."

"And is that what we'd do if we went to the boudoir—something constructive about ushers—"

"Well, of course, we might get around to something else constructive."

Margaret hesitated. She knew that if she consented to go with him, the gratification he already felt at the success of the evening would be enormously increased. He was now convinced that, as a hostess, she was unexpectedly competent and resourceful and, as a prospective daughter-in-law, more than satisfactory in every respect; the conviction was still lacking that she was a normal woman awakened at last to the normal instincts which would permit her to respond to her suitor; and, despite the stabbing thrill of pain and pleasure, she was not ready to so convince him. She knew—Nicolas had as good as admitted it—that if she went to the boudoir with him, he would not keep his word, he would kiss her after all, the way he had done that first night and perhaps—what was it he had said?—"go on from there." She looked up at him and shook her head and, suddenly, there were tears in her eyes.

"It's been perfect for me, too—so far. Don't let's spoil it, Nicolas."

"I didn't intend to spoil it. I merely hoped to crown it," he said. Then, releasing her completely, he turned and walked over to Esther. "I want the next dance with you," he said tersely.

11 ❧

"Miss Marg'ret, dey's a gennelmun at de do' say he gotta see you."

"Annabelle, I told you I couldn't see *anyone*."

"Ah knows, Miss Marg'ret, but dis gennelmun say he gwine stan' right dere till you comes. An' he's got two odder gennelmun wid him. Dey's out pokin' roun' in de yard, like dey wuz huntin' somepun you got hid dere."

Margaret had already been up for several hours, but she was still in her bedroom, and still only partly dressed. She had not been able to sleep, so she had had an early breakfast and decided to spend the first half of the morning putting her clothes in order, thus making space in her closet and bureau drawers for all the beautiful new things Esther had brought her, as she discarded many of the dilapidated old ones. Annabelle would have been delighted to help, for reasons not altogether disinterested: it was her experience that, when ladies embarked on such an undertaking, their maids were likely to benefit, if such maids stood watchfully by and exclaimed with admiration over some item that their mistress was beginning to eye with disfavor; and though her new employer's normal wardrobe did not seem to offer the rich rewards of some she had seen—being, indeed, rather scanty and shabby—still there would probably be something worth gleaning. There might even be some trifle in the vast contents of the big boxes that had come from New York which did not suit Miss Margaret's fancy or which escaped her notice. But Annabelle was doomed to disappointment: Miss Margaret had a headache and she did not feel like talking; it would be easier to go through her things alone, and decide for herself what she wanted to do with them, than to give directions to anyone. Besides, she did not intend to work steadily; she would spend a few minutes sorting and arranging and then she would lie down for a few minutes; she might even go back to bed, unless her head felt better. And when, despite this verdict, Annabelle still lingered hopefully, Margaret told her, rather sharply, to pick up the breakfast tray and go back to the kitchen, where she was really needed.

Annabelle felt aggrieved. She welcomed the ring of the doorbell which presaged another gift or another visitor; and when the gentleman at the front door told her so firmly that he proposed to stay there until he saw Miss Porterfield, Annabelle was delighted at the excuse for getting back to the bedroom and seeing what, if any, promising progress had been made with the contents of the closet and the bureau drawers.

The news that there was someone at the door who declined to leave until received might possibly have been passed over without excitement. Reporters were notoriously importunate and aggressive, and Nicolas had warned Margaret that she might expect to be confronted with them at almost any time now and that she must not let them wear her down. But strange men poking around the lawn were something else again; such trespassing on personal property, such a violation of privacy, were not to be tolerated, not for an instant. She snatched up a dress that she had casually tossed over a nearby chair, and which happened to be the "hideous thing" Esther had persuaded her to discard the day before in favor of a smart little knitted number and, flinging it on, pelted down the stairs, with Perdita at her heels, her head throbbing harder than ever with haste and rage. Then she threw open the door, which Annabelle had closed in the face of the persistent caller, and belligerently confronted the thickset, determined looking man who stood there, at the same time endeavoring to prevent Perdita's pursuit of his companions.

"What do you mean by this intrusion?" she demanded. "And what are those other men doing on my lawn? They are acting as if they expected to find a body buried there!"

"I'm terribly sorry, Miss Porterfield. I'm Kent Curtis, Chief of the White House Secret Service, and the others are with me, working under my direction. We've been informed that the President and Mrs. Maynard are planning to attend your wedding and the reception here tomorrow evening and were given to understand you knew we'd have to go over the premises, inside and out, some time today. We've already been to the church and the Vestry House and the churchyard and I think the inspection of your grounds is almost finished. That had to be especially thorough, because your beautiful boxwood is so thick that it —well, it makes a most effective screen. And we've already checked the front steps and feel they're quite secure. We had to be certain because, in some old Virginia houses, they're pretty shaky. But of course we didn't want to go into your residence until I'd seen you personally and assured myself this wasn't an inconvenient time for you."

"Oh, Mr. Curtis, do forgive me! Won't you please come in? I—I didn't understand at all! If a message were sent to me, it must have reached here when I was out or asleep, or something and my—my staff isn't very experienced. No one working for me would have had any idea what Secret Service meant and I may as well be honest with you— it didn't occur to me that any special precautions would be necessary. Of course, it should have. But this is the first time a president has been to Hills' End since Jefferson Davis came here after the Battle of Manassas and, naturally, that was before my time!"

The corners of Kent Curtis' mouth twitched slightly, but his answer was becomingly grave: he and his men would try to disturb her as little as possible, he assured her, as he accepted her invitation to enter; but it would be necessary for them to familiarize themselves with the entire house; not only the ground floor, but the family bedrooms and guest chambers, the servants' sleeping quarters, the kitchen, basement and attic. After doing this, they would make suggestions about any other special aspects of the situation which required careful attention. For instance, did she have plenty of fire extinguishers? If not, he would see to it that some were installed where they might conceivably be needed; almost any old house presented a fire hazard, but of course it was not a reflection on her if she had not realized this. He felt sure there was a well from which water could be pumped, but was there enough hose to reach any distance? That was something else she might easily have overlooked, but she was not to worry. . . . He would be checking with the Fire Department at Alexandria, in any case, at the same time that he checked with the local police about handling any traffic on the roads that might be necessary. And were the floors highly polished? Was there any danger that one of the rugs might slip? This was what he meant, in a general way. Next, they would decide at just what points the special agents should be stationed; with all the valuable antique ornaments and books there were in the house and all the costly wedding presents coming in, Miss Porterfield really ought to welcome their attendance on her own account, he reminded her, stooping over to pat Perdita.

His speech was soothing, his manner deferential; Margaret had more cause to be chagrined at the thought of the way she had greeted Kent Curtis than at anything he or his assistants did or said; but it took them some time to make their survey, ask their questions and offer their suggestions. First, about the service. Would her own regular staff be taking care of everything or would there be caterers? In the former case, he would accept her word for it that her faithful retainers were reliable, that there were no subversive elements among them; in the latter, he would have to check with the catering establishment. Her "regular staff," until two days before that, Margaret told him blushingly, had consisted of just one old colored woman, Cassie Preston; now, because Dr. Hale had insisted she needed more household help, Cassie's niece Annabelle, who had opened the door for Mr. Curtis—or, rather, who had declined to open it—and Annabelle's husband Rufus had come to Hills' End, too, and would be staying there; for the wedding, all their relatives would be on hand; Margaret did not believe any of them so much as knew the meaning of the word subversive and, though she couldn't classify them as "faithful retainers," she had known most of them, except the very youngest, all her life, as they lived near by; she thought Mr. Curtis would describe them as "good old-fashioned darkies"; they would handle the wedding supper themselves. . . . Well, he was willing to take her word for it that they were reliable, Mr. Curtis said. Cassie, the one who had lived there all along, was the cook, wasn't she? He would have just a word with her, or Miss Porterfield could do it for him if she preferred, to let Cassie know there would be one special agent stationed in the kitchen, to be sure everything served to the President was all right. In this case, that was only a matter of form and he'd like to be sure the old woman wouldn't be upset by it. . . . Another special agent would be at the house in advance to inform the hostess just when the President would arrive. . . . Why, but *I'm* the hostess, Margaret said in some confusion and, of course, I can't leave the church until. . . . No, no, of course not, Mr. Curtis said reassuringly; but the bride and groom are the first to leave the church and then the immediate family. Naturally, out of courtesy, if for no other reason, the President and Mrs. Maynard would remain in their pew until those had gone and this would give plenty of time. Then Mr. Curtis would suggest Miss Porterfield—that was to say, Dr. and Mrs. Hale—should be at the door to welcome the President and Mrs. Maynard—the same door by which he, Kent Curtis, had come in; and that the other guests should be ushered in the side door, where perhaps Dr. Page and Mr. and Mrs. Waldo Hale would be near at hand to receive them. . . . Now, if he could just have the guest list, so that the guests could be checked off as they arrived. Margaret was terribly sorry, but it wasn't fully made out yet; she and Dr. Hale had tried to complete it, but there had been so much to do and so little time to do it. . . . Yes, yes, Kent Curtis understood perfectly, but she *could* have it ready to submit to one of his men the first thing the next morning, couldn't she? That was when both the "inner perimeter" and the "outer perimeter" would be formed. The inner perimeter would be the circle of special agents close to the house; the outer perimeter would be the circle of men on the other side of the boxwood. They would have to come early in order to be sure that no crasher could secrete himself in some curve of the boxwood and not be discovered. They would know their entire situation and, inside the house, the special agents would be "spotted" so that the President could be easily watched as he moved from room to room. Kent Curtis assumed he would be staying for about an hour. . . .

As all this went on, Margaret's headache had grown steadily worse. The combined facts that presents and telegrams continued to arrive at such a rapid rate she did not even have time to open them; that Perdita barked every time the doorbell rang; that the library and drawing room were increasingly cluttered; that the telephone never stopped ringing, but that no reassuring call came from Nicolas did not help to calm her. And, when Kent Curtis and his assistants had left, after accepting her proffer of coffee, and Cassie came to the library and reminded her that not one word had been said about lunch, that no one in the kitchen knew what Miss Margaret wanted to eat herself or how many people would be eating with her, the distracted girl burst into tears.

"I don't want anything to eat. Why do you keep asking me that when you ought to realize I don't want anything? And I don't know how many other people will be here. I haven't heard from Mr. and Mrs. Steinmetz or Mr. and Mrs. Hale or Dr. Page or—Dr. Hale the entire morning. For all I know, they may be back in New York or Vermont or Charlottesville or Peru by now."

Cassie sat down heavily beside Margaret and, with the corner of a not irreproachable apron, tried to wipe away the latter's tears. "You actin' like you ain' got good knowledge," she said, lifting Perdita into her lap and petting her. "Heah you not only got all de cake you kin eat, aftah you done gwine hungry dis lon' while, you got hit frosted. Iffen none o' dem fine folks ben to see you yet dis mo'nin' hit's cuz you acted so plum' tuckered out las' evenin' dey figures you needed yo' res', an' Ah reckon you does. Iffen dey tried to call you, how dey gwine do hit, wid dat foam ringin' ev'ry minute, wid odder folks askin' kin dey take yo' pitcher, an' fool things like dat? You oughtta git right back in de bed an' stay dere till you feels bettah."

"I don't believe I'm going to feel any better. I seem to be feeling worse and worse all the time."

"Den hit's like Ah says, you ain' got good knowledge. You oughtta be right down on yo' knees thankin' Sweet Jesus fo' all He done fo' you an' give you since He sent Mistuh Nic'las a-co'tin': a frien' like Miz Steinmetz, bringin' you mo' pretty clo'es dan you can evah weah out, an' dat kin' lady an' gennelmun, proud to have you fo' dere daughter, an' a real prince to marry you."

"I know, Cassie, I know. And I'm ashamed of being so cross and so unreasonable, truly I am. But I can't help wishing, if it were the Lord who sent Mr. Nicolas courting, that He didn't tell him to give me a little more time. You know I hadn't seen Mr. Nicolas in years and years and then suddenly he appeared out of nowhere and gave me just five days to get ready to marry him."

Cassie snorted. "You didn' have to say yes, did you?" she inquired cogently. "He give you a chance to say no. Co'se, you'd have ben an awful fool iffen you had, but he give you de chance. Mebbe you don' know hit, honey, but dere's plenny girls don' have no chance to say nuthin', once a man makes up his min' he wants dem, specially iffen he thinks dey might trifle wid him. He don' give dem five days to get ready fo' him. Mah firs' baby's pappy didn' do none of dem things. Ah wuz walkin' home aftah dark, through dat li'l stretch of woods 'tween de Big House an' de qua'tahs an' first thing Ah knew he had me down on de groun' an' wuz pullin' off my clo'es."

"Oh, Cassie, how dreadful! I'm so sorry for you! I never knew anything like that ever happened—I mean to one of our own people, on a place like this."

Cassie smoothed her apron, which had ceased to serve as a makeshift handkerchief. "Reckon hit happens in plenny places to plenny people," she said calmly. "An' hit don' hurt none—aftah dat firs' time."

"Do you mean to say there were other times?"

"Lawd yes, honey! Aftahward, seemed like dat man couldn' let an evenin' go by, all summah, widout comin' alon' dat same path."

"But why didn't you do something about it? Why didn't you

complain? You could have found a way to be defended and safeguarded from such a scoundrel."

"Lawd, honey, dat's w'at Ah'm tryin' to tell you! Ah didn' want to be defended from dat man. Ah went alon' slow, draggin' mah feet, so he wouldn' have no trouble catchin' up wid me. But by'm by, yo' pappy catched us togedder an' say we wa'n't to carry on dataway no mo', not on his proppity. But he knowed you can' go agains' nature, not iffen yo' youn' an' got yo' health. He knowed us'n carry on somewheres de same way, lessen he give us a cabin of our own an' asked de preachah to marry us. So dat's jus' w'at he done. He give us a right nice cabin happened to be em'ty, cuz de no'count niggahs who ben livin' in hit had gone off to work at East Lawn fo' mo' money, 'stead of stayin' wid dere own white folks. Co'se dey wuz kin o' mine, but not close, thank de Sweet Jesus, so 'twuz good riddance ev'ry way when dey quit. One nice thing dey done, dey planted sunflowahs. Give me de idee. Ain' you nevah noticed, honey, dere's always flowahs roun' de cabin wheah my po' ol' cousin 'Randa live now?"

"Yes, I have, but I didn't know—"

"Dat wuz de one Mistuh Herbert give Zeke an' me," Cassie said proudly. "At firs' we kinda missed dem evenin's in de woods, but aftah awhile we got used to bein' togedder indoors. Den de firs' thing we knowed mah Jesse wuz on de way. Co'se dat wuz a lon' while fo' yo' time, so mebbe you ain' nevah heard dat he were de bigges' baby evah bo'n on Hills' End. Two days an' three nights hit wuz befo' Ah finally turn him loose, hollerin' to heaven all de while. But jus' like de odder, bo'nin' babies ain' so ha'd aftah de firs' time. Ah ain' sayin' Ah wan't skeered when Ah knowed Ah wuz in de fam'ly way again, de very same spring. But Neel'yus, he wuz smallah, an' he come pushin' alon' so fast Ah couldn' get my breath to scream much befo' he slipped right into de world. . . . W'at's de mattah, honey? You white as a sheet! Come lon' upstairs, Cassie gwine put you to bed an' see you get a good long res'."

"May we come right in? We hoped we could help some way."

Margaret struggled to her feet. Mr. and Mrs. Hale, both beaming with good will, were already standing on the threshold of the library and eagerly making suggestions, almost simultaneously.

"The twins have gone sightseeing with that nice young Mr. Lassiter who was here last night. He's going to take them to lunch, too, but he promised he'd have them at the church in time for the rehearsal. And I thought perhaps I could help you with your clothes. I heard you say you were planning to give away some, now that you're going out of mourning, and I know that nice Mrs. Steinmetz has brought you everything you need for your trousseau, so you'll have to do some reorganizing and it's always easier when two women can do it together."

"And *I* thought, while you and Mother were busy with frills and furbelows, I might get after those fine guns of yours and give them a good cleaning. I hope you won't take it amiss, Margaret, when I tell you they're in great need of one. Of course, you couldn't be expected to realize that and, anyway, you've had other things on your mind. But they're rusty and they're just plain dirty. I stopped on my way out here and got me a gun-cleaning kit, complete with everything I'll need, Outers make. You ought to keep one handy here all the time. When you and Mother come back downstairs, I'll show you what a good job I've done. I thought if Cassie here would send me in a snack, I could eat while I worked and maybe you and Mother would have one in your room. That way, we wouldn't lose any time. And just forget about the doorbell and the telephone in the meanwhile. Annabelle can attend to those."

"You're wonderfully kind and thoughtful. You would be a great help to me—both of you. But, as far as the telephone's concerned, Nicolas might call, so I think—"

"No, he called *us* and said to tell you he'd be at the church, promptly at six. He's been dictating to Lester Wendell all morning, trying to clear up the backlog of correspondence. Just as soon as the announcement of an expedition appears in the newspaper, his mail is flooded with letters from all kinds of people who want to go along. This morning there was one from a barber in Buffalo and one from a chiropractor in Chicago. Nick said at least they had the merit of being alliterative. All these aspirants have to be told that the personnel of the expedition has already been selected, so much as Dr. Hale regrets, and so forth and so forth. Then there are all the thank-you notes to people who've been of real assistance in one way or the other and formal letters of appreciation to the Peruvian Government and to the New York group of the Explorers Club—the head division. He has to acknowledge the honor of being allowed to carry the flag which was presented to him Sunday and promise to send pictures that show it flying over his camp. Well, there were lots of other letters, but that will give you an idea of Nick's homework. He's also been in touch with Mr. Bates—that's your rector's name, isn't it?—and they agreed it would be better to have the rehearsal before dinner, rather than afterward, because then you could have a good time without watching the clock and worrying that you might be keeping Mr. Bates up too late. The Steinmetzes thought that was a good plan, too. We haven't meant to go over your head, my dear, in coming to all these decisions. We just wanted to make things easier for you when you had so much on your mind already. We hope you realize that."

She did realize it, Margaret said and she spoke sincerely, stifling the little nagging disappointment because Nicolas had not himself been in touch with her; and she was duly grateful for the elder Hales' kindness. She had so many new clothes that she had been staggered by the attempt to put them in order and confessed she hadn't got anywhere with it; and she knew the guns were in dreadful condition, but there hadn't been anyone available to take care of those, either. At the end of two hours, her gratitude was even greater than it had been when she first expressed it. Mrs. Hale made short shift of creating order from the chaos in which she found Margaret's wardrobe; the beautiful new stockings, undergarments and nightgowns, separately and neatly piled, were lying in bureau drawers with small bags filled with dried lavender tucked in among them; and the coats, furs, suits, dresses and negligees were suspended on padded hangers in the closet and *armoire*. When all this was done, she suggested that, as it had apparently been some time since Margaret tried on the ancestral wedding dress in which she planned to be married, it might be a good idea for them to get it out of the chest, or wherever it was, and make sure it did not need altering or mending. So they went together up the steep attic stairs and dragged from under the eaves a cowhide trunk, bound with metal and strapped with leather. Margaret unlocked this with a rusty key and, raising the lid, disclosed a tray covered with linen diapering; when she turned this covering back, almost reverently, the century-old bridal finery was revealed.

The dress was made of brocade, which had doubtless once been snow white, but which was now ivory with age. It had the full skirt and tight bodice which Nicolas had visualized; however, as Margaret had warned him, it was not designed to leave the shoulders bare, but to cover these completely; it was fastened down its entire length from neckline to hem with a double row of tiny buttons, looped together with silken threads, and closed, just below the throat, with a turn-over collar of soft lace. The same kind of lace edged the bell-shaped sleeves and formed the border of the filmy veil. A band of waxen orange blossoms divided the part that would be thrown back from the face at the end of the marriage ceremony from the cap which would remain in place as the bride went down the aisle; and this band widened at either end to a cluster, so that, all in all, it formed an exquisite headdress. Short white glacé gloves, clocked white silk stockings and narrow, low-heeled white satin slippers completed the ensemble; and a prayer book and hymnal, bound in white leather, had been carefully placed in the folds of the sheet.

"Well, it's certainly the most beautiful wedding dress I ever saw in my life!" Mrs. Hale exclaimed, as Margaret shook it out to its full length and held it up for inspection. Then, looking at it more closely, she added a little doubtfully, "But, like I said, I think you ought to make sure you can get into it. Girls used to have smaller waists than they do now, even slim girls like you."

"I know. But I did manage all right when I wore it in the pageant, though I admit I wasn't very comfortable. Perhaps you remember that, a few years ago, there was a brief vogue for wearing corsets again and I got hold of a new one and was laced into it. It wasn't a regular coat of armor, like the old-fashioned kind, but it served the purpose. So I thought it would again. I've saved it. It's here, underneath some other things."

Margaret draped the diapering over the back of a nearby chair and laid the wedding dress and veil carefully across it. Then she lifted another dress from the tray and, with less solicitude, tossed it across the open lid of the trunk. Mrs. Hale leaned forward to survey a crimson satin, belted with an embroidered black velvet sash, to which Margaret seemed to be paying such slight attention.

"Why, my dear, this is a beautiful dress, too! In fact, it's magnificent! And it looks as if it belonged to the same period. Did it?"

"Yes. That was the second day dress."

"The *second day dress?*"

"Yes. Brides always had them in Virginia. I mean, well-outfitted brides. Didn't they in Vermont?"

"I don't think so. I never even heard of one before. Did it have some special significance?"

"Yes, of course. You see, the second day the bride had to we : something different. I mean, she wasn't—well, a girl any more. She was a married woman. So this was to prove—"

Margaret had stopped, flushing scarlet and hastily resuming her search for the corset. Mrs. Hale spoke to her very gently.

"I'm sorry, my dear, to have seemed so stupid. But there's no reason why you should be embarrassed. She was proud to be a wife, wasn't she? This dress is just as beautiful as the other, in a different way, and just as symbolic. Let's take this one down with us, too, and try them both on. Nicolas would want you should wear it if he knew about it. And you can, very easily, since you're staying right here in your own house and don't have to worry about being conspicuous."

So Mrs. Hale and Margaret went back to the latter's room with the wedding dress and the second day dress and all the accessories, including the corset, and the fittings took place. Though Mrs. Hale chatted cheerfully all the time and said she often helped the twins with their clothes, nothing could alter the fact that the ancestral dresses were very tight and the corset an instrument of torture and an ancestral chemise very scant covering for a girl who was not accustomed to having a stranger around when she was not fully clad. But, as far as providing for the next two days was concerned, Mrs. Hale was more than equal to the situation.

"Let me have a closer look at those dresses, will you, my dear? Well, it's just as I thought—good big seams. Pass me a pair of scissors and let me rip those under the arms. Now give me a needle and thread and I'll baste them up again in two shakes of a dead lamb's tail. Then you can try on the dresses once more. Of course, it's bound to show a little, where we've let them out, but who's going to notice, with your veil and everything, in candlelight? And the next day, no one will be seeing you but Nicolas and I'll warrant he won't be looking for underarm seams in that crimson dress."

So, if not actually in two shakes of a dead lamb's tail, at least in a very short time, the two dresses were satisfactorily altered and, when Mrs. Hale and Margaret went downstairs, it was to find Mr. Hale beaming even more broadly than he had been when they left him. The old flintlock musket was a treasure, he told Margaret. He knew Lafayette had given some French *pistols,* very much like it in general character, to the poorly equipped colonists; but this gun was of even earlier manufacture. When they talked before, she hadn't mentioned this handsome Kentucky rifle; to his way of thinking, that was an even greater treasure. Did she know how the stock happened to be striped? Well, of course, it wasn't a happenstance at all—when wood with a curly grain wasn't available, plain stocks were "flame-grained" by wrapping twine soaked in saltpeter spirally around the wood and, when this was burned off, there was that tiger-stripe pattern! And would she just look at the silver inlay and the ornamental patch boxes! Some places, these rifles were still used in shooting matches and the "buffs" still loaded them just like in the good old days. As she knew, the dueling pistols were French, too. In fact, comparatively few were of American manufacture, though some were made in Philadelphia by Henry Deringer, Jr. and Richard Constable. Hers were a matched pair of Le-Faucheux percussion, complete with loading accessories; Mr. Hale knew of only one pair that could compare with them and those were in the West Point Museum. Did Margaret know that pistols primarily designed for dueling were never ornamented with gold or silver, like those designed for other uses? The reason was that there must be nothing which might catch the sun and distract the dueler from his purpose. Dueling pistols were simple, finely made, functional arms which "pointed." It was speed that counted. The first shot carried the day.

"So when that jealous husband Nicolas was talking about came home unexpectedly, everything was probably all over very quickly?" Margaret asked, trying to speak lightly.

"No doubt about it, no doubt whatever," Waldo Hale said conclusively. "I only hope the survivor, whichever he was, also happened to be the better man of the two. As I said, I wonder if the jealous husband wasn't some to blame himself, going off and leaving his wife instead of cherishing her, like he'd sworn at the altar to do. Well, that's enough about duels. Here's a shotgun, looks like one my father had, made by W. and C. Scott and Son. Probably your father, or maybe your grandfather, shot ducks and geese with it right from your front lawn. But the barrel's laminated now. It would be foolhardy for anyone to shoot it with modern ammunition—might blow right up in his face, and don't you forget that. Now this sword that was used at Seven Pines—have you noticed here on the counterguard the pelican feeding its young? Isn't that the coat of arms of Louisiana?"

"Yes, it is."

"And see the inscription on the blade: 'Dufilho, N. O.' That must have been the manufacturer of the sword in New Orleans."

"Yes, it must have been, but Great-grandfather Porterfield could never find out anything about him. Years after the war, when he was in New Orleans on business, he tried to locate Dufilho, but apparently he'd been dead a long time and nobody seemed to know anything about him or his sword factory."

"Come now, Waldo, that's enough about weapons and such like," Mrs. Hale interposed. "We'll all have us a nice cup of tea and then I want Margaret should go upstairs and take a rest before she starts for the church. There isn't another thing she needs to do—the house looks lovely and smells so good what with the flowers and the things Cassie's cooking, I can't hardly tell whether it's roses or wedding cake I keep sniffing. I may snatch forty winks myself before I change my dress. Nick said he was sure I'd be welcome to freshen up in the spare room, so I've got what I need right with me. . . . Mercy, is that the doorbell again? Well, let's pretend we don't hear it. I've a mind to tell Annabelle if any more presents come, just to pile them up in the hall for now and let me take care of them tomorrow, if that's all right by you, my dear. I'm real good at making lists."

With an ever-growing sense of obligation to her prospective parents-in-law, Margaret docilely drank her tea, took her rest and ignored the doorbell. But she was unable to dismiss from her mind forebodings which the story Cassie had told her with such relish had done much to intensify; and she was further troubled with recurrent qualms about what manner of greeting she might expect from Nicolas when they met at the church. The abruptness with which he had left her the night before, in the pause between dances, had passed unobserved by every-one except herself for, almost at the same moment, her uncle Virginius had benignly claimed that now it was his turn, that she needn't pretend that she thought he was too old to waltz; and after that someone proposed a Virginia Reel and the evening ended on a note of joyous hilarity. Practically everyone kissed everyone else good night and, in the pleasant general confusion, the fact that Margaret was not singled out for an especially ardent and prolonged embrace had, presumably, been unnoticed. At all events, if there were any surprise, because Nicolas did not find a pretext for lingering when the other guests finally announced their intention to depart, there was no illtimed jesting about it. Margaret had reason to hope that not only good manners had prevented this.

At the church, however, the situation would be entirely different. There would be only a few persons present, and the occasion would be free from all disorders and confusion, would, as a matter of fact, be rather solemn in character. Nicolas and his father, his ushers and the rector would make up one little group; she, Margaret, with Uncle Virginius, and Esther and the twins, would make up the other. They would greet each other in the somewhat hushed way that seemed natural for conversation in churches, and then Mr. Bates would tell them just how and where the two different groups should come in, and how and where they should proceed to the altar and leave it. Because the hush would seem natural, perhaps it would also seem natural, not only to her but to everyone else, that Nicolas should greet her rather formally. Desperately, and with chagrin because of this desperation, she hoped so. When the greeting turned out to be casual rather than formal, her relief was unbounded until, late at night, she began to worry because it *had* been so casual.

For Nicolas did not seem to feel the least overpowered by the solemnity of the occasion or aware of any awkwardness in his relations with his fiancée because of the abrupt manner in which he had turned away from her after they had been dancing together. He was already standing near the altar with his group, chatting companionably with Mr. Bates, when Margaret entered with her group; and he nodded pleasantly and said he and his father and Mr. Bates would go back to the Vestry House and come in again by the side door, so that Margaret could see exactly how this was going to be done the next day. As soon as she saw them standing again where they were now, she was to start up the righthand aisle on Uncle Virginius' arm, behind the ushers and the twins and Esther, exactly as she would be doing twenty-four hours later; and then, after Mr. Bates had gone over the marriage service with them, meanwhile cautioning them not to say "and thereto I plight thee my troth" and himself omitting the pronouncement which declared them, Margaret and Nicolas, man and wife, he and she would start down the other aisle together. It was really all very simple. In fifteen minutes they could be on their way to Washington for dinner. They would let Sam and Esther make a quick getaway because the dinner party was theirs, and even as accomplished a hostess as Esther liked to put around place cards and pass judgment on the flower arrangements at the last moment. Nicolas would take the younger ushers in his car, as long as he had brought them out to the church, and he supposed this automatically meant the twins would crowd in on him, too. Margaret and Uncle Virginius and Mr. and Mrs. Hale could all go in the Hales' Hertz Rent-A-Car, as Uncle Virginius had very properly dismissed the taxi that he should never have taken in the first place. Now that this was all so easily settled, should they get on with the ceremony?

Perhaps it was because Mr. Bates seemed to feel Nicolas was handling everything in the best possible way and wanted to co-operate with him that the brief rehearsal actually bore no resemblance to a "ceremony"; or perhaps it was the other way around, perhaps Mr. Bates had told Nicolas before her arrival that they were to be very careful to remember that this was *only* a rehearsal. At all events, it seemed to Margaret that every time she started a sentence, the rector said hastily, "That's plenty. Don't say the rest. Wait until tomorrow." Then she was in the Hertz Rent-A-Car with Mrs. Hale sitting beside her, telling her that she had never seen such a beautiful little church, and Mr. Hale and Uncle Virginius were in the front seat exchanging similar small talk. And presently, they were all in the Steinmetz suite at the Mayflower and there were a great many heavily scented flowers and a great deal of bubbling champagne and the rooms were dreadfully hot and everyone was talking at once again. And she wished she could go home and go to bed and not say another word to anyone. And suddenly Nicolas came and put his arm around her shoulders and said, "Look here, you've just about had it. I'm taking you back to Hills' End."

Then they were in his car and, as soon as they were out of the heavy traffic and on the comparatively free stretches of the Shirley Highway, he put his arm around her shoulders again, but he did not talk to her at all and she was conscious of great gratitude mingled with her exhaustion. She must even have dozed a little, for she was slightly startled when Nicolas eased the car to a stop and she knew they must have reached Hills' End. But she did not try to protest when he lifted her from her seat with as little effort as if she had been a small child and carried her upstairs and lowered her carefully onto her bed. Then she was aware that he was standing beside her looking down at her, though with just what kind of an expression, she could not guess; and she thought that, perhaps, she should try to sit up and put her arms around his neck and thank him, not only for bringing her home, but for doing it in exactly the way he had, without talking to her or kissing her or anything. She realized dimly that it would have pleased him very much if she could have done this, and still more dimly that if she had, some of the tension between them would be gone. But by the time her thoughts were sufficiently clear to result in action, she saw that Nicolas had moved over to her dressing table and seemed to be doing something there, though just what it was she could not see and really did not care. Next she realized that Nicolas was gone and that she had not even known exactly when he left; but that because she had let him leave like that, the tension was still there.

12 ❦

" 'Dearly beloved, we are gathered together here in the sight of God, and in the face of this company—' "

The hush which had been so curiously lacking at the rehearsal had come at last. The *Lohengrin* wedding march had ended, not with a series of chords growing softer and softer, but with startling suddenness, and Margaret was more conscious of this portentous stillness than of anything else in the church—the gleaming whiteness of walls and pews, pulpit and altar; the flickering candlelight; the fragrant flowers; more conscious than of any*one* in the church—Nicolas and his father, the robed rector, the bridal attendants, the President, the diplomats, the senators and scientists, and the wives of all these persons. One small cold hand was still slipped through Uncle Virginius' steady arm, but she had ceased to feel its support. In a minute there would be a still greater hush, when the rector paused and asked if there were anyone present who could show just cause why the ceremony should not go on. No one would answer. The hush would become, if possible, more all-enveloping than before, it would engulf everyone in the church. And yet she, Margaret, knew there were all sorts of reasons why the ceremony should not go on and, if she were not such a coward, she would say so, then and there, in a clear firm voice, to answer the admonition, " 'I require and charge you both, as ye will answer at the dreadful day of judgment when the secrets of all hearts shall be disclosed, that if either of you know any impediment, why ye may not be lawfully joined together in Matrimony, ye do now confess it.' "

She should confess it, not because there was any legal handicap, not because Nicolas already had a wife or she already had a husband; but because, in another minute or two, they would both perjure themselves by saying they were taking each other for better for worse, for richer for poorer, in sickness and in health, to love and to cherish, till death did them part. Nicolas had no idea of loving and cherishing her until they were parted by death; he intended to begin "acting like a husband" that night and to keep on doing so for such time as they were together, only until he was sure of a son. If she conceived immediately, which she knew was what he hoped, perhaps their actual marriage would last only five days and nights. She had known from the beginning that this was his plan; he had told her so quite candidly; still she knew that it did not enter his head that he should be the one to interrupt at this point. But she should have been appalled at the mere thought of such perjury, even if nothing else about the so-called courtship had appalled her. In as far as she could, she herself would remain true to her vows; she would never have another husband, much less a lover. She would keep herself only for Nicolas, to the day of her death, even if that meant living for years like a widow. But her faithfulness would not atone for the perjury she was permitting Nicolas to commit and which it had never occurred to him to consider a crime. At the very moment the rector was asking him the inevitable question and presently Nicolas would make the inevitable answer and it would be her turn.

" 'Margaret, wilt thou have this Man to thy wedded husband, to live together after God's ordinance in the holy estate of Matrimony? Wilt thou love him, comfort him, honour, and keep him in sickness and in health; and, forsaking all others, keep thee only unto him, so long as ye both shall live?' "

Her affirmative answer was as inevitable as her bridegroom's, but it was made in a whisper so low that, with additional panic, she was afraid she might be asked to repeat it. However, Mr. Bates seemed wholly unaware of her terror and her anguish. He was proceeding quite calmly with the service and did not seem to mind in the least because the vows which constituted perjury were pronounced so clearly and resolutely by the groom and murmured almost unintelligibly by the bride. She had been comfortably sure, beforehand, that the word obey was no longer included in the bride's vow; but she was now seized with an unreasoning fear that, like the one about the blessing of children, it might be used or deleted at the discretion of the officiating clergyman and that she might have to repeat the word in the next pledge. Her mother had told her that there were two possible interpretations of this: its general meaning and its special application to a husband's marital rights; and then Emma Porterfield had gone on to tell her daughter a hideous story, based on the second interpretation. It was of this story Margaret was thinking now, all she could think of.

" 'Who giveth this Woman to be married to this Man?' "

Uncle Virginius was taking her small cold hand and placing it quietly in the strong warm hand which Nicolas was already holding out to her, and presently he was clasping hers firmly as, a clause at a time, he repeated the words that the rector was putting into his mouth. Then it was her turn again and she was doing the same thing; and she had hardly finished when she was aware that Mr. Bates was taking a ring from Waldo Hale and "delivering" it to Nicolas, who in turn was again taking the small cold hand which he had so briefly "loosed" and was slipping a circlet of diamonds over the finger for which it was intended and from which the diamond and sapphire circlet had been removed and given into Esther's temporary safekeeping. And Nicolas was saying in a voice even clearer and more resolute than the one in which he had spoken before, " 'With this Ring I thee wed, and with all my worldly goods I thee endow: In the Name of the Father, and of the Son, and of the Holy Ghost. Amen.' "

She must be fair, she must remember that, as far as wordly goods were concerned, Nicolas was not only just but generous. He had thoughtfully and efficiently prepared for her material welfare; and he had far surpassed such prudent provision, when it came to gifts. *Gifts!* That morning when she went to her dressing table, she had found out what Nicolas had been doing there the night before. He had been writing a note, which he had propped up against a heart-shaped box covered, like the much smaller box which had contained her engagement ring, in dark blue velvet; and he had carefully placed this where she could not fail to see it. The note ran:

> "I hope I shall not guess wrong as many times about the location of my lost city as I have about propitious occasions to give you your wedding present. When I suggested going to my 'boudoir' after the dance, I honestly did not mean to anticipate any of my nuptial privileges—only to have the pleasure of fastening your necklace the first time it was put on. I confess that I was very disappointed because you wouldn't give me the chance and I apologize because, on account of this disappointment, I behaved very badly afterward. However, I thought we might retrieve our lost opportunity when I brought you home from the Steinmetz party and that hasn't seemed to work out, either. So please put on the pearls yourself and wear them to our wedding.
>
> "P.S. I am not sure just how I should begin a note like this or how I should sign it, so I am omitting both the salutation and the closing."

Yes, it was true that Nicolas had behaved very badly at the dance, but when Margaret read the note she understood why and she was more than ready to forgive him. She hoped he was equally ready to forgive *her*. If she had gone to the "boudoir" with him, of course it would have been the most natural thing in the world for him to put on her necklace; and then it would have been equally natural for her to lift her face to his and they would have kissed spontaneously, without any discussion about it, and the kiss would have been followed just as instinctively by an embrace. After that, there would have been no question as to how he should begin or close a note to her. It would have begun "Darling" and it would have ended "With all my love." She was to blame because the note had no beginning and no ending. A normal man did not address his bride as "My dear Margaret" on the very eve of their wedding or sign himself "Cordially yours." She knew that Nicolas must have looked at her, as she came up the aisle toward him, to see if she had put on the necklace herself, and it would hardly show under the turn-over lace collar with which the dress was finished at the throat—just a little bit in front where the tabs of the collar did not quite meet. Even if he did see it, things were not the same as they would have been if he had put the necklace on himself and, perhaps, they never would be. . . .

At all events, he had now put the circlet of small diamonds on her finger and was still holding it firmly in place long after he was supposed to have "left" it during the prayers which came before the rector joined her right hand to Nicolas' right hand and pronounced them man and wife. "Our Father" was a respite, but a respite which did not last long. The next prayer was for the faithful fulfillment of the covenant just made and Margaret knew there would be no such faithful fulfillment. Then came the petition, which could be omitted or included, just as the officiating clergyman preferred, and which Mr. Bates had preferred to include.

" 'O Almighty God, Creator of mankind', who only art the well-spring of life; Bestow upon these thy servants, if it be thy will, the gift and heritage of children. . . .' "

At last she was praying, too, not repeating words that were put into her mouth and which she did not have the courage to reject, or words which she spoke automatically, because she had done so every night of her life ever since she was three years old. She wished that this prayer need not have been made publicly by a clergyman, that Nicolas might not have been given the opportunity to recognize the important place it had achieved in the solemnization of matrimony. But with her whole heart she hoped that it might be answered, that there would be not only the son on which Nicolas had set *his* heart, but a family which would bind him and her together and take from her the sin of perjury. . . .

" 'Those whom God hath joined together let no man put asunder.' "

Mr. Bates was now addressing himself not to the bride and groom, but to the company at large and, after a few introductory and relatively inconsequential remarks, he was pronouncing to all his listeners that Nicolas and herself were now man and wife and they were kneeling together to receive the final blessing. . . .

"That's it, darling. Now I help you get to your feet and you take my arm and we go down the aisle together, smiling to right and left as we go."

The whisper sounded as nonchalant as if he were suggesting a stroll in the garden after tea, instead of the final rite in a time-honored ceremony. Margaret had been so absorbed by the intensity and fervor of her personal prayer that she had been only dimly aware of the fact that another hush had engulfed them after Mr. Bates had finished speaking and the organist had not yet begun to play Mendelssohn's March. But there was nothing dim about her awareness of the fact that Nicolas had called her darling, in spite of everything. So he must have seen the necklace after all, if not when she came up the aisle then afterward, when they were kneeling side by side. Her lifted veil disclosed a smiling face and the smile was first of all for him.

13☙

"Were you really pleased, Nicolas? Was everything all right?"

"All right! Everything was perfect and you know it!"

"I wanted it to be. But having the President was such a responsibility."

"Well, after all Kent Curtis took care of that."

"Of the President's safety, not of his enjoyment."

"You didn't need anyone to help you take care of that, darling."

There was no mistaking the pride in his voice or the satisfaction in the expression with which he looked down at her. They were still standing near the front door where they had personally bade their guests good night. Now the last of these were gone and the sound of departing cars had grown fainter and fainter.

"Do you want me to lock up now or don't you bother?"

"Of course I do. What a question! Just think how long Cassie and I have been living here all alone!"

"Well, you're not alone now and you won't be any more. As a matter of fact, the bolts on this door are ornamental, but I don't think they'd be much of a handicap to a really determined burglar. But here goes. What about the lights in the drawing room?"

"Annabelle can see to those."

"Of course she can, but why don't we turn them out ourselves? We don't need them any more—or Annabelle and the rest of the staff, either. Why don't we thank them for all they've done to make the evening such a success and let them get off to the kitchen to talk things over?"

"That's exactly what we should do. Afterward, we'll go to the library, which is so much cosier than the drawing room, and talk the evening over ourselves." Briefly, she gave a few directions and seconded Nicolas' words of appreciation to the smiling servants. Then, after they had drifted away, with profuse expressions of gratitude and good will, she turned to the library. "Mother and I always used to come in here after a party, to talk it over," she said. "Sometimes I think that's the most fun of all—talking it over, I mean."

"I agree, on general principles; but this wasn't just a party, you know. It was a wedding. We're married now, remember? I do want to talk to you, but not about the evening. Isn't it all right if I begin to act like a husband?"

"I—I reckon so."

"You *reckon* so! Haven't I kept my part of the bargain to the letter?"

"Yes, Nicolas, you have. And you've been very kind, very thoughtful, very generous. I'm sorry if I haven't seemed to meet you halfway."

"Then aren't you going to keep your part?"

"I'm going to try. But I'm not sure what you want me to do first."

"I want you to sit beside me and listen very carefully while I talk to you. And I want you to look at me while you listen. If the library's the place you'd rather go, I suppose it's as good as any."

One arm was already around her and, as soon as they were seated, he turned toward her and kissed her lovingly, then with his free hand tilted her head so that their eyes met. Though he did this gently, she knew he intended to hold her like that and have her face him until he finished what he had to say and if she tried to move or avert her gaze, he would somehow prevent her from doing so.

"If you'd been willing to do things my way, this last week, my next move would be to ask you to go upstairs and get out of that dress," he said. "It's a beautiful dress and, what's more, it's *your* dress—if it had been made on purpose for you, it couldn't have been more becoming or more suitable. I'm sure it's just what you'd have chosen, if you'd had time to choose—except that a new one wouldn't have been so close fitting and so well reinforced." He tightened his hold on her waist and smiled. "My God, all I can feel is whalebone, when I want to feel you. And I'll bet you're laced within an inch of your life. If I'm not mistaken, you're terribly uncomfortable in that dress."

"No, not terribly." Her answer came breathlessly, but this was not wholly because of the tight lacing. "Your mother was very kind and thoughtful, too," Margaret went on; "she let the dress out for me—as far as she could."

"But that wasn't far enough to make it an easy fit, now, was it? Come on, darling, tell the truth!"

"Well—"

"Well, so if things had been going my way, I'd have liked you to dispense with all your ante-bellum attire at this point and change into one of those flowing, filmy negligees that I'm sure Esther brought you. Then *I* could have dispensed with this damn tail coat. After that, we could have sat here in front of the fire for a couple of hours, exchanging endearments, and I'd have been perfectly satisfied, knowing the night was yet young and all that. But the trouble is, we haven't exchanged enough endearments to make them seem natural to you, so instead of enjoying that interlude with me, as a foretaste of greater delights to come, you'd go on dreading that complete surrender which I honestly wanted to make easier for you and which I thought I could. Now I know that I can't and I want it behind you, instead of ahead of you, for your sake as well as mine. So I think you'd better follow your mother's advice and 'submit' to your husband tonight—I promise you'll never have to do it again. But we won't have any happiness together, Margaret—*you* won't have any happiness—until you're through with your dread of what you called menacing mysteries. You can't seem to overcome that dread yourself, so I've got to do it for you. Afterward, we *will* be happy together. Please believe me, darling."

He kissed her again, very lovingly. Then he released her. Once more she caught her breath. But this time she did not try to answer, which did not matter, because Nicolas did not care whether she did or not.

"I want you to go upstairs and get ready for me," he continued quietly. "I'll join you presently and, as soon as we're together, I'll clear up those menacing mysteries very quickly, if you'll help me. Once I've got through to you, they will cease to exist. Lord knows I don't want to hurt you and I hope I won't have to, very much or very long. You may hate me for a little while, but when you get over hating me, you'll know this was the way it had to be—for us. You may even be glad this was the way it was."

She would never get over hating him, she would never belive that was the way it had to be, she told herself bitterly, when at last Nicolas lay sleeping beside her. But at least, he would never be able to say she had failed in compliance, even when the pain with which she was suddenly pierced was followed by invasion that went deeper and deeper into her being, until it seemed no part of it was her own any more.

But now at last she was released and Nicolas was asleep, so he would not hear the sobs which she did not need to suppress any longer. And when he waked, she would tell him that she did hate him, that she would never get over hating him. He had lied to her when he told her he did not want to hurt her. But at least he had told her there would never be any question of submission between them again and she would remind him of that promise. Unless she had already conceived, she would not give him his son. No, she must do that because she had promised, just as she had promised to submit. But she would let Nicolas know how she hated keeping her promise—both promises, and it would be she who would ask for a divorce. . . .

How long she lay quivering with shame and rage and pain she never knew. It seemed a great while and all the time Nicolas lay close beside her, sleeping so soundly that he did not move at all. And then vaguely she realized that she was growing drowsy, that she was not conscious of much shame or rage or pain any more, that she must be drifting off to sleep herself.

When she woke, the room was flooded with sunshine and Nicolas was still lying close beside her. He was not touching her, but he was looking at her with an expression of tenderness that she had never seen on his face before.

"You've had a good long sleep," he said pleasantly. "I'm glad. But I've been awake for some time and I've enjoyed lying here, looking at you, because you're very beautiful. Do you hate me?"

"Of course I do. I always shall."

"Are you sure?" he asked gently.

She did not understand why, but she found she was not sure after all. She was forced to admit to herself that Nicolas had told the truth when he said, since she could not herself overcome her dread of menacing mysteries, he must do it for her or they would never find happiness together; because there was no other way, he had constrained her surrender. And now there were no more menacing mysteries; she was released from them, as he had told her she would be.

"I don't seem to be sure," she said at last. "Before I went to sleep, I was. I thought I could never forgive you, that what you'd done was unforgivable. But now—now I think perhaps what happened was the way it had to be. Not for everyone, but maybe for us."

"Only perhaps? Only maybe? If I'd sat in front of the fire with you for hours, caressing you gently, wouldn't you still have been just as unwilling to let me go further? If I hadn't made you promise not to resist me, wouldn't you have tried to fight me off, after we were in bed together? And then wouldn't we still be exactly where we were last night before we came upstairs, still strangers warring against each other, instead of where we are now, united lovers?"

Her answer came hesitantly because it came reluctantly, but when it did come it was truthful.

"Yes, I'm afraid so."

"And if I'd let you go back on your promise, would you have had much respect for me, either as a man or as a husband?"

"Perhaps not."

"Please stop saying perhaps. Say yes or no."

"But—"

"I've asked you before not to say but."

"Then I suppose the answer is yes."

"I'd have rather had that without the suppose, but I'll accept it. Because I think you're almost ready to forgive me. Am I right?"

She did not answer instantly and he did not try to hurry her. But, as she lay beside him, she had not only a growing sense of release from dread, but a sense of release from futility. Whatever happened next, the arid empty years were behind her now, never to return. All her resentment was engulfed by the rich reward of this knowledge.

"Yes," she said at last. "Yes, you are right. I am ready to say I've forgiven you—if there should really be any question of forgiveness. I'm not sure about that, either. I not only don't hate you any more, I have a feeling that doesn't seem to be connected with forgiveness. I can't describe it to you because I've never had one like it for anyone before, but it *is* almost being glad of what happened since it was you who made it happen. If it had been anyone else that would have been different—and dreadful. But since it was you—"

"May I tell you what I think?" Nicolas asked quietly. "That this feeling means you're ridding yourself of a false image—the dim and distant hero who was a creation of your own fancy—and the equally false image of an ill-intentioned, predatory male who wouldn't keep his distance. You're falling in love with a real person at last. You're beginning to recognize me as your man, just as I recognized you right away as my girl." He came closer and put his arm around her again. "Now that you've told me that, I think I ought to tell you something. I might have made it easier for you last night. Not at first. I couldn't help hurting you for a minute—you must know that. But do you remember I told you, after the first time I kissed you—it was really the only time until last night—that I enjoyed it so much more than I expected I found it hard to stop what I was doing? That time I did; but this time I didn't—I couldn't. The desire had become a need. Not just a need for gratification, but a need for *everything* you have to give me. And you've filled that need completely. I'm very grateful to you, Margaret, for marrying me. I'm honored at having you for my wife. Why, darling, what's the matter?"

For she was crying. He leaned over her, murmuring words of tenderness and comfort as he kissed her and tried to wipe away the tears. But she was already smiling through them.

"Do you mean," she asked incredulously, "that you didn't keep me all that time just to show me that you had the right to do it? That it was because you *wanted* me?"

"Good God, Margaret, of course I wanted you! I keep telling you, you're very beautiful, you're very alluring!"

"But I never thought I was beautiful, I never thought I was alluring! I thought I was just an unattractive old maid!"

"Well, you never were unattractive, though you certainly did your best to make yourself look that way; and just as certainly you're not an old maid any longer. What's more, being a bride is very becoming to you—so becoming that I'm having the greatest difficulty in keeping my hands off you. Merely having my arm around you hardly counts."

"And you didn't insist on doing it—just because of the baby, either?"

He burst out laughing. "That's why we got married, isn't it?" he said lightly. "So that you would have a baby. Of course you must have. In the light of your experience as a married woman, do you think we could count on one in August?"

"I hope so, Nicolas."

"I hope so, too, but I may as well tell you I forgot all about the baby last night. I forgot everything in the world except that I had you in my arms and that nothing and no one could stop me from making love to the most wonderful girl in the world. I hope you won't mind if I admit I think I'm on the point of forgetting it again. I told you only the first time would be hard. Now I want a chance to prove that to you."

14 ❧

"Nicolas, don't you think that perhaps we ought to get up?"

"Well, I don't know," he said lazily. He had been lying on his back, with his hands clasped behind his head, but now he turned toward her and kissed the cheek nearest him. "I'm finding it very pleasant to spend the morning in bed," he went on. "It isn't even lunch time yet. Perhaps you don't realize that, if you'd been a Creole instead of a Virginian, not so long ago either, you wouldn't have left your nuptial chamber for at least a week, probably more, after your wedding. And that your bridegroom wouldn't have done so, either."

"Yes, I've heard so and I wondered if it could really be true. Because

I didn't see how any people with any pretensions to refinement—much less any loving parents—could subject their daughter to such an ordeal."

"You mean because the poor little bride hadn't ever seen her fiancé alone and didn't have even five days' grace to get used to the idea of having him act like a husband?"

"Yes, partly that of course, mostly that. But then there were other aspects of the situation—"

"Not many bathrooms in those days? Well, I believe there was usually a *cabinet de toilette* adjoining said nuptial chamber, so that the bride and groom didn't have to perform what they euphemistically called the acts of nature in each other's presence and, presumably, a slave emptied the slops. But I admit the aspect of the situation which you've called to my attention couldn't have improved the setting for the acts of love with which the young couple were evidently supposed to be preoccupied."

"How can you say I called it to your attention?" Margaret said indignantly. "Since you knew all about those revolting Creole customs, you must have thought of it dozens of times yourself! And, obviously, the slaves didn't come to do only what you just mentioned! The laundry had to be taken care of, the meals had to be brought in. If the Creole bridegroom never left the room any more than his bride, he wouldn't have waited on her the way you waited on me this morning, Nicolas!"

"Well, after all, I wanted to show off the new dressing gown Mother gave me—that was my trousseau! So it seemed natural, once I had bothered to put it on, to go to the back stairs and call to Annabelle that I wanted her to bring our breakfast up to my boudoir. Then I got quite a kick out of bringing it the rest of the way myself and sharing a tray with you."

"That wasn't the only reason you did it, Nicolas. You knew I'd be embarrassed, having Annabelle come in and seeing us in bed together. Of course I'll get used to the idea, but it's still so soon. It was very thoughtful of you. You are thoughtful. And—and very engaging."

"So you've decided I'm not an utter brute after all?"

"That wasn't a sudden decision. I never thought you were."

"Never?"

"Why, if I'd thought that, I would never have agreed to marry you!"

"No. But since you did agree, you've had some bad moments." He slipped one arm under her shoulders and let it slide down to encircle her waist, but still without pressure. "To revert to the Creoles just once more before we get up," he said smiling, "I understand the bridegroom not only expected a frightened bride, who tried to fight him off, but insisted on one. In fact, there's a well-authenticated story of a man who demanded a legal separation, because the girl had been responsive to his first advances; he couldn't believe they were the first anyone had ever made to her. I don't think much of his powers of penetration. Granted that he hadn't seen much of the poor girl, he ought to have been able to size her up better than he evidently did. Now my problem was just the opposite. I was so sure I was the first that I didn't want my bride penalized for her inexperience. But nothing I could say would persuade her. . . . All right, all right, we're not going to talk about that any more. And it is getting near lunch time. I'll be off to snatch a shave and a shower and then go on to my boudoir. At least I suppose that's what you want me to do, though of course I'd much rather stay here and watch you dress after you've come out of your bath. Or did your mother tell you that no lady ever let her husband do anything of the sort, even if he so far forgot he was a gentleman to suggest it? Yes, I was afraid so. Well, I won't press the point just now. I see you still blush. Very attractive, as I've told you before. Dangerously so right now, when you're so hellbent to get up."

"If I don't get up, I can't show you my second day dress and your mother thought you'd be interested."

"I never heard of a second day dress and I don't believe she ever did either, until you told her. Now you'd better tell me."

"It's the Virginia substitute for what the Creole bride wore—or didn't wear—the day after her wedding. It was usually very beautiful. Of course, a colored dress."

"I see. Is yours the same vintage as your wedding dress?"

"Yes. They belonged to the same bride. But the second day dress *is* low necked."

"One improvement. But stiffened with whalebone? And very tight around the waist? And trailing on the ground?"

"Yes to all those questions."

"Then, if it wouldn't hurt your feelings, I'd like very much to have you show it to me, but I'd rather you didn't put it on until evening. Then you might wear it to dinner. I think it would be rather fun to sit down at a candlelighted table, set with old glass and silver and china, and see you sitting opposite me, wearing your second day dress. All that would be quite in keeping with pleasant tradition. But I hope you'd find it so stiff and so tight that you'd be glad to get out of it into something comfortable. And, meanwhile, I think we'd have more fun if you put on something a little more suitable for sauntering in the garden than your famous and symbolic second day dress. It's a glorious day. Since nothing I've told you seems to predispose you in favor of Creole bridal customs, we ought to spend part of the afternoon outdoors."

It was, as Nicolas had said, a glorious day, mellow with the warmth of Indian summer; and, after a leisurely luncheon, they sauntered out to the garden, taking with them Perdita, who romped joyously at their heels, almost frantic with delight at release from her banishment to the service quarters. Although there had been so much rain and a long succession of drab days, there had been no actual frosts and unseasonable warmth had followed the early chill. The flowers had taken on fresh vigor and brightness in the autumn sunshine. Some of the late roses were actually putting out new buds, pansies had reseeded themselves and were velvety in their purple; the ageratum was as blue as it had been in midsummer; and the chrysanthemums and asters were at the height of their glory. There was no use in gathering any, because the house was already overflowing with flowers; but it was pleasant to wander along the paths and discuss plans for further development of the borders. Margaret found a four-leaf clover and slipped it in Nicolas' buttonhole for good luck.

"More good luck, you mean," he said with the smile she found so beguiling. "The best luck I've had in a long time was marrying you. Incidentally, I'm very pleased that you allowed me to persuade you to save your ancestral second day dress for evening. That outfit you have on is exactly right for an afternoon stroll. In fact, it's a knockout."

"It's what Esther calls a smart little knitted number," Margaret observed with satisfaction. "I believe it's one of those Italian things that looks simple and costs a small fortune. While we're on the subject of clothes, I like yours, too."

"Any preference among them?"

"Well, of course you looked superb at our wedding."

"My dear girl, what an adjective to apply to a man! Besides, I don't wear full dress for months at a time when I'm ranging around in the Andes. If I hadn't just been getting into practice again at the White House and the Peruvian Embassy, I'd have probably looked about as superb as a head waiter."

"You never would look like a head waiter and you don't need practice to make you look just right in any kind of clothes. When you wear charcoal gray suits and white shirts, there isn't a wrinkle anywhere and the shirts are so white they glisten."

"You talk as if most of the men you'd known wore rumpled clothes and dingy linen."

"No, I don't mean that, but there is a difference," Margaret persisted. "Anyway, you asked what I liked best of all and I'm coming to that, but you keep interrupting me. I think it's those tweeds you have on right now. They look like the sort you read about in English novels."

"Perhaps for a very good reason—that they are. I have very extravagant tastes when it comes to clothes—tastes I hope you'll share. Couldn't you bring your complimentary remarks to a climax with praise of my pajamas? They're custom made, too, the best Italian silk, just as your dress is the best Italian knitted goods, so I'm even with you."

"All right. Then that's a good place to stop talking about clothes. There's something else I wanted to talk about anyway."

"Just as you say. Shall we wander along toward the Virgin's Bower, which we will now rename the Bride's Bower, and see how the traveller's joy is coming along in this nice warm weather? That might be a good place to pause for conversation."

"I think so, too."

When they reached the arbor, they found the nice warm weather had, indeed, produced a fine effect on the traveller's joy; the vine had some new buds and, also, a new fluff of seeds and both Nicolas and Margaret agreed this was a good omen. Margaret settled down in the old swing made of grapevine and Nicolas swung her back and forth, higher than she had ever gone before, so high indeed that, if she had not known he would tease her for timidity, she would have asked him to call a halt. But he guessed, easily enough, that she would prefer less adventurous soaring and gradually brought the swing to a standstill. Then he kissed her and told her again she was the most wonderful girl in the world and that he would lie at her feet, which was really where he belonged anyway. The grass was nice and warm. Perhaps, after she got tired of the swing, she would come and sit there beside him.

"I've been wanting to ask you some questions. I'm afraid if I came and sat down beside you I might get diverted."

"You probably would. So let's go ahead with the questions, if they're important, and have the diversions later. I may not be able to answer everything you ask me and I may not want to, even if I am able. So, in either case, I wouldn't. But there's no reason why you shouldn't ask."

"Do you realize you've never told me much about your work? Just that you hoped to discover a lost city?"

"Yes, I realize it. We've had a good many other things to discuss and not much time to do it in."

"I know. But now there isn't much of anything left we really need to discuss, is there? I mean, about us? So, I'd really like to hear more about you."

"I'm not in the mood for talking. I find it very relaxing, lying here in the sun. Naturally, I'd enjoy it even more if you'd come and sit beside me."

"And would you go on feeling relaxed?"

Nicolas laughed. "You're learning fast, aren't you? No, of course, I wouldn't. Well, you have a perfect right to ask about my work. What aspect of it interests you most?"

"Every aspect of it interests me. And all I know, so far, is that the first time you came to see me your equipment was already on its way by ship, in charge of your assistant, who's a good fellow named Pete Hart, and that it was then too late to change the date you'd planned to meet him, because the whole setup was so complicated. Oh no—after that I also heard Pete Hart had trouble with the customs at Callao about releasing some of the equipment, though this had never happened before, and you couldn't get out to see me when you expected to because you'd been obliged to go to the Peruvian Embassy to straighten things out. But it was your father who told me that—you didn't. Your father also told me about your fan mail. But I still don't know what sort of equipment you had to take. I don't know whether Pete Hart is your only assistant or whether your secretary Lester Wendell is the only one flying south with you or whether you pick up additional members of your expedition after you get to Peru. I don't have the least idea what your schedule calls for, though I suppose a lot of traveling. Where do you go first?"

"First I go to Lima, where I stay one night. I'll spend it with my polo-playing classmate, Ildefonso Parra, his charming wife Marina and their six or eight charming children. I lose count because there's a new one every time I go there. They live in a house that's even more beautiful than this one. I'll telephone you from there as soon as I get in."

"And I'll be waiting for the call. Tell me about the Parras' house."

"Well, it's in the new part of the city which means it has lawns and gardens around it, instead of being built flush to the street with an interior patio like the houses in the old part. The Parras' grounds are about as big as a ball park and they have a wall around them. You enter by a gate—no, it isn't exactly a gate for it isn't made of iron grillwork you can see through. It's a huge solid wooden door studded with big iron knobs and it's opened for you by a man who would be called a gatekeeper in England, because there what he opened would really be a gate. The man who fulfills the same function here is called a *portero*. The Parras' *portero*, Luis, is about a hundred years old and he doesn't do much any more except totter out from his own little shelter near by, grinning and bowing, to let you in; and then he closes the door after you, still grinning and bowing. The place wouldn't seem the same without him."

"And what happens after you get inside this solid wooden door?"

"Why then you go along a curving driveway bordered with flowers, with great expanses of flower-strewn lawns on either side, until you get to a porte-cochere surmounted by a statuette of Santa Rosa; and from there you enter a small vestibule, with not more than two or three priceless paintings and tapestries hanging on the walls and not more than two or three magnificent marriage chests of painted leather and *bargueños* inlaid with mother-of-pearl standing around. But, unless you especially want to see Marina's elaborate *nacimiento,* made of snow-white *Huamanga,* the famous Peruvian marble, you don't linger in the vestibule. Marina rather collects collections, if you know what I mean: La Granja glass and jade ornaments and Spanish colonial silver stirrups —the kind the unprincipled veiled ladies called *tapadas* used; and so on and so on. These are all in plain sight in the drawing rooms beyond, but the *nacimiento* is kept enclosed except during the twelve days of Christmas. Then it is beautifully illuminated and glistens like snow. And on Twelfth Night the Three Kings come out of seclusion and take their places by the manger, along with the Holy Family and the shep-herds and the angels and the animals. It's really a very charming sight. I must get you an antique Peruvian *nacimiento* if I can find one. You could make a place for it in the drawing room, couldn't you?"

"I probably could, if I knew what it was."

Nicolas laughed. "The same thing as a crèche, a *precipio,* a Nativity scene. Don't tell me you haven't heard of them! I believe it was St. Francis of Assisi who first—"

"Of course, I've heard of them; I haven't heard them called *nacimientos,* that's all. But I've seen two or three, though we don't have one at Pohick Church and I've never had one at Hills' End. I'd love to."

"All right, I'll see that's taken care of. Now, so far, we don't seem to have got beyond the vestibule at the Parras' house. Do you want me to go on?"

"I can't wait to have you."

"Well, next, if you turn to the left, you go into a paneled library, where all the books are hand bound, either in vellum or embossed leather, and kept behind glass; and, if you turn right, you go into the dining room which will seat thirty or forty quite easily and has some very fine family portraits. If you go straight ahead, you'll come to a whole succession of drawing rooms, each more elaborate than the last and each containing at least one of those collections I mentioned. An inner gallery runs all around these drawing rooms on the second story and on the outside is a portico which runs all the way around them at ground level. That portico is a very pleasant place to have drinks."

"I should think it would be. And what is there upstairs besides this inner gallery?"

"Well, what would you expect? Bedrooms and more bedrooms; mostly with their own private sitting rooms, which, however, are not called boudoirs but *salitas;* and enormous bathrooms. The beds really are something—very elaborately carved and heavily gilded. They gleam, they glisten, they invite, they actually beckon—and they never were meant to be slept in alone, which, alas! is what I shall be doing in one of them next week."

"You could still change your mind and take me with you."

"No, I couldn't. Don't let's spoil this perfect afternoon with an argument about that. You know it's a closed question."

"All right. I won't. . . . But I still don't know where you think you're going to find the lost city."

"If I knew where I was going to find the lost city, there wouldn't be any problem. There wouldn't be any question of discovery, either, because it wouldn't be a *lost* city."

"Of course, I realize you don't know where you're going to find it. But you must be aiming in the general direction of some place."

"I am, but that doesn't necessarily prove anything, either. Hiram Bingham was looking for the city of Vilcabamba when he found the citadel of Machu Picchu."

"And he never found Vilcabamba?"

"Yes and no; in Bingham's mind, Machu Picchu *is* Vilcabamba."

"And, in your mind, nobody else has found it, either?"

"No."

"So that's what you're hunting for?"

"It's one I've considered."

"But not the *only* one you've considered? Not the one you're aiming for now?"

"No, not primarily."

"Oh, Nicolas, we're not getting anywhere! Do try to be a little more definite!"

"I didn't realize you were such a curious woman, darling."

"It's not that I'm actually curious. It's that I care so much about you I care about everything you're doing."

"Margaret, if you speak to me in that tone of voice, I shan't be able to refrain from making love to you. I'm greatly touched that you should care so much. All right, let's begin with the dry details and then get on to the glorious objective. There'll be six of us in the expedition: myself, Pete Hart, my mechanical assistant, who's gone ahead and who acts as recorder and photographer; Lester, who has architectural ambitions, Inca style, who, as you know, is flying to Lima with me; and three Andean professionals—Estéban Mamani, geologist, and Pedro Mendoza, botanist, both of Cuzco University; and Julio Gomara, leading archeologist of Bolivia, but now in exile and attached to Arequipa University. They will all get leave of absence from their respective universities and join me in the field. Lest you should picture them as graybeards, let me tell you here and now they're all younger than I am, except Gomara. It doesn't take as long in Latin America to reach the status of full-fledged professor as it does with us."

"You don't have a doctor?"

"No. Bingham sometimes had as many as three on his staff and it used to be very generally the custom to have at least one. Now we just get a message to the nearest settlement and ask to have a sick or injured man flown out."

"But isn't it dangerous to be without medical supervision all the time?"

"Dangerous? What's danger? Crossing the street, slipping on a rug, eating a bad oyster! We all know the elementary rules of sanitation and take first aid supplies and standard remedies with us. . . . Well, to go back to the staff: even if we don't have a doctor, we do have a cook, Li Chan, Chinese as you'd guess by the name, not Indian, as I'm sure you expected; if you'd ever eaten in the native Chinese restaurants of Lima, you'd know why. And naturally, we have carriers, half a dozen or more Indians at a time, hired at the nearest sierra towns, not permanent members of the crew. Are you following me so far?"

"Yes, fairly easily. Now I want to know how you travel."

"Magic carpet."

"Nicolas, please be serious!"

"It is serious. Consider the topography of the *montaña*—or do you know anything about it?"

"Not much, I'm afraid."

"It's a geography of negatives. No easy slopes in my zone, no naviga-ble rivers, no through trails for jeep, horse or burro. Some man has to do all the hefting. The Incas had manpower by the thousands. We don't. As I told you, we have no permanent crew of carriers. There's always a turnover among the *peones,* because they have the hardest job of all."

"But, Nicolas, Lima's right near the ocean. I do know that much. And that's where you land when you get off your plane. You don't worry about slopes that aren't easy or rivers that aren't navigable or trails that are impassable—until you leave there. And you haven't yet told me where your zone is. You've got to tell me how you get there from Lima."

"First I go to Cuzco."

"How?"

"Lester and I go by plane, comfortably. We leave Lima at six in the morning and when we get to Cuzco the bells are ringing for nine o'clock Mass. Pete doesn't have it so easy, though his hardships are mitigated by Li Chan's cooking. He drives a truck overland and it takes him four days."

"What's in the truck?"

"You name it, we probably have it: sleeping bags and insect powder; machetes and nylon rope; hammocks and portable two-way radios. And so forth and so on. Do you want me to go into more detail or is that enough to give you an idea?"

"It's enough to give me an idea."

"Glad to hear it. Because it's pleasant here, but after all I don't want to stay all night in the Bride's Bower, telling you what Pete has in his truck, when I'd much rather be in the bride's bedroom. . . . Well, the fact that it takes Pete four days to drive to Cuzco means he'll already have left Lima when I arrive there, because we're trying to get a head start before the worst of the rains. That's why I'll stay over only one night in Lima myself. Pete has not only arrived in Cuzco, but has organized and marshaled the whole group. I'll get there just in time to have my picture taken as its director for the two Cuzco newspapers, before leading my men with intrepidity north—northeast."

"Where to, Nicolas?"

It was so long before he answered that she realized he was hesitating how to do so. She knew he would have preferred not to tell her any more than he had already—indeed, that he would not have told her this much if she had not pressed him and if he were not eager to make her feel he, too, would be willing to make concessions, that she was not to be alone in that. When he finally did speak, it was very slowly, as if he were weighing his words as he went along.

"I told you I was 'considering' Vilcabamba," he said. "Well, that's true—at least, it's partly true. But it isn't my lost city. I know how to get that far, or at least I know how to get to the solid ridge by that name. Vilcabamba's part of history. For that reason it's a minor objective. There's no magic to it. My real objective is farther afield. Possibly it's only a dream, but it's a magic dream."

"El Dorado?"

"No. Right area, wrong dream. You'll remember El Dorado was all about a realm of gold, centering on a mountain lake and ruled by a gilded hero who lured Spaniards past the safe sierra to lead them astray in the jungle. The *conquistadores* believed in El Dorado all right. A colonial governor was appointed for the region and any number of men tracked a whole continent to find it, among them a governor-designate who was killed at a jungle encampment, along with his lady love and some loyal officers, by an insubordinate sergeant. But they never found either the gold or the hero or the lake. And no wonder. These didn't exist. They don't exist. They were as mythical as the Midas legend and vaguely akin to it. And the search for them wasn't inspired by anything better than greed for gold. But I believe that, somewhere in the zone of Andean Amazonia, there really is a region, or at least a city—"

"Does it have a name?"

"Yes. I never meant to tell you or anyone, except the members of my expedition, what I was looking for. But it does have a name. Its name is Paitite."

"Are you the only person who ever believed in it?"

"No. Some Spaniards, led by a certain Captain Pedro de la Egüi, went looking for it in the seventeenth century—and failed to find it. But one of Egüi's followers, Juan Recio de León, returned to Spain with a memorial which he laid before the Council of the Indies and made a recommendation that a new expedition be formed. I have a copy of the memorial. It's one of my greatest treasures. I'll show it to you some time."

"Before you leave?"

"I can't do that, it's in a safe deposit box in my father's bank. But I'll get it out when I come back and we'll look at it together. Perhaps then I can show you how I've traced my own route by Recio de León's."

The same faraway look had come into his eyes that Margaret had seen when he told her some day a road in Peru would be named for him just as one had been for Bingham. "Besides," he went on presently and more realistically, "Recio de León declared he had seen hatchets and knives which Indians in the Peruvian jungle near Cuzco claimed they had received in trading with other Indians—from Paitite. Its name isn't a secret. It has always lingered in popular fancy and every now and then it appears on a map—on the heights of Pantiacolla. It even had a titular Spanish governor, just as El Dorado did, though none ever reached there. But, as a matter of fact, I'm not the only one in our own time who's gone looking for it."

"Then why do you think you could find it when no one else could?"

"Because in modern times the others—the ones I know about anyway —have made the Andes a field of learned observation instead of becoming a part of them, as I have—just as I was part of the Green Mountains and the White Mountains when I was a boy and they were part of me. I don't go forward just by scholarship and stones."

"You mean you follow your star?"

He shook his head. "I know you say that symbolically, so in one sense perhaps I do, though if you were talking Andean vernacular, instead of Virginian, you would speak of following the moon goddess, rather than a star. But mostly, like the Indians, I follow what's closer to me, what's more real to me. I'm not a great scientist, I never pretended to be. I'm lucky to be able to go on drawing from wartime Navy training. Besides, I know the meaning of clouds and mist, rain and streams and waterfalls. I can follow their lead and I'm going to. Where? That's still the secret of the Andes. I have to learn it. To find what? The hidden paradise of

Paitite. When? At the appointed time, whenever that is. I told you the
first time I came to see you that, if three proved to be my lucky number,
I'd soon be on top of the world in more ways than one. I don't know
whether it is or not—"

"But you're going to try to find out? You're going to push your
luck?"

"Yes—to the utmost limit." He smiled and shook his head as if to
forestall any further questioning. "That's all—there isn't any more—
at least not right now. The rest of the story will have to await discovery.
But, though you may not realize it, the fact that I've told you this
much is the highest compliment I could possibly pay you. It means I
have complete confidence in you. So, if you care as much about me as
you say you do, you might prove it by getting out of that swing and
coming to sit next to me just for a few minutes."

She knew it would not be for just a few minutes, but she also knew
she could not refuse; indeed, it was unthinkable that she should.
Nicolas had not only shared his precious secret with her; he had
revealed himself to her as never before. She no longer saw him only as
the adventurous explorer of her rapt but unenlightened imagination,
but as the searcher guided by the elements, the discoverer who dared to
dream of magic and fix his sights on mystic realms. She slid from the
swing and dropped easily down beside him. The hunters' moon was
shining brightly overhead when they went back to the house.

15 ❦

The weather was not as pleasant on Friday as it had
been on Thursday, but then, Nicolas said, there was no reason why
they should expect it to be. It was still unseasonably warm, but it was
muggy and lowering, with occasional rumbles of distant thunder and,
every now and then, a shower which threatened to become a downpour
and then stopped as suddenly as it had begun. Nicolas didn't care
whether they were outdoors much or not, though he did want to check
the stables again for immediate and complete renovation. Of course, he
wouldn't make any visible changes in the old barn—that was really a
museum piece. But he ought to see what condition it was in.

"It's in dreadful condition. I can tell you that right away."

"Then all the more reason why I ought to go there to decide on necessary repairs."

"Is that the only reason you want to go there?"

"It's a perfectly sincere and valid reason. But I'll admit there's another. I don't think our honeymoon would be complete unless we took a tumble in the hay."

"Nicolas, that's a terribly vulgar expression."

"It may be a vulgar expression, but it can be a glorious experience. An old barn, deserted except for an occasional bird flying through a broken window, high above the rafters, and long shafts of dusty sunshine streaming down from them gives a marvelous feeling of secrecy and space. And soft, sweet-smelling hay makes a delightful bed. You shouldn't think of one just in terms of an ancestral four-poster."

They had left their pleasant luncheon table and gone into the drawing room to open and inspect the additional presents which had come in that morning. Margaret laid down the twenty-seventh silver dish she was listing and spoke rather gravely.

"But Nicolas, someone might come in."

"There won't be anyone to come in. With your permission, I'm going to send Rufus off to do the grocery shopping and he's the only person on the place so far who might even imagine he had any business there. Besides, the big door will be bolted and that's the only place you can get in. What's more, it wouldn't occur to either Annabelle or Cassie to look for you there. They'd have just the same mistaken idea you have—that ladies and gentlemen don't make love in the hay."

"Or in the middle of the afternoon."

"Look here, we made love in the middle of the morning yesterday. That ought to have been enough to convince you that it isn't a privilege which can be enjoyed only at night. And I've reminded you before that my plane leaves at noon next Tuesday and, as we weren't being married until evening on Wednesday, that left us just Thursday, Friday, Saturday, Sunday and Monday for both day and night. You didn't mind when I worded my reminder that way, and Friday's half gone already. Surely you knew I'd create every opportunity I could to make love to you, even if I didn't confine you to one room, like a Creole!" And, as she made no immediate answer, he asked persistently, "Didn't you?"

"I did realize that since we had such a short time together you'd want to make love to me—often. I—I want to have you. But I don't think I realized you'd want to keep creating opportunities. Nicolas, please don't ask me to go to the barn with you."

"Why not?"

"Because, from the way you talked about a bed in the hay, I couldn't help knowing you'd been in one before."

"I haven't been in one with you. That's what counts, as far as I'm concerned. It's what ought to count with you, too."

"Oh, Nicolas, you can't think how cheap it makes me feel to think you'd want to treat me as if I were—well, the kind of girl you'd have done that with before! It's bad enough to know you've had affairs, how many I don't know. But I did suppose that at least the women with whom you'd been involved were what we call ladies, even if they weren't chaste. I didn't think they were the sort you tumbled in the hay. And now I know there must have been some of those, too."

"Look here, I guess we do need to have another serious talk. I thought we were all through with those, but it seems we're not."

So far, he had been standing while he helped her undo packages, refusing to sit down beside her on the stiff little Empire love seat, where she was surrounded with tissue paper and boxes. He had claimed that, at best, this was the most inappropriately named piece of furniture with which he was acquainted and that, at worst—specifically, in its present state—it was actually unusable for a man of normal size and normal habits. He had said all this jokingly; but now, as he drew up a chair so that he could face her, he spoke in the hard voice she had not heard since the morning he had accused her of trying to cheat.

"You knew all the time there had been affairs," he said. "I told you that in the beginning. If you thought they made me ineligible as your suitor, that was the time to say so. You objected to plenty of other things in the next few days, but never to those. And I certainly didn't tell you they had all been with what you rather archaically call ladies, though I did mention one or two—maybe two or three—with so-called social equals. But you wouldn't have recognized as such the somewhat uninhibited teen-agers who went to the same rural school I did when I was growing up; neither are social equals always available in the more remote reaches of an explorer's range. What I did tell you was that, if I had lived more continently than most men—and I believe I have—it wasn't because I wouldn't have preferred to live otherwise; and sometimes I followed my preference. I also told you I had an inherent aversion to sex combined with commercialism, though I have great respect for each, kept apart. I might have added that I have an even stronger objection to venereal disease, but I was still trying not to be too crude in my language. So all that adds up to the fact that I've never been a patron of bawdy houses. But yes—there have been some episodes in haylofts, as well as in bedrooms. I didn't realize there'd be such a gulf between them in your mind. There isn't actually, except that the illicit affair in a hayloft is apt to be a lot less sordid and artificial than one in a bedroom. You're not dodging a suspicious husband or snoopy servants; you're not cheating, unless your companion's married already and, in my experience, she wasn't—or unless one of you is cheating the other. What's more, you find you're not dependent on a lot of trappings to make the act of love so natural that it's practically inescapable. That's what I want you to find out."

He paused, but only long enough for emphasis and, when he went on, he was still speaking in the hard voice which, to her ears, carried overtones of accusation. "You've come a long way in a short time and you've won my everlasting admiration and respect because you have. But you still feel love-making needs just the right setting at just the right time and that it must be safeguarded with certain concessions to what you still think of as modesty. You don't want me to stay in the room while you dress and undress, so I haven't; but there must be a special sort of happy intimacy between a man and his wife, when they share a room all the time, when he isn't relegated to a place with a silly name like a boudoir. You don't want me to see you without a nightgown—in fact, you want to wear one all the time you're in bed, whether the room is dark or not and, so far, I've let you. Of course, it's just a froth of chiffon and lace, but it's *there*, between my chest and your beautiful breasts. If, before I leave you, I could get you away from all that nonsense, if I could make you see it's silly and inconsistent, I'd have done almost as much for you as I did when I cleared up those menacing mysteries, not to mention at all what I'd have done for myself."

Again he paused, this time longer, so that she would have a chance to break in if she wanted to; but she had bowed her head and was not looking at him. He suspected that she was crying again, but this time he made no move to wipe away her tears. "Theoretically, I know a girl likes to think she's a man's first love and, just to gild the lily, she thinks she'd like her bridegroom to be as inexperienced as she is," he said, rather satirically. "Precious few of them are, by the time they're of legal marriageable age, whatever that is—certainly not by the time they're thirty-five; and, practically, I'm not at all sure it isn't better that they shouldn't be. Anyhow, you knew how it was, as far as I'm concerned, and if you're going to begin now to act as if you couldn't bear to be in the hay with me, because you suspect, and rightly, that I've been there with someone else, you might just as well begin to act as if you couldn't bear to have me get into bed with you."

Once more he waited for her to answer and once more he gathered that she was silently weeping.

"You're my wife," he said and now his voice was not hard any more. "I've never had a wife before, so probably I make mistakes about the way I treat you. But it isn't because I hold you cheap. You've given me a new standard, Margaret. I've discovered that desire isn't lessened when it's combined with respect and admiration—it's enhanced, it's glorified. I know I'll be faithful to you, even though we'll be separated so much, because no other woman could bear comparison with what

you've meant to me since you became my wife. You're infinitely precious to me, darling. That's why I want to share with you every
wonderful experience that I think could add to your happiness, as well
as mine, even if I've had one something like it before, in what seems
to you the wrong way and in what I know now is a lesser way. After
I've gone, I want you to remember, happily, everything you and I have
done together, without thinking what I might have done with someone
else, or when or where. And I honestly believe you will, if you let me
crowd these few days and nights with so much mutual joy, that there
won't be room in your mind or your heart for anything else—as there
won't be in mine."

"Oh, Nicolas, will you please *stop!*"

"What do you mean, will I please stop? I've stopped several times, to
give you a chance to answer back if you wanted to."

"I couldn't. I can't now. But please don't talk to me any more."

"What do you want me to do?"

"You must know."

Nicolas went all over the barn, both inside and out, making careful
notes of what needed to be repaired. Then he put these in his pocket
and said that, the next morning, he would order lumber and other
things that were needed. Afterward, he closed the great doors, where
laden wagons had formerly come in and out, and where they would
again, the next summer, because Hills' End was once more to be run as
it should be. The sun streamed in long dusty shafts from the high
windows, just as Nicolas had said it would; but except for the places
these shafts illumined, there was only twilight. And there was a deep
stillness and a spaciousness that seemed like the spaciousness of the sea,
though otherwise there was no reminder of the ocean. Nicolas had
brought a blanket with him from the house, carrying it folded over his
arm; but Margaret had not noticed it particularly because it was the
same color as his tweed coat, and he had laid it aside while he made his
careful investigations. Now she saw that it was a rather shabby old
blanket, that had been stored away in the closet of the boudoir since
her mother died; but it was a large blanket, because it had been meant
for a double bed, and it was thick, too; no wisps or prickles could come
through it. After Nicolas had spread it out for them, he asked Margaret
if she were cold and, when she said she was not, he asked her if he
should take off her dress or whether she would rather do it herself.
He did not pretend that there were any complicated fastenings, as there
were on the second day dress, and that she might welcome help; he
simply made it clear that he wanted it removed and that it would be;
and though he spoke of the dress, she knew he meant more than that.

She still had not realized he would expect this and it came as a shock to her. She did not think he had a right to take such a revelation for granted; it not only offended her sense of delicacy, it made her feel he was overestimating his prerogatives; and she did not believe he would force her to do violence to her feelings. But when she drew away from him a little and tried to put this into words, she found she was tongue-tied, not because she was frightened but because she began to sense there was some reason why he wanted her to do as he had asked; and, though she could not comprehend what this was, she did comprehend, very soon, that the reason was not a gross one. And slowly, very slowly, while Nicolas made no further move toward her, she grasped the healing fact that he felt there was a vital element still missing in their marriage, because they had not yet come together as primal people had done and that, until they did, they would not have fulfilled in its entirety the divine command that they should cleave together and become one flesh. Perhaps he also felt that only when they did would they be able to fulfill the rest of that command: to be fruitful and multiply. If he did, there was a double reason why she should not deny him.

"You would rather be the one to do it, wouldn't you?" she asked.

He took her hands and clasped them in his. "Thank you for understanding, Margaret," he said quietly. And she knew he had divined everything that had been passing through her mind, that she could not close this to him, any more than she could decline to do his bidding. But the sense of shock was gone. She had shrunk from his assumption that he had as much right to reveal her person as to enter it; now one seemed as natural as the other, for he acted on his assumption in such a way that she was exalted and not shamed by it—slowly and carefully, almost reverently, without speaking to her at all. Some vital element, hitherto lacking, had, indeed, been added to their relationship by the revelation which was his doing and she wanted him to know that she realized this, that she was not startled or offended any longer. She had ceased to fear that no part of her being would remain wholly her own; she merely feared that it would not become wholly his. She still did not know how to put her feeling into words and, in any case, it did not seem the moment for speech. But, as he bent over her, she raised her hand and shyly stroked his cheek. It was the first time she had caressed him spontaneously and, sensing his pleased surprise, she drew his face down closer to hers and whispered, "I understand now."

"What, darling?"

"Everything you tried to explain before you brought me here. And everything that's happened since. Belonging to you has a new meaning."

"I hoped you'd feel that way."

"And this time you don't have to wait for me to 'get ready' for you, do you? I'm ready now."

He saw that the time had come when she was able to meet passion with passion, but he did not instantly grasp that she wanted to do more than this. She was so deeply moved because he had been able to overcome her false modesty, by sheer will power, that she was yearning to have him overcome her separate identity by sheer physical power. Something deep within her demanded his dominance and, inevitably, her self-abandonment acted as a spur to primitive male instinct. At last, appalled lest his triumphant virility should oppress her past all endurance, he slackened his hold and looked down on her with solicitude, only to find that she was gazing at him with eyes of love.

"Now I belong to you for always," she murmured. Then her joyous subjugation merged into blissful semiconsciousness. She raised her arms so that she could put them around his neck and her face so that she could kiss him; and, sighing like a tired and contented child, she fell asleep.

The rain, which had been threatening all day, came at last. The distant rumbles of thunder had become loud claps and, every now and then, lightning flashed through the barn. Nicolas did not know whether or not Margaret was afraid of thunderstorms, though he doubted it; but he lay still until he was sure her slumber was so profound this one would not wake her in any case; then he pulled on his clothes and put her shoes in the pocket of his tweed coat, with the notes he had made hours earlier. Next he tucked her neatly folded garments close to her and wrapped the blanket around them and her. Afterward, he went to the great doors, unbolted them, and assured himself that the rain was over. Then he opened one door wide enough for him to carry Margaret through it. There was no one in sight, but he did not feel any special concern lest someone should appear and surprise him with his burden. He believed that he could get to the house and up the stairs unobserved and he was right. He laid Margaret gently down on their bed and covered her; then he put her clothes away where he thought they belonged and rang for Cassie.

"Miss Margaret is very tired," he said, with a calmness he was very far from feeling. Then, as Cassie gave a startled exclamation, he added quickly, "Not hurt or ill or anything, just tired. She's having a good sleep and I think you'd better not disturb her by touching her or the bedclothes. The rain has cooled the air enough to have a fire, so I'm going to light one here and have my supper beside it. I'd like you to bring it to me on a tray—you, not Annabelle. And you'd better put some good strong broth in a thermos bottle and make some sandwiches. Perhaps later on Miss Margaret might be hungry."

Cassie turned toward him, mumbling something unintelligible and, momentarily, he thought she was going to defy him and go to Margaret, or at least to upbraid him in vehement speech. But presently she turned again and went out of the room, still muttering to herself. He lit the fire and sat down beside it, with no other light in the room except what came from one small shaded lamp. Eventually Cassie brought him a delicious supper, which he left almost untasted and, when she came to remove his tray, she brought another set with a thermos jug, a cup and saucer and some small sandwiches carefully wrapped in oiled paper. She looked reproachfully at the delicacies she had provided for him and which were still untouched. When she came into the room the first time, he had quickly sensed her antagonism to him and her concern for Margaret. Now he was equally quick to sense her change in mood, even before she spoke to him.

"Don' you fret yo'self 'bout Miss Marg'ret, Mistuh Nic'las," she said soothingly. "Ladies—Ah means ladies w'at's ben brung up careful like she were—is apt to swoon when dey firs' married. But hit don' harm dem none. Dey comes out o' dey swoons rested an' lovin'. You gwine see."

"Miss Margaret hasn't swooned, as you call it," he said sharply. "She's having a good sleep, that's all."

"Ah shure am sorry, Mistuh Nic'las, iffen Ah'se 'fended you. All Ah wanted wuz you shouldn't fret."

"I'm not fretting. I didn't happen to be hungry, but thanks for the nice supper, just the same. Good night, Cassie."

She asked respectfully if there were anything more she could do for him or Miss Margaret and then she said good night and went away. Nicolas had heard about swooning, under similar circumstances, but had set it down to an old wives' tale. And certainly Margaret had not fainted—he would have recognized the symptoms of such a loss of consciousness. But his concern deepened as time went by and the only sounds in the room were the licking of the flames and Margaret's quiet breathing. A man had no right to exhaust his wife merely because he, himself, was inexhaustible. For the moment he did not remember that Margaret's exhaustion had been building up for days before they were married, that he himself had observed it then and had tried to prevent her from continually overtaxing himself; he laid her prostration entirely to what had happened that afternoon. For the first time, he had not tried to spare her from his weight, but had lowered his body until the whole burden of it rested on hers; and the spearhead of a conqueror could be a devastating weapon if his captive were a yielding prisoner.

His troubled thoughts persisted, but at last he undressed and got into bed, taking care to lie as far as possible from his wife, who still had not moved. The night wore on and daylight began to filter in through the curtains. He had not slept when Margaret stirred and spoke in a bewildered whisper.

"Where am I? What happened?"

"You're in our room, darling, in our bed. Nothing has happened except that you went to sleep in the barn and I brought you back to the house without waking you."

"But I still have the blanket around me. I can feel it."

"Because I didn't want to disturb you by taking it away. I folded it around you when I brought you here. I can take it away now, if you'd like me to."

"No, no, I like the feeling of the blanket. It's a nice soft blanket, isn't it? Have I been asleep a long while?"

"Rather a long while. But you were very tired. I think you ought to try to sleep some more."

"I won't have to try very hard. I'm still very sleepy. But I need to go to the bathroom."

She slipped out of bed and, as she pattered across the floor in her bare feet, he folded the blanket and laid it carefully on the chaise longue. She had never before referred to any urgent bodily function and it pleased and relieved him that it now seemed natural for her to do so. When she returned from the bathroom, she climbed back into bed, still quite without self-consciousness, and rubbed her eyes.

"I keep getting sleepier and sleepier. But I'm hungry, too."

"I thought you might be when you waked up. I have some nice soup here for you and some sandwiches."

She accepted the steaming soup from him and drank thirstily, soon holding out her cup to be refilled and suddenly Nicolas thought of the great iron *landriers,* surmounted by casseroles, which formed part of the equipment in certain bedrooms of old Norman houses. It was in the casseroles that the *bouillon de la mariée* was prepared and given to the bride the morning after the telltale sheets had proclaimed that her marriage had been consummated. Now that he had seen Margaret sitting up in bed to savor her soup, veiled only in her long unbound hair, Nicolas could visualize the medieval scene, as it must have been enacted many times in old manor houses, and wanted to share the image with her. But when she had emptied her cup again, she lay down, refusing the sandwiches; apparently she was still more sleepy than hungry.

"It isn't time yet to wake up anyway, is it, Nicolas?"

"No, darling, and it won't be for hours and hours."

"I'm glad. That is, I would be if I were sure you wouldn't get tired of waiting for me to wake up and go away."

"Not a chance."

"But you seem awfully far away. Won't you hold my hand again, the way you did when you said, 'Thank you for understanding, Margaret'?"

"Of course I will. So go back to sleep."

"I want to. Now that I know it all came true."

"What came true, darling?"

"About cleaving together and becoming one flesh. You made it come true. And then the rest did, too. My desire was to my husband and he ruled over me just the way God told Eve it was going to be. I'm so glad. Oh, Nicolas, I can't tell you how much I love you! And now I know there will be a child."

16♋

It was Saturday, and there would be only two more full days after this one.

Rain was falling steadily now and, though Nicolas and Margaret took Perdita for a quick run, they agreed the house was a pleasanter place to linger than the grounds. Nicolas had already declared he would have nothing more to do with wedding presents: Margaret could finish listing those after he was gone; he simply could not face any more superfluous silver. But he would be glad to help her reorganize the library, to which he proposed to add a number of books on South America; there was a lamentable lack of these—all he had found so far, besides Nicolas Hale, was William Prescott and the latter represented only one side of a many-faceted and splendid story. ("You have been keeping track of me, haven't you? *Realms of Glory* and *Full Fathom Five* are positively dog-eared! Why didn't you interrupt me when I was giving you all that flap about waterfalls and golden bells—right in the middle of my proposal, too!") Madriaga and Ybarra were among the immediate musts for modern writers and, of course, Bingham; later in the day he would telephone Brentano's and see what they had on hand. Then he would fill in the gaps when he got to New York and Lima. Meanwhile, the rest of the books needed almost as much attention as the guns had before his father took those in hand. He carefully reassembled sets of classics, in which the separate volumes were out of sequence, and which were haphazardly divided and jumbled in with lesser literature. He paused now and then to read something he particularly enjoyed or to call Margaret's attention to it, so she could read it later; she was amazed at the scope and catholicity of his reading; the ease with which he located passages he had liked especially and his delight when he came across a rare first edition or an unusually handsome binding. She willingly, but rather absent-mind-edly, helped him sort and dust and he soon saw she was only half-listen-ing when he read aloud to her.

"What's the matter? Don't you enjoy Keats?"

"Very much. But I want to ask you some more questions. They're weighing so heavily on my mind that I can't seem to concentrate on anything else."

"There may be some more questions, but there aren't any more answers. I've already told you everything I know myself about my schedule."

"This isn't about your schedule—that is, not exactly. I want to know if explorers don't take their wives with them on their expeditions sometimes?"

"What makes you ask?"

"Because, from something Mrs. Madison said, I thought they did. And I thought if other explorers could—well, perhaps you could, too."

"Well, I can't. And, even if I could, I wouldn't."

"You mean you wouldn't want me with you on an expedition?"

"That's exactly what I mean." Nicolas clapped together the pages of the book he was dusting and slammed it, rather than placed it, on the desk beside him. "I have an inherent objection to female partic-ipants in a voyage of discovery," he went on emphatically. "Evidently Bingham had the same feeling—anyway, he never took his wife with him. I don't deny that some women are themselves quite notable explorers, who've done very well on their own, and that there have been some husband and wife teams who have done good work, too—the Oliver Gilchrists, whom you met at the Madisons' luncheon, are among those. But the unmarried female explorers have headed their own expeditions if they wanted to. I want to head my own, as Bingham did, and the husband and wife teams have usually been at it for years. They started out together in a small way, at the same time, with the same interests, and they've kept the same interests as they've gone along to bigger and better things. You and I didn't begin the way they did. You're nearly ten years younger than I am. You were still in school when I became an explorer. The only reason I knew you fairly well as a debutante was because we were both at the Schaeffers' house a lot when Esther's father was Assistant Secretary of Commerce. You were there as her schoolmate and I was there seeking financial backing for my earlier expeditions. Normally, I wouldn't have been considered in your age bracket for parties, though of course I'm very glad I was. Then I never saw you again until Esther and Sam were married. And what had you been doing in the meantime? Living like a recluse on this plantation!"

"You know why, Nicolas."

"Yes, I know why and it's all to your credit. But it's no sort of a preparation, either mentally or physically, for roughing it around South America. What started you off on this tangent? You told me yourself at that memorable wedding—I mean Sam's and Esther's, not ours—that you didn't see any reason why an explorer's wife shouldn't be contented, during his absence, provided she had a comfortable, pleasant place to stay. And this is not only a comfortable, pleasant place, but it's one you love very much, one where you've always preferred to stay. It never so much as crossed my mind you'd want to go with me. What's happened to change yours?"

"Loving you so that I don't see how I'm going to live without you."

"Look here, you mustn't say things like that to me, darling. I've told you so before. I can't take it."

"But it's true. I didn't know how much I was going to love you. You'd been my hero for a long time, but that wasn't like having you for my husband. You said yourself I'd dismissed a false image and found a reality and, of course, it's the reality that counts. As a matter of fact, I didn't know much about love anyway, even last Wednesday. I thought I did, but I didn't really. And now it's Saturday and you're leaving on Tuesday. I can't bear the thought of losing you."

"Then don't think about it. We'll go on packing happiness into the days we have left, just as I told you we would; and then there'll be that grand send-off in New York and you'll have lots of fun with Esther, going to the theater and buying clothes and—"

"Would you mind very much if I didn't come to New York?"

"Would I—why, of course I would! Not have you at my farewell party? Not have you at the plane when it takes off?"

"I don't think I'd be much of an asset at a party, feeling the way I will. And I'm sure I'd disgrace you by breaking down and crying at the airport."

"But, Margaret, if you don't come with me, we'd have one less day and night together. And you're beginning to feel, just as I am, that we haven't got much time left. Besides, how could I explain why you didn't come with me?"

"You could say I didn't feel well. It wouldn't be nearly as much of an untruth as those lavender lies you told your parents. Or you could telephone Sam right now and ask him to call off the party. I think he'd understand. And, instead of going to New York Monday, you could stay here until early Tuesday morning and then take a plane that would connect with the one for South America."

"If the weather were all right!"

"If the weather weren't all right, the plane to South America wouldn't be going either. You know that. And you know if you were a little late they'd hold it for you anyway."

"You've got it all figured out, haven't you, Margaret?"

"Yes, I have. Would going to that party, which will last until all hours and be crowded and noisy, like all the Steinmetz parties, mean so much more to you than staying here alone with me and having another long lovely day and night to ourselves?"

"You know it wouldn't. It's just that I hadn't thought of it that way."

"But won't you, Nicolas? Because if nothing I can say will persuade you to take me with you—"

"You're not going to spoil our last days by teasing, are you? Because it won't do a bit of good and it might do a great deal of harm."

"No, I won't tease about that if it really is hopeless."

"It really is hopeless, Margaret. I've got a job to do. I've promised a lot of people, including my financial backers, that I'll do it and what's more, I promised myself, which is just as important. You wouldn't have the slightest respect for me if I didn't carry on. . . . Shall we go back to Keats?"

"No, not quite yet. I am going to tease about the other because I believe, if you think it over, you'll admit I have a right to decide about that trip to New York."

"Maybe I will. Anyhow, I'll think the matter over. Now, come and sit down beside me and listen to this. You didn't seem to care much for Keats, so let's switch to Byron. Of course, your hair is golden and not raven, but otherwise 'She Walks in Beauty' seems to fit. By the way, I've been meaning to ask you to promise me you won't ever cut your hair."

"Why, I never had any idea of cutting it!"

"All right, but promise me anyway."

"I promise anyway. But please, in return, promise me that you won't make me go to New York."

"All right, you insufferable nagger. Now listen:

" 'She walks in beauty, like the night
    Of cloudless climes, and starry skies:
And all that's best of dark and bright
    Meet in her aspect and her eyes:
Thus mellowed to that tender light
    Which Heaven to gaudy day denies.

" 'One shade the more, one ray the less,
    Had held impaired the nameless grace,
Which waves in every raven tress,
    Or softly lightens o'er her face;
Where thoughts serenely sweet express,
    How pure, how dear their dwelling-place.

" 'And on that cheek, and o'er that brow,
　　So soft, so calm, yet eloquent,
　The smiles that win, the things that glow,
　　But tell of days in goodness spent.
　A mind at peace with all below,
　　A heart whose love is innocent!' "

He reread the last lines, dwelling on them and closed the book. Then he kissed her and stroked her hair with a lingering touch. They stopped sorting and dusting and sat quietly together in the firelight, as the daylight faded.

17 ℘

It was Sunday and there was only that day and one more.

They had not discussed plans for either one. But when Nicolas discovered that Margaret had taken it for granted they would go to church, he made no objection, though he confessed he would not have thought of doing so until he found out she considered it an integral part of a Sunday schedule and he was genuinely pleased at her next suggestion.

"Church is over about twelve. I thought we might drive down to Charlottesville and drop in on Uncle Virginius. He'd be terribly pleased if we did. It's a beautiful day again and I'd love to have an outing with you. We could take a picnic lunch with us and eat whenever we felt like it at one of those wayside rest areas with a rustic table and benches. There are lots of them in Virginia. We could talk about all sorts of things. There's one story I've been wanting very much to tell you, but I had to wait for just the right time."

"And I've been waiting for just the right time to tell you one."

Nicolas was glad, after they reached Pohick Church, that he had so readily agreed to going with Margaret to the morning service. She belonged there, he would think of her as being there every Sunday while he was away; and he could visualize her feeling for her faith much more clearly than if his presence in this setting had been limited to the Sunday their engagement was announced, when she was extremely self-conscious, and to their wedding and its rehearsal; for now he saw her quietly resuming the accepted pattern of familiar and beloved ritual. Also revealing was the exchange of greetings and plans with her friends and neighbors, from whom she had slipped away as quickly as possible the previous Sunday, but to whom she now introduced him proudly, though shyly, as her husband when they went out into the churchyard after Morning Prayer. These were the people with whom she would be carrying on her accustomed activities in the Ann Mason Guild and the Altar Society; and one of the elderly ladies assured her she could count on immediate reinstatement in the Garden Club after all. Now that he had met them and taken their measure, he was well content to feel these would be her associates. Surely, once he was gone, she would see for herself that it was much more fitting she should remain among them than to go to strange lands. He completely forgot she had told him how empty her days were, of anything that really mattered, before he came.

Several of their fellow churchgoers had spoken to them of the fine spread the Sunday papers had given their wedding, which reminded them they had not even thought of looking at any news items themselves. They stopped at Stratford Court House and bought an armful of New York, Washington and Richmond papers, all of which had devoted at least one page to pictures, beginning with the shots taken at the church and ending with those made in the gun room: the President and Mrs. Maynard arriving at the church; the bride arriving at the church; the bride and groom leaving the church together; the bride and groom with the President and Mrs. Maynard, the Vice President and Mrs. Bruce, the Assistant Secretary of State for Latin-American Affairs and Mrs. Lambert, the Ambassador of Peru and *Señora* Román, and Mr. and Mrs. Bingham; the bride and groom with members of the wedding party; the groom's parents with their celebrated son and their new daughter-in-law; the President toasting the bridal couple; and the bride cutting the cake with the sword that had been used at Seven Pines. Margaret was delighted with them all and Nicolas slightly amused that she should take so much pleasure in them. Since he had refused to give her time on their wedding night to "talk the party over," he had not realized how exciting and gratifying she had found the presence of so many celebrities, especially the President and his wife, at the wedding. Now her enthusiasm led to another idea.

"Do you realize that I myself haven't a single picture of you? What am I going to do when my Peruvian friends wait expectantly for me to take out my wallet and show them snapshots of my bride?"

"You're going to tell them you don't carry snapshots around in your wallet, as of course you don't."

"True enough. But I'd like a really good picture of you, what I believe is called, in the trade, a 'portrait,' to frame in Peruvian silver and put on my desk or my bureau, when I happen to have either of those commodities at my disposal. I grant that isn't often, but it's a nice idea just the same. Please go to Harris and Ewing or Bachrach or some such place and get some portraits—a lot of them, and airmail me the proofs."

"Portraits are terribly expensive. Are you sure you have plenty of money?"

"There is no such thing as plenty of money. But I have enough for a few photographs and I hope I'll have enough for a real portrait of you one of these days, by the best painter we can find. It would do wonders to lighten up that long row of ancestors in the dining room. Some of them are rather on the gloomy side."

"You don't appreciate them, that's all."

"I appreciate you, anyway."

The inspection of the wedding pictures reminded them that they had delayed discussion of the wedding reception because, though they agreed that talking over a party afterward was often more fun than anything else about it, Nicolas had called Margaret's attention to the fact this wasn't *just* a party, but the celebration of a marriage, and had insisted that, instead of sitting before the fire and cozily chatting, she must go upstairs and "get ready" for him. Since then, there had been so many other things to discuss. Now, at last, as they drove, with no sense of haste or urgency, along the pleasant road that took them deeper and deeper into Virginia, the propitious moment to review the great event seemed to have come.

"I agree with you about Mrs. Bruce, Nicolas. There *is* something almost dazzling about her. She completely outshines Mrs. Maynard, doesn't she?"

"Yes, I'm afraid she does. There are rumors of a little natural jealousy on that score. It just isn't done when the President's wife and the Vice President's wife are concerned. At that, Miriam LaGuarde has more class than either one of them."

"New York class!"

"All right, you snooty Virginian! Now, turning to the less deadly of the species, whom did you like best?"

"Tom Herbert."

"Well, well! So you're not so snooty, after all! You pass over the Cabinet, State Department and half a dozen other important branches of the government in favor of a mere newspaperman."

"He didn't seem to me so very mere."

"He isn't, either. You're right about that. I'm certainly glad you and he hit it off. As I told you before, I think you'll enjoy going to the parties he and Sally give."

"I've already accepted an invitation from them for next Sunday."

"Good. Their food doesn't come up to yours, but it's pretty fair at that. They rather specialize in Near Eastern dishes, like cous-cous, grape leaves and peanut soup. But, incidentally, it was a grand idea to have eggnog as well as champagne, and there never was such a wedding cake as the one Cassie made for us!"

"I'll tell her you said so. She'll be terribly pleased. And weren't you glad we had all our people come in and sing for us the way they used to do at the Christmas parties you liked so much?"

"Of course I was, but 'Canaan Land' got me down; it was almost more than I could take."

"Because Peru's your 'Canaan Land,' isn't it, Nicolas?"

"You're too good at guessing. But I'm not so confident the Sweet Jesus is going with me. If He were, I'd be a lot surer of finding my lost city."

They continued to discuss various aspects of the wedding reception, and rather tardily realized they had nearly reached Fredericksburg without considering a place where they might like to stop. Since almost all the rest areas were already occupied, Margaret suggested they should turn off the main road and go down the less traveled one that led to Stratford, Lee's birthplace, and other historic houses on the Northern Neck. It really did not matter whether or not they ever got to Charlottesville; they had not told Uncle Virginius they were coming, so he would not be disappointed; what really counted was their chance to talk together. Again, Nicolas agreed and the place they finally found suited their mood completely, and it was after they finished lunch that Margaret and Nicolas told each other their stories.

He asked her to tell hers first and listened very gravely while she did so. She said it was the one that had flashed through her mind in the midst of the marriage ceremony and had given her a moment of such foolish terror, because of her unreasoning fear lest the word obey might be included in the vows she had to make. Her mother had told her that, of course, the word could be used in a general sense; but Emma Porterfield had added in a whisper that the commandment applied especially to the physical relationship between husband and wife, which she explained only by saying it must always be governed by the husband's wishes. And then she had gone on with a dreadful tale about a man—a Southern gentleman—who whipped his wife, because she was reluctant to have him exercise his marital rights, and wrung from her a confession that this was because she was afraid she might become pregnant again and she had suffered such agonies when her babies were born that she could not face childbirth again. So then he told her he would teach her how to overcome those fears: he would whip her every night until she begged him to stop because she would be thankful enough to accept his advances if they saved her from further lashing. He used the same whip on his wife that he did on his dogs. Sometimes the children would stand outside their parents' locked door and hear their mother's pitiful promises never to fail in her wifely duty again, if he would only spare her. By-and-by their old colored nurse would come looking for them and hurriedly take them away and put them to bed and tell them, with tears running down her cheeks, they must not grieve, because there was nothing they could do to help their mother and, above all, they must never let their father know they had heard what was happening. The next morning he would greet them brightly, sit down at table with them, see that they had a hearty breakfast and then take them out with him on the plantation and give them a delightful day. He was so kind to them it was hard for them to believe he was really unkind to their mother and they convinced themselves they had more or less imagined what they had heard behind the locked door. Their father told them their mother was not very strong and that she was resting a lot because she wanted to give them a baby brother or sister, so they must not be surprised if she stayed in her room most of the time. Of course, now she was hoping she would conceive because that would free her from nightly cruelty; her husband wanted more children and he would not do anything which might injure the unborn. But weeks went by without deliverance and, finally, it came by death. And then of course it was announced that this lady had died of a heart attack, but the truth leaked out and the children grew up knowing their father was a murderer. "And ever since I heard that story, I've cringed at the word obey," Margaret said as she finished it.

"It's a terrible story. I don't wonder that it affected you very strongly. But may I tell you why I think your mother told it to you, Margaret?"

"Yes, of course."

"I take it your father wasn't a cruel man?"

"*Cruel!* He was one of the kindest, gentlest men that ever lived! I worship his memory and so did my mother. He saved her in every possible way. He knew she wasn't strong and that she shouldn't have heavy family cares."

"I see. I think possibly that's why you were an only child—that she succeeded in convincing him she wasn't strong enough to have any more children, just as she convinced you that you mustn't ever leave her. She told you that story to frighten you—it isn't the sort that a wise and loving mother tells to a sensitive young daughter, unless there's a special reason for it and, in this case, there could have been only one special reason. I won't say it may not be true; I suppose there are sadists in Virginia as well as in other places, though elsewhere they wouldn't be called Southern gentlemen. Be that as it may, I think she wanted to make you believe there were so many terrible things which could happen to you, if you married, that you'd never consider doing so, at least as long as she lived. And you didn't."

"Nicolas, you're not being fair to my mother. She was a very saintly woman."

"Maybe. Anyhow, you're right in believing I shouldn't try to spoil your image of her. I wouldn't have said what I did if I hadn't wanted you to stop cringing at the word obey. After all, it's part of a man's oath to love and cherish, just as it's part of his wife's, and if he did that, his rule couldn't be harsh, much less cruel, could it? He wouldn't be likely to be unreasonable about asking her to obey whether the word was comprehensive or meant just one thing. Would he? My guess is that some of those Victorian women were so 'refined' they insisted on regarding sex as a sentiment, instead of a vital force, and maybe they did need to be reminded of a husband's rights once in a while—in a normal way. Not just in bed, either. Everywhere about the place. A man who's worth his salt wants to be the head of the house, and he ought to be, whether the house belongs to him or his wife. Don't you agree with me?"

"Of course, I do. And I hope you'll never feel, Nicolas, that because this one happens to be mine—"

"I know I never shall. But would you really have worried if the word obey had still been in the marriage service?"

"Yes, Nicolas, I would have—then. Of course, I don't now."

"More than you were worrying anyway? I honestly don't see how that would have been possible! Aren't you glad all those worries are behind you now?"

"You don't know how glad."

"Good. Now let's talk about something else. Perhaps I might get on with my story."

He brushed away some leaves that had fallen on the rustic seat and lighted a cigarette. "As a rule, I don't believe in dwelling on past history," he began. "But this time I'm going to. I'm going to tell you about a girl I fell in love with when I was just a kid myself. It can't do any harm now and it may do some good in clearing up one or two things that still can't be evident to you and that, heretofore, I haven't had a very good chance to explain. I'm very grateful to you for not trying to hurry me into explanations.

"After my freshman year, I got a job on a farm for the summer. My father wasn't as well-to-do then as he is now and I was trying to meet most of my college expenses myself. This was the best paying job I could get. I worked just like any other hired man, four a.m. to eight or nine p.m. No one in Vermont in those days had heard about minimum wages and forty hour weeks; but none of the young people I knew

minded long hours, either. Very often, when we went to a party at the
village hall, we didn't go to bed at all. We danced all night and then at
four o'clock the men started milking and the girls started doing whatever they were supposed to in the house—cooking breakfast, getting the
wash ready to hang out, that sort of thing.

"There were plenty of girls to go around, when it came to dances, but
I thought I was awfully lucky because it seemed perfectly natural to
everyone that I should be the one to take the daughter of the farmer I
was working for, since I was living at his place anyway. She was the
prettiest little thing I'd ever seen, in a kittenish kind of way, just naturally cute and cuddly. When we were at the dances, she had lots of
different partners, because that was before the craze for going steady
developed into an unwritten or maybe a written law that a girl
shouldn't dance with anyone except her date. But I had my innings on
the way to and from the village hall and, more especially, the nights
when there weren't any dances. Those were the nights that she and I
tumbled in the hay.

"I told you, the first time I came out here last week, that I'd never
wanted to get married. That wasn't quite true. I was crazy about
this girl and I wanted very much to marry her. It never occurred to me
that what we were doing wasn't leading to exactly that—as soon as we
were both old enough, as soon as I'd finished college and got a little
money saved up. Once in a while I worried a little about what might
happen if I got my girl pregnant—not on moral grounds—I wasn't
conscious of doing anything immoral. But, if she were going to have a
baby, of course we would have had to be married right away and that
might have meant the end of college for me. But she didn't seem to
worry and, presently, I didn't either. I was only eighteen and she was
my first love. I mean that literally. She was about the same age, though
she looked younger, and it didn't occur to me for a long time that I
wasn't first with her, too.

"Of course, I ought to have guessed. If any of the other fellows had
wanted her very much, they wouldn't have stood back and let me take
her to all the dances, simply because it was a logical arrangement as
long as I was working on her father's farm. The reason I didn't have
any opposition was because all the other boys in that crowd had had
her already. They'd got tired of her cute, kittenish ways and the
impartiality with which she shared them.

"It wasn't until another outsider came along that there was a show-
down. We got through haying without any extra help, but when
threshing began, we needed more, and another college student
appeared on the scene. He was smitten just as hard and just as fast as
I'd been. But I took it for granted I had the inside track and didn't
worry until Maisie—that wasn't her real name, but it'll do—suggested

that the newcomer and I might take turns as her escort to parties, and didn't seem to have as many free evenings as she used to for taking a stroll, which eventually led to the barn, the nights there weren't any dances. So I told this other fellow he'd better make himself scarce, because Maisie was my girl and we were going to get married. And what do you think happened then? He laughed at me—and so did she.

"I took it pretty hard. I stayed the rest of the summer and went on with my work. But I didn't go to any more dances and I knew all the rest of the crowd was laughing at me. Sometimes the laughter wasn't even hushed up. I was a general object of ridicule for having been such an easy mark, because of my own innocence. If I'd played around like the rest of the boys, it wouldn't have happened—at least that was the inference. I was hurt through and through. I vowed then I'd never trust another girl and that I'd never marry. I never have trusted another girl, and I never have wanted to marry one—until I met you again. Then I knew I could trust you completely and, presently, I wanted to marry you more than I wanted anything else in the world, except to find my lost city.

"But the funny thing about all this, the thing I hope you won't ask me to explain, because I'm not sure I can, is that I've always remembered what that barn was like, and that part of the memory has been a happy one. I've always had a queer dream, at the back of my mind, that some day I'd find another like it, and someone who'd go to it with me, and this time it wouldn't be someone who was cheating me. I didn't think of that someone as my wife, because I didn't intend or expect to have a wife, but I did keep looking and hoping for the right person as my companion. And all these years the looking and hoping have been in vain. Maisie never had a successor—of that kind. The only tumbles in the hay I ever had were with her. But somehow, Friday, I felt my long wait was over. I remembered you told me, the day we met in New York, about an old barn where hay had been stored for a long time and that it was still soft and sweet smelling and I suddenly knew I'd found the girl I'd looked for all these years, the girl who'd make my dream come true, and she did."

He had told his story through, without stopping, looking straight ahead of him and speaking in a voice which, for him, was singularly toneless. Now he threw away his cigarette and turned to her with the tenderness which always moved his wife so deeply.

"You did more for me that afternoon than you realized, Margaret," he said. "Besides accepting me as your husband in a truly Biblical sense —which, of course, was the greatest thing—you also assuaged a long harbored sense of injury. That was a lesser thing to do, but still it was one that was very important, as far as my joy in living is concerned. They're all gone now, the resentment, the hurt, the shame of having been the dupe of a wanton. And only a woman like you could have driven these feelings away—a woman whose 'love is innocent,' but at the same time very confident and very strong—almost sacrificial. I've never liked the expression 'she came to him as a virgin.' It's the husband that comes to the wife, who 'goes in unto her and knows her,' to revert again to the beautiful Biblical language that has such significance to both of us. I'd already gone in unto you and it had meant everything in the world to me that no man had been able to do that before; but I hadn't really known you until I found in you the supreme fulfillment which I had believed no woman could ever give me."

"And you did?" she asked in a hushed voice.

"Yes, yes, yes. I don't know anything else to say. There aren't words for me to put it more strongly."

"But we don't need to put it into words any more, do we, Nicolas?"

"Not any more. We know each other."

After that, they thought of more stories they wanted to share. Nicolas had not yet told Margaret about the *landriers* and the *bouillon de la mariée* and this seemed a perfect time and place to do so; and, ever since he had said he thought they should have horses on the place again, she had longed to tell him how much this would mean to her, because of the riding she had done with her father; but she had hesitated, because Nicolas was doing so much for her, she did not want to suggest, even indirectly, he should do any more. The subject of horses brought them to the Huntingtons at East Lawn; Nicolas was very indignant because these *nouveaux riches* had gone to the wedding ceremony at the church; it had been impossible to turn them away there without making a scene; but the Secret Service had done so at the house, because their names were not on the guest list, and he was glad of it.

"I hope you'll keep on turning them away," he said. "Somehow, I don't like to think of you having any connection with East Lawn since it changed hands."

"There's no reason why I should have, beyond the point of cool courtesy."

"Well, keep it cool, whether it's courteous or not. I don't want those social climbers bulldozing you."

The leaves continued to fall gently from the oak trees above Margaret and Nicolas and he brushed them away and lighted one cigarette after another and still the two went on talking. Then there was a long companionable silence, which seemed as intimate as their speech had been, and Margaret looked up at Nicolas with an expression which showed she had had a welcome surprise.

"Do you know something, Nicolas? We're friends, as well as lovers! If we weren't, we couldn't talk with each other this way or sit together without talking and still feel closer and closer."

"I thought maybe we'd find that out—about being friends, I mean. It doesn't surprise me as much as it seems to surprise you."

18 ❧

They went no further than the quiet place they had found. It did not matter, they said to each other again, because they had never told Uncle Virginius they were coming and there was not enough time to share with anyone else.

So they spent a long afternoon telling each other stories and discovering they were friends as well as lovers. Then they drove slowly home by moonlight and dined again by candlelight and, afterward, they made a further discovery: another vital element had been added to their marriage by their newfound friendship. Because of it, love-making no longer needed preparation or prelude; it had been freed from domination on the one side and from subjection on the other and had become mutually confident, mutually spontaneous and mutually joyous. Over and over again, after they had gone to sleep in each other's arms, they waked to find fresh wellsprings of delight.

And now it was Monday and this was the last day and night.

Nicolas and Margaret wandered through the garden again, with Perdita at their heels, and sat in the arbor again, but not very long; they were too conscious of the fact that it was the last time, so they decided on something different. They went into town to do the last errands together and followed the river on the Memorial Drive as far as Mount Vernon; but, surreptitiously, they both kept looking at their watches and saying to themselves, "Another hour has gone and another and another"; and by tacit agreement they went back to Hills' End, because, after all, that was the place where the remaining hours would mean the most to them. Then Nicolas called the staff, both the servants already working in the house and the additional employes he had engaged to work on the grounds—Mingo, Tam, Reason and Esau— with Rufus as their foreman, and told them again all the things he expected them to do while he was gone; but, above all, they were to take good care of Miss Margaret. They promised solemnly and faithfully and went their ways and Nicolas and Margaret sat down to another candlelighted dinner. Cassie had outdone herself. She had provided terrapin stew and wild turkey with rice dressing, spoon bread, trifle and jelly roll; but neither of them ate much. Then they went to bed and Nicolas told Margaret he could see she was very tired and that she must try to sleep, but he knew very well she could not and neither could he. Nevertheless, when he at last withdrew from her, she did not cling to him, begging him to keep her just a little longer and, when he left her, she was still dry-eyed. It was not until after he had gone that she gave way to grief. But when Cassie came to her room, hours later, the old woman found her still crying as if her heart would break.

"Don' you grieve so, honey," Cassie said soothingly. "Ah knows jus' how hit be—when you loses yo' man, yo' own man, ain' no comfort nowheah in dis wide world. But you ain' really lost yo's. He ain' dead, like mine is. He comin' back to you. An' he ben thinkin' 'bout you lots already. He got to de airport early, so he tol' Rufus to wait 'til de plane come in, he wuz goin' write you a lettah he wanted Rufus to fetch back. Heah 'tis. You sit up an' read hit an' presently you gwine feel bettah. When you does, you ring yo' bell an' Ah'll bring you a nice breakfast my own se'f an' Ah'm gwine bring Perdita to you. Co'se you don' know hit yet, but she's gwine be a heap of comfort an' company to you."

Margaret had already snatched the letter away. She sat up in bed and tore open the envelope.

"Darling—

"I hoped you'd be asleep when I left you this morning, or at least happily drowsy the way you were once before, after we'd been very close to each other for a long while. But this time it didn't work out that way. I suppose it couldn't, because I wanted it too much and, sometimes, that's dangerous. (It's all right to want something a lot, but not too much.) I was very proud of you because you didn't cry and didn't even hint again about wishing I would take you to Peru with me, just let me keep on making love to you until the very last minute, without saying a single word that would spoil it. But I'm afraid that, since I left you, you *have* been crying and thinking a lot about Peru; and I've been thinking, not of one word *I* hadn't said, but of three which I ought to have said long ago. So I'm writing this letter on purpose to say them now and I don't think they'll spoil anything for you:

"I love you.

"I told you that I admired and respected you more than ever—of course, I always had admired and respected you—because you hadn't gone back on your promise to marry me on five days' notice and let me act like a husband as soon as we were married. That's true, I do. I know you were terribly tempted to back out all along the line. And you didn't. You went through with it. It took no end of courage and a great sense of obligation to a pledged word. I should have told you I realized all this and then I should have added: I love you.

"I told you repeatedly I wanted you, meaning that I desired you, and that I kept finding you more desirable all the time. That's also perfectly true. I want you so much at this minute that it's taking every bit of will power I can summon not to come back to you. But it's a good thing I've plenty of will power for, if I did come back now, you'd despise me, because you know as well as I do that I ought to go and do my job. And having you despise me would really be something I couldn't take. I told you I couldn't take it when you said you cared so much about me you cared about everything I was doing and when you said you loved me so much you didn't see how you were going to live without me. Instead of telling you I couldn't take anything like that—which, of course, I could—I should have come right back at you and told you I loved you so much I cared about everything you were doing and that I didn't see how I was going to live without you. I don't see and I don't intend to try. All that silly talk about making sure of a son and then calling quits on the whole thing is off. We're married for richer, for poorer and all the rest of it. I wasn't committing perjury when I said that, though I know you thought I was. I wasn't half as nonchalant about the whole thing as I tried to sound, to cover up the way I really felt, and that was another silly thing for me to do, I should have let you see then I already loved you, that I had, almost from the beginning.

"I was afraid I was going to, that first evening—I say afraid because, as you know, it hadn't been part of my plan. Then, when I thought you were going back on me, I said to myself, well, what the hell, of course I don't love her, anyway. But you didn't go back on me. I should have told you then that I loved you. But you wouldn't let me act like a suitor and that bothered me for two reasons: first, because it hurt my pride that I wasn't persuasive and attractive enough to overcome the scruples which were due partly to your mother's misguided notions and partly to your natural reserve and, secondly, because I knew things would be harder for you in the end that way and I didn't want things to be hard for you. But my hurt pride and my aversion to your scruples didn't keep me from loving you quite a lot. And from the moment you confessed to me, the morning after our marriage, that you didn't hate me, that there was nothing to forgive, that you were almost glad that was the way things were—well, ever since then I've loved you so much it doesn't seem possible to me any husband ever loved his wife that much before.

"I told you I'd never ask you to submit to me but once and then I made you do it a second time when I asked you to go to the barn with me. I don't mean it was submission in a physical sense because, though we'd been married only two days, you were all through with your fears of menacing mysteries. But it was a demand for submission in another sense, because you felt I wouldn't ask you to take a tumble in the hay with me unless I held you cheap. Of course, you were mistaken in that. As you've found out since, I hoped and believed you could and would help me to overcome an ancient grudge, and you have, so that I've already nearly forgotten I ever held it. And, as I tried to tell you beforehand, what I wanted most of all was to have you find out that a luxurious bedroom wasn't the only place appropriate for the act of love and that a big secret barn might be a very wonderful alternative. I can think of other places that might be: rough little camps beside blue lakes and great open pastures high on hillsides and the depths of immense forests where pine needles, instead of hay, would make a bed. Perhaps some day we'll be together in places like those, too. But, at the moment, the barn seemed the best place to prove my point and I believe I was right. I know it was hard for you at first, but you didn't say so or show it in any way and I loved you all the more on that account. But I also know—at least I believe—there was something about the primeval quality of our surroundings that affected you as strongly as it did me, in the end. You couldn't have looked and acted the way you did unless it had. I'll never forget how beautiful you were, lying on that shabby old blanket. I hadn't supposed you could look any more beautiful than you did the morning after we were married. But I was mistaken. I'll never forget, either, how you joyfully yielded yourself up to me so that you would 'become all mine' and the way you told me it would be for always. I hadn't supposed that any sense of possession could be more triumphant than the first one. But I was mistaken about that, too. I ought to have said I love you, over and over again, that afternoon and I didn't say it once. Even if I'd never said it before, I should have said it then. But I'm saying it now. I love you, Margaret, I love you, I love you.

"I hope when you're alone at Hills' End, thinking over these five days and nights we've had, you won't feel we've spent too much of them in being together, in the full sense of the word. And I hope that no one will ever say anything to you, heedlessly, that will make you feel again there is something shameful about sex, because sex itself is never shameful, only the abuse of it; and what we've done is to reveal its glories to each other. Not all of them—five days and nights weren't enough for that; but enough, I hope, to make their afterglow bright for us until I come back to you. I've told you over and over again I needed you and I hope you won't feel I am presumptuous in saying I believe you needed me, too; and the wonderful thing about it is that we found each other. The first splendor of that discovery would have been dimmed if we'd denied ourselves a single moment of the rapture for which we yearned; and rapture, at this stage of our marriage, was physical union. Of course, we haven't assuaged that yearning yet. At this very moment, I'm longing desperately for you and you're longing desperately for me. But it isn't because we haven't made the most of all the time we did have. And thank God, it isn't as though we didn't have years and years of life together ahead of us. Naturally, there'll never be another five days like these —probably it would be a mistake if we tried to duplicate them. But there'll be other days with their own wonders, either like those we've had already, or new ones that keep on making life perfect and complete.

"This time, I haven't left a present for you because it seemed to me that, if I did, it might look as if I were trying to repay you for all you've given me and that is beyond money and price. I've been thinking a lot about that big blazing Colombian emerald I mentioned and I'd decided not to wait and give it to you when our son was born, but to ask you to go with me to Cartier and choose the setting for it right now. But when you begged not to go to New York with me, I knew that was out and, even if it hadn't been, I'd have changed my mind for the reason I've mentioned. But I'll send you a little present from Peru every now and then just for the fun of it, not for any special reason or occasion. There are some quite lovely things in Peru—gems and furs and a very soft white marble called *Huamanga* that makes charming statuettes and, once in a while, it's possible to find a wonderful old Inca ornament of gold. If you think of something you'd especially like, I hope you'll let me know. If not, I'll follow my own judgment.

"This is a long letter and still I haven't said half the things I wanted and meant to say. And now my plane, which was late—but not late enough to make me lose my connection in New York—has just been announced and I haven't even time to read through what I've written and correct careless mistakes like misspelled words and left-out commas and that sort of thing. But I know there's nothing basic in it that I want to change and I've time to write just one more sentence before I seal the envelope and thrust it into Rufus' hand and dash out to the runway.

"I love you, Margaret."

II ❧ NICOLAS

"One may fall but he falls by himself—
  Falls by himself with himself to blame;
One may attain and to him is the pelf,
  Loot of the city in Gold or Fame:
Plunder of earth shall be all his own
Who travels the fastest and travels alone."

—From Rudyard Kipling, *L'Envoi* to
The Story of the Gadsbys

Scene of action: Lima, Cuzco and various outlying parts of Peru, with interludes in Washington and Virginia

Time: Autumn, 1953 to Autumn, 1957

Principal characters (added):

Ildefonso and Marina Parra, Limenian friends of Nicolas Hale

Fray Gregorio, Dominican monk of Quillabamba Mission; afterward bishop

Dr. Juan Labrador, Rector of San Marcos University, Lima, and his wife, *Doña* Ana

Members of Nicolas Hale's expedition:
Pete Hart, Nicolas Hale's assistant and an old friend
Li Chan, Chinese cook
Julio Gomara, exiled Bolivian archeologist, of Arequipa University
Esteban Mamani, geologist, of Cuzco University
Pedro Mendoza, botanist, of Cuzco University
Cipriano, Quero Indian, one of the carriers
Walter Ruiz and Clodomiro Vasquez, graduate students of Cuzco University

Dr. Carlos Castel, volunteer lay physician at Dominican Hospital, Quillabamba

Sister Teresa, Dominican nursing Sister

Antonio Astur, Royalist veteran of the Spanish Civil War, now living in Atalaya, and his wife, Fátima

Dr. Haskins, Washington specialist in obstetrics

Irvin Powers, Chairman of the Foreign Relations Committee, U. S. Senate

Lieutenant Teodoro Toledo, Peruvian Air Force Pilot

* Warren Holtz, South American representative of the Hiller Company

Ethan Watkins, a New England lawyer

Perpetua Quispe, a Machiguenga Indian girl, and her son

Dr. Rafael Villarán, civilian representative of Peruvian government

Harry Davis, pilot-mechanic

Jorge Ibarra, Faucett representative at Quince Mil, and his wife, Doris

Mr. and Mrs. Edgar Huntington of East Lawn Plantation, Virginia

19

Over the Andes came a burning ball, the sun of the tropics, god of the Inca, first igniting high patches of ice, then setting fire to a whole sea of cloud.

Nicolas had managed to doze in the cool plane between the sticky airports at Panama and Guayaquil, where the passengers had been required to leave the plane while it was serviced; now he wanted a long look at the Andes. Years before he had been repelled by the first sight of the coastal *cordillera* because of its barrenness; now the same barrenness had a strange attraction for him; but most of the time it was veiled, for the plane rushed and dipped and scudded into a sea of cloud. When the glitter on the surface of the cloud gave way to dimness and moisture streaked the windows, he knew that in a few instants the plane would dive through the eternal mist which overhangs Lima; and suddenly the city lay there, cut off from the sun, drab in contrast to the richness of the green in the few outlying farms. Even the ocean, as the plane circled, looked dull. Then the plane touched ground and he was looking out on the marble and glass solidity of the passenger terminal at Limatambo.

As he stepped out of the plane, he looked searchingly at the sea of faces above him on the open terrace of the terminal. Even at this distance, it would be easy to identify Ildefonso Parra, if his friend were there, for the polo player stood out in any crowd because of his height, his lean grace and the distinction of his bearing. Then a familiar voice called from below, *"Bienvenido, Señor explorador!"* and Nicolas saw that Fonso, to whom guards represented only petty officials to brush off quickly and nonchalantly, was already standing at the foot of the gangway and almost instantly the traveler was engulfed in a hearty *abrazo*.

"Que tal! Good to see you!" he said heartily. "But why didn't you let us take a taxi? It's a shame to get you up at cockcrow to meet a couple of rumpled, unshaven derelicts who've spent sixteen hours in rapid transit through space. Oh, sorry—this is Les Wendell, architectural aspirant, actual man Friday."

"Sea bienvenido también, Señor Les! Nick, you know there is no cockcrow in Lima and we don't let our friends ride in taxis. What

about letting a porter carry some of those bundles, unless they contain crown jewels? Anyway, come along to the customs. Everything's set, we'll be out of there in a matter of minutes."

"It wasn't a matter of minutes for poor Pete. He had a devil of a job getting the equipment through."

"Well, it'll be different this time, you'll see."

As if to verify Ildefonso's assurance, the uniformed Chief of Customs greeted Nicolas by name and waved him on with a "glad-to-have-you-back-Doctor." Then they were on their way to the car, where Emilio, the chauffeur, was already holding open the door and, in no time at all, the baggage was neatly stowed away and they were starting for town.

"I'd forgotten about the ubiquitous habits of your cocks," Nicolas remarked, as they sped along at the breakneck speed normal to Peruvians. "I should have said 'in that darkest hour just before dawn' or something equally descriptive of your sacrificial offering at the altar of friendship. I hadn't forgotten about the jacarandas though—they weren't out when I left and I've been looking forward to seeing them again, not just because that purple bloom is so beautiful, but because it means spring has come."

"Spring, but we still have *garúa*," Ildefonso replied, as Emilio brought the car to a halt, took from the glove compartment a set of windshield wipers and, somewhat belatedly in Nicolas' opinion, attached them. He realized the fiction that it never rains in Lima must, at all costs, be maintained; but he was relieved to find the existence of heavy mists was recognized. "Now what's back of all these headlines and featured announcements about an estate in Virginia and a wedding in a historic church and a beautiful bride?" Ildefonso went on. "You might have taken time to drop me a line yourself instead of letting me read about all this in the papers. I take it you really are married?"

"I am, indeed. But it all happened so suddenly—"

"Yes, I gathered that. However, did you ever do anything without haste?"

"This isn't the most appropriate moment to talk to me about haste, considering the speed at which we're charging through traffic. Remember, Lester's never been here before, he's actually quaking with fright. Couldn't you at least persuade Emilio to stop for a traffic light?"

"Certainly not. Traffic lights are still too much of a novelty for us to take them seriously. Besides, my instructions were to get you to the house as quickly as possible. Marina's dying to hear all about the great romance with presidential trimmings. Meanwhile, you might tell me—"

"I can't tell you anything while we're zigzagging around like this.

All my thoughts are concentrated on the probably vain hope that we may avert a crash. There, I was afraid so!"

The skidding car, braked instead of accelerated, had slid into a school bus, which had just stopped to pick up additional passengers. The collision was without actual violence and no damage was done to either vehicle; but both Emilio and the bus driver leaped out of their seats to exchange vehement insults, while the youthful passengers of the bus, delighted at the diversion, scattered over the sidewalk, shouting and screaming as they chased and pummeled each other from sheer exuberance. With exemplary, if exceptional, celerity, a uniformed policeman appeared on the scene, notebook in hand, and began rapid-fire questioning. Idlefonso grinned rather ruefully and, shaking his head, turned toward his guests.

"Well, it looks as if I would have to let you take a taxi after all. It seems indicated that I should stay here long enough to show respect for the law, if not actually to prevent a fight and gather up a few truants. See you both later. Meantime, make yourselves at home and let Marina brief you on the people she's invited to meet you at lunch. I know the American Ambassador's among them—the new one. Of course, there's been a new one since you left, all of six weeks ago."

"If you don't mind, I'll rescue one small suitcase from that neat stack in the luggage compartment and I imagine Les would like to do the same," Nicolas said drily as he rose, picking up his briefcase and his miscellaneous small bundles. "I'm thinking rather longingly of a shave and a shower and some clean clothes and, if Marina's throwing a party, we'd both prefer not to look so much like tramps, anyway. No, don't interrupt Emilio—it would be a shame to check such a flow of eloquence. Les and I can manage all right by ourselves."

A cruising taxi had already approached the scene of action and, having cautioned the driver that they would be pleased if he moderated his velocity, Nicolas and Lester climbed into the cab with the most essential items of their baggage and were soon jolting along toward the business district, which was just coming alive for the day. As Lester gradually recovered from his qualms over Limenian methods of transportation, he observed with interest the Indian fruit vendors squatting at the street corners, the lottery sellers hawking their wares, the alert, diminutive newsboys, almost invariably very small children, and the itinerant peddlers of toys and sweets. Nicolas, to whom all these were an old story, paid them scant attention; but he stopped the taxi on the Plaza San Martén to leave his card and Lester's with the marine on duty at the United States Embassy, giving instructions to have these delivered to the new Ambassador; and he called a second halt when he saw with relief that a favorite florist on the Calle Beza was already open for the day: if Marina were having a luncheon, she would want to use for her centerpiece white roses, which she had shorn of their stems and arranged in a shallow brazier of dull colonial silver; and, though there were quantities of roses growing in her garden, he would feel he had failed in the appropriate beau geste as a privileged visitor if he did not intuitively provide this special offering. Yes, some white roses had just come, so fresh the dew was still on them, a tiny Indian woman told her first customer of the day with pardonable pride; and Nicolas, seeing that the freshness was not exaggerated, decided to take the flowers with him, rather than run the slightest risk of having them arrive late for the party. In consequence, what with his packages, he was overladen by the time the great iron-studded door, which served as the entrance to the Parras' grounds, swung open to receive him; and he was glad there was hardly an instant's delay, after he had been admitted by the smiling *portero,* before he had drawn up to the porte-cochere and the butler had rushed out to relieve him of part of his paraphernalia. Nevertheless, he did not regret his hasty last-minute purchases nor the fact he had brought them with him; for just inside the entrance was a beaming mestiza in a starched white uniform with a wide-eyed baby in her arms and beside her two toddlers, who flung themselves on Nicolas with rapturous cries of welcome, bear hugs and eager inquiries as to whether or not he had brought them presents.

"Why, of course, I have *regalitos* for you! Did I ever forget?" (He had come dangerously near to doing so this time, but they need never know that!) "Jaime, stop grabbing at me like that! Isabel, give me a kiss and *then* we'll see what's in the biggest package! And both of you say *bienvenido* to the *señor* who's with me right away. Where are your manners?"

"It's all your fault, Nick, that they forget those—you spoil them most outrageously!" Marina had come up behind them, so swiftly and lightly that Nicolas had not heard her approach. Now she held out both hands to him and, shaking his head to indicate he could not take them because his were still full, he kissed her lightly on the cheek. Accepting the caress with no sign of self-consciousness, but without returning it, she went on, "And what wonderful roses! Just what I wanted! How like you to spoil me, too! But what's the meaning of your arriving like this? Where's the car? Where's Emilio? Where's Fonso?"

Briefly, Nicolas explained, interrupting himself to present Lester, who was standing by, looking and feeling somewhat superfluous and strangely helpless. Instantly, Marina turned to him, the personification of gracious solicitude. She was afraid he would have a very bad impression of the family, after such a disorderly greeting, she said, speaking with a charming accent in careful English. It was fortunate the elder children were at school—if they had been present, too, there really *would* have been a riot! She was having him shown to his room at once, his suitcase had already been carried up, coffee and fruit—papaya and chirimoya—would immediately be sent to him. No one else used his bathroom, he could soak or shower all the morning if he wanted to. Luncheon was not until one-thirty, perhaps he would like to take a nice long nap after his uncomfortable night. She would have him called, so he need not worry lest he should be late. Yes, she was going to send Nick to his room also, but not until she had asked him a few questions.

"And not until you give me a chance to get to the telephone," he said firmly. Then, as Marina looked slightly surprised, he added, "I promised my wife I'd call her as soon as I got here. She'll begin to worry if she doesn't hear from me pretty soon."

"Of course. How thoughtless of me! But you haven't given us time, Nick, to realize you're married! We should have had an extension put in your room. Would tomorrow be too late? Yes, I know, Fonso said you were off for Cuzco immediately. Well then, I'll take you to the library and leave you there."

"No need to leave me right off. It'll take some time for the call to come through. And I'd rather have that question and answer period behind me than ahead of me." He felt strangely disinclined to discuss his marriage with Marina, much as he liked her; it was not only too recent and intimate an experience; it had proved an overwhelmingly vital one, difficult to explain, impossible to interpret. He would probably sound brusque, even cold-blooded, if he did not make the equally great mistake of sounding casual in his presentation of feelings and actions which had been deeply emotional. "I don't know about Lester, but that suggestion of a nap has a very strong appeal to me," he went on, as he followed her lead into the beautiful book-lined room furnished in Cordovan leather.

He put in his call and sat down beside the telephone, cigarette in hand. Marina, after lighting a cigarette, too, curled up in a big chair facing him. She was unquestionably one of the prettiest women he had ever seen and so light of movement and ingenuous of expression that he found it almost impossible to remember she had been married at least ten years and was the mother of five children—or did that wide-eyed baby make six and was it a boy or a girl? Marina wore her blond hair in a page boy cut with a soft bang over her brow and soft curls over her shoulders. Her candid gaze was always slightly tinged with surprise, as if she had not been expecting what was being said and done around her, but as if, far from being displeased with whatever this was, it had added to her joy in life. Her color was fresh and rosy and she had the good sense to leave it alone—Nicolas doubted that she even used lipstick—and her figure was as young as her face. She dressed with deceptive simplicity, in monotone wools and crepes, round-necked,

short-sleeved and casually girdled. Throughout October, like most of
her feminine associates, she wore only purple, honoring the festival of
El Señor de Los Milagros, and neither issued nor accepted invitations;
her unquestioning faith lent itself easily to the acceptance and obser-
vance of traditional Limenian feasts and fasts, such as the veneration
of this miraculous image. During the rest of the year, she revealed a
preference for such soft colors as fawn and cream; and, though she entertained lavishly herself and appeared at all the social functions she
was expected to attend, she was conspicuous for the apparent artless-
ness of her clothes, rather than for their elegance. Nicolas, who had
always appreciated her attractions without being stirred by them, found
himself wondering for the first time whether or not the childlike
quality of her charm ever changed. If not, there must be hidden power
to it, or it would never have sufficed to hold a sophisticate like Ildefonso
Parra all these years—and that it had sufficed him, to a degree very rare
in a Latin husband, Nicolas did not allow himself to doubt. But
perhaps it was the women who gave least evidence of power who most
possessed it. He thought of Margaret, of the way she had been misprized
by their fellow guests at the Schaeffer-Steinmetz wedding, of the
wellsprings of beauty and loving-kindness and passion which he had
unsealed. . . .

"About those questions," he said, speaking, as he had feared he
might, with more abruptness than courtesy. "I told you I wanted to get
them over with."

"Yes. Well, of course, we're consumed with curiosity. What made
you suddenly decide to get married?"

"I wanted a son," he said curtly. "I have for a long time—a legitimate son who'll carry on my name and, I hope, my work. But I didn't
dream I'd find a girl who'd be willing to marry me just on that basis.
And then I did."

"Then you did *what?*"

"Then I did find one. At least, in accidentally renewing my acquaintance with a very fine girl I hadn't even seen in years, a chance remark
disclosed the fact she didn't think marriage on that basis was such an
impossibility after all. So I proposed to her and she accepted me. We
were married five days later. And five days after that—namely yesterday
—I left for Peru. My schedule was already so hard and fast that I
couldn't change it at this late date. But naturally, despite lack of time,
I hope my marriage isn't going to fail in its primary purpose."

Marina's habitual expression of mild surprise had suddenly changed
to one closely akin to shock. "But Nicolas!" she protested. "I think
what you're saying is simply dreadful! Here we've all been supposing
that this was the culmination of a great romance, that you'd finally
persuaded a beautiful girl, whom you'd loved in vain for a long while,

to marry you, that the reason you'd never married before was that there wasn't room in your heart for anyone else."

"That's what you were supposed to suppose. That's the story that's been given out to the public—not just to the public, either. Even to my parents. But I thought it might save an indefinite number of explanations if I told you and Fonso the truth first, instead of last. So I have. That is, I've told you the truth. You can relay it to him."

"But Nicolas—" Marina began again.

"However, I will add, in the hope of making you feel better than you obviously do at this moment, that I haven't yet told you the whole truth. To my very great surprise—and somewhat to my chagrin—I fell in love with my fiancée before I'd been engaged to her for an hour. That is, before I said good-bye to her for the first time. And the last time I said good-bye to her—as my wife, not as my fiancée—I didn't think I was going to make it. It didn't seem as if I could bear to leave her. But of course I had to."

"You didn't have to do anything of the sort!" Marina burst out indignantly. "You could have brought her with you. You could have taken her along as far as Cuzco. She would have loved it there. Not just the Inca walls and the lovely Spanish colonial overlay—the Indians in their bright costumes, the women with their babies on their backs, the soft furs, the wonderful woven rugs and ponchos. Any girl would have loved seeing all that for the first time on her honeymoon, with her bridegroom to show her everything and buy her presents and sit with her for a long time while they ate their evening meal. And afterward—while you're in the jungle—she could have stayed here, with Fonso and me and the children. You know perfectly well we'd have been delighted to have her. And since you really do love her after all—"

"Yes, I really do love her after all. But I've come to Peru to find a lost city, not to make love to my wife. I don't suppose you read Byron, do you, Marina?"

"You mean that English poet who was such a roué? No—I wasn't allowed to before I was married and since then I've been living poetry, instead of reading it."

"Charmingly put. I hope Fonso realizes you feel that way and is suitably grateful. Nevertheless, the English poet who was such a roué was nobody's fool. And among the many wise, if unprincipled, things that he said about the tender passion is included the truthful statement that while 'man's love is of man's life a thing apart, 'tis woman's sole existence.' "

The telephone rang and Nicolas picked it up. There was the usual intermediary series of blurred questions and answers before the connection over long distance was established. Then Nicolas was saying, "Hello there, Margaret! I'm keeping my promise to telephone you as soon as I got here!" Next there was a sound like a gasp of joy and relief before there were any words and then a woman's voice, tremulous but very clear and sweet.

"Oh, Nicolas, I thought the call would never come through! I've stayed in bed all morning, waiting for it. I didn't dare move for fear I'd miss it. And before you say another word to me and before I say anything else to you, I want to tell you I'm sure no woman in the whole world ever had such a wonderful love letter as the one you wrote me from the airport. I'm keeping it right close to me and every hour or two I read it over again. Of course, I know it by heart now, but that doesn't make any difference. Oh, Nicolas, my darling, how am I ever going to live without you?"

Marina slipped quietly out of her big chair and left the library, closing the door after her. There were tears in her eyes as she did so.

20 ❧

Though Ildefonso was himself an urbane and witty host, he and everyone else habitually referred to the functions given at the Parras' house as "Marina's parties" and, like all her parties, the luncheon to celebrate Nicolas' return to Peru was a great success.

Pisco sours were served in the great drawing room with the vitrines containing her priceless collection of La Granja glass at one end and Chinese jade at the other; luncheon was in the long dining room with the portrait of Ildefonso, dressed with casual correctness for polo, at one end and, at the other, the portrait of his ancestral *conquistador* in shining armor; and coffee was on the tiled terrace, facing the garden of a hundred roses, with the wall, on which was depicted the story of Santa Rosa de Lima in *azulejos,* beyond it. The new American Ambassador, Alvin Todd, enjoying the hospitality of a Peruvian house for the first time, was duly impressed and voiced his appreciation candidly. He had just been transferred from Helsinki, with Morocco as a previous post, and was not yet thoroughly adjusted to Lima; but he felt certain that, as soon as he had succeeded in coping with his third unfamiliar language in five years, he would really enjoy himself. His wife, the only woman present who was wearing a hat and sensible shoes, was less sure of this; she had found the trip from Finland so wearing that she doubted if she would ever feel really rested again. Moreover, she would be separated from her children for Thanksgiving and that was always a trial. She took a little leather folding case from her capacious handbag, which was designed to accommodate not only her passport, but the other important documents testifying to her freedom from venereal disease and recent vaccination and showed snapshots of her family to Fonso, at whose right she was seated, and to Fray Gregorio, a huge, bearded Dominican monk, who was on her other side. Letty, she explained, was already in college—the University of North Dakota; Sam, Hilda and Morty were still in school. These pictures had been taken by their father when they were last all at the beach together; the sun had been very bright and focusing had been something of a problem; still, all things considered, the likenesses were very good. Both Ildefonso and the monk expressed polite interest and Mrs. Todd began to brighten.

The other guests included the natty Minister of Foreign Affairs, the dignified Rector of San Marcos, and the slouching correspondent of *Time* magazine and their respective wives, all noticeably well dressed, but otherwise self-effacing. There was also a sprightly spinster whose charm and vivacity made her a great social favorite; a portly widow of uncertain age whose ears and fingers were loaded with enormous diamonds and who took a voluble interest in welfare work; and a rather sullen looking, but potentially beautiful, girl who had been invited on the theory that Lester might draw her out. Barring the ambassadorial couple, the Dominican, and this girl, everyone present was an old friend of Nicolas and, normally, the general pleasure expressed in the renewal of acquaintance would have been mutual. This time, however, he found his marriage was of such absorbing interest to all his fellow guests except the Todds, who had never heard of him before, and Fray Gregorio, who had heard a great deal about him on other counts, that, as soon as possible after luncheon, he maneuvered for himself a seat between the Ambassador and the monk, not because either had any special attraction for him, but because he thought they represented his best chance of escape from prying questions. As it turned out, Fray Gregorio also had questions to ask him, but these were not about Margaret.

"I understand you're about to start on a new expedition in the Cuzco area, Dr. Hale. Will your route take you past our mission at Quillabamba? If so, perhaps I might impose on you by asking you to take a parcel there for me."

"Of course, I'd have been glad to, Father, if I'd been going that way. But I'm approaching the jungle via Paucartambo."

"Ah—and is there some special reason for this choice?"

"Yes, and surely you must know what it is. In the dry months, there's a wind that comes funneling up the Paucartambo Canyon so fast and furiously that it's punishment to face it. Moreover, lower down, beside the same ridge, it rains all the time anyway."

"You couldn't have waited and taken *our* easier route at a more propitious season?"

"Yes, of course I could have. But I didn't want to. I'm not very good at waiting—ever. And, this time, I had everything so well organized, with a staff so willing to accommodate itself to my time, that I decided to be on my way."

"I see. Well, if you should ever take the other route—"

Nicolas laughed. "If the route I'm following now leads me where I want to go, I probably shan't be experimenting with any others—that is, not in the foreseeable future. I'll be in the happy position of having 'conquest achieved and search fulfilled at last.' "

"I see," the monk said again, more thoughtfully this time. "Well, I merely wanted to let you know there'd always be a welcome for you and your staff at Quillabamba, or at any of our jungle missions, for that matter. . . . Now I'm afraid I must ask the Ambassadress to forgive me if I fail to observe protocol and leave before she does. It's so pleasant here that I'm not surprised she's lingering. But I left an overcrowded desk and I must get back to it."

Nicolas was glad to see the monk leave. He did not understand just why the big Dominican had irritated him, yet he was conscious of irritation. Perhaps it was merely because of the assumption that he would be glad to carry bundles when he was already overburdened, as was always necessarily the case at the beginning of an expedition; or perhaps it was because he thought he detected a criticism, both of the route he had chosen and the season in which he had elected to take it. Well, his time in Lima was too limited to waste in worry because he had not found congenial a religious he might never see again—though something told him this monk had become a frequent and welcome visitor at the Parras' house and that, since he had long enjoyed this enviable position himself, they were bound to continue meeting. Meanwhile, he had not forgotten that Allan Lambert, the Assistant Secretary of State for Latin American Affairs, had entrusted him with a confidential message for Dr. Labrador, who was a close friend of Lambert's Spanish father-in-law, the Duke of San Ricardo. This was hardly the time and place to deliver it, but, after all, Nicolas was leaving early in the morning—he should be able, easily, to make some plausible excuse for withdrawing to the library with the rector. He nodded to Pancho Murray, the *Time* correspondent, who caught his signal, excused himself to the Minister of Foreign Affairs, and, bringing along his liqueur glass, joined Nicolas beside Mr. Todd. Thank God it was the political picture in Washington with which these two were primarily interested and not his personal one, even though the wedding at Hills' End had fitted into a twin frame; so he chatted casually about the increasing jealousy between the President and the Vice President, the growing strain between the White House and Capitol Hill, the inaction of the Appropriations Committee in the House of Representatives and the popular resentment over the latest decision of the Supreme Court. Then, feeling well satisfied with the *entente cordiale* he had helped to establish between the new ambassador and the seasoned journalist, with adroit handling of these bromidic subjects, Nicolas chose a moment when they had become involved in a heated discussion and drifted toward the Rector of San Marcos University.

Evidently, Dr. Labrador was expecting not only Nicolas himself, but the message from the State Department. At all events, he rose, saying he was going to follow Fray Gregorio's lead and beg to be excused; but he hoped Dr. Hale would give his wife and himself the pleasure of his company for tea that evening. There would be no other guests; he understood the travelers were off again in the morning, so they would want to get to bed early; and, in any case, after the copious feast and the brilliant company they had all just enjoyed, anything more than the simplest fare in the quietest setting would be unthinkable. Nicolas agreed; he would be at the rector's house promptly at seven and he would, indeed, be glad to get to bed early. The sullen looking girl, whose expression had gradually been changing for the better, had come across as far as Lester was concerned: one of her friends was giving a small "coctel" that evening; she would be very pleased if *Señor* Wendell were free to escort her to it. . . .

"Of course," Nicolas said heartily, as Lester looked to him for encouragement. "But go rather light on the cocktails and remember we have to be up and doing at five. See you then if I don't before."

It was a relief to have Lester so easily disposed of and a further one to find that the Parras had planned to attend a family wedding, taking all the children except the baby with them, before they knew the exact date of Nicolas' arrival, and would not insist he should go with them, since he was obviously disinclined to do so. Marina's manner was exceptionally cool as she said this; it was not difficult for Nicolas to guess she considered his conduct deplorable, as far as his bride was concerned, and that she had no idea of pretending otherwise, in order to conform with the amenities. Moreover, in relaying the story to her husband, as Nicolas had given her permission to do, she had evidently infected him with her opinion, for his manner also lacked his usual conviviality. Nicolas shrugged his shoulders. As far as he was concerned, they were welcome to their viewpoint; it did not change his; and having emphatically told himself this, he spent the two hours, which intervened before he started for the Labradors' house, in writing a long letter to Margaret.

Unlike the Parras, the Labradors lived in the old part of town and, when Nicolas reached the center of the city, he stopped at an antique shop, where he found a charming seventeenth century *nacimiento* in polychrome, and at a jewelry store, where he found a pear-shaped aquamarine pendant, with earrings and brooch to match. He gave the necessary instructions, in both cases, to have these purchases sent to a customs broker, who would take care of the requisite formalities and pay the duty when the statuettes and the jewelry arrived in the United States. Then, after leaving the second shop, he dismissed the car and walked through a succession of narrow streets to the Labradors' house.

This occupied almost half a block and, though shops had encroached on the corner opposite, a small open plaza and a beautiful baroque church respectively graced the third and fourth sides. The mansion itself presented blank façades to the street; the shutters were closed and the doors were massively paneled. But on one of the panels was suspended a brass knocker in the shape of a lady's hand, realistic even to the point of the ring on the tapering middle finger. Nicolas rapped with it, reflecting that if he had not seen the knocker many times before, it would have seemed like a liberty to use such a delicately feminine symbol for such a vigorous purpose. Almost instantly the heavy opaque door opened, and he passed through the *zaguán*, or entryway, and stood on the threshold of one of the most beautiful patios in the New World, even more beautiful, or so it seemed to Nicolas, now that he saw it at dusk, than when he had seen it illuminated with candles for an important reception. The *azulejos* with which it was walled lined it on all four sides of its entire height, and the house was one of three stories, surmounted by a flat roof. Across these blue tiles now fell the soft shadows of early evening. Around the second story ran a gallery, adorned with hanging plants whose greenery had deepened in the twilight; and in the center of the patio stood a fountain which made a soothing sound. Otherwise, the place seemed engulfed in silence as well as shadow—a silence so pleasant that Nicolas wished he did not have to break it. The manservant who had opened the door for him seemed aware of the visitor's mood and stood quietly by, waiting without impatience for Nicolas to speak. It was the latter who finally said, "I think Dr. Labrador is expecting me."

"Certainly, *Señor*. He is awaiting you in the library. Have the goodness to ascend this way."

Nicolas mounted a long flight of red-carpeted stairs and in due course came to the enclosed gallery which surrounded all the living quarters on the street side and represented the theory, prevalent at the time the house had been built, that it made for coolness in summer and warmth in winter. Practically, it also kept out more daylight than Nicolas would have thought desirable if this had not streamed in abundantly from the patio. The library, the *salón* and the dining room all benefited by this; so he assumed did various other apartments which he had never seen. The Labradors, he knew, still lived in patriarchal style; they all came together for meals, but the rector and his wife had their suite, the largest, on the right of the stair landing, while the families of their two married sons occupied similar suites, each with its own *salita,* located some place on the further side of the library. Nicolas was not sure just where, for the house was so vast and its floor plan so complicated that he had never thoroughly mastered this. . . .

"You are very prompt, Nicolas—a North American virtue which we Latins would do well to emulate," the rector said, as he came quietly into the library. "Find a chair that will suit you and light a cigarette, if it would please you to smoke while I read the communication you have brought with you. Then we will talk it over, if it requires discussion, and afterward my family will join us for tea."

Nicolas took an envelope from his coat pocket and handed it to the rector; then both men settled themselves comfortably. There were some parakeets in a large metal cage which stood in the gallery near the library door and for some moments their twittering made the only sound, except for the turning of pages. Then the rector replaced the letter in its envelope and looked up.

"I assume you know what the Assistant Secretary of State has written me?"

"No, *Señor* Rector, Allan didn't volunteer any information and, naturally, I didn't ask."

"Mr. Lambert seems to think you might be of service to both your country and mine, in ways additional to those of exploration."

"I hadn't flattered myself that those were especially useful. Allan just said there was something of semi-official nature he wanted to communicate to you, as an old friend of his father-in-law's, and that he thought it might be simpler in the end to send it by me, rather than through regular State Department channels."

"I see. Well, in that case, I should like to think the contents over at my leisure and perhaps discuss them, quite informally, with some of my political friends in the higher echelons, before I do so with you. Then, after your return from your expedition, we will have a meeting of minds. Meanwhile, on my own responsibility, I should like to ask you if you would consider giving a series of lectures at San Marcos before you go back to the United States?"

"I appreciate the compliment. But I'm not sure just how long it's going to take me to reach my objective in Peru or how fast I'll have to hurry back to Virginia for personal reasons afterward. Would it be satisfactory if I promise to give one lecture this coming season, but that we agree to postpone the series until some later date?"

"Disappointing, but understandable. If that is your decision, I shall accept it. And now I shall tell my wife and daughters-in-law that we are ready for tea."

The three ladies entered the room together and the thought flashed through Nicolas' mind that if such divergent types could live together in harmony, this would be a miracle except in Spain and Latin America, where the difference in tastes and habits seemed to create few difficulties between the generations. *Doña* Ana, the rector's wife, whom he knew already, very definitely belonged to the old school. Since she had married in her teens, she was probably not now past her middle forties; but she looked much older, though her pale skin, as free from wrinkles as it was from cosmetics, was wonderfully soft and clear and her dark eyes wonderfully expressive. Nicolas had never seen her when she was not wearing a black dress, elegantly but conservatively cut; and her black hair, now slightly and becomingly flecked with white, was wound about her fine head in a heavy braid which gave the effect of a coronet. The diamonds in her ears and on her fingers were of the finest possible quality, but they were not conspicuously large, and she wore no other jewels except a small cross, also made of diamonds, which fastened her delicate lace collar at the throat. Both the younger women, on the contrary, had on a great deal of make-up and both had short hair, artificially blonde and rather fantastically arranged. Both wore jangling gold bracelets and rings set with semi-precious stones which, in size, would have dwarfed a bishop's. Their bright-colored, sleeveless dresses had very short skirts and very tight belts and their inconsequential sandals revealed toenails painted a flaming carmine. Nicolas was presented quite informally to "my daughter-in-law Micaela; my daughter-in-law Yolanda"; he did not instantly grasp which was married to the elder son, Rafael, and which to the younger son, Vicente, who came in separately a little later—slim, sleek, well-mannered young men, with neither the intellectual force of their father nor the reserved grace of their mother. It was not until all were seated in the dining room, with as much ceremony as if this had been a formal dinner, instead of a family tea, that Nicolas realized Micaela must be Rafael's wife, because she was placed at her father-in-law's right; and presently she began toying with her ice cream, which proved that, in one respect at least, she was a rebel against established customs. Nicolas did not blame her; personally, he had always found it a rather trying dish with which to begin a so-called afternoon tea; and he thought, with nostalgia, of that first tea at Hills' End, with its hot buttered toast and its homemade jam and its fruit cake, which he and Margaret had eaten so cozily beside the library fire. Of course, tea would follow the ice cream in a few minutes now—tea without lemon, and with the little fancy sandwiches which he despised and a huge *torta,* dripping with mocha frosting. It did not have a great deal to commend it at best, from an Anglo-Saxon's viewpoint; and after the ice cream it was even less appetizing than it might have been. No, decidedly, Micaela should be forgiven. . . .

"Yolanda is trying to persuade us that we should do something about our roof," *Doña* Ana was saying. "She insists if we had it partly paved and partly planted, it would make an ideal terrace."

"Yolanda has been getting a lot of gringo ideas since we went to the States," Vicente remarked rather acidly.

"*Querido,* I'm always glad to have you express yourself freely," *Doña* Ana said mildly. "But this time it was actually a gringo opinion I was seeking—if we can properly designate as a gringo anyone who has identified himself with Peru as thoroughly as our guest. What do you think of Yolanda's idea, Nicolas?"

"That it's excellent. The view over the city must be superb. I should think you'd enjoy having tea there."

"Yes, the way other people do, instead of sitting around the dining room table like this and beginning with ice cream, which nobody who's really up-to-date wants," Yolanda said triumphantly, glancing first at her sister-in-law's plate and then at their guest's.

"My dear child, I know we are hopelessly old-fashioned," *Doña* Ana said, still very mildly. "And I think Papa and I will continue to have our tea here and to begin it with ice cream. But Nicolas is right; the view from the roof is superb. It seems too bad that we should not use it to better advantage than we do at present."

"In case you don't know what Mama means by that," Yolanda remarked, as she turned toward Nicolas, now feeling more and more emboldened, "our roof, and most people's roofs in Lima, take the place of your New England attics. Everything we don't want or need any more finds its way there. Papa's old silk hat, Micaela's frayed pink slippers, the baby's high chair after it's broken."

"My dear, you exaggerate a little. But there is some justice in what you say. If Papa approves, I shall be glad to consider the question of a terrace. You and Micaela could entertain your friends there, while Papa and I spend quiet evenings in the library. And I know that is what he and Nicolas are planning to do now."

"Some other time—soon, I hope, *Doña* Ana. But tonight I'm going to ask you and the rector to excuse me. I have fulfilled my mission— that is, I have seen a mysterious letter with which the Assistant Secretary of State entrusted me safely to its destination; and I have had the honor of coming to your beautiful home again and enjoying your hospitality. But I am making a very early start for Cuzco and I did not get much sleep on the plane. So I have promised myself to make up for it tonight. Otherwise, I am afraid I should not prove a very alert leader of my expedition."

Nicolas took a courteous and unhurried leave, reflecting, as he did so, that perhaps after all there was more conflict in these patriarchal establishments than he had supposed. But the reflection, although it shattered an illusion, did not trouble him much; and, as he had hoped, he was back at the Parras' and ready to retire by ten o'clock. But his vague feeling of irritation had returned; though this was no longer with Fray Gregorio. He had kept telling himself when night came, he would be delivered both from curious questioning and carping criticism, not to mention family feuding, and this was true enough. But it had not occurred to him that he might be the prey of a new loneliness and a new yearning. Margaret had been almost constantly in his thoughts since he left her, but, once he was actually on his way, these had not been so poignant that he could not keep them in abeyance. Even the dark hours of his flight, more wakeful than restful, had brought with them no special sense of deprivation; he did not associate her intimate presence with a seat on a crowded plane. Now that he was alone, however, in the privacy of a luxurious chamber, with no prospect of a passionate prelude to slumber in the arms of a desired woman, he was conscious of frustration such as he had never known before. This was not the time for sleep, it was the time for ecstasy. He himself had said to Margaret, in speaking of the golden beds at the Parras' house, "They gleam—they glisten—they invite—they actually beckon—and they were never meant to be slept in alone!" Only a fool would have failed to realize a man could not leave the wife to whom God had joined him, making the two one flesh, with the same emotional impunity that he left a light-o'-love. And he had been just such a fool. The expression *"une nuit blanche"* had always seemed to him lyrical, but ineffective and faintly amusing. It would never do so again.

21 ೪

Faucett, like most airlines, liked to have its patrons on hand well in advance of the time a flight was called; it differed from others, however, in that the time of such a call, though definitely announced beforehand, was more often than not subject to change without notice. If, at six-thirty, there were rain at Cuzco, the plane waited until visibility was better; if visibility did not improve, the plane did not leave at all, and there was not another until the next day, when the same thing was likely to happen again. Cautiously, Nicolas had refrained from mentioning this feature of their planned progress to Lester, hoping against hope that today would be one of those when the plane took off on schedule. His hopes proved vain. Having reached the airport at five-thirty, to be in good season for a six-thirty flight, they were informed by a squawky loud-speaker that there had been a delay, that there would be a weather report at eight. . . .

"You mean we just have to stick around in this trap for two hours and a half?" Lester inquired indignantly.

"That's right."

"And what happens if the weather report isn't favorable for starting at eight o'clock?"

"Why, we don't go today, that's all."

"My God, can't we go this afternoon? Surely you don't mean you got me up at an ungodly hour for the second morning in succession, this time to no practical purpose?"

"It's too soon to decide it's to no practical purpose. We have to learn to take our chances philosophically and this is one way of doing it. Meteorological conditions aren't favorable later in the day. And, speaking of ungodly hours, you'd better start to think nothing of keeping them two mornings in succession. The chances are they'll be the rule rather than the exception. The only way to get around that is to keep very godly hours the evening before."

"Well, I did last night. The party was still going strong when we left. I don't think Carmen was at all pleased at being taken home so early. And I certainly wasn't keen on doing it."

"If we don't leave Lima this morning, you can call her up and see if she'd like to go dancing with you tonight. Of course, you might have to invite the whole family. I never met Carmen before, I don't know whether her people belong to the conservative or the liberal school. But you can always try. I might remind you, however, that you and Clarissa seemed to be hitting it off so well in Virginia, I gathered you had staked out some sort of a rather purposeful claim in that direction. Romance always seems to be catching at weddings; that's one reason I've avoided them so long. Now, as Clarissa's much elder brother, perhaps I should warn you not to trifle with her young—very young—affections. Sweet sixteen and quite possibly never been kissed—unless you did it. The best families of Woodstock, Vermont are conservative."

Lester growled in his throat and plunged off in search of coffee and reading material. The airport presented to him a scene of completely incomprehensible and equally reprehensible confusion. Over the

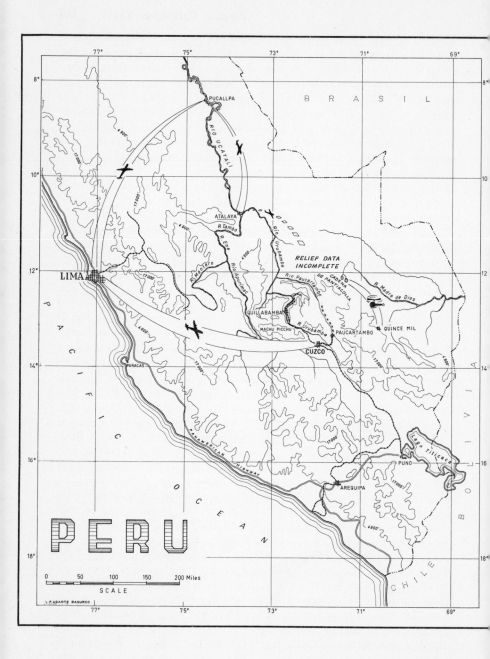

PERU

SCALE

0 50 100 150 200 Miles

L.F. UGARTE BASURCO

raucous speaker came the announcement of a second delayed flight—
Pucallpa—pending a weather report; other flights, which were leaving
on time—some along the coast, some into the sierra—were called.
Meanwhile, the overnight plane from Miami came in and the
passengers in transit for Buenos Aires explored the concourse and
bought silly souvenirs at outrageous prices. All the Faucett planes but
two had left by the time the international plane continued on its way
south; but strangely enough the crowd, which included a staggering
number of small children, appeared as great as ever; it did not seem
possible so many persons could have come to see their friends off or to
welcome them back, but otherwise there was no accounting for such
milling multitudes. Aside from the unmistakable tourist groups and
numerous priests, who might either belong to these or be on their way
to their mission bases, most of the swarm was made up of Indians or
mestizos; though he was quite free from racial prejudices, this added to
Lester's sense of strangeness, as he had not previously realized their
preponderance in Peru. He felt lost and bewildered and he was
aggrieved at Nicolas' unsympathetic levity.

It was quite true he had "hit it off" so well with Clarissa Hale that
there had been some mutual promises of correspondence, which was to
lead to future meetings, and that a few innocent caresses had been
exchanged. Now Lester was also attracted to the beautiful *Limeña*
whose sullenness had evaporated under his skillful handling of the
situation and who was considerably more sophisticated than Clarissa,
though he had been careful not to take advantage of this. He had also
made an honest attempt at moderation, as far as drinking was
concerned; but yesterday's had been his first experience with pisco
sours and, because of their smoothness, he had underestimated their
potency. He now decided to keep as far from Nicolas as possible until
the plane started—if it ever did!—in order to avoid further unwelcome
comments and disclosures; and he succeeded so well in this attempt that
Nicolas was obliged to plunge through the crowd, in his turn, to round
up the truant and breathlessly inform him the weather had cleared
after all, the flight had already been called and they'd be the last
persons on the plane if they didn't actually miss it. . . .

They managed to make it, although the door slammed behind them
before they were far enough from it to reach their seats and they were
glowering at each other and muttering mutual accusations as they took
these. Moreover, it appeared Lester's troubles were only just beginning; he had eagerly accepted the gum and the cotton that were
offered him by a flight attendant, but his ears had already started to pop
and soon they were really hurting. Then he had scarcely taken time to
notice the slender rubber tubes, which ran from the wall to the
gathered pocket fastened to the seat in front of him, when a trim stew-

ardess approached him briskly, removed the cellophane covering from the tip of the tube and placed it in his hand, motioning toward his mouth and nose. Above the noise of the engine he shouted a question which the stewardess and Nicolas answered almost simultaneously.

"Oxygen. You'll need it any minute now. We may fly as high as twenty-three thousand feet."

"You mean the plane isn't pressurized!"

So this was one more thing Nicolas forgot to tell me, Lester said to himself resentfully; instead of enjoying the scenery, which ought to be terrific, we devote all our attention to sucking in oxygen! His sense of injury increased with the pain in his ears and his shortness of breath. Nicolas, with his tube casually tucked into one corner of his mouth, was unconcernedly reading the scare headlines of *La Prensa*, and, with equal unconcern, glancing out from time to time at the magnificent panorama of snow-capped peaks. Though the flight attendants watchfully patrolled the plane, supplying cellophane masks to passengers for whom the tubes did not supply sufficient oxygen, Lester among them, Nicolas was showing no more sympathy for his wretched secretary than he had at the airport; and, as the plane finally bumped its way to the ground, he found his attention riveted to an article about the danger of fire in tropical forests. Before he had unfastened his belt and prepared to descend, Lester, thankful at the prospect of escape, had already struggled out of his seat and charged down the gangway. Then, as he stepped to the ground, he fainted dead away.

Three persons, apparently unrelated—the flight stewardess, a cargo handler and a medico—immediately converged over his prostrate form. Nicolas had paused at the open door of the plane to acknowledge the welcome Pete—conspicuous in a crowd of small, dark men for his bright red hair and tremendous size—was signaling from the gate and would have stumbled over his unconscious secretary when he himself reached the ground had he not been motioned aside by the alert stewardess. At the moment, there was nothing he could do except stand helplessly by, admiring the speed and co-ordination of the succor, administered as a matter of routine to any passenger who was a victim of mountain sickness; and, with uncharacteristic docility, he followed along as his secretary, still unconscious, was carried back into the plane. But when the stewardess announced that Lester would, of course, automatically be flown back to Lima, he protested.

"There's no of course about it in this case. The *señor* isn't a tourist, he's my secretary, here to accompany me on a scientific expedition. This is his first experience with high altitudes, but he'll snap out of his *soroche* in a day or so. In fact, he's got to."

"What do you mean '*soroche*'?" Lester, his consciousness returning in waves, caught Nicolas' last words and struggled away from the oxygen apparatus. "It wasn't mountain sickness that did me in, it was fright. I wouldn't even try to fly a reconnaissance plane between the walls of that canyon wedge we've just been through."

"Well, you won't have to—Korea is behind you now. Remember? That's one thing to be thankful for anyway. What you're in for now is a different type of endurance test. See if you can't make it to the gate by leaning on me. Pete'll be foaming at the mouth if we keep him waiting much longer."

Pete was indeed "foaming at the mouth," not merely with impatience, but with annoyance. "Send the kid back to Momma, let her give him smelling salts," he said in a scornful aside to Nicolas, as the three went from the gate to the baggage counter, with Lester still leaning limply against Nicolas. "Everything's all set for a quick start tomorrow. Gomara is here, comfortably quartered at the Hotel Ferrocarril and raring to go, as I am. I left him with Mamani and Mendoza, all making bets Rector Lobo would keep you here two or three days, so you could give a lecture at the university, if you accepted his invitation to be his house guest. They even have a title for it—'The gringo drive for success, as applied to short cuts in archeology.' You'd better avoid him and lie low with us at the Ferrocarril. Of course, I've got a room for you there, too. Also for the sick child. Incidentally, who's going to take care of him? We're all asked to a cocktail party at the Geminianis' this evening. The handwritten invitations came by special messenger, along with one to use the walled area of the Esperanza factory for the expedition staging zone, and you don't decline that kind any more than you do an invitation to an embassy."

"Thoughtful of you to bolster my ignorance of etiquette, but it seems to me I've heard something of the kind before in connection with the White House. And, being interpreted, this means explorers in my category don't decline invitations from university rectors, either. So I go to the Lobos' directly after the luncheon of the Lions Club, where I've already agreed to speak, and I'll handle the question of the more serious lecture with adroit mendacity subsequently. You and I and our learned associates will, of course, go to the cocktail party later and, meanwhile, you will take charge of the staging zone, which ought to keep you out of mischief for the greater part of the day. As for Lester, I'll call a doctor before we leave the airport and myself see the patient safely in bed at the hotel, with a nurse and a canvas oxygen bag alongside, prior to going on to the Lions' den." Lowering his voice and turning slightly aside, Nicolas added, "And you'd better forget about sending the boy home to Momma. If you knew the Wendell matriarch, you wouldn't consign him to her tender mercies. She's definitely the type that tells her son to come home with his shield or on it."

Pete muttered something vaguely argumentative without being actually defiant, rescued from the jumble on the counter the hand baggage Nicolas and Lester had brought with them and, while Nicolas was telephoning, supervised its removal to the trim taxi he had waiting. During the brief drive to the hotel, conversation was at a standstill: Pete, having spoken his piece and been snubbed, needed time to prepare a further barrage of statements and suggestions; Lester, who was feeling sicker by the minute, did not dare to open his mouth for fear the mere act of doing so would precipitate the active nausea which he was trying hard to keep in abeyance; and Nicolas had unwillingly noted the exotic beauty of the soft furs and colorful fabrics which Indian vendors hawked at the airport exit. Marina was right, Margaret would have loved to see these, she would have been delighted beyond measure by the gift of a striped poncho or a fluffy rug; and the curved wall of the Incaic Temple of the Sun, now serving as the apsidal base of the Church of Santo Domingo, the only historic monument near which they passed, would have awakened a different kind of astonishment and admiration. Margaret, he knew, had traveled very little—even that one trip to Europe, so joyously and generously planned for her by her wealthy friends the Schaeffers, had been sacrificed at the altar of filial duty. And now that Nicolas might have been the one to share with her some of the world's unique wonders, which he knew so well and could interpret so brilliantly, he had stubbornly refused to do so. He was glad there were no more extraordinary sights to add to his disconcertion before the taxi drew up with a dash at the nondescript entrance of the Hotel Ferrocarril.

Rooms were in readiness for Lester and himself, as Pete had promised, and, though these were small and bare, they were clean and Nicolas succeeded in getting Lester into a narrow bed, equipped with heavy blankets, cold coarse sheets and one hard pillow, before the arrival of the doctor and, what was even more of a relief, before the threatened catastrophe of retching and vomiting. The mestizo physician, after explaining at some length that one of his brothers had been to the United States, but that his own training had been local, and taking Lester's temperature with a thermometer which required five minutes to register, made a routine examination and repeated the advice given on the airplane to the effect that the sooner the patient returned to sea level, the better for all concerned. Then he prescribed some medicines, which it would be necessary to get from a pharmacy, as he had brought none with him; and, leaving this errand to someone else, took a courteous but casual departure. A nurse, it seemed, would be along later and would bring oxygen with her; but the exact moment when this succor might be expected was left very much in doubt.

Nicolas located Pete, told him to go for the medicines and, also, to inform their "learned associates" he would come to salute them as soon as he could leave his patient and to send word to the Lions he might be a little late for lunch, but that he would join them as soon as possible. Then he sat down on a high hard chair—the only one provided for Lester's room—and found it increasingly uncomfortable as the morning wore on. It was some time before Pete returned with the medicines—the first pharmacy he had tried did not carry them. In fact, he had been obliged to chase all over town and, as Nicolas very well knew, he was needed at the staging zone for the loading of the truck, so he would be on his way there now. He would, however, leave it in time to attend the cocktail party.

"And just whom are you planning to leave in charge then?" Nicolas inquired sarcastically, as he poured lukewarm water into a glass and handed it to Lester along with a couple of capsules which he shook from a box.

"Li Chan, of course. He likes to sit around, sharpening his bowie knife. I've had him acting as watchman for the truck while he's been doing that and he might as well keep on, unless you want him to take your place here."

It was Nicolas' turn to mutter something vaguely argumentative, but he let Pete depart without further futile discussion, resumed his hard seat and gave himself up to thought. Mercifully, Lester was beginning to be drowsy; if he could get a good sleep, he might still snap out of his *soroche* in time to leave Cuzco the next morning. If not, provided he were still unable to travel but visibly on the road to recovery, the others could leave without him; and, though there was no regular bus service, some means could be found of getting him to Paucartambo later. The expedition would have to pause there, in any case, while securing carriers and mules—just how long was problematical. Nicolas did not need Lester's help during this period. The main thing was to have him fit for the long drag ahead, when that began. . . .

Nicolas had almost given up all hope of the nurse when a tremendous pounding on the door brought him to his feet and sent him rushing to answer the summons, but not soon enough to prevent it from shattering Lester's peaceful doze and precipitating another violent attack of nausea. The nurse, thus unceremoniously presented to her patient, set down her canvas bag, told the *mozo* who had conducted her to the room to hurry off and dash back with a basin, and applied herself to making do with a towel until his return. Nicolas conscientiously waited until the worst was over, instructed the nurse to ask for anything she wanted, informed her when medication had last been given, and told her he would look in again later in the day. Then he tipped the *mozo* who was lurking in the hall, sincerely eager to be of service, and made his escape to his own room in search of a clean shirt before tardily presenting himself to Mamani, Mendoza and Gomara. He found them contentedly ensconced in the bar where they were drinking local beer; and, after ordering coffee for himself, he passed the time of day with his colleagues for a few minutes, before going on to the club where the Lions held their meetings.

As he had feared might be the case, he was a little late in arriving and nearly all the members were already in their seats, from which they rose to salute him with a formality suitable in welcoming a distinguished outsider. When one of their own organization appeared tardily, however, he was greeted with a loud roar instead of some milder form of recognition and, the first few times he heard this, Nicolas, who had been quite unprepared for the literal way in which the Lions hailed their fellows—the *Hermanos Leones*—found himself involuntarily starting from his seat. He had intended to make his speech mildly humorous, but weariness, preoccupation and anxiety about Lester had combined to dull his usually ready wit; he was chagrined, but not surprised, to find his remarks courteously but unenthusiastically received and thankful that it was possible for him to plead the necessity of looking in on his invalid and paying his respects to the rector before going on to the cocktail party.

The invalid was peacefully sleeping and it appeared the rector and his wife were also going to the cocktail party and were expecting Dr. Hale to accompany them. They informed him his friend, Mr. Hart, had stopped by to say he and the "learned associates" were going on ahead and Nicolas groaned inwardly; this meant Pete would get a head start on the cocktails and that he would keep on drinking as long as the party lasted, or at least until he could be dragged away. Nicolas could only hope the liquid refreshments would be on the sparse and simple side, but he realized the hope was a forlorn one. The Geminianis were enormously rich and their estate, located in a eucalyptus grove on the outskirts of the city where earlier an Inca palace had stood, was among the show places of Cuzco. It was unthinkable that the entertainment should not be on the same scale as the establishment.

He and the Lobos arrived late, not only to find the party in full swing, but to discover Nicolas' fears, rather than his hopes, had been realized. The huge living room, pervaded with the pleasant scent of eucalyptus coming from the logs burning in the great fireplaces at either end of it, was filled with guests, among whom a veritable corps of white-coated menservants were circulating with laden trays. The hostess, a striking blonde, as modern in manner and dress as the younger Labradors, was outstanding among the more conservative ele-

ment of Cuzco society, as represented by both town and gown; and
Nicolas could not help wondering if, in the circles where she and her
husband moved, people spoke of Faustina's cocktail parties just as, in
Lima, people spoke of Marina's luncheons; for the young host, whom
Nicolas knew already as the pleasant and unpretentious heir to a vast
fortune, seemed to have been swallowed up in the crowd, as he was
nowhere in evidence. At the moment of Nicolas' arrival, Faustina was
coping competently with Pete, whose compliments had already taken
on a drunken glow, but Nicolas was conscious of her unvoiced relief at
his intervention. Without delay, he corralled a professor, whom he
recognized as Cuzco's most brilliant light in the field of archeology,
and who happened to be standing near at hand awaiting his own
opportunity to pay compliments; however, he was immediately pressed
into service to take Pete on a guided tour outdoors which should thoroughly include niches, terraces and traces of antique irrigation. Nicolas
was hardly through congratulating himself on the success of this
maneuver, when he himself was approached by two more professors
who eagerly inquired whether or not it would interest him to become a
staff member of an expedition they were hoping to carry off in the dry
season past Paucartambo and—

"I've already organized an expedition of my own going in that direction immediately," he said, again recognizing he was not showing his
best side. Ashamed of his brusqueness, he added quickly, "But tell me
about yours. I'd be greatly interested—"

Oh, it was only a hope, they said vaguely, and drifted away. He knew
that he had offended them and in an effort to make amends, he asked
the next professors who came up (My God, how many professors were
there in Cuzco, anyway? And aren't there any male guests at this party
whose occupation was a little more on the frivolous side?) if they would
not drop their classes and join him in his forthcoming venture. They
stared at him in ill-concealed amazement. Once more he had said the
wrong thing: a Cuzco professor, unless he had special leave of absence
like Mamani and Mendoza, could no more drop his classes within a few
weeks of the final examinations before the December closing than he
could fly. Of course not, Nicolas said hastily; he was all twisted around.
He had not been back in Peru long enough to remember the seasons
were reversed; that the months when the university was not in session
were December to April, instead of June to September, as in the
United States. He greatly regretted his stupidity. Would they please
excuse him?

By this time, the cocktail party, like all of its ilk, had become so noisy
that, in the general babel, it was impossible to distinguish clearly what
anyone was saying; and Nicolas was thankful that the Lobos, who were
rather on the austere side, wished to leave early, since this wish

represented a means of escape from a scene which, through no fault of the charming Faustina or her pleasant husband, was growing increasingly distasteful to him by the minute. Mamani had managed to get Nicolas aside and tell him Gomara had removed Pete from the terrace, where he had gone on accepting an unlimited number of pisco sours, and taken him back to the hotel. The removal had not been difficult, because, by then, Pete had been so drunk he could hardly stand; but the Bolivian was afraid that, as soon as he had made a partial comeback, he would go out again, in search of far less desirable company than the elite gathering at the Geminianis'; perhaps, it would be just as well for him to go to Pete's room at the hotel and report back. Would he mind going to Lester's at the same time, Nicolas asked; if Gomara would do this, it would save him, Nicolas, a trip back to the Ferrocarril, and he hated to confess it, but he had had it.

Gomara willingly undertook the commission. Pete, he was glad to report, in the note he sent around to the rector's house, was out like a light. So, more innocently, was Lester. Gomara would like to stress the word innocent: the replacement nurse, fully dressed in dark woolen clothes and with her head tied up in cellophane, was sleeping soundly in the twin bed beside Lester's. Gomara did not think she would represent temptation.

22 ❦

Nicolas had estimated that a long night's sleep and plenty of black coffee the next morning might have a curative effect on Pete's hangover; and, though the road from Cuzco to Paucartambo—the first stop in their long journey—was a rough one, the total distance was only a little over a hundred kilometers, not such as to obligate them to an early start. He had been less hopeful about Lester, who had certainly been dreadfully sick. As a matter of fact, he was twenty-four, but he looked and acted much younger; Nicolas still thought of him as a boy, and not a particularly vigorous one at that. He was fair skinned, with a tendency toward deep blushing when embarrassed; very slightly built and too tall for his weight. His exceptional intelligence, his eager interest in every phase of Nicolas' work and his sincere devotion to his employer, rather than his physical condition, had seemed to qualify him for inclusion in the expedition; but Nicolas doubted if Lester had the stamina to make a quick recovery from any sort of severe attack.

Nicolas was therefore agreeably surprised when he answered a knock at his door, before he had gone down to breakfast himself, and found his secretary standing outside.

"I think I can make it, sir."

The "sir" was a further welcome surprise. During the earlier days of their association, when Lester was "fresh out" of the army, it had come naturally enough—indeed, his student days were not so far behind him that it had ceased to seem a logical form of address to higher authority. But its use had gradually become less frequent and, though Lester referred to his employer as Dr. Hale, in speaking of him to others, he generally stopped short with "you" in direct conversation and occasionally lapsed still further and used the informal abbreviation of Nicolas, though even Margaret had hesitated over this; it was, she had said laughingly, too literally a *nick* name! Wisely, Nicolas had decided not to make an issue of the matter; now he was glad he had not. Apparently, Lester's sense of the fitness of things was reasserting itself.

"I think I can make it," he repeated. "I'm still a little lightheaded and I start panting if I try to move fast. But the nausea's gone and I've drunk some coffee. Is there anything I ought to try to do before we start, besides getting my own things together? That's done already. After all, there wasn't anything to pack but my shaving kit, my pajamas and the shirt I wore yesterday."

"Well, good for you! No, don't try to do anything else. Sit down and take it easy while I have breakfast and round up the others. I'll call you when we're all set. We've got the loan of a station wagon from the rector, and his son Ignacio is going along with us to drive it over and back. We're staying with cousins of theirs in Paucartambo, so Ignacio's glad of the pretext for visiting them. I'll send you and our learned associates, as Pete calls them, with him and go myself with Pete and Li Chan in the truck." He hesitated a minute and then went on, "Perhaps I'd better warn you that Pete may not be in the best possible mood this morning. He very willingly accepted quite a number of toasts at the cocktail party last evening and, unfortunately, he's the genial type that gets ugly afterward. Pete's too valuable to me when sober, which, after all, is most of the time, for me to interfere or moralize when he goes on a bender. So, *hasta luego.*"

Pete proved to be sullen but sober and, as soon as Li Chan had selected an ample supply of fresh vegetables from the well-stocked Cuzco market, the group was on the road with everyone else in good spirits. The start of the trip was downhill, through Cuzco's own beautiful green valley, where the scattered farmhouses had gardens abloom with roses, the roadside was aflame with yellow broom and the fields were planted with corn and potatoes. Then the expedition was climbing toward the puna, the desolate rolling uplands so high that only the scant *ichu* grass grew there; but, just as they reached the highest point, the sun broke through the clouds, gilding the drab slopes with its radiance; and, when the inevitable rain came, later in the day, it softened the perspective, enriching the verdure and deepening the shadows in the second valley toward which they were heading. Lester turned toward Mamani, who was seated next to him, with a long drawn out breath of excitement.

"What a revelation this whole ride has been! I never imagined such a series of chiaroscuros before!"

"I am pleased to see you appreciate the beauties of my country," Mamani answered formally but cordially. "Unfortunately, your compatriots do not always do so. Also, to see you are feeling so much better than when we started. I confess I was somewhat concerned about you."

"Better! Why, I've practically forgotten I was ever sick. . . . What are those queer stone mounds we keep passing now?"

"Chullpas—prehistoric tombs. A town—the one we're headed for—has stood here since very ancient times. And, as we go farther along the valley, you'll see that this becomes very fertile. Just that could account for its continued habitation. There's a stretch of fruit trees calculated to make a man's mouth water, just looking at them. But you won't have to wait long for refreshment—you'll be offered apples and probably oranges, too, as soon as we get to the Lobos' house and, before that, you'll have a treat of a different sort: you'll see the eighteenth century bridge—*época Carlos III*—your good taste will enable you to appreciate. I should also call your attention to the unique construction of the town as we go through it. It's built like a maze."

"Isn't that unusual construction for a Spanish colonial town?"

"It certainly is. Most of them were built in the form of gridirons. Lima's a perfect example of that. But the wind was a major consideration. If you were here in the dry season, when it comes sweeping up the valley, you'd find out for yourself why the Spaniards constructed in such a way as to make Paucartambo itself a windbreak."

When they crossed the high arched bridge into the town, the thinning rain carried with it a fragrance of orange blossoms; but this was presently engulfed in the less agreeable scents of mud and wet straw, as they went twisting and turning down the narrow unpaved streets, flanked with red-tiled, white-walled houses. There were no people abroad and no lights; only the flickering flame from a few lamps and candles, seen here and there as a window or door was occasionally opened, shone through the fast falling dusk of the tropics and revealed the presence of secluded families. Pigs and chickens, resentfully grunting and cackling, scattered at the approach of the travelers, but not fast enough to completely avoid casualties. As the truck drew up at the entrance of the Lobo house and a heavy door swung open to give access to the patio, Nicolas leaped down from his high seat and offered a limp white rooster to his waiting host.

"We've not only come to visit, we've brought our supper with us!" he said laughingly, as he accepted and returned an *abrazo*. "Not to mention a cook to take part of the burden from your capable staff!" Li Chan, descending in his turn, took the rooster from Nicolas, bowed and drew back a little, awaiting further instructions. "You remember Pete Hart," Nicolas went on, indicating his assistant, "he was with me the last time I came here."

"And could hardly wait to get back, not only to see *Señor* Lobo, but my other valued friend, *Señor* Juan Angel," Pete hastened to say. "I hope he is still carrying on his magical experiments and that I can again enjoy a convivial evening with him, hearing about them while I sample his lavish hospitality."

Lobo stiffened slightly. He himself was a prominent citizen, temporarily in political disfavor for opposing the current dictatorship in Peru, but essentially a pillar of law-abiding rectitude. The Angel to whom Pete so blithely referred was a notorious Communist, whose uncanny gift for grafting various kinds of fruit trees had met with amazing success, but who was no more highly esteemed on that account by the conservative element in the locality than if he had devoted all of his time, instead of merely his evenings, to the bottle. The fact that he controlled, to a very large degree, the available supply of carriers and mules would, of course, necessitate dealings with him on the part of the expedition's leader; but, in Lobo's opinion, these dealings should be confined to business matters, handled by Hale, and not stray into the social field to include his assistants.

"Juan Angel is still making his usual experiments," Lobo said coldly. "Whether they are magical or not, I suppose time will tell. Personally, I'm not much interested in freaks of nature and, needless to say, I do not follow along with anyone who preaches the gospel of Lenin. Besides, I had hoped that you, as well as the others, would be *my* guest this trip, *Señor* Hart. The rooms are in readiness and so is the baked guinea pig, which has been under preparation all day. We will keep the cock for tomorrow. And remember, *ésta es su casa*." Lobo turned away to embrace his cousin Ignacio and greet the other newcomers as the station wagon swerved into the patio; and, at almost the same moment, a bent, frail old man, who ignored the rest of the group, shuffled into sight and made straight for Pete.

"You'll excuse me, I know, *Señor* Lobo," Pete exclaimed, hailing the interloper with delight. "The magic must be working all right—

otherwise how would my good friend divine the exact moment of my arrival and come to carry me off to his orchard-encircled home? *Vamos, amigo mio!"*

"Damn it, stay where you are!" Nicolas muttered under his breath, clutching Pete's arm, only to be easily shaken off. Unless he were to create a scene, there was nothing to do but let the renegade go, mingling apologies for him with introductions of the others. It was, he reflected a little later, perhaps just as well there was one less man to accommodate, especially if that one were in a quarrelsome mood; for all the others had been quartered together and Nicolas was the only one who had been given a small neat room to himself. For this, he was duly thankful. He did not want to talk to anyone, to meet any more problems. Those would have to wait for the morrow. He could not logically say, "Sufficient unto the day is the evil thereof," for it had been a fairly easy one, as days on an expedition went. But he was tired, bone tired, without any real reason for it, so far as he could see. He had even been spared the effort of making labored compliments to his hostess, for the lady of the house, far from being the center of attraction like Marina and Faustina, had conformed to local tradition and kept to her place in the kitchen, so he had hardly seen her; and, as soon as he could, after the bounteous feast in which the promised baked guinea pig had been succeeded by a thick brew of cheese and potatoes, seasoned with rosemary and red pepper, he excused himself on the ground that he must write to his wife. Actually, he had not intended to do so; it was not in him just now to write Margaret such a letter as he had done before, and he was afraid another, in a different vein, would seem like a sad letdown. Then, wisely, he decided she would prefer almost any kind of a letter to none. The one candle on his bedside table gave all the light available in his room and the table itself was the only space on which it was possible to lay out a sheet of paper. He sighed, lighted a cigarette, and sat down to write.

"Darling—
"This should be a long, measured letter, full of hopes and promises, but I'm setting off on my quest in a black mood. It's raining, of course, and the rains have a chill of winter, instead of a tang of spring, so I can't accept them cheerfully; and though the wind is a mere breeze, compared to what it'll be later on, it's whistling around this low-eaved house and rattling the loose windowpanes like an ill-intentioned ghost. I know I shouldn't allow all this to depress me, but it does. What's more, Lester has been desperately sick and, though he seems to have made a quick recovery, I can't bank on its being a permanent one. Pete was drunk last evening at a very select cocktail party given by the elite of Cuzco and will get still more

disgracefully drunk tonight at the home of a notorious Communist, who lives in a small house set in the midst of a great orchard on the edge of town. To my intense embarrassment, Pete has insisted on staying with this character (who, despite his bad habits, is by way of being the local Luther Burbank) instead of with Paucartambo's leading citizen, along with the rest of us, and the chances are he won't be any good tomorrow. And there's a lot to do before we can leave here. Gomara, who's a very devout Catholic, doesn't want to push off before Monday anyway—the little old church here is the last one where he'll have a chance to hear Mass in heaven knows how long. As this is Friday night—does it seem possible to you it's only three days since I left you? It doesn't to me!—we'll probably need that much time anyhow to get ready for the next lap of our journey. No matter how carefully I think I've planned beforehand, some things have to be left behind when we get this far, and those need to be crated or sewn into sacks; then we have to find a tarpaulin to cover them. We're welcome to a corner of our host's storeroom, but its roof leaks, as does every roof around here—it's impossible to create a rainproof shelter. We're also leaving the truck here; my host has asked me whether or not I minded if he used it temporarily for a chicken house and, of course, I had to say he could. The first thing tomorrow we must start making an inventory, which will include fresh victuals and the *cañazo*—raw alcohol—and coca leaves that constitute the Indians' wages. That job calls for the united efforts of all hands and the cook and I mean this literally. Li Chan will be doing his share all right, but from present indications Pete won't be.

"Paucartambo is the last point I expect to reach in a long while where there's a post office and, technically, you could address mail here, in care of my present host, Manuél Lobo. But the University of Cuzco, Facultad Ciencias, would be better. For safety's sake, I'm sending this letter back to Cuzco for mailing through the good offices of the rector's son, Ignacio, who came over with us in his station wagon, which was a great convenience, as far as space was concerned, and will be returning tomorrow.

"When we leave here we go on muleback and for two or three days we'll still come across scattered farmhouses, now and then, where the Paucartambo Sierra gives way to the *Ceja de Montaña* (eyebrow of the jungle). (I'm enclosing a little sketch to show you this route.) After that there are only two words—*Noche Triste*—marked on the regional map. Are they meant to designate a place—or a mood—or an event? Something like the tragic night when Cortez almost lost Mexico before he finally and fairly won it? No, evidently not—just some local loss, so remote to memory no one even knows what kind of a loss. And beyond Noche Triste nothing is marked, though there have been futile expeditions to that region before. The existing trail goes on, out toward the Valley of the Urubamba, in the zone where that river has dug its way from the sierra down to the jungle, but we go where no trail is marked. The map shows the *Macizo de Tocate* (the massif of Tocate), the *Cadena* (mountain chain) *del Paucartambo* and the *Cadena del Pantiacolla*. But these terms have no real meaning yet, because actually they're still parts unknown. Perhaps when I come back, they *will* have a meaning, because I'll be the first to go up there and find, for you and me, something that's magic.

"Meanwhile, every night is a sad one—a *noche triste*—for me, because I'm separated from you. I'm glad to believe—and, I hope, justified in the belief—that in one way, at least, the separation isn't as hard on you as it is on me. If there'd been an extension in my room, I'd have called you Wednesday around midnight; but there wasn't and I didn't want to go back to the telephone in the Parras' library and risk seeing raised eyebrows and hearing jocund remarks

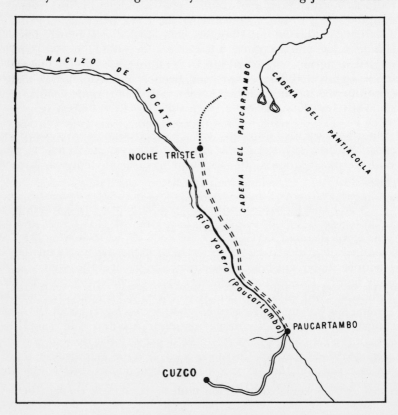

because of a second call from Lima to Virginia in a little over twelve hours—'Lo, Benedict the married man!' (I got enough of that as it was!) And there's no such thing as a direct connection from Cuzco to Virginia, only from Cuzco to Lima, so last night a call was completely out of the question. And now, of course, I'm far from telephones that reach any place, any time.

"In my first lonely wakeful hours, I began thinking of that wonderful French expression *'nuit blanche.'* Do you know it? Probably not, for all your nights have been white, not from sleeplessness but from innocence—until you met me!—so it wouldn't mean as much to you, even if you had come across it, as it would to someone to whom it had another connotation—as it did and does to me. Now I'm past the point of finding *nuit blanche* a strong enough description for what I'm going through. I've remembered something else I read some place, I've forgotten where, describing complete despair and saying it overtook its victim *'pendant l'angoisse d'une profonde nuit'*—'during the anguish of a profound night.' And then, of course, there was the 'dark night of the soul,' as interpreted by John of the Cross, one of the greatest saints who ever lived. I believe it was not only suffering of the soul he understood so completely, but suffering of the flesh as well. The two are interrelated, they can't be wholly separated, or at least that's what I feel. And however it may be, this letter is written with suffering, during the anguish of a dark night, through which no gleam of brightness seems to shine, nor will it until I cease to yearn for you as I do now. And when can that be, if ever?"

He rose abruptly, throwing down his pen and pushing away the paper. But he knew he must not close the letter on such a note as this. With equal abruptness, he sat down again and added a hurried postscript.

"Don't take all this too seriously. When we're actually under way, I'm bound to feel better. So far, I haven't felt as if I were getting anywhere because Lester and Pete, each in his own way, have so successfully diverted my attention from exploring, but soon they'll both be straightened out. I do so hope you'll spend the holidays with my family. I know they want very much to have you and, besides pleasing them and me, I honestly believe you'd enjoy it. I bought you a few presents in Lima that ought to reach you about the same time you're generously providing for 'Chris'mus Gif'' at Hills' End. (You'll have to anticipate the demand for it, so that you can get to Woodstock by Christmas Eve.) I hope and believe they'll please you and that, as you arrange the ornaments and wear the jewelry, you'll remember they were sent to you by a husband who loves you very much.

"There, that's better," he said to himself. Then he signed and sealed the letter and went to bed.

23 ❦

They were six days out of Paucartambo and the "black mood" in which Nicolas had written Margaret had grown deeper and deeper.

He recognized that there had been too much haste in the beginning and, with so little time for co-ordination among the different elements of which the expedition was composed, he had not expected everything to go smoothly; that would have been too much to hope for. On the other hand, he had not expected everything to go wrong, and this was exactly what had happened. No, that was not quite true. On the whole, the weather had been better than he thought it would be. Night after night, the sky had been spangled with big splashy stars, while the moon, which at first had been only a small rollicking crescent that set before they made camp, had become a smooth effulgent oval, spreading its silver beams over their tents and the boulders and bushes surrounding these. Moreover, morning after morning had been clear and nothing could have been more beautiful than the brief periods of brilliant light when the fresh-washed hills shone in the sunshine. But aside from that. . . .

Even before the expedition left Paucartambo there had been a disturbing incident: when everything else was in readiness and the mules had been brought in from the pastures above the town, Nicolas instructed all members of the expedition, which was much larger than he had originally planned, to come first to the corral where the fifteen cargo mules were being loaded, to make sure personal and professional gear was properly handled. This order was followed without question except by Mendoza, who slipped away to the adjacent corral, where the seven saddle mules had been herded. There he climbed up on a wet fence and clapped his hands so hard that the resultant sound was as sharp as the snap of a whip. Despite the suddenness of the crack, only one of the mules jumped and Mendoza chose to interpret this as a sign of singular alertness. When Nicolas came to find out why the botanist was not with the others, Mendoza pointed to the animal in question and announced triumphantly, "That mule is mine!"

With polite sarcasm, Nicolas inquired why the botanist should have the first choice. Because he would have special work all along the way, was the explanation; he would often have to go ahead hunting for specimens. Nicolas was tempted to make a serious statement of policy to the effect that no one was entitled to special favors; that all must draw lots. But he was in a hurry to get started, the propitious moment for argument passed and the best mule became Mendoza's.

Then, from the very first, the full-blooded sierra Indians of Quero had been restive. Nicolas realized the antagonism he had so unwisely roused in Angel, to whom he had been obliged to look for his supply of both carriers and mules, had resulted in his being given the worst the Communist controlled. Nevertheless, if there had been no language difficulty, Nicolas would have been able to placate these men; but they chose not to understand his schoolbook Quechua. A few unceremoniously disappeared, which left extra burdens on the others and the grumbling increased. If it continued to do so, there might be a stampede. Indeed, it seemed as if one were already impending when the expedition reached a deep torrid canyon in a gap of the sierra where gnats were a source of torment. The Queros carried their bright-colored, woollen ponchos, instead of wearing them; then they scratched the insect bites on the exposed parts of their bodies and crazed themselves. Gomara, who had studied their way of life, tried to convince them that, when their ankles stung, they must scratch not those but some unaffected place, say their elbows. He could not, of course, explain the reason for this: that scratching only made a bad spot worse in the end, whereas, if it were let alone, the sting would gradually subside. But he did remind them that they descended into a valley of their own, where there were also gnats, to harvest *yuca*, papaya and bananas. Yes, in their own valley, they admitted, but even there they had to hold their breath until they could rush back to their uplands. They demanded permission to do so now and, with the utmost difficulty, were persuaded to remain.

While remaining, however, they withdrew more and more into their sullen and secretive selves. Nicolas was convinced that somewhere along the way the expedition was now taking lay a landmark which would clarify their route or serve as a clue to future discoveries; but no amount of questioning could persuade the Indians to enlighten him. This did not surprise him; he knew they resented sharing with the *viracochas*, as they called the foreigners who were considered superior beings, the deepest mysteries of the Andes. He had encountered just such bafflement once before when his carriers had refused to go further, telling him the very air of the zone he was requiring them to enter was permeated with poison, that vegetation and streams were rank with it. He had defied them and plunged on alone—and it was then and there, deep sunk in a pool behind a waterfall that he had found the golden bell to which so much of his present fame and fortune were due. If he could persevere now, if he declined to be discouraged or daunted, a still more glorious discovery, still greater fame and fortune lay ahead of him.

As he kept telling himself this, he also reminded himself there was no sound reason why he should be discouraged or daunted. After all, the condition of the trail was no more surprising to him than the evasive silence of the Indians. He was used to following a track so steep that every step hurt, if he were going on foot, or to dismounting, if he were riding, to help his mule get from one pocket of bog to another. Suppose the trail did vanish for stretches, vaguely reappearing at last beyond some almost impassable expanse of muck? Suppose he could not tell, as he stepped into this, whether his foot would sink in an inch or a yard? Suppose this state of quagmire did go on and on, even near the top and that, while he was trying to struggle through it, he tripped over the hidden roots of dwarf trees and stumbled and fell? Suppose the earth all the way up this ridge lay in pockets of rock where the water stayed until it evaporated? That was all part of the game. That was what you let yourself in for when you decided to become an explorer, when you declined to be satisfied with two major discoveries and insisted on going on to make a third which would be supreme. As Nicolas told himself this, the ridge finally smoothed itself, just as dusk was falling, then climbed, angling into the sky. It was too late to go on that night, so an early camp was called. Tomorrow would be another day and perhaps an easier one.

But the Indians and the trail presented by no means the only problems. Lester spoke almost no Spanish, Mamani and Mendoza almost no English. Nicolas and Pete on the one side, Gomara on the other, did their best to maintain an even balance between the two languages and somehow include everyone in general conversation. But this was far from easy when there were so many other important things to consider. Lester felt he was being slighted because of his youth and inexperience; Mamani and Mendoza felt they were victims of the gringos' imagined superiority. Instead of teamwork, there was mutual jealousy and resentment, and Mendoza, with his advantage in having the best mule, took to straying far ahead or far behind, accommodating himself as if on a private botanical stroll.

What was even worse, Pete and Lester were at loggerheads and their mutual antagonism was increasing by leaps and bounds. To begin with, the fault had certainly been all on Pete's side. When he did not put in an appearance, the morning after the group's arrival in Paucartambo,

Nicolas had trudged out of town to Manicombe Azul, the downstream
farm of Juan Angel and, having been denied entry at the gate, hauled
himself over the wall and dropped down among the fruit trees, while
Angel stood cursing him for damaging an "apple-pear" tree and an
"apple-orange" tree. Without stopping to argue with him, Nicolas
forced his way indoors, where he found Pete in a drunken stupor on the
floor of the dark study, which had a bust of Lenin in one corner and a
school map of the Soviet Union on the wall; and, after failing to rouse
his assistant by slapping and shaking him, Nicolas finally forced an
emetic pill into his mouth. The result was an attack of nausea even
more violent than the one Lester had suffered two days earlier because
of mountain sickness and Pete, with vengeance in his heart, determined
to square things with Nicolas, not only by getting drunk again himself,
as soon as the expedition was under way, but by getting Lester drunk
with him. Accordingly, he invited the latter to drink from a barrel of
cañazo with him on the ground there was nothing like it to help him
through a day's work. When this argument met with doubt, the taunt
of "coward" met with immediate success. Lester had unwisely admitted
to Pete that he had really been frightened on the flight from Lima
to Cuzco and that even the urban traffic in Peru was a source of alarm
to him. He had regretted the confidence almost immediately; but the
harm had already been done and he was eager to undo it as far as he
could, by showing a braver spirit than Pete; presently, both were far
gone under the influence of the raw liquor, brought along as part of
the pay for the Indians, who were, however, permitted to drink it
only as it was measured out to them. They now squatted stolidly by,
watching the two white men as these began to weave about, every
now and then, aimlessly pummeling each other. The blind blows
were without intentional violence, but one of them hit Lester on the
jaw and he began to sputter with blood from a bitten tongue. Pete
burst into wild laughter at the notion that he was such a successful
boxer, and Lester stumbled and fell. Nicolas, who had been briefly
away from camp, futilely following the fresh trail of a bear, crashed in
on this disgraceful scene and hastily decided the best way to put an end
to it was to pick up Lester, who was still unconscious, and carry him to
his pup tent. Once convinced that the boy was sound asleep, Nicolas
left him to himself and went back to Pete, on whom the reaction of the
alcohol was, if anything, worse. He could not be bullied first and babied
afterward; he could not be kept from helping himself more and more
copiously from the barrel and, the more he drank, the more hilarious
he became. He told smutty stories, he sang, he shouted, he invited
everyone within earshot to join him in his guzzling and, despite
Nicolas' efforts at control, the camp soon became the scene of wild
disorder. Gomara, the devout Catholic, the pathetic refugee, hitherto so

self-effacing, so grateful for every kindness shown him, inquired, demandingly, why he and his university colleagues could not have a share of the good cheer. Were only Anglo-Saxons entitled to it? Were Latins to be classed with Queros? Of course not, Nicolas protested. Well, in that case. . . . So, presently, Mamani and Mendoza were drinking, too, Mamani avidly, Mendoza more hesitantly. "Perhaps someone had better stay sober," the botanist suggested, glancing around him.

"You're not intimating I'm drunk, are you?" Nicolas asked curtly.

"No, certainly not," Mendoza answered in a shocked tone. "But you can't be everywhere at once, watching everyone at once. If any of this liquor should fall into the hands of the Indians—"

"It won't."

But in the morning, despite Nicolas' watchfulness, an extra barrel of raw alcohol *had* fallen into the hands of the carriers and at least a quarter of them were out of service—some because they had already run away and some because they simply could not stand up, much less undertake a day's work. As the expedition got off to a late start, the latter were paid off in coca leaves and left behind to recover at leisure and then find their way home. The jeers and insults of their fellow Queros who were going on floated back to them. Lester was unable to talk, even to swallow hot liquids, because of his raw, ripped tongue. Pete had a painful hangover. Only Nicolas and his Latin associates were glad to break camp.

But even their good spirits were of brief duration. Never, in Nicolas' experience, had a trail been so arduous. At some points, it mounted to the very top of the ridge; then it dropped into a canyon; then it mounted again. The men climbed and climbed, descended and descended, climbed again. None of Nicolas' maps, whether regional or international, showed the contour of the ridge; and these had also proved unreliable as an accurate guide to altitude; so he had come to depend on readings of his altimeter for this, until Lester dropped the instrument, which was broken in the fall. However, the thin chill in the air and the absence of vegetation were proof positive they were traveling at heights which exceeded ten thousand feet and progress was becoming more and more taxing and laborious. And finally, on a misty day when they had climbed since daybreak, they came at noon to a point where the ridge fell away abruptly, on both sides of the trail, and this led only to the edge of a lagoon.

For Pete, who was in the lead at the time, one look at the water was enough; he was more than ready to say this was it, he was going to turn back. Lester, haggard from pain and humiliation and obsessed with the idea that his tongue might be infected, forgot his grudge against Pete long enough to enter into hearty agreement with him that the expedition was over.

"It isn't anything of the sort. Start preparing the underwater equipment."

The mist was beginning to lift a little and, as he shouted his defiant instructions, Nicolas was peering through it, trying to estimate the probable distance to the further end of the lagoon. This seemed to be fairly long, possibly as much as a thousand feet. Its water was opaque, and if it were deep as well as dense, everything would indeed point to its impassability. Nevertheless, Nicolas cautiously started to edge into it, though one backward glance at Gomara was enough to tell him the Bolivian agreed with Pete, that this should be the end of the expedition. But he also noticed that the Quero carriers, no longer sullen and silent, were conferring among themselves; and suddenly the one called Cipriano, after hurriedly crossing himself, rushed after Nicolas and, seizing him by the arm, forced him to stop. Then, gesturing wildly, the Indian burst into excited speech: that way, the *viracocha* was headed for dangerous waters; but there was another way through them, a safe one. He would take it and let the *viracocha* follow after.

Releasing Nicolas' arm and turning slightly to one side, the Quero began to advance through the obscure waters. He moved slowly but steadily, with no evidence of doubt as to the security of his footing on the stones of some submerged causeway. With the same steadiness, Nicolas followed after him, wading through water two or three feet deep, without once slipping. He did not stop until he and the Indian had reached the middle of the lake. Then he turned and shouted a challenge to the others.

"Come on in, the water's fine! What are you waiting for?"

"To see whether or not you get all the way across," Pete shouted back.

There was only one possible answer to this and it was not made in words. Without another backward glance and without stopping again, Nicolas followed the Indian to the far end of the lagoon.

For the first time since leaving Paucartambo, Nicolas was experiencing triumph. Now, knowing the others were already deeply shamed, he could afford to be generous. In his best schoolbook Quechua, he expressed his gratitude to Cipriano and persuaded the Indian to lay aside the habitual burden carried on his back and secured around his forehead by a *pretina,* which apparently it had not occurred to him to remove before starting over the lake. Then Nicolas gave orders that the Quero was to return and lead not only the other men, but the mules as well, across the invisible causeway, just as he himself had been led. The men crossed quickly and with surprising ease; and though it took longer and represented more of a feat to deal with the mules, this was also skillfully and persuasively done, as some of the other Queros now proved willing to be helpful. With no show of impatience, Nicolas awaited their safe arrival and he greeted his associates without arrogance or resentment; in fact, he even went so far as to inquire what they thought the next move should be. Personally, he would like to remain at least one full day beside this lagoon, exploring it, getting underwater photographs, writing a report of his findings. The others, with an abrupt about-face, were all for pressing on, though not all for the same reason. According to Mamani, the findings would amount to nothing in any case; the causeway, though unquestionably Inca built, was part of a common thoroughfare; the fact that none of them had known of its existence and had been halted by it proved nothing in the way of actual discovery. Pete, on the other hand, was especially vehement in arguing that this was beside the point. Discovery or not, the causeway had been built to facilitate progress toward a more important destination and the sooner they found out what it was, the better. Both recommendations gained force when the Quero carrier who had been sent on ahead came back to report a sharp descent in the trail, steep but not otherwise difficult. They made an early camp and Nicolas finally decided on a compromise: he would get up at dawn and devote the morning to diving and photography; unless he found something especially arresting, they would break camp the next afternoon.

The arrangement proved acceptable to all concerned. Nicolas convinced himself that it would be profitless to linger any longer at the lagoon: the water was too murky for successful photography and the causeway, unremarkable in itself, was the only submerged structure. Mamani gloated over his correct prophecies; and Pete was off to a fresh start. Nicolas led a grateful group downhill and, as the descent continued, everything went well. Rain fell only lightly and intermittently and, as far as the countryside was concerned, they might have been entering Paucartambo. Yellow broom made a bright border for the trail, corn was waist high and potato plants a mass of white and purple blossoms along the terraced plots of scattered farms; and, at these farms, it was possible to secure a few eggs, and even fowl, for the unkempt, hut-dwelling Indians who lived on them raised poultry as well as crops, and were disposed to friendliness—indeed, they offered to share their squalid living quarters with the *viracochas,* and only the realization that they were more hospitable than cleanly prevented acceptance: anyone from the lowlands was all too subject to the typhus transmitted by lice, to which these Indians had built up immunity.

Li Chan had felt that he lost face because he had not been allowed to help prepare the feast at Paucartambo and, since the group left there, had nursed his grievance to the detriment of his art. Now his spirits rose with the chance to prepare succulent fare in keeping with his own ingenuity and standards. Refreshed by an easy day and a restful night, restored by nourishing and appetizing food, the expedition at last began to show the *esprit de corps* for which Nicolas had so long and so vainly hoped. . . .

And then they reached Noche Triste, the place which Nicolas had told Margaret in his letter would mark the end of the known trail.

In itself, there was nothing depressing about it. To be sure, instead of the clustering huts, encountered at intervals during the last few days, there was only one in sight. But the Indian couple who occupied this received the expedition gladly and offered to share with its members such hospitality as a hovel and a shed could afford. Quartering in the hovel was declined for the usual reason—fear of contagion—but the shed was more than welcome for storing and sorting the stock of the expedition, part of which must now be left behind. Nicolas, who had learned wisdom by experience, allowed none of this work to be done unsupervised and did not try to have it done too hastily; but he also took time to talk with their host, whose name proved to be César and who was unusually loquacious for a sierra Indian. He volunteered two pieces of information that Nicolas found useful: first, that he himself knew the jungle, having worked rubber in his early years, and would be willing to hire himself out as guide; and second, that the Machiguenga Indians, who would eventually be found in the jungle far below Noche Triste, were resentful when their territory was invaded by large groups of outsiders, whoever these were. A smaller group the Machiguengas might actually welcome, out of curiosity; and this welcome would be warmer if gifts were brought along; but twenty-odd persons—no, that was too many. They would get no help, they might even be attacked.

Nicolas pondered the situation, lying awake in his pup tent. A week earlier, he would have welcomed an excuse for sending not only Mamani and Mendoza, but Pete and at least half of the Indians back where they came from. He had been sick of muttered complaints against "gringoism" and sicker still of drunken bouts. But since the discovery and the passage of the causeway, there had been such a change in the atmosphere that he hesitated to do or say anything that might recreate strain and thus lead to something worse. Besides, for the first time in his entire experience as an explorer, he had begun to feel there was actually a bond between him and one of his carriers, based on something stronger than the mutual needs of master and man. This feeling, too, had begun at the causeway: ever since Cipriano had grasped his arm to prevent him from wading into the murky water, and then had led him safely across the submerged passage, he had noticed that the Indian had found pretexts for coming and staying closer to him than to any of the others; also, that Cipriano not only spoke with increasing frequency, but seemed to be struggling for some further expression to which he had not yet been able to give tongue. Whatever happened, whatever anyone advised, Nicolas intended to keep this Quero with him; and keeping one Indian made it harder to choose among the others. If some left of their own accord, that was one thing; if he dismissed some and kept others, that was quite different. He must think the problem through with the greatest care.

After tossing and turning for hours, he finally fell into fitful slumber, riddled with dreams. He was searching for something, reaching for something and, when he had almost grasped this, it eluded him. No, of course, it was not some thing he was searching for, grasping for, he decided with dimly returning consciousness; it was Margaret and she was thousands of miles away, he would not see her for months, he would not even hear from her for weeks. Well, it was his own fault, he told himself savagely; he could not have given up his expedition, but he could have brought her to Peru, he could have kept her with him that much longer before he left on this wild goose chase, he could have rejoined her that much sooner. He had told himself already, night after night, that only a fool would have thought he could leave such a wife without paying dearly for it; but this was the first night he had actually thought he was paying *too* dearly. She had been a living bright reality and she had been his. He had given her up—for what? A fantasy? The mental image of a nonexistent realm? To pursue a will-o'-the-wisp? To seek the pot of gold at the foot of the rainbow? The next time anyone suggested that the expedition should end, he would agree. It had all been a mistake, everything was a dismal failure. There were no more lost cities or, if there were, they were not worth trying to find.

Rest that night was out of the question. Nicolas finally shrugged himself out of his sleeping bag, unfastened the flap of his tent and stepped into the open. After the darkness inside, the light was dazzling. There was not a cloud in the sky and the rising sun had flooded it with a radiance that was reflected on the mountain peaks toward which the unknown trail led. The way was still obscure. But beyond that obscurity, in all its glory, lay the promised land of his dreams.

He heard the sound of soft footsteps coming close to him and then halting. Next he was aware of Cipriano standing beside him. The Indian's eyes were fixed, as his had been, on the distant vision of that magic mountain, Macizo de Tocate. But presently the Indian turned and, instead of looking at the mountain, looked at Nicolas. His steadfast gaze was mirrored in Nicolas' eyes. There was no need of words between them.

24 ೮

Later that day Nicolas called his group together and, after remarking with a smile that he was not trying to imitate Pizarro on the Isle of Gallo, he made a statement: he was leaving early the next morning for the jungle with César as his guide. The mules could not be used on the unmarked trail, so they would now be sent back to Paucartambo, in charge of such Indians as would like to leave; he would no longer try to keep any of them against his will. (He knew, after the morning's revelation, that he was safe in saying this; Cipriano would never desert him now.) As far as his associates were concerned, they were also free to make their own decisions; he knew the first week out had meant very tough going, tougher than he himself had expected or led them to expect; if the discovery of the causeway and the easier week which had followed did not make up for the first hardships, he would understand. There would be no ill feeling on his part.

The Indians withdrew, to converse in guttural tones, as was their habit. Mamani and Mendoza exchanged glances. Then Mamani cleared his throat and spoke for them both.

"To tell you the truth, Dr. Hale, my colleague and I have become somewhat worried about our classes. True, we both secured official sanction for official leave from the university, as you know. But neither of us has felt satisfied with our replacement. And we had not expected the expedition would require such effort or be of such duration. As you yourself have admitted, the first part of the trail was much more arduous than we had foreseen and took much longer to cover. The submerged causeway is interesting, but only as an Inca relic still in use. Frankly, your search no longer seems essential to us, in connection with our own scientific status. We should like to be back in Cuzco to resume charge of our classes for the final examinations just before Christmas and shall, therefore, be glad to take advantage of your courteous offer to release us from further participation in the expedition."

"Well, I don't remember hearing you say, when I first asked for your co-operation, that you and Dr. Mendoza weren't satisfied with your replacements or that you were putting any limit on the amount of time you could spend with the expedition. And, of course, your departure will leave me without either a geologist or a botanist. But, as I've just said, it's up to you. Perhaps you would be kind enough to mail a letter to my wife from Cuzco, if I can dash one off some time today; this is the last chance I'll have to send her one for a long while."

"Of course, it will be a privilege. And any other small service we could render you in Cuzco."

"Thanks, I guess that's all. And now, what about you, Dr. Gomara?"

"I am not unduly fatigued, I have all the time in the world, and I am not worried about my classes. Moreover, I'm convinced the most interesting part of our trip is still ahead of us."

"Pete?"

"Them's my sentiments. I mean about the interesting part of the trip. And thank God I don't have any classes to worry about or feel the necessity of pretending I do because I'm a coward. Of course, that causeway's going to lead, sooner or later, to something else."

Pete spoke with hearty conviction and Nicolas' heart warmed to him. This was the old Pete, the one he had known and loved for years; the one who slipped from grace when not much was at stake, but who stood by when he was really needed; the one who could and would say the things which he, Nicolas, should not say because he was the leader, but which he was glad to have said by someone else. Grinning, Nicolas nodded his appreciation and turned to Lester.

"What about you, Lester?"

"You must know, sir, that I never had the slightest intention of leaving you."

There was a mild rebuke in the civil, formal reply. Well, Nicolas said to himself, probably he deserved it. He would make up to Lester for his own lack of courtesy and lack of confidence later. But just then Cipriano came forward to report on the Indians' decision: all but six were ready to stay with the expedition.

"Good! Six should be able to look after the mules very capably. They can also look after Dr. Mamani and Dr. Mendoza. The rest of us will leave at daybreak for the jungle."

Although his decision was accepted then, the afternoon did not pass without a considerable show of hesitation on the part of both Gomara and Pete. Lester limited himself to the remark—based on his experience in Korea—that of course the really easy way to reach their goal would be to go in by parachute. If they were only, here and now, a few hundred feet above their present position, aboard a comfortable Faucett DC-4, heading northwest, they could be over the saddle-shaped heights of the Macizo de Tocate in five minutes.

"You remind me of the old gag about the two hungry tramps who were discussing a hearty breakfast," Nicolas said drily. " 'If we had some eggs, we could have some ham and eggs, if we had some ham.' We haven't got a comfortable Faucett DC-4 at our disposal, worse luck, or any parachutes, either. We have to go by trail."

"But we don't even know for sure there is one," Gomara remarked mildly, glancing in the direction of their objective. The heights which had stood out so clearly at dawn were now hidden by massive clouds, and the panorama was reduced to an expanse of green sierra above green jungle. Even if the gray clouds should disperse again, revealing the violet peaks beyond, the sight of the trackless intervening wastes was appalling in its implications. Nevertheless, Nicolas's retort was quick and sharp.

"You mean we don't know *where* it is, that sitting here we can't even guess where it might be. Just the same, there's bound to be one and its whereabouts will be known to the savages we'll meet in the jungle. Besides, the way probably isn't as hard or as long as it looks. We may not have to climb up to the very top of the massif; the way to the lost, hidden, secret city may well be around—and beyond. . . ."

"You certainly make it all sound like a conducted tour around London, under the direction of Thomas Cook," Pete said sarcastically. "I'm still with you. But what if these savages we're so sure to meet are afraid of this lost, hidden, secret city that's become such an obsession to you? What if it's taboo as far as they're concerned? Jungle-dwelling Machiguengas are quite capable of setting up a taboo against something left by sierra-dwelling Incas. What's more, the Indians we meet may turn out not to be Machiguengas at all. We might have a chance with them, even if César has warned us they're unfriendly except to small groups. They're a good sized, spreading tribe. They admit missionaries along the Urubamba River and some of them even send their children to school at the Dominican jungle headquarters in Quillabamba. But the Indians we meet, if we do meet any, may turn out to be Cogapacoris, the savages no outsider has ever visited. And we don't know anything about them, except through the trembling references of their Machiguenga neighbors, which certainly aren't reassuring."

"Certain you don't want to go back to Cuzco with Mamani and Mendoza, or at least as far as Paucartambo with the six defecting Indians and the mules?" Nicolas inquired, speaking still more sarcastically.

"Well, I might think it over again, now that you've given me a second chance."

"Do, by all means. But, as I said before, I'm leaving at daybreak tomorrow in the other direction."

At dawn the air was fragrant with the scent of balsam, a welcome tonic for all jaded spirits, including Pete's. But the trail was no longer easy anywhere. Fallen trees, thorny and decayed, blocked the path and in some places it was impassable, as far as walking was concerned; the only way to cover it was by jumping or by getting down on all fours. The clouds made an opaque curtain over the Andean world as César led the expedition further and further, at headlong speed, until they had descended so far that they were engulfed in a deep ravine. When the sun came out, at noon, it was already very hot and low enough to invite the plague of a full-scale attack by jungle gnats. This was the point from which they must again ascend and Gomara seconded Cipriano's plea to Nicolas that they should begin to climb at once. The way was steep and, as César warned them with his parting instructions, they could not expect to go up as rapidly as they had come down. But they were at last definitely on the clustered foothills of Tocate. From now on all they would have to do would be to climb.

"Yes, that's all we have to do now—climb!" Pete remarked, as he watched César's retreating form; and, in the next days and weeks, the same words became his scathing theme song. If the group advanced as much as a kilometer a day, they were lucky. For their progress was an inch-by-inch battle with *paca,* the yellow-green sword grass with sharp, double-edged leaves, which grew taller than a man and so thick that men could hardly walk between the stalks and also so resilient they sprang back after a machete stroke, to frustrate and wound again. Nicolas called on all hands to clear a trail through the *paca,* for if it were not cut down it would engulf them; it might even make them forget their way, their plan of advance. With his usual eagerness and industry—and, unfortunately, his usual lack of skill—Lester immediately went at the *paca* with a vengeance, in order to set the Queros a good example; it was only a matter of minutes before his bare knuckles were gashed as though he had thrust his fist through a window. For the next few days he could neither work nor hunt, and was obliged to content himself to practicing, left-handed, with a lariat—an occupation which served no useful purpose. But, afterward, he learned to approach the growing *paca* with his head covered and his shoulders low to the ground and, by avoiding the double-edged leaves, to chop the stem at its base.

Above the *paca* rose, in rich and great variety, the tall green trees of the jungle; but these presented no menace and not too much of a mystery. Through them a way could surely be found, once contact had been made with some nomad Machiguenga; and every now and then there was a clearing among them. If the expedition came to any of these, on one of their rare bright mornings, the view to the rear would open up to something familiar—the ridge of Paucartambo, the smoke from César's farm. They could not see the saddle-shaped summit of

Tocate because they were on the slope of the low ridges climbing up to that pinnacle; but this was as it should be, this was in itself reassuring.

Every afternoon it rained with a vengeance and the nights began wet and, for the most part, ended wet. Occasionally, the downpour ceased shortly before dawn and, when this happened, Gomara quietly slipped from the tent he shared with Pete, for this was the time that offered the best hunting conditions and he was the crack shot of the expedition. He scanned the skies for the high-riding Southern Cross and blessed himself by it. Then he started out, rifle over his shoulder, to return with partridge, venison or bear. It taxed the utmost skill of Li Chan to do justice to these with a kerosene burner. But it was thanks to Gomara that the expedition feasted on a series of delicacies, instead of porridge for breakfast, rice and jerked meat for lunch, and stew for supper. Lester wasted good ammunition trying to match the Bolivian. But the first hit he made, after a fortnight of vain attempts, proved to be a hawk —worse than useless, since it was no good for food and the restive Indians fought as to who should wear its feathers.

Mutiny was a constant menace and, though it was still an unfulfilled threat, the expedition was never free from its lurking shadow. Then one day Cipriano, who had been absent collecting medicinal bark, came bounding back into camp, holding one hand against the side of his head: an arrow had grazed his ear. Instantly, he was surrounded by his fellows, shouting and stampeding: this was the beginning of the attack they had been warned they might expect; the man who had shot that arrow would be followed by others; not only their ears would be bloodied, but their bodies. Cipriano alone remained wholly unmoved: the wound was very slight and it was accidental, he insisted; the arrow had not been aimed at him, but at some animal a hunter was pursuing; presently, this hunter would come in search of it and they would make friends with him; after that he would lead them where they wanted to go. Ever since César had left them to shift for themselves, they had been hoping for contact with the lowland Indians, the friendly, resourceful Machiguengas. Now this hope was about to be fulfilled. . . .

He was still trying to calm the other Queros, still trying to reason with them, when the *paca* parted to disclose a painted Indian, armed with bow and arrows, and naked except for a knotted jungle fiber around his middle, from which hung a hatchet. Instantly realizing he was surrounded, he glanced furtively from side to side and then stood motionless, awaiting whatever action the other Indians might take. A glance sufficed to show he was apparently not a wilful aggressor; indeed, the Queros, who had ceased to shout and were muttering instead, whispered that he "smelled of fear" and themselves ceased to feel any as they came crowding around the motionless man. But Nicolas was shouting now.

"Look at that hatchet! It's *stone!* This is no Machiguenga! God Almighty, it can't be—but it is! It's a Cogapacori!"

The words ended in a shout of triumph and, smiling exuberantly, Nicolas held out both hands to the savage. Instantly, the man stiffened. The identification of him had been correct; the friendly greeting had been a mistake. He belonged to a tribe which considered its name, if applied from the outside, an insult, even a challenge. It would now obviously be necessary to placate him, after all, and not only necessary but desirable; the hatchet which hung from the knotted jungle fiber was unquestionably an example of Stone Age culture and wherever that had come from would be more like it. If only this man's good will could be secured, he could indeed lead the way to the discovery of the greatest treasures the expedition had dared to hope of finding.

Sudenly the savage, moving for the first time since his arrival, reached out an exploratory hand and touched Nicolas' belt.

"Give it to him!" Gomara whispered excitedly.

"My God, what'll happen if I do that! I can't go around the way he does!"

Nicolas had pulled away, a hundred reasons for not giving up his belt, from which hung both his pistol and his bowie knife, flashing through his mind. However, since he had extra knives, he detached the one he was wearing and offered it to the Indian, who accepted it indifferently and went on fingering the coveted belt. Nicolas peeled off his shirt and offered that; again the acceptance was one of indifference. Lester, inspired by the idea that a counter-attraction to the belt should be provided, had rushed off to see what he could find and, returning with a loaded sack, began to empty its miscellaneous contents on the ground.

"Not everything we have, not all at once like that!" Nicolas shouted, but he was already too late. The savage had leaned over and swiftly scooped up a bolt of cheap blue cotton, some mirrors and some lipsticks. Unfortunately, he had not noticed that there were fishhooks among this numerous treasure; he pierced his finger and, dropping everything he had gathered, dodged his way through the Queros and vanished from sight as quickly as he had come.

Nicolas acted almost as rapidly. He picked up the blue cloth and made it into a neat bundle, outlining a plan as he did so. One of their group would go into the woods alone, bearing this bundle and seeking out the Cogapacoris. Once they had been found and the good will offering accepted, the expedition would be sure of the Cogapacoris' friendship and would have the natives of this region for guides. They were in the upland woods, where the Queros would feel more and more at home, and there must be trails which only the Cogapacori knew which would lead straight to a major discovery.

"Major, your hat!" Pete exploded.

"But I'm sure of it! That stone hatchet! There's nothing like it now in the Andes or along the Amazon."

Nicolas continued to argue with enthusiasm and conviction: his plan was right, the timing was right, and major discovery did lie up there— between the massif of Tocate and the ridge of Pantiacolla. But the opposition was unanimous. Expedition officers and Quero carriers were in complete agreement: they had made an enemy of the warrior scout; they could expect no mercy if they forced their way into his people's lair; they had all witnessed the scene with this savage and they were sure he would think he had been poisoned by fishhook witchcraft; he would arrange a hostile greeting. . . .

"Shut up, God damn it, shut up every one of you! Of course, I'll be the scout, that's what I meant to do all the time, none of the rest of you will run into any danger. You can make out all right here for another week, even two weeks. If I'm not back by then, you can report me lost in action and someone else can take the Explorers' flag back to Washington."

"For God's sake, Nick, let up on the cheap heroics! If you'd only had the brains to give that so-and-so that damn belt of yours, you might have made a friend of him, instead of enemy, and there might be some sense in what you're saying. As it is, the only sane thing for us to do is to break camp and get away from this zone before the whole Cogapacori tribe comes here in full force."

"All right, all right, go back if you want to. I'm going forward. You'll admit it's too late in the day to start off in any direction before tomorrow. But we can spend what's left of the afternoon getting ready and, in the morning, I'll take the high road and you'll take the low road and so on and so on."

"Whatever road you're taking, I'm taking too, sir. And unless I'm terribly mistaken, that's what at least one Quero will do, too."

Nicolas wheeled around. In the same noiseless way that Cipriano had approached him at sunrise, the day they left Noche Triste, the Indian had come up beside him now and was looking at him with mute appeal. In some way, Nicolas' purpose and the purpose of the others had been made clear to him and, like Lester, he had made his own decision. A sudden mist blurred Nicolas' sight and he found it hard to speak.

"All right. I told my wife three would be my lucky number some time. I see the time's right now."

Gomara got up at three, instead of four, the next morning. There was a moon and the Southern Cross, near its zenith, stood forth like a key to a sky of hieroglyphics. According to his habit, Gomara blessed himself by it and, this time, he gave thanks as well. The dawn would be clear,

the day good. If Nicolas were determined to plunge off into the unknown, at least he should not start until he was provided with good
fare. Gomara had hopes of a fat *paujil;* he had shot one before and Li
Chan had quickly transformed it into a roast which Nicolas had
pronounced better than the turkey it somewhat resembled could possibly have been. Well, he would relish such a roast even more on the
rough road he was now about to travel. And he would have two good
men and true to share it with him.

As Gomara quietly skirted the Indians' part of the encampment, he
was amazed to see a light there and hurriedly changed his course.
Several of the Queros had left the primitive shelters they built for
themselves and were gathered around a still form lying prostrate on the
ground; others were fast approaching the same place. As Gomara came
closer and the group parted a little, he saw that the man lying on the
ground was Cipriano and realized, with horror, that the man must be
very ill, possibly dying; if he had chosen merely to sleep in the open, his
fellows would have left him undisturbed. Gomara hurried forward and
knelt beside him while the others, all of whom held the white man in
great respect, made way for him and enlightened him.

"The arrow. It was poisoned. If we had gone forward, as the leader
commanded, we would all have met our death that way."

Yes, they would all have met their death this way. But, because
Cipriano had met his this way, this night, Nicolas and Lester would not
meet theirs. Cipriano had not guessed, in the beginning, that his life
was endangered; he had believed, as he said, his ear had been grazed
accidentally and probably he had still believed this when he let it be
understood he, too, meant to go forward. But afterward—afterward,
when he knew the wound was mortal, he had not revealed this, he had
not bewailed his fate, he had been a willing victim.

It would do no good to call Nicolas now. Cipriano was long past
speech, past consciousness or even transitory recognition. Gomara
continued to kneel beside him, repeating, in as far as he could
remember them, the prayers for the dying, then the prayers for the
dead. Cipriano had been a Christian, he had crossed himself before he
led them safely across the causeway; and he had died a good death.
"Greater love than this hath no man that he lay down his life for his
friend." There should have been a priest there to give him absolution,
to see him safely on his way to heaven. But since there was none,
Gomara would do the best he could and his final service was to help
with the burial. The Queros, with gratitude, accepted his offer to do
this before they silently stole away.

Nicolas, in his tent, heard an unfamiliar noise and reached for his
pistol. César had told him about an old puma who could no longer

catch its normal food and, in desperation, turned on the weakest and most treacherous prey—man. There was a scuffling noise, but that could be any small animal or number of animals. Anyway, he was exhausted. If some emergency arose, he would be called and he would instantly be out among the others, on his feet, setting things right. But no one called him and he slept on and on, far past his usual hour. When he finally roused and looked at his watch, he cursed himself for his sloth. Today, of all days, he should have risen early to start on his great adventure. He sprang up, but even before he opened the flap of his tent, he became aware of unnatural silence. Lester was sitting outside, apparently waiting for him. No one else was in sight.

"What's happened? Where is everyone? Where's Cipriano?"

Lester did not answer and Nicolas saw that he could not. It was not merely a sore tongue that kept him from speaking now. He was choked with tears.

"Damn you, don't sit there crying like a baby. Tell me."

But when Lester had told him, Nicolas found that he was crying, too.

He wanted to be by himself, he did not want to talk to anyone. His staff understood the depths to which his chagrin and his grief were taking him. Pete's prophecy, to which Nicolas had refused to listen, had proved all too true—it was a hostile Cogapacori whom they had met, not a kindly Machiguenga; and the meeting had been a prelude to tragedy. Nicolas had lost a dream—he would never find out now whence the stone hatchet had come, he would never lead his expedition triumphant over the Macizo de Tocate. And he had lost a friend. . . . The others would have left him undisturbed in his tent had he chosen to stay there. But they understood, too, when he said he would have stifled if he did that, he must get out in the open. If he did not go far, there would be no danger. . . .

He realized he was being watched as he left the camp. His friends did not really believe he would try to go forward—that would be futile folly after what had just happened. Indeed, it would be something worse than that: it would make a mockery of Cipriano's death, for then the sacrificial offering of his life would have been in vain. Nevertheless, Nicolas was not to be trusted in his present mood; his sense of bafflement might be so strong that it obscured his reason and drowned his grief. If it were, he was quite capable of madness.

He himself was not sure, when he started out, what direction he would eventually take. For some time, he walked slowly and aimlessly along the cleared path. He had told the truth when he said he wanted to be alone, that he did not want to talk to anyone. On the other hand, he did want to think things through. That was what he was doing now. And presently his confused thoughts clarified. He knew what he wanted to do, what he ought to do, what he was going to do. Even if it proved that he was a madman and an ingrate, even if it were the last act of his life, he was going on. He would be an explorer to the very end.

That Lester was following, he did not notice until he turned and worked his way into the virgin *paca* below the trail. Immediately, the jungle became hot and oppressive and, though he was not aiming to extend a clearing, he worked harder yet, trying to squeeze his way along. This was the only way to approach the Cogapacoris who might have a camp, a settlement, very close. . . . It was only after he had lost his footing and, despite his frantic struggle to save himself, fallen in a landslide of rocks and earth into the crashing branches of some trees forty feet below that he looked back and dimly saw the boy on the ground above him. He shouted, "Stay *up* there, damn it—you'll get hurt if you don't!" Then he blacked out. His last thought before he lost consciousness was that, if this were the end, he would never know if he and Margaret were to have a son.

25 ༃

Nicolas regained consciousness slowly and, to begin with, only in waves, as if he were coming out of ether. First he vaguely realized, not only that he was still alive, but that he was not mortally injured, just bruised and bleeding and that he seemed to be ensnared in the branches of a tree into which he had fallen. Then he blacked out again. The second time he drifted back to reality, he was aware that someone was trying to yank away the entangling branches that imprisoned him. This attempt at rescue gave fresh impetus to the landslide and, together with rocks and trees and mud, he was hurled farther and farther down a deep ravine and over a narrow waterfall. In this sharp descent he once more lost consciousness and when he came partially to himself for the third time, he was lying on a ledge below the cascade and failed to recognize the identity of the man who was bending over him.

"Where did you come from?" he asked thickly.

"The same place you did."

"Lester? I told you to stay where you were."

"I know. But I had to come after you to see if I could help. Instead, I only made things worse. The second landslide carried us twice as far as the first."

Nicolas was still not sure he understood, but he began to make a determined effort to do so. "Well," he said groggily and slowly, "since you're here, maybe you can get me to my feet. I seem to be so damn dizzy."

After several vain attempts, he did manage to stand, but he still could not do so, unsupported, and minutes, which seemed like hours, passed before he was able to take a step forward. Then, still silently and with infinite difficulty, the two men began to pick their way down the ravine. Neither dared say what Lester already knew and what Nicolas was slowly grasping: that there was no way back, no hope of rejoining the expedition. From now on, it was merely a question of survival.

Sticking to the bed of the narrow stream, they stepped or slid from one slippery rock to another; but here at least they were free from obstructing *paca* and, as they approached another waterfall, the woods receded enough to disclose an outside world of mountains, thick and green and steep, on the other side of a canyon. Working his way to a rock at the edge of this cataract and lying belly down, Nicolas studied the sheer drop of fifty feet or more and shook his head.

"I'm not going to admit that this or anything else can really stop me for long," he said, speaking clearly for the first time. "But I've got to admit that it has for the moment. I wish I knew how a Machiguenga would tackle such a drop. I believe even one of them would be hard put to find a way."

"Maybe you're forgetting something," Lester said, almost cheerfully.

"Do you mean I should remember a man who thinks he is lost in the jungle never really is if he can find running water and follow it?"

"No, not that old saw." For the first time, Lester actually grinned and pointed to the coil of rope at his belt. In the course of his many hours of practice with his improvised lasso, he had become so attached to it that he kept it with him all the time. Now, fastening one end to a rock-jut and using it as a scaling line, he reached a ledge part way down the drop. After Nicolas had reached there, too, Lester released the pulling pressure and, as the slipknot came loose, the rope fell after them. This brought them halfway down, in the pelting middle of the waterfall, and Lester managed to find the right jut for a second descent; but the stream which they finally reached was so swollen by the heavy rains that its volume of water represented an even greater peril than the vertical drop and they did not dare try to go on. It was not until late in the afternoon that there was a break in the weather and, as sunlight streamed through the trees, Nicolas made his way to a cave near the edge of the river.

"The water may be lower in the morning," he said, sniffing. "I don't like the way this place smells—it must be the lair of a gamey old puma.

But if it weren't for that, I'd say we'd found a good place to spend the night. Anyhow, let's light a fire which might keep him away and would give us a chance to dry our clothes. We can rest awhile and take stock of equipment."

"Maybe it would be a good idea to have a look around first," Lester suggested. "Here's another surprise for you—I've got a flashlight, as well as a lasso. How's that for equipment? If your guess about the puma's home is a good one and he happened to be there, he might not give us the kind of welcome we'd really enjoy."

"My compliments on your equipment. And right you are about making use of it."

Their investigation of the narrow cave revealed it as both dry and empty and, while Lester went in search of something which might serve as firewood, Nicolas was persuaded to lie down and rest. He was so spent that he was past argument about helping. The blood had dried where his skin had been gashed, but the bruises throbbed and he ached all over. When Lester, still irrepressibly cheerful, returned with an armful of branches, Nicolas was unable to match his mood.

"Only a Machiguenga could get a flame out of those damp twigs," he said. "Bet you a dollar they never ignite."

"You just lost a buck to old eagle scout Wendell," Lester retorted, puffing away at the base of his mounded firewood and grinning triumphantly when it caught. Even though they had nothing to cook, its light added a cheerful note to their quarters and its warmth enabled them to dry their clothes. They stripped and dried first their underwear, then their corduroy pants, flannel shirts, windbreakers and boots. Lester was so drowsy that he nodded while he busied himself with this task and, when it was finished, almost instantly fell asleep. Nicolas, though even more exhausted, fought to keep himself awake while he tried to size up their situation.

No man in his right mind, even though well equipped, would have voluntarily placed himself high on a mountain jungle where the only Indians were wary and unapproachable, where there was no transport route, no road, no recognizable trail; and neither he nor Lester was *well* equipped. Lester, when he plunged after Nicolas, had been carrying nothing but a bowie knife besides the happy accident of both a flashlight and a lasso. Since Nicolas, when he started out, had intended to begin his search for the Cogapacoris, he carried a lightweight knapsack, equipped with such supplies as standard drugs for snakebite, burns and dysentery, in addition to vitamin pills and a few trinkets with which he hoped to intrigue the first savage he met. But he recognized only too well that these were meager safeguards in his present peril. He had jeered when Margaret asked him if it were not dangerous to go into the jungle without a doctor. "Danger? What is danger? Crossing the street, eating a bad oyster, slipping on a rug!" Now his own words came back to mock him. If you were hit whlie crossing a street, an ambulance picked you up and took you to a hospital; if you ate a bad oyster, you telephoned your doctor; if you slipped on a rug, you shouted until someone else in the house heard you, if you could not even manage to crawl over to a sofa. But here there were no hospitals, no telephone, no doctor, no sofa. *There was nothing but jungle.* As he lay listening to the jungle sounds—the clinks and whirs and clicks made by discreet creatures who kept out of sight—Nicolas knew he would never again use the word danger carelessly or scoffingly.

Mercifully, the recognition of his peril was not weighted with either despair or fear. He refused to admit defeat in his purpose to follow the Cogapacori, to find his lost city, to rejoin Margaret, to see his firstborn son; and, as he weighed the hazards to survival against the will to live, which was so strong within him, he felt the power to prevail reborn. But he must move fast, he must keep moving and so must Lester, if their drive were to overcome their obstacles. It was still dark, but, if their flashlight revealed waters that were receding, they could start on their way again, not waiting for morning and, with the help of the lasso, they could descend, keep on descending, never stop.

He learned over and shook his inert companion, but to no avail. Lester was, literally, dead to the world. Until he roused from his profound sleep, it would be better for him, Nicolas, to sleep also, to conserve and restore his shattered strength. . . . But the sense of danger permeated even his deep dreams and when Lester, half awake at last, muttered incoherently, "What's that growling? Is the puma coming home?" Nicolas was instantly alert. *Growl of a puma, was it? A jaguar, much more likely and much more dangerous. And, if the beast had eaten early, he wanted to get back into his lair, where they were, before daylight, which was just coming on.*

"No such luck," Nicolas snapped. "Pumas don't growl that way. And we'd better not keep our host, the jaguar, from his sleep. . . . Let's hope we meet only bushmasters from now on," he added, with another attempt at lightness, as they made their way below the waterfall which had detained them overnight. Hunger had now become a gnawing pain, which Nicolas' vitamin pills had done nothing to assuage, though thirst, at least, was no problem, for the muddy stream which was their plunging avenue of escape also supplied their drinking water. But Nicolas, who was still unsteady on his feet, kept grabbing at the boles of one tree or another for support and, more than once, clutched a trunk with thorny bark and gashed his hand again. He swore, partly from annoyance with himself for not watching out and partly with pain from the thorns, and then stopped swearing to call, with the same determined lightness as before, "Make a note, Lester: leather gloves, several pair, for the next trip."

"My God, the *next* trip! Hadn't we better see how we make out on this one before we begin talking about another?"

"No. If we keep talking about another, if we keep planning for another, we'll make it. *'L'audace, l'audace, toujours de l'audace!'* There's a lot of truth in the old French slogan for success."

But *l'audace* alone was not all sufficient. The next day the lasso broke and Nicolas, who was following Lester down over a knife edge of rock, fell into another thorn tree. Again, he was badly scratched, for though his body had been protected, to a certain degree, by his clothing that was now torn and there were fresh bruises, especially on his right hand. His increasing weakness made him intolerant of pain and carried with it not only increasing irritation, but the first discouragement that was so deep he had hard work to rise above it. If he couldn't manage to hurry, his exploring days would soon be over and his lost city would be found by some youngster, some husky youngster like Lester, possibly Lester himself. Momentarily, he forgot that Lester, far from being considered husky, had been viewed as a poor risk for the expedition, because of his physique; it was his other qualities that had made him eligible. Well, he was displaying all those other qualities now and unexpected endurance as well. Nicolas was suddenly jealous, and jealousy, added to weakness and irritation, made him speak sharply, instead of gratefully, as Lester helped to disentangle him from the thorn tree.

"Damn it, man, don't shove me. Can't you see I'm on the edge of a cliff?"

"Sorry, Nick. I was so excited, I didn't notice. I just wanted to ask, could we eat that?"

Lester was pointing toward a huge bear, which stood on his hind legs, just below them, ripping a green palm apart. Vehemently, Nicolas shook his head.

"No, we couldn't eat *that!* Even if we could shoot him, how could we skin him and cook him?"

"I didn't mean the *bear*. I meant, could we eat what he's eating?"

"Well, we might at that."

Nicolas was instantly ashamed of having spoken so grudgingly, but if Lester had taken his tone amiss, he did not show it. He picked up a stick and threw it at the bear, who growled and lumbered out of sight into the thick vegetation. He might, of course, be lurking somewhere near, but the refugees were hungry enough to take a risk. They clambered off the ledge and down to the chonta palm, which had conveniently been split open by the bear and offered its pulpy heart as a perfect lunch for man as well as beast; after devouring it, the men felt infinitely better and the effort of continuing down the mountain ravine became correspondingly easier. Moreover, Lester had discovered that the long lianas, which now appeared on many of the trees, made excellent substitutes for the lost lasso. Actually, in some ways, they were even better, since they offered disposable scaling lines of practically any length; the next descent the two men made, which proved to be their last, took them straight into a waterfall at a point where the brook leveled off and, for the first time, ran silent.

The trees, which had been such an obstacle in their downward climb, were now only a brooding presence, a screen marking the sides of the stream's avenue; and their endless greenery, as they crowded together, resulted in perpetual twilight, except when this deepened into complete darkness. But Nicolas and Lester could now move without encumbrance, walking knee deep, sometimes waist deep, in the brook until it joined another and the resulting stream became too deep and strong for wading. When this entered a dark river, a lonely tree-haunted river at the bottom of a canyon, the lianas which hung from many of the trees became useful in a new sense—as binding for the raft the two men managed to hack from light *topa* trunks.

Since they had no machetes, it took them all morning to chop six sections of smooth *topa* logs, each some ten feet in length, with their bowie knives. These they laid side by side in a calm eddy of the stream with two crosspieces of heavier wood fore and aft, lashing each log to either crosspiece. "We can't help reaching civilization before long," Nicolas said, as the raft came clear of a battering descent of rapids and they saw the river ahead lie unobstructed. "Surely we've advanced far enough around the top of the Macizo de Tocate to come out by one of the other rivers, the Ticumpenía or Timpía."

"Bet you that dollar you owe me this is still the Paucartambo," Lester retorted. "No other river would have the deliberate malignancy to hold us in one place like this."

"Are you crazy?"

But it was true. The river was holding them in one place—on a flat expanse of water which revolved as though it were a wheel. "Good God, this isn't possible," groaned Nicolas, the third or fourth time the raft had gone around after he had begun to watch. On the smooth surface of the water no circle was visible, but it was there and they were caught on it. It projected halfway out into the river from the left bank, while the righthand half of the river flowed freely along. Lester began to pole frantically with the slender tree trunk, which had served him as a paddle, in an effort to slide the raft into the unimpeded current, but Nicolas' hands were so lacerated that he could only scoop at the water in an ineffectual way. Whenever they were within a few feet of success, the greater revolving force pulled them back. On the shoreward side of the circle, they sometimes floated close enough to touch but not to grab the rock wall, which had been cut into a marble-smooth half cylinder by centuries of running water; and, as Lester paddled more and more furiously in an effort to free the raft, his pole slipped from his grasp. . . .

Daylight faded and rain came with nightfall, as the two men sat helplessly huddled together, each a silent prey to increasingly depressing thoughts. Lester had confidently boasted, when he lashed the raft together with lianas, that they would hold forever. But continuous bumping over the rocks of the rapids had loosened the vines and now he could feel the logs shifting uneasily. If this went on, he reflected gloomily, the whole raft might come apart under them; hastily, he tried to secure the lianas more tightly. Instead, he succeeded in loosening some of them still further and breaking the one by which Nicolas' boots were held, and these floated away.

By morning, the rains had raised the level of the river and suddenly their turntable became a mere curve in the current, carrying the raft rapidly downstream with it. Unexpectedly, as they raced through the misty dawn, a whole army of parrots and macaws and orioles took off before them in separate squadrons. No wonder the Inca was interested in this zone, Nicolas thought, as terraces came into sight along the shore; proof positive of how far the Inca reached for tribute; colored feathers were more prized than gold. And these terraces were cultivated. Where there were terraces still under cultivation, there would be farms. Where there were farms, there would be human beings, succor, food, shelter. Nicolas flung up his arms and shouted aloud in triumph.

"We've made it! This is it! Now we've only to reach the shore!"

As he spoke, the damaged raft fell apart beneath them, hurling them, amidst the rocks, into the wild stream. The violent current rushed them past the first clearing; then, on a curve of the canyon, they were caught in a friendly eddy and brought, without effort, to a bank where two dugout canoes were tied. By first grabbing and then clinging to these, they managed to reach the shore, hallooing as they struggled out of the water. Their call was almost immediately answered, and they saw a bevy of small Indian boys running toward them, with dogs leaping at their sides, and then men and women coming from a nearby hut. Lester rushed forward, so eager to proclaim both their desperate need for food and their harmless intentions, that he did not realize Nicolas was no longer close beside him until he heard a loud cry of pain and turned to look back.

Stepping ashore, Nicolas had received a lashing wound, deep in his right instep, from a stingray.

26꙰

Nicolas seemed to be rising from some great depth, rising and then sinking again and, somewhere along the line, he must be hitting his foot against a hard substance, because otherwise why should such sharp shooting pains be coming from it? Could it be a well that engulfed him and, if so, what was he doing in it? No, it could not be a well, for, in that case, he would be dripping wet, he would feel the water streaming off him, he would be choked by it. Of course, it might be an abandoned well, one that had long since fallen into disuse; but this would not explain his presence there, rising and falling, rising and falling again, and hitting his foot against its stone wall.

He had not tried to open his eyes, while this strange sensation obsessed him, but now that it seemed less potent, he was trying to struggle toward clearer thought and more rational feeling. He realized then that he was not going up and down in a well, but lying on something indefinable, but solid and secure. He put out his hands and touched a fabric of some sort, coarse and cool, and it lay firmly on something else —whatever it was that he himself was lying on. Then somebody took hold of one of his questing hands and held it in a firm but gentle grasp. It was when Nicolas felt this grasp that he opened his eyes and groped for recognition of the face belonging to the man who was bending over him. It was—no, it couldn't be—yes, it was—that Dominican he had met at Marina's luncheon a thousand years ago and to whom he had taken an unreasoning dislike. Fray Gregorio, was that his name?

"Where am I?" Nicolas muttered thickly.

"In the Dominican Hospital at Quillabamba, my son."

"Why?"

"Because you were wounded on the instep by a stingray and the wound became infected. And, before that, you had suffered other injuries."

"When did all this happen?"

"In the weeks after your fall. You fell with a landslide."

A landslide—yes, he was beginning to remember now. He had fallen and fallen, not in imagination as he had just been doing, down a deep well, but in reality with a landslide. Then he had lost consciousness. Presently, he had realized that Lester was there, too. Then they had started down a ravine and had finally reached a river. They had made a raft which fell to pieces and by-and-by they had reached a farm where they had been kindly received and fed on *yuca*. But, in the meantime, they had been very hungry. Somewhere he had gashed his right hand and been wounded by a stingray and after that there had been a great deal of pain followed by helplessness and repeated waves of unconsciousness. He had lain in a hut, which had a roof but no walls, so that it was open to wind and rain and his bed had been merely a palm mat on a mud floor. The occupants of this hut and, apparently, others near by were tame Machiguengas, very friendly and merry, but unintelligible to him when they talked to each other in their strange dialect. They could (when they felt like it) understand both Spanish and Quechua; but it was not until they realized how much the lack of communication troubled their sick guest that they softened.

Nicolas knew he had lain in the hut for a long time and then he had been lifted on the back of a mule and in that way transported somewhere, evidently to this hospital, though he had a dim recollection of other places along the way. But how long that had taken and where he had been in the meanwhile, he had no idea. He knew he must have been very feverish, for he remembered feeling as if he were burning up; and probably he had been delirious, too, though of course he would not know about that. . . .

He tried to organize his thoughts so all this would be clear to him and the effort made him drowsy. He did his best to fight off this drowsiness because he did not want to feel, again, that he was rising and falling in a well and hitting his foot against something that hurt. But, this time, instead of dreaming about a well, he dreamed about a landslide and that he was worrying about something which had no direct connection with the question of mere survival, which was the only big question at that crucial moment. And then suddenly he remembered what it was: he had thought he had been mortally injured in the fall and that he would die without knowing whether or not he and Margaret were to have a son. He still did not know. The Dominican had told him where he was and why and he was slowly beginning to understand about all that; but he still did not know about Margaret and the baby and, as of now, *this* was really the most important question, just as he had thought it was before. He opened his eyes again. The Dominican was still sitting quietly beside him.

"How long have I been here, Father?"

"Several weeks."

"And you said the stingray and other injuries happened in the weeks before that, after the landslide. That was some time in December—I think. So now it's what? January?"

"A good guess. It's February, but only early February—the fifth, to be exact."

"February!"

"Is there something about the month of February which is especially displeasing to you, my son?"

"It isn't that. It's—it's—"

He tried to go on and found that he could not. He would not have known how to explain to a priest about Margaret and the baby, even if his mind had been entirely clear, even if speech had come easily to him: he did not see how a priest could understand this yearning for a wife and an unborn child. But while he was struggling for expression, Fray Gregorio spoke again.

"Perhaps I can help you, my son. Our mutual friends have told me you were married shortly before you left the States. Of course, you are distressed because you have not heard from your wife and at the thought of her anxiety and the harm this might do her if she had not heard from you. I assure you she has been advised that you are safe and that we have every reason to believe you are on the road to recovery. And we have letters from her to you."

"You have letters *here* from my wife? How on earth—"

"It seems you wrote her from Paucartambo and told her to address you at the University of Cuzco. At Cuzco they heard when you were brought here and, as some letters were already awaiting you, these were sent on immediately by messenger. Others have arrived since. There has been no problem. Perhaps you did not remember that Ildefonso Parra has a tea plantation near here. Although Marina never comes here on account of the primitive conditions and the insects, Fonso is among our most congenial neighbors and one of the most liberal supporters of the Mission—that is why I always manage to see him and his wife whenever I go to Lima; and when Ildefonso is here I see him often—more frequently than ever these days, because, naturally, he is much concerned about you. And then there is your faithful secretary, Lester Wendell, who has never left Quillabamba since he brought you here to us. At first, he stayed at the little hotel, but we invited him to move to La Granja, our primitive Polytechnic Institute. He comes twice a day to inquire for you. Tomorrow, if you continue to improve, perhaps our mission doctor will permit you to see him."

"I want to see him very much. But first—first I must see those letters!"

"Yes, of course. If you do not feel their contents will be so private that you would not wish anyone but yourself to see them, I will read them to you—gradually. Or, if you would rather wait and read them yourself, I will ask our mission doctor how soon he will permit you to do so."

"You wouldn't let me read one—just one, right away, without waiting to ask him? A Christmas letter?"

Fray Gregorio appeared to hesitate, but only for a moment. Then he asked a question.

"You were married when, Nicolas?"

"On the tenth of November."

"But, if I am not mistaken, it was on the sixteenth of November that I met you at Marina's luncheon. Do you mean to tell me you left for Peru five days after your marriage?"

"Yes."

"Was that wise—or kind?"

"No. It wasn't either wise or kind. But that is what I did. I didn't care whether it was or not. I didn't realize beforehand how much I was going to love my wife. I married her because I wanted a son—that was the only reason, at first. But I've missed her so that, until you drugged all the desire out of me, I thought I'd go crazy. And now I think I'll die if I don't know she's all right."

The words came tumbling from his lips so fast he could not stop them. He did not try to stop them. He could not tell what impelled him to bare his heart in this way to a man whom he thought he disliked, a man who, only a moment before, had questioned the wisdom and kindness of his conduct. He only knew the need of confession was so great it could not be denied. He did not guess that Fray Gregorio had listened to such outbursts hundreds of times before, both under the seal of sacramental secrecy and without it.

"I have the letters here with me," Nicolas heard the Dominican saying quietly. "I think this is the one you want first—it is postmarked Woodstock, Vermont, December twenty-fourth. There, I will slit it open for you and spread out the pages. Let me prop you up a little, so you can see to read. You are right. We should not wait to ask the doctor and when your nurse comes back we will not tell her what we have done. We will be very quick and you will know what is in your letter before anyone can stop us!"

Nicolas took the letter with fingers that were trembling with more than weakness and read it with vision so blurred he was obliged to keep laying it down to wipe the tears from his eyes. But, long before he had finished, his heart was bounding with joy.

"Dearest Nicolas:

"This is the happiest Christmas Eve of my life. If only you were here, it would be a perfect Christmas Eve. But then, nothing is ever *quite* perfect, is it? Even in those five days and nights we had together there were what you called some bad moments, and I'm glad there were, because, otherwise, I never would have known the supreme joy of all the rest. So some day perhaps I'll understand why it was better that Christmas should be this way, too—I mean, why we should be separated by thousands of miles, instead of being close together, why you won't even get this letter with all its good news until long after New Year's.

"As you'll see by the postmark, I followed your suggestion and their urgent invitation and came to spend Christmas with your family. (I came for Thanksgiving, too, and *what* Thanksgivings you New Englanders do put on!) I have brought Perdita—who goes almost wild with joy over the snow—with me both times and, this trip, I brought the *nacimiento* you sent and which arrived most opportunely. Better still, I was able to bring them the same good news I am sending you: Dr. Loomis says there is not the slightest doubt in his mind that I am going to have a baby.

"Of course, there never was the slightest doubt in my mind, anyhow. I'm not going to remind you when I told you I knew, because I'm sure you'll never forget about that, or anything connected with it, any more than I shall. But I realize feminine intuition isn't always considered reliable, so I began going to Dr. Loomis as soon as I had a sound reason for believing I was pregnant and that wasn't because I kept fainting away or losing my breakfast or anything unpleasant like that. I never felt so well since I can remember and your mother and father and the twins all agree I look a hundred per cent better than I did at the time of the wedding. (And why shouldn't I, now that I'm no longer a desiccated old maid, with nothing to look forward to except a long succession of barren years, but a triumphant married woman, who's proved her capacity for fertility almost overnight—well, anyway, within three nights, if my hunch is right—and who knows all the rest of her life is going to be rich and rewarding?)

"I would like to have our baby at Hills' End, since that is where all the babies of my family have been born for generations, but Dr. Loomis is insisting I should go to a hospital and has made the reservation for August 5th, just in case Nicolas, Jr. should take it into his head to hurry into the world a little earlier than he's expected, which it seems sometimes happens. Under the circumstances, it's to be hoped he doesn't decide to come very early because, after all, we did get married in a great rush and some horrid old gossip would start saying, after she counted on her fingers, etc., etc. And when everything is so beautiful and normal and—yes, I'm going to say perfect, I'd hate to have that happen, wouldn't you?

"Of course, your parents are thrilled at the prospect of their first grandchild and your mother is planning to come and stay with me, in the good old-fashioned way, when the baby is born. The twins are also terribly excited about being aunts. And, speaking of the twins, did you get the impression that Clarissa and Lester were getting along extremely well together and that something might come of that, too?

"I'm going to save all the rest of the news for my next letter, since anything else would be an anticlimax after what I've just told you. Tomorrow, when we all go to church together, and hear those wonderful words, 'For unto us a child is born, unto us a son is given,' they'll have a new meaning for us. We'll be thinking not only of the Divine Child, about Whom that was written, but about our own, given to us because we followed our Heavenly Father's command to become one flesh and whom we must teach to follow in His Son's footsteps.

"With all my love, your wife
"Margaret."

When the letter fell from Nicolas' trembling hands, he was weeping almost uncontrollably. But Fray Gregorio recognized the tears as those of joy even before Nicolas muttered, "It's all the best, the very best in the world, the best it could be. But tell me, Father, isn't there some way I could get a message to my wife, I mean right away, so she'll know I've had this letter and how happy it's made me?"

The Dominican appeared to ponder. "If you will tell me what you want to say, I will send someone with the message up to Huadquiña, where there is a railroad telephone," he said presently. "There they can telephone into Cuzco and from Cuzco it can be telephoned to Lima where it can be cabled. Would that do?"

"It would be wonderful. I want to say, 'Christmas letter joyfully received. I am safe, I am getting well and your news makes me supremely happy. If it were possible for me to love you more than I did already, I should do so now.' Is that too much? I don't mean would that be too expensive, I don't care what it costs; I mean, is it too much for all the people who'll have to read it to get it straight?"

Fray Gregorio smiled. "I'm afraid it may be, but we will do our best with it. If we make a few mistakes, I believe the general purport of it will still be clear to your wife. Now you must get some sleep and, when you wake, you must make the acquaintance of your doctor and your nurse and show yourself a tractable patient, so that you will make more rapid progress from now on. But I shall soon be coming to see you again and we will have another talk. Meanwhile, God bless you and keep you—you and the wife you love so dearly and the child who is to be the precious first fruit of this love."

He raised his hand in blessing and, as he did so, Nicolas noticed, for the first time, the glitter of a great ring. "I shouldn't have called you

Father, should I?" he asked apologetically. "I should have said Excellency or *Monseñor*. But I didn't know. Were you always a bishop? I mean, when I met you before, weren't you just Fray Gregorio?"

"Yes, Nicolas. It is only since then that I have been called on to succeed the very great and good man we have lost here at Quillabamba. And it is quite all right for you to call me Father. After all, I call you my son."

He smiled and turned away. As Nicolas watched the departing figure, still simply clad in graceful black and white Dominican robes, he wondered how he could ever have thought he did not like this man, whom he was now very close to loving. But his wonderment did not keep him wakeful. This time, he did not try to fight off drowsiness, but sank gratefully into it and slept dreamlessly for a long while. When he waked, he had no sense of strangeness in his surroundings; the wide window spaces, the walls of slates, the tin roof, all seemed vaguely familiar. The nurse, Sister Teresa, came in and she, too, looked vaguely familiar; Nicolas wondered how often she had ministered to him in various ways: a stocky, capable Dominican nun, the type who, had she been an English Sister, would have told him plainly that she did not propose to put up with any nonsense. She now fed him broth, scooping the last spoonful from the bowl and watching him while he swallowed it. Then she left briskly, to look after the other patients in the ward: three Machiguengas, one fighting a losing battle against snakebite; one who had traveled on a raft with a missionary family and caught a child's cold, which had quickly become pneumonia; and one who seemed to be making a slow but satisfactory recovery from tuberculosis. Before she left the ward, Dr. Castel, a tall, bearded lay surgeon, arrived and she returned to Nicolas' side and stood by, the personification of efficiency, while he examined his patient and made a guarded report of his findings.

"You are certainly very much better," the doctor said in a tone of relief. "I think we can at last dismiss the fear of gangrene. I assure you, it has been a very great fear and it would have meant amputation."

"Yes, I know. And that, in turn, would have meant the end of exploring—the kind to which I'm committed."

"Exactly. I'm glad to see you can face facts. Therefore, I shall go on to tell you that there is no reason, as conditions now stand, to suppose your days of exploring are over for good; but they are certainly over for the first half of this year. The stingray slashed to the bone, which was thus exposed and which became infected and it was a long while before you had proper treatment."

"What happened in the meantime?"

"Lester Wendell left you at Cahuide Farm on the Yavero River, where you got ashore, and went to the nearest mission, Chirumbia on the Urubamba, for a mule. It took him four days to reach there and, of course, the same length of time to get back to Cahuide. Then, with you lying helpless on the mule, more time was used for the return to Chirumbia. We have no hospital there, so the next step was to get you to Quillabamba. There's a good trail, on the right bank of the Urubamba, so after that was reached, you were within two days of your journey's end, and that last lap was made partly on a truck, instead of on muleback. Just the same, unless there's something wrong with my arithmetic, two weeks were used up between the time Wendell left Cahuide to get the mule and you were finally lifted out of the truck at the door of the hospital. So, even without counting the time at the farm, I think you'll agree you went quite a little while without medical attention."

Nicolas was sure that his own arithmetic, as well as his geography, was unreliable on these various points, but that did not matter. He and Lester would straighten them out together later on. What did matter was that he was getting better, despite the long neglect of the infection. He asked for further reassurance and Dr. Castel supplied it.

"The infection is now subsiding and we can look for a slow healing process. You will not be able to walk normally for at least a month; you may be able to hobble around with a crutch before then if, in the meantime, you take all the rest you need. You have more than the stingray from which to recover. Besides, there were wounds made by thorns, which were neglected so long they became infected. Then there was near starvation followed by malnutrition; *yuca* is not the best possible diet for a fever patient. And, finally, there was such complete exhaustion that this in itself might have meant a very long period of convalescence to a man less vigorous than you are. I must congratulate you on your physique."

"Thanks. . . . So this fine physique might enable me to start hobbling around, as you call it, about the first of March and perhaps have me walking normally by the first of April?"

"Yes. And I should think you might leave here by May, provided you had comfortable means of transportation and that you did not try to cover immense distances."

"All right, I'll agree to your schedule if you'll also agree to something. There are a number of letters here from my wife. So far, I've seen only one of them. I want very much to see the others."

"Well, if you do the reading a little at a time—"

"I don't know just what you mean by that, but if I find I'm getting tired, I'll stop and rest before I go on. I also want very much to see my secretary, Lester Wendell. I understand he's staying at La Granja, that he's been coming faithfully to see me every day, all the time I've been unconscious or delirious or whatever. I probably wouldn't be alive at all if it weren't for him. He followed me when I left camp—"

"Yes, I've already heard the story. There's no doubt he deserves a tremendous amount of credit. I can understand that you want to express your gratitude and also to review with him the details of your joint adventure which still aren't wholly clear to you. At the same time, I must urge you to conserve your strength."

"It'll be easier for me to do that when the clarification you just mentioned has taken place. Moreover, I'd like enormously to find out what happened to the rest of my expedition when Lester and I started, quite accidentally, on this great tangent of ours. I haven't had a report on that yet, either."

"Then let me relieve your mind on that score immediately. Your other companions all made their way safely back to Cuzco. Dr. Gomara and Mr. Hart have taken a house there and have installed Li Chan as their cook. They are all in good health and, as soon as you are well enough to see them, they will come here to visit you and receive your instructions as to what you would like to have them do next. Meanwhile, they charged us here to tell you the flag of the Explorers Club is safe. They had to abandon a good deal of their equipment because, for a long while, they had no carriers. But that flag never went out of Gomara's keeping. It's standing, furled, in a corner of his room at Cuzco, waiting for you to fly it again."

For the second time that day, Nicolas' vision became blurred with tears and for several minutes he did not trust himself to speak. Then, in a fairly steady voice, he said, "That's good news. I hope you'll let me see Gomara soon, but meantime, can't I see Lester Wendell?"

"Yes, tomorrow, if I find, when I come to see you then, that you have continued to improve as much as I expect."

"And what am I to do the rest of today?"

"Lie still and think about that letter from your wife. I have no doubt you'll sneak another look at it when you're not being watched. I've got forty patients here, some of them desperate cases. I can't give any one of them as much individual attention as I'd like, even with all the co-operation I get from the good Sisters. And, believe me, you've been monopolizing a great deal of my time for a long while now."

He nodded and went on to the next bed, with Sister Teresa trotting along beside him. Evidently, the poor Machiguenga who was suffering from snakebite was a very sick man, sicker than Nicolas liked to think. Here he was, making a good recovery, lying in comparative ease with Margaret's letter under his pillow and the prospect of reading other letters and seeing Lester the next day. An afternoon rainstorm made a rattling attack on the corrugated roof and the loudspeaker in the street outside announced a change in the movie program for the next day: *The Red Rider,* episodes seven, eight and nine; come one, come all. None of this was disturbing or distressing. Nicolas slept again.

27

When Nicolas woke, it was morning again, a beautiful clear morning that gave promise of many good things. The first of these was breakfast, a real breakfast of papaya with lime juice, tea from the Parras' plantation and fresh-baked bread with cottage cheese that the nuns had made themselves. He persuaded Sister Teresa to let him feed himself and, while he was eating, he reread Margaret's letter, which seemed even more wonderful to him the second time than it had the first. Next there was a bath of sorts and a clean hospital shirt and the promise of the shave and the haircut which he wanted so much, for he would never feel really clean until he had them; and, by that time, he was ready to drowse again, without urging, straight through to dinnertime. Dinner was the white meat of chicken, finely minced into white rice, with just enough cream sauce to moisten it and make it tasty, and more tea to wash it down. And then, before he quite willingly took another nap, he read the letter Margaret had written early in January, after her return from Woodstock.

She was still in the best of health and—except for missing him—in the best of spirits. She went regularly to church, she had resumed her work for the Altar Guild, and she was enjoying the meetings of the Garden Club, which was already beginning to plan its spring program. She had been asked if she would be willing to have Hill's End included in the tour of historic houses during Garden Week and she had given an enthusiastic consent, after first consulting Dr. Loomis, who had agreed, without the slightest urging, that the effort would not be too much for her. But her interests and occupations were by no means wholly local any more. The Herberts had given her a standing invitation to their Sunday night suppers and she had compromised by saying she would go there every fortnight, but that on the alternate Sundays she would have parties herself. Gordon Holmes was still pursuing his research of Virginia butterflies and, though Margaret could not understand how he could be doing so very successfully at that time of year, he seemed to think it was better to stay in one locality, namely the one where he was, rather than to keep going from place to place.

Besides, he was actually planning to do what Nicolas had jokingly
suggested: that is, to make an especially intensive study in Fairfax
County; he was a frequent and welcome caller at Hills' End. Margaret
had been to a farewell tea in honor of Manuela Reeves, the President of
the Woman Geographers, who was just starting off for some jungle
herself, but there had been such a confusion of voices, with all the
Geographers talking at once, that it had not been clear to Margaret
whether this was in Peru or elsewhere. She had been to the opening of
Congress, as the guest of Mrs. LaGuarde, and afterward they had had
lunch in the Senate restaurant with Mrs. LaGuarde's father, Senator Powers, and several other senators. Senator Powers was simply
charming, he must have been a real heartbreaker in his youth. Margaret
was enclosing a clipping from the *Star* with Betty Beale's account of
the opening; Nicolas would see that she—Margaret—was mentioned as
among those present in the Senator's Gallery. And, oh yes—she was
invited to the Diplomatic Dinner at the White House on the twenty-
sixth and she was going to wear that gold brocade Esther had given her
for her trousseau. It was a sheath and she had been a little afraid she
might not be able to get into it by the end of January, but there had
not been any visible change in her figure so far and Dr. Loomis had said
there would not be for another month at least and even then it would
be very slight. With the brocade, she was going to wear the beautiful
aquamarines which Nicolas had sent her—the gold of the dress and the
blue of the stones set each other off. Esther kept teasing her to come up
to New York and perhaps, just for the sake of peace, she might do so a
little later on; but really, she was finding life so exciting where she was
that she hadn't the slightest desire to go anywhere else. Right now, she
was closing her letter because Mrs. Bruce, who was prettier than ever,
was having an At Home that afternoon and had asked Margaret to pour
from six to six-thirty. Then she and the other pourers would stay on for
an informal supper party afterward and the Vice President and the
Speaker of the House would both be there. . . .

Nicolas smiled when he read the letter and he was still smiling when
he fell asleep again. How quickly Margaret was finding her way back to
the social scene from which she had withdrawn because of her father's
death and her mother's invalidism, and how easily and well she fitted
into it! But she was still a good deal of an ingénue. Obviously, it did
not occur to Margaret that Gordon Holmes' continued interest in the
butterflies of Virginia might have anything to do with her. Well, the
biologist would be as harmless a *cavaliere servente* as could be imagined
and certainly Nicolas could not expect her to be without one—or more
—throughout his long absences. As a matter of fact, Senator Powers,
who was a widower and indeed a charmer, might be more of a menace
to a distant husband's peace of mind; his heartbreaking ventures were

not all in the past, according to reliable rumor. The next letter—or the next one after that—would probably tell about the White House dinner. Nicolas was glad Margaret was going to wear the gold sheath with his aquamarines. She would look beautiful. But then she had looked beautiful in everything she wore, once he had got her out of those dreadful old black sacks she had been wearing at first. And he would be pleased, rather than otherwise, when her figure did begin to change, because that would mean . . .

He drifted off into happy dreams of all it would mean and when he woke again Lester was sitting beside his bed, good old Lester, looking better than Nicolas had ever seen him look, and that was not only because of the joy in seeing him, but because the boy had begun to fill out, on the good food he was getting at La Granja, and had more color in his face, too, not to mention a very broad smile, instead of a hesitant shy one. Because there was so much they wanted to say to each other, they had hard work knowing where to begin; and, actually, Nicolas started by saying what seemed to Lester quite inconsequential: he must not forget to write Margaret about all those butterflies they had seen in the jungle. As Nicolas had hardly appeared to notice the butterflies when they were in the jungle, Lester did not immediately see the connection and said so; so then they both laughed and Nicolas told Lester about Margaret's letters and read him the paragraph about Clarissa in the first one. Well, the boy had not forgotten how to blush, despite his astonishing advance toward maturity; he turned a deep crimson and stammered something unintelligible but happy and then they were off to other topics.

"Now that I'm so much better, you ought to get to Cuzco once in a while. You were cheated out of seeing anything of it the day we were there, between Lima and Paucartambo, because you were so deathly sick; and you were tremendously interested in the colonial architecture —at least, that's what you told me beforehand. Besides, I understand Gomara and Pete have taken a house there; you could stay with them and a pleasant time would be had by all. I want them to come out here, too, as soon as I'm allowed more callers."

"Until then, there's all the more reason why I should stay here. Besides, I thought that presently you might like to dictate a little— letters and things like that, the parts that weren't too private. You could fill in the other parts by hand."

"Excellent idea. I understand the message I sent yesterday went off by personal messenger to Huadquiña, forty kilometers from here, and from there by railroad telephone to Cuzco, from Cuzco to Lima by regular telephone and, finally, by cable from Lima. The bishop admitted it might get slightly garbled along the way. I'd forgotten that Lima and Tacna are the only two cities in Peru where you can send a cable. My family's going to find that hard to believe and so will Margaret. You might drop a few lines to them, explaining the situation. As far as I know, there isn't any little one-horse town in either Vermont or Virginia where you can't send a cable if you feel like it. When you get to Cuzco, you can reduce this complicated Peruvian system of transmission by one half and that'll be all to the good. Also, I could give you a list of presents I want to give Margaret and you could get them for me. So I really think you'd better go."

"If there were just one other person to drop in on you, I wouldn't hesitate so much."

"What do you mean, one other person? There's the bishop, and he's very much of a person, in case you haven't discovered it. And there are three full-fledged priests, three lay brothers and nine nuns here besides. I'll gradually get to be friends with all of them. Moreover, I shouldn't be surprised if Fonso turned up here, too. In fact, I wish you'd telephone him and ask him if he couldn't make a special trip, if necessary, so that I can get the clothes I left at his house. Naturally, I don't mean white ties and tails or even dinner jackets, but just about everything else. One of the major confessions I felt compelled to make, when I married, was that I have very expensive tastes when it comes to dress, and that these tastes include an addiction to custom-made pajamas of Italian silk. I've had enough of these scratchy hospital shirts to last me a long while and, when I start getting out of bed, I'll need a dressing gown and slippers, even before I can get into tailor-mades."

Lester could not suppress a smile; there was certainly more than a touch of the paradoxical in Nicolas' tastes and habits; he was willing to wear sweat socks, corduroy pants, a khaki shirt and a leather windbreaker, with a minimum of washable underwear, for weeks, even months on end, when these were indicated because of exploratory conditions; but the minute he returned to civilization, even civilization as represented by a jungle mission hospital, he wanted the ultimate in luxurious wearing apparel. Nicolas saw the smile and laughed.

"All right, set me down as a disciple of Beau Brummell, instead of a disciple of Hiram Bingham, if you want to," he said good naturedly. "As a matter of fact, Bingham has always been extremely well turned out himself, whenever I've seen him. So attend to that telephone call as soon as you get to Cuzco. Incidentally, I've been thinking a good deal about Fonso lately. It seems he comes quite often to his tea plantation near here, but that Marina never does."

"Surely you don't think there's a rift there?"

"Oh, no! But the bishop says a Lima wife—I mean a wife in the Parras' social bracket—wouldn't think of coming to a place like Quillabamba. Of course, there are all kinds of plausible reasons: they have a large urban establishment that requires her constant supervision, not to mention a large family ditto. But I can't help suspecting that the prevalence of insects and the absence of diversions may have something to do with the situation, too—not to mention the wretched railroad down from Cuzco; and I keep remembering that Margaret would have gone anywhere in the world with me, if I'd only have taken her, whatever the hardships were that she had to face. It's my own fault she isn't here with me right now."

"Then why not send for her?"

"Don't believe for a moment that I haven't thought of that, too—with a good deal of longing. But I don't want her making bumpy landings in airplanes and riding over rough roads this year. So the next best thing is to keep as closely in touch with her as I can. When you come to see me tomorrow, I'll have another short circuit message to send and when you get back from Cuzco I may be up to dictating. But I'm afraid I'm not, just yet. I seem to want to sleep most of the time. And I'm working up quite an appetite, too—for something besides *yuca*."

"What about chonta?"

"Well, I still think quite tenderly of that. I'll never eat another hearts of palm salad without remembering the one luncheon of our trip. And another thing I like remembering is those brilliant birds we saw over the river one day at dawn, that whole army of parrots and macaws and orioles."

"What about our host the first night? Do you think tenderly of him? Was he really a jaguar?"

"I don't think tenderly of him and I'm positive he was a jaguar. No puma ever smelled quite that bad or growled quite that loud."

"I'm sorry you never had a chance to get acquainted with our *real* hosts, the ones at Cahuide Farm. They were awfully kind to us. I can't say I greatly enjoyed drinking *masato* from the gourd that served as a loving cup. It was bad enough to watch our male hosts drinking out of it first, without knowing that our female hosts had prepared it by munching *yuca* until this formed a paste and then mixing it with water as needed. But no one could say I wasn't game. I'm all in favor of observing local rules for etiquette. But I had a good time fishing and swimming and there was one Machiguenga girl, plump and giggly, that seemed quite ready to be my personal guide, both in public and in private."

"Since you're so strong on local etiquette, I gather you didn't take advantage of this readiness."

"No—not unduly. Someone warned me that might be inadvisable."

"The understatement of the year. Now, if you don't mind, I wish you'd set me straight as to just where that farm was and how we got from there to here."

"Well, you know our old friend, the Paucartambo, becomes the Yavero after a while. Same river, different name, just the way the streets act up in Lima and throw you off from block to block, because you can't imagine what became of the one you were on. And by-and-by the Yavero flows into the Urubamba—of course, you know that. Cahuide is located just a little way above that confluence. Seems it was established about fifty years ago by merchants whose interest in the zone was the collection of wild rubber by Machiguengas. When the boom collapsed, the settlement dwindled. . . . My, but this is a proud moment for me, teaching you something!"

"I am very sorry, *Señor* Hale, but I must ask *Señor* Wendell to leave you now. It is again time for you to take nourishment."

Sister Teresa had come upon them unperceived while they were deep in reminiscence. But now she spoke with a degree of authority which both men knew it would be hopeless to dispute. They nodded good-by to each other and, as Nicolas humped himself up on his pillow, in order to hold his tray more easily, he noticed, for the first time, that the bed next to him was empty.

"Where's my neighbor?" he inquired casually, as he looked with appreciation at the eggs and orange juice on his tray.

"It is to be hoped he is with God and I believe he is," Sister Teresa said soberly. "He was a good boy, one of our best for carrying messages. He died in the night. Often there is no recovery from the bite of a bushmaster."

Nicolas was happily surprised to find that the days in bed did not drag at all. During the intervals between eating and sleeping and reading and rereading Margaret's letters, he enjoyed his visits from the bishop and the doctor, both of whom he found he had reason to like and admire, though he enjoyed them more when they visited him separately than when they came together. On the latter occasions, they fell into juvenile jibes at each other's *procedencia*. The Basques, to hear the doctor, were a tribe of heavy-footed fools; the Catalans, to hear the bishop, a nation of shopkeepers.

One day the two were engaged in banter of this sort beside Nicolas' bed, when a barefoot man stole noiselessly up behind them, without coming into their sight, and they were startled by the sudden exclamation, "Franco was wrong to keep either Catalans or Basques in the country at all!" Having made this authoritative statement, the newcomer burst into their midst and went down on his right knee to kiss the bishop's ring before rising to exchange a hearty *abrazo* with *Monseñor* and then another, even more enthusiastic, with the doctor. Both bishop and doctor were obviously delighted to see this man and simultaneously began a rapid fire of questions in which his answers:

". . . started out from . . . never again. . . ." were more or less
engulfed. Meanwhile, Nicolas, whom the three Spaniards quite ignored
while catching up among themselves, was completely in the dark as to
the significance of this strange encounter; and, as he studied the newcomer—a man of medium build and commonplace features, remarkable
only for his scarecrow appearance—he was perplexed as to why the two
dignitaries should make so much of him. Some moments elapsed before
the bishop turned to Nicolas and, with no apology for the delay,
introduced him as Antonio Astur, with no further identification than
that supplied by the comment that Franco's real trouble lay in having
been obliged to direct a war by relying on Royalist captains so
bloodthirsty by nature their natural habitat was the Amazon jungle.
Then all three left, arm in arm.

With his new found faculty for dropping off with every lull in the
conversation, Nicolas promptly fell asleep, to discover with interest
upon waking, that the bed next to his was no longer vacant and that
Antonio Astur, scarcely recognizable now that he had bathed and been
to the barber's, was its new occupant. He felt privileged, he said
pleasantly, to have this unexpected opportunity of making Dr. Hale's
acquaintance; he hoped the latter's health would permit them to while
away otherwise tedious hours with friendly talk. As far as he was
concerned, nothing much was the matter with him; he was only following Dr. Castel's advice that he should have bed rest while undergoing
certain tests for diet and resistance; and he would like to assure Dr.
Hale the bishop had jestingly misrepresented him: it was true that he
had been a Royalist officer in the Spanish Civil War; but it was not
true that he had come to the jungle because he was bloodthirsty. Quite
the contrary. He had had more than enough of bloodshed, not only on
the firing line, but on the home front. He had lost both his wife and his
child in a hideous way and he had come to the jungle not to destroy,
but to forget and to rebuild. He had taken his degree in Architectural
Engineering at the University of Barcelona and had begun the practice
of his profession in Madrid just before the beginning of the Civil War.
He had managed to cross the lines, he had served throughout the war,
and then he had left Spain to accept a position as Engineering
Consultant at the University of Buenos Aires, which he lost in the wave
of xenophobia after Perón became dictator. It was then he decided he
had had enough of so-called civilization, as well as bloodshed, and he
had come overland to Cuzco and Quillabamba, making friends at each
of the Dominican missions, all the way down the Lower Urubamba.
When he came to Atalaya, situated where two rivers meet and form the
great Ucayali, he settled down for good. His first activities had been in
logging virgin zones back along some Urubamba tributaries and, as this
had proven profitable, he intended to go on with it. But now that he

had acquired property in Atalaya and put up buildings, he hoped to expand further by raising Zebú cattle and utilizing the regions he had cleared for pasturelands. Among the buildings he had put up was a house, modern as to equipment, but, in architecture, an adaptation of native style, with a high thatched roof, open walls and a raised hardwood floor. He was planning to marry again, a river girl this time, of mixed Portuguese and Indian background. She had been to the local school maintained by the Franciscan nuns, she was sixteen, and she was very pretty. He was taking the marriage very seriously; that was why he had come all the way to Quillabamba, on purpose to ask the bishop to marry them. Atalaya belonged to a Franciscan missionary province, where Dominicans should not intrude, except for special occasions, because the different Orders were not without their jealousies, which was sometimes regrettable. But his marriage was to be a special occasion. He would be much honored if Dr. Hale would attend it.

At this point, Sister Teresa came in with her usual inexorable edict about the necessity for "nourishment" which, as a matter of fact, proved to be an appetizing supper, to which Nicolas did full justice. But he was sorry the conversation with Astur had been cut short; he had found it not only interesting, but exciting. He knew that even to go *down* the Urubamba was a sporting danger, that the foreigners who had done it were less than a dozen in fifty years, but no one had ever described to him a trip *up* the same river, and Astur had nonchalantly made it, not because he was an explorer, but because he was a prospective bridegroom and wanted his old friend, the bishop at Quillabamba, to officiate at his wedding! Nicolas waited, with ill-controlled impatience, to hear the details.

Astur was more than willing to oblige at the next opportunity for conversation. As he himself had said, he had hoped that talk with Nicolas might help him to while away many hours that, otherwise, might have been tedious; he was not even uncomfortable, much less really ill, therefore talking did not tire him; and he so quickly discovered a kindred spirit and a natural equal that they were soon using first names and the familiar *tú*. He had taken a month for his trip, he divulged, starting out from Atalaya with a heavy dugout canoe and a solid Evinrude motor. He left the outboard below the Pongo de Mainique—a deep gorge cut by the river through a wedge of rock, as Nicolas doubtless knew—and exchanged his heavy dugout for a light one, which he and the Machiguengas who were with him were scheduled to portage around the Pongo; but the Machiguengas, unpredictable as a jungle sky, simply vanished. So Astur had abandoned the dugout—since, of course, he could not carry it alone—and had come dragging along on foot in full flood season, up around the Pongo and other perilous places, with nothing left to sustain him except his dignity as an hidalgo and his determination to go to Quillabamba and personally ask the bishop to marry him.

Astur interrupted his narrative to give Nicolas some sound advice.

"Listen to me, *amigo*," he said earnestly, "it's a mistake to rely wholly on Machiguengas. They carry to perfection, but when you least expect it, if they encounter something they consider an obstacle, though you don't see it as such, they quit, they disappear without a word."

"So do the Queros," Nicolas replied in bitter reminiscence. "As far as I can make out, the only real difference between the two is that the Queros wear bright-colored, woollen ponchos and the Machiguengas wear striped brown cotton *cushmas,* which are shaped just like ponchos, but sewed together under the arms. We didn't have but one out of Paucartambo who had any conception of perseverance or loyalty and he was killed with a poisoned arrow by a Cogapacori scout. The bishop swears by Machiguengas and I know he's already begun collecting them for my next expedition. I'm afraid it's too late to change. If it isn't, what kind of carriers would you suggest, Antonio?"

"Mestizos—available along the Ucayali for cash. They're capable of hard work and much more trustworthy than the Machiguengas, except in one respect. I can get some for you if you want me to."

"What's the one respect?"

"In a Machiguenga camp, they go after the women."

"I don't want that kind of trouble," Nicolas said with finality. "I'm bound to have plenty of others. So I guess it's the Machiguengas for me."

Astur shrugged. "Just as you like. You asked, so I told you. As far as I'm concerned, I'm not going to depend on anyone but myself. I'm going to make the whole trip, both ways, by outboard motor the next time I come to Quillabamba."

"You're crazy."

"Maybe. Want to bet on it?"

Nicolas was perfectly willing to bet on it and when Astur left the next day, to return to Atalaya by trail, raft and dugout, they were still joking about their wager. Nicolas was sorry to see the Spaniard go and gave him a farewell *abrazo* of friendship. Astur had proved more than good company; he had made numerous observations, like the one about the mestizo carriers, which suggested future exploratory procedure; and he had given a picture of life in the jungle, only vicariously connected with exploration, which also furnished much food for thought. The chance acquaintance gave promise of a lasting association; certainly, if it were possible to attend the wedding, he would do so; if not, he would visit the newly-married couple later on; he wanted to see for himself this domestic establishment, this loyal and legal alliance between a man of culture and a river girl, which the former seemed so sure was to provide lasting happiness.

Nicolas missed his new-found friend, but now that his head was clear and he was relatively free from pain, he was beginning to make plans for the future. When Lester returned, full of enthusiasm over his visit to Cuzco, Nicolas was ready to discuss these with him.

"Dr. Castel says I'm doing fine, but he still insists I won't be doing much walking this season. So that set me to thinking about a new schedule—that and the remark you yourself made, a while back in Noche Triste, if we had an airplane and some parachutes at our disposal, we could be over the Macizo de Tocate in about five minutes."

"And so—" Lester asked excitedly.

"Well, we could do our organizing right here and we could begin now—or rather, as soon as Gomara and Pete can come up here and, as far as Dr. Castel is concerned, that could be next week. The expedition could start from here—part of it, anyway. The bishop tried to talk to me about a schedule like that, way back when he and I met at Marina's luncheon, and I shut him off, stupid boor that I was. But, since then, he and I have talked about it here."

"But I thought you said you wouldn't be able to walk, that is, any distance, this spring."

"I shan't. Gomara would be my deputy leader and Pete would be my second in command. That is, if I could wring a solemn promise from him that there'd be no benders. If he made a promise, I believe he'd keep it. But it would mean going on the wagon completely, all of you, so that he wouldn't be led into temptation. Would you mind?"

"I suppose I would, a little. But if that's what it took to keep Pete with us, I'd be willing. You'll be glad to know he and I have completely buried the hatchet."

"Good enough. Now another condition: you and Pete have got to talk Spanish, not once in a while, all the time, except when you and he are alone. I don't want any more bruised feelings about Anglo-Saxon superiority and gringo talk. Not that I feel it's justified, but there it is."

"Well, that condition doesn't frighten me, either. I've been studying hard all the time you've been laid up. I forgot to mention it before, but Fray Martín has been giving me lessons. He's an excellent teacher. I can burst out into Spanish any time you want me to, if you'll just steer clear of subjunctives and conditionals for a while longer. How Pete will feel, of course, I don't know, but, after all, he likes to talk and, if he finds all the rest is silence unless he bursts out into Spanish, too, my guess is that he'll do it."

"Right you are. . . . Well, besides you and Gomara and Pete, I think there'd better be some graduate students from the university, not professors this time. I think they'll have more staying power."

"Now it's my turn to say good enough and right you are."

"You'll have good Machiguenga Indians for carriers from the beginning. You'll leave here in May without me along; but I'll be here to see you and your Machiguengas and your mules get off to the right start."

"Not by truck this time?"

"The truck could be loaded aboard a freight car in Cuzco, off-loaded at Huadquiña and used locally here; but that hardly seems worth while when the Dominicans have offered not only the best Machiguengas, but the best mules. You'll go mounted for the first week, down into the jungle, up over a sharp ridge and down to the farm of Lacco, which overlooks the gorge of the River Paucartambo. Leaving the mules there, you'll cross the Paucartambo and start climbing. Personally, for old times' sake, you might keep an eye out for signs of our own recent transit. You'll make for the ridge top, and these Machiguengas seem to know an Inca way which we, with our sierra Indians, from Quero, missed. Sticking to the ridge top, you'll make your way north and, if the weather is good, as it mostly should be, you'll have two landmarks ahead—the heights of Tocate on the left and the ridge of Pantiacolla on the right. Like this!" He drew a piece of paper from the drawer of his bedside table and quickly made a little sketch, which he handed to Lester, who studied it and nodded. "Your principal concern," Nicolas

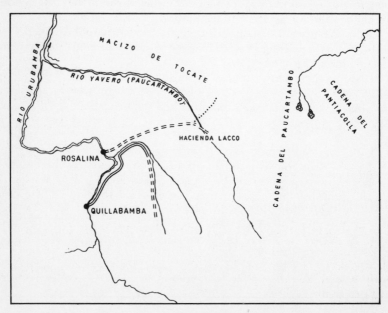

went on, "will be to find a lagoon somewhere on the heights of Pantiacolla and establish a base camp suitable for our future operations."

"And what will you be doing in the meanwhile?"

"I'll stay on here until late May, when Dr. Castel has promised to turn me loose to go home. Then I'll kiss you boys good-by until the first part of September—by which time I should be one hundred percent operational. I will come in by hydroplane from Atalaya to that lagoon where the rest of you will be. Then we'll begin to develop our plans to find the secret city."

"Better and better, the further you go. But what are you going to be doing between the time we leave here in May and before this pregnant meeting?"

"That, my dear friend, is exactly what I am coming to, in my usual dull slow fashion. Nothing could be more apt than your use of the word pregnant. I'm going home to be with my wife the last few months she is in this interesting condition. Your next job is to make a reservation for me with Panagra: Lima—Miami—Washington, late May. I shall hasten on to Virginia and remain there until I have welcomed my son and heir and seen him and his mother both safely back from the hospital and comfortably installed at Hills' End."

28

The sign, "No Smoking—Fasten Your Seat Belts," went off. Nicolas unbuckled the confining strap, lighted a cigarette, and settled back comfortably in his seat on the first lap of his homeward journey.

The fact that he was not especially tired, much less sleepy, was proof positive of his improved condition. Convalescence was behind him now; he limped very little when he walked; and he knew in years to come he would treasure the memory of the time he had spent among the Dominican Missionaries. They and their doctor, as well as their extraordinary guest, Antonio Astur, had been his prudent advisers and had become his firm friends. The longer he stayed with them, the more reason he had to respect and admire the work they were doing, for the material and physical, as well as the spiritual, welfare of the people who came to be nursed at their hospital and taught at their Polytechnic Institute and the girls' school supervised by the nine nuns who cooperated in their labors.

Fonso came to stay briefly at his tea plantation and brought with him the clothes which Nicolas had specified as necessities, to which, by way of emphasizing his opinion of his friend's foppish tastes, had been added a few extras of his own selection: pajamas printed with ballerinas, Gipsies and Eskimos; bed slippers fringed with small gilded bells; a dressing gown that shaded from bilious yellow to sickly green. Nicolas put them all on and demanded more of the same; Fonso had completely spoiled his hitherto conservative tastes, he complained. Sister Teresa received something of a shock when she saw her prize patient thus arrayed for the first time; but, to his surprise, she entered jovially into the jesting spirit of the occasion.

Pete had also come briefly to visit, insisting on making his headquarters at the hotel, though the hospitality of La Granja was offered him, just as it had been to Lester, who had so gratefully accepted it. There was nothing at La Granja, Pete insisted, that could lure him away from his enjoyment of the orange juice at the hotel; it was the best orange juice in the world and surely, since Nicolas had insisted he should go on the wagon, the former would not begrudge his second such an innocent beverage as orange juice. Was it really the orange juice that so intrigued him, Nicolas asked good-naturedly, or was it the spectacle of a small boy climbing the big tree in the patio, whenever Pete said he was thirsty, and throwing the fruit to a little girl who stood below, waiting to catch it in her apron? Well, perhaps that was partly the reason he wanted to stay where he was, Pete admitted; but certainly Nicolas should not begrudge him this source of innocent merriment, either. Nicolas laughed and said, hell no, he did not begrudge Pete anything, he was so damned glad to see him again.

When Pete had practically exhausted the hotel's supply of ripe oranges and his departure therefore seemed imminent, Nicolas persuaded Dr. Castel this would be a propitious time for his own trip to Cuzco: Lester hesitated to interrupt his conscientious studies with Fray Martín; and Pete would be a made-to-order companion for the journey and host for the visit. So he, like Lester before him, enjoyed a sojourn in the charming old house with the three-foot walls and the four patios, which had entranced his secretary and, like him, wandered at will around colonial Cuzco, remarking that he preferred to reserve Inca ruins for exploration and concentrate here on the still gloriously uninjured monuments of Spanish colonization. Though he could reasonably plead he was still not strong enough to attend cocktail parties or give lectures, he dined informally and most pleasantly with the Geminianis and renewed his cordial association with the university, finding his only difficulty in choosing graduate students for the next expedition lay in the number available for selection. He finally decided on two local boys, Walter Ruiz, a young botanist who had been an honor student throughout his course at the university; and Clodomiro Vasquez, a youthful geologist whose grades had been only average, but who came with a high personal recommendation from the Geminiani family, his employers while he was earning the money to pay for his education.

When Nicolas returned to Quillabamba from Cuzco, Walter and Clo went with him and, a few days later, Gomara, Pete and Li Chan joined them, not without some regret at leaving the picturesque house which had proven such pleasant and comfortable headquarters for several months. Twenty Machiguenga carriers, recommended by the bishop, had already been chosen for the expedition, along with twelve mules for cargo and six for mounts. Nicolas' convalescence had given him ample opportunity to work out the details of the equipment with great care and thoroughness; it had been mail ordered from Abercrombie and Fitch and eased through the Peruvian customs by the combined efforts of the American Embassy staff and Ildefonso Parra. Nicolas was satisfied that, as to both quality and kind, it could not be improved; and though everything in the way of personal necessities—tents, sleeping bags, mattresses and so on—had been bought in quantities of seven, providing for each member of the expedition with one to spare, it had still been possible to keep the individual burdens light with the increased number of carriers.

All the members of the Dominican Mission—the bishop, the priests, the lay brothers, the nursing nuns—and many of the students at the Polytechnic Institute and the girls' school came to watch the expedition start and wish it Godspeed. The bishop gave it his blessing and then stood, with his arm around Nicolas' shoulder, until they had watched it wind its way out of sight. There had been no defections among the Machiguengas this time; on the contrary, there had been great eagerness to join; and several men, who were wearing preternaturally clean *cushmas*, blew vigorously on their *pututus*—the conches made of woodland snails which gave forth a low penetrating sound—to advise their friends they were on the march and the marching was good.

The first radio message came through from Rosalina farm that same night. Everything had gone well all day and everyone was still in good spirits. The expedition had been supplied with more fresh fruit and eggs than it could use; it had also picked up a few extra carriers, who had listened to the lure of the conch shells and hastened to join their friends. The next message, sent the following night from the Chirumbia Dominican Mission on the farther side of the Urubamba, was equally reassuring; and, since several days must now elapse before there could be one from Lacco, Nicolas decided the time had come for him to leave Quillabamba and find out whether or not it would prove practicable to pick up messages in Lima. He had already been warned that direct reception from the expedition might be difficult there and had arranged, by military telegram, that, if this proved to be the case, Antonio Astur would act as an intermediary and Fonso, long a ham radio operator, would send Nicolas the results of the reports by air mail. Accordingly, as soon as it was evident his doubts had been well founded, Nicolas' radio was sent by military plane to Atalaya, along with the silver "toilet set"—brush, comb and mirror—which Nicolas guessed, and rightly, would be the type of wedding present particularly pleasing to Antonio's sixteen-year-old bride; and, before he boarded his plane, Nicolas had the satisfaction of hearing, at the Parras' house, the news—which continued to be good—from Lacco and learning that Fátima was indeed delighted with the "toilet set."

He enjoyed the few days he had in Lima, not only the visits with the Parras and the Labradors, but the activities connected with his lecture at the University of San Marcos and his association with its staff. Because of these, he had been the Labradors' house guest for part of his stay and had observed, with amused interest, both the deletion of ice cream from afternoon tea and the first steps toward the transformation of the mud roof from a bizarre open attic to a paved and flowering terrace. Obviously, youth must be served in Lima as well as elsewhere.

He was still without definite information as to the contents of Allan Lambert's letter, that he had delivered to the Rector of San Marcos University, and intended to ask some discreet questions of the Assistant Secretary on his return to Washington. But Labrador had inquired casually as to the possibility of his accepting an official connection with the Peruvian government—not exactly like the one for which Dr. Albert Giesecke, now an attaché at the American Embassy, had shown such aptitude as Director General of Education, but one of similar nature, based on familiarity with the needs of isolated regions. Nicolas had replied that, for the time being, he had all he could do trying to run an expedition by long distance control and, simultaneously, making the effort to fulfill his new role as a Virginia country gentleman. The rector, still speaking casually, said they would take up the matter again when Nicolas was less preoccupied.

Festivities at the Parras' did not center around one of Marina's luncheons this time, but around the baptism of another baby, their fifth boy. The wide-eyed infant Nicolas had seen in its nurse's arms on his arrival in November was now, inexplicably, a toddler; he had not realized babies developed so fast or that large numbers of them were so nonchalantly taken for granted. Marina must already have been pregnant at the time of his previous visit, but neither she nor Fonso had mentioned it; doubtless, when he returned in September, she would again be in the same interesting condition. It seemed as natural to her to have more and more children as it did to breathe.

Although Nicolas had not been able to suppress some pangs as he watched the expedition start off without him, the disappointment, because he had not been able to go along, was not as lasting as he had expected. In the first place, he was on his way to his home, his first since he had left his parents' roof fifteen years before; that in itself was a wonderful feeling: to have a home of your own and a very beautiful one at that. And waiting to welcome him in that beautiful home was Margaret, his dearly loved wife. All the news he had had from her was good. She continued to be in the best of health and, though she was now six months along, she still had no reason to be so self-conscious about her appearance that she and Nicolas could not go out together in Washington society until the end of the Little Season, if that was what he would like to do; and, after that, of course they could entertain their friends in a quiet way at Hills' End. Everything Nicolas had wanted done on the place, in the way of improvements and developments, had gone ahead well, though, naturally, it would go faster still when he was there to supervise it; and when he left she would be ready to lead an active life again, taking over the responsibilities for crops and livestock where he would be forced to relegate these to her, because of obligations elsewhere.

Nothing that Margaret wrote had ever indicated any resentment over his projected return to Peru in September and this made him grateful for more reasons than one. He had a profound distaste for any uncompleted job and, as far as his lost city was concerned, that was still in this category. He was not given to knickknacks of any kind on his desk, even when one was available, which was seldom; but, wherever he went, he carried a card in his wallet on which was printed the prayer of Sir Francis Drake, composed on the eve of attacking the Spanish Armada:

"Give us to know that it is not the beginning but the continuing
of the same until it is entirely finished which yieldest true glory."

This undertaking was not "entirely finished"—nothing like it. He proposed to carry on until it was.

Besides, private conversations with the bishop during Nicolas' long convalescence had given additional impetus to his quest for the lost city. *Monseñor* had told him some available Machiguengas had offered to guide any expedition to a section of the Vilcabamba ridge, where they swore there were taboo Inca ruins; and the bishop, out of affection for Nicolas, urged him to make this his objective, so that he might be the lucky one to get official credit for the discovery. This advice was worthy of serious consideration, especially as, a few weeks earlier two young Englishmen, Sebastian Snow and Julian Tennant, the former with some exploratory ventures already to his credit, had arrived in Lima with the declared intention of going on to Vilcabamba in search of ruins which they believed to be there. But, as Nicolas had told Margaret when he first shared his secrets with her, Vilcabamba had never made a strong or convincing appeal to him as a final objective; its narrow *cordillera* was not characterized by the lagoons he was after and, therefore, could not provide the ultimate magic of which he was in search. During the course of the conversations, when the bishop had been talking about the probable feasibility of finding Inca ruins on the Vilcabamba ridge, he had disclosed that the Machiguengas also knew of three other ruins across the Urubamba River or on the ridge of Pantiacolla; that one of these ruins was submerged in a lagoon and was known as the "House of the Sun of Gold"; but that they had been reluctant to explore these themselves, not for fear of Inca taboo, but out of healthy respect for the living tribe of Cogapacoris. It was on this region, as Nicolas had also confessed to Margaret, he had long set his sights; the question had not been where he wanted to go, as far as he was concerned, but how and when best to get there; and he had learned, early in his career, that one of the surest ways to find out what you can do is to eliminate the things you cannot do. He now knew, from bitter but valuable experience, that the Paucartambo-Noche Triste route was not for him. All right, at this very moment, he was getting ready to try the Quillabamba-Lacco route. Despite the tragic loss of Cipriano, he was still ready to confront the Cogapacoris; and he was quite undaunted by the fact that, unlike the tongues of the Queros and Machiguengas, theirs was completely unknown. He had read that, on a recent expedition made by Frenchmen in the Orinoco region, the first successful contact with the savages had been through a tape recording of Mozart's music. After all, there was nothing new about that; it was with music that San Francisco Solano had charmed the savages over thousands and thousands of miles of hitherto unexplored territory, in the course of his missionary journeys, when his battered violin and his singing voice were his only means of communication. Very well, Nicolas would try "a concourse of sweet sounds" on the Cogapacoris. Personally, he enjoyed Victor Herbert. He would get some records the first time he went shopping in Washington.

He had been doing quite a little shopping in Lima and he realized he might have a tussle with the customs ahead of him when the plane arrived in Miami. Guayaquil, with its interruption to his well-ordered thoughts, was behind him now; but Panama was still some distance off and he could dwell with leisurely satisfaction on the presents he had bought for Margaret. A suitable specimen of *Huamanga* alabaster had taken some searching; but at last he had found a snow-white crucifixion, about eighteen inches high, for which he could visualize exactly the right place, surmounting a carved cabinet in one corner of the drawing room at Hills' End. He had bought it without haggling over the price, which was steep. Then, just as he was leaving the shop, which dealt largely in antique jewelry, his eye happened to light on a magnificent amethyst necklace. The stones, which completely encircled the heavy gold chain, were large, dark and brilliantly polished; they constituted a regal ornament, and Nicolas could not help wondering to whom it had originally belonged and how it had found its way into an antique shop; there must be both drama and tragedy in its story. He hesitated a little; the necklace would not be suitable for Margaret to wear until she was older and more matronly of figure and bearing; the pearls and aquamarines he had already given her were much more appropriate. But he could picture her wearing the amethysts at their son's wedding, for instance, perhaps at their own silver wedding. He left the shop with the necklace, lying on the original yellowed white satin lining of its worn velvet box, safely stowed away in his coat pocket.

Later that same day Marina had modeled for him several beautiful vicuña coats, in different styles and shades. Eventually, he chose one in natural color that could be worn either flowing loose or tightly belted. His mental picture of Margaret as she would look, wearing this coat as she strolled about the grounds at Hills' End, when cooler weather came and she was again her own slim self, was a very pleasant one. And the coat had cost only forty dollars. Admittedly, he had hesitated over his next extravagant purchase—a chinchilla cape as costly as the amethyst necklace. But it semed so exactly the right fur and, in the form he had bought it, so exactly the right style for Margaret—soft and rare and elegant—he had allowed himself to be tempted.

Perhaps, now that he was by way of being a family man, he should be a little more careful of what he spent, especially as the recent abortive expedition would not furnish material for another book which might rival *Realms of Glory* and *Full Fathom Five* in sales. He had confidently expected that it would. He had become so used to the role of best-selling author, it had not occurred to him this might be a memory rather than an actuality. But of course the setback was only temporary; his own "House of the Sun of Gold" was still ahead of him as a discovery, as a book, as a series of lectures; the slight postponement was nothing to worry about. Meanwhile, thanks to Pancho Murray, the *Time* correspondent in Lima, that weekly had featured his "great adventure" with Lester and, as a result, *Collier's* had asked him to write an article, possibly two, about it. He would do this as soon as he reached Virginia. *Collier's* paid very well—the amethyst necklace was easily taken care of, with quite a good deal to spare. (Perhaps that should be set aside for hospital bills?) For the time being, Nicolas would dismiss any disturbing thoughts about the cost of the chinchilla cape from his mind. . . .

He did this so successfully that he slept peacefully all the way from Panama to Miami, even though he knew, at the latter point, dawn would be coming up like thunder and that the thunder of the customs officials would be even harder to take.

"Ladies and gentlemen, we are now approaching Washington. Please remain in your seats until the engines have stopped. Be sure you have not left any of your personal possessions. We hope you have enjoyed your flight and that we shall soon have you for our passengers again."

Nicolas could see them all before he reached the door and before he was at the foot of the gangway, they were crowding around him—the reporters, the photographers, the faithful friends: Alfredo Román, Allan Lambert, Charlie Madison, Tom Herbert; also, more to his surprise, Kenneth Bruce, Irvin Powers, Jerome LaGuarde, Gordon Holmes. His back was slapped, his hand was wrung, he was pelted with questions, overwhelmed with exuberant expressions of welcome. It was useless to protest that, this time, there was no story, that he hadn't discovered anything, that he had been invalided home while another man, a better man than he was, took charge of a new expedition. . . .

"What do you mean, no story? *Collier's* has you under contract, congratulations and all that, but no high-hatting, please! What's the last place you heard from by radio? Say that again, will you? Lacco? What's that, another lagoon? Oh, just a farm? Come on, Nick, you're among friends, don't act so shy."

"Boys, he's still limping and he must be dog-tired. Let up on him for today, can't you? I want to get him out of here as fast as I can, see him started on his way home."

Nicolas heard the kindly aside with mingled gratitude and chagrin. It was good of Allan Lambert to shield him like this; it was humiliating to know he needed shielding. But he accepted Allan's arm, which might have been offered merely as a gesture of friendliness, but was more likely one of visibly needed support, and made his way past the barrage of cameras and notebooks to the place where Rufus was waiting for him. Before he reached this point, the more important dignitaries had already taken leave of him and Tom Herbert had relieved him of his checks and gone to claim his baggage. With some of the others out of earshot, he could ask questions himself.

"How come I rate Bruce and Powers? I don't know Bruce all that well and Powers I hardly know at all."

"I imagine you'll be seeing a good deal more of both in the foreseeable future. Imelda and Miriam have both taken a great shine to Margaret."

"Good! But it wasn't the distaff side of the family that was represented here."

"There weren't any distaffs as long as Margaret decided not to come —very wisely, of course. If there had been, Mrs. Bingham would have come—the grand old man is still going strong, but he isn't quite up to standing around in airports any more. Naturally, he'd want you to come and see him. And I think you can take it for granted the VP and the great solon are in accord with the views held by the former's wife and the latter's daughter. And you must have gathered Gordon Holmes is probably going to spend the rest of his life ostensibly chasing butterflies in Virginia. . . . Well, there's Rufus grinning a broad welcome and here comes Tom with the baggage. Good God, discovery or not, you must be in the money if you could spend what that indicates in excess weight. I'll be seeing you—in fact, I believe Milagrita and Margaret already have something cooked up for Sunday night."

"Just a minute! I've still to find out what was in that mysterious letter you gave me for Juan Labrador. Can't you give me a hint?"

"All in good time, my friend, all in good time!"

Allan was gone and Nicolas was wheeling quietly along in his own car, except for Rufus, which was the way he wanted it to be. Of course, Margaret had been right in waiting to have him all to herself when she welcomed him, and he did not feel disposed to ask questions about how things were going at Hills' End; he would see soon enough. As it was, he could hardly believe his eyes when the car turned in at the gate. The memory of how the place had looked that dreary November day when he had first returned there was still a vivid one: the rusty gate, sagging on its hinges; the unkempt land, sodden under the downpour of rain; the unpruned trees bare, the driveway rutted, the flower beds overgrown with weeds; the arbor with the scraggly vines no longer worthy of their beautiful names; the house, with its broken shutters and peeling façade, a dim ghost of its erstwhile splendor. Now the gate that opened to receive him was neatly divided in two upright grilled parts, black and glistening; the May sunshine lay bright over the closely cropped, velvety green lawn, through which a smooth driveway wound its graceful way; the trees were feathery with their fresh leaves, the flower beds a mass of bloom. And the house! Had he said anything about having it painted, had he provided money for the work? Of course, he should have, but if he had, that was forgotten. Nevertheless, it was now gleaming, its walls a radiant white, its shutters a glossy green; it rose behind its encircling box and among its sheltering trees with such freshness added to its dignity, it seemed, in itself, to personify the new life that was burgeoning there. . . .

Suddenly there was a happy bark and Perdita tore down the steps and flung herself against the car, demanding entrance. And in the doorway Margaret was standing, Margaret with her shining eyes and her shining hair and love rising from her heart to her lips.

29

It was a new experience to be the head of a house—not a privileged guest, not an importunate suitor, not an insatiable bridegroom; but someone who belonged, who had responsibilities both toward the establishment he had rehabilitated, where he was now the host, and toward his beloved wife, who was soon to bear his child. It was a time for direction, for management, for administration, as far as the estate was concerned, the more concentrated because the period he could devote to this was limited to the months he would be in Virginia. It was a time for hospitality, which must be unfailing and gracious, but which still must be kept within certain bounds lest it impose an extra burden where there must be none at present. It was a time for tenderness and loving-kindness toward a prospective mother whose condition now precluded any repetition of the uncurbed intensity of his previous relationship with her.

As far as his role as a squire was concerned, Nicolas found his responsibilities strange rather than burdensome. There was nothing in his New England boyhood, much less in his experience as an explorer and a leader of expeditions, to fit him for the limited pursuits of a Virginia country gentleman, though Margaret assured him he looked and acted the part to perfection. Quite possibly, he might *look* it; he could not help knowing he was well-built and well-favored and that he had an almost unfailing instinct for wearing the right clothes. He might *act* it, for, after all, it would be strange if, by this time, he did not know how to adapt himself to any kind of situation. But that did not mean he *belonged*.

It occurred to him that, if everything had not been running so smoothly, if there had been more of a challenge, or even if more personal effort on his part had been required, conditions might have seemed more natural. In New England he would have taken some part in the manual labor he was directing; he did not know a single Vermont farmer who failed to share, while he supervised, the work of his hired man. But the Negroes at Hills' End would have been aghast at the spectacle of the boss in a hayfield, except as a spectator. A little light gardening, a bit of pruning here and there, carpentry that achieved the status of cabinet work—those were all right; but beyond such trivia Nicolas saw he must not go. Without exception, the staff he had assembled for work on the grounds and in the house was doing a good job, facilitated by weather which had been favorable to crops, vegetables and flowers. Moreover, Margaret was exhibiting great gifts as an executive and an administrator and she did not need his help to run the place; her authority and judgment were everywhere accepted without question.

In the perfectly ordered house, the domestic routine permitted long lazy mornings in bed, candlelighted suppers and superb cookery for every meal, whether Nicolas and Margaret were alone or innumerable guests drifted in. To Nicolas' relief, these did not include their next-door neighbors, to whom he had taken such a strong dislike, for the Huntingtons were spending the summer at their Norman *haras;* but there seemed to be no limit to the other visitors who were attracted to Hills' End. The Herberts accused Margaret of having stolen their thunder, as far as Sunday night suppers were concerned. Not at all, she protested vehemently; everyone had been so kind and cordial to her, during her first loneliness after Nicolas' departure, that she had to think of something to do in return, and a revival of the old-fashioned parties in the gun room seemed the easiest and most natural. And since more people could come on Sundays. . . . All right, all right, the Herberts said good-naturedly, they understood—and they meant what they said. But, without question, there was a new luminary among local hostesses, and Nicolas could not help remembering "Marina's luncheons" and "Faustina's cocktail parties" and wondering rather wryly how long before he would be hearing about "Margaret's Sunday night suppers!"

There were moments when it was hard for him to realize this splendid woman and the shy, repressed girl he had met at the Schaeffer-Steinmetz wedding less than a year earlier were one and the same. She was certainly revealing great talents as a hostess, as well as an administrator, and he had every reason to be pleased and proud of the place she had made for herself among his friends and of the distinguished additions to this circle which were her achievement rather than his. The mild surprise he had felt at finding the Vice President and the Chairman of Foreign Relations among those who were waiting to welcome him at the airport would probably have died down, after Allan Lambert's easy explanation of their presence, if they had not continued to be so much in evidence. The Vice President, from choice as well as policy, never went anywhere without his wife; Senator Powers was less habitually accompanied by his daughter who, after all, had her own social responsibilities as the wife of the President of the National Geographic. That Gordon Holmes had wholeheartedly accepted his position as *cavaliere servente,* whether Margaret was aware of it or not, Nicolas had sensed from the time he received her second letter; and it was this same letter, he remembered now, that had made the inclusion of the senator's name seem less harmless and natural. At the moment, there was nothing to fear from that direction. Margaret carried herself with such grace and dignity that her condition, though now unmistakable, was not yet disfiguring; and she had consented, for Nicolas' sake, to go with him to official dinners and other festivities of the Little Season which he especially wished to attend; just as he went regularly to church with her, because she took it for granted he would, though this was one of the duties of a country squire which rather bored him, but he was careful not to say so. Anyway, in a few weeks, she would be going out only among their close friends and confining her invitations to these. They were almost at the end of the Little Season and Nicolas was always with her, no matter where she went or whom she received. But what about the following winter, when he would be gone and the Big Season would be in full swing? Should he perhaps make some jesting remark about the unreasonable jealousy of absent husbands and wolves in sheep's clothing? He thought it over and decided against it. Obviously, Margaret had not the slightest idea that Senator Powers might be regarding her with a covetous, rather than a kindly eye and, quite as obviously, her love for Nicolas himself was still close to adoration. It would be almost an insult if he put notions and suspicions in her innocent mind which did not belong there.

The first air mail letter from Fonso came in when Nicolas had been only a few days at Hills' End, but when the unfamiliarity of his present role had already begun to tell on him; and the mere consciousness that he was not out of touch with his expedition gave him more solid satisfaction than anything that had happened since his return, except his welcome home, although the report contained no news of exceptional value. Lester had talked by radio with Antonio from camp on the right bank of the Paucartambo, across the river canyon from Lacco. The expedition had been delayed at Lacco, first by the transfer of all cargo from mules to carriers, whose numbers were still increasing; second, by getting in extra supplies of eggs and fruit, while these were still obtainable; and third, by the unseasonable rains which had temporarily made it impossible to ford the river; but they had finally got across. The third cause for delay had not been very philosophically accepted. "Rains in the rainy season you accept, but rains in the dry season make a man sorry," Fonso commented, with wisdom, toward the end of his letter. Then he added that Lester had praised him for suggesting that boots for the members of the expedition should be made by Cúneo of Lima, instead of being mail ordered from Abercrombie and Fitch like everything else. The boots were made of good leather, handworked throughout and had a balance of lightness with solidity in extra layers of sole, to take the cleats. Climbing where they were now without cleats would have been impossible.

The next news that arrived was not only good but thrilling: for several days atmospheric and meteorological conditions had been bad between Atalaya and the jungle ridge of Paucartambo, but they were now improved and Antonio had talked by radio with Lester the same morning the letter was written, for Antonio had immediately reported to Fonso. Lester could not say for sure whether or not the expedition had crossed the trail of the previous year, because the *paca* grew thicker than ever after having been cut. However, there was one thing he could say for sure and this was that they had found an Inca way, a route of stone; it was broken, it was overgrown, it was more of a curiosity than an aid to progress, but it showed unmistakably that they were on the right track.

Nicolas showed the letters to Margaret as they came in and was happy to find she took an intelligent interest in their contents and that, far from begrudging him the ties which bound him to Peru, she rejoiced that these were not severed and that there was no prospect they need be. She had accepted without discussion the fact that only his temporary disability had justified his prolonged absence from his expedition at this time and his decision that he must rejoin it as soon as was feasible after the birth of the baby. Moreover, she had never again expressed the desire to accompany him. Apparently, she realized the question of doing so had been automatically answered; even if she could have gone herself to the wild and trackless lands where he was headed, she could not possibly have done so if she were burdened with an infant in arms; and, if the present exploratory venture led to discovery, her husband's future absences could be better timed and less prolonged. Decidedly, everything was working out for the best.

The first jolt to Nicolas' feelings of complacency about the expedition was given not by any bad news from Fonso, but by some probing from Waldo Hale who, accompanied by his wife and twin daughters, came to spend a long Fourth of July weekend at Hills' End. The reunion was a joyous one and Mrs. Hale—Grandma Hale, as she already insisted on calling herself—found it difficult to decide whether her son's presence at Hills' End or the primary reason for it caused her the more satisfaction. But when they had all feasted on salmon and green peas until they could not possibly eat another morsel, and the twins had blithely gone off with Burt Lassiter and a pleasant youth he had introduced as a suitable substitute for Lester, Waldo announced that he was sure the ladies would like to lie down until the heat of the day was past and, meanwhile, he and Nick would keep each other company in the gun room.

To Margaret, there seemed nothing sinister about the suggestion; she did not find the heat oppressive and she was not in the least tired; but she felt sure her father-in-law belonged to the school which taught that expectant mothers should "put their feet up" for a certain number of hours a day, just as her mother-in-law agreed with Cassie they should "eat for two." It gave her pleasure to humor him, in view of his never-failing kindness and generosity to her. Nicolas, however, was not deceived; he was certain his father had some ulterior motive in making sure they would not be interrupted. The bedroom doors were hardly closed and the house sunk in the deep quiet of midafternoon when he found his suspicions were all too true.

"I was real pleased that you and Margaret invited us all to come down for the Fourth," Waldo began. "Because, if you hadn't, I'd have felt called upon to ask you to run up to Woodstock, just for a day or two, and I'd have hated to take you away from Hills' End, the way things are right now. But I'm kind of bothered by a letter I've got here from the credit department of a firm in New York City, name of Abercrombie and Fitch. It was addressed to you, but I opened it, like I do all the mail that comes to you in my care at the bank, because I thought, seeing the letterhead, it was just one of those bills I always take care of for you out of your checking account with us when you're off in the wilds. Well, this wasn't a bill, after all. It was a nice polite letter, calling your attention to the fact that their latest statement must have escaped your notice. The letter went on to say you were one of the firm's most valued customers and all that and, of course, your credit with them was okay—"

"Well, if that's the case, there's nothing to worry about, is there?"

"Maybe not. But I looked around and I couldn't find any bill, overdue or otherwise, from this Abercrombie and Fitch. If it was sent to you in my care, same as your bills usually are, I don't know what's become of it."

"It wasn't sent to me in your care, the way my bills usually are. I knew there wasn't enough money in my checking account with you to pay it and that this would worry you. It was sent to me in care of Fonso Parra in Lima. I thought I'd manage to take care of it somehow pretty soon, that you wouldn't need to know anything about it. I didn't realize Abercrombie and Fitch would address a letter to me in care of your bank, though of course it's easy enough for them to find out the connection between us. I thought they'd just let the account run for a while. I didn't dream they'd want such prompt payment."

"Have you got you a checking account or a savings account at some other bank I don't know about, Nick?"

"No."

"And this bill that hasn't been paid was rendered May first?"

"Yes."

"It's for quite a sum."

"It certainly is."

"Well, just how were you planning to take care of this sum and when?"

"I hadn't got as far as planning. As you know, I've been laid up for quite a while and things like bills have got ahead of me. Give me a little time, can't you?"

"You've already had quite some time. Ever since May first. You won't be able to get credit much longer if you keep on spending money like a drunken sailor, instead of living within your means and putting something aside for your child's college education," Waldo said, speaking more sharply. "It shouldn't be necessary I should remind you, Nicolas, this bill has got to be paid right away."

"Very well. Then perhaps you'll tell me how."

"You're not expecting any money from your publishers?"

"Why should I? I haven't sent them anything since *Full Fathom Five*. Royalties are still coming in from that and *Realms of Glory*, as you know, but, as you also know, they don't run to very large figures any more—just hundreds, not thousands. I've drafted a couple of articles for *Collier's* since I came to Virginia, but I haven't sent them off yet. I've been trying to get adjusted here and that's taken more time and effort than I realized it would. However, I can buckle down and get the script off in a few days—and I will. *Collier's* pays promptly, so pretty soon I'll have a couple of thousand to the good. But, as you don't need to point out, that won't go far on this bill."

"This bill isn't all I'm worrying about. Who's underwriting this new trip of yours, anyway? The Schaeffer-Steinmetz combination?"

"I think it's safe to expect some help from that quarter—help, but not complete underwriting. We've been expecting Sam and Esther down for a weekend. I thought when they came I could talk the situation over informally with Sam. Often that's the best way to handle the old men."

"Well, do you think Sam and Esther will be down this next weekend?"

"The next or the one after that."

"Good Lord, Nick, you can't put this Abercrombie and Fitch outfit off for an uncertainty when you owe them a sum like this. What about Yale University? What about the National Geographic Society?"

"Dad, to be bromidic, you know as well as I do nothing succeeds like success and nothing fails like failure. If I'd found my lost city this last winter, they'd all be crowding around, inviting me to make my next discovery under their auspices. And I could name my own price on advance royalties for the next book and a series of lectures. As it is, I can't do anything of the sort. You'll have to arrange some kind of a loan for me at your bank, using stock as security. Pay this damn bill as soon as you get back to Woodstock and send me a note to sign. That'll have to be it for now—except that, while we're on this sore subject, I'd better tell you to make the loan big enough to cover my pay roll, too. My staff hasn't complained and it won't. But the two new boys haven't been paid at all yet and I'm two—or maybe three—months in arrears with all the others. I guess it's time we took care of them, too."

"You talk as if the amount of stock you had was about the size of Rockefeller's. You seem to be forgetting a good share of your income is going right smack into the upkeep of this place. If you sell too much stock, you'll have to reduce Margaret's allowance."

"Like hell I will. I don't need to tell you she's done wonders with it. Somehow, she's squeezed out the money to have the house painted, and several other odd jobs taken care of that I hadn't provided for, because I didn't think of them, though I should have. If there's not enough income left after we've met the expenses we've been talking about, I know you'll tide me over. You may play the heavy father about everything else, but, when it comes to Margaret, I know damn well you'll see she gets everything she needs. Look here, don't you think she's been banished to her room about long enough? Unless we have company, she and I usually get out to the grape arbor about this time, now that we're not going to Washington so much any more. I read aloud to her and she sews. A flowering vine, appropriately called traveller's joy, covers the trellises that arch over our heads. Perdita lies curled up at our feet. Very Victorian—or maybe very ante-bellum—I don't know. But, anyway, very pleasant. You and Mother don't count as company, so of course we'd be pleased to have you join us if you'd like to. Usually, we have supper out there, too. And then we just sit and talk until it gets dark. I've spent so much time where there isn't any twilight, it just seems as if I couldn't get enough of being out in it. It's the loveliest period of the day and the most restful. I'm going to enjoy it while I can."

Sam and Esther were not able to make it over the next weekend; anyhow, they had decided it would be more fun to come when they could see the baby, so there was no immediate chance for an informal

conference about Schaeffer-Steinmetz co-operation with the present expedition; and it was, perhaps, inevitable that the next letter which
came in from Fonso should be the first which did not contain good
news and it arrived while Nicolas was still feeling depressed over his
conversation with his father. Though it had taken Margaret some time
to find this out, Waldo Hale had never needed to be told that his son's
apparent nonchalance was often actually a cloak to very real concern;
and he was deeply concerned now. The latest message from the expedition was sent not by Lester, but by Gomara, who reported there was
rain at least every other day and that the cold at night was so intense
the Machiguengas were becoming restive and, instead of bringing in
more and more of their friends, as they had done at first, were threatening to quit altogether. And how could the expedition move without
them? They not only carried everything, now that the mules had been
sent back to Quillabamba from Lacco, they opened every foot of the
way. This had to be along the ridge tops, even though it meant great
drops, great ascents and, along every ridge, a curious condition of no
real footing, for it was covered with matted vegetation, the result of
constant rain and mists. Cutting away the vegetation took forever, as
the roots grew over one another, much as in a mangrove swamp, but
four or five times as involved. Cut away one snake-like set of roots, and
you come to a sharp rock; cut away still another snake-like set of roots,
and you come to nothing, just more rotten matted growth of the same
kind, further down. Add to this that the intertwining roots were not
only snake-like, but snake-inhabited and you have another happy
aspect of travel for the summer tourist.

Gomara thought it would be worth while to give the Machiguengas
some of the trinkets destined for the Cogapacoris—pure bribe of course,
but he was disturbed. The disturbance was the greater because a chance
meeting with some nomad Machiguengas had become a battlefield;
they had been obliged, or claimed they had been obliged, to defend
their females from Pete's gross attentions. Gomara thought they were
exaggerating, but there was no doubt their suspicions had been
aroused, that harm had been done. . . .

This time, Nicolas did not show Fonso's letter to Margaret; it could
only distress her, to no avail. But, though she did not ask questions, he
knew she was puzzled, and possibly hurt, when the mail came in and he
did not share it with her. He himself was deeply disturbed. If this
incident had happened earlier, at Rosalina or Chirumbia or even
Lacco, Pete could have been summarily dismissed from the expedition.
Now it was too late; he could not be turned loose in a freezing wilder-
ness, with chances ten to one against survival; but, somehow, he must
be warned that, if there were any repetition of his indiscretions, his
days with the expedition would be numbered. In the meantime, of

course, the Machiguengas must be placated; Nicolas was thankful it could still be done with trinkets, as far as the carriers were concerned, and he could only hope no more nomads would be encountered.

Fortunately, the next communications brought nothing but good news: the Machiguengas had not deserted after all and, thanks to the dexterity of their labor force, a way had been kept open. They had to be given their heads when they claimed this way was good, that way bad. The way they thought was bad was toward the *rising* sun, in the region where the lagoon of Nicolas' dreams might well lie. The expedition had learned from them this was in the heart of the Cogapacori territory and that the precarious welcome upon those heights depended on the good will of that tribe. When they could come in greater force, the Machiguengas, who were brave, hoped to try the test of a pitched battle and then the heights of Pantiacolla would be Machiguenga and not Cogapacori any more. Right now, the Machiguengas had to be prudent and so they led them toward the *setting* sun, sure that by doing this they could locate *another* lagoon, one they knew existed and which would serve as the desired headquarters until their leader could rejoin them.

The almost unbearable excitement and suspense resulting from this letter were partially assuaged by a cable: "Gomara reports lagoon found. Details follow air mail." And, though Fonso's next letter began, "Prepare for a disappointment if you expected an announcement of the desired discovery," Nicolas was exultant at the news. According to Gomara, the lagoon, hitherto known only to the Machiguengas and lying on the heights of Pantiacolla was almost too good to be true. It was a big lake, six hundred feet long, at least, and full of superb fish. Li Chan was in seventh heaven and turned out one culinary delight after another; and, since the lake was a treasure for him, they were provisionally calling it Li Chan Lagoon, though of course Nicolas might want to name it something else—possibly Moonstone Lake, for it had the soft beautiful translucency of that gem, though it lacked the complete clarity of Nicolas' dream lake and it contained no treasure for anyone except the cook. But it was good to be there, living by it. They had found solid ground around it and the domestic-minded Machiguengas had tried planting *yuca* seeds in the hope of having their own favorite food freshly available. They were happy and wanted still others of their tribe to join them there, so that more Machiguengas could also enjoy the fishing and hunting. The altitude was under four thousand feet, easy for all to tolerate. There was no question that the base could serve satisfactorily for a long while. . . .

Here at last was some joyful news that could be shared not only with

Margaret, but with Hiram Bingham, with Alfredo Román, with Allan Lambert, with Charlie Madison, with Jerome LaGuarde, with Tom Herbert. Román insisted they must have a party at the embassy to celebrate the foundation of the camp at Moonstone Lake; and, as Margaret was now very near her time, the celebration took the form of a stag supper, to which not only Nicolas' special cronies, but several high-ranking officials, among them both Bruce and Powers, were invited. The Románs' chef was very generally reputed to be the best in Washington, not excepting the one at the White House; and though there were some who contended the cellar at the French Embassy was better, this opinion was met with skepticism. At all events, the so-called "supper" took on the proportions of a Lucullan feast and was presented, all the way from service plates to finger bowls, on utensils of Peruvian silver. As the company, which ended by including no less than thirty well-wishers, left the dining room, with its priceless paintings of the Cuzco school, the host suggested that, instead of remaining in the drawing room (where the priceless paintings were works of Murillo and Goya!) they should have coffee and liqueurs on the terrace, where there was a pleasant breeze. And presently Senator Powers managed to draw Nicolas aside for what he designated as "a few moments of confidential chat."

"It's hard to get you to myself, Nicolas, you're always so surrounded. But there's a matter I've been wanting to speak to you about for some time and, unless I could persuade you to have dinner alone with me some night soon, I think perhaps this is as good a chance as I'll get."

"It's very kind of you and, of course, normally I'd be honored, as well as delighted, to have dinner alone with you. But, just now, I don't like to leave Margaret any more than I can help. I wouldn't even have come here tonight if Alfredo and Allan hadn't shown such insistence, I just couldn't refuse. So, if this would be a good time for you—"

"Just as I thought, just as I thought! Naturally, you begrudge every moment you spend away from that lovely wife of yours. I'd feel exactly the same way if she were mine. In fact, I don't see how you steel yourself to continue your exploratory ventures. But since you do—"

"For a long time I didn't have any choice as to whether I'd continue them or not. I was so deeply committed to my sponsors I had to go on. That was still true when I was married. It doesn't happen to be true at this moment. But now that I'm so near my goal—or have every reason to believe I am—I've got to justify the faith others have had in me and I've had in myself."

"That's natural, very natural. But did I understand you correctly— you're not committed to anyone at this moment? I mean, to any sponsor?"

Nicolas' throat suddenly seemed to go dry. He answered with difficulty.

"I believe I can always count on the friends who first had confidence in me—Mr. Aaron Schaeffer, the former Assistant Secretary of Commerce, and Mr. Samuel Steinmetz, Sr., the father of my roommate at college. I haven't had a chance to discuss this with them since my return, but I'm expecting to soon."

"However, to give a definite answer to my definite question, you're not *committed* to them, are you? To them or to anyone else?"

"No, Senator, I'm not."

"Well, that was what I understood and what I was rather hoping. You see, I've had some talk with my son-in-law and he told me he wasn't deeply interested in your further search for submerged treasure. Jerome's a good boy, but sometimes he strikes me as lacking imagination—vision—whatever you choose to call it. Of course, I'm not criticizing him. In his position as head of the National Geographic, he needs to be prudent. But, occasionally, he seems to my daughter and me a little overcautious. This is one of the occasions."

The dryness in Nicolas' throat was getting worse. Now he did not even try to answer.

"It was a real grief to my wife and myself that we never had a son," Senator Powers continued, speaking with great gentleness. "But now that I am a widower, my daughter Miriam and I are very close to each other. We have discussed the subject of your discoveries at length, and it is because of her interest in it, as well as mine, that I am bringing it up tonight. We would be very much gratified—very much honored, to borrow the word you were kind enough to use a few minutes ago in connection with me—if you would permit us to underwrite your present expedition. It would be done in the same spirit we would have shown anything undertaken by a son of mine, if I had been fortunate enough to have one—a son of mine and, of course, a brother of Miriam's. When the new discovery of which you feel so confident—and, may I add, we share your confidence—is an actuality, we can, if you wish, make some financial adjustment which would permit you personally, or your publishers in your behalf, to take over part of the expenses. But that is a situation we can handle when it arises. Meanwhile, Miriam and I would have to insist, if you accept our offer, that there should be no question of help from Mr. Schaeffer or Mr. Steinmetz, from Yale University or the National Geographic Society. The undertaking would be known as the Powers-Hale Expedition and would go forward, I am sure, to success under our joint powers—there, I did not mean to make a bad pun! What do you say, Nicolas?

Shall we call together our friends, who are now scattered here and there over the terrace, and tell them what we have decided to do?"

It was all done too quickly, far too quickly, Nicolas knew that. But he had not been able to resist the mesmeric effect of the senator's offer. Within five minutes after it had been made, Powers had asked their host to call the rest of the company together; and, with the same grace and ease which characterized his more formal and public utterances, had told the select group he and Nicolas had become partners, and that they wanted their mutual friends, now gathered together under such favorable circumstances, to be the first to know this. He stood with his arm around Nicolas' shoulder while he was talking, as poised and easy of manner as he was of speech, and irresistibly charming. Nicolas was conscious of the intentness with which Kenneth Bruce was watching and listening. There were rumors afloat that, jealousy between their wives had reached such a point, when Maynard came up for re-election he wanted to change his running mate and that, given his choice, he would select Powers. He would have taken Powers the last time. But then the latter had not been open to persuasion—he did not want to leave the position in the Senate to which he was so well suited, even to his very name—on which he made puns. But, perhaps, another time. . . . Bruce recognized in him a formidable rival, that was evident. And Nicolas had won him as a friend, a supporter, an advocate. Nicolas? Or Margaret? That, of course, was the corroding question. He preferred to leave it unanswered. He could only hope no such question had been raised in the mind of anyone else. If it had, there was certainly no hint of it in the general acclaim, in which Jerome LaGuarde took a conspicuous part. Nicolas' friends would not let him go home alone. They must all accompany him to Hills' End for a nightcap, for several nightcaps, for another round of congratulations and then another. He was afraid they would disturb Margaret and he slipped upstairs to tell her this was a very special celebration, that he couldn't stop now to tell her about it, but he would do so in the morning—well, later in the morning. She, however, was sleeping so peacefully and profoundly she was not even aware of the jubilant sounds in the gun room. Nicolas went back to the celebrants, and the sky was already bright with the burning sun of another July day when he said goodbye to the last of them.

Thirty-six hours later Waldo Hale telephoned his son that a hundred thousand dollars had just been placed to his credit from the joint account of Irvin Powers and Miriam Powers LaGuarde. Waldo wanted to know how come? Nicolas said he would explain later. Meanwhile, would his father please take care of that sum due Abercrombie and Fitch?

30❧

"Lima, Peru
July 25, 1954

"Dear Nick:

"Perhaps I will be taking some of the gilt off your gingerbread by sending you a tearsheet from the *Peruvian Times* and some clippings from *La Prensa, El Comercio,* etc. along with this letter. But, after all, it's better you should hear the news as promptly and as accurately as possible than to have it leak out in one form or another to upset you later. I hope you'll be able to feel the latest news from your camp, which continues to be very good, will more than offset the other.

"Yours ever,
"Fonso."

Nicolas unfolded the enclosures with care. The article in the *Peruvian Times,* captioned EXPEDITION FINDS RUINS AFTER ARDUOUS JOURNEY INTO THE URUBAMBA COUNTRY, covered a whole page and was written with a dateline of Urubamba, July 23, by a well-known journalist, Guild Walter, who had accompanied the explorers on the first lap of their journey. "News of the latest ruins to be discovered in Peru was brought to Lima last Friday, July 16, by an expedition composed of two Englishmen and a North American," he read. "The group includes Sebastian F. Snow, 26. He is a veteran of five expeditions to South America and the author of a book, '*My Amazon Adventure*,' which was published last November in England. Originally from Devon, Snow attended Eton and is a Fellow of the Royal Geographical Society of London.

"The other Englishman in the party is Julian W. F. Tennant, 29. An ex-Guards officer who has traveled extensively in many parts of the world including Africa, Australia, Canada and the United States, Tennant is a Director of C. Tennant Sons & Company, Ltd., one of the oldest merchandising houses in London. William H. Glasgow, 26, of East Orange, New Jersey, is the third member of the expedition which he joined in Lima. A U. S. Naval Pilot during and after the war, with service in Saipan and other parts of the Pacific, Glasgow also was a Panagra pilot for three years before resigning to go into business here."

So far, there was nothing upsetting about the article. Though Nicolas had not previously been acquainted with the curricula vitae or known that a third member had been added to the party, he had learned about the Englishmen's project before leaving Quillabamba and had, therefore, been somewhat influenced in making his own plans. He resumed his reading.

"Since the journey from Cuzco to the point on the Urubamba River which the expedition wished to use as a base camp is highly hazardous, because of whirlpools and rapids, it was decided to start from Pucallpa. The latter part of May, Snow, Tennant and Glasgow flew to Pucallpa and then spent several days at the Yarina Cocha camp of the Summer Institute of Linguistics from whom they chartered a plane for the first portion of the journey."

Yes, of course, that was what they would have done, what he would have done himself in their place. Now he wanted to know what they did next. He read rapidly on, skimming over some details, but missing no salient points.

"A site on the Urubamba known as Timpia or Campo Domingo was selected for a base camp. . . . Since it was necessary to make two flights to transport members of the party and supplies, we were able to accompany the first one. . . . The plane . . . followed more or less the course of the winding Ucayali. . . . After an hour or so we landed at Miaria, a settlement on the Urubamba. . . . While the men refueled the plane from gasoline drums stored in a nearby hut, we explored the small village, a collection of thatched-roof huts on stilts. . . .

"Gassed up once more, the plane gathered momentum for the take-off. . . . Almost three hours after we left Yarina Cocha we . . . came in for a landing at Timpia. . . . The next afternoon we returned to Yarina Cocha as the expedition prepared to go upstream . . . to Pangoa. Later we learned they were unable to negotiate the Pongo de Mainique. . . ."

Nicolas laid down the article, smiling to himself. So they had not been able to "negotiate" the Pongo de Mainique which Antonio had conquered singlehanded! He read on with increasing interest.

"Another Institute plane was secured to fly them to Pangoa. There lives a fabulous man known as Fidel Pereira, 71, who is part Spanish and part Machiguenga. . . . Through [his] efforts, the group was loaned . . . eight Machiguengas to assist them in transporting their supplies and equipment.

"After twelve days of climbing, the expedition discovered the ruins they were seeking. According to Mr. Tennant, they are on a mountain at an altitude of between 7,000 and 8,500 feet, in a virtually unmapped region near the headwaters of the Mantaro, Seringaboni and Picha rivers. Two-and-one-half to three miles in circumference, this mountain commands a view of the surrounding countryside. The fortress-like ruins were reached after a three-hour climb through the jungle from the banks of the Mantaro River (not to be confused with the big Montaro River in northern Peru). . . .

"Jutting out from the slopes of the mountain at intervals were rock balconies or projections. The group brought back to Lima some of these smaller stones, which bear chisel marks, a pottery drinking vessel about seven inches high and a stone hatchet head."

So they had actually secured a stone hatchet head—the treasure that had escaped Nicolas on the occasion of his expedition's great disaster! For the first time since he began to read, he felt the stirrings of jealousy and uneasiness.

"An evaluation of their discovery is being left to archeologists and geologists, Mr. Tennant declared, adding that none of his party has had training in these fields. Whether or not these ruins are the legendary Paititi remains to be seen but it appears evident from the description of them and the photographs taken that an important discovery has been made."

Unquestionably, that was true. Nicolas was genuinely sorry for the hard luck that had prevented them from pursuing their investigations. Well, perhaps another expedition would be formed, either by them or by someone else as a result of what they had found. Some of the clippings seemed to suggest this. He could not afford to have anyone beat him to the draw at this stage of the game. The sooner he could get back to Peru, the better. He must convince Margaret of this. He took the tearsheet, clippings and Fonso's letter to the arbor and read them aloud to her.

"You do, don't you?" she asked anxiously, when he was through reading.

"I do what?"

"You do feel the news from the lagoon outweighs the news from Pangoa."

He did not answer instantly and she gathered this was not because he was unwilling to do so candidly, but because he found his feelings hard to explain. "Perhaps I should be more upset than I am," he said at last. "These men were operating under the auspices of the Royal Geographic Society. The *Peruvian Times,* a very reliable weekly, *El Comercio* and *La Prensa,* the leading dailies, have given them quite a play. I haven't noticed anything in the American press, but I could have missed it. I'll look more carefully. I don't underestimate the importance of the discovery that's been made. I believe it is important, and that others, equally important, will continue to be made by these men or other explorers—other than myself, I mean. As a matter of fact, last December, while I was thrashing around in the *paca,* a Peruvian expedition penetrated deep into the forests of the Amazon, looking for the elusive city of Manoa, which these explorers thought was in Paitite. The quest was carried on among the Piros Indians of the Kosnopala region and something may come of it yet. I don't see how such discoveries can help happening, with all the undiscovered riches there are still in Peru. But my lost city isn't a citadel—it's a palace and its dependencies." He hesitated a moment and then went on. "My friend the Dominican bishop thinks that some Machiguengas he knows and trusts can find the way to three Inca ruins across the Urubamba River and beyond the ridge of Pantiacolla and that one of these is known as the 'House of the Sun of Gold' and that this is submerged. I've told you before that I've always set my sights on Pantiacolla and that I believed three was my lucky number. I've also believed my lost city was not buried, but submerged. Now I believe I'll find it in the lagoon the bishop told me about."

"I don't understand how a city could be at the bottom of a lake."

"Of course it wasn't built at the bottom of a lake, but with the amount of volcanic action there is in the Andes, the level of the land changes, sometimes quite suddenly. Over the centuries it has changed a good deal. And I know the first imperial Inca architect was a lover of water, just as I am. He'd have built near a lake or a river or a cascade and now some of the palaces are submerged. At least, that's the way I see them."

The same faraway look had come into his face that she had glimpsed when he first talked to her about his work and she had recognized him not only as the adventurous explorer of her dreams, but as the searcher, guided by the elements, the discoverer who dared to dream of magic and visualize mystic realms.

"Of course, the lagoon where my staff is now isn't the one of my dreams," he went on. "I'm glad it isn't. It would have been a bitter blow to me if one of my own associates had found it first. But I'll find it, probably not too far from where they are now, as soon as I go back. And I know you'll understand the sooner I can do that, the better, in view of this discovery."

His thorough search through New York and Washington papers revealed no reference to the Snow-Tennant expedition, nor did he find Jerome LaGuarde or anyone else connected with the National Geographic Society excited about it. This was a good sign, as far as Nicolas was concerned. The third member of the expedition had been an American, which should have stimulated national interest if the discovery had been regarded as really important. Nicolas wrote to his British publisher, asking to have London press clippings sent to him and, while awaiting their arrival, tried to possess his soul in patience, but he was restive. He not only thought it was advisable that he should return to Peru, he wanted to go back. He had not previously said so and, until this news had reached him, he had been careful to keep from Margaret the fact that this was not only a case of yearning, but a case of need. Gomara, kind, gentle and wise, still lacked the force requisite for a leader. If he, Nicolas, had been there, he could have stilled the Machiguengas' murmurings about the cold; it would not have been necessary to bribe them with the trinkets which would be greatly needed, very soon, for other purposes. And Pete would not have dared to endanger the safety of all by his folly; Nicolas had put fear into him and this had curbed his drinking; Nicolas would have put fear in him again and there would have been no "gross attentions" to the females of a nomad tribe. For the time being, the Machiguengas were contented and Pete was subdued; but there was no telling how long this state of things would last. Besides, if the expedition were now close to its ultimate goal—and Nicolas firmly believed it was—he wanted to take no chances of having someone else make the great discovery. This, as he had confessed to Margaret, would indeed have been a bitter blow.

Despite his cautiousness, she now knew all too well she would not be able to hold him, once her ordeal was over, and that she would not be able to bring him back to her again until he had found his sunken palace. She could only pray that this might be soon. . . .

She had wanted, as she had written him, to have her baby at Hills' End, and she had never been able to still Cassie's mutterings because she had not persisted, against Dr. Loomis' advice, in preparing to do so. But she could not afford to take any chances, when this child meant so much to Nicolas. She even consented when Dr. Loomis advised a Washington hospital, and a specialist in obstetrics, greatly as she herself would have preferred to remain nearer home, if not actually at home, in the care of her faithful old family physician. She insisted, however, that in some ways her wishes must be respected: except as a last resort, no instruments were to be used; under no circumstances to hasten the baby's birth and thereby shorten labor. She would gladly accept an anesthetic to ease pain, but only with the assurance it should never be so deep as to permit tampering with the conditions she had made. Yes, she knew the baby would be a large one, that she had perhaps been unwise because she had not curbed her appetite. But she did not think so. She thought she was very fortunate because she had been so healthy and happy throughout her pregnancy. If this meant she had to pay for her healthiness and happiness by a hard delivery, she would willingly do so. They would see she had great powers of endurance.

She had told the truth. Of course, it was not customary, any longer, to let a woman go so long in labor; but then, though this was slow and arduous, still, as the specialist was forced to admit, it was "completely normal." The patient did not exhaust, much less endanger herself; her estimate of her own endurance proved accurate. She had maintained she did not want Nicolas to come to the hospital where she had gone so unwillingly herself; what possible good could he do there? The only thing that would upset her would be the thought of him sitting around in an ugly waiting room, among other anxious men who were fingering dog-eared magazines or going out for an extra drink. If she knew he were comfortably reading in the library, comfortably eating his supper, comfortably lying in bed whether he slept or not, she would have nothing to worry about. As a matter of fact, she did not have much difficulty in overpersuading him; Nicolas himself did not see that a hospital waiting room would make much sense.

He did, however, take the initiative in calling the hospital more than once, before he himself was called. He kept receiving the same answer, "Everything is perfectly normal and we think in another hour. . . ." The third time this happened, he answered angrily.

"What do you mean, another hour? Have your clocks all stopped in there? Let me speak to my wife's doctor!" The answer came with prim precision: "Dr. Haskins cannot leave his patient at present. You will be advised when there is anything new to report. Meanwhile, everything is perfectly normal."

Nicolas slammed down the receiver and did not lift it again until the long-awaited call came in. With relief, he recognized the pleasant reassuring voice of Dr. Loomis, instead of the cold tones of that automaton, the head nurse, or the pontifical mandates of the specialist.

"Great news for you, Nicolas. Margaret has come through like a Trojan and in the best possible condition. The baby's perfect in every respect, nine pounds, a little larger than we wanted, but no harm done, except it's taken a little longer to get her safely into the world than if she'd been smaller. Come on in and have a look at her as soon as you like. You'll be delighted with your beautiful new daughter."

31 ❦

Just why it had never occurred to him the baby might not be a boy, or why someone else, to whom it must have occurred, had not reminded him of this, Nicolas could not imagine. His disappointment was all the more bitter because he felt he should have been spared, either because of his own good sense, or—if he had none, which was apparently the case—by the good sense of his mother and his wife, both of whom had plenty. Mrs. Waldo Hale, who was delighted with her granddaughter, did not hesitate to let him know, in tones more forceful than he had ever heard her previously use, that he was behaving very badly, and that she hoped to heaven he would not betray to his wife, by so much as a look, the feelings which he had expressed, without reserve or control, in talking to his mother. She need not worry, he told her, speaking angrily in his turn; the very first words Margaret had spoken, when he was finally allowed to see her, revealed the understanding that the nonfulfillment of his hopes for a son had been a hard blow. She had not forgotten it was this hope, and this hope alone, which had been responsible for his decision to marry—a fact, of course, of which his mother was unaware, but with which he had candidly acquainted Margaret in the beginning. True, he had fallen in love with her almost immediately and this love had transformed his original insensitivity; but he knew she felt she had failed him in not giving him his heart's desire and, far from "betraying" the feelings which had so upset his mother, he had been at great pains to assure Margaret she had not failed him in anything and that he knew she never would. She was the most wonderful wife in the world, the baby was a knockout, he thought the idea of naming her Cynthia for his mother was an inspiration, that they must have a bang-up christening party as soon as Margaret felt equal to it. As he spoke, he leaned over the bed to kiss away the tears from her brimming eyes and she had put her arms around his neck and drawn him closer to her.

"I'm sorry I'm so silly, crying like this," she said softly. "Somehow, tears just seem to come. My nurse says it's nothing but a sign I'm still very tired and, of course, I am. But I can't help grieving—on your account, I mean. I know how you counted on a boy and I just wouldn't let myself believe we wouldn't have one—this time, I mean. But, Nicolas, the next time—"

Cynthia was only two days old and Margaret was still so weak after her long hard travail, she could not control her tears and still she was ready to talk about the "next time." Nicolas had resolved he would carefully refrain from doing so until she was stronger; but that did not mean he had not been thinking, wondering, hoping—and now she had taken the initiative, as he might have known she would. She was ready, she was willing, she was eager to give him his heart's desire, at whatever cost to herself. He could depend on her to do it. And, involuntarily, he began to weigh one claim, one desire against another. He needed to rejoin his expedition, he wanted a son. How long could he delay his return to Peru? Every day that he put this off increased the seasonal hazards of travel; and though a letter received from his British publishers told him that, aside from two brief pieces in the *Daily Tele-*

graph, there appeared to have been no notices in the London papers about the Tennant-Snow expedition, there were still chances of rival discovery. How soon could he go back to his wife? Every day that a woman's convalescence from childbirth was artificially hastened, toll might be taken from her later on. At all events, it was unthinkable that he should leave until she was safely and comfortably installed at home again. Then they would see.

There was, however, something else that had not occurred to him and this was that the advent of a baby would completely revolutionize the design for living at Hills' End.

His mother was the first to enlighten him. She did not approve of modern obstetrical procedure and she thought it outrageous that Margaret should be discharged from the hospital within a week after Cynthia's birth; she had hardly been able to restrain her indignation when Dr. Haskins had told her, if he had been following standard practice, his patient would have been sent home in four days, since her delivery had been "normal," though, due to her own willfulness, it had been long and her convalescence was a slow one.

"Of course, when there is a Caesarean or an eclampsia or some other difficulty like a breech presentation, we keep them longer," he said, so pontifically that Mrs. Hale realized he felt she needed to be put in her proper place, which was *not* that of an interfering grandmother. "But, fortunately, nothing of the sort entered into the present picture. However, Mrs. Nicolas Hale declined to accept advice about restricting her diet, so her baby was much larger than we recommend. Furthermore, she exacted a promise from me that I would not use high forceps under any circumstances, except to save the baby's life—she said nothing about saving *her* life, so, despite my promise, I should have exercised my own judgment about that, as any physician, except perhaps some misguided Catholic, would do. I am glad to say high forceps were not necessary, though it looked for a time as if they might be and, certainly, everything could have been made much easier for Mrs. Nicolas Hale if low forceps had been used. She was obsessed with the idea the infant might be injured, and brought it into the world herself, with only whiffs of ether to help her over the very worst at the end. The result is that she is still exhausted and she has not been able to take the usual strengthening exercises. Consequently, she will need to have professional care for some time longer. Two excellent practical nurses, Miss Hilton and Miss Hogle, have consented to go to Hills' End. They will ride out in the ambulance with their patient and I am sure you will see that proper provision is made for their comfort while they are with you. They will let you know at what hours they require their meals—in the dining room, of course. We are very fortunate to have them. It is increasingly difficult to find professional nurses who are willing to undertake private practice, because of its many disadvantages."

"You mean to tell me that my daughter-in-law, who's perfectly healthy, except that she's exhausted—and I don't mind telling you I like her spunk!—and who's got a perfectly healthy baby, is coming home with *two nurses!*"

"But, Mrs. Hale, surely you understand that even practical nurses now operate on a twelve hour schedule! The old arrangement, by which a nurse could count on resting only when her patient was doing so, has long since been discarded. However, no doubt your daughter-in-law has already taken steps to secure a reliable English nanny and, as soon as she is in residence at Hills' End, we can probably reduce the professional staff to one practical nurse. But, for the moment—"

The specialist left the sentence unfinished and, after he had given a few supplementary directions about sleeping arrangements, made it clear he considered the discussion at an end. Mrs. Hale, with some doubts as to how her news would be received, returned to Hills' End and broke it as gently as she knew how.

"The night nurse will sleep on a cot in Margaret's room. We're to move the cradle in there. The day nurse is to have the guest room across the hall—the one where I am now. I'm to move up to the third story."

"And just what is supposed to become of me?" Nicolas inquired sarcastically.

"Why, you're to sleep in the boudoir, of course! You'd have had to do that for a while anyway. You must have realized that."

"I'm afraid I didn't. I took it for granted a married man could sleep in the same bed with his wife, if he wanted to, except when she was actually in a hospital."

"Not when she's just had a baby! Why, Nick, I thought you had more sense! There's still things that have to be done for her—it's hardly a week yet. And then there's the baby, nursing at ten and again at six."

"Ten at *night!* Six in the *morning!*"

"Of course. Maybe also at two in the morning—that depends partly on the doctor's school of thought and partly on how the baby's doing. After Margaret gets her strength back, she'll just reach over to the cradle and lift the baby into bed with her and—"

"How long does the baby have to nurse? At a time, I mean?"

"About twenty minutes. And, besides that, it has to be changed and, if it cries, it has to be burped."

"*Burped?*"

"Put over someone's shoulder and patted on the back until it gets rid of the wind that's giving it a little pain. That doesn't take long, usually. Of course, some babies do cry a good deal. You did. You screamed and screamed, even when there wasn't a thing the matter with you, as far as we could see. You had your father and me plain tuckered out."

"I take it you didn't have two nurses to ease all these burdens for you."

"I did not. I had one and she was a treasure. Never thought she was overworked, either, on twenty-four hour duty. Slept when you and I did and got plenty of rest that way. But then I wasn't rushed to a hospital after the pains had started and then rushed out of it when I was still half under ether. I stayed right in my own good bed, while I was having my babies, and two full weeks afterward, and then I got up and began to do things, little by little. Just hung my feet over the side of the bed for a few minutes the first day and the next sat up in a chair for half an hour and the next—"

Nicolas brought the conversation to an abrupt end before Mrs. Hale considered it finished, just as Dr. Haskins had done on a similar occasion and she went off to tell Cassie about the impending changes that must be made in household arrangements. The laden ambulance arrived late the next afternoon and, amid scenes of considerable confusion which were intensified by Perdita's barking, Nicolas calmly lifted Margaret off her stretcher and carried her upstairs to the room where the cot and the cradle had already been installed.

"I understand I'm banished," he said good-naturedly. "You and I will talk about that later, when we get rid of some of these experts. Meanwhile, I'm leaving you to the tender mercies of whichever one is supposed to be on duty right now. I confess I haven't got it all straightened out in my mind yet. But if you want me, don't hesitate to call me. You've still got a bell that will bring Cassie to you PDQ and Cassie'll get me. Great to have you home again, darling."

He kissed her and left her, not without some misgivings. He had a feeling that the total unsuitability of Hills' End for a professional nurse's home, even temporarily, would be made evident before nightfall and he only hoped the evidence would not be laid before Margaret. Neither Miss Hilton nor Miss Hogle had dreamed that every bedroom would not have its own private bath, much less that there would be only one to a floor and they would be expected to share this with Mr. Nicolas Hale. It would, perhaps, be better, after all, if Mrs. Waldo Hale would return to the room she had previously occupied and let Miss Hogle have one on the third floor. No, that would not do, either; it would involve going over too many stairs. It was so seldom *any* stairs were a problem nowadays with elevators practically everywhere. The stairs would be *very* bad for Mrs. Nicolas Hale, too. They were very long and very steep. She would not be able to go over them at all for at least another week, perhaps another fortnight, and then only *once a day.* Possibly Mr. Hale would move to the third floor; then, at least, there would be only ladies to use the one bathroom on the second. Mr. Hale felt, since all the arrangements had been made in accordance with Dr. Haskins' instructions, they should not now be changed? Well, of course, the bathroom situation had not been clearly explained to Dr. Haskins. Mr. Hale would be glad to explain it? Well, that was kind of him, but Dr. Haskins did not like to be called in the evening, except for some emergency and, as Mrs. Nicolas Hale seemed to be resting quietly, there was no real reason. . . . Only, might Miss Hilton and Miss Hogle point out it was already past their regular supper time? The Hales dined at *half-past seven?* No, that had not been explained to them.

Most of these problems were presented first to Mrs. Waldo Hale for solution and with increasing perplexity, fast mounting to distress, she relayed them to Nicolas. "I'm so afraid Margaret will get wind of all of this," she said unhappily. "Here we were told the whole idea of these experts was so she shouldn't get overtired. If she hears them complaining, she'll be upset and that'll be a lot worse for her than just getting tired."

"I had exactly the same idea. I think perhaps I'd better have a talk with the experts. I don't know if it's in order to invite them to have a drink with me—probably not. Maybe I'd just better have one myself, to build up my strength, and let you tell them I'll be glad to see them in the library whenever it would be convenient for them to come there. They needn't be afraid of both leaving Margaret at the same time. As I've pointed out to her, she can still ring for Cassie whenever she feels like it."

He mixed his own drink, lighted a cigarette and gave thought to the situation as he smoked and drank. When the two "experts," somewhat taken aback by his message, appeared at the library door, he rose, invited them to be seated and, without preamble, embarked on the statement he had been turning over in his mind.

"I understand you're having some difficulty in adjusting yourself to conditions at Hills' End," he said pleasantly. "I'm very sorry and I'm sure my wife would be sorrier still if it came to her ears. We all realize how important it is for her to be completely free from care or anxiety just now, and she wouldn't be, if she thought anyone staying in her house was discontented or uncomfortable. So I shall have to ask you both to say nothing to her tonight which could possibly upset her and if, in the morning, you still feel dissatisfied, I'll try to explain this to her. I think *I* could do it in a way that wouldn't upset her. Then I'll have a chat with Dr. Haskins and also with Dr. Loomis who, after all, is our regular family physician. They may think, as I'm inclined to, that perhaps it would be better if you didn't remain. This happens to be a house where there aren't any servant problems and our present cook was my wife's nurse when she was a baby. Now she's dying to be my daughter's nurse—insists she's got one of her nieces so well trained as a cook that this girl, Emmeline, could take over in the kitchen. Then my mother's here with us now, as you know, and she's very fond of my wife and tickled to death with her granddaughter. She's a very capable woman, she's had three children herself and she's helped lots of other women take care of theirs. I can't resist confessing to you that, if you both left, there'd be great rejoicing in at least two quarters and I don't believe my wife would be in the least bit the worse for it."

As a result of this conversation and those which took place with Dr. Haskins and Dr. Loomis the following morning, Miss Hilton departed, in a state of affronted dignity. Miss Hogle, however, elected to stay on, provided it was understood she was to be on duty only at night and that, during the daytime, she was to occupy the guest room undisturbed. Again, Nicolas decided that an interview was indicated.

"I think it would be better, Miss Hogle, if you took over day duty. I understand that you find the stairs very hard and if you need help with the trays you can have it. But, if you follow my suggestion, you could show my mother and Cassie just how you do things and, if they don't follow directions after you're gone, that won't be your responsibility. Meanwhile, Cassie can be the one to sleep on the cot in my wife's room. It would be easy enough to call you if anything went wrong—not that I believe it's going to. Incidentally, you needn't worry about the stairs as far as my wife is concerned. I've often carried her over them and found it a pleasure."

With very little further adjustment, the new schedule was effected and, at the end of another week, Miss Hogle surprised them all by saying she would be glad to remain as long as they needed her. She understood there was not going to be an English nanny, after all, so perhaps it would be better if she made no plans for immediate departure. At this point, Margaret herself was cautiously consulted for the first time and, without the slightest hesitation, said she appreciated Miss Hogle's willingness to co-operate. But, actually, what was she doing that could not be handled now without her help? Nothing, Mrs. Waldo Hale and Cassie hastened to insist. Annabelle carried up the trays and welcomed the chance this gave her to look in on the baby. Margaret was still forbidden the stairs, but Nicolas would carry her over them as soon as she felt like going down to her meals and, meanwhile, she was up on her chaise longue most of the day and was back to tub baths. Grandma delighted in bathing Cynthia, who was a model baby, sleeping soundly without burping from a ten o'clock to a six o'clock feeding. Cassie only needed to change her, take her to her mother and put her back in her cradle after she was nursed. Aside from that, there was nothing for her to do.

"Except act as a watchdog," Nicolas suggested, when he and Margaret were alone again and it had just been decided, amicably, that Miss Hogle was to leave at the end of another week, as Sam and Esther would then be making their long delayed visit and would be needing the guest room. It was twilight, the time Nicolas enjoyed so much, and he was sitting near Margaret on the little gallery that led from the upper hall, where a wicker couch had been placed, so that she could be as much at ease there as in her own room. He left her very rarely, but that afternoon he had been into Washington for a conference with Allan Lambert about the progress (or lack of it) of his exploratory ventures, and, when he came back, he had tossed a package into her lap, which proved to contain a necklace of moonstones, encircled and separated by small diamonds. The large emerald, about which he had written her when he left in November, had not been mentioned again; it was understood between them that this was to be saved for the birth of their son. But he could not let Cynthia's birth go by without some visible token of tenderness and the necklace, which had been made to order at Galt's, had just been finished.

"Nicolas, you must stop giving me expensive presents! I know you can't afford it, even if you don't," Margaret protested.

"I know. I ought to be saving up for Cynthia's college education. Father's reminded me of that already. I promise I won't give you another present until I can afford it—or until some special occasion indicates it. I want you to keep thinking of me at Moonstone Lake— and of the hidden lake we've still to find. The moonstones are for this one—the diamonds for the next."

"Then wouldn't it have been better to wait until you found the next one before you gave me this necklace?"

"No. The more I spend, the more incentive I have to afford it. Besides, my check from *Collier's* has come and it's larger than I expected. What's more, they've put me under contract for all the articles I write after I get back to Peru, whether there's any immediate discovery or not. So you see I'm as good as in the money already."

He smiled so engagingly that she could not bring herself to reprove him further and, as he fastened the necklace around her throat, he pressed his face against hers and told her he was glad times had changed, that he had not been obliged to leave this one on her dressing table, as he had her pearls, because she was afraid he would take liberties if she let him put it on. However, as a matter of fact, perhaps she ought to be afraid of the same thing now—that was why it was just as well to keep Cassie in her room as a watchdog.

"What do you mean?" she asked lightly.

"Can't you guess?" he asked, less lightly. "All right, as long as Cassie's in your room—*our* room—I won't have the nerve to come charging in there, until Dr. Loomis says I may. Cassie would be quite capable of throwing me out. If you were alone—well, I might yield to temptation. Who knows? We hear an awful lot about nature being hard on women and, on general principles, I agree. But sometimes it's hard on men, too—especially when they've lived continently for a long while and know they've got to do so again. Somehow, there ought to be a provision that would keep them from wanting their wives."

It was the first time he had put his yearning for her into words, and he instantly cursed himself for a selfish, sensual brute, for the quick tears, which were still a betrayal of her failure to regain her strength, came into Margaret's eyes.

"It'll only be a few more weeks, Nicolas."

"*A few more weeks!* In a few more weeks, I've got to be on my way back to Peru. I ought to be on my way back now."

"Have you had bad news you haven't told me about?"

"No. The latest news was exciting, but it wasn't actually alarming. One day recently, after a sudden rainstorm, the camp was surrounded by Cogapacoris, who, contrary to what we had been told to expect, were delighted to meet the *viracochas*—so delighted, they decided not to make war on their traditional enemies, the Machiguengas. Instead, they invited our Machiguengas—about thirty of them—to take part in contests, fishing and hunting both. The Machiguengas are actually more skillful than the Cogapacoris when it comes to the use of bows and arrows and one wise old Machiguenga warned the others not to show too much superiority. They didn't, so everything turned out for the best."

"Then you're not worried?"

"No, not actually. The same wise old Machiguenga warned the *viracochas* it would be better to act as if there were no women among the Cogapacoris. As long as that warning's heeded, I don't believe I've anything to worry about."

"But you're afraid it won't be?"

"I can't help it. Pete's been indiscreet once already since I came home. I didn't tell you about it then, I didn't want to worry you before the baby was born. Now I guess I have to tell you, to explain one of the reasons I'm getting uneasy. After all, what can I expect? The oldest man on my staff, Gomara, is only forty. The others range from their early twenties to their early thirties. They're not longing for their wives, because none of them is married. But they can't be expected to go on forever without longing—well, for something in the way of feminine companionship. When I get back, I'll see that they take vacations, turn and turn about, so they can go where there are women of their own kind. Lester's found a girl he likes in Lima, Carmen somebody or other, a perfectly suitable *novia*, which is what I think he'd rather have anyway. I'm not sure he isn't also keeping a rather warm place in his heart for Clarissa and I don't know anyone I'd rather have for a brother-in-law. Whichever way that turns out will be all right. But as for the others, except Gomara, who's that *rara avis,* a natural celibate—"

He broke off abruptly. "To get back to where we started," he went on after a minute, "I was terribly touched, terribly moved, when you told me, of your own accord, just two days after Cynthia was born, you realized I was disappointed because she wasn't a boy, but that the next time. . . . It showed a lot of courage for you to say that, so soon after what you'd just been through, and it showed something else—that you love me a lot more than I deserve."

"No, no, darling—not a lot more than you deserve. That couldn't be possible. But a great deal, so much that—"

"So much that you'd welcome me if I came back to you?"

"Of course."

"Any time now?"

"You know I'd *welcome* you any time, Nicolas. It isn't a case of welcome. But I have just had a baby and now I'm nursing her. I'll speak to Dr. Loomis again. I don't believe he realizes how soon you've got to leave."

Again Nicolas cursed himself for a selfish, sensual brute and said she must do nothing of the sort. Then the arrival of Sam and Esther created a diversion and he forgot about it. Both guests were slightly aggrieved; Nicolas should have known, they said, that of course their respective fathers would have stood back of him again. He did not need to begin peddling his wares here, there and the other place; above all, he should steer clear of an old satyr like Powers. He had not done any peddling, Nicolas retorted indignantly. Nothing could have surprised him more than the senator's spontaneous offer, made in behalf of his daughter, who had become one of Margaret's best friends, as well as himself. After all, he, Nicolas, had been in Virginia ever since late May and in all that time Sam and Esther had not found it convenient to come to Hills' End. It was all very well to say they were waiting to see the baby —they could have come twice. The tension was further increased when Esther said, with the same frankness that had characterized her expressed wish to be Margaret's matron of honor, she would like to be one of Cynthia's godmothers. She understood that, in the Episcopal Church, girl babies had two, so that would give Margaret a chance to ask still another friend beside herself. Yes, that was so, Margaret had replied, with some embarrassment. But there were some restrictions, she was not sure just what, she would have to ask Mr. Bates. Unequivocally, Mr. Bates declared that the member of any Trinitarian church would be eligible, since all subscribed to the same creed which they must promise the child would be taught. He was very sorry, but unfortunately, unless he were mistaken, Mrs. Steinmetz was a Jewess. Margaret was sorrier still that the explanation of this provision was her responsibility. It was a relief when the visit, to which she had looked forward with so much pleasure, came to an end.

The day after their guests' departure, Margaret told Nicolas casually that Cassie was not going to sleep in her room any more. He smiled and said she was an angel and all that, but he had resolved he would not take advantage of Cassie's absence—that is, not yet. He kept his resolution until another letter came in from Fonso Parra.

Rural delivery did not reach Hills' End until afternoon and, the day the letter came, Nicolas had gone to the White House to attend a reception given by President and Mrs. Maynard in honor of a Latin American delegation representing eight countries, including Peru. Before he left, he had seen Margaret, who was no longer confined to her bedroom and the balcony, comfortably settled in the arbor and told her not to wait supper for him, as he probably would be delayed, if not in one quarter, then in another. She had followed his suggestion and, when he rejoined her, with expressions of regret because his premonition had been all too accurate, Annabelle had already taken away the tray and Margaret was sitting with the unopened letter in her hand, looking anxiously down at it.

"I suppose I have to give this to you, don't I?" she asked.

He glanced at the familiar stamp and the postmark. "I'm afraid you do," he said regretfully. He took it from her and read it very slowly, before returning it to her without comment: Pete Hart had disregarded the warning that the *viracochas* would do well to ignore the presence of women in the Cogapacori camp. He had gone there and put a necklace of colored glass around a girl's neck and given her a tiny mirror. That, in itself, did not seem very serious, of course. But the same wise old Machiguenga, who had given them such good advice in the beginning, had now told Pete, very respectfully, that a gift for a girl must first be given to a male who, in turn, would see to it that his woman got it in the *viracocha's* behalf. This method of bestowal would be taken as a compliment; the other way was taken as an insulting advance. And Pete had only laughed and gone on his willful way. This meant that, at any moment now, there would be trouble—grave trouble.

For a long moment, Margaret and Nicolas sat silently, looking into each other's eyes. Then she gave the letter back to him and left him to reread it, quietly and alone. She did not need to be told that, when he had done so, he would come to her.

He could not have tried harder to be gentle, to remember that it was a long time since they had been together and that this, in itself, would make her supersensitive. Besides, perhaps giving birth to a baby affected a woman both physically and emotionally in some way which he did not know about, and which might make it almost as hard for her to have him "act like a husband" as it had at first. Moreover, far from feeling, as he had on their wedding night, that the more masterful he seemed, the more compassionate he would actually be, he knew this was the time for infinite loving-kindness. If he had needed to overcome the least resistance or shrinking, however instinctive or involuntary, he would have wooed her patiently, he would have kept on trying to be gentle, to remember. But speedily as he had come to her, she was already awaiting him, and everything about her bespoke her joyous readiness to receive him. He had not even envisioned, much less expected, such perfect pliancy, such serene accessibility. Without urgency, much less constraint, with almost unbelievable swiftness, she was again wholly his; and he knew he need not release her until his first fierce hunger had been appeased and that he could return to her again and again as long as his vital need for her persisted. From the moment he touched her, there had been complete understanding, complete spontaneity, complete harmony, all beautiful beyond belief.

In the morning, the soft stirring of the baby in the nearby cradle made him aware, for the first time, of another presence. How did it happen, he asked, as Margaret lifted Cynthia into their bed, he had not known when she did this the night before? Because you were already so sound asleep at ten o'clock you did not hear her asking for her supper, Margaret said smiling; had he forgotten how early he came in from the arbor? No, nor why, Nicolas said, smiling in his turn; but he must have waked again after that, because. . . . Yes, a little after midnight and then *Cynthia* was sleeping soundly; see, they did not disturb each other in the least! Nicolas regarded the baby thoughtfully and with more appreciation than he had before; she had quantities of soft hair, as dark as her mother's was blonde, and there was already a sturdiness about her which transcended mere infantile rosiness. She drank avidly, her tiny hands pressed against her mother's flesh, as if to knead it; she was not old enough to really do that yet, Margaret said, but at the rate she was going, it would not be long before she did; no matter how much there was for her, she would demand more. She was very strong, gaining almost a pound a week, developing fast.

"Why, she's a perfect vampire!" Nicolas said. "No wonder you don't get your strength back!" Then, suddenly softening, he tried to put into words his deep feeling that there was no hunger of whatever kind Margaret could not and would not assuage for those she loved and that the sight of this black-haired child she had given him at her white breast, after he himself had lain against it through most of the night, made him more than ever conscious of all he owed her, all he could never repay. How could he blame the baby for draining her strength? That was what he had done, over and over again, and what he would continue to do. He must not say such things, Margaret told him gently; he did not drain her of strength and neither did Cynthia. They tested it and she was so proud they did not find it wanting that it was renewed. And it was Nicolas who had given her this child, not she who had given it to him. He had transfigured her life and made it fruitful instead of barren. And this was only the beginning of that rich fecundity. When he came home the next time—

"What then?" he asked eagerly.

"Why then Cynthia'll be a big girl, won't she? Perhaps as much as six months old?"

"I hope not. I hope I'll be back long before then. But that isn't what you started to say, is it?"

"No, I've forgotten now what that was. But I'll never forget what you said to me just now. You have a way of making me feel that being a wife and becoming a mother isn't something almost any woman could do. As if it were something very special."

"It is very special, the way you do it. In some ways, you must be like Juliet."

"Juliet?"

"Yes—don't you remember what she said to Romeo:

'My bounty is as boundless as the sea,
My love as deep; the more I give to thee
The more I have, for both are infinite.'

There aren't many women, Margaret, who have it in them to bestow infinite bounty. Evidently Juliet did. That's why her story has lived through the centuries. And you do. You have. You always will."

Later in the morning, while they were still in bed, he asked her impetuously how quickly she could arrange for the christening party, which they had agreed should take place before he left, and she assured him, without the slightest sign that this might be an effort for her, that it could be done at once.

"At least," she said smiling, "I don't know that we could take all the precautions Mr. Kent Curtis would feel necessary to assure the safety of President and Mrs. Maynard. As far as I know, the steps are secure, the rugs don't slip, the well works and the servants have no criminal records. But my confidence in all of this might not be great enough to satisfy the White House Secret Service."

"The Maynards won't be here. Having proved yesterday that they're

Good Neighbors, they're leaving tomorrow for New England, where it's lovely and cool, instead of staying in Washington, where it's lovely and hot. So we can start with the Bruces at the top of the list. Probably it's just as well. The *entente cordiale* is getting more and more strained between The Great Man and the VP. . . . Are we all set for sponsors?"

They had already asked Martina Román and Milagrita Lambert to act as godmothers, Margaret reminded him, as she picked up the telephone, and both had graciously accepted; they now signified their availability for the following afternoon, provided this were convenient for Mr. Bates, who was next consulted and who replied it was *more* than convenient. The question of a godfather, which had seemed to require more thought, was still unsettled, and Margaret suggested that she thought Senator Powers would be very much pleased if he were invited to act in this capacity and that, in view of his generosity and interest, it would be suitable to ask him. Nicolas hesitated, fortunately not long enough to have his hesitation obvious and, as Margaret had predicted, the senator expressed the greatest possible pleasure at their invitation. Chauncey, the incomparable Alexandria grocer, was also reached by telephone; he would immediately send out as much caviar and pâté de foie gras as Mrs. Hale wanted, and he would also get in touch with the state liquor store and arrange to secure two cases of champagne and one case each of Scotch and bourbon for those misguided souls who preferred to drink whiskey, even at a christening. With these details settled, Margaret rang for Cassie, who assured her Emmeline would "get going" on the christening cake within an hour and, since that would be snow-white and towering, there must also be devil's food cakes, richly dark and flat by way of contrast. Then, of course, two big hams, two big turkeys, two big rib roasts of beef, chicken patties, tomato aspic, lobster salad, Parker House rolls, peach ice cream, raspberry sherbet, coffee, fruit punch—well, if Miss Margaret thought of anything else she wanted later on, she was just to ring again.

"I even have just the right dress," Margaret said, slipping out of bed. "I had some sent on approval from Pasternak's because I didn't want Esther to say it was time I had new ones and start giving me a second trousseau. As it was, she brought a lot. But I've one creation I chose myself, right after you gave me the moonstone necklace. Wait a second, I'll model it for you." In a matter of minutes, she was standing before him in a gauzy white dress, shot with silver and silver-girdled. "Don't you think it's lovely?" she asked enthusiastically.

"As you are. It's a good thing I don't mind having you outshine me. No one is even going to know I'm among those present."

"Everyone is going to know. You'll wear that wonderful new suit of yours, the black Italian silk. We'll contrast each other, like Cassie's cakes!"

So Cynthia, a vision of infantile loveliness in an ancestral christening robe which was a foam of fine lace, was baptized at the beautiful old stone font of Pohick Church; and, afterward, there was a gala gathering in the house and on the lawn at Hills' End, with a surprising number of congenial spirits in attendance, considering how little notice it had been possible to give them. The weather was perfect, the grounds at the height of their late summer luxuriance, and Tom Herbert, who had an accordion, offered his services as strolling player. Cynthia, still good as gold, was handed from one gushing guest to another, as these stood about in small friendly groups sipping champagne. Then she was borne away by the beaming Cassie, who had also dressed with care for the occasion, in a soft, full, flowered muslin that had once belonged to Mrs. Robert E. Lee's personal maid and had somehow found its way to Hills' End from Arlington with a few other minor heirlooms. When Cynthia's bedtime approached, Cassie marched majestically toward the house with her charge, fully aware of the complimentary remarks that followed them. Then, cradling the baby in her arms, she sat crooning old lullabies until Margaret came to rob her of her precious treasure.

Margaret and Nicolas said good-by to their guests at the door, just as they had at their wedding reception and again Margaret asked if everything had been all right, if Nicolas had been pleased and, again, he told her everything had been perfect and she knew it. Then he laughed and said that, theoretically, it was impossible to improve on perfection, but in one way the christening *was* an improvement on the wedding reception: this time he knew Margaret was not dreading to see him alone after it was over! She did not shed unwelcome tears any more; she was right, her strength was renewed; Nicolas was right, her bounty was as boundless as the sea. She laughed, too, and they were very happy together. The festive atmosphere of the party continued to pervade their consciousness and that night they were able to forget that this was borrowed time, that their reunion was only an interlude between two long periods of separation, that, at any moment, a dreaded message might come and bring it to an end.

It came in cable form the next afternoon:

Cogapacoris have kidnapped Pete. Machiguengas have deserted. Lester insisting on foolhardy trip downstream alone in hopes of retrieving losses. Expedition threatened with complete disintegration. How soon can you get here?

Fonso.

32 ❧

There was always some reason to hurry. Now that he had reached Atalaya, now that he had found a warm welcome in the house with the high thatched roof and the open walls and the raised floor which his friend Antonio had built for himself and his bride Fátima, Nicolas would have enjoyed lingering there, at least for a few days. He would have liked to visit the clearings which Antonio had converted into pastureland; he would have liked to learn more about the breeding of Zebú cattle; above all, he would have liked the luxury of long, leisurely conversations with a kindred spirit, the kind in which he and Antonio had indulged when they were fellow patients at the Quillabamba Mission—not conversations about things which must be done and how and when best to do them, but about abstract ideas and ideals. Instead, he must be off to the camp at the lagoon without a single hour of unnecessary delay.

So far, he had made good time. He had been able to get immediate reservations by plane from New York to Lima via Panagra and to make good connection from Lima to Pucallpa via Faucett, despite a schedule which did not provide for daily service. According to Fonso, who also regretfully informed him that radio contact had been most unsatisfactory the last few days, many of the local flights had not only been starting late recently, but some had been turned back to Lima shortly before they reached their intended destinations, because of weather unpropitious for landing. Nicolas was thankful that nothing of that sort happened now; besides having every practical reason for haste, he could not help feeling Fonso's welcome had lacked its former exuberance and that his hospitality, though as lavish as ever, also lacked something of its old warmheartedness. This did not occasion either surprise or resentment. After all, Pete and Lester meant nothing to him personally; though he could and did regret the trouble they were causing Nicolas, their fate could hardly be a matter of deep concern. Besides, Nicolas' exploratory ventures were getting to be an old story to his Limenian friends; he could not expect them to feel the same enthusiasm and excitement about these that they had when his expeditions were a novelty, especially if they failed to achieve their objective, like the latest one. In addition, he knew Marina thought he had treated Margaret very badly from the beginning, and that this new departure, when he left her with a baby only a few weeks old, was insult added to injury; Marina's viewpoint had, of course, influenced Fonso's; and, though the latter had been faithfulness itself, in his role of ham radio operator, it was inconceivable that he should not be relieved at the prospect of dropping it as an obligation, rather than a pastime, which he would be able to do as soon as Nicolas reached Atalaya. Under all these circumstances, though no one voiced any lessening of affection or any reason for this, Nicolas had no desire to linger at the Parras' house; he was thankful, on every score, when his plane left Lima on time to the minute and landed him at Pucallpa before noon the same morning.

This was the place where flight by commercial airlines ended, as far as Nicolas was concerned, and also the place where he must arrange for a chartered hydroplane. He was already informed as to the possibilities for doing this, and they were encouraging, for there were actually two between which he might be able to choose: the Summer Institute of Linguistics, sponsored by the University of Oklahoma, and located on the shores of nearby Yarina Cocha, had at its disposal for its extensive jungle activities no less than ten planes of one sort or another. Their pilots, like everyone else on the "Yarina" staff, were there because they believed in the spiritual side of the work; they undertook the material service of charter flying only as a sideline, and the decision as to whether or not they should undertake a commission involving risk lay with each individual pilot. Understandably, these men were not disposed to have much to do with a project which was not both sound and safe and Nicolas could not conscientiously say that his was either. However, if the Linguistics turned him down, he could appeal to the Peruvian Air Force, which by recent disposition had made available for charter flights out of Pucallpa one of its Cessnas, based at Iquitos. A Peruvian Air Force officer might well be more venturesome than an American volunteer worker. At all events, such a contingency was worth looking into.

Nicolas had decided to try the Linguistics first and had wired ahead, asking if he could come to Yarina Cocha for a conference. The response could not possibly have been more cordial. Luther Moulton, the Director of the Institute, was waiting for him at the airport and drove him quickly away from the ugliness of Pucallpa to the beauty of the Linguistic settlement on the oxbow of the Yarina. Luncheon at the cafeteria was followed by a brief visit to the print shop, which Nicolas made quite willingly, despite his feeling of urgency in regard to a plane; he could not help being impressed by the astonishing achievement of producing primer textbooks involving numerous bewildering languages, not to mention the gospels in any required dialect; and the obvious sincerity of his interest and admiration facilitated his approach to the subject of his flight. The director heard him through courteously: as he understood it, Dr. Hale needed a hydroplane, not only to take him first to Atalaya and then to a camp at some lagoon on the Pantiacolla range, but to remain there for local sorties? Yes, he thought that could be arranged, but first he must consult his pilots and see which, if any, would undertake the mission and, if so, what the charge would be. Dr. Hale understood, didn't he, that this was the way they operated? Good! Well, then, until the next morning. Eight would be a good time. A bus was now available for the return to Pucallpa and the same bus would bring the visitor back to Yarina Cocha the next morning.

Nicolas had hoped the whole thing could be settled that same evening and he could be on his way to Atalaya bright and early the following day. As things turned out, he could have been, but for his sense of fair play. When he checked in at the Hotel Mercedes, he found that an officer of the Peruvian Air Force, who had already learned by aeronautical grapevine of his requirements, was awaiting Nicolas in the bar, ready to offer his services. He introduced himself as Lieutenant Teodoro Toledo and announced he was ready to fly anywhere, any time, at five hundred *soles* an hour.

"I'd certainly like to take you up on that right now," Nicolas said with genuine regret. "But Dr. Moulton has promised to let me know at eight tomorrow morning whether or not one of his pilots would be available. He's been very decent to me—very hospitable. So has everyone at the Institute. I'm not really free to accept another offer until I've heard from him."

"I understood you were in a hurry. That's why I waited here for you tonight. I could have you halfway to Atalaya by eight A.M."

"I realize that. And you're right, I am in a hurry. But while this other arrangement's pending—"

Toledo shrugged his shoulders and rose. "In that case, I might as well start back to Iquitos at dawn."

"On the contrary. You might as well stay here until I return from Yarina Cocha. I'm perfectly willing to pay you for waiting that long if you want me to. But you can still get to Iquitos tomorrow, even if you do wait for me. It isn't going to take long to get my answer."

Toledo shrugged again, emptied his glass of beer and left the bar with a casual good night. Nicolas still had no idea whether or not the pilot meant to wait for him and spent a restless night, worrying for fear he had turned down a good chance for an uncertainty. He worried still more the following morning: Toledo was nowhere to be seen when he himself started for Yarina and the answer there was negative: in this case, the chief pilot had made the decision and, as a matter of policy, felt such a series of flights as Dr. Hale required did not come within the limitations the Linguistics had set for themselves. He was very sorry.

Nicolas was sorrier still. Toledo had apparently carried out his threat

of returning to Iquitos; at all events, he had checked out of the Hotel
Mercedes and left no message about coming back. A long dull day
stretched out endlessly before Nicolas. Fortunately, extremes of temperature did not usually bother him much; but Pucallpa's heat was
something special. The town had outgrown its first sprawling state,
when the choice mango trees planted in the small park off the *malecón*
by Joseph Hockings, an American missionary who was also a botanist,
were the only feature in its entire panorama which provided a touch of
beauty. Unlike all other provincial towns in Peru, it did not begin its
building around a *Plaza de Armas*, but it had an unpretentious and not
unattractive residential neighborhood and a row of shops that catered
to a population sufficiently prosperous to support two banks, two motion picture houses, and two hotels, in addition to several bars and
restaurants. What was more, it had fourteen sawmills, which made it
the lumber center of Peru, and was the only point on the South American continent where the Atlantic-Amazon cargo could be off-loaded
directly onto a truck bound for the Pacific. Traffic came upstream from
Iquitos by barge or big launch and downstream from Atalaya by
smaller launch; from Lima by both truck and airplane. It was developing a sense of tourist trade, personified by Foster Lopez, the prosperous
owner of the Hotel Mercedes and—in quite another way—by a few
local Indians who posed as jungle Indians, painting their faces, sticking
combs in their hair, and yelling, "Money, money!" to the camera buffs
who excitedly tried to photograph them.

Nicolas was always glad to while away a few hours watching the river
craft from the *malecón,* and he had long been on friendly terms with
Lopez, who cordially invited him to lunch; but the shipping and the
visiting did not fill enough time to quiet his restlessness and he had just
decided to return to Yarina Cocha and beg the chief pilot to reconsider,
or at least to take him as far as Atalaya, where he could get in touch
with his camp by radio, when Toledo re-entered the bar with exaggerated nonchalance and asked if Dr. Hale had come to a decision.

There was more than a touch of insolence in his manner and
Nicolas' first impression of the lieutenant had already undergone a
considerable change for the worse; but the latter's offer was still open
and, though it was now made in modified form, it was still too good to
turn down. Toledo, who now volunteered the information that his
American friends called him Teddy, was no longer ready to go any
place, any time; he now wanted it understood that the flight to Atalaya
was to be made the following morning at dawn and the one to the
lagoon the day after, also starting at dawn and allowing for a layover of
only one day. There were to be no deviations in route and any
additional flights were to be made at a slight increase in cost—say a
thousand *soles* an hour, instead of five hundred. With the feeling that

some of the gilt was off the gingerbread, but the gingerbread was still substantial fare, Nicolas accepted.

At five the next morning there was a gentle tap at his door and a man with a flashlight opened it part way to say quietly, "Five o'clock, sir." Nicolas had passed another restless night; even his long periods of early rising had never taught him to sleep soundly as long as he could, if he had to be up and doing betimes. There was no electricity in the hotel at this hour, but by the time Nicolas was ready to leave it, the light of the new day, which definitely separated it from the night, was already gaining strength, though the sun had not yet begun to prove its full powers.

The single motor Cessna, red and silver, lay moored beyond the *malecón*, on a mudbank among piles of lumber and refuse, shacks and smaller craft. Just upstream lay the *Elena*, tug of the Ganzo Azul, and the *Samuel*, tug of the Booth Line. The Cessna was tiny—not even as long as a dugout canoe—and half a dozen boys were sporting muddily about its pontoons. Teddy greeted Nicolas with the casual—and inaccurate—observation that he was late and turned to bark at his mechanic, "*Rápido!*"

Gunning the engine, Teddy took his time taxiing upstream. The mechanic, Fidel Soto, was busier than the pilot, as he studied the flow for floating obstructions. Pucallpa drifted away, the *Elena*, the *Samuel*, a hundred motorboats and dugouts and launches, then the rising wall of dry and dusty mud. In a heavy way, the plane began to hurry, pivoted on its pontoons to face upwind, downstream. Nicolas, on its starboard side, could not even see Pucallpa, only the distant eastern shore of the river or jungle. The engine roared and the Cessna retraced its taxiing route, straining, without success, to rise. Teddy hesitated, then decided to continue far down the stream, through sections of river surface no one had studied. Then suddenly they were airborne and a porpoise flipped, as if to wish them good luck!

The Cessna made a wide turn and Teddy set his course south, upstream. His first checkpoint was an oil refinery, glittering under the rays of the early sun; then behind them lay the town, ugly and sprawling and dusty. The heat of another despairing jungle day must by now be encompassing the Hotel Mercedes and Nicolas had a sense of escape, for cool air cascaded over him from a welcome ventilator. The Cessna was holding its south heading, and the Ucayali was also ascending south via endless meanders. They were flying low, yet clouds came and sifted and grazed between them and the river. This was the dry season, so the river was studded and scarred with sandbars. Off to the right went the tributary Pachitea and there lay one recognizable town, Masisea; beyond it the upper Ucayali was as sparsely populated as Antarctica. The dark green jungle, here and there, cut a swath of light green and beyond this and the sifting, grazing clouds lay a blue mist. The haze thickened. Rain? Not today, but soon. The drought seemed meaningless. Only the horizon made sense. Its one sharp line in a scene of parabolas. A twist of river, a twist of jungle, a twist of cloud. . . .

And then they circled Atalaya, where there were a few blocks of simple jungle houses, a single tower church and a plaza of green right by the river—the Tambo, just above its juncture with the Urubamba. On the plaza, a *fútbol* game broke up under Nicolas' very eyes, the players taking off to race along a trail shaded by banana fronds, as they hurried to meet the plane. Teddy had taxied idly for only a few minutes when a bevy of the young athletes appeared on the run and caught the mooring line from Fidel. He promptly leaped ashore, asking the pilot's leave to go on ahead, in order that he might lose no time in looking up the police sergeant who was an old crony of his and whom he seldom had a chance to see. Teddy was also in a hurry; he must report in with the Military Infantry Battalion Number Nine at once; but before the mechanic and the pilot were actually out of sight, Antonio had emerged from the banana-shaded trail with a shout of greeting.

"Here, give whatever you're carrying to one of those boys," he said, as he released Nicolas from a hearty *abrazo*.

"Not a chance. I've carried it in my own lily-white hands all the way from New York. I shan't risk having it smashed in the last quarter mile of its journey. I'm delivering it personally to a certain *Doña* Fátima. But, first of all, I've got to hear the news from camp."

"Of course. I'm going to give it to you as we walk along toward the house. And I'll tell you right away that it's all good. I talked with Gomara at six this morning, and if the reception hadn't been unusually clear, I couldn't have made out what he was saying—he was so excited: Pete is safely back at camp."

"Thank God! He isn't—mutilated?"

"Not in the way you've been fearing—and with reason. It's a miracle that he isn't, after flouting tribal morality in the way he did. But he's so disfigured by facial tattooing no woman will ever voluntarily look at him again and, I'm afraid, very few men. Almost automatically, his life is bound to be a lonely one from now on. I'm sure I don't need to ask you to treat him with great forbearance—especially as he repentantly realizes that, if it hadn't been for his wanton folly, you wouldn't have had to leave home as soon as you did."

"Don't worry. Pete's been his own worst enemy for a long time. But, as far as I'm concerned, he always has been and always will be my friend—one of my best. What's the rest of the news?"

"Li Chan was disappointed because you couldn't get to the camp in time for lunch; it seems he had already killed the fatted calf for you, figuratively speaking; in this case, it was a wild pig. He'll try to have something equally choice tomorrow, but can't guarantee it. The students are behaving themselves and being generally useful, though, actually, there isn't much they can do right now. As for Lester, you've nothing to worry about."

"Well, thank God for that, too. As you know, I gave strict orders that he was on no account to abandon Gomara, Li Chan and the boys, after Pete was kidnapped and the Machiguengas deserted; but I couldn't help being afraid he'd start off on some foolhardy trip of his own, to see if he couldn't catch up with the Machiguengas and persuade them to come back."

Antonio coughed slightly. "Well, it seems your strict orders weren't transmitted fast enough. Gomara and Li Chan saw him as far along as the first cataract, a drop of nearly a thousand feet. They let him down by nylon scaling line and, through signaled jerks from below, understood he had made the first drop safely. After that, they didn't have any news of him for several days and I didn't, either."

"Talk about mutiny on the *Bounty*," Nicolas said sarcastically, "not only is there always some obscure reason why there's a delay in receiving my orders, but all hands then turn to help the prize mutineer defy them. However, I take it you've heard from him since, as you've assured me I've nothing to worry about, as far as he's concerned. I'd be glad of a few details."

"I will hasten to supply them. Lester next encountered three sets of smaller cataracts, but the river toward which they led—the Ticumpenía—was low in volume, and he was able to make the descent easily, as he was well equipped with more scaling line and all the proper tools."

"Provided with almost uncanny thoroughness, I'd say, for a man who'd taken such a sudden departure."

"Really, Nicolas, your sarcasm seems not only ill-directed, but ill-timed. I'm not the one who mutinied and though it is quite true that Lester did so, this was from the best motives and it all had a happy outcome. He met Machiguengas along the lower course of the Ticumpenía, but none of *your* Machiguengas—the ones he was after. They guided him to a field station of the Summer Institute of Linguistics, located at the mouth of the next Urubamba tributary downstream, and the resident American couple gave him every possible attention. By radio they advised Yarina Cocha of the situation and I, in turn, was alerted. Then they loaned Lester one of their own dugout canoes with a good outboard motor. They also supplied him with a river guide who would know the two places for portage and would pilot the dugout back. Lester ought to be turning up at my house almost any time now, perhaps today, and I suggest you show some forbearance to him, also. You're his little tin god on wheels and we will do our best to comfort and cheer you, *amigo*, Fátima and I. That is my house, just ahead of us, the one with the porch. Of course, porches do not belong

on jungle houses; but I wanted one on mine, in memory of my home in
northern Spain. And there is Fátima, standing at the top of the steps,
waiting to receive us."

Nicolas had not been without curiosity concerning the impression
which Antonio's bride would make on him and it was a very pleasant
one. She was wearing a fresh muslin dress, which reminded Nicolas
vaguely of those the twins had worn to dancing school when they were
little girls, except that it was longer. Unlike them, however, she did not
wear patent leather slippers and white socks, but gold sandals, which
might have seemed inappropriate, considering the simplicity of the
white dress, had they not complemented her long gold earrings and
heavy gold necklace. Her magnificent black hair, plaited in two braids
which had been brought forward over her breast, hung well below her
waist; and, with a pang far more poignant than mere memory, Nicolas
thought of Margaret's hair, which he had made her promise never to
cut. To be sure, that was as fair as Fátima's was dark; the resemblance
was only in its abundance and in its beauty. But with the poignancy
still unallayed, Nicolas thought of Margaret's as it had veiled her when
she lay on the soft old blanket in the barn and when she sat up in bed
to drink the *bouillon de la mariée*. While he was last at Hills' End,
the nurse had confined it, as long as she could, in just such braids as
Fátima was wearing; but Nicolas had managed, those final nights at
home, to loosen it himself, to see it spread out over the pillow and then
to stretch out his hands and wind it softly round his knuckles and draw
it—and Margaret—closer to him. Was that, he wondered, what hap·
pened to Fátima's braids, in the conjugal chamber of the house An·
tonio had built in Atalaya?

Bringing himself swiftly back to present realities, he smiled and
bowed and held out his package. Fátima accepted it, smiling in return
and betraying her pleased astonishment.

"Another present? Oh, *Don* Nicolas, that is too much! You have al·
ready given me a present, a beautiful one! I cannot wait to show it to
you, displayed on the table that Antonio made on purpose for it."

"I want to see it. But first you must open this one. The other was
your wedding present. Now I am bringing you one because you have
been kind enough to receive me as your guest. Such an offering is
customary in my country."

She needed no second urging. The two men stood by, exchanging
amused glances, as she undid the wrappings with the eagerness of an
excited child—the heavy brown paper, the corrugated cardboard, the
shavings and cotton, the final tissue. When a red glass bowl was at last
exposed in all its splendor, she gave a delighted cry and held it at arm's
length to admire it.

"Oh, how beautiful! Oh, how rare! It must have the place of honor on top of the refrigerator. Thank you, thank you, thank you!" She passed the vase to her husband, with a word of caution that he was not to drop it and seized Nicolas' hand, the better to show her appreciation.

"Policarpo!" she called, to some invisible but obviously accessible servant who suddenly appeared. "Fetch me the drinks from the refrigerator." Then, before giving a tiny boy time to pass a tray set with glasses of *chicha,* she added, "And, afterward, bring me some fruit."

"Where on earth did anyone get a name like Policarpo?" Nicolas inquired, as he seated himself and accepted a cooling drink of *chicha,* which Fátima told him she had made herself that very morning from dried corn brought in from the sierra.

"I got it at the Mission." The small servant, returning with one banana so noiselessly that Nicolas had not heard him, was answering for himself. "The padre named me after the saint on whose feast day I was born and, when I was kidnapped and sold for a shotgun, all I kept was my name." He disappeared in search of more fruit and, as Fátima followed him, to make sure he understood his instructions this time, Antonio said regretfully, "It's a cruel matter. Father Alegre has protested vehemently against it, but so far to no avail. The river people profit by the low grade of civilization in the various tribes, which permits them to steal one another's children and sell them into regional slavery. . . . I could no more break up the system than I could persuade my wife to put the refrigerator in the cookhouse, instead of the living room," he went on with a slight smile, "and you may be sure Policarpo himself thinks a shotgun is worth a lot and that a boy is lucky to be valued so highly. And he really is very well off here with us—he works part time and studies part time. . . . Now we've talked on and on about conditions at the lagoon and what is happening here. It is time we talked about Virginia and Margaret and Cynthia. You left them well, I hope?"

"Oh yes. Margaret seems to tire very easily, something new for her. She's nursing the baby and that, apparently, uses up a lot of strength, especially when the baby gains as rapidly as Cynthia. Of course, I don't know much about obstetrics and pediatrics. But Cassie, our old colored cook, keeps muttering that 'everything goes to the milk' which, being interpreted, evidently means Cynthia's benefiting more by this deal than Margaret. Supposedly, it's very rare that a baby's weight, when it's a week old, isn't less than when it was born. Cynthia's was more; and since then she's been racing along at eight ounces a week, instead of four—the standard amount. Again I'm only quoting, but that's what I was told."

"You were told quite correctly. I haven't forgotten about such things, though they are far away and long ago, as far as I'm concerned."

Nicolas looked up in surprise. Antonio had never referred to his life in Spain since the day he had briefly and bitterly said, "I've had enough of bloodshed, both on the firing line and on the home front. I lost my wife and child in a hideous way. I've come to the jungle not to destroy, but to forget and to build." He had certainly built and, in so doing, had obviously achieved happiness, as well as success. But he had not forgotten, after all. Something that had been said, though it all seemed rather trivial to Nicolas, rather dull in fact, had awakened memories of the wife and child that were killed—a loss for which even his lovely young bride could not compensate.

"She is very dear to you, this little Cynthia of yours, isn't she?" Antonio went on.

"Why, yes. Though, of course I couldn't help being terribly disappointed that she wasn't a boy. If I could only be sure she'd have a brother, I'd feel better about it. And I might have had such an assurance if you hadn't sent for me so urgently. At least, I might have been sure another baby was on its way. And it doesn't seem as if I could possibly have such bad luck as to have a second daughter when I want a son so much!"

Antonio rose and crossed the room, laying his hand on Nicolas' shoulder. "*Amigo,* you are tempting fate when you talk like that," he said gravely. "You should thank God every night on your knees that you have a little daughter. And if He sends you another, you should thank Him for that, too, because it will mean your wife is still alive, that she can bear you more children. She has not been murdered, she and her first girl-child, leaving you bereft. When you go into the jungle, it is of your own free will that you part from your family; when I came into the jungle, it was because I had been parted, through no fault of mine, from everything in the world that I held dear."

33 ❧

Nicolas was sorry he could not leave for camp that same afternoon. Though his feeling of haste had been allayed, he was now a prey to a general feeling of malaise, much the same as that of which he had been aware in Lima; he no longer desired to linger for leisurely conversation. He kept telling himself that the opinion of his friends, whether implied—as in the case of Fonso—or outspoken—as in the case of Antonio—should not matter; he was annoyed to find that it seemed to. As far as his wife was concerned, his conscience was clear and, as far as his work was concerned, his purpose was fixed. He had more than lived up to the obligations he had undertaken when he married; Margaret herself had been the first to say this and she had done so repeatedly. And he had other obligations: to the men who were waiting for him at the lake, not only to those who had served him so faithfully, but to the poor black sheep who had gone astray and needed him more than ever now; to himself as an explorer and a leader; and to the great causes of geography, science and history.

His departure from Virginia, though he regretted its abruptness, had not subjected him to the same emotional upheaval that had racked him when he left Margaret the first time. She had understood his fierce hunger to reclaim her as his wife after his long months of continence, and not only had she never denied him; she had shown herself tender and approachable while she was still the prey of the inevitable lassitude which followed childbirth and was prolonged by nursing the baby; and, as soon as she knew his departure was imminent and inevitable, she had insisted that their intimate relationship must immediately be resumed. He realized, in so ministering to his needs, she had disregarded the advice of her physician and that, theoretically, he, Nicolas, should not have permitted her to do so. On the other hand, she would have reproached herself all winter, if her failure to conceive quickly again had been due to her insistence that her husband should be "considerate"; moreover, being Margaret, she would also have felt her power to attract him irresistibly had lessened, that she was not as desirable in his eyes as when he had first possessed her.

As it was, she knew he had never needed and wanted her more than in their brief period of reunion; and her rapturous reception of him, her spontaneous and sustained accessibility had satisfied, for the time being, the requirements of demanding virility. There had been no *"nuits blanches"* since he left her. But, if he were to be exposed to domesticity as represented by married couples like Fonso and Marina, Antonio and Fátima, there was no telling how long his temporary respite from unfulfilled desire would last. He wanted increasingly to get away from all well-ordered homes where feminine influence and conjugal intimacy were dominating forces. He wanted to reach his camp, far beyond the limits of standardized gracious living, unrestricted by the amenities, thoroughly male, not only in personnel, but in atmosphere; to set things straight, to reach his goal, and then to return free to the wife whom he had at first visualized only as a means to an end and who had become the lodestone of his life.

He sought out Toledo, who had obviously decided to do more than "report" at Infantry Battalion Number Nine, since he had settled in

there for a prolonged game of cribbage, with individual cigarettes as
stakes. Making a gesture that was apparently habitual, the pilot
shrugged his shoulders; their agreement had been to start at dawn the
next day, hadn't it? Very well, that was when they would next meet—at
Astur's house, where he would pick up his passenger; or, if Dr. Hale
preferred to start a little later, say at seven, he was willing to concede
that much. He had learned that the radio conversations took place at
six and, of course, it was desirable, from every viewpoint, to have the
latest report. Meanwhile, even if he himself had been disposed to start,
he had no idea where to find Fidel who, as Dr. Hale well knew, had
gone off with the police sergeant, an old crony of his. What was more, it
was beginning to rain. Yes, the sky had been a clear blue a minute ago.
But that *was* a minute ago.

Nicolas had no choice but to accept the inevitable and the rest of the
day passed pleasantly enough. Although Fátima apologized for the
luncheon, because she had only fish, nothing as exciting as wild pig to
offer, actually the meal was delicious—a superb soup of *boquichico*
followed by baked *zúngaro,* and fruit for dessert; and she had made
every possible provision for his comfort, providing a hard bed, as well
as a soft hammock, in his room, so that he could follow his preference
between them.

"What about a *lupuna* tree?" he asked jestingly.

"A *lupuna* tree?" she repeated in a puzzled voice.

"Surely a river girl like you must have heard of their bizarre magic!
Anyone who sleeps under a *lupuna* betrays the memory of its secrets by
a special shadow in the eyes. Don't tell me I've been mistaken,
thinking I saw it in yours! And that, therefore, you might provide me
with a *lupuna* tree, as well as a bed and a hammock, so that I could
have a similar experience."

"Don't tease her, Nick, she can't follow you when you talk like
that," Antonio said quietly, as Fátima looked from one man to the
other, still betraying her bewilderment; and, putting his arm around
his wife, he smoothed her beautiful hair away from her forehead and
kissed her. "In fact, this isn't the time for talk, anyway," he went on,
turning to Nicolas. "You need a siesta, after all the hard traveling
you've done and all the anxiety you've undergone. Take your choice,
as Fátima suggested, between a bed and a hammock, but get into one or
the other without any more idle chatter."

Usually, Nicolas would have scorned this suggestion, but this time he
accepted it gratefully. He was not only very tired; he did not enjoy
standing by, watching another man caress his wife, when he, Nicolas,
had put two oceans between himself and his own. He could tell, from
that caress, that Antonio felt much the same about Fátima's hair as
he did about Margaret's. He left them abruptly for his own room,

chose the bed rather than the hammock, and slept most of the afternoon. In fact, it was already so dark in the room when he waked, he did
not immediately identify the dim figure sitting quietly in one corner.
Then, with mingled relief and irritation, he realized that it was Lester.

"History seems to have a way of repeating itself," he said rather
grimly, without any other form of greeting. "If you can find some kind
of a precipice to leap over, you do it, whatever the orders are to the
contrary. It's a good thing you're not still in the service—you'd be shot
at sunrise. And, if I take a good long refreshing sleep, the first sight to
disturb my waking vision is apt to be the spectacle of you hunched up
in a chair beside my bed."

"You were damn glad to see me the last time," Lester replied
without abashment. "And there's no use pretending you aren't this
time, too, because I know you are. Besides, I've news for you. I arrived
in Atalaya safe and sound about two hours ago and, after checking with
Antonio on the general situation, I went and had a talk with Teddy.
This was while you were having that nice long sleep. Teddy's in better
humor than when you last saw him, now that he's been winning
cigarettes at cribbage all day. So he's agreed to make a special flight to
the camp tomorrow and—"

"What do you mean, a special flight? That's what he'd agreed to do
anyway."

"Yes, of course. But now he's willing to make *two* flights without
increase of price per hour."

"That would still make five hundred extra. What's the use of
squandering all that money when we're short as it is?"

"Because, if you and I go separately, we can each take a fresh supply
of medicines and other necessities, especially ammunition, without
overloading the plane. Now that the Machiguengas are gone, we can't
depend on their archery any longer, to get game. If we had all such
commodities at the camp, we could stay on there, almost indefinitely,
even through rains. We've got a fine site now, as you'll see, nothing
like the makeshifts we had to put up with most of the time before. And
I have a feeling we're not so far from *the* lagoon—I mean the one of
your dreams. Of course, I'm only guessing, but there seems to be a
whole coronet of them along the ridge and I believe you're in the right
region at last. When success may be so nearly within your grasp, you
don't want to close down and leave just because one of us gets
dysentery and you haven't got any medicine for it or something else
that will sound equally bromidic in your reports."

"If one of us gets dysentery, he'll be treated with *ojé* bark and that'll
fix him up. Just the same, what you say about weight makes sense. I
don't want to stay here another day, but I suppose one more or less

doesn't really matter, now I know that poor devil Pete's all right, or as nearly right as he's ever going to be. And I suppose your latest insurrection might at least have the practical value of helping Teddy find a more direct route to the camp than if he were groping his way over wholly unknown territory."

"I was coming to that. My modest services might really be of some use. I know now there's a sure approach to our camp by ascending the Urubamba almost to the Pongo de Mainique, then its tributary, the Ticumpenía, easily identified by waterfalls."

"All right, you win. Go and tell Teddy you're his passenger tomorrow and leave me in peace."

"Fair enough. 'I am gone, sir, and anon, sir, I'll be with you again.' "

The radio report the next morning was highly favorable and, to Nicolas' agreeable surprise, Teddy was back in Atalaya by noon, receptive to the idea of making a second flight that same day. They had had a little trouble, he reported, with clouds issuing from the Pongo de Mainique, but they had spotted the river Ticumpenía and kept it as contact guide without difficulty and he was confident he could do it again; in fact, he was actually eager, rather than reluctant, to be off before the weather changed. Nicolas took a hasty farewell of his kind hosts and, within an hour after Teddy's return, the Cessna was circling over the town again, before heading toward the camp. All too soon, Toledo regretted his hurried decision. Clouds began to form over the treetops and he could hardly tell where the Urubamba lay, much less identify any tributary. He would have insisted on returning to Atalaya if he had not seen an opening in the cloud blanket in the east. He was still in a zone with which he was familiar and he knew this kind of a break in the weather was unusual. For the next hour, he made an erratic flight, trying to keep in visual contact with the ridge which clouds now obscured. Then suddenly, off to the east, another gap in the mist lay bare the ridge, and Toledo steered for it. Unlike most of those in the jungle, it did not rise to a razor edge; on top, it leveled off to something that was not woods, but water.

"We're way off course," he said desperately. "I've got to turn around."

"Damn it, you can't do that now. I have to have a closer look at that lagoon."

"I'll make a note of its location for future reference. It'll be easy to identify for its crescent shape, its clearness and its setting in a deep cleft. But it won't do you any good to have a closer look at it. We can't possibly land there."

"You've got to. If all you've seen is its shape and its clarity, you haven't looked very carefully. Can't you see shadows? Shadows that prove there's a causeway in that lake, a very real causeway?"

"What you see is just a discoloration," Teddy said curtly.

"It's nothing of the sort. Fly closer." The order was peremptory.

"I tell you, I can't," insisted Teddy. "I've either got to take you on to your camp or go back to Atalaya. It's almost three o'clock already."

"You were the one who suggested making an afternoon flight. And now you're damn well going to do what I tell you to. I'm not going back to Atalaya and I'm not going on to camp until I've had a closer look. It won't hurt you to go just a little closer and just for a second." And, as Teddy hesitated, Nicolas shouted, "You can't call that a mere discoloration!"

While they were arguing, they had floated almost directly over the lagoon, just as a shredded cloudbank beneath them parted in its entirety, to reveal not only a submerged causeway, but a submerged palace, iridescent in the slanting glare of the westing sun, unquestionably the "House of the Sun God," the first of the three Inca ruins described by the bishop. Nicolas leaned forward and seized the pilot's shoulder.

"If you don't land me there, I'll kill you."

"And what good would that do you? You can't pilot a plane. And I can't land on any unknown, unmapped lake among mountains I can't identify, no matter what you think you see there. What's more, I won't. I've got a flight plan and I'm following it. If you make any more threats, I'll report you to the police."

"And if you'll put me down on this lagoon now, instead of getting killed, you can name your own price! Two thousand, three thousand, four thousand an hour!"

Again Teddy hesitated. Nicolas' grasp was still tight on his shoulder and he knew, all too well, that desperate men, in their rage, would risk destroying themselves if such destruction would also mean that of the man who had reduced them to such a state of fury. Besides, the view was still undimmed and now he also saw, or thought he saw, submerged structures of some sort, a causeway, perhaps even a palace. But whatever they were, they would only make landing more difficult.

"Five thousand an hour, Teddy Toledo!"

"All right, I'll put you down there."

Suddenly the hum of the motor was hushed and then silent. The plane skimmed the water so close to its surface that Nicolas could see window cavities covered with green algae in the palace. Then the engine caught again and the steady descent became a twisting climb.

"What in hell are you doing?" he shouted.

"Can't you see for yourself? The deal's off. I could have set us down, but I never could have got us out again. The crescent's too short."

"Too short for *what?*"

"Too short for the straight run I need for a takeoff. What's more, the jungle walls around are too steep."

"You could have tried!"

"I did try. But I know when I'm licked, even if you don't. Take your hand off my shoulder and shut up. If you don't, we head back to Atalaya. It's what we ought to do, anyway. It's too late to try hunting for your camp. I wouldn't even know where to look, a cloudy day like this."

For some minutes the mechanic had been making the sign of the cross and muttering to himself, "We're out where no plane should ever stray," while Nicolas swore and Teddy plunged ahead. Now Fidel had suddenly burst into excited speech.

"*Mi teniente,* isn't that the Pongo de Mainique over there, to the left?"

Teddy glanced in the indicated direction. Sure enough, another opening in the white sea of cloud low over the green sea of jungle revealed the vast vista of the last great Andean ridge along the Urubamba.

"My God, I believe you're right. If you are, the Ticumpenía lies just short of it, and we're not too far from the camp after all. It's worth a try."

Quickly, Teddy dropped through the level cloud blanket and close, very close below were the trees of the right jungle ridge. He flew along, almost touching its crest and soon their own lagoon with the camp beside it and the Explorers Club flag flying over this came into their range of vision.

They were all waiting to welcome him: Gomara and Lester, Walter and Clo and Li Chan, wreathed in smiles; and, facing him unflinchingly, poor Pete, who would never really smile again. A swift glance was enough to tell Nicolas that the praises of the camp had solid foundation in fact—as solid as the camp itself, which stood on a belt of good arable land that made it entirely habitable. Some planting had already been done there and the crops, though abandoned by the Machiguengas, still showed signs of careful tending. Probably Walter, the botanist, who had brought along some seeds for experimental planting, was responsible for that. Nicolas must not forget to thank him for his successful efforts. He must not forget to thank *all* those who had so diligently worked during his absence and so faithfully awaited his return; and he must be very careful what he said to Pete, choosing not only his words, but tempering the tone of his voice. For the moment, however, he found he could not say much of anything, either to Pete or to the others. He wrung their hands and muttered something about being glad to see them and then something about having to leave them for a few minutes. After that, he asked which tent was his and walked swiftly away.

"What on earth—" Lester began, and started to follow him. Pete pulled him back.

"No you don't, not this time. Something's happened since we talked to him this morning. Perhaps Toledo can tell us what it is."

His words were not meant to be threatening, but, even if he had not spoken after the manner of a powerful man who expects a swift and convincing answer when he asks a question, his disfigurement rendered his very presence terrifying. Teddy did not shrug his shoulders nonchalantly this time; his reply betrayed some nervousness and it was prompt, courteous and suitably regretful.

"I'm afraid I can. The weather was fine when we left Atalaya. I suggested the afternoon flight myself, so I've got to take the responsibility for it. But we ran into heavy weather and got way off course. Then suddenly the clouds parted and there was a lagoon—not this one, not even one anywhere near it—that is, I don't think it is. I've no way of being completely sure. And Dr. Hale swore he could see things in it. First he talked about a causeway and then about a palace." He shouted something about a 'House of the Sun of Gold.'

"And you couldn't see anything?" Pete cut in.

"At first, I thought it was just a discoloration. And then, afterward— yes, I think perhaps there was something. But I couldn't land there. Dr. Hale offered me five thousand *soles* if I would and I could have used that much money all right. But the landing just wasn't possible. We were lucky to get back on course, to reach here safely." He paused a moment and then went on defiantly, "I might add that he threatened to kill me."

"And I might add, you're damned lucky he didn't!" Pete exploded. "After all these years, after all the bad luck Nick's had through no fault of his own, when he's gone on, patient and persevering—and then to actually *see* the fulfillment of his dream and not be able to reach it! If you'd landed him on that lagoon, if he really saw what he thought he did and could prove it, he'd have been hailed as the greatest discoverer of our times! What's more, he could have gone home to his wife, 'conquest achieved and search fulfilled at last,' as he was always saying it had to be before he could stop! *You might have taken the chance!*"

Instinctively, Pete took a step forward and, again, though no physical threat was intended, just as instinctively, Toledo stepped back. Gomara came between them and put a gentle hand on the arm of each.

"Pete, you are forgetting that the lieutenant is our guest," he said quietly. "Our poor leader has, indeed, had a terrible disappointment, a terrible blow. He will want and need to be alone for a time, to recover from it and, since he does not pray for himself, I shall pray for him. But, meanwhile, Li Chan has prepared a little feast for us. You and your mechanic must share it with us, Teddy. And, of course, you must stay tonight. We have an extra tent, the boys will put it up immediately. Unquestionably, you did only what you thought was right."

Gomara's good counsel prevailed. Teddy and Fidel were received as welcome guests, and no further reference was made, in their presence, to the mishaps of the day. And not until very late that night, when everyone else was in bed and asleep, did anyone intrude on Nicolas' solitude. Then Lester lifted the flap of his tent and went in.

"Were you asleep, Nick?" (Sir had now been left far behind them.)

"What do you think?"

"Pete and I have been talking and—"

"In Spanish, I hope. Or was that another order that's been disregarded?"

"No, it's been faithfully kept. But you said, 'except when we were alone at night,' and that's the way it was this time. Anyway, while we were talking, I got an idea. I thought maybe if I told you about it, you'd feel better."

"Then do, by all means. I can't imagine anything that would make me feel worse."

"Is there any reason why we couldn't have a hydroplane of our own?"

"Several. You remind me of the old story about the village minister who told his congregation there were thirteen reasons why they couldn't have a new roof on the church. The first of these was that they had no money. That being the case, the other twelve didn't matter."

"Haven't we any money?"

"We have some, of course, but we don't have anywhere nearly as much as we need. Senator Powers underwrote this expedition very generously; but I was already in debt and then I spent more money on equipment than I ever have before. So what I have on hand isn't going to buy a hydroplane and there are reasons why I feel I shouldn't ask the senator for more money."

"Well, what about Schaeffer and Steinmetz?"

"Sam claims they're offended because I didn't go to them this time. I waited, as long as I thought it was prudent, for them to approach me—in fact, I began to wonder how on earth I was going to manage, because I had a huge overdue bill from Abercrombie and Fitch and, until Powers made his unexpected offer, I thought I'd have to borrow on my securities to meet it. I can't go back to Schaeffer and Steinmetz now because the one condition Powers made, about helping with the expedition, was that they shouldn't have any part in underwriting it— he wants the credit for that himself. Besides, I don't think it would have done any good to approach them, even when I was free to do so. I think Sam's talk about hurt feelings is more or less pride—or imagination. His father and father-in-law have stopped thinking about me as the kid who was just getting started, whom they enjoyed helping to finance in the first place, and have got used to thinking of me in terms of a best-selling author and a popular lecturer who ought to do a good deal to-ward financing himself. That's the way I've been thinking, too—until lately. Now I haven't any best-selling book on the market and, after what's happened today, there's no telling when I will have. So, pretty soon, they're going to begin thinking about me in quite another way— as a washout when it comes to exploring. They're rich and generous, but they aren't primarily philanthropists. In other words, they like to help make a success a bigger one, but they don't care much about bolstering a failure. And I've been pretty extravagant, as far as my personal expenses are concerned. I'm not sorry. All the money I've spent for luxuries were luxuries for Margaret and if any man's wife ever deserved them, she does. But that doesn't alter the fact that the money's been spent."

"All of it?"

"No, of course not all of it. What's got into you, Lester? I thought you said you had some great idea to share. All you've done so far is to ask questions."

"Well, I thought, if we had *some* money, we could get us a hydroplane. I mean, we could rent one. We wouldn't have to buy it. We could rent one at a reasonable figure from the Linguistics."

"They've already made it clear they don't *want* to rent us a hydro-plane. They don't consider our venture 'sane and sound' and they're damn right about that, too."

"They don't want to rent us a hydroplane with a *pilot*. As far as I know, we haven't asked them to rent us one *without* a pilot."

"And what would we do with it then? Keep it as a parlor ornament?"

"No. I'd pilot it."

"*You'd* pilot it!"

"Why not? Of course, I've never been checked out in a hydroplane, but it belongs to the same breed as the slow reconnaissance plane I flew in Korea. So I don't think it would take me very long to learn. I could go to Yarina Cocha and take lessons and, at the same time, one of our students could be trained as a possible mechanic. You could stay on here, doing what you could with Gomara, Pete and the other student to help you. I'd fly back to Pucallpa with that So-and-So Teddy the day after tomorrow—I believe that's the time limit he's set, without raising his rates sky high—in fact, I don't see any reason why we shouldn't make it tomorrow, instead. Then you could get rid of him that much sooner and I'd get started on my lessons that much sooner. When I return, a full-fledged pilot, you can let the others go—those that want to. But I bet some of them would stay on. Anyway, you and I could."

"How long?"

"As long as we had to. As long as it took before we could make a landing on that lagoon you saw today and get to the submerged causeway and palace. Perhaps it wouldn't take very long. Teddy has kept muttering that he would make a note of its location for future reference. I'll check with him the first thing in the morning to make sure he has, while it's still fresh in his mind. Besides, though the Machiguengas have left us, they kept talking about a route to a lagoon east of here, the route they wouldn't take in the beginning because they said that wasn't a propitious time—remember? But, before all this trouble started about the women, they were planning to open a trail right to the top of Pantiacolla. Maybe we can find it without them, given decent weather, for we ought to be able to see a lagoon of any size down over Pantiacolla and that might be the very one you want. If we can't land there in a hydroplane, maybe we can do it with a helicopter. They don't need much of any room for a takeoff and I could learn to fly one of those, too. I bet you could raise the money for a helicopter if you were driven to it. Wasn't it Grant who said he was going to fight it out along those lines if it took all summer? We can do the same."

There was a long silence. Then Nicolas stretched out his hand and, in the dark, found Lester's.

"You're right," he said as he gripped it. "We can."

34♥

There was another silence, not so long as the first one; then they began giving definite shape to their plans. When Lester finally left the tent, to discuss these with the rest of the staff and Toledo, Nicolas lay quietly in his sleeping bag for a little while, his mind as active as his body was motionless. Then he rose, lighted a candle and, seated on a box which had originally held K-rations, wrote a comprehensive letter to Margaret, not only telling her everything that had actually happened, but dwelling on his profound depression after his abortive glimpse of the lake and his hope that Lester might have found a practical way to overcome it.

"We know now my dream city exists, that it isn't a figment of the imagination," he went on. "That's not just something, that's a great deal. But we still have two handicaps to overcome and there's no telling how long it will take to do this, especially with the rainy season coming on. The first is that the lake's very well hidden, in a cleft between mountains; even in fairly clear weather, we might fly over it half a dozen times without seeing it, unless we were flying very close to the sierra, and that's a tricky thing to do, the winds being what they are. The second is that, even after we've located it again, it's going to be hard to land there. We'll try, of course, as soon as Lester gets his license. But if Toledo hasn't exaggerated the difficulties—and there's no real reason why he should have—we may not be able to do that with a Cessna or any other plane we can hire. We may have to wait until we can buy a helicopter. And where the money's coming from to do that, I haven't the remotest idea.

"I'm writing you all this, darling, so you'll understand it may be longer than I expected before I can get back to you, and why. I know you realized when I left that, this time, I didn't mean to come back until I'd either established the fact my dream city wasn't where I thought it was; or that I'd found it and, with the camp on Lake Moonstone a going concern, I didn't think it would take too long to do one or the other. Well, of course, just before I left, I found out the camp wasn't a going concern any longer. But there wasn't time to discuss that phase of the situation with you, I had to take off in such a hurry. However, I knew I could count on you to size it up and see it might prolong my absence. Now that we know the lost city is (approximately) where I thought it was, a mistake or even an uncertainty about that won't affect my schedule any longer. But the fact that it's been seen, without any tangible proof of this, and the further fact it's been seen only from the air, without being entered, may affect the schedule still further. Naturally, I shan't rest, day or night, until I have entered it. And I can't believe conditions at the camp are so much worse than before the Machiguengas deserted that the situation's hopeless as far as the trail is concerned. Some of them who claimed they knew the way to my lake—our lake—may come back. With their lack of dependability, which is the worst of their qualities (because otherwise they're very good and were very happy here) I don't see why that couldn't happen. It's a poor rule that won't work both ways. And, anyhow, they've said my lake—our lake —lies to the east of Moonstone, so we can blaze our own trail, weather permitting. Also, the Cogapacoris may still be the ones to lead us there, as I thought they would from the beginning. After all, there's the tangible evidence of the stone hatchet. And, perhaps, in time they'll forget their grievance against poor Pete. He didn't actually do any harm and they've had the satisfaction of wreaking a terrible revenge for a mere indiscretion. What's more, I may be able to get hold of some of the mestizos Antonio recommends so highly for lightening manual labor. I wish I'd done that in the first place, not so much to lighten labor, but so they could act as intermediaries between us and the pure blooded Indians. Of course, I'm playing this blind, but I can't help feeling they might have found out more about the trail than we have by ourselves.

"Lester will mail this letter in Lima. I'm insisting that, as soon as he's made arrangements in Pucallpa to rent a plane and take lessons, he should have a few days off, to see the girl he likes, go to a few movies, etc., whatever suits his mood, before starting in on his training. He's put in a year now without anything faintly resembling a vacation, except for the few days he spent in Cuzco and those (as far as I know) were devoted entirely to colonial art and architecture. Clo is going with him; he seems the best mechanic material and he's perfectly satisfied to have his fun in and around Pucallpa. Now that Toledo knows the way, I believe he'll agree to come back here, some day when the weather is favorable, to get Gomara and Walter, so they won't have to wait until Lester has his license to have their time off. At all events, Lester's going to try to make a deal with him to do that. Walter needs and wants a break for fun as much as Lester and Clo and it's a long time since Gomara's had a chance to go to church. (If we could only have a resident chaplain on our staff, I believe he'd stay here indefinitely and contentedly!) Pete and Li Chan and I will hold down the fort. I'll be talking over the radio every day, or almost every day, with either Pucallpa or Atalaya and I'll find ways of getting letters to Lima. (Under the circumstances, I'm sure to have lots of willing postmen!) I suggest you always write me in care of Fonso, who will also be able to find willing postmen coming in the opposite direction. Cable service in Peru remains fantastically limited for a civilized country, but Fonso will deal with that, as well as with the mail."

The flap of the tent opened and Lester stood in the doorway, staring at the sheets of paper which Nicolas had dropped, one by one, to the ground as soon as he had covered them with rapid writing. "For God's sake, Nick!" he exclaimed. "Haven't you been asleep at all?"

"No. I'll sleep after you've gone. But I wanted to be sure, not only of getting this letter off with you, but of saying everything in it that I wanted to. I think I have, just about. Are you all set?"

"Just about, also. . . . I don't know whether or not you'll feel you want to have another talk with Toledo before we take off."

"Why? Did you have trouble getting him to agree about coming back for Walter and Gomara?"

"No, he was willing to do that, provided they'd agree to go with him any time he came and without any advance notice."

"As, of course, they did. So then what?"

"Well, about those notes. He said he'd make some for future reference, on the location of your dream lake."

"He certainly did. And you said you'd ask for them, while you were making up the rest of your schedule."

"I asked for them, all right, but now he claims he was so upset and exhausted last night he forgot to make them. And this morning— well, he hasn't forgotten he promised to do it, but he's forgotten exactly what he ought to say. He claims that, what with your bribes and your threats and your manhandling, he got so rattled he doesn't think any notes he made would be reliable. He thinks it's much better for you to start again from scratch." And as Nicolas sprang up, swearing and heading outside, Lester laid a detaining hand on his arm. "Hold on, it won't do any good to attack him again or even to make him sore by reminding him he's a fourflusher and all that. If you do, he'll probably welsh on coming for Walter and Gomara. So I think you'd much better not have a talk with him. I just didn't want the unwelcome news about the missing notes to seep through after I'd left, that's all. I thought I'd better tell you how things are."

Inevitably, Nicolas found the next few days dismal. The insects were a constant source of irritation, and he was thankful he had told Lester to get some additional headnets; how it could have happened that he didn't order enough in the beginning, he could not imagine, though of course it was never possible to calculate everything exactly. . . . Rain fell almost incessantly and, lacking the Machiguengas' facility for starting fires, no matter if the wood with which they had to deal was sodden—a facility only the absent Lester shared!—it was hard to keep these going. Nicolas would have liked to tramp around in the woods, as those close to the camp were free both from *paca* and the rotten roots which had previously rendered progress difficult at different times; and the only thorns were those on a vine which produced an acid fruit called *cocona,* a distant cousin of the tomato, that provided juice and vitamins and might prove a valuable addition to camp menus; but every time he went out, he came back drenched to the skin and decided the game was noth worth the candle. Gomara and Walter were preoccupied with happy preparations for departure. Pete, shamed and silent, made it clear he did not want to talk with

Nicolas about his downfall or even to see him any more than could be helped. With his withdrawal, Nicolas' best chance for human companionship was gone, for, if Pete had not shut himself away, Nicolas could have talked to him as one old friend to another, about his own troubles, with a freedom he would not and could not use in talking with the others: his anxiety about money matters; his uneasy feeling that he had not fitted into the prescribed pattern for a Virginia country gentleman and that he never would; his disappointment about his son; his consciousness that he would soon be yearning in vain for his wife. As it was, he had no outlet for his thoughts and feelings and they churned around inside him, giving him no peace. Only Li Chan remained calm, cheerful and completely competent; three times a day, with clockwork regularity, he set an excellent meal before his so-called betters.

Antonio had assured Nicolas he would be glad to continue daily talks with the camp, and his sincerity was so obvious that Nicolas did not hesitate to take him at his word, as he had in the case of Fonso. But at the moment there did not seem to be anything much to say in response to the Spaniard, though the news from the latter was all good: Lester had radioed from Pucallpa that he had been able to make arrangements both for flying lessons and airplane rental and was going on to Lima, where he expected to stay only two or three days, as he realized that time was of the essence. Clo was already beginning his practice as a mechanic and was enjoying that as well as less serious pursuits. So far, so good. Then, much sooner than they expected him, Toledo was back at Moonstone Lake, for the weather at Pucallpa was better than it had been at camp until the actual day of his arrival, when the sun came out with dazzling brightness. Before this had faded, Gomara and Walter were gone, too.

Nicolas had confidently hoped when he and Pete were alone the latter might be more responsive to friendly overtures; instead, he became increasingly withdrawn. At last, desperately lonely himself and knowing that Pete must be even more so, Nicolas tried to force the issue by going to his old friend's tent, after everything was quiet for the night, with the intention of suggesting he should bring his own sleeping bag in there, so they might keep each other company.

There was no answer when he lifted the flap and spoke, as he thought, with a commendable mixture of cheerfulness and appeal: "Hi! What about chewing the rag for a while, the way we used to?" Well, at least Pete was not bothered by insomnia, Nicolas reflected; he was dead to the world already and it was no time at all since they had finished their supper. Nicolas called a second time and went a little closer. Pete, lying on his back in his sleeping bag, did not move. The light in the tent was dim, but not so dim that Nicolas could not see the pitifully disfigured face. At least it was not distorted by suffering; there was even a certain peace about it. Partially comforted by the thought that slumber had brought release from humiliation, Nicolas went back to his own tent, thankfully realizing that he himself was already drowsy.

It was broad daylight when the consciousness that he was not alone brought him back from semi-slumber to wakefulness. Li Chan was standing beside him, silently weeping. Involuntarily, and with uncanny swiftness, Nicolas thought of that other morning, months earlier, when he had wakened late and had gone out of his tent to find Lester weeping; he had angrily charged the boy not to sit crying like a baby, but to come out with what had happened. This time, when Nicolas asked Li Chan a startled question, the cook only shook his head, still silently, and then quickly left the tent before Nicolas had time to slit open the envelope that came sliding into his hands and pick up the key that fell to the ground.

"Dear Nick"—he read, with steadily increasing horror—"I know you'll say I took the coward's way out and it's true. But then I lost the capacity of fortitude long ago. If I hadn't, I wouldn't have become a drunken bum or a fornicator. I didn't start out that way, but you don't need me to tell you I've gone from bad to worse.

"I understand when you first told Margaret about me, you said I was a good fellow, that you hoped she'd meet me some time. Well, she'll never meet me now, so perhaps you'll manage to let her keep on thinking that I was—once. Of course, it's Lester who's really the good fellow I started out to be, the man I called a coward. He'll stand by you through thick and thin. He'll never disgrace you. He'll get you to your lake.

"I'd still like to feel though that I had a hand in the discovery. I've got a little money saved up, I'm not sure how much, but I think it's enough for what you need. In fact, I'm sure it is. I want you to buy a helicopter and name it Pete. Then I'll be with you on the great day Lester will share with you. Otherwise, I wouldn't be. I'd have gone on being a source of shame and trouble. I can't stand that any longer.

"You were never told about the worst thing I did, because that happened very soon after we left Quillabamba and you still weren't in shape to hear anything but good news, so the bad news was hushed up. I saw a girl washing clothes in a stream—you know how they pound them on stones—and I went after her. There was something about her, the way she looked leaning over, that just got me. They said I raped her, but that isn't true; she could have whacked me with a stone, easy enough, and she didn't, so that means it wasn't rape. I'll bet any number of loving, legitimate husbands have used more

force than I did, deflowering their shrinking brides. This girl not
only didn't fight me off, she didn't want to. But Gomara said I'd
behaved like a Russian soldier in an occupied town and made me
sign a paper, accepting parenthood for any child born to Perpetua
Quispe as a result of this encounter, and leave her all my pay. He
agreed not to tell you about it if I would do all this, so I did, though,
at that point, I thought he was going too far. Then he went on to say
that, if the Cogapacoris ever got wind of this, they would destroy the
entire expedition and I began to think he had something there. I still
do. I believe they did get wind of it. I don't believe it was the mirror
and the string of beads I gave another girl months later that led to
my kidnapping; I think it was this other thing and I'm damned glad
I was the only victim. But if the Cogapacoris never come back to help
you find the lake, it will be all my fault.

"To be completely honest and, at a moment like this, a man wants
to be, there's another reason why I can't go on. I didn't mind staying here as long as I didn't have to, for any cause except that it was
part of my job. But now that I know I can't face the world again,
because the world would instinctively avoid facing me, I can't
endure the prospect of tomorrow and tomorrow and tomorrow at
Moonstone Lake, or some other place equally far from civilization. I
might easily live for another forty years, if what I'd be doing could
be called living. You might be able to stand looking at me and so
might Lester and Li Chan, but I know that even Clo and Walter find
it hard to do, though they've done their best not to let me see this;
and new men coming in wouldn't be able to conceal their repug-
nance; so the place for me to hide is underground and it means
something to me that I'll still be a whole man when you bury me. At
least I've escaped the fate of Abélard and a few others less famous,
who've been punished for their sins the way he was, instead of the
way I was.

"Now please don't get it into your stupid old head that the
helicopter will be bought with blood money if you do as I ask. What
I have saved up isn't from insurance—in fact, I doubt if you could
get an insurance company to pay you anything, under the circumstances. It's mostly good old Tel and Tel stock and I could turn
it over to you alive as well as dead—probably easier. And don't
imagine, either, that you're robbing anyone else. I haven't got a near
relative in the world. Among my belongings, you'll find a copy of my
will, which was made out three years ago, and the only difference
between my wishes then and now is that then I didn't care what was
done with the money and now I do. Everything's completely in
order. As you'll see, the will was drawn up by our mutual friend,
good old Ethan Watkins (who also ought to be able to handle all

legalities for you) and witnessed by three leading citizens of Woodstock. The original, along with stocks, bonds, mortgages, etc. is in my safe deposit box at your father's bank and I'm enclosing my key to it in this letter. Watkins has a duplicate key, so there shouldn't be any delay or difficulty about getting access to the box. Anyway, I'm suggesting you go straight to Woodstock, report my death and get things started. With no one to contest the will, it shouldn't take long to set the wheels in motion. So go ahead and buy that helicopter and don't come back to camp until you have it.

"What I'm going to do as soon as I've finished this letter will be quick and painless—just swallowing a little pill I've known about for a long time and then lying down and going to sleep. I must have known I'd need it some time or I wouldn't have bothered to find out about it in the first place or to keep it with me always. There won't be any mess to clean up. My life was a mess. My death will be a clean thing.

"Yours to the end,

"Pete."

35 ଓ

It was too late to reach Antonio by radio that day and Nicolas was thankful for the respite. If he had dared, he would have kept the latest tragedy of the expedition a secret, for he knew when Walter and Gomara heard of it, they would feel they ought to return to camp as soon as they could get there; also, that Lester and Clo would share this feeling, were it not for the fact that the sooner they could operate independently, as far as aircraft was concerned, the more helpful they would be to their leader. However, a suicide was too great a tragedy, and had too many ramifications, to lend itself easily to concealment; Nicolas realized he must advise Antonio of what had happened as soon as possible, and trust to his silence, if silence seemed permissible to the Spaniard under the circumstances.

Antonio, reached at six the following morning, responded both sympathetically and practically as Nicolas had known he would. Should he assume that the burial had already taken place? Of course, it was unfortunate there had not been more witnesses, but that could not be helped. Nicolas had found the will and it seemed to be in order? At least, that was to the good. In Antonio's opinion, Nicolas would be

well advised to start back as soon as feasible, to clear the will and select
the helicopter himself, though probably arrangements for the purchase
could be made in Lima. How long a vacation were Gomara and Walter
supposed to have? Two weeks and one was gone already? In that case,
no doubt Nicolas would feel better in the end if he did not call them
back ahead of the stipulated time, though the intervening period at the
camp would certainly be very hard for him to endure. And it would not
be very much longer, would it, in all probability, before Lester and Clo
got their licenses, since they had left before the others and Lester had
had previous experience with flying? Perhaps Nicolas would think he
should wait until all of them were back at camp and that, when he left,
Li Chan should also leave and remain in Lima while Nicolas was in the
United States. After all, he had not had any time off in more than a
year and he had sustained a terrible shock in finding Pete's dead body.
He should be given a chance to recover.

Nicolas gave careful thought to Antonio's advice and suggestions and
realized that all were good. But the next week proved an even more
nerve-wracking experience than the Spaniard had foreseen, since Li
Chan, normally so completely impassive, was even more unstrung than
Nicolas. He wept and did not pause in his cooking to stop the flood of
tears that fell into his pots and pans; he talked to himself in some
strange dialect, whose very sound was unfamiliar to Nicolas; he
wandered off into the woods, heedless of the pelting rain, and was
absent for so long at a time that Nicolas feared he might be lost or that
lurking Cogapacoris might have captured him; he spent hours
squatting beside Pete's grave, sometimes silent, sometimes chanting in
weird singsong. Nicolas did not dare to reason with him, for fear of
upsetting him still more; and, as his own loneliness increased, he began
to wonder how soon he, too, would show the strain and in what
ominous way. He found himself counting the days and then the hours
before he could logically expect to be rejoined by at least part of his
staff.

Although two weeks had indeed been set as the limit for the vacations which Gomara and Walter were to take, this had necessarily been
a tentative arrangement, since, as far as anyone could foresee, they
would have to depend on Toledo's willingness and ability to bring
them back. But Nicolas, listening hard and scanning the sky for the
sound and sight of a plane, had a welcome surprise: it was not Teddy's
Cessna that he heard and saw, but one of the Linguistics' Pipers, with
Lester triumphantly at the controls, Clo grinning beside him and
Walter and Gomara as his happy passengers.

The general elation was, necessarily, short-lived; for once, bad news
had not traveled fast and Antonio had succeeded in keeping the dreadful secret of Pete's suicide, which now came as a shocking surprise to

his erstwhile companions. But at least they had all returned refreshed and invigorated and, in the case of Lester and Clo, with a sense of real accomplishment. Grief-stricken as they were by the tragedy that had befallen the expedition, they were in better condition to bear up under it than Nicolas and Li Chan, and soon their presence had a tonic effect: unbidden, Li Chan went to his cookhouse and began the preparation of a festive meal; while Nicolas gathered the others around him and asked them to be frank in expressing their views on the best move to make next.

Without a dissenting voice, they agreed with Antonio: there was every reason why Nicolas and Li Chan should get away, none why they should remain. The likelihood that a rival expedition might come into the area during the wet months could be discounted, and Nicolas would be back well before the change of seasons. Meanwhile, if there were any fear at the back of his mind that Lester might discover the dream city in his absence, Nicolas was to forget about that; Lester would use the hired plane only for necessary trips to get supplies from Atalaya or Pucallpa, which would give him all the practice he needed, and the next one would be with the first break in the weather, when he would have his boss for a passenger—and it would mark the proudest moment in his life. But, for the most part, he and the others would just sit tight at the camp and keep it going.

"Don't be such an ass," Nicolas said sharply. "I *have* discovered the lost city—the fact that I couldn't get into it is only incidental. Of course, you must keep on trying to get to that lagoon, both by trail and by air, and report your progress, if you make any, to Antonio, with instructions to publicize it. I'd a little rather be the first to use the underwater equipment, actually to move along the submerged causeway and push the algae away from the palace windows. But if you can get lakeside, with Clo as a witness, if you can swear you've done it and you're ready to prove to any doubting Thomases who may come along that you've seen the causeway and the palace, you'll have advanced our project to a point where no one can challenge its ultimate success."

"Well, I guess you're right at that. I didn't see it that way before, but I do now. I heard you make a joke once about getting to Cuzco just in time to have your picture taken for the two newspapers as the leader of an expedition, after your staff had laid all the groundwork for it. If you really want it that way this time, maybe we'll have to see about getting some photographers and reporters up here."

The next break in the weather came two days later. Never had the lake been so beautiful or the name Nicolas had given it so fitting. The somber weather of the previous afternoon had been followed by a morning of mingled shower and sunshine, with wonderful effects of light and shade, which ranged from gray and purple, so dark as to be almost black, through cold glittering greens and blues to pale tints of pearl and violet. The lake, like a great moonstone, lay quiet beneath an opalescent sky; then, suddenly, it rippled like quicksilver under diamond rays. For some moments, Nicolas stood gazing at it in silent rapture; when he turned to Gomara, who was standing close beside him, the archeologist's expression revealed the same sense of enchantment.

"That's the way the other lake looked," Nicolas said. "Only it was clear, instead of translucent, its waters sapphire, not moonstone. And then it glowed, as if shafts of topaz were streaming down, touching the hidden treasure and revealing its gold. No vision you've ever had of heaven could be half so glorious. I wish I didn't have to leave, I wish we could go searching for it right now. But we'll see it together when I get back."

"Please God!" said Gomara, crossing himself.

The flight from Lake Moonstone to Atalaya with Lester at the controls was smooth and uneventful and the welcome awaiting the travelers, though inevitably shadowed by their grief, as genuine as ever. Moreover, Nicolas again found Antonio a knowledgeable advisor, as well as a congenial companion, and went on to Lima much better informed than before his visit.

"A helicopter may well prove your solution for a landing on or beside your dream lake," Antonio said. "Of course, it's tragic that, since Pete could have provided the money for it anyway, he didn't do so alive, instead of dead, and share your great moment when you get to your final destination. But I can understand his desperation and his shame, so let's pray that an all-forgiving God may do so, too, and that he may rest in peace, despite his sin of self-destruction. Now let's leave it at that and go on from there. How were you planning to get the helicopter to Moonstone Lake?"

"Why—I hadn't thought out the details very carefully. Would it be brought boxed to Lima and then assembled and flown from there?"

"Much too far, even without going into the handicaps of topography. Normally, a light helicopter doesn't fly more than two and a half hours on a load of fuel."

"All right. It could be taken boxed all the way, couldn't it?"

"Not if you're picturing that box fitting into the Piper. Besides, this operation calls for an entirely new route. You've got to stop thinking in terms of Atalaya and begin thinking about Quince Mil, which is much nearer Moonstone Lake. You'll charter a C-84 at Lima from SATCO and it will take you and the helicopter, still boxed, to Quince Mil. That's where your new whirlybird will be assembled and from there it *can* be flown to Moonstone. The distance is well within its range."

"This situation seems to be a little more complicated than I expected. If we do things that way, who's going to fly the whirlybird? Lester can't fly two planes at once."

"Very true. What's more, Lester doesn't know anything about flying helicopters—yet. I'm not saying he can't eventually learn. He's a smart guy and his experience in Korea stood him in good stead when he started his lessons with the Linguistics in Pucallpa. I've heard by the grapevine he was very quick to catch on. But, for the time being, you'll need a special pilot-mechanic and, if I'm not mistaken, you'll have to bring him with you all the way from the States. I can't be sure, but I believe there are only two native helicopter pilots in Peru and, naturally, they couldn't be spared for any length of time from the Ministry of Public Works, with which they are connected, though I don't need to say the Peruvian Government is always very co-operative in such cases. And I'll tell you who'll give you the information you need— Warren Holtz, the representative of Hiller Brothers in Lima. He's a very pleasant fellow and he has all the answers. Go to see him as soon as you get there—and that, I take it, will be as soon as ever you can."

"You're right, Tony. This is one of the times when you really do have to speed the parting guest. But I'm no end grateful to you for putting me on the right track before I displayed my ignorance to someone who wouldn't have been as tolerant of it as you are."

"There's no reason why you should have known all this before or, as a matter of fact, any of it. Maybe, ten years from now, helicopters will be pretty generally used in Peru. But you're pioneering, as well as exploring, as far as they're concerned."

The two men parted, more than ever conscious of the enduring warmth in their friendship. Less than twenty-four hours later, Nicolas was in Lima, where he immediately telephoned, first to Margaret and then to his father. With the former's ready approval, it was decided he should go straight to Woodstock from New York to "put the wheels in motion," as Pete himself had suggested. Then Nicolas would not have to leave Hills' End again for some time; all the next formalities in connection with Pete's estate could be fulfilled in his absence and there would, inevitably, be quite a wait before he could actually lay his hands on enough money to pay for the helicopter. This point being settled, he promptly presented himself to Mr. Warren Holtz. As Antonio had predicted, Nicolas found the agent the soul of helpfulness. Yes, the information Dr. Hale had received from *Señor* Astur was entirely correct, as far as it went. If Dr. Hale decided on a Hiller and would himself like to get a factory check-out in Palo Alto, the company would be glad to let him have this. It might come in handy some time, in case of an emergency; but certainly he should arrange to bring a pilot-mechanic with him to Peru and keep him there for the present.

Frances Parkinson Keyes   293

Mr. Holtz was sure any number of pleasant, competent young men would jump at the chance, and there was no question that such an addition to the staff of the expedition was required. A helicopter needed four or five hours of maintenance for every hour of flight. It would carry two persons, besides the pilot-mechanic; it would use seventeen gallons of gasoline per hour and, in addition to its normal supply, it could have two long-range tanks, holding twenty gallons each, strapped to its sides. Luggage racks could also be strapped to its sides. No doubt Dr. Hale had already made arrangements for fuel storage at Moonstone Lake? Well, of course, that would have to be the next step. But Mr. Holtz was sure everything was going to work out just fine. He'd read one of Dr. Hale's books, *Quest for Gold,* was that the name of it? He had enjoyed it. Too bad the '53 expedition had met with such bad luck. He was sure the '54 expedition would do better. . . .

"Well, I hope so," Nicolas said a little doubtfully. When Lester had said, if they couldn't make it with a hydroplane, they might succeed with a helicopter, the suggestion had not appeared to indicate too many complications. Now it seemed they were to approach Moonstone from a new air base, they were to add a pilot-mechanic to the staff and they were to make permanent arrangements for refueling—in fact, there seemed to be no end to the details involved, let alone the expense. *Expense!* That was another item, still to be discussed. Pete had said in his suicide note, "I've got a little money saved up, I'm not sure how much, but I think it's enough for what you need. In fact, I'm sure it is." But could Pete have realized the Hiller would cost thirty-five thousand dollars—the price Mr. Holtz had quoted—and that this did not include transportation or the salary of a pilot-mechanic or a storage tank for gasoline? "A little money saved up" did not usually mean sums sufficient for all this. *Sums!* There he was up against them again. It would be embarrassing, to say the least, if, after returning to the United States, Nicolas found the legacy would nowhere nearly cover costs of purchase and maintenance.

He managed to take his leave of the pleasant and efficient Mr. Holtz without betraying too much anxiety and, irrationally, but characteristically, spent the remainder of the afternoon shopping. He wanted Margaret to have gold jewelry like Fátima's and, after a considerable search, he found some pieces that pleased him, as well as some gold sandals. He had actually remembered, in the course of their telephone conversation, to ask her what size shoes she wore; and, though he had not failed to catch the note of extra surprise in her voice when she answered, he was not sorry he had taken the time for so seemingly trivial a question, when he had such important tidings to tell. Very often, if they were to be alone for dinner, she did not dress completely after her evening bath, but over her nightgown wore a graceful, loose fitting garment that she called a *robe d'intérieur,* claiming its more usual designation as a hostess gown was a misnomer, for it was not the sort of thing you wore when you were a hostess, but when you were *en négligé,* which made its French name all the more appropriate. Nicolas could visualize how charming she would look in a jewel-colored *robe d'intérieur* made of velvet, and set off with the gold jewelry and the gold sandals. She had beautiful feet, slim and white, with high arches. Perhaps he could persuade her to dispense with stockings when she wore the sandals.

The flight to New York was comfortable and uneventful, and Nicolas, who was utterly exhausted, managed to sleep a good part of the way. An almost immediate connection with Northeast Airlines brought him to Lebanon the same day he landed at Idlewild and his father was waiting to drive him to Woodstock from the small New Hampshire airport. The countryside was at the height of its autumn glory, with all the lower hills ablaze with gold and scarlet and some of the higher points lightly powdered with snow; normally, this splendor would have had a special appeal for Nicolas after the drab drizzle of Lima. But he was still very tired and he was impatient to do what he had come for and get back to Virginia and Margaret.

"Land o' Goshen, Nick, you can't get into the bank tonight!" Waldo said, in some exasperation. "We closed at three, same as always. 'Course, we could have asked Watkins to have supper with us, but it wouldn't have hurried things up, as far as the will's concerned, that is, not any to speak of. And Mother and I, we thought we'd kind of like to have you to ourselves, for once. It's been quite a spell. . . . Not that we wouldn't have been tickled to death to have Margaret, too," he added hastily. "Margaret and Cynthia and, if Cynthia isn't the prettiest baby I ever saw, I'll eat my hat. What I meant was, Mother and I wanted just a family get-together at first. She's looking forward a lot to seeing you, Nick. It's kind of quiet at the house these days, with the twins gone."

"*With the twins gone!* Where on earth are they?"

"Why, they're at college! We told you, 'way back when you got married, they were going to college this year! Don't you keep any kind of track about what your folks are doing? Better not let Mother know you forgot. She'd get the notion you're losing interest in everything except that lake of yours."

Nicolas promised he would not confess that a news item, as important as one concerning the twins' departure for college, had escaped his memory and, on the whole, he believed he showed the proper degree of interest in such other pieces of information as his parents had to impart. As usual, they were more disposed to tell him about local happenings than to hear what was happening in Peru; and, though this attitude of mind was faintly amusing to him, it had long since ceased to annoy him. He listened with attention and was unsparing in his praise of the supper that had been prepared for him. But he was thankful when he could escape to his old room and crawl into the spool bed where he had slept as a boy. Almost immediately he fell into blessedly dreamless slumber and was still sound asleep when his mother came in to rouse him with the news that Ethan Watkins was downstairs.

"My God, what time is it?" he asked groggily, as he struggled to sit up.

"Why, it's 'way past eight! Ethan thought you'd want to see him in good season."

"Dad said there wasn't any point in trying to talk with him until the bank was open."

"The bank will be open by the time you get there. You and your father and Ethan can walk over there together. It seemed more neighborly to ask Ethan to come here first, especially after he told your father maybe he ought to have a look at that suicide note before he opened the safe deposit box. He's drunk two cups of coffee and eaten two doughnuts already, while he's been waiting for you. After all, he had his breakfast quite some time back, and Sarah Watkins is a fine woman, but she isn't the best cook in Woodstock, by any means."

"The best cook in Woodstock is, of course, right here in my room," Nicolas said with sincerity. "Somehow I'd forgotten you got under way quite so early though. I'll be down as soon as I can, but I do have to shave, whether I wash much or not. We can't have Ethan Watkins rashly concluding that explorers necessarily look like tramps. It wouldn't advance my cause much if he did, and I imagine he's slightly suspicious of me, anyway. After all, I don't do any of the accepted things to earn a living and I neglected to join the First Congregational Church before I started out on my peculiar career."

While it was not quite correct to say Ethan Watkins regarded his new client with suspicion, it was true that he regarded him with reservations and was disposed to proceed with caution. He read the suicide note through twice, following its lines one by one with his index finger, pausing several times in his reading to ask questions and for a longer time when Pete's choice of words in such a serious document shocked him to a degree that brought him up short. At last, having said that he must have a copy made and that, probably, Nicolas would like to come to his office while this was being done, later in the day, he consented to proceed to the bank. There, having opened Pete's safe deposit box with his key, in the presence of Waldo, Nicolas, the cashier and the teller, he carried it carefully to the Board Room. Then, dismissing the cashier and the teller, he asked to see the copy of the will Nicolas had with him and compared this, also line by line, with the original, to make sure there had been no changes. Having satisfied himself on this score, he asked whether or not Nicolas had formed any estimate as to the size of the legacy.

"All I know is that Pete said he was leaving everything to me, that the money was mostly in Tel and Tel stock and that there'd be enough to buy a helicopter, which is what he wanted me to do. A helicopter costs thirty-five thousand dollars. That doesn't include the expense of transportation or of upkeep, but Pete may not have been reckoning on those additional items."

"I can't say a helicopter seems to me like a prudent investment for a sum like thirty-five thousand dollars," Ethan Watkins observed disapprovingly. "Let alone allowing more for transportation and upkeep. Not that I can stop you from using the money that way, when it says right there in that suicide note it's what Pete wants you to do. But maybe there isn't thirty-five thousand available."

Nicolas thought he detected a note of hope in the lawyer's voice. "You'll be able to tell, won't you, when you've looked at the securities?" he inquired.

"I'll be able to make an estimate—a rough estimate, pending a formal appraisal. But you understand stocks and bonds vary considerably in value."

"Even Tel and Tel?"

"That doesn't vary as much as some, though it does vary. However, I've got the latest quotations here—brought a newspaper along with me. I'll look these securities over right now. No use of your counting on that helicopter if you can't have it anyway. It's hard for me to believe Pete Hart could have been a man of means."

"I can't for the life of me see why, Ethan," Waldo said with conviction. "He never spent anything to speak of. That's one of the best ways to stay in comfortable circumstances. He didn't throw money around like a drunken sailor, the way some do."

Nicolas decided it was wiser to let this aspersion pass and, for the next few minutes, the only sounds in the room were the almost inaudible ones of documents being changed from one pile to another and the slight rustle of the newspaper as Watkins consulted it before making miscellaneous notes and adding up figures. He did this with such painstaking deliberation, Nicolas was tempted to ask if he were having trouble with his arithmetic. But at last Watkins put the securities back in the box, closed it and again surveyed his figures before speaking.

"I guess there's no way I can keep you from making that imprudent investment," he said regretfully. "Near's I can make out, there's quite a considerable sum represented here. But of course you won't be able to lay your hands on it yet awhile. I'll file the will in the Probate Court today with a petition for its allowance. As far as we know, there aren't any other interested parties, but there's always lots of things we don't know. We can't take chances."

"Well, if no other interested parties turn up, what then?"

"Then I write you a letter and tell you so. You can start looking for that letter in about a month."

"And after that I'll get the money?"

"That's right—some little time after. Pete's creditors have got six months in which to present their claims to the Commissioners. I don't dare pay legacies until I'm sure I won't be left with insufficient funds to pay those creditors."

"I'm almost sure Pete didn't have any creditors."

"Maybe you are. But it doesn't do, when you're dealing with the law, to be almost sure. I don't know but what I might let you have part of the legacy after six months. It would depend on how things looked."

"Well, supposing they looked pretty good?"

"Well, supposing they looked pretty good, I'd be inclined to consider a request from you to pay you enough, so's you could buy this helicopter. Of course, I'm not saying I'd do it. But I'd consider it."

"Then I take it you've calculated there is going to be more than thirty-five thousand available, sooner or later?"

"Yes, I'm kind of afraid there is. I'm kind of afraid there may be more than sixty thousand involved. That would mean a federal tax return would have to be made and a federal tax paid. It'd slow things up a little more."

Nicolas pushed back his chair and rose. "I think I'd better take the first plane I can get back to New York," he said. "The longer I listen to you, the more it sounds to me as if I could die of old age before I get a cent of this money. I need that helicopter for my work. I need it a lot more than you seem to realize. Pete knew that I did. He thought he was making it possible for me to get it. What makes the whole thing seem worse is that, if he hadn't committed suicide—if he'd just sold some stock and given me the money—I could have gone ahead and bought it right off. I'll write you a letter, asking you to let me have fifty thousand dollars, as soon as you can clear that much. And you needn't answer until you can send me the check. Now, if you'll excuse me, I'll go back to the house and say good-by to my mother."

36ಀ

Only six weeks after leaving Hills' End, presumably for an indefinite absence, Nicolas was back there again.

Certain elements of his return were, inevitably, anticlimactic. He had vowed, both before and after his departure, meaning every word he said, he would not come back until he had made his great discovery and could proclaim its importance to the world. Now, though he could claim he had *seen* the lake of his dreams and, though he was sure it was the site of a submerged causeway and a palace, he could not say he had verified this conviction with underwater equipment. Therefore, though his report was not received with incredulity, neither was it hailed as a triumph of exploration, nor was it bolstered very much because he had returned on account of an unexpected legacy, the result of a major tragedy, which would enable him to secure the means, hitherto lacking, that might well complete conquest in the very near future. It was perhaps only his imagination, but it seemed to him very few persons were interested in hearing his story and that LaGuarde and Powers were actually avoiding him. Though the social season was already in full swing, with the Anteaters giving fantastic luncheons and at least half a dozen cocktail parties scheduled for each evening, he and Margaret did not often have to decline a dinner invitation because they were already engaged, whereas, the summer before, when "everyone" was supposed to be out of town, they had been obliged, with genuine regret, to decline a great many because of conflicting dates; and, though the Sunday night suppers at Hills' End were still largely and eagerly attended, Nicolas had the impression that an increasing number of the guests were Margaret's friends rather than his. Obviously, the celebration at the Peruvian Embassy had been premature; his best advisers admitted that probably it would have been better not to regard the foundation of the camp on Lake Moonstone as a definitive factor in discovery. No more celebrations were planned in his honor, and both the press and his publishers took a very dim view of the situation from a newsworthy standpoint. He supposed there must have been other moments in his career when everything fell as flat as it did now, but, if there were, he could not recall them; and a letter from Ethan Watkins did not materially raise his spirits:

"Woodstock, Vermont
"November 15, 1954

"Friend Nicolas"—it ran—

"You said you didn't want I should write you until I could enclose a sizable check. Just the same, your father and I both thought you wouldn't take it unkindly if I should let you know the will was allowed, right on time to the minute. This being the case, maybe in another six months I'll be writing you again, to tell you I might consider letting you have part of your money. As I already told you, I was kind of afraid the estate might come to more than sixty thousand and it has, so if you want to throw away thirty-five thousand on a helicopter, I guess I won't be able to stop you.

"We have been having heavy snows and half the town is abed with bad colds, but so far I am as usual.

"Hoping you are the same, I remain
                                        "Ethan Watkins."

"Evidently you're going to have me on your hands all winter," Nicolas said, tossing the letter over to Margaret without further comment.

"Why, that's wonderful, isn't it, dear?"

"I don't deny it has some good points. But I'm afraid a minimum of seven more months at the lake, before I show up with the helicopter, is going to seem pretty long to Lester and the others."

"They must have known there'd be some delay about turning the money over to you. And then, if I understood you correctly, weather conditions wouldn't have been favorable for you to return before May at the earliest."

"That's right. But this way I won't be returning before July."

"I'm selfish enough to be very glad, Nicolas."

He made an honest effort to prevent her from seeing that he was not glad at all; but his private life suddenly had the same lack of radiance as his professional life. If he could have foreseen his prompt return, so perfectly timed to mark a renewal of intimate relations with his wife, he would, of course, have waited the extra weeks; there would have been nothing in his attitude toward her which would have indicated a degree of importunity that could lead her to disregard her physician's advice and subject her to the risk of a second confinement so soon after the first. Now he was annoyed with himself because he had done so and his annoyance increased, rather than diminished, when he learned Margaret again had a "sound reason" for believing she was pregnant.

"Has Dr. Loomis told you so, or is this just another intuition?" Nicolas inquired, hoping it was the latter and that, this time, she might be mistaken.

"Dr. Loomis did tell me so, but I also had another intuition," she told him, speaking rather shyly, not because she felt the news itself called for reticence, but because she feared she saw signs that her "intuitions" might become the subject of raillery if she laid claim to having them repeatedly. "I believe it happened even more quickly this time—the evening when you had the first bad news about Pete and we came in early from the arbor. I was sure, even before you went to sleep, and I was very glad, because I knew you thought you might have to start back to Peru right away."

"That's what I should have done, the minute I got the letter, without waiting for the cable and without leaving the bed in the boudoir for yours. . . . How can you say you're really glad? If I'd waited until now, at least the babies would have been nearly a year apart—possibly all of a year. It's to be hoped you're not inevitably going to conceive the minute I touch you."

"But Nicolas, I thought you'd be glad, too! I thought that was what you wanted, that I should conceive instantly, whenever we were together, at least until we had a son. You want one so much and you had no idea, when you left, you'd be back for months and months."

"That's all true enough, but—well, I can't help wishing there weren't the prospect of another baby right now."

"It needn't make any difference. I mean, when you came home in June, I was seven months along and, of course, then. . . . What I'm trying to say is, since I've just started, if I actually have started, we can be together as much as you like. We don't have to be careful about hurting the new baby, not for ever and ever so long. I asked. Nicolas, don't tell me you're not glad."

"Certainly, I'm glad. But everything is so at sixes and sevens."

"I know, I know. You've had one piece of hard luck after another. But, darling, I'm sure everything's coming your way from now on. Naturally, you can't bring poor Pete back to life, but you're going to get your helicopter and your submerged palace and then, presently, you'll have a message from me, telling you we have a beautiful *ten* pound son! And, meanwhile, we'll be together all the time. We won't have to keep thinking you're leaving in five days, as we've done twice, that we've got to make very minute count, because there are so few of them. We'll have leisure to enjoy each other in all sorts of ways—reading aloud and taking walks and playing with Cynthia and seeing our friends. And, of course, making love whenever we feel like it, as much as we feel like it, but without that dreadful sense of urgency and haste."

"I didn't think it was dreadful. I thought it was exciting."

"I used the wrong word. Inescapable would have been better."

"Did you want to escape?"

"No, certainly not. I'm expressing myself very badly. All I'm trying to say is I'm very, very happy to have you home and I know everything about it is going to be wonderful."

Nicolas wished he could have been equally certain of this. He hoped he was concealing from Margaret the fact that it bored him very much to go to the services at Pohick Church every Sunday morning, and that her correlative activities, such as those connected with the Altar Guild, held no charms for him whatsoever, even conversationally. The same was true of the Garden Club. He was appalled when she suggested that, perhaps, he would address one of the meetings on the flora of the Andes. The truth was he had never noticed them particularly, any more than he had the butterflies, and was amazed to find that, by hearsay, Margaret was more familiar with them than he was. *She* had better make the speech, he said; but no, it was Nicolas they wanted. Why, he had often gone on lecture tours, what was there so different about this? He could not brutally say his lecture tours had been merely a highly profitable commercial venture, whereas, in this case, he took it the members of the local club considered they were paying him a compliment by asking him to address them; but he did say, rather bitterly, it was the artifacts he had found he talked about, not the flowers; and Margaret knew, only too well by this time, there was nothing new for him to say on his chosen subject.

Cynthia had continued to gain prodigiously during his absence and he admitted she was a very fine specimen of infancy. Her skin was beautifully soft and rosy and she had not lost the thick fuzz of black hair which had covered her head when she was born. Margaret told him it was not unusual for babies to lose this first hair and pointed with pride to the lengthening growth on Cynthia's well-shaped little head. Her eyes would not be blue much longer, however; they were going to be dark, just like her father's. In fact, her resemblance to him was striking already. Nonsense, Nicolas said, all babies looked alike; but, as he observed this one more closely, he could not deny there was something about her. . . . And, when his mother produced his first photograph, taken when he was only a little older than Cynthia, he had to admit that, except for the difference in their clothes, the picture might well be one of his daughter.

Like most healthy, well-fed babies, Cynthia cried very little and, though Nicolas could not truthfully say he considered the cradle a welcome addition to the conjugal chamber, he was silent on the subject as long as the late evening and early morning feedings were the only source of disturbance to him and those, through Margaret's careful management, a very slight one. But, shortly before Christmas, when

Cynthia, instead of going back to sleep with clocklike regularity, as soon as she had been fed, began to whimper from time to time and then to scream regularly, he voiced his irritation.

"Isn't there something that can be done to keep that child quiet?"

"Yes, I'm afraid there is."

"What do you mean, *afraid*? I should think it would be a relief to you, as well as to me, to have her shut up."

"I mean, I'm afraid I've got to wean her. And I was so proud of being able to nurse her. But she isn't getting enough any more."

"Nonsense, she's been greedy from the beginning! I told you, the first time I saw her with you, she was a perfect vampire."

"It's the new baby who's beginning to be greedy now or, rather, who's demanding his rights. I've been lucky to keep on with Cynthia this long. But, after all, I'm nearly four months pregnant. I'll have to begin giving her a bottle. She may not mind too much, if I can do it gradually, that is, alternating breast and bottle feedings. On the other hand, she may fight the bottle. Dr. Loomis and Cassie both say that sometimes happens."

"Well, let's hope it doesn't happen this time."

He tried to keep the annoyance out of his voice. The information that the "new baby" was already complicating matters, as far as the "old baby" was concerned, was as startling as it was unwelcome. There had been no reason, before his marriage, for Nicolas to take an interest in gynecology, and it seemed to him it was now affecting the pattern of his life in more ways than was rational. And, for several reasons, he did not like the reminder that Margaret was already nearly four months pregnant. During the next few days his annoyance mounted. Cynthia exhibited a degree of fury over the proffered bottle that he would not have supposed possible in so young a baby. She beat at it with her tiny fists as one bloodcurdling scream after another issued from her small pink mouth. For the first time since she was born, she lost, instead of gaining weight; apparently, the formula which had been selected for her did not agree with her, even in the small quantities that could be forced down her reluctant throat. Margaret was deeply troubled and her anxiety added to the disturbances in her physical condition; her breasts were painful and she began to run a low fever. At this point, Nicolas delivered an ultimatum: the cradle was to be moved into the guest room and Cassie, not Margaret, was to watch over it. When Cynthia discovered that, no matter how long she howled, she would have to accept the bottle or continue to go hungry, she would capitulate. There was one thing he would say for the kid, she was not stupid; she would catch on sooner than her mother or her nurse believed possible.

She was not stupid, but she was almost unbelievably stubborn. As she continued to scream, Margaret became more and more unnerved and pled with Nicolas to bring Cynthia to her; there was still enough milk in her breasts to pacify the baby, if not to nourish her and, once quieted, she would be easier to deal with. Margaret herself would feel better if the weaning were not precipitated in this way, which probably accounted for her fever. For the first time, she and Nicolas quarreled. He not only refused to bring Cynthia to her or to let Cassie do so; he effectively prevented Margaret from getting out of bed and going to Cynthia herself; tears, appeals and denunciations all left him equally unmoved.

The battle raged for nearly a week. At the end of that time Nicolas won, but it was a Pyrrhic victory. Cynthia accepted the hated bottle, but drank so little of its contents that she continued to lose weight for some days more. Finally, force of habit and a change of formula improved the situation and she began to gain again, though not at the rate she had before; and Nicolas could have sworn she looked at him with infantile animosity, whenever he went near her, though, at the same time, he told himself the very idea of this was fantastic. Margaret's fever continued and Dr. Loomis agreed that, as far as she was concerned, it would have been better if alternate breast and bottle feedings had been kept up a little longer. He was afraid, perhaps, he had erred, in not insisting they should be. But it had seemed best, at the time, to do things in Nicolas' way. . . .

The cradle was not brought back into the conjugal chamber and Cassie continued to take competent charge of Cynthia. Margaret's fever passed and Nicolas had her to himself again. But, to his surprise, the insatiable desire for domination, the fierce hunger for possession that had been so hard to satisfy or even appease, no longer obsessed him. He still wanted to "go in unto" his wife, freely and frequently, with a minimum of preliminary caresses and a maximum of retentiveness; but, having done so, he was not hounded by urgency until he had done so again. Instead of recognizing this intermittent sense of sufficiency as a normal development in the sustained marriage relationship and welcoming it as a release from tension, he resented it as a sign of a marked change in Margaret's attitude toward him. She was as approachable as ever, but there was a listlessness and apathy about her which had not been there even during her slow convalescence after Cynthia's birth.

He himself had said then that, between them, he and Cynthia had drained her of strength and reproached both himself and the child he had given her because this was so. She had replied they made her so happy that joy helped her to renew it, and he not only knew she believed this, he believed it himself. Now he feared, if he repeated his statement, she would not deny its truth. He knew it was not wise to put this fear to the test, but somehow he could not refrain from doing so when a moment presented itself that seemed singularly propitious.

It was now seldom warm enough outdoors to make much use of the arbor, and they were sitting after dinner in the library, before a cheerful fire, while Nicolas read aloud and Margaret sewed. They both still enjoyed a quiet evening spent in this way and the library was more often than not their chosen center, partly because it was so pleasant in itself and partly because it had come to have so many associations with their life together. It was here that Nicolas had proposed to Margaret and first made love to her and, on their wedding night, it had been the anteroom to their bridal chamber. It was here he had first read aloud to her and asked her to promise she would never cut her hair, after telling her that, like Byron's ladylove, she "walked in beauty." He still felt she did, he still reveled in her hair and, to his immense satisfaction and somewhat to his surprise, she had been as much pleased with the gold sandals as with the gold jewelry he brought her from Peru; she had readily fallen in with his suggestion that she should "dispense with stockings" when she dressed informally for her evenings alone with him. There was a precedent for such a costume, she told him smilingly: as late as the turn of the century, ladies, even very conservative ladies like her mother and her grandmother, were in the habit of "getting into something loose" at the end of the day, when they were at home alone with their husbands. Of course, then it had meant removing the rigid corsets into which they were laced and perhaps a few of their multitudinous undergarments before topping the remainder with a *robe d'intérieur*. Now there were no more corsets and very few undergarments to remove. But the total effect that met the eye was much the same. And the house was so lovely and warm that a nightgown was all she really needed under the jewel-colored robes Nicolas liked so much. She was tired by dinner time, it saved a great deal of effort not to dress for a second time after her bath, to be all ready for bed when they went upstairs. Nicolas thought he had never seen her look lovelier than she did during these evening sessions in the library; the gold jewelry and the gold sandals gave just the finishing touch to attire that was already charming.

Generally, as Nicolas read, Margaret made some comment on her own initiative, from time to time, which revealed her attentive interest in what she was hearing or, if Nicolas invited one, expressed a ready and intelligent opinion. But, tonight, it was so long since she had spoken, he gathered she was hardly listening and, when he looked at her, he saw that her expression was even more listless than on any other occasion he could remember. He paused in his reading, his finger still marking the place where he had stopped.

"You don't act like yourself, Margaret."

"That's not strange. I don't feel like myself."

So she was not even going to pretend, this time, that everything was all right! This was so completely out of character, he should have been warned. But, having started, he persisted.

"What seems to be the matter?"

"Do you expect me to feel the same as I did before I was forcibly separated from my baby?"

"You mean, before I kept you from giving in to that fractious child?" he asked in genuine surprise.

"Yes, that's just what I mean."

"You're holding it against me because I did what I knew was best for you and for her?"

"You can put it that way if you like. You don't *know* you were doing what was best. Dr. Loomis says now—"

"Well, he didn't say it then. At least, if he did, I certainly didn't hear him."

"He didn't commit himself one way or the other. And you were looking for an excuse to get Cynthia out of our room. You didn't want to share me, even with our child. You wanted me all to yourself."

Nicolas closed his book and laid it on the table beside him. They had been sitting on opposite sides of the fireplace, as the lamps were so placed that this gave them both the best light, him for reading and her for needlework. Now he crossed in front of the hearth, stopping to turn out the light by his seat and putting another log on the fire before making room for himself beside her on the sofa.

"Margaret, aren't you glad I want you that much?" he asked in a tense voice.

"No. Not now that we have a child, now that we're going to have another. I'd rather you wanted Cynthia with us. If she'd been a boy you wouldn't have acted this way."

"If Cynthia had been a boy, you wouldn't have been pregnant again so soon. You could have gone on nursing him. I didn't object to having Cynthia in the room until she began to make a nuisance of herself."

"I'm not by any means sure I wouldn't have been pregnant again so soon. You wanted a son, but you weren't thinking wholly about that when you came back to bed with me."

"I can't help asking you again, aren't you glad I want you that much?"

"I always have been until now. You know that."

"And you're not any more?"

"I've told you, it ought not to be just you and me any more. It ought to be you and me and our children."

"Margaret, you're begging the question. Aren't you glad I find you just as desirable as when I married you?"

"I don't believe you do."

"For God's sake, why not?" he asked, all the more vehemently because what she said was true and because he did not want to face it.

"I don't see how you can. I'm not as desirable. I'm tired and I'm half sick and I'm unhappy and I show it."

"You're *unhappy?*"

"Has it taken you all this time to find that out?"

"You've been unhappy ever since the night I wouldn't bring Cynthia to you or let you go to her?"

"Ever since the night you held me down to prevent that. You told me, when we were married, I'd have to submit to you once, but that I'd never have to do it again. You haven't kept your word. I hate people who break their promises."

"I haven't broken any promises. When I said I'd never ask you to submit to me but once, we weren't talking about keeping you from doing something that was bad for you. We were talking about something quite different and you know it. You don't hate me. You told me that before and, when I asked you if you were sure, you had to admit you weren't."

"This time, I am sure."

"Margaret, you're not well, or you wouldn't say that. You love me, you love me dearly, as much as I love you, which is more than I ever loved anyone else in my life, more than I thought I had it in me to love anyone. As I've told you before, you're infinitely precious to me. If you thought I found you less desirable, it was only because you didn't seem to want me as much as you used to. You've accepted me, but you haven't welcomed me, you haven't invited me. I haven't been able to imagine why not. That is, I knew your strength had been sapped in all sorts of ways; but that never made any difference before. You were never too tired to receive me with rapture. I didn't dream the trouble was because you were still angry with me, that you thought you had so much reason to be. Please forgive me. Please act like yourself again."

He put his arm around her waist and, with his free hand, began to stroke her hair. Then he pressed his cheek gently against hers and turned his head until their lips met. She did not draw away, but neither did she return his kiss. He stopped stroking her hair and reached for the second light. Except for the fire, the room was engulfed in friendly darkness.

"Do you remember what happened when we first sat on this sofa together?" he asked. But the question was only a murmur, for his lips were still close to hers.

"Yes."

"Tell me the way you remember it."

"You kissed me."

"And then?"

"Then you said, 'No, I'm afraid that had better be it for tonight, after all.' "

"You *have* got a good memory! And the next day you told me to explain and I said—"

She did not answer.

"What did I say, Margaret?"

"You said that you'd enjoyed kissing me so much more than you expected that you thought you'd get even more enjoyment if you went beyond kissing. You said it would have been the easiest thing in the world to put me down on the sofa and go on from there. You thought perhaps it would have been better that way: it would have saved a lot of needless talk. But second thought convinced you you'd shock me and hurt me and that you wouldn't get any lasting satisfaction out of it."

"This time, there isn't going to be any second thought. And we are going to save a lot of needless talk. I'm going far beyond kissing and I do expect to get lasting satisfaction out of it. I hope I'm not going to shock you or hurt you, for I certainly don't want to. In fact, I'd be a lot happier if you could act as if you wanted me the way you used to. But I don't intend to have you make any more mistakes about whether or not I still find you desirable. And I don't believe you will after tonight."

37 ❦

"Dr. Hale? Just one moment, please, the White House is calling."

Nicolas held the receiver to his ear during a brief succession of short clicks, meanwhile motioning to Margaret, who had come into the gun room with a question, that he could not answer her just then. With surprise, he recognized the President's penetrating voice even before Maynard had identified himself, speaking in his usual precise fashion.

"What about luncheon with me today, Nicolas? On a tray in my office? One o'clock, if that's a good hour for you."

"Couldn't be better. Thank you very much, Mr. President."

"Allan Lambert will be here, too. He's been quite urgent in suggesting we three should get together, without other guests."

"No danger I'll be the one to make a crowd?"

"You know I wouldn't have asked you in that case. Good-bye now."

"Have you any idea what this is about?" Margaret, who had heard as plainly as Nicolas, asked excitedly.

"Not the slightest. Allan has been making hints for a long time about something so indefinite that I couldn't even guess what he had on his mind. Labrador, the Rector of San Marcos, has been just as full of hints and just as vague. But I haven't heard from either of them lately. That is, as you know, I've seen Allan from time to time, though not as much as usual; and since he hasn't made any reference to this mystery, I haven't felt inclined to do so, either. Perhaps it's to be revealed at last, but why under presidential auspices, I wouldn't have an inkling."

"Will you tell me all about it when you get home this afternoon?"

"Yes, if I am free to. I can't imagine it's top secret. But, of course, it could be. What are your plans for the day?"

"Well, as long as you're going into Washington, I think I will, too. Miriam's been asking me to set a day for luncheon. I could call her up and see if she happens to be free on such short notice."

"This would be just a ladies' luncheon?"

"I don't know. Why do you ask?"

"Because, as you must have noticed, both Senator Powers and Jerome LaGuarde have been giving me the cold shoulder ever since I got back, and that's almost four months now. I was wondering if you'd felt the frost, too."

"No, they've been very cordial to me, as always. But—well, I have thought there was a little strain about something. However, if there is, Miriam would be just the person to ease it and, if she is free and if either her husband or her father is to be at home, naturally Miriam will say at once that, of course, you must come, too. It will be rather fun to say you can't, because you're lunching at the White House."

"Maybe you've got something there. . . . Rufus can drop me off and take you on to Georgetown. Then he can come back for me and, afterward, I'll join you. I imagine your conference will be longer than mine." Nicolas grinned and held out a detaining hand. "What were you starting to say when you found the Great Man had a prior claim on my attention?"

"Only to ask if you'd like terrapin for supper."

"Of course. You know that without asking. Sure there wasn't anything else?"

"No, not for the moment. Let me go, Nicolas, so I can telephone Miriam."

There it was again, the feeling that, instead of welcoming his caresses, she only tolerated them and that, at a moment like this, she might well have lingered a little, instead of rushing off to get in touch with a woman doubly allied to men who apparently were ready to put him in the class with Dr. Cook. There had never been another outburst like the one on that memorable night in the library; though he could not have failed to convince her then that he still found her desirable, to his chagrin, she had made no similar effort, as far as he was concerned. That his pride should be hurt by outsiders was hard enough to take; that his wife should be doing it, too, was insult added to injury. She seemed perfectly well again, as far as he could judge, and Cynthia was blooming and showing a ravenous appetite for orange juice and various gloomy looking strained foods besides milk. She was fast outgrowing the cradle, sat up, unsupported, in her carriage, banging a rattle against its sides, and expressed both joy and rage with equal vehemence, even though she as yet lacked words to do so. Certainly Margaret could not still be holding against him a difference of opinion in which his will had prevailed, but which had done neither her nor the baby any lasting harm!

Miriam was free, Margaret reported as she came back to the gun room, where a big desk had been installed for Nicolas and where he did much of his paperwork, as he still regarded the boudoir with scorn because of its designation, though he could have had much greater quiet and seclusion there than downstairs. She was already dressed for town, very becomingly, in smart black that set off her new chinchilla cape to perfection. He had not realized it was so late; he would have to hurry with his own dressing and, on the drive to town, he kept glancing at his watch with some anxiety: the White House was one place where it would not do to be even minutes behind time. Fortunately, they arrived at the northeast gate with one to spare, and were met at the main entrance to the Executive Offices by Bill Simmons, the portly, dignified old doorkeeper who had served several presidents before the present incumbent. Allan was already there and various members of the press immediately pounced on the visitors, eager to learn and record the purpose of their call. Nicolas laughed and shook his head.

"You boys know as much about it as I do. Maybe more. . . ."

"Then can't you help us out, Mr. Secretary?"

"Sorry. This is one of those times for hope deferred. Besides, time is of the essence right now."

The sound of a striking clock confirmed his statement and there was no further insistence. As Simmons opened the door to the President's private office, a large oval room, carpeted and curtained in green, Maynard rose from behind a massive and rather cluttered desk to greet his visitors. The telephone was surrounded by gold stars, one for every state; large, silver-framed photographs of Mrs. Maynard in the dress she had worn for the inaugural ball, of the Maynards' daughter in bridal white and the Maynards' son in the uniform of a Captain of Infantry and the Maynards' grandchildren in less formal attire were scattered among various party emblems; and offerings from the latest civic groups received, though doubtless subject to removal in the near future as superfluous, added to the disorder of the moment. A large globe stood on one side of the desk and two chairs upholstered in deep red were drawn up on the other. The President was putting on weight, Nicolas noticed, and he looked tired; there was very little color in his lined face; the old ruddiness, the deceptive look of youthfulness were fading fast. He touched a bell and food, in metal warming ovens, was wheeled in. Maynard hardly waited for them to start eating before broaching the subject at hand.

"I don't see any reason why we shouldn't get right down to business, Nicolas," he said, as soon as the brief greetings were over and the trays had been set before them. "I know you didn't have any idea why I asked you to come, beyond the fact that Allan thought we should have a three-cornered conference, and I suppose you've been turning various possibilities over in your mind. Well, let's put an end to your speculation. How would you like to be United State Asmbassador to Peru?"

It was quite true that Nicolas had been turning various possibilities over in his mind, but the President's abrupt proposition was not among them. He had not been so surprised since Margaret had agreed to marry him and, for a moment, his astonishment left him speechless. The President continued to demolish his steak, quite as if nothing more important than the weather had been under discussion. Allan Lambert lighted a cigarette and leaned back a little in his chair, grinning amiably. Somehow Nicolas found it easier to speak to him than to Maynard and, disregarding not only protocol, but the standard code which requires that the person who asks a question should be the one to receive a reply, he turned to the Secretary.

"Don't tell me this is what you and Labrador have been whispering about for a year!"

"No, Nick, it isn't. Maybe we'll come to that later. Meanwhile, suppose you answer the President's question, instead of asking me any more just now."

"You'll have to excuse me, Mr. President," Nicolas said apologetically. "You took the wind out of my sails so suddenly—"

"Yes, I realize that," Maynard said, buttering a roll. "But things haven't been running as smoothly as I'd like in our embassies south of the border and, though Allan had other plans for you, he now seems to think you're the great white hope as far as our Latin American posts are concerned—especially as far as the post in Peru is concerned. We've had several political appointees there who didn't speak a word of Spanish and wouldn't try to learn—enough of them to do damage between the career men who were all right in their way, but didn't weigh much. The present incumbent's a pretty good one, as you know, conscientious and all that, though he isn't brilliant. I'd be willing to keep him, but he wants to resign because his wife's discontented—claims she never gets to first base with Peruvian women. Now Margaret —" The President pushed back his empty plate and began to drink coffee, pausing between sips to make one point after another. "Margaret would not only get along with Peruvian women, she'd charm them—Peruvian men, too. She'd give more prestige to our embassy than it's had in a long while. She's a natural born hostess in the grand manner. I don't suppose she speaks Spanish, but I'd be willing to bet my bottom dollar she'd learn, mighty fast, too. And you not only speak Spanish like a native, I understand you speak—what is it, Allan? Oh yes, Quechua and two or three other Indian dialects. You're on intimate terms with the ruling families, like the Parras, and the intellectuals, like Labrador, the Cerro de Pasco crowd, the missionaries, Protestant and Catholic both. You know the country like the back of your hand—the out-of-the-way places, the psychology of the inhabitants, the history way back to pre-Inca times and through Spanish colonialism right up to the present. I don't see why I didn't think of you myself. . . . Well, what do you say?"

"I can't say anything, Mr. President. I'm too staggered."

"Well, isn't everything *I've* said true?"

This time, it was the coffee Maynard pushed away before lighting a cigar. Nicolas realized that, as far as the President was concerned, the lunch hour was nearing its end.

"Most of it is," Nicolas said slowly. "That is, of course your estimate of Margaret is entirely correct—she would give prestige to an embassy or any other place, for that matter. I do speak Spanish and some of the dialects. Ildefonso Parra and I were classmates at college and have been friends ever since and I'm close to the university crowd in both Lima and Cuzco. But there's one thing you've said that wasn't entirely accurate. I don't know all of Peru like the back of my hand. If I did, I wouldn't be searching for something I haven't found."

"Some submerged treasure in a hidden lake off in an unexplored, half legendary region! Good God, what does that amount to? You talk like a visionary, instead of a hard-headed, practical New Englander. You're not even sure the treasure exists!"

"No, I'm not. That's just the trouble. If I were sure, if the job were done, if your offer had come after it was. . . . Maybe I'm not as hardheaded and practical as I ought to be, even if I am a New Englander. After all, I've strayed a long way from Woodstock, Vermont. But I have a congenital objection to leaving anything I've started unfinished. I've got to find that lagoon or die in the attempt and I mean that pretty literally. However, as a matter of fact, I don't expect it's coming to that. I think I'm pretty close to success. I've every reason to think so. I've got a good base camp with good men in it. I've actually seen the lake with the submerged palace, though I haven't been able to land there. Now, thanks to a legacy, I'll have the means to do it. I've got to go on."

"So the answer is no?"

"Mr. President, you know how honored I am by your offer. But, in my place, wouldn't you do the same thing?"

"You seem to be having difficulty today, Nicolas, in giving me direct answers. Is it no?"

"I'm sorry, Mr. President, but it has to be."

The President laid his half-smoked cigar down on a brass ashtray embellished with various weird figures. Then he touched a bell and rose. He looked even more tired than when Allan and Nicolas had come in. *He really is taking this Good Neighbor failure hard,* Nicolas said to himself. *I suppose I could have helped. But, after all, it isn't my fault he's in trouble down there. . . .*

"I'm sorry, too—sorry and disappointed," the President was saying. "This is the first time anyone's turned me down on a proposition like that. I must be losing my powers of persuasion, which doesn't augur well for the next campaign. Goodby, Nicolas—best of luck with your lake. . . . Better make it this time again tomorrow, Allan. We've got to get this thing settled and out of the way. There are plenty of other matters pending, even more important."

"I suppose I've offended him," Nicolas said to Allan as they walked away.

"I would not say that exactly. His own word—disappointed—is a better one. He really wanted you for that job and so did I. Now I'm afraid he wouldn't go out of his way to grant you a favor, if you should happen to want one. It's always safer to be in a position to ask."

"But you understand, don't you, Allan?"

"Yes, I understand, though I'm disappointed, too. However, I'm still hoping to make use of you in the way I originally had in mind, before this brainstorm."

"How much longer before you're going to break down and tell me what that was?"

"I'm not sure. However, one thing is sure—it won't be now. I've got to beat it back to my own office. There's another nice little revolution brewing in Santo Domingo and I'm supposed to have all potential belligerents pacified before cocktail time. Give my love to Margaret. And, as the President said, good luck with your lake."

"Can't I give you a lift?"

"No, it's just a step to the State Department and the walk's good for me."

Allan nodded and walked briskly away, again good-naturedly shaking off the thwarted press. It was the first time, as far as Nicolas could recall, that he and Allan Lambert had parted when the latter had not said something about getting together again as soon as they could, if possible, for dinner. He could not help feeling the omission meant that his ties with the Assistant Secretary of State were becoming either strained or loosened, as he suspected they were in several other cases, and the realization was depressing. When he reached the La Guardes' house, he reluctantly accepted an invitation to come in for coffee; Miriam and Margaret were just finishing their first cups and would be glad of an excuse for seconds. He added nothing to their cheerful chatter and, in response to an eager question from Miriam, answered lightly that she knew better than to ask why the President had wanted to see him; and, after he and Margaret were in the car, he shook his head and then nodded toward Rufus when she revealed similar curiosity.

"Did you enjoy your luncheon?" he asked, effectively changing the subject.

"Yes, it was very pleasant."

"I take it you didn't see Powers or Jerome?"

"Just for a few minutes before lunch. We all had cocktails together. The men were both going to some big Press Club doing. Senator Powers stopped by to pick up Jerome."

"Rather a zigzag route, wasn't it? The Capitol to Georgetown and then on to 14th Street?"

"The Senate wasn't in session today. It adjourned out of respect for some senator who suddenly died—I didn't even hear who—so Powers hadn't been to the Chamber."

"Did either he or Jerome say anything about me?" Nicolas inquired. And, as Margaret, in her turn, glanced at Rufus, Nicolas continued, "This is different. There's no reason why you shouldn't go on."

"Jerome referred casually to those two Englishmen—Tennant and Snow, were those their names?—and said someone was always imagining he'd discovered Paitite, but that the National Geographic didn't take it seriously. It never failed to be all smoke and no fire. He didn't mention you directly."

"He didn't need to, if he said that. What about Powers?"

"I'm afraid you're not going to like this, Nicolas. I'd rather not tell you."

"Oh, for God's sake, go ahead! I'd have to find out what it was sooner or later, wouldn't I?"

"Perhaps not. Perhaps he'll get over this feeling. But he seems to think that, when he told you he didn't want Schaeffer and Steinmetz to contribute to the expedition, you'd understand he didn't want anyone except himself and Miriam to do it. He thought they were to bear the full responsibility for it. He said he'd have given you extra money for a helicopter, if you'd asked for it. He didn't know you needed one. I tried to explain that you didn't, either, until you found out the difficulties of landing with a hydroplane. But he's afraid now you'll tack Pete's name on somewhere and this won't be known solely as the Powers Expedition."

"Of course, it'll be known that way. How dumb can you get? Poor old Pete wasn't looking for publicity like this headline hunter."

"But he doesn't want Pete's name even on the helicopter."

"Well, it's damn well going to be and I'll tell Powers so myself the next time I see him. Also, that he doesn't need to send me messages by my wife. That's why he stopped by to pick up Jerome—so he could use you as a cat's-paw."

Margaret opened her lips to answer and then thought better of it. The rest of the drive was made in silence. After they reached Hills' End, Nicolas went to the sideboard and poured himself a stiff drink, though habitually he still maintained afternoon was not the time for alcohol. Then, refilling his glass, he went to his desk in the gun room and began opening his mail. Margaret, puzzled and a little hurt, came and put her arm around his shoulders.

"Can't you tell me now what happened at the White House?" she asked softly.

"I don't feel much like talking after what you told me about Powers. However, I suppose I may as well tell you now as later. The President offered me an ambassadorship."

"An *ambassadorship!* Where?"

"Where do you suppose? Peru, of course."

"Oh, Nicolas, how *wonderful!* Now our family can be together!"

"I turned it down."

The gaze with which she regarded him was at first unbelieving and then stricken. He saw that her lips were trembling and that she did not trust herself to speak. He threw down the letter he had just opened and rose, angrily.

"I'm an explorer, not a diplomat, and I happen to feel my job is important," he said with heat. "So do plenty of other people. I don't believe you could find half a dozen well educated persons in Washington, let alone the whole country, who could tell you the names of our ambassadors to Peru since 1911. But every one of those same persons would know all about Hiram Bingham and Machu Picchu. My discoveries have been compared to his already. Pretty soon they're going to surpass his. The President's a politician and he's in a jam with his Good Neighbor Policy; he'll continue to be unless he changes his tactics. He thought I had all the answers for him. Besides, he may really have believed he was paying me a compliment, though he knows as well as I do that, except in the cases of career diplomats, ambassadorships generally go to salve the feelings of some senator who couldn't get re-elected or some old ward heeler who's been useful in a campaign. He's made plenty of such appointments himself. Maybe he was trying to salve *my* feelings, because I haven't got any further than Moonstone Lake, and do me a good turn while he was doing himself a better one. If that entered the picture, he ought to have known better. Anyway, Allan Lambert should have. He's a gentleman and a scholar. At least, I've always thought so until today."

Margaret continued to look at her husband without speaking. He turned away from her and started toward the dining room, his whiskey glass, now empty for the second time, in his hand. Then abruptly, he faced about.

"I told you in the beginning we wouldn't be together constantly," he said with increasing vehemence. "As it is, we've been together a lot more than I expected—a lot more than you expected. I should think that would satisfy you, that you wouldn't be such a poor sport about a situation you accepted as satisfactory. Apparently, you're still toying with the idea that I'll take you with me to Peru. I shan't. Do you hear me, Margaret! *I never shall until I make my discovery.*"

"Yes, I hear you."

"Perhaps Maynard could be persuaded to send you to Peru as ambassadress. I don't believe it would take much persuasion. He mentioned that you'd give great prestige to the post if I had it. He didn't say anything about my giving it prestige. Then you could go to Peru on your own—you and Cynthia. Of course, I wouldn't decline to take the same ship, though it might lead to complications as to protocol."

"What you've said is fantastic. But I know you were only joking."

"There's many a true word spoken in jest. You'd better give the matter some thought. With all the prestige you enjoy in the higher echelons, you probably could pull it off and that would be a way for you to get to Peru right now—the only one, as far as I know. Incidentally, I didn't fail to notice those two new books you've brought into the library—*Alaska Challenge* and *Jungle Wife*. Where did they they come from?"

"Mrs. Madison gave them to me."

"Yes, I know she's tried to put ideas into your head from the beginning. The next time I see her, I'll tell her she might as well stop. And if you've had any idea I might enjoy reading aloud to you out of those damn books, or that I'd even consider doing so, you'd better forget it."

"I didn't have any such idea. I think our evening sessions in the library have about served their purpose anyway, don't you, Nicolas?"

"Just what do you infer by that? Is it meant to be a dirty dig about my acting like a caveman? I had to do something to bring you to your senses. I told you I didn't think there'd ever be any doubt in your mind, after that night, as to whether or not I desired you, and I don't believe there has been."

"No. But you also told me, when we were first married, that I'd given you a new standard: that you never realized before desire could be combined with respect and admiration. You didn't act that night as if you either respected or admired me. You acted as if you were determined to teach me a much needed lesson—in a rather coarse manner. Your methods were very different in the old barn. I've always treasured the memory of those."

38❦

"Woodstock, Vermont
"May 20, 1955

"Friend Nicolas:

"Yours of the tenth received and contents noted. I suspicioned you might have been looking for a letter from me, as the six months were up a week ago yesterday. However, I thought best to stay on the safe side, as I was never one to favor being left with insufficient funds to meet an obligation. Though you were convinced Pete Hart didn't have any creditors, at your age you've probably learned there's nothing so uncertain as a dead sure thing. Just the same, no claimants have shown up and things are looking pretty good otherwise, so I don't know as I can keep you any longer from making that imprudent investment you're so set on. Near as I can recall, you talked first about $35,000 for a helicopter and then you went on to say that didn't provide for transportation and a pilot and Lord knows what else besides and began to mutter about $50,000. Well, the $50,000 is available all right and a considerable sum besides, so your father wants I should tell you, as far as that is concerned, there's no reason why you can't start for Palo Alto and make any arrangements you see fit for that crazy purchase. Just the same, personally, he doesn't think you should leave home right now and neither do I. He tells me your wife is in the family way again and pretty close to her time; also, if you weren't going to use the money for another month that would be a good thing as far as the interest is concerned. But I presume you'll want to go ahead and I would take it kindly if you would answer by return mail and oblige yours truly,

"Ethan Watkins

"P.S. I sure hope you get a boy this time. I hate to think of a fine old family like the Hales daughtering off."

Nicolas threw the letter down on his desk and, in a futile gesture of exasperation, tore up the envelope and flung the scraps into the wastebasket. "Daughtering off!" It was years since he had heard the old colloquialism and, in the past, it had not irritated him, because it had no special significance for him. Now it did. The new baby was due the first of June and he was convinced, as he thought Margaret was also, that it would be another girl. If he had dared to hope that it would be a boy, and that its birth would mark a tenderly memorable moment of rapprochement between Margaret and himself, he would not have considered leaving for Palo Alto as soon as he got his money. In the absence of any such hope, that was exactly what he intended to do.

He read through the letter a second time to make sure he had made no mistake. Then he picked up the telephone and made a reservation on a plane leaving for California the following day. He had already familiarized himself with the schedules of the principal airlines. He next opened the drawers of his desk, one after the other, and checked their contents to make sure he was overlooking nothing that he would need to take with him. He kept them in reasonably good order at all times and the checking was really a superfluous precaution; but it was in line with the many things he did every day, all of which were equally trivial. Since nothing of importance was required of him, he fell back on the unimportant, or he would have gone crazy with inactivity.

The Huntingtons were at last in residence again at East Lawn and, if Nicolas had been willing to meet their overtures toward neighborly relations even halfway, he could have had his choice of a mount from their stables, joined the Belvoir Hunt, and attended the convivial Hunt dances and breakfasts on Saturday nights and Sunday mornings. Besides, he would have been warmly welcomed for dinner and bridge any night he chose to go to East Lawn, taking Margaret with him. She would willingly have shown herself more friendly. It was the Huntingtons who were lonely now, she insisted; even though they had been invited to join the Belvoir Hunt (at her private suggestion) they were only on sufferance and they knew it. The time had come to give them a chance to show that, even though they were social climbers, they could learn, sooner or later, how to fit in. But Nicolas, who was not much of a horseman or a bridge player anyway, continued to condemn Edgar Huntington as a beefy boor and his wife as an empty-headed twitterer. He consented, reluctantly, to their inclusion in one of Margaret's Sunday night suppers and went, with even greater reluctance, to one of the Huntingtons' showy, ill-planned dinners. After that, the two couples met at church, where the services bored Edgar as much as they did Nicolas, but which both attended to please their wives; it was the only bond between them and it remained an unspoken one. Little by little, the Huntingtons also found their way to the informal gatherings where established churchgoers met for juleps and cocktails before going home to their respective Sunday dinners. But, as yet, the rich New Yorkers had never been among those who managed to remain for dinner itself, either at Hills' End or any of the other nearby plantations and Nicolas was glad of it.

Tardily, and only to fill the place of a speaker whose plane had been delayed, he was invited to address the National Geographic. But he was only too well aware that his slides were inadequate, and that he had lost the knack of making a speech at one and the same time easy and informative. He did no better at the Explorers Club. The last of the articles for which *Collier's* had contracted was now written and he proofread it again, just to make doubly sure it contained no typos, after he had put his desk in apple-pie order. But the afternoon was still young. It would not take him more than an hour, at the outside, to pack and he must find something else to do before he went upstairs to take his suitcases out of the storeroom where they had been neatly stowed away. His latest letter from Lester, which he had answered the day before, was already in his briefcase, but he took it out and reread that, too, by no means for the first time.

The news it contained was so important that Lester had flown all the way to Lima on purpose to mail it: after a long dull stretch of months, when nothing had actually gone wrong, but when the weather had been so consistently bad that no progress had been made toward further discovery, either, a few Machiguengas from Lacco had come to the camp of their own accord. They had come looking for Pete, half-vengefully and half-hopefully. Among them were two women, one middle-aged, the other quite young and quite pretty. The young one, whose name was Perpetua, had a baby—a *redheaded* baby. And when she learned Pete was dead, she grieved and grieved. So he had told the truth in his letter—not that Lester had ever doubted it: he had not raped her, she could have fought him off with a stone, she didn't want to, she wanted him. Nobody needed to be told the baby was Pete's, it looked exactly like him, even if it was half Indian, and it was the cutest little trick any of them had ever seen. They were all crazy about him and, somehow, Gomara had persuaded his mother and grandmother and male relatives he must be baptized, so Lester had flown him and

Perpetua down to Atalaya and Antonio and Fátima had arranged everything for a ceremony at church, where they acted as sponsors, and had a christening party at their house afterward. Of course, the baby had been named for his father, so now there was another Pete Hart and he would be the expedition's mascot and their link with the Machiguengas. Since the group from Lacco had been so warmly welcomed and there had been no question of denying the baby's paternity—on the contrary, he had been made the pet of the camp—there was much friendly feeling and it would spread. Presently, some of the other Machiguengas—the ones who knew the trails farther east—would return and the final thrust toward the magic lake might be made any time. If it was not, it would be when Nick came back with the helicopter. Soon victory would actually be within their grasp.

Nicolas did not tear up the envelope in which this letter had come. He carefully replaced the sheets on which Lester had written and sat for some moments, drumming his fingers on the orderly top of his desk, and trying to calculate just how long it would take him to get back to Lake Moonstone. There was the flight across the continent, both ways; the necessary time for the factory check-out at Palo Alto, which he supposed would be at least a week, probably two; then transportation of the helicopter and the pilot by ship from San Francisco to Callao, twelve days, without counting the time necessary to make a connection with a scheduled sailing. Of course, Nicolas must come home and stay there long enough at least to see the new baby and assure himself of Margaret's satisfactory convalescence. But if everything went according to Hoyle, the confinement and sailing date would almost coincide, and he would stay at Hills' End for the period required for the voyage and then fly down and make connections with the pilot and the helicopter in Lima. He would arrange by cable with that capable agent, Warren Holtz, to have his C-84 all ready to make a quick getaway to Quince Mil. But even so, by the time the helicopter was assembled and they were actually on the last lap of the trek to Moonstone Lake, he would have used up more than a month before he could see that redheaded little boy who was to be the living link between the Machiguengas and the expedition and, hence, a fellow discoverer.

He was beginning to wonder if, perhaps, he had made the worst of his many mistakes in feeling not only that he must marry, but that he must marry a gentlewoman in order to provide the right sort of mother. Maybe it would be Pete's son, not his, who would eventually carry on his work. If he had not lived selectively, even when he did not live continently, before his marriage, if he had done long ago what Pete had done only last year, he might by now be teaching a sturdy little urchin his ways. A half-breed? Well, a mestizo; but the other more derogatory term was almost never used in Peru. A bastard? No, again the term was too harsh. A natural child: a child he had begotten on the grassy bank of a river which flowed quietly by over its smooth stones, when he had taken an unresisting girl in his arms and gone in unto her with no struggle on her part and no force on his. He could not have come closer to nature than that. . . .

The sound of infantile rage, not far from the gun room, brought him back abruptly from conjecture to reality. Cynthia was resisting the efforts of Bernice—the latest of the nieces whom Cassie had pressed into service—to bring her into the house for her supper, after spending several hours in the arbor with her mother. She did not wish to get out of her gocart. Bernice was bending over her and had managed to get the confining strap undone; but beyond that, she had not been able to go. Cynthia kicked and beat with her fists, meanwhile screaming as if she were being murdered. Nicolas went quickly to the open door, descended the steps and picked her up, still beating, kicking and screaming.

"Be quiet, you little hellion!" he said angrily, setting her down on the floor. She stopped screaming, turned her head to give him a malevolent glance and started swiftly toward the stairs. She crept everywhere now, with astonishing rapidity, and had begun to pull herself upright by clutching a chair or a table, and even to take a few tottering steps now and then before falling down and howling, not because she was hurt, but because she was thwarted in her attempt to go farther. She could not, of course, safely engineer the stairs, and Nicolas rushed after her and picked her up again, this time unable to resist the temptation of slapping her buttocks. Just then, Margaret, who had followed the progress of the gocart at a more leisurely pace, came into the house.

"Please don't do that, Nicolas," she said gently—too gently. Nicolas had come to recognize the tone as one denoting a conscious and difficult effort at self-control. "Give her to me."

"She's much too heavy for you to carry and you know it," he said brusquely.

"I won't carry her. I'll walk along slowly and she'll creep beside me. Meanwhile, Bernice will get her supper ready. As soon as Cynthia sees it, she'll quiet down. She's hungry, that's all the matter with her. I should have sent her in half an hour ago. But it was such a lovely afternoon and I'll have so few more with her that. . . ."

Margaret left the sentence unfinished and smiled down at Cynthia. As predicted, the baby crept along rapidly and contentedly beside her mother as soon as Nicolas lowered her to the floor. Margaret turned back to smile at him, too.

"You see," she said, still in that very gentle voice.

"Yes, I see. As soon as you're absolutely sure you've got her quieted down perhaps you'd join me in the gun room. I'd like to talk to you for a few minutes."

"She'll go along with Bernice now that I have her started. I can come to you right away."

It was very often the gun room, instead of the library, which they used now. A comfortable chair was kept, drawn up near the desk, and Margaret sat there, off and on, when Nicolas wanted to talk with her, in the interludes between his paper work. She did not usually bring sewing or knitting with her any more. The interludes were apt to be brief, not because he was pressed for time, but because she was. For one thing, Bernice needed a great deal of supervision; for another, Margaret needed a great deal of rest, and she was advised to stay out of doors as much as possible now that the weather was so pleasant. She had found her second pregnancy much more trying than her first. Though she had again been free from nausea and other unpleasant symptoms, there were some less obvious that had been hard on her. She did not complain; in fact, her very patience, like her very gentleness, seemed to Nicolas an unspoken rebuke. She looked and acted tired all the time.

"Yes, dear?" she said, as she seated herself.

"I finally heard from Watkins. I can have the money any time. That is, fifty thousand dollars of it."

"Oh, I'm very glad! So you'd like to leave for Palo Alto right away?"

"Unless you'd rather I didn't."

"No, I'd much rather you did. I know how eager you are to get started, how necessary you feel it is to go back to Peru."

It isn't really all that necessary, he said to himself. *Everything is going well at camp and we ought to have almost three months of good weather ahead of us. If I can't get to my submerged palace in that length of time, I'd better give up exploring and resign myself to being a Virginia country gentleman after all. The trouble is, I want to go back. For one thing, I want to see that redheaded kid of Pete's.* Aloud, he said, "I can stay here a couple of weeks anyway, after I get back from California. I have it all figured out. When I've seen the pilot and the helicopter safely aboard a freighter in San Francisco, I'll come back to Hills' End. Then, a fortnight later, I'll take a plane and make connections with them in Lima. The only hitch is that, if the baby were early, or I were delayed in California, I might not be here when you went to the hospital."

"I'd much rather you weren't. Husbands are an awful nuisance in a hospital."

"And you really don't mind having people misunderstand?"

"Misunderstand?"

"My absence. Feel I ought to be here."

"Well—as long as you and I don't misunderstand, as long as we don't feel you ought to be here, it really doesn't matter, does it, what anyone else thinks or feels?"

"I suppose not. . . . I can get space tomorrow on United to San Francisco. Perhaps I'd better take it."

"Perhaps you had."

He almost wished she had said, "You've taken it already, haven't you, Nicolas?" If she would only say something like that, it might start a quarrel and a quarrel could clear the atmosphere. But she left the room, without saying anything else, to supervise Cynthia's supper. Except for that one vehement outburst, when she had told him for the second time that she hated him, Margaret had never said the wrong thing, that is, the thing that was deliberately unkind or disturbingly observant or even tactless. Though she had never actually retracted those angry words in speech, of course he knew that she did not hate him; that she loved him; she showed it in many ways. But perhaps it was the almost infallible courtesy which he lacked, the instinct for graciousness in both word and deed, that made him jealous of her.

He was now obliged to admit to himself that he was jealous of her, for qualities superior to his own, just as he had been obliged, the year before, to admit his jealousy of Lester for the same reason. It was jealousy that had made him behave so inexcusably when he had been offered an ambassadorship and the President had spoken about Margaret's prestige, instead of his own. It was jealousy that made him resent Powers' generosity, not jealousy because he thought Margaret would be unduly attracted by a distinguished and fascinating man, but because it was not Nicolas' qualities, but Margaret's, including, but by no means solely, her pleasing femininity, that had stimulated Powers' interest in the expedition. And it seemed more and more likely that Powers would be his party's choice for Vice President and that, this time, he would not refuse the nomination, which would bring him pretty close to the throne, if not to the throne itself. It was an open secret that Maynard had had another heart attack. Involuntarily, a phrase from the Bible story of Esther flashed across Nicolas' mind: "The one whom the King delighteth to honor." That would be Margaret if Powers became President. And suddenly her husband's jealousy became a soaring flame.

But this was not all, he told himself more and more angrily. Margaret had not come back to the gun room, she was now putting Cynthia to bed, though Bernice was perfectly capable of doing this. He was jealous of Cynthia, too, of his own child, because she had created division and not cemented unity between Margaret and himself. And he could foresee greater division, more disunity, when the new baby came. Again there would be nurses to placate and annoying questions as to who should sleep where and a nursing schedule which must take precedence over everything else. He would have given anything—anything, that is, except his purpose of discovery—if he could have set back the clock, if he and Margaret could have returned to those days and nights when they first found each other, and found nothing wanting, when there had been no disappointments, no jealousy, no controlled patience on her part, no eagerness to escape on his. For with the finding had come fulfillment for them both, such fulfillment as neither had dreamed beforehand would be attainable in marriage and, for a long while, the act of love was one of supreme rapture for both. Was it all his fault that the radiance of their relationship was dimmed? Had the mistake he had made that night in the library, when he was only trying to prove how much he desired her, been such an affront to her delicacy and her dignity that she could neither forgive nor forget it? That was one way in which Margaret failed him—she neither forgave nor forgot anything easily. He had told her he was sorry, that it had honestly never occurred to him that she would consider what he had done coarse or crude, and she had accepted his apology. But nothing had been the same between them since. It was tragic that, after the finding and the fulfillment, there should be such spiritual separation, such a breakdown of mutual understanding and sympathy and trust. The division was far more disastrous than any which could be wrought by distance and, as he sat alone in the gun room through the deepening dusk, it seemed to him there was no way of bridging it.

It still seemed so when he left Hills' End for California the following morning.

39 ❧

"The first thing I'm supposed to tell you is that you're not to rush off to Quince Mil," Fonso informed Nicolas as soon as they had exchanged the first *abrazo,* and a few jesting remarks to the effect that meeting planes, on which Nicolas was a passenger, was getting to be almost a full-time occupation for his friend.

"Why? Has there been any trouble about getting a C-84?"

"None at all. It's standing by already loaded, except for you and your baggage. Holtz and I saw your new toy and its operator safely through the customs yesterday, with a minimum of trouble and delay, and then we got the toy hauled from Callao to Limatambo. I thought probably you'd want to check on it and say hello to your pilot, who watches over his charge like an anxious mother with her first child, before we went into town. But we're not to dally. Labrador's waiting to discuss a very important appointment. The President wants to see you before you go off again into the wild blue yonder."

"The President! What for?"

"I haven't the least idea. Labrador has, though. I'm to drop you at his house, instead of taking you home with me, worse luck. We wanted to show you the new baby right away, before you had time to brag about yours. Incidentally, you haven't even told me her name yet."

"Her name's Audrey and I wasn't going to brag. But go on, you and Marina can't have another baby by now! It's a biological impossibility."

"You're a great one to talk! Our two latest are fifteen months apart. What about yours?"

"You had six already. Ours was a once in a lifetime happening."

"Well, give yourself a little more time and be a little more constant in your attentions to your wife. At the rate you've begun, under the handicaps of separation, I'd say you'd soon be in a position to give me considerable competition."

They continued to badger each other as they walked along to another part of the field, where they found Harry Davis, the pilot-mechanic, waiting beside the C-84. Yes, the helicopter was already aboard, he told Nicolas, they could start whenever Dr. Hale said the word. He understood that meteorological conditions were better in the morning, also that Dr. Hale would not be free to start that day. Perhaps the next? Nicolas would have to let him know. While they were talking, Fonso bethought himself of the responsibilities of a host, which had temporarily slipped his mind.

"Now that you and Nick have made connections, I hope you'll come along with me, Mr. Davis," he said cordially. "There's no point in your waiting around here until we find out what he's going to do. Everything's under control. I'm still hopeful that Nick can break away from presidential and academic pressure and join us later. Anyway, I think my wife and I could make you feel more at home than the Labradors. Their house has been declared a public monument and it's very imposing and traditional and all that, but I think you'd find ours more fun."

"Go ahead, Harry. Fonso's right. I'll be with you as soon as I can. Meanwhile, take it easy and enjoy yourself. You'll have plenty to keep you busy later on."

Nicolas had never before seen the Rector of San Marcos show signs of excitement; but this time Labrador was waiting for his guest in the patio, unable to restrain his impatience until they could get upstairs.

Though the drizzly chill of mid-July had settled over Lima, two rattan chairs had been placed near the fountain, with a small coffee table between them, and Nicolas discovered that this was where he was expected to hear whatever Labrador was so eager to tell him.

"I hope this appointment you've made for me is going to bring me better luck than the last one I had with a president," he said rather ruefully, as he seated himself. "That one caused all sorts of ructions, both at home and abroad."

"Yes, so I've heard. Allan has written me quite frankly. Believe me, he thought he was doing you a favor in suggesting that you be offered the ambassadorship. Ninety-nine men out of a hundred would have leaped at it. But he saw your side. He realizes now that something more in line with what we visualized for you at the beginning would suit you better personally and be just as helpful to both governments."

"I hope you'll excuse me if I remind you that you and Allan have been talking to me in riddles ever since the fall of '53. That'll soon be two years."

"I know, I know. But these things take time to arrange."

"As far as I can make out, Maynard and Lambert dreamed up the ambassadorship practically overnight."

"I know, I know," Labrador said again. "But this is Lima, Peru, not Washington, D.C. And it took a *resolución suprema* to effectuate this appointment."

"*What* appointment?"

"Yours. As Director of a Special Survey of Cartography. You'll be working with the *Servicio Geografico del Ejercito* and there'll be at least one civilian government representative on the survey with you, probably a surveyor."

"Hold on a minute. I haven't accepted the appointment yet. I've got myself a helicopter, I've put an American pilot-mechanic on my staff, I'm on my way to Moonstone Lake, via Quince Mil, hell bent, if you'll excuse the expression, to find another lake. I haven't time or inclination to undertake anything else. I think maybe you'd better tell your President that I appreciate the honor he's doing me and all that, but—"

The rector held up his hand. "My dear Nicolas, I must be the one to say 'just a minute.' Of course, we know all about the helicopter, the American pilot-mechanic, Moonstone Lake and so on. But can't you see how wonderfully this new appointment dovetails in with what you're doing already, what you want to do in the future? Henceforth, your exploratory ventures will all be made with official approval and official co-operation. The Peruvian government and your own government will both be backing you to the limit. If you need more money, you can have it. If you need more time, you can have it. If you need more help, in the way of personnel, you can have that, too. Far from interfering with your activities at Moonstone Lake, everything will be done to facilitate and expedite your final discovery. If that happens to be made quickly, you can rest on your laurels for a time while you accept universal plaudits, sign contracts for more books and set other people to drawing maps. On the other hand, if weather conditions or anything else delay the discovery, you can establish your headquarters wherever you choose in Peru, under favorable conditions and, so to speak, make maps yourself while awaiting developments."

As the rector went on talking, Nicolas began to see, at first vaguely and then more and more clearly, the advantages of the suggested office. Even the title—Director of the Special Cartographical and Geodetic Commission—had a ringing sound. It was salve for his wounded feelings, a challenge to his efficiency and enterprise, a spur to his soaring spirit. Within twenty-four hours, cables would be carrying an announcement of this appointment, and everyone he knew in Washington, from the President down, would be reading it and talking about it. He looked across at Labrador, and the expression on his face bespoke his grateful acceptance of the offer, even before he put this into words.

"What time is the President expecting to see me?" he asked.

"He knows you're in a hurry to be off. But it happens that tomorrow morning a new ambassador is presenting his credentials, with the usual elaborate ceremony—cavalry escort of sixty from the Bolívar to the Palace, trumpeters, horse-drawn carriages for the envoy and his entourage—well, you know the ritual. So you'll have to wait until after that is over, namely until about eleven. Then you'll make your entrance to the *Palacio de Gobierno* with less fanfare from the *Calle de Palacio*, passing through the *Puerto de Honor*."

"Whose honor?"

"I must have known once, but I seem to have forgotten. It doesn't matter. You will, of course, be formally attired, and that you always enjoy. You will walk up some stairs, and then you will go down a hall until you find a rather nondescript porter, sitting in front of an unimpressive door."

"It doesn't sound much like the White House."

"It isn't in the least like the White House, either in physical resemblance or in the results you may expect from your interview. In the former case, those were obviously anything but satisfactory; in this case, they will be noticeably so. . . . Around this nondescript porter, you will see a bevy of persons all seeking interviews, most of them vainly. But the porter has a list and your name will be on it. You will therefore be shown into the *Sala de Edecanes*."

"What language is that? *Edecanes*, I mean?"

"Spaniards often accuse Latin Americans of corrupting their language—in most cases, unjustly. In this case, the charge would be justified. *Edecanes* is a corruption of the words *Aides de Camp*. In their *sala*, you will find assorted military personnel, plus typists. You may have a short wait there, but eventually you will be shown into the President's office by the *Aide-de-Camp de Servicio*. This is a large, rather gloomy room with heavy draperies and a huge crystal chandelier which is the brightest thing in it. You will find the President seated at a carved desk under a portrait of Pizarro. He will greet you with great formalism and you will answer in the same vein. But in fifteen minutes everything will be over. The *resolución suprema* has already taken effect. You will leave the august presence with a new title and a new position."

"And can I start for Quince Mil as soon as I have left it?"

"That would be most inadvisable. You should remain at least long enough to meet the officers with whom you'll be associated in the Military Geographic Service—you must make an appointment and call at their headquarters. You must also arrange a meeting with the civilian government representative who's going to work with you. And what about the preliminaries for organizing your office?"

"And meanwhile, the C-84 is out there in the field, already loaded, and costing me so much a minute! Besides, every day that I lose of good weather lessens my chance of discovery this year! If I'd only known about this job sooner—"

"My dear Nicolas, you are the factual embodiment of the mythical man who wanted to eat his cake and have it, too! You have already waited seven months to receive the money for your helicopter and you have devoted another month or more to its purchase and its shipment, meanwhile spending a small fortune. Surely you can wait a few more days and spend a few more hundreds in order to perfect a plan which should crown your career! If necessary, the helicopter can be unloaded and stored and you can get another C-84 when you need it. Probably that would be the best plan. You can then meet your new associates and organize your new office with less sense of haste and your Limenian friends can see something of you before you are lost to them again. *Doña* Ana is anxiously awaiting you at this moment. I hope you won't find it too chilly for an al fresco luncheon on the roof. You will see that my daughter-in-law's wishes have prevailed and my wife and I are ready to admit that a great improvement has been made in our establishment."

Admittedly, the rector was right: Nicolas did want to have his cake and eat it, too. He always had, he probably always would. In like measure, he probably would never learn to take complete satisfaction in any given situation or combination of situations. His formal audience with the President, and the equally formal "coctel," in another wing of the Presidential Palace, at which he was singled out for special attention, were of course gratifying occasions. So were the press notices in both the Peruvian and the American papers and the congratulations with which he was showered, both by everyone he saw and by practically everyone else he knew, but whose absence from the triumphant scene made it necessary to send these by letter or cable. But he would have found this all the more rewarding if he had not been champing at the bit to be on his way to Quince Mil. He made his courtesy call at the headquarters of the Military Geographic Service and met the principals with whom he was to be associated, who were quite ready to lend him office space until he could secure exactly what he wanted and who also wished to give a cocktail party in his honor. With difficulty, he finally convinced them that, since his appointment had come as a complete surprise, he must attend to a few personal matters before he could settle down to work with them and he would deem it a favor if they would delay the party until his return to Lima—at a date which he was careful not to specify too exactly. Dr. Rafael Villarán, the civilian representative of the government assigned to assist him in the survey, was also volubly and cordially at his service. Never, it seemed to Nicolas, had he known Latins so eager for organization and industry. It was, he told himself, entirely out of character and, personally, he would have been more pleased to have them typically procrastinating.

It was, of course, inevitable that the Labradors and the Parras should both give dinners for him and that these should last until very late at night. He had no time for correspondence during the day, and there were at least two long letters which he must write before he left Lima, neither one of which could be composed hastily. The first of these, naturally, must go to Margaret. The new baby had not come early, so he had arrived at Hills' End in plenty of time to accompany his wife to the hospital. Then, without enough delay to cause anxiety, he had received the expected but unwelcome news that she had given birth to another daughter, whom she wanted to name Audrey, partly after some rather remote ancestress and partly because she liked the sound of it. Audrey was smaller when she was born than Cynthia, since Margaret had not "eaten for two" this time, and her confinement was easier; but it was almost immediately obvious that supplementary bottles would be necessary to augment the maternal supply of nourishment. As far as Nicolas was concerned, this was all to the good: Audrey, who was much more docile than Cynthia in any case—and, incidentally, much less plump and sturdy—would take bottles as a matter of course, from the beginning, and there would be no painful scenes later on. But Margaret was disappointed; she had looked forward to nursing Audrey all summer at least and, again, she was very slow about regaining her strength. She seemed averse even to making the slight effort of getting out on the balcony, though it was so much cooler there than in her bedroom. Nicolas had the impression that she consented to the move, once a day, largely because she did not want him to think she did not appreciate his readiness to carry her back and forth; but he also believed her lassitude was such that she would not be sorry when she did not have to consider his feelings. She had not once intimated that she wished he could delay his departure and though, if she had, he would of course have told her this was impossible, he could not help feeling slightly aggrieved because she had not. It seemed all too evident that she was resigned, to say the least, to his departure. And there had been another significant omission: she had not drawn his head down on her breast, almost as soon as she had recovered from the anesthetic, and whispered, between her tears, that she knew he was disappointed, but the next time. . . . She did not ask to see him until Audrey was nearly a day old and then, bringing up no other subjects, she had talked quite calmly and impersonally about arrangements for going back to Hills' End.

These had worked out smoothly, though the trip by ambulance had proved very tiring. And he had left her in good hands. His mother was at Hills' End again and the practical nurse they had found this time was a great improvement on the ones they had had before. There had been no problems to solve, no ruffled feelings to soothe, as far as she was concerned. She was brisk, competent and kindly. Margaret liked her and so did everyone else in the household; it seemed possible that she might remain for quite a while, that real devotion would develop between her and her patient.

So, all in all, there was no question now of the sort of letter he had written Margaret when he left before; but, just the same, one must be written before he went far beyond the easy reach of postal communication; and, in some ways, it would be harder to write than the others, not because it would be so weighted with insatiable longing, but for the very reason that it would not, and that the lack of it would not disturb her. How did you write to a woman, who was your wife and whom you loved and respected, but who could get along very well without you and without whom you yourself could get along very well? It would be almost like writing to some pleasant friend with whom your connection had once been rather close, but from whom you had become divided without anguish by time and distance. And not quite like that, either, for you had no special obligations to such a friend and he had many to Margaret. He must express his sense of this as best he could.

"Dearest"—he began and hesitated. But no, that was still the way to begin. There was no one dearer or nearer. The trouble was that even the dearest one in the world was not dear or near enough.

"I have not telephoned you because I have been afraid the message would go through at just the wrong time, when you were sleeping or trying to sleep and I know how much you need your rest. But you have learned from my cable that I had a good flight and I was glad to learn from your first one that everything was going smoothly and well at Hills' End. I also appreciated the second one, congratulating me on my unexpected appointment as Director of a Special Survey of Cartography—if it hadn't come as a complete surprise, of course, I'd have told you about it before I left Hills' End. At the moment, I'm almost overwhelmed by the stir it has created, not only among my personal friends, but in the press and in official, scientific and social circles generally. I haven't begun to acknowledge all the flattering messages that have poured in, because I've been kept so busy making and receiving courtesy calls and going to parties—even the American Embassy threw one! The President's 'coctel' was really something. Sentries stationed all along the *Desamparados* side of the palace, facing the Rimac, were apparently very suspicious that someone might crash the party. After driving through the grilled entrance, we couldn't move more than a few feet without being required to stop and identify ourselves! Liveried footmen were stationed at regular intervals all the way up a very long, very broad marble staircase. At the top of this was a hall two stories high, leading into a French style drawing room—the type Peruvians especially admire—and on into an immense reception room, where white-gloved, tail-coated servants were passing the inevitable pisco sours and literally thousands of *bocaditos* (hors d'oeuvres) to a very distinguished group of guests, all assembled and accounted for before the President put in an appearance, just as they are at the White House. At first, it was all pretty stiff and solemn, but after a while we had a chance to escape into the patio, which is located between the dining room and the salons. It has the usual central fountain, surrounded by potted plants, attractive though unimaginative, but its tiling is quite noteworthy. I found this a very pleasant place to linger for, of course, I can't deny that all the remarks I kept hearing about a well-deserved honor were music to my ears. But I know I'm not as sensible about the honor as I ought to be, for I'm impatient to be off for Moonstone Lake—and whatever lies beyond. But I do realize it *is* an honor and that the work in connection with it will keep me occupied and interested during the months when weather conditions make active advances in exploration impossible or nearly so.

"Still another phase of the situation, however, is that, in order to do a really good job, I'll have to stay pretty constantly in Peru. For instance, there was no reason last summer why I couldn't stay at Hills' End: my injuries made it impossible for me to take a long overland trek; I had to leave that to my staff. But they wouldn't have made it impossible for me to superintend the scientific making of maps. Again, since camp was already established and the bad weather had already set in when poor Pete committed suicide, there was no reason why I shouldn't stay at Hills' End while I waited around to get the money from my legacy. If the legacy had come a year later, I'd have flown back to see my lawyer—and of course to see you—but I'd have been honor bound to spend most of the waiting period on my job here.

"Probably you've realized every bit of this already, but, for the record, I wanted to say it myself. It isn't an easy thing to do, because it's equivalent to saying we'll be separated even a great deal more than I foresaw when I asked you to marry me. On the other hand, it's easier than it would have been if I hadn't gathered that you don't mind being separated from me as much as you did at first or as much as you thought you always would. Please believe this isn't said by way of reproach. I can't pretend it doesn't hurt my pride a little to feel you can get along so well without me; but it wrung my heart when I thought you couldn't. And I'd rather have my pride hurt than my heart.

"Personally, I don't mind the geographical separation of land and ocean as much as I do what, for lack of a better word, I'll call the spiritual separation. I thought about this a good deal before I left Hills' End and I've been thinking more and more about it since. It doesn't seem to me as if we understood each other as well as we did when we were first married and with that lessening of understanding has necessarily come a lessening of harmony. I won't say lessening of love for I don't need—I hope—to tell you that I love you dearly and that I have confidence in your love for me. But if you can think of anything that would bring us closer together again, in the ways that count the most, I wish you would tell me. Because I want very much to keep close to you, darling."

He read the letter through and hesitated. Should he confess his jealousy of the superiority which he recognized? Should he apologize again for anything and everything that had offended her in his attitude toward her, not only as far as their most intimate relations are concerned, but in other ways as well? Should he send some playfully fond messages to the babies? It might help if he did any or all of these things. But perhaps they could wait until he saw how Margaret answered this letter, until he wrote her in reply. It was already long past midnight and he was resolved to write another letter, on quite another subject, before he went to bed, and he was getting off for Quince Mil early in the morning. He signed this one, "Best love to you and the little girls," sealed it and drew another piece of paper toward him.

"Dear Mr. Watkins:

"I am pleased to report that the pilot, the helicopter and I have all arrived safely in Peru and I have kept well within the $50,000. In fact, I figure I still have enough to handle operating expenses for the immediate future, though Harry Davis, my pilot-mechanic, gets a thousand a month, and that's a bargain, possible only because he was interested in the job. Usually, a pilot alone gets a thousand.

"Now, if you are in a position to tell me the total amount of the estate, I should be interested in hearing it, especially since I feel, as things have turned out, that Pete would not have wanted me to be his sole beneficiary after all. I have learned, since I last wrote you, that he left a posthumous son. There is absolutely no doubt that the child is his—in fact, he signed a paper agreeing to accept paternity if a child should be born to a girl named Perpetua Quispe within ten months of his relations with her. He died without knowing that there had been such a child, but the baby's mother has now brought him to my camp at Lake Moonstone. According to the reports I have received, he has bright red hair and bears a most extraordinary resemblance to Pete in other ways as well. He has been informally adopted by the members of my staff and duly baptized with his father's name. Perhaps later on he may be legally adopted by someone, but meanwhile, in any case, proper provision must be made for him, so I hope you will see your way clear to establishing a trust fund which will take care of his maintenance and education. I am aware that, in some states, an illegitimate child cannot inherit from his father. I do not know whether or not Vermont is one of these. It doesn't matter. Morally I think he should and I know Pete would have felt the same way in this case. I think I have a right to use whatever I need from Pete's legacy to facilitate discovery. But I don't think I have a right to use it for the upkeep at Hills' End or to provide for my own children until Pete's is taken care of.

"I shall appreciate a reply sent in care of Ildefonso Parra, Apartado 1976, Lima, Peru.

"Very sincerely yours,
"Nicolas Hale."

40 ❦

Fonso had jestingly referred to the helicopter as Nick's new toy and, actually, the delight the latter took in it was not unlike a child's excitement over a novel plaything. While taking his factory check-out at Palo Alto, he had given the mechanism such serious attention that his preoccupation with this had absorbed him completely. But now that he had mastered its main points and Harry Davis was in control and prepared to deal with every detail, Nicolas could give his enjoyment free rein. With difficulty, he restrained his impatience while the helicopter was being uncrated and assembled at Quince Mil and, during the two days consumed by this process, he hardly left the grassy airstrip where it had been landed. Warren Holtz had accompanied Nicolas and Harry on their flight from Lima and, together with the pilot of the C-84, had supervised Lester and Clo, who had flown down from Camp Moonstone to welcome their errant leader, and various local mechanics in their labor, until this was well under way. As soon as Holtz pronounced the job completed, Nicolas climbed into the cabin, settled himself comfortably and, gazing around him in every direction, called out to everyone within earshot that the degree of visibility provided was almost unbelievable. Then he insisted that he and Harry must go up in it at once, to see if it really worked, even though they were coming right down again, since it was too late to continue their trip and go on from Quince Mil to Lake Moonstone that day. (And this really wouldn't be lost time, as it would give them a chance to have PETER HART painted on its side and let the paint dry overnight.) So Harry took the controls with the air of humoring youthful enthusiasm and the helicopter performed the completely normal feat of rising a short distance from the ground, to the accompaniment of loud noise, and then shooting straight up in the air. As abruptly as he had started it, Harry halted it and turned to Nicolas, his amusement at the latter's exuberance unconcealed, and asked which direction they should take— the boss had only to choose—north, south, east or west; in the twinkling of an eye, the helicopter would be going that way.

"I don't care which way we go. The thing that really gets me is no matter what, you can stop, just like that, and stay suspended as long as you want to. I suppose we might circle over Quince Mil, now that we're just above it—that won't take long. Then we'll go down and let the boys have a ride. It was selfish of me to fly off like this, just for the hell of it. But I couldn't seem to help it."

The helicopter came down, more slowly than it had mounted, blowing dust around as it hit the ground. Nicolas sprang out with the same rapidity that he had climbed in and flung one arm around Lester and the other around Clo, who were fortunately standing close enough together to facilitate this dual embrace.

"Do you know, the first time I ever talked to Margaret about exploring, I told her the way to do it in the kind of territory I was trying to cover was by magic carpet. And she asked me to please be serious! I went on teasing her, telling her that I had to deal with a geography of negatives, rivers that weren't navigable, slopes that couldn't be climbed, trails too narrow for jeeps and even for horses and burros—if there *were* any trails! It's no wonder she was puzzled as to how I ever got anywhere. And I don't need to tell either of you that it *has* been a problem. But it won't be any more. We've got a magic carpet at last. Go, take your turn on it. There's room for both of you, besides Harry. . . . And what about you," he added, turning to Jorge Ibarra, the local manager of the Faucett Airline, who had come to meet the C-84 when it landed on the grassy run that served as an airfield and had spent considerable time with them ever since. "Wouldn't you like a ride, too?"

"Thanks, Dr. Hale, but choppers are an old story to me. Glad to see you're so pleased with yours, though. What about coming to the house for supper again?"

Nicolas accepted with thanks, but not without some misgivings lest he be taking advantage of the agent's hospitality, which had been almost continuous since the arrival of the C-84. As soon as this had discharged its passengers and its cargo, Ibarra had said, "Anything my wife and I can do to make you feel at home? There's nothing I need to stay here for much longer. Our DC-3 that makes the run between Cuzco and Maldonado in good weather left here before you got in, and it'll be back here on its return flight to Cuzco any minute. Quince Mil isn't much of a place, as you must have gathered, just seeing it from the air, and we haven't much of a house, but if you and your friends would care to have me show you around and take supper with my wife and myself. . . ."

Nicolas had expressed his appreciation of both offers, at the same time asking for permission to delay giving an immediate answer to the latter. First he must get to the Mission; he and the Dominicans had been great buddies ever since he had spent several months with them at Quillabamba and he believed the Brothers were planning to put up him and his party. He supposed the Mission kept early closing hours; but if they wouldn't create a disturbance, getting in late, they'd be delighted to come for supper. Could he let Ibarra know a little later? It shouldn't take long to walk to the Mission and find out its schedule.

Ibarra had shrugged. "It doesn't take long to walk anywhere in Quince Mil. It was quite a place once. I suppose you know it got its name from the fact that a reported discovery of gold brought fifteen thousand prospectors here."

"No, I didn't. . . . I assume the report was unfounded?"

"Evidently. Though there's still a lot of undiscovered gold in Peru."

Nicolas was not sure whether the agent's retort was prompted by rumors of the chopper's mission, or whether it was merely a chance observation. As a matter of fact, it would not be strange if the former were the case; it could no longer logically be regarded as something they must try to keep a secret. He was half inclined to do a little probing and find out just how far rumor had gone when the incoming Faucett plane required Ibarra's attention. The Piper had been moored on the Marcapata River, at a point not far distant from the grassy airstrip and, having arranged for its supervision, Lester and Clo, as well as Nick and Harry, accepted Ibarra's guidance into town, leaving Holtz and his helpers in charge of the helicopter. The location of Quince Mil, among the lowest foothills at the base of the Andes and close to the jungle area, was scenically pleasant; but the only attractive sights that met their eyes as they strolled along the unpaved and malodorous street were the regional costumes of a few altiplano Indians and the brilliant tropical fruits which did something to redeem a small, unclean market place, where withered, discolored potatoes, carrots and cabbages were otherwise the chief stock in trade. Most of the unpainted houses which they first passed on a street not over a block long were built on stilts, a few with roofs of corrugated zinc, but many of them thatched. The next street to which they came—and, as it proved, the only other one in Quince Mil—ran perpendicular to the first and was, so Ibarra informed them with a rather wry smile, "The main business thoroughfare." This was lined with dejected blue and pink buildings, one of which was a general store handling gasoline and similar commodities, and another, Ibarra's office, with living quarters behind. His invitation to come in for a drink before continuing on to the Mission was gratefully accepted; and presently they were joined by a rather stocky young woman with a mop of sandy hair, a pleasant freckled face and a cheery smile which revealed beautiful teeth. Her cotton dress, evidently once a bright blue, was rather faded, but it was a good fit and it was freshly laundered. She was carrying a tray set with well-filled glasses and a plate of cookies and Ibarra presented his guests to her in a voice ringing with love and pride.

"This is my wife, Doris," he said. "I didn't know how she'd take it, when I found out this was where I was going to be sent, just after we were married. But she said she knew she'd like it and, if she's changed her mind, she's never said so. She's giving you the traditional *chicha* to drink, because that seems to belong, in Peru, unless you're having pisco sours. But the cookies are made from her own recipe. She's a wonderful cook, as you'll see if you'll give us the pleasure of your company for supper. Maybe you'd like more to eat right now, Dr. Hale. I don't think you had much of a lunch—those were pretty sad looking sandwiches you brought along from Lima. And you were too much interested in seeing the chopper uncrated to eat them anyway."

They wouldn't spoil that wonderful supper by eating anything more now, they all decided, but they would get along to the Mission as soon as they had done justice to the *chicha* and the cookies, to make sure it would be all right for them to return later on. One of the Brothers, Fray Ambrosio, proved to be an old friend of both Nicolas and Lester: he had been at Chirumbia when they went through on their way to Quillabamba; and though Nicolas' desperate illness at the time had rendered his recollection of the encounter rather vague, it was vivid with the others and they vied with each other in trying to refresh his memory. Of course, it would be entirely convenient, as far as the Mission was concerned, for their guests to come in at any time, he assured them, as did his companion, Fray Cristofo; they must not miss such a treat as *Señora* Ibarra would give them with her fine supper. But they must first take time to see where they would sleep—nothing very luxurious, but then they hadn't expected that!—and to pay a visit to the chapel, of which the Brothers felt they had a right to be proud. And could their guests really stay for two days? Well, they were doubtless impatient to be off, but their loss was the Mission's gain. When they left, the Brothers would come to bless the helicopter and wish its passengers Godspeed.

The supper that night proved more than worthy of its advance notice and the evening a pleasant one. It might seem advisable, Nicolas told Ibarra, for him to open an office in Quince Mil himself. He was not sure yet how many he would need, in connection with his Cartographical Survey, besides the main one in Lima and, of course, one in Cuzco; but he thought it highly probable that he would want one still nearer Camp Moonstone. He intended to put special emphasis on more detailed and accurate maps for this part of Peru. Did Ibarra realize how large a section of the operational navigation chart, published by the Aeronautical Chart and Information Center of the United States Air Force, was still labeled RELIEF DATA INCOMPLETE? Well, one of his chief concerns was to reduce the size of that section. And there was nothing like being near your objective when you were working. Ibarra heartily agreed. He would certainly be glad to see another office opened in Quince Mil, one that was not concerned with Brazil nuts, rubber or lumber. In the event of such an opening, he hoped that Dr. Hale would not leave all the work to his associates, but would spend much time there himself. And what about Mrs. Hale, Doris wanted to know? Wouldn't she be coming, too?

"I'm afraid not. She has a brand-new baby and another not quite a year old, so it wouldn't be practical."

"Oh—but we have brand-new babies in Quince Mil, lots of them. I'm hoping to have one myself before long."

She spoke quite without self-consciousness and it was obvious she felt no more anxiety about the conditions which might surround her confinement than she felt discontent about those under which she was living. Nicolas looked around the bare little room and failed to visualize Margaret in such quarters. The group was seated on collapsible chairs at a portable zinc table which had been unfolded to make it large enough—in a pinch—to accommodate six. There was not enough matching china and glass to go around and the battered cutlery had lost whatever luster it might once have possessed. A sofa of sorts and a matching armchair preempted one side of the room. There was nothing more in it and no space for anything more. Beyond were a bed alcove and a primitive kitchen. The house contained no plumbing—indeed, from the walk they had taken, Nicolas concluded that the town contained none. Life there was not only without beauty, it was without elemental comforts. What was the background, he wondered, of a girl who accepted it happily? He was glad when a chance remark of Lester's led to information about this.

"Jorge and I met when I was at Simmons and he was an exchange student at Tufts. I'd hardly ever been out of Boston until I came to Peru. My, that was a thrill! I haven't got over it yet. I don't ever expect to."

The next night Jorge and Doris had again been the travelers' hospitable hosts and, far from seeming weary in well-doing, they were emphatic in their expressions of regret when the time was fixed for departure. The whole town, or so it seemed to Nicolas, came to see him and his staff set off: the Dominican Brothers, the Ibarras, the manager of the general store and his numerous family, the mestizos employed in the rubber and lumber industries, the stray Indians from the altiplano. The Piper took off first, circling until the chopper could shoot up to follow it. Then they were away, over those regions "where the data was incomplete," headed for Lake Moonstone.

To Nicolas, it was a flight of sheer enchantment. The very next day— or, at the very latest—the day after that, he and Harry and Lester would be in their pontoon-equipped helicopter on their way to that crescent-shaped lagoon with the long-sought prize hidden in its depths. And, as soon as they had located it, with careful relation to the camp this time, they would land there and then they would get out their underwater equipment and he would begin his diving, his photography, his search for treasure. There was no reason why Lester and Harry and, for that matter, Clo and Walter and even Gomara, should not be taught to dive, too. Now that Cousteau had revolutionized underwater swimming with his aqualung, what had once been a daredevil risk was now a joyous adventure. Why, there were actually resorts in the south of France already where opportunities for skin diving were regarded almost in the light of a routine tourist attraction! The next thing Nicolas knew, the crescent-shaped lagoon would be receiving travelers who had made the trip by helicopter from Quince Mil, where they had been comfortably quartered in a pleasant inn; they would descend to the sunken palace and tour it with the same freedom and ease that visitors had for years been touring the Grand and Petit Trianon! And though he shrank a little from connecting this grand and magical palace with commercialism, it was something, after all, to know that his financial worries would soon be at an end—and forever. . . .

Again he saw the flag of the Explorers Club flying over his camp and then the chopper came straight down with its slow, steady movement and, as the dust that it stirred blew away, he saw Gomara and Walter and Li Chan waiting near by—Gomara and Walter and Li Chan in a group of Machiguengas in their striped *cushmas*. One of the Indians touched the shoulder of a young woman standing beside an older one and turned her around, so that, instead of facing Nicolas as he got out of the chopper, she had her back to him. And from the shawl fastened there he could see the head and shoulders of a baby: a baby with a round, unfrightened face and large questioning eyes and a shock of bright red hair.

Serious searching did not begin the next day. There was too much to do, unpacking food and clothing, medical supplies and other gear, setting up an extra tent for Harry, distributing presents, reviewing the major happenings during the period of separation, mapping out a definite plan for immediate action for the future. Nicolas had hoped there might be more progress to report, both on an overland trail to the lagoon and on promising glimpses from the air; but the Cogapacoris who had never reappeared at camp and the Machiguengas who had recently joined the staff there were not the ones who had claimed to be acquainted with the region. Besides, the good weather had been very late in starting: advancement on foot had been difficult, when it was not actually impossible, and flying had been dangerous. But now the weather was fine again, the leader was back and there was that beautiful new bird to take them wherever they wanted to go.

The general attitude of the Machiguengas was so contented and friendly that Nicolas felt this more than compensated for their failure to be helpful about the trail; and, despite their inclination to devote a good deal of time to slumber, they had been helpful in other ways. Without any definite orders from Gomara, indeed, quite on their own initiative, they had gone about the slow and difficult task of chopping, hewing and burning select tree trunks for the construction of several dugouts. They had kept the camp so well supplied with fish, which they pursued with bows and arrows instead of hooks, lines and sinkers, that neither Gomara nor Li Chan needed to angle, except for the pleasure this gave them; and they had continued and expanded the planting of *yuca* and corn which their predecessors had begun and abandoned. Again they had proven their undependability, not by their desertion this time, but by their sustained attachment. And, quite as unpredictably, Pete's seduction of Perpetua, though this had led to the mutilation which impelled him to suicide, had also led to the creation of a bond between his people and hers.

The baby was now six months old, large for his age, as his father doubtless had been, and bubbling over with infantile merriment. Most of the time his lips were parted in an engaging grin and a satisfied chuckle frequently escaped them. As soon as he caught sight of someone he liked—and he liked everyone, just as everyone liked him—he waved his arms in excited welcome, somehow disengaging them from his mother's confining shawl. The men had begun to lay bets as to how soon he would creep and then toddle along beside them. Not without difficulty, they had persuaded his mother that he must be frequently washed; he was a child of the river, they pointed out; his father would have insisted on having him kept clean as a water spirit and, since his mother was his guardian spirit, she must be clean, too. The argument had force; she bathed in the lagoon, holding fast to her baby. The men remained apart, respecting her privacy as they at all times respected her person; but the distance between the white men's tents and the Indians' shelters had never been so short, either figuratively or literally. Lacking a house, the camp had nevertheless become a household, a partnership, an entirety.

Nicolas was swift to sense this. He had brought all the usual types of presents for the Machiguengas—beads, mirrors, lipsticks, knives, bolts of bright cloth—but he had added toys for Petie, earrings for the women and—mindful of how disastrous the lack of an extra one had once been—belts for the men. All these were presented with due regard for tribal etiquette and were gratefully received. Still more felicitous was his suggestion that the Machiguenga men should each have a ride in the new bird and that, after this, Perpetua and her mother, and any of the other women who were not afraid, should ride, too, turn and turn about. Perpetua's presence in the copter automatically meant Petie's, too, and, when they had their ride, Nicolas was the extra passenger.

The next day, Nicolas, Lester and Harry left early to begin "the serious search." He was determined not to be disappointed, Nicolas told his staff before he started, if they did not reach their objective with enough time to spare so that they could be sure of getting back to camp before dark. After all, they had no notes on the lagoon's location, nothing to guide them, except instinct and hope. It was nearly a year since Nicolas had made the abortive flight with Toledo; his memory, even if it seemed clear, might well be playing him tricks. But the miracle happened: they had been in the air for less than an hour when he shouted, "Go slow, Harry! I think we're almost there!" And the words were hardly out of his mouth when a crescent-shaped lagoon came into sight, clear as crystal, sparkling in the sun, set in a deep cleft of jungle walls.

"That's it, that's it!" he called out, almost strangling with excitement. "Get down there, Harry, get down there!"

"Take it easy. That's what I am doing."

The helicopter descended, as easily and surely as if it were making a routine landing, and came to rest in the shallow water beside the shore. Nicolas was already tearing off his clothes, reaching for his aqualung, his wet suit and his flippers; and the engine was still vibrating when he wrenched the door of the cabin open and slid into the water. There was not a ripple on its surface and it was so clear that Lester and Harry could see him as he glided, with effortless grace, farther and farther into the distance. The sunken structure toward which he was headed, following the causeway which led to it, veiled as it was with algae, was revealed, even to their inexperienced eyes, as an unmistakable relic of Inca grandeur.

They looked at each other without speaking, because the intensity of their feeling made it impossible for them to put this into words. What Nicolas' feelings must have been, as he parted the algae obscuring the palace windows and disappeared within it, they could not even imagine.

Their breathless wonder still held them speechless when they saw him coming back, swimming more rapidly this time. "Thank God I brought my camera along!" he exclaimed, clambering up the side of the cabin. "Quick, hand it to me. I'm going back!" And, as Lester seized the pressurized Rolleiflex and thrust it through the door, Nicolas grasped it and was gone again, waiting only to call back, "Don't worry if I'm away a long while. You'll be able to see the streams of bubbles coming from the back of the regulator even when you can't see me.

This time, there isn't going to be any doubt whether I found what I was looking for or what it was."

The jewel-colored bubbles were both very beautiful and very reassuring. Lester and Harry had occasional glimpses of Nicolas, for he was taking pictures outside the palace, as well as inside. When he finally returned, he was clutching not only his camera, but a stone hatchet; and though he stretched out an arm to hand the camera to Lester, before hoisting himself up, he clung to the hatchet. And he was hardly in the cabin when he began to speak so hurriedly and vehemently that the words tumbled over each other and it was almost impossible to follow them.

"I've got it, I've got my stone hatchet, the proof I needed that we're on the right track! Not that I needed any more proof myself, but some old fossil may. And I can bring up half a dozen of these and any number of other things, much more important, much more beautiful. But I shan't tell you all about it now! Get going, Harry, get going! We have to get this on the radio to Ibarra, to Astur and on to Fonso. The news must be on every hook-up tonight and in every newspaper tomorrow morning. 'Nicolas Hale discovers Inca palace and causeway submerged in Andean lagoon on Pantiacolla ridge.' I've done it! I've done it! I always said I would and I have! Now I'm ready to tell the world."

An hour later, everyone at the camp was examining the hatchet, listening to his story, sharing in the triumph and showing, each in his own way, that he was rejoicing with his leader. Gomara's exultation took the form of fervent prayers of thanksgiving: Clo and Walter danced the Cuzco equivalent to a pas de deux; Li Chan prepared a feast; the Machiguengas marched around the lake playing their flutes and conches. Nicolas was deeply touched by these varied expressions of congratulation, but his emotion did not prevent him from remaining at the radio until all the connections he wished to make had been successfully effected. Ibarra and Astur took the news as differently as Gomara and the Machiguengas. Ibarra was sure at first that Nicolas was jesting; it took moments of precious time to convince him that this was no practical joke. Astur, on the other hand, had always believed that nothing would keep Nicolas much longer from his objective and, recently, Fátima had had an intuition which made her sure that the discovery was not far off. Perhaps she had slept under a *lupuna* tree after all, though her intuition was not actually a dream. Did Nicolas remember how he teased her about the *lupuna* tree and how she had not understood then? But she did now.

The following morning reports on the initial radioed messages began to come in. Astur had heard from Fonso: all the regular networks had carried the great news; it had made the first page of *La Prensa* and a wire from Washington assured him that it would be in the *Star* and the

News that night and in the *Post* the next morning; a similar wire had arrived from New York and of course wires of congratulation had already begun to pour in, sent in his care and the Labradors'. One was from Nick's publishers: how quickly could they count on getting the next book? Another was from a lecture bureau. Would Dr. Hale consider a nation-wide series of addresses the following winter? He could set his own price. He was to answer these queries as soon as possible.

Yes, of course, but first of all they must get back to the lagoon and that must have a name of its own now, too. Emerald or Sapphire would do for the time being; but it was not enough, as in the case of Moonstone, to call it after a precious jewel, because its waters were gemlike in color; the name must also suggest the sunken palace and the triumph of discovery. Well, Nicolas would be thinking that over while he considered how much time he could spare from the work to which he was committed with the Peruvian government, besides that which he meant to devote to his private interests at the lagoon. Surveying and sounding must begin at once—he would see if he could not get Rafael Villarán, the civilian representative of the government, assigned to help him as Director of the Special Cartographical and Geodetic Commission, up to the camp and, perhaps, a second assistant. Meanwhile, he and his own staff would begin this work, in which they all had some experience. And, of course, as he had already planned, Lester and the others must be taught the principles of skin diving. Was it beyond the realm of possibility that some of the more intelligent Machiguengas could be taught, too? He did not know. It was worth a trial.

But soundings and surveying and lessons in skin diving would all have to wait a few days at least, as far as he was concerned. What he wanted most of all was simply to get back into the water of the lagoon, to feel its coolness and its clearness and cleave through its clarity to the palace that was no longer lost because he had found it. He wanted to dive down quickly, so that he would not lose a second in getting to it and then he wanted to swim slowly in and out of its window cavities, reveling in its size and in the erstwhile splendor which it would be his proud privilege to restore.

He took Gomara with him when he made his second trip and sent Harry back for Clo and Walter. They must all see the wonder of it, glory in this wonder, before they began their work; but they would not postpone this after today. Harry went back and forth. "Taxi service?" he said, grinning. It was late afternoon before Nicolas, who had left Camp Moonstone early in the morning, consented to return there.

In the evening, two of the dogs, which had been quietly snoozing, began to show signs of restlessness. They stretched lazily into an upright position, padded around in circles, and then lay down again, growling intermittently and not loudly. This was repeated several times. Then they jumped up, barking and tearing back and forth from one end of the camp to the other. Their respective owners, who had also been sleeping after a successful hunt, roused themselves and did their best to quiet the dogs, with only indifferent results; the growls continued in a subdued way and so did the uneasy movements.

During the afternoon, Nicolas spent an hour or so alone in his tent and by the time he sat down to supper with his staff, the dogs' restlessness had proved infectious. The Machiguengas had not retired to their shelters for the night as early as they usually did; they stood around in little groups, talking in low tones and glancing in the direction of the table where supper was being served. Two or three of them started forward, as if intending to come and speak to Nicolas or one of the staff and, after a slight hesitation, rejoined their own groups. When this had happened several times, it attracted attention.

"I have a feeling those people are troubled about something," he said, as he pushed back his plate and lighted a cigarette. "Would you have any idea what it is, Julio?"

"They're a little worried over the way the dogs are acting."

"Why should they be? Is there any significance to it?"

"Sometimes. But there's not a thing we can do about it—except pray. I have my own special prayers for such a disturbance. I shall say them."

He seemed disinclined to talk any more and Nicolas did not press him. It had been a highly gratifying day, but a rather wearing one. He took a turn around the camp, stopping to have a last look at the baby, who grinned and gurgled and waved his arms. Then Nicolas went to his tent and undressed. Within five minutes he was sound asleep.

He was wakened by a low rumbling sound, alien to the complete stillness which usually encompassed the camp at night. It grew no louder and, had it not been for its abnormality, he would have given it no more thought other than a passing one of puzzlement as to its origin. But it continued and, presently, it semed to Nicolas that there was a lack of stability in the ground beneath him; it was not actually shaking, but it seemed to tremble. Then the sensation ceased and he had almost decided he had imagined the whole thing, when he felt the movement again, so much more violent this time that it could not be laid to an illusion. The earth was jolting and jarring and the dislodged rocks which encircled the belt of good earth around the lagoon were tumbling down; above the violent noise that they made came the crashing of trees and the rushing of water. One of the loosened rocks hit Nicolas on the chest and, as he sat up, struggling to remove it, another hit him on the back. Then he was thrown clear from the tent onto the heaving lane outside and he could hear sounds of shouting, and shrieking and wailing, human sounds mingling with those of disrupted nature. Afterward, in the moment of uncanny stillness which came with the shock's abrupt ending, a baby crying. . . .

In the midst of all this horror, here was something for which Nicolas could give thanks. If Petie were crying, he was not dead, he was not even badly injured. No matter what else the earthquake had done to the camp, it had not killed the baby. Everything but that, whatever it was, he could face.

41&

He struggled to his feet, shouting as he did so, "Don't be frightened! It's all over! There's nothing to be afraid of!" He could only hope that he was managing to make himself heard above the shouts of others, the shrieking and wailing and crying. He had often been told that Latins, no less than Indians, panicked at the slightest tremor, and this was obviously more than a tremor. How much more, he did not yet know; but if he were practically unhurt so, probably, were others—the noises he heard did not sound like those of the dying, but of the terrified. If he could only reassure them, if there were no stampede, no injuries due to rash actions, not to the earthquake itself. . . .

Thankfully he realized that he would not have to deal with total darkness as well as abject terror. A waning moon shed its mild light over the wrecked tents, the flooded path beyond them, the troubled waters; and it revealed no fissures, where the gaping earth could have engulfed human beings; there were no buildings to topple over— another cause for thankfulness—and the outlines of both helicopter and hydroplane were visible—they might be damaged, but they were not lost. All this he grasped with lightning swiftness and immeasurable relief. And, in the same instant, he saw that Harry was also struggling to his feet, albeit with difficulty, and that Lester, who had apparently not been hurt at all, was already charging in the direction of the Indian quarters. That was as it should be: the Machiguengas must be pacified first of all. Nicolas would get to them, too, as rapidly as he could. But he had never been able to run fast since his stingray wound and, in any case, as he hitched along, he must pause to speak to Harry and Gomara, Walter and Clo and Li Chan. He was responsible for them, too. Harry first.

"I guess something hit us. Are you all right?"

"I guess something did. But I guess I am."

"Good!" Gomara next. But his tent had fallen on top of him and no sounds came from underneath it. Nicolas tugged hard at the sodden canvas, calling his friend by name.

"Julio! Can you hear me? I'll have you freed in a minute."

"Here, let me help." This was Clo, coming from the opposite direction. If he were hurt, it was not seriously. There was no time to ask. Between them, they must free Gomara. And, as the last of the canvas was pulled away, he tried to sit up, stifling a moan and crossing himself. Then he opened his eyes, recognized Nicolas and spoke with quiet authority. "You must leave me, *querido,* and go to our Machiguengas. They are the ones who need you. I do not."

"But we don't know yet how much you're hurt."

"I'll stay with him until we find out," Clo said quickly. "But *Don* Julio is right, you must go on to the Indians."

"What about Walter and Li Chan?"

"We'll have to hope they're only frightened. We'll get after them as soon as we can."

Walter was not dead, that was certain, for, as Nicolas hurried past his tent, he could hear hysterical sounds which might be either wild laughter or wild weeping. Nicolas pressed on, as impatient with these signs of unmanageable fear as he was to minister to greater needs. The wailing and shrieking were not so loud now and Petie had stopped crying. But the male Machiguengas had gathered around Lester and were variously shouting and muttering to the accompaniment of frantic gestures. Obviously, Lester's efforts to calm them had begun to take some effect, but not as much as he had hoped. Perpetua and her mother were standing a little apart, with Petie as usual tied in the sheltering shawl. Both women were quietly weeping. Beside them stood Li Chan, impassive of expression as one of his own idols, but muttering words of cheer and comfort. Nicolas went straight to Perpetua.

"I'm counting on you to help me with your people," he said impellingly. "If you tell them you have believed me when I say there is no more danger, they will believe you. And you must believe me. You know I would not let you do anything that would endanger your child. He is our mascot and yours. We must unite to keep him safe. Therefore, you must not take him away from here, where the danger is now past, until we see what damage has been done elsewhere, what is still threatening. Do you understand me, Perpetua?"

She raised her head and he saw that she was no longer crying. Although she did not answer in words, he could see that her eyes were trustful.

"I know that when there is disaster in one place your people rush to seek another," he went on. "This time they must not do that. When a *temblor* strikes, it often does so in several places close together. It has already struck here. Though we cannot be sure, we have reason to hope that it will not strike again here soon. The two shocks that came close together were probably all there will be at Camp Moonstone, perhaps for years, perhaps forever. But we do not know what has happened on the rest of our *montaña*. As soon as possible, I shall go with our helper who makes the new bird fly and find out. We will take one of your men with us. If we find a place he thinks is better for you and your baby and your mother and all your people, we will take you there. It is a promise. Meanwhile, I want you to stay here. Will you do it?"

Very slowly, still with her trustful eyes fixed on his face, she nodded.

"Then go with your mother and your baby and tell the men what I have said. And remember that you loved your baby's father and that I did, too."

The habit of obedience was strong within her and she trusted him. She went to the male Machiguengas and said to them what Nicolas had told her to say. None of her people listened to her without argument or objection. Some of them would not listen at all. It was not a woman's place to tell warriors what they ought to do. A few of them left before daylight, though one of them had a broken arm, and they were not seen or heard from again. A few others, with minor injuries, lingered through the day and then disappeared into the darkness to find their own medicine men. But several still remained and helped the white men to repair the damage. Gomara's back was injured; it still was not possible to tell how seriously. He was moved on a stretcher to a dry place and put under an improvised shelter. There he lay motionless and uncomplaining, his rosary between his fingers. Walter's hysteria continued; he seemed quite incapable of pulling himself together. He was led to another dry place, as far as possible from Gomara, made to lie down and given a tranquilizer; from time to time one of the others went back to check on him. Such cases had been known to go berserk; it was a relief to find that he was slowly responding to medication and quiet.

The hydroplane, which had been moored in midlake and buffeted by the full force of the waves, had been damaged but not destroyed; the helicopter, which had been nearer the shore, had been dashed against this and the engine had been clogged with mud and debris. Lester and Harry were putting all their time in repair work on these. Meanwhile, Clo helped Nicolas get the deluged tents dried and set up again and, with infinite patience, Li Chan had made do to feed them all with such foodstuffs as he had been able to salvage from the wreckage of his kitchen.

At the end of two days, Harry announced that it would be safe to take the helicopter on a short flight. It was agreed that, first of all, they must get in touch with civilization, from which they had been entirely cut off, since they were unable to use their radio. They must let their families, friends and associates know that, though marooned, they were safe, and that they would be able to carry on, even under difficulties. They must restock their sadly diminished larder; they must get Gomara to a place where his injured back could have treatment. Possibly the Dominican Brothers at Quince Mil could do all that was necessary for him; if not, he could be put on a plane for Cuzco, with one of them in charge. At all events, Quince Mil was obviously the place to go first and, since Gomara was still unable to sit up and would occupy more space lying down, no one else could go in the helicopter with him and Harry. The trip to determine the scope of the earthquake would have to await another day.

Nicolas was the first to recognize this and he had never found it harder to control his impatience; that he was able to do so was a moral victory of which, a few years earlier, he would not have been capable. To a great degree, however, he was rewarded by his staff's appreciation of his attitude and, characteristically, Gomara urged him to go first to the other lagoon, which they had decided should temporarily be called the Golden Lake, rather than by the name of any jewel. It would relieve them all, he insisted, if they could know everything was well there; and, as far as treatment for his back was concerned, one day more or less would not make any difference. But Nicolas stood firm; first things must come first. And, in this case, first things were Gomara's welfare, food supplies and communication with the outside world—in that order.

Nicolas was up and doing at daybreak, helped to lift Gomara into the helicopter, where the best makeshift bed they could manage was already installed, and did all he could to make the injured man comfortable. Then, pausing only to watch the take-off, he resumed his supervision and participation in the task of rehabilitation. No more Machiguengas had left and Perpetua and her mother both helped the men with the work. By the time Harry returned, a great deal had already been accomplished: most of the loose stones and earth had been cleared away and the tents were habitable again. The waters had receded and Clo had been able to make considerable headway in repairing the hydroplane. Walter, who was slowly recovering from his shock and was deeply ashamed, apologetically tried to help. Everyone was in greatly improved spirits and Harry was able to improve these still further: since he had no passenger for the return trip, he had been able to bring everything with him that they would need for some time to come in the way of foodstuffs and other supplies. Ibarra and Doris had been more than helpful about securing these from the general store and

Doris had turned to and baked not only her famous cookies, but several of her other specialties to send along. Ibarra would get messages both by radio and military telegraph to families and friends and was hopeful that direct communication with the camp would soon be reestablished. Gomara had stood the trip well and had been warmly received at the Mission. Brother Cristofo had considerable medical and surgical skill; in fact, he was generally believed to have "healing hands." He thought rest, hot cloths and massage, together with a certain brew of herbs, in which he had great confidence, taken internally, would do wonders for Gomara; but if there were no improvement with a week, he himself would accompany his patient to Cuzco. Last but not least, Harry's tinkering with the helicopter had apparently been all that it needed. It had gone like a breeze. He took it for granted that he and Nicolas and Lester would be off for Golden Lake at dawn.

Of course, he did not really need an answer nor did he expect one. He was already at the controls when his passengers joined him and everyone else at the camp was on hand to see them off. It was a beautiful day, one of the clearest that any of them could remember in that region; it would be perfect for underwater photography and exploration. Meanwhile, the helicopter would fairly zoom through the air. They would be at their destination in a matter of minutes.

Nicolas was the first to speak. "You couldn't have got off course, could you, Harry?" he asked, a dry throat making it almost impossible to utter the words. Harry shook his head and began the drop between the jungle walls enclosing a deep cleft.

There was no mistaking them for walls different from those they had seen a few days earlier, despite a treeless scar on the side of one. No others they had passed rose so sharply and steeply. But at their base lay no crescent-shaped lagoon of crystal clearness. Only a tangled mass of rocks and trees and mud. It was all too evident what had happened: the water-soaked soil, which had been suspended on the steep slope, had become dislodged by the earthquake and had slid down to the bottom of the defile, filling the lake.

Without a word, Harry set down his craft on the edge of this quagmire and waited, his own sense of frustration and destruction so overpowering that he could not even imagine what must be passing in the mind of Nicolas Hale. Lester made a swift involuntary movement, almost like one a woman might have made to show her sympathy toward a man she loved in his hour of supreme trial. Then he checked himself. This was a moment that Nicolas would have to meet alone.

He got out of the helicopter and looked around him, not only at the encircling walls of the cleft, but at the debris beneath him. Immediately, he sank almost to his knees in deep mud. He struggled to his feet and turned back to his companions.

"We've got a shovel with us, haven't we? All right, hand it down to me!"

He grasped the extended shovel and pushed it into the mud. It sank, nearly to the handle. Wading a short distance, he pushed the shovel down again and, once more, it met with no resistance. The greatest difficulty in penetrating the surface of this mass, at least as far as he had covered it, would obviously be in sloughing through the mire, not in driving through masses of hard rock. So far, so good. He looked around him again. Some of the uprooted trees had been carried to the opposite wall of the canyon in an almost upright position, as if they had ridden on top of the slide without overturning; several large boulders were lodged on the opposite wall. Moss still clung to the upper side of these, indicating that they, too, had not been overturned. As he looked up at the broken ledge of rock and the sky beyond, he could reconstruct in his mind what had happened: an overcropping dike of volcanic rock had been dislodged by the earthquake and the water-soaked debris had come flowing down the mountainside with trees and remnants of the dike riding on top. It was evident that the water had arrested the impact of this slide because the lake could still be outlined by a deep depression, indicating that the debris covering the lake had settled after it had come to rest. He turned back to the helicopter and, when he spoke, there was not a break in his voice.

"The 'House of the Sun of Gold' is still down there—undamaged," he said with conviction. "This kind of an overlay isn't heavy, except for the few rocks and trees on top of it and it won't take us long to clear those off. A lot of old volcanic ash has fallen, but that's comparatively light. All the rain we've had will have helped, too—the earth is watersoaked, it isn't much more solid than a swamp. Besides, the buoyancy of the water will have broken the impact of the slide and the window cavities of the palace will reduce the effect of its weight. We three start work right here and now, hauling off rocks and trees. We work as long as we can see. At daybreak tomorrow, we start bringing help from camp. Harry will taxi the helpers back and forth. Some of the Machiguenga boys are small and light. He can put two of them in the place one of us would use up. That'll get more help here quicker. As soon as the radio's working, we get through a message to Antonio to send us some of those mestizos he recommended for hire. We establish an additional camp here, equip it, provision it. We work every daylight hour until we get to the 'House of the Sun of Gold.' It may take us years, but we do it."

42 ❧

The news of the disaster at Golden Lake reached the United States while Margaret was still trying to frame an answer to the letter Nicolas had written her at the Labradors' house, just before going on to Quince Mil. If he had only included the extra passages over which he had hesitated and then decided to leave for another time—the confession of jealousy, the apology for anything and everything that had offended her, the playful messages to the babies—she would have been not only placated, but touched. She would have made light of the jealousy, welcomed the apology, enjoyed the messages; and she would have written in return, saying that, of course, she loved him; that she did not blame him for being annoyed when persons who should have known better exaggerated her qualities; and that she should not have made a mountain out of a molehill as far as Cynthia's feedings and the episode in the library were concerned, even if she had been exhausted and upset. But the absence of the fond and contrite overture, which the missing paragraphs would have represented, left her at a loss, because there was no satisfactory substitute for such an omission. She could truthfully say she understood that his new official position would require his presence in Peru and she could refrain from saying—as he had not done so—that, since this position would oblige him to establish working centers in at least two or three Peruvian cities, there would no longer be any sound reason for saying it would not be feasible for her to join him there. It would have been one thing for him to say this when he was constantly in the jungle or the sierra; it was quite another when he would be going back and forth between these remote points and civilization. Lacking any recognition of this, on his part, she did not know how to suggest they should come closer together; as she saw them, the geographic aspects of the case were closely allied with the spiritual, whether or not Nicolas admitted this.

A telephone call from Fonso brought her the bad news. It had been delayed in reaching Lima because, with the radio at Camp Moonstone still out of commission, it was not until the second trip could be made to Quince Mil that Nicolas could send a report; then not only Ibarra, but also Antonio and Fonso had been alerted. Fonso spoke reassuringly and with admiration: no one had been killed and only one person— Gomara—seriously injured; some of the Machiguengas had deserted, but more had remained; the camp was not damaged past repair; Fonso shared Nick's belief that the submerged palace could be salvaged and praised his friend's resolution to carry on; he knew it would be a long hard process, but he did not believe it was hopeless.

"Is there any way you can get a message to Nicolas from me?" Margaret asked tremulously.

"Not until his radio's repaired; and then not directly. But I can get messages to Ibarra and Antonio Astur and they'll relay these as soon as they reestablish connections. I'll keep you informed just as completely and regularly as I possibly can. Meanwhile, do try not to worry."

Despite his advice, she could not reconcile herself to this severance, to this silence. Actually, it was only a few days before Fonso telephoned again to say he had been in touch with Astur, who said he had already sent efficient mestizo workers to Nicolas and that Nicolas had been able to notify him of their arrival. The radio was repaired and the helicopter was most appropriately designated as being worth its weight in gold. The hydroplane, though of no use at Golden Lake—which they were still calling that—since there was no place for it to land, was doing helpful taxi service between Moonstone and Quince Mil. Gomara had been taken to the Cuzco hospital, but this was more of a precautionary measure than anything else. He had resigned his position at the University of Arequipa and would remain with Nicolas indefinitely, as of course Lester would, too. Clo and Walter would have to return to their postgraduate studies sooner or later, but no definite date had been set for this; Cuzco University was disposed, as an institution, to do everything it could to help Nicolas in his extremity and both Mamani and Mendoza would return to him whenever he said the word; they regretted that they had ever left him. Nicolas himself was physically fit and keeping all flags flying; the fallen trees were already cleared away and good headway had been made with the rocks.

Margaret kept in touch with Woodstock, relaying news to Nicolas' father and mother as rapidly as she received it herself and, before long, she had a letter from Waldo, written surreptitiously at the bank: wouldn't Margaret bring the babies and come to stay with the old folks for a spell? Mother was taking all this talk about earthquakes pretty hard; perhaps Margaret could help him, Waldo, convince her that the danger was over now and, anyway, the babies would take her mind off Peru. Besides, it would do Margaret good to get out of the heat of Virginia.

She readily agreed to make the suggested visit; it would be easier to stand the strain if she did not have to do so alone. She would drive, bringing Cassie with her and allowing plenty of time for the trip. She was all ready to start, when she was suddenly called to Charlottesville: her uncle Virginius had had a heart attack; she was his only relative and he was asking for her. So she went south, instead of north, and, since she was still nursing Audrey, despite her earlier fears that she might soon have to stop, this meant taking one baby at least and it was really easier to take both with Cassie than it was to arrange for a separation.

The sojourn in the old family house on the outskirts of the University grounds was inevitably a sad one. Her uncle represented her only remaining tie with the previous generation, whose standards and habits and tastes were so largely responsible for her own, and it was a tie of affection, as well as tradition. Margaret knew that Virginius Page had loved her as he would have loved the daughter he never had and, though he could not take her father's place, she knew he had tried to and she loved him in return. Moreover, her marriage had brought them closer together than they had ever been before; Virginius had been pleased and touched because she had asked him to give her away, and had made a point, in Nicolas' absence, of coming to see her often and staying with her at Hills' End, rather than at the Metropolitan Club, as formerly. She would miss him very much.

For a long time, his house had been the residence of a bachelor who had no incentive to make it cheerful and attractive. It was overcrowded with monumental furniture and curtained with heavy draperies and the shadows which obscured it seemed to deepen every day as the inevitable end approached. A certain amount of paralysis had set in after the heart attack and it was so hard for Virginius Page to talk that, though he kept trying, Margaret with equal persistence urged him not to. It wrung her heart to see his pitiful efforts and she realized only dimly that there was some special thing he wanted to tell her; therefore, it was not until after he died that she really understood she, too, had a legacy. Her uncle had made her his principal heiress. He had been tormented by the tardy fear that he had not been sufficiently alert to the needs of his widowed sister and her child; now he hoped to make at least partial amends for his oversight. That was what he had been trying and trying to tell Margaret in the desolate days before his death.

She remained in the shadowy house for another week after the funeral, putting everything to rights and receiving visits of condolence. By that time, the midsummer heat of Virginia was at its worst and, when she and her charges reached Vermont, the abrupt change in climate resulted in bad colds for all the travelers and some murmuring on Cassie's part about catching her death. But Margaret was not sorry she had gone ahead with her interrupted plans. It was, indeed, obvious that her mother-in-law, who had been so kind to her from the beginning, really was in need of the diversion the babies could supply, to keep her from worrying about Nicolas; and Margaret had been right in believing that her own anxiety would be easier to control, when she had a chance to discuss the havoc wrought by the earthquake in several of its phases. One of these was its financial aspects; they all knew that Nicolas would need money and more and more money; and, sincerely as she mourned her uncle, Margaret had a measure of relief in saying that, as soon as his estate was settled, she would not need to accept anything more from Nicolas for the upkeep of Hills' End. His entire income could be used for the furtherance of the excavation.

"Well, that's good news in a way," Waldo told her. "He'll need quite a sum to carry on, that's for sure."

"Isn't it good news in every way?"

"I presume so. But we don't want to be hasty in our judgments. You don't know yet just how you're going to make out, do you? Why don't you come to the bank and talk things over with me there? I never did like bringing money matters to the dining room table, along with corn on the cob and green apple pie."

She did not quite follow his line of reasoning, but the next morning she went, willingly enough, to the bank, where he led her into the Board Room and closed the door. "I didn't want to say this before Mother," he told her. "She worries about Nicolas enough as it is, without my saying something she hadn't thought of. Maybe you haven't, either, and won't thank me for putting it into your mind. But I'm not certain sure it would be such a good thing for Nicolas to think he didn't need to support you."

"Why not?"

"Well, it could work out two ways. Mind you, I'm not saying it would, only that it could. He might think, if you didn't need his money, he'd be justified in pouring more and more into this lake of his, and I'm not sure that's prudent beyond a certain point. I think he ought to keep a sense of obligation to something else—somebody else. And then, on the other hand, it might hurt his pride to have you show him you didn't need him. That would be bad in a different way. What you and Nick need is something to keep you together, not something to pull you further and further apart. Isn't it, Margaret?"

"I'm afraid so."

"Well, I don't want to pry and I'm glad to say Mother's never suspicioned a thing. I don't want she should. As I said before, she's fretting too much as it is. And it never so much as crossed her mind that there might be anything peculiar about your marriage. Now don't make any mistake. I think the world and all of you and the babies. I couldn't ask my only son should have a nicer wife or cuter children. It's Nick that's had me concerned from the beginning. Railroading through a wedding like it was a crooked bill in a state legislature! Traipsing off to Peru when he hadn't been married but five days! Taking on because Cynthia wasn't a boy like you'd given birth to a spastic or something! Not noticing Audrey any more than if she'd been a kitten! Leaving a pretty young woman to live by herself months at a time! That's what worries me most of all. I tell you, every now and then, I have a nightmare about those dueling pistols of yours."

Margaret managed to laugh. "Why, Father Hale, I never should have believed you'd have bad dreams or, if you did, that you'd think they meant anything, except you'd eaten too much corn on the cob and green apple pie! And you're too hard on Nicolas, really you are. I'm afraid I have been myself. I'm afraid I said some things that hurt his feelings before he went away. I'm afraid I didn't always show him how much I love him. I had a letter from him that sounded—well, a little unhappy. I mean, about him and me. I'm sorry there's been no chance to answer it."

"I'm not. I don't want you should go eating humble pie with Nick, Margaret. If you said something to hurt his feelings, he must have done something to hurt yours first. Let him be the one to come around. Just because you're worrying about him isn't any reason to let him act like he shouldn't. And, as far as that goes, you haven't any call to worry about him, you or Mother, either. He's doing what he wants to. Leave him alone and he'll come home, wagging his tail behind him."

Waldo drummed on the table with his fingers, just as Nicolas often did. Then he drew a letter from his pocket. "I don't see any call to tell Nick that you've had a windfall, too," he said. "Of course, you won't have a chance right away, anyhow, and, when you do, break it sort of easy. Whichever way he takes the news, it might make trouble. And he isn't going to need the money he sets aside for you, not for quite a spell. I've been meaning to show you this letter before it was mailed to Nick in care of Ildefonso Parra. Lord knows when he'll get it. But, anyway, it's written and what it says is fact. Ethan Watkins wrote it, but I was breathing right down his neck when he did it. I've got Nick's welfare and his needs at heart, too. So you just set your mind at rest about money for that digging they're doing down in Peru."

"Friend Nicolas"—Margaret read—

"I understand the postal service is nothing to brag about down where you are, but I hope this letter will reach you some way.

"Most folks here figure your latest setback was just another thing you had coming to you, because you were bound and determined to go off to a foreign country that takes earthquakes about the same way we do crops, instead of counting your blessings and staying in the place where you were fortunate enough to be born. However, it's natural your father shouldn't look at it quite that way and he has asked me if, under the circumstances, I wouldn't just as lief release another sum to you out of your legacy from Pete Hart. I can't say I'd just as lief, but the money's there, a lot more than we thought, and I presume I can let you have what you need for the present, anyway, if you can get word to me where and how to send it. Meanwhile, I hope you'll manage somehow. I'm bound to say I like your gumption.

"Yours truly,
"Ethan Watkins."

The "digging" went on until mid-September. Then the incessant rains made further progress at Golden Lake impossible. Harry returned to Palo Alto, as Nicolas and Lester were now both licensed pilots and flights were limited in both extent and number. The hired mestizos were paid off and given leave of absence until the following June; they departed well satisfied with their wages and promising to return. The Machiguengas who had not deserted after the earthquake did not desert now, either; they had come to regard Lake Moonstone as their natural habitat and, little by little, others of their tribe joined them. Gomara had already asked to be taken back there to stay. He was greatly improved, though he still could not do any work and it was doubtful whether he ever could again; but he was loved and respected by all the Indians and his authority was never questioned. He could act as Nicolas' deputy during the latter's absence. From now on, Clo and Walter would take turns remaining with him until active work at Golden Lake could be resumed. Meanwhile, Nicolas and Lester had established the first headquarters for the survey at Cuzco, in the same charming old house with the endless patios where Gomara and Pete had lived while Nicolas was convalescing at Quillabamba. Rafael Villarán, the civilian representative of the government assigned to assist in the survey, came to stay with them; and Li Chan, happy to be back in a real kitchen, fed them royally. They were able to keep in frequent, though not constant, touch with the camp by radio and, during an occasional break in the weather, to go there. One such break came just before Christmas and they loaded the helicopter with as many presents as they thought it could safely carry and provided a real celebration for the Machiguengas. Then, still more laden, they boarded a Braniff plane for Washington.

Margaret had gone to great pains to make the house at Hills' End look as Nicolas first remembered it, gay and glossy with holly and laurel, an immense yule log in the gun room fireplace, a huge tree in a corner of the drawing room, red candles on the dining room table and every mantel; and, besides these time-honored decorations, the *nacimiento* Nicolas had given Margaret two years before was given the place of honor. Stockings were hung for both babies and they were almost smothered with presents; Audrey looked about her with wondering eyes and Cynthia, who now ran tirelessly and rapidly everywhere, kept adding words to her limited vocabulary, "Pretty!—lights!—star!" This year the Woodstock Hales had come to Hills' End and that gave an added incentive for long celebrations. There was not only the enormous Christmas dinner and eggnog and beaten biscuits and fruit cake on hand at all times for all comers; there was also a dance every night when the twins were not going somewhere else. Lester, who was that *rara avis,* a native Washingtonian, was shamefully neglecting his own family, whom he had not seen in more than two years; it was beginning to look as if the absent Carmen might well have cause for jealousy. But Clarissa herself gave her rival the right of way.

"You're grand for a date, quite a few dates," she informed Lester. "But if you've got anything else on your mind, you'd better forget it—unless you want to give up Peru. If you decide to do that, you might let me know."

"I can tell you right now that I shan't play any mean tricks on your brother," Lester replied with some heat.

"If you're trying to say you're going to shovel right along beside him, year after year, as long as he wants to keep on digging, we'd better talk about something else. Maybe Margaret likes playing patient Griselda—and maybe she doesn't. If I were Nick, I wouldn't be too sure of it. Anyway, I'm sure I wouldn't."

So that was that, but neither of them allowed it to cast any gloom over the general merry-making, as far as they were concerned, or as far as the company at large was concerned. Festivity was in the air. Kisses were snatched under the mistletoe, jazz was mingled with carols and spirituals, the coming of dawn was no reason for going to bed. And if Clarissa were not in the mood for romance, at least as far as Lester was concerned, Narcissa made up for this. She blithely announced her engagement to Burt Lassiter and thereafter the two exchanged fond endearments without the slightest self-consciousness. The contagion of love making spread from the parlor to the kitchen and presently there were courting couples on both sides of the house. Only once did Waldo Hale succeed in drawing Margaret aside long enough for a serious talk.

"I'd admire to know whether you did like I said," he told her.

"About what, Father Hale?"

"About your money."

"Well, more or less."

"What do you mean, more or less?"

"Nicolas asked me about Uncle Virginus' will. It was a perfectly natural question. I'd have thought it strange if he hadn't asked. So I told him I'd been a beneficiary, but I didn't know yet to what extent, which is true. He was perfectly satisfied with that answer. After all, it's only five months since my uncle died. Nicolas didn't know how much money Pete had left as soon as that, and this will's a lot more complicated than his was, what with bequests to charity and servants and the sale of the Charlottesville house and all that. The executor has let me bring the family heirlooms home. I've put the silver and linen away for the girls' trousseaux and I'm trying to find a place for the portraits and furniture. You may have noticed a few extra pictures and tables here and there, but most of them are still in the attic. We were pretty well stocked at Hills' End already. I've been wondering if Nicolas couldn't use some of these things in Cuzco, now that he has such an interesting house there. But I don't like to suggest it, for fear he'll think there was some kind of an *arrière pensée*." And, as Waldo looked a little puzzled, she added, "I mean, for fear he would think I was hinting I want to join him."

"I don't see why you shouldn't hint, if you're a mind to."

"Well, because, as you have guessed, there's been a little strain. I don't want to add to it. I know Nicolas wants to be completely free for his work and he can't wait to get back to it. He's explained to me exactly what's been done so far and what he's planning to do next. It's the first time he's ever tried to make me understand and I'm very much pleased. He says it's been possible, right along, to remove debris in the helicopter and dump the trees and rocks and mud in another ravine. They got rid of the trees and most of the rocks quite fast; but, except for the removal by helicopter, everything was done by hand labor at Golden Lake last summer. The shoveling wasn't hard in itself because the mud was so soft. But it was also so wet it kept running back into the holes that were dug almost as fast as they'd been made. And, naturally, it was just about impossible for the men to keep their footing. They were knee-deep in the mire most of the time. So now, as soon as Nicolas goes back to Peru, he's planning to buy a gasoline pump."

"I see," Waldo said, making a mental note that here was something else which would require money.

"The pump will be put over the area where they think the palace is," Margaret went on, speaking proudly, like a child who has learned a hard lesson. "And, after the mud begins to dry out, they can make much more rapid progress. Though, in one way, it'll be harder, because the shovels won't go in so easily. But, in another, it will be much less discouraging, because the same work won't have to be done over and over again."

"And what happens to the water after it gets pumped out? It's got to go somewhere."

"Yes, and I think the answer's terribly interesting. Of course the palace wasn't built at the bottom of a lake—a lake was formed there, nobody knows how long ago, by another earthquake and its outlet was clogged by an earthen dam. They've got that released already and some of the water's draining off. After they've installed their pump, they'll also build sluice boxes along the borders of the lake and the water will run through those to the natural outlet. When Nicolas first began to explain, it sounded awfully complicated. But now I think I understand exactly what's going to happen: eventually, he'll succeed in clearing the complete area."

"Well, I guess I understand, too—more or less. But I understand he's leaving as soon as the twins' vacation is over. If he can't do any of this until next summer—our summer, I mean—"

"That's just it. When summer comes he wants to be completely free for this work. So, in the meanwhile, he must devote all his time to the Cartographical and Geodetic Survey. I know Nicolas doesn't want the babies and me in Peru. He put it in a nice way. He said, seeing me at Hills' End over this Christmas makes him surer than ever this is where I belong. Last Christmas, things weren't going so well. That was when we differed about Cynthia, when I was expecting again and probably was a little difficult. Now Nicolas is full of praise for everything—the food, the decorations, the entertaining, my looks, my clothes. We haven't quarreled since he came home or even argued. Everything has been pleasant—on the surface. But I can't help having the feeling that, if you and Mother Hale and the girls hadn't been here, if Christmas hadn't been in the air. . . . Perhaps strain isn't the right word any more. But there's some undercurrent that frightens me just a little."

"Don't let yourself get frightened. Just hang on. It'll come out all right one of these days if you hang on long enough."

"And long enough means until Nicolas unearths his palace and I have a son?"

Waldo appeared to turn this over in his mind. Then he nodded. "I presume that's about the size of it," he said. "But don't you let it get you down. You've got just as much gumption as Nick has, only it's a different kind."

43 ❧

The next time Nicolas came home, the Waldo Hales were not there and Christmas was not in the air.

He had good reason to be discouraged. He had now been working for two years and a half at Golden Lake and, though he had met with no actual setbacks, progress had been painfully slow. The surplus water was seeping off, but drainage could not be hastened, for the soil had to be kept moist, in order that it might be comparatively easy to move and still not so wet that the original drawbacks persisted. One pump had proved insufficient for the work. It had been necessary to buy two more and it seemed to Nicolas that all three were seldom in good condition at the same time. The level of the morass had been greatly reduced— possibly by half—but they were still nowhere near rock bottom.

Moreover, though no official dissatisfaction had been openly expressed with his cartographical survey, he could not help knowing, from his own feeling about it, what the feeling must be elsewhere. Until he could produce a map on which the words RELIEF DATA INCOMPLETE could be triumphantly erased, he would not feel he had justified his appointment. More particularly, he would not be ready to rest on his laurels until he had inscribed the word PAITITE in golden letters on the site of Golden Lake. And this was still only a dream.

His relations with the *Servicio Geografico del Ejercito* were courteous, but they could hardly be described as cordial. The centers he had established were all functioning—in a languid fashion. Villarán had been succeeded by another representative of the Peruvian government, who did not pretend to be anything but a figurehead. Scientific organization had sunk to the level of shadow boxing.

And then there was that question of expense. . . .

Nicolas drew his salary regularly, but reluctantly, feeling he really did not deserve it. It sufficed to meet the cost of maintaining the centers, but there was nothing left over to help with the cost of excavation. Labrador had assured him, when he accepted the appointment, that he would never be short of money again, that from then on both his own and the Peruvian government would always be ready to help him finance his work. But neither had come forward with an offer and he did not intend to ask for funds except as a last resort. Now it looked as if he had almost reached that point.

He had radically reduced his staff. When Clo and Walter had stretched their leave to the utmost limits and returned to Cuzco University, he had not replaced them with other graduate students. He and Lester had carried on with hired mestizos and volunteer work from the Machiguengas. Perpetua and her mother had never left Camp Moonstone and neither had half a dozen of the Indian men and boys. Others amicably came and went. Gomara presided over them, their demigod. Petie, now a sturdy two-year-old, remained the darling and mascot of the camp. As the trust fund that Watkins, at Nicolas' instigation, had established for the child was more than ample for his present and foreseeable needs, it was also used toward the maintenance of the camp, since this was his home. But Nicolas had established rigid boundaries as to what such maintenance meant. Some of the cost of running the helicopter, yes, for without it the camp could not have been kept provisioned and otherwise equipped; but a careful record was kept of the trips made for these purposes and those made to the cartographical centers. (The hydroplane had long since been returned to the Linguistics; they managed without it.) Lester's salary and the hire of the mestizos, no. They were not directly ministering to Petie. And he was running out of the wherewithal for those, not to mention the wherewithal for the extra pumps, the extra gasoline, the extra food. His return to the States was prompted not by a desire for a break in his work or any special yearning to be with his family, but by the necessity of finding a way to continue it.

Just how he was going to do this was still not clear to him. Nothing would have induced him to ask Powers for more money; and he was almost equally reluctant to approach LaGuarde, both because of the latter's relationship to Powers and because of his position as head of the National Geographic, whose indifference to his work had so long irked Nicolas. Sam Steinmetz, who was now independently wealthy and would not require co-operation from his father and father-in-law, was of course a possibility; but Nicolas shrank from admitting to a former classmate that he himself was in straitened circumstances when the classmate in question was rolling in money; and Watkins' misprisal of exploration had, from the first, been a thorn in his flesh. Perhaps he should go direct to Yale—universities always had hidden funds on which they could draw. Or, if his alma mater was inclined to take a dim view of his achievements, perhaps one of the other institutions of learning, which had so eagerly showered him with honorary degrees, might be persuaded to come forward.

For several days after his arrival at Hills' End, he did not broach the subject of his mission and Margaret forebore to question it. Obviously, though still bent on perseverance, he was very tired and very discouraged and it was not hard to guess that money might again be a problem. At last, unexpectedly, a moment seemed propitious for mentioning her uncle's legacy, not in connection with what he needed, but with what Cynthia wanted. This indirect approach might possibly be the best one; Margaret was hopeful that her father-in-law would feel, at this point, she was justified in making it.

Cynthia was a beautiful child, with a bush of dark hair, large dark eyes and very red cheeks. She was now three years old, large for her age, physically tireless and mentally alert. She was also headstrong, demanding and impudent. She completely dominated Audrey, who was gentle and subject to small ailments, which prevented her from competing with her active sister or even following the latter's lead. Most of the time she played quietly by herself, attracting little attention and making no trouble for anyone. But Cynthia and Nicolas had clashed almost from the moment of his arrival. She plainly resented his presence, which puzzled her without intriguing her, and addressed herself almost wholly to her mother, ignoring him as much as possible. Both little girls came to the table for the midday meal, which was timed for them to take naps afterward and still be ready for an early bedtime at night, though, as far as Cynthia was concerned, the readiness was more or less theoretical. When she came in for lunch, she had already been up and doing for hours; she was voraciously hungry and inclined to be fractious, which was the only way in which she ever showed fatigue. Nicolas thought her table manners deplorable and her petulance exasperating. When she complained that she was tired of the old swing, that Audrey would not toss beanbags with her and that it was a long while since she had had anything new to play with, he spoke to her sharply.

"You already have more toys than any other child I ever saw," he said. "If you haven't had anything new lately, it's because there's nothing left to give you."

"Yes there is. Mommy can give me a pony."

"If you contradict me again, I'll send you away from the table. Your mother can't afford to give you a pony. They cost a great deal of money. Besides, you're too young to have one."

"No, I'm not."

Nicolas rose and took her by the arm, not roughly but angrily. "You heard what I told you," he said. "Go to your room."

Cynthia wriggled out of his grasp and flounced away from the table. But, when she reached the door, judging this to be at a safe distance from her father, she turned for a parting shot before she went pelting up the stairs, too fast for Nicolas to catch up with her, and slamming the nursery door behind her.

"Just as soon as you've gone away again, Mommy will get me a pony," she shouted.

Out of consideration for Margaret, who did not believe in corporal punishment, Nicolas suppressed the impulse to follow her and spank her soundly. But his self-control did not stretch to the point of silence on the subject of Cynthia's insubordination. "For God's sake, isn't there anything you can do with that child before she becomes a public nuisance?" he inquired.

"I hope so," Margaret said mildly. "I'm trying. And I really don't think a pony is such a bad idea. It might help her to work off some of her surplus energy, which is one thing that's the matter with her. I began to ride when I was three—just around the yard at first, of course, with someone leading a very gentle pony on a halter. But you get the feel of having a horse under you that way and pretty soon riding is second nature. I'd already thought of getting her a pony, though I hadn't told her so. Unless you'd really much rather I didn't, I believe I will."

"You know I've never interfered with the way you spend your allowance. This time I'm going to. I not only don't approve of gratifying that naughty child's every whim, I haven't any money to spare for extra expenses right now. The cost of the pony itself is only the beginning. It has to have a saddle and a bridle and presently Cynthia would think it ought to have a harness and a cart. It has to be fed. It has to be cared for."

"Yes, I know. But I'd be very glad to take care of all those items myself."

"What do you mean?"

She hesitated. Perhaps this was not the best moment, after all. Then she decided to go on.

"You've never asked me a second time about Uncle Virginius' will," she said. "He remembered me very generously."

"Yes?" Nicolas answered. Despite its form, the reply was a slightly bored question rather than an affirmative. He rose from the table, lighting a pipe, and strolled toward his desk in the gun room, after giving Margaret time to precede him and start Audrey off for her nap. "I thought I noticed a few more grim portraits and uncomfortable chairs scattered about," he said, sitting down and drumming on the desk with his fingers.

"We'll eliminate any you don't like," Margaret said, taking her usual place beside the desk. "But I wasn't referring to pictures and furniture. Uncle Virginius was quite a wealthy man—much richer than we realized. And his house has been sold for a very substantial sum to the University."

"I suppose you mean the University of Virginia?" inquired Nicolas, to whom Virginians' designation "the University," as if there were only one in the world, had always been irritating.

"Yes," Margaret replied imperturbably. "That sale brought in enough money to establish trust funds to educate both little girls. Of course, I can't touch any of that."

"Of course not. But I'm surprised he thought it was necessary to educate them. He wasn't much concerned about your education."

"That's exactly why he was concerned about theirs," Margaret said, still imperturbably. "He felt he hadn't done enough for me and he tried hard to make amends. It was very pathetic. And he had quite a little property aside from real estate. He left bequests to the University of Virginia and several charities and to both his old servants. The rest of his money, he left to me. Not outright. I can't spend capital, except partially, in an emergency. But I can have an income, adequate for anything I reasonably need."

"What do you call an adequate income?"

"Well—just about what you've been giving me." It was on the tip of her tongue to add, "A little more," but wisely she refrained and added instead, "Tax free."

"You mean about eight thousand a year?"

"Yes, just about. Insurance and things like that can be paid for out of the estate, just as you've been doing and there's enough extra to meet the cost of other things you've paid for, instead of having me take the money out of my allowance—heat and lights and things like that. So I hope you'll let the executor take care of all those from now on. And I've been wanting to say—"

"That you don't need my help any more? That you're completely independent of me? Not only as far as taxes and insurance and other extras are concerned, but as far as everything is concerned?"

"I don't need your *money* any more. That's very different from not needing your help any more. I do need it. I do want it. And I certainly don't want to be independent of you. There's nothing I'd like better than to be a Victorian clinging vine. But until we live in a way that would make this possible—"

"We can't live in a way that would make this possible."

"I know. I should have said that *since* we can't live in a way that would make this possible, I wish you'd take the money you've been giving me and use it toward the expenses of excavation. It would make me very happy. It would give me a feeling that I was helping you in your work. I never have felt that way, so far. I've been terribly sorry not to."

"I appreciate your offer. But a man doesn't like to feel he can't support his wife."

"Your father was afraid you'd feel that way. But—"

"*My father was afraid I'd feel that way!* You talked this over with my father before you talked it over with me!"

"Neither of us planned to. You see, I was in Woodstock just after Uncle Virginius died and—"

"Your uncle Virginius died more than two years ago. Do you mean to say—"

"I meant to say exactly what I did say. I knew then that my uncle had left me some money, but I hadn't any idea how much. Remember how it's been with Pete's money. It's only recently that I've known—"

"How recently? Didn't you have any idea when I came home for Christmas more than a year and a half ago?"

"Yes, I had some idea then. But there didn't seem to be a good chance to talk about it, with everything else that was going on, the house so full of noise and people and Clarissa refusing to get engaged to Lester and Narcissa insisting on getting engaged to Burt and all."

"But you did have a chance to talk it over again with my father, with all this going on?"

"Yes. He managed to find a quiet moment. But you and I never seemed to have any quiet moments."

"As I recall it, we still slept together—just as we're doing now."

"Yes, we still slept together—just as we're doing now. I didn't think those were the best times to talk about finances, either."

She hoped that he would not pursue the subject from this angle, and it was a relief to her to find out he was as reluctant to do so as she was to have him, though whether or not this was for the same reason, she could not tell. She had been glad—gladder than she thought he realized —to welcome him back to her bed. She could not help believing that, like most men, he thought women to be less dependent than they themselves on release from the urge of passion; and doubtless, she told herself, this was true among the uninitiated of her sex, who were much more numerous before marriage than their male companions. But once they had had the full experience of love, if they were young, healthy and fond of their husbands, didn't they usually suffer if they were deprived of it? Certainly she had. The "twelve days of Christmas" had been all too few for her, though they had seemed enough for Nicolas; at least there had been no expressions of unassuaged yearning when he left her. And, for the first time, her passion had not been productive; she felt she had failed in fecundity. Was the lack of the erstwhile glory in their relationship the cause or the effect of this? She did not know. She only knew that she longed, unspeakably, to keep him with her this time until they had recaptured a little of that lost ecstasy, until she could say again, "Now I know that I am going to have a child." And, instead, he would be gone as soon as he had found the means to carry on his work. Instead of giving him a son, she must give him freedom.

She left him sitting at his desk and went upstairs. Later in the afternoon he came to her and told her he appreciated her offer, that he was sorry if he had seemed surly and ungrateful; his "black mood" had nothing to do with her; he was sorry that she must suffer for it. And that night, when he took her to him, the urgency she had missed was there again and instantly she was all his.

The next day she was happier than she had been in a long time, and the happiness deepened when he told her he would accept her offer, that she would, indeed, be helping him in his work by making his money available for it and using hers for the upkeep of Hills' End. An unexpected call from the Huntingtons, with an invitation to dinner so urgent that they could not think up excuses quickly enough for declining it, marred the afternoon; and the evening itself did nothing to mend matters. There was too much to eat and too much to drink and, afterward, there was bridge for much higher stakes than the Hales could afford. Margaret was aghast when she heard Nicolas consenting to five cents a point. And on the way home she could not refrain from saying that her anxiety had spoiled the game for her.

"If you'd lost, it would have taken weeks and weeks to make up the deficit."

"There was no reason why I should have expected to lose. Huntington was half seas over before we even began to play and he kept right on guzzling one whiskey and soda after another until he couldn't tell a deuce from an ace."

"Just the same, it was risky. And I hate to see you take money from—"

"From whom?"

"From someone you've never acknowledged as a social equal. Somehow, it doesn't seem like what the English call cricket. Besides, you've never wanted Edgar Huntington at Hills' End; and before we left, you told him you were certain he'd be waiting to take his revenge, that we'd have to set an evening for him and his wife to come to us later in the week. Doesn't that mean you expect to win more money from him?"

"It does, indeed. I don't see why I didn't think of this get-rich-quick stunt before. I don't like bridge, but I know what to do with cards. So do you. And you've been urging me ever since I can remember to be more neighborly to the Huntingtons."

"I don't call it being neighborly to invite them to dinner just to get money from them."

"Look here, Margaret, they're tickled to death to be invited. When word gets around they've been to Hills' End, they'll be invited to other places to dinner—at last." He put his arm around her and kissed her. "Don't preach to me, darling," he said. "You know you took me for better, for worse, for richer, for poorer. And this is one of the worse times, one of the poorer times. But I want you a lot and I hope you want me."

What could she say, what could she do? Tell him that, of course, she wanted him—and, the next day, invite the Huntingtons to dinner, sit silently by as he won and won and won again and finally accepted a check from Huntington so large that she wouldn't even look at it, so large she knew he made it out unwillingly. Not that he couldn't afford it. But he was humiliated because twice in succession he had been defeated by a man who didn't claim to be much of a bridge player, because this man, who had never willingly invited him to dinner before, had deliberately trapped him into a contest where they were not equals. He seemed to hesitate a little as he made out the check and for a dreadful moment Margaret was afraid he was going to say something insulting, half in jest and half in earnest: that the cards must have been marked, that Nicolas must have maneuvered a surreptitious glance. Instead he laughed, good-naturedly though a little unsteadily, and said good night.

"It's fortunate we can't have any more games," he said. "If we could, I'd be bankrupt. But the wife and I are off to Normandy tomorrow. I've heard of a man that I think is just the ticket for a studmaster at East Lawn—licensed vet and all that, fine family, too, but poor as a church mouse. He needs a job and I want to latch onto him before somebody else does. If I get him, I'll let him take over here for a while and we'll go to Paris and the Riviera, maybe around the world. We'll send you a postcard now and then. 'Having a grand time, wish you were here.' But I wouldn't really. I'd know you could fleece me in Hong Kong just as good as you did in Virginia."

It was too bad they were planning such a long absence from East Lawn, Margaret said courteously, if not sincerely. Such a beautiful place, she hated to think of it vacant—

"Oh, it won't be vacant! We'll keep it fully staffed. In fact, we're planning to enlarge the stables. And one of these days we'll be back. Meanwhile, you might like to meet the studmaster, if we get him. He's one of those real swells, the kind you like. Not lowbrows like us, who aren't much good to you as neighbors, except to beat at bridge. Well, good night, good night. . . ."

"Nicolas, aren't you ashamed?" Margaret asked in a low voice, as soon as their guests were out of hearing.

"No. Are you?"

"Terribly."

"I'm sorry. This money has given me a lift and quite a lot of ideas. As soon as I get back to Lima, I'll join a bridge club. There are plenty of them and I'll ask Fonso which he thinks is the best for me. Meanwhile, I'll ask Allan Lambert which he thinks is the best one in Washington. Then I'll start playing the stock market and go back to Peru either broke or well heeled."

"Nicolas, please—please!"

"Listen, Margaret," he said. "I don't believe you know what it's like to work and work and wait and wait for an objective that will make you rich and famous and fulfill your heart's desire and then lose it when you think it's actually within your grasp. There's no reason why you should and probably I can't expect you to understand why I feel I've got to get to that sunken palace, no matter how long it takes, no matter if it's the only or the last thing I ever do. But it is the way I feel and it is the thing I'm going to do. If I can't do it one way, I'll do it another. I'm sorry if you don't like the only way that seems to occur to me right now, but this is one of the things I have to decide for myself. I asked you several days ago not to preach to me. Now I'll ask you again. Because, if you preach, presently we'll argue and, if we argue, presently we'll quarrel and that couldn't do any good and might do a lot of harm. You've got to let me lead my own life."

"All right, Nicolas, I'll let you lead your own life. But perhaps you'd better not try to share it with me any longer, even as little as you have so far."

Inevitably, the argument came next and then the quarrel. The next morning, Nicolas abruptly left Hills' End. But neither he nor Margaret realized until long afterward that the words spoken in reproach and anger that night had marked a definite parting of the ways.

III ❦ JACQUES

"For in this lies the power of love; that is joins and unites separate spirits, so that they conform to each other as if they were one."

Closing words in diary of María Vela,
a 16th century Spanish nun.

Scene: Virginia and Washington
Time: Autumn, 1959

Principal characters (added):
Jacques de Briare, studmaster at East Lawn Plantation
Victor, his nine year old son
Cynthia Hale, four year old daughter of Margaret and
   Nicolas
Audrey Hale, three year old daughter of Margaret and
   Nicolas
The Ambassador of France and Madame de Josselyn

44 ❧

"Don't worry, darling, I'm sure Felix is going to be all right."

"What makes you so sure, Mommy?"

"Well, you see I've heard M. de Briare's wonderful with horses, that he can do anything with them or for them."

"More than Dr. Drake could have done?"

"Yes, I think so. Anyhow, I hope so. That's what we're going to find out right away, for here we are."

They had turned swiftly into the driveway at East Lawn. The foreman's house had originally been the lodge and was therefore located just inside the gate. It was pleasantly lighted and from it came the sound of music. Someone was playing the piano and evidently two persons were singing, for a childish voice blended with an excellent tenor. Margaret switched off the engine and leaped out of the car, with Cynthia scrambling after her, and pounded hard on the front door with the brass knocker. Instantly, the music ceased and there was a sound of rapid footsteps crossing the floor. Then the door was flung open to disclose the striking figure of a man with one arm protectively around the shoulder of a curly-headed little boy.

"Good evening," the man said courteously. "Won't you come in?" The English words, though markedly accented, came readily. Then, with the sudden recognition of his unexpected visitors, Jacques de Briare went on, even more cordially, "Why, it's Mrs. Hale, isn't it? And—Cynthia? Or is Cynthia the little one? What a delightful surprise to have a visit from you! Victor and I were just wishing we had someone to enjoy our fire with us. We think it's quite a splendid one!"

He half turned, as he spoke, toward the huge fireplace directly behind him, where large logs were indeed blazing brightly. The door had opened directly into the living room and, despite her haste and distress of mind, Margaret had not failed to notice its tasteful and valuable furnishings. The fine portrait of a beautiful woman, set off by a background of dark paneling, surmounted the mantelpiece, and large bookcases, filled with richly bound volumes, flanked this on either side. It was years since she had been in the old lodge, but she remembered

371

it as being quite without any sort of distinction; she had been very far from expecting such a glowing interior or one which bespoke so much culture.

"Thank you very much," she said hurriedly. "But I'm sorry to say we haven't come to make a social visit." The thought that it was strange Jacques de Briare should have thought she *had* flashed through her mind, but it was quickly dismissed for more urgent considerations. "My little girl's pony seems to be sick—very sick," she went on, with increasing hastiness. "He's rolling around in his stall and he's banged his head against something and injured one of his eyes. Every man on the place has left—you know how it is on a Sunday afternoon! And I've called our own veterinarian and several others on the telephone and can't get an answer anywhere—again, the Sunday problem! I know it's presumptuous of me, but I thought that perhaps—"

"*Voyons, chère Madame,* what are neighbors for if not to help each other? Of course, I do not know that I can do for Cynthia's pony what it needs, but certainly I can try! You have your car here? Then may I come with you, to save time, instead of getting mine out? Victor, run quickly and bring me my small kit with the hypodermic syringe and find Tim and tell him to come at once to Hills' End with a stomach pump and mineral oil. Meanwhile, *Madame,* with your approval, I think I'll give the pony an intramuscular shot in the neck if I feel he needs it to relax him. My French certificate as a *vétérinaire* has already been approved here."

"Even if it hadn't, I'm sure you'll do the right thing."

"I appreciate your confidence. Come, let us be on our way."

He moved almost as quickly as he spoke and, as soon as Victor had come running with the kit and they were in the car, he leaned forward from the back seat to speak reassuringly to both mother and daughter. "You are right about these Sunday afternoons, *Madame,*" he said. "There could be battle, murder and sudden death and no one would be the wiser until afterward—unless one took precautions beforehand. That is what I do. I keep at least one man on duty, twenty-four hours a day, at the stables. Fortunately, the Huntingtons allow me so much financial leeway that I am able to run my department at East Lawn more like a Norman *haras* than a Virginia plantation. The horses are much too valuable to risk a loss by oversight. . . . As I am sure your pony is too, *chérie,*" he said, patting Cynthia on the shoulder. "Don't worry. I'm sure everything will be all right."

"Mommy said it would be, if we could find you."

"So I shall have to prove she was not mistaken, shan't I? What is your pony's name?"

"Felix."

"What a nice name! Did you think it up yourself?"

"No, Mommy thought it up. She told me it meant happy and she thought it was ap-ap something. A long word. I don't remember the rest."

"Appropriate? That *is* a hard word. I have trouble with it myself! What color is Felix?"

"Brown. I think brown is a nice color, don't you?"

"Very nice—one of the nicest."

"There's some white on him, too. And he's very shaggy."

"I take it he's a Shetland and a Shetland should be very shaggy. He must be a beautiful pony. I can hardly wait to see him. And, fortunately, here we are, almost to Hills' End, Cynthia. It is Cynthia, isn't it?"

"Yes, my sister's name is Audrey. You didn't make a mistake about her being the little one."

"I shall remember. And I shall try not to make any mistakes about Felix, either. So that you will not be upset when you see me getting to work, I will tell you exactly what I mean to do. I shall probably have to pass a tube into his stomach to see if it is inflated by gas and then I shall inject a gallon of mineral oil with carminatives in it by means of a stomach pump through the tube. This will not hurt him. It will relieve him. Tim will help me—he's studying to be a vet himself."

It was evident to the anxious child from the moment he entered the stall that there was immediate rapport between man and beast. De Briare had hardly touched Felix when the agonized thrashing became a quieter movement and, presently, the pony stood almost still, as if trustfully awaiting release from pain. The hypodermic quickly did its good work and by the time Tim arrived with the stomach pump and the oil, Felix was entirely tractable. "It's too bad horses can't vomit to get rid of their colic the way little boys and girls get rid of their stomach aches," De Briare said sympathetically. "When horses throw up it means their stomachs are already ruptured. But Felix is going to be all right. Now I think I'll give him a second shot. In the vein this time— chloral hydrate."

De Briare glanced at his watch and patted Cynthia's shoulder. "Do you see the time? In twenty minutes I'll ask you to look at my watch again. Because I think by that time Felix will almost have stopped having cramps."

He was quite right. In fact, a quarter of an hour had hardly passed when the situation had changed so radically that the improvement was almost unbelievable. Cynthia flung her arms around De Briare and hugged him ecstatically.

"Oh, thank you, thank you, thank you!" she cried. "You've saved my pony's life! You're the most wonderful man I ever saw."

"*Voyons*, Cynthia, I am not all that wonderful. Felix might have recovered, even without my help and Tim's—you must thank Tim, too. But your pony would have been in pain longer. I'm glad I could spare him that."

"You've saved his life," Cynthia persisted. "Didn't he, Mommy?"

"It seems that way, darling, Margaret said. "But if it embarrasses him to have us say so, we mustn't keep on doing it. . . . I'm afraid your beautiful fire will have died down," she said, turning to De Briare. "But my faithful Cassie—who doesn't desert me on Sunday afternoons —will surely have kept one going for us in the library. Won't you join me there for—well, whatever you like to drink at this hour?"

"With pleasure. Of course, I'll want to check on Felix again after a while and, meantime, a little refreshment would be very welcome. Could it be coffee? I'm still the old-fashioned type of Frenchman who would like to say, even if he doesn't obey that impulse, 'No, thank you, I'm quite well!' when he's offered tea."

"Of course, it can be coffee—for you and me. And perhaps cocoa for Victor and Cynthia. Or does Victor drink *café au lait* already?"

"He does with me—more *lait* than *café*—*bien entendu!* But with Cynthia, he will of course drink what she does—it will seem more like a party that way. And, after all, it is much more ap-propriate for him, as he's only nine. But since he has no mother, I am afraid that details of diet do not have as much attention as they should."

Margaret took her guests to the house and ushered them into the library, where Cassie had, indeed, kept the fire burning. Then she went off to find that faithful old woman, her thoughts in a state of some confusion. It was ridiculous of her to be so relieved because Jacques de Briare did not want tea—or rather, ridiculous because of the reason for her relief: namely, that tea was what Nicolas had wanted when he first came to the house and, somehow, she did not like to think that any other outstandingly attractive man, on his first visit, would want the same thing. She did not want the visits to resemble each other in any way, even so seemingly an insignificant way as tastes in beverages and thus bring Nicolas poignantly to her mind. On the other hand, the manner in which De Briare had spoken of his motherless son's condition had been upsetting. The reference had seemed casual enough, a half-jesting excuse for a man's lack of care in matters to which his wife would have given scrupulous attention, but somehow Margaret knew it was not really casual. There was deep feeling there, a sense of loneliness, an unhealed wound—exactly what she was battling with herself.

The coffee and cocoa were brought in by Bernice, Audrey's nurse, together with fruit cake and cookies; and when she had set up the table in front of the fire, she went to get her charge, who had taken a much longer nap than usual, after a fretful morning that seemed to presage some slight indisposition. De Briare made friends with Audrey as easily as he had with Cynthia, and when Bernice returned again, to remove the tray and say that it was bedtime for both little girls, he begged that they should be allowed to sit up a little longer; it was so seldom Victor had a chance to see other children.

"Perhaps he would like to go with them to their playroom for a little while," Margaret suggested. Again she had the impression that the remark she had just heard was not a casual one, that it voiced loneliness and sadness. "There is no reason why the girls should go to bed right away, especially as Audrey has had such a long nap," she went on. "But perhaps Victor would find their toys were the kind he had already outgrown, and girls' playthings, rather than a boy's, in any case."

"Oh no, *Madame!* I should like very much to go! Papa, please let me!" Victor had already laid down the picture book, whose pages he had been eagerly turning, and now he looked gratefully toward Margaret and pleadingly toward his father.

"We mustn't impose on the hospitality of Hills' End too long, Victor," De Briare said gently. "If we did, perhaps they wouldn't let us come again."

"But of course you must come again! Run along, children. . . . How can you use such a word as 'impose' after what you have done for us today?" she asked, turning to De Briare, as the three youngsters scampered away together.

"That was different—an answer to a call for help—what one neighbor would always do for another, if possible, as I said before. This, if I'm not mistaken, *is* a 'social visit'."

"Of course, it's a social visit," Margaret replied, flushing a little at the slight emphasis he had put on her expression.

"And I am, of course, enjoying it very much, as is Victor. But just the same, in this case we *should* be careful not to impose. We must be very sure we are welcome."

"What can I say to convince you of that?"

Margaret and De Briare had both begun to smoke after drinking their coffee and now he leaned forward to light a fresh cigarette for her before he answered. "I'm not sure you need to say anything," he said eventually. "You have been very cordial, very gracious. But somehow I cannot help feeling that perhaps, if you had not needed my help, you and I would never have progressed beyond a bowing acquaintance, that you would never have offered me coffee in your charming library. The Huntingtons told me, before I came, that you had never been on friendly terms with them, that I must not expect you to be on friendly terms with me and my little son. Forgive me if I have been gauche in saying this, if I should not have said it at all. I am still very much a stranger here. I try not to make mistakes, as I assured Cynthia. But I am certain I do, very often."

"I can't imagine your saying anything that was gauche," Margaret said. She spoke with complete sincerity. At the same time, she realized that the situation was, indeed, slightly awkward; she might very well be the one to fail in delicacy and tact if she tried to explain it. "The Huntingtons are comparative newcomers here," she began, cautiously feeling her way along. "And Virginians, especially Virginians who've lived on the same place from one generation to another, aren't, I'm afraid, always as cordial to outsiders as they ought to be. I believe it's like that sometimes in France, too, isn't it? I mean, the old families —"

"Yes, *Madame,* it is that way in France. Nearly always. I myself have seen it happen, many times."

Of course, you have, Margaret said to herself. *That's the kind of family you belong to yourself. De Briare is one of the oldest names in France. If the French counterparts of the Huntingtons had moved next door to the current De Briares, the latter wouldn't have been cordial, either. Perhaps that's comparable to what actually did happen. It was the Huntingtons themselves who moved next door and perhaps the De Briares had to pocket their pride, because they were poor, and send the heir to this great name to a Virginia plantation so that he could earn some money to help them keep their own haras.* "As a matter of fact, I did call on Mrs. Huntington as soon as she came here," Margaret managed to go on, without—or so she hoped—betraying too much of her thoughts. "She returned the call. But when I invited her to tea, she didn't come, and I rather had the impression she wasn't interested in pursuing the acquaintance. I didn't blame her in the least. She was in residence at East Lawn very little and this was before I was married. I was in mourning for my mother and I lived very quietly. Hills' End was badly run down. There was nothing about it or me that could have appealed to Mrs. Huntington."

"Not even the fact that you were very lonely?"

Margaret colored. "You're reasoning just the way my husband did," she said, surprised at her own candor. "Because, afterward—"

"Afterward, you married a very famous man? And the place was no longer run down, but beautifully kept up? And a great many prominent persons, including the President of the United States and his wife, began coming here? So then the Huntingtons decided they wanted to come, too, and your husband discouraged the visits? Wasn't that the way it was, *Madame?*"

"More or less. I really never attached much importance to the situation myself, M. de Briare. But since my husband felt so strongly about it and since I've tried very hard to respect his wishes—"

"I am sure you have. And, needless to say, I admire that effort very much. But since Dr. Hale feels so strongly about the Huntingtons—and, believe me, I understand his feeling—do you think he would be pleased to have you let down the social bars between Hills' End and East Lawn in favor of a studmaster who happens to be a good veterinarian?"

"*Monsieur!*"

She spoke indignantly and she had risen, to find him already on his feet, regarding her with a searching gaze not untouched by faint mockery. Unlike Nicolas, he was not much taller than she was; it was easy for him to look her straight in the face and this was what he was doing now.

"Would he?" Jacques de Briare repeated. "Of course, I shall return to the stables again this evening and tomorrow as well; probably the day after also, to make sure all is well with Felix. That Dr. Hale would want me to do—would expect me to do. I shall go to the stables and then I shall report to you at the house. That would be a professional call. But after the necessity for these professional calls has passed, what then?"

With chagrin, not unmixed with anger, Margaret realized that she did not know how to answer him. Obviously, she could not say that Nicolas would recognize him as a gentleman, whereas there had been no such recognition as far as Edgar Huntington was concerned, and that this made a difference. Besides, did it make enough difference for Nicolas to want her to welcome in his absence, as a frequent visitor, an unattached and extremely attractive man, even if that man were obviously lonely and sad? She could not, in all honesty, tell herself that it did. Her answer, when it came, seemed to her so inadequate that she was amazed to find it satisfactory to her caller.

"In my husband's absence, I must make my own decisions," she said. "I shall be very glad to welcome you and Victor at any mutually convenient time."

"I am greatly honored by your decision," Jacques de Briare told her.

45 ❧

"Mommy, why doesn't Victor come to play with us?"

"Cynthia, it's only three days since he was here the last time."

"Oh, Mommy, it must be longer than that!"

"No, dear, it isn't. It only seems longer."

Seems longer to you, of course she should have said. She did not want to admit, even to herself, that it also seemed longer than this to her. Jacques de Briare and his young son had so quickly and so easily become part of the normal pattern of life that the days when they did not come to Hills' End were already the ones which were outstanding and somehow incomplete. The morning after Felix' seizure, De Briare had driven over early to make sure the pony was all right and had driven back in the evening for the same reason. Both times he had gone up to the house to make his favorable report, but he had done so very briefly, pleading the pressure of work when Margaret had urged him to stay for coffee. The next day he had come on horseback with Victor and had found Felix so completely recovered that he expressed the opinion it would do no harm for Cynthia to ride him, if she wanted to; he and Victor would go with her, just as an extra precaution. An hour later she had returned jubilant. Never, she said with unconscious cruelty—for hitherto she had ridden only with Margaret—had she had such a wonderful ride. Couldn't she go riding every day with M. de Briare and Victor?

"Of course not, Cynthia. Mr. de Briare's much too busy to make a practice of taking you riding. It was very kind of him to take you this once."

"Well, couldn't he take me just once more?"

"I am sure that could be managed." De Briare had spoken before Margaret could answer. "You are not riding yourself nowadays, *Madame?*"

"Yes, usually I ride with Cynthia. I used to ride a great deal with my father. Then there were a good many years when I had no one to ride with me and no horse to ride. So I have been grateful for renewed opportunities. Besides, Cynthia has no one else to take her."

"You mean I didn't have, until Mr. de Briare and Victor came. But now I have. You don't need to go with me any more, Mommy."

Again that unconscious cruelty! And again Jacques de Briare stepping smoothly into the breach.

"Your mother is right in believing I wouldn't have time to take you every day, Cynthia. And Victor won't be able to go every day, either. I'm arranging to send him to school in Alexandria. Anyway, now that we're sure Felix is all right, of course you and your mother will be riding together regularly, as you were before Victor and I came. But if, for any reason, she can't go with you, let me know, and I'll see what can be managed. And perhaps all four of us could go together, once in a while, if your mother, as well as yourself, would give Victor and me that pleasure."

Margaret was grateful to him for not letting the fact that Cynthia was no longer dependent on her hurt too much—so grateful that she fell in with the suggestion, without giving it too much thought, that all four might ride together sometime in the future. This point having been settled, De Briare did not decline to stay for coffee and, as they drank it and chatted about various inconsequential things, somehow a day and an hour were set for an excursion. So they had taken a long ride, mostly along forest roads, where Margaret had not been for quite a while and which she was overjoyed to find still undisturbed by the new superhighways. And when they returned from this ride, late and healthily tired, it was, of course, the most natural thing in the world for De Briare and Victor to stay for supper.

Three days had passed since then and it seemed longer than that, as Cynthia had said. Now she was continuing her insistent talk.

"You're not listening, Mommy. I was saying that, even if I couldn't go riding with Victor every day, I'd like to have him come here every day. So would Audrey. Wouldn't you, Audrey?"

Audrey agreed, as she usually did with anything Cynthia suggested, and then contentedly left the room, as Bernice appeared in the doorway and reminded her that they had planned to go and see Perdita's new puppies. She was a quiet and biddable child. Cynthia, who was neither, stood her ground. Margaret sighed.

"Cynthia, we keep telling you that Victor's father is a very busy man. He hasn't time to bring Victor to see you every day."

"Victor doesn't need to have his father bring him. He can come by himself. He said so. He said he could come any school day, late in the afternoon, and on Saturdays and Sundays he could come earlier and stay longer. It would be nice if you would invite him to have supper with Audrey and me on school days. Sunday mornings he goes to church with his father in Alexandria, but you could invite them both to Sunday dinner. And Saturday he could stay all day."

"Cynthia, Victor wouldn't want to come here as often as that or stay as long when he did come. If he's going to school, he'll soon be making friends of his own age, boys he can play games with. You and Audrey are just babies to him—girl babies. He doesn't want to be bothered with you."

"He does, too! He doesn't think we are babies! He doesn't care if we are girls! He wants to pretend we are his *sisters!*"

There was no question about it, Cynthia was rapidly working herself up into one of those childish rages with which Margaret found it difficult to cope, and which had so infuriated Nicolas when he was last at home, while leaving him quite as inadequate as his wife in dealing with their elder daughter. She never said she was sorry for any of her misdeeds, and she did not respond, in a normal childish way, to either gentle persuasion or any form of discipline that had been tried. If she were deprived of her supper, she went haughtily to bed without it; if she were shut up in a closet, she remained there, stonily silent, until she was released; if, as a last resort, she were spanked, she shed no tears, either while she was being paddled or afterward; she merely looked with scorn at her assailant, as if daring him to try once again if he thought he could make her cry. Margaret was strongly opposed to any and all of these measures and wept bitterly when Nicolas, exasperated beyond endurance, insisted on resorting to them; children needed all the nourishment they could get; a little girl might easily suffocate in a closet; corporal punishment was a cowardly and cruel weapon for an adult to use against a child. Nonsense, Nicolas retorted, with irritation; Cynthia was plump as a partridge; it would do her no harm to miss an occasional meal; it would take a long time to exhaust the air in any of the big closets at Hills' End; and, as far as corporal punishment went, he had been sent out to the woodshed more than once when he was a boy, and Margaret would certainly agree that his parents were neither cowardly nor cruel. Of course, she would, Margaret admitted. But methods of rearing children had changed since his day.

"You make me feel as old as Methuselah when you say that. Even if I am getting on, I don't propose to be bulldozed by a three year old child."

"How do you propose to prevent it? None of the measures either of us has tried has done any good."

"You're too easy on her. If I could be here all the time, I'd soon have her toeing the mark. She doesn't see enough of me."

"Well, you know I'm not going to dispute that last statement."

Such discussions brought with them nothing but bitterness and, as she sat, sorrowfully reviewing the last one before Nicolas' latest departure, Margaret forgot, for a moment, that she had a new instance of Cynthia's willfulness with which to deal and that this time, as usual, she must somehow do it alone. The defiant little figure, still planted firmly in front of her, recalled her to the present emergency without offering any solution for it.

"Cynthia, Mommy's very tired. She doesn't feel well. When you came in she was just going upstairs to lie down and see if it wouldn't make her head feel better. We'll talk about Victor tomorrow. Please go and see the puppies."

"I've seen the puppies twice today already."

"Then do something else. Whatever you like. But don't tease me any more right now."

It was quite true that her head ached. She had always prided herself that she was not a victim to any of the favorite forms of malaise in which women took refuge when they did not want to be bothered. But at least she was not pretending: the migraine was all too real and this was not the first time she had suffered with it. Perhaps she should consult Dr. Loomis, for there were other adverse symptoms besides migraine; she was "edgy," she tired easily, she felt vaguely dissatisfied with life in general and some aspects of it in particular. She was longing, equally vaguely, for some sort of a break in its monotony. She did not try to define what sort of a break this might be.

Having watched Cynthia heading unwillingly in the general direction of the stable where Perdita's latest family was installed, Margaret gave a sigh of relief and went upstairs, unbuttoning her dress as she did so. Then she kicked off her shoes, turned back the coverlet and lay down on her bed, grateful for its comfort and the encircling silence. She had been sleeping badly of late and she almost never took naps in the daytime; now, to her surprise and relief, she began to feel drowsy. If she could sleep for a little while, perhaps, when she waked, her headache would be gone. And then she would try to think what was to be done with Cynthia, who was certainly growing more and more willful every day.

Meantime, instead of going fast asleep and instead of thinking about Cynthia, her semiconsciousness was permeated with thoughts of Jacques de Briare. After the ride the four of them had taken together, they had eaten their supper in the gun room and, like her father-in-law, her latest guest had expressed interest in her "collection," especially in the dueling pistols. She told him, as she had told Waldo Hale, that she did not know their history, but she understood they were valuable, that there was a pair very like them in the museum at West Point, but that they were a rarity in the United States. De Briare asked for permission to take them out of their box and examined them with thoughtful interest. Then he looked up with a smile.

"I think perhaps I can tell you something about their history," he said. "I am so glad you kept their box, because that will help us. Dueling pistols, as you have probably been told before this, were never ornamented—their purpose was strictly utilitarian! But this does not prevent ornamentation of their container." He pointed to the coat of arms, surmounted by a coronet, stamped in gold on the cover of the leather box and then, taking off his signet ring, handed it to her. "The device seems to be the same," he said, still smiling. "If I'm not very much mistaken, these pistols belonged to my great-grandfather."

"Surely you're joking!"

"No, *Madame,* I am serious."

"But how do you suppose they happened to get here?"

"Perhaps for much the same reason that I did. Their owner needed money. There were rich Americans in France at that time, just as there are now."

"Do you know anything more about the pistols' history?" Margaret inquired, hoping the embarrassment he had caused her by his candid answer was not too visible.

"I think so."

"Will you tell it to me?"

"Some time, perhaps. Not today."

"Would you—would you let me give them back to you? Please do! It would make me awfully happy if you would. I feel they really belong to you—not to me."

For a moment he continued to finger the pistols without answering. Then he closed the box, laid it aside and shook his head. "Not today," he said again. "Some time, perhaps—if you would still like to have me when I have told you the rest of their history. But now it's time we went back to The Lodge. Come, Victor."

It was not until after he had left that Margaret realized she was still holding the signet ring which he had handed her, so that she could compare its device with the one on the box that held the dueling pistols. She could not pursue him and tell him he had forgotten to take it back. She would have to keep it until the next morning. By then, he would certainly miss it and return to get it. Meanwhile, for safety's sake, she took it upstairs and laid it on her bedside table. Apparently she did not do this as carefully as she should have for it rolled off and fell clattering to the floor. She picked it up and put it on. It was too loose, of course, but not so loose that it did not stay on her forefinger. Again, for safety's sake, she let it stay there all night. When De Briare did not return for it the following morning, she wrote him a note, which she dispatched by Rufus, and told him that the ring was quite safe; she was afraid he might think he had lost it. When could she expect him to reclaim it? His reply took the form of a personal call, but not until late the following day and, meanwhile, she had been constantly aware of the ring.

"I knew it was in good hands," he said. "The very best. I should have been delighted to have it remain there. Indeed, perhaps I should confess I did not actually forget it. Shall we say I overlooked it? But, if you insist, I will take it back now."

"Of course, I insist," she said. But she wondered why it was so hard to say this quietly.

This had happened three days ago. Now she was startled by the sound of voices in the front hall: a man's voice, with an unmistakable accent and a child's voice, also unmistakable. She swung off the bed, slipped on her shoes, buttoned her dress and, without giving her disheveled appearance a thought, started down the stairs. Before she was halfway to the bottom, she was aware of Jacques de Briare smiling up at her, just as Nicolas had stood smiling up at her so long ago.

"Victor and I have again been honored by a visit from Cynthia," he said lightly. "He and she have had *gouter* together and have looked at some old picture books together; apparently, they have both enjoyed it very much. But, as Cynthia came this time without her mother, I thought it wiser to inquire whether or not she had mentioned, at home, her intention of making this visit and found that she had not. After questioning her a little further, I found that her mother supposed her to be with her nurse and that her nurse supposed her to be with her mother. Under all the circumstances, I thought perhaps I should escort her back to Hills' End, much as Victor and I would have liked to detain her."

"Cynthia, I'm ashamed of you. Go to your room at once. . . . M. de Briare, what can I say? Except that, as you must know, I'm deeply embarrassed."

"Isn't this perhaps one of those times when it's better not to say much of anything? Wasn't it one of your own Presidents—Coolidge, I believe—who replied, when a presumptuous young journalist expressed the fear that some silly article he had written might have been disconcerting, 'Nothing *you* could say, young man, could possibly embarrass me.' Surely, nothing anyone could say or do could put a great lady like yourself in an embarrassing position."

"You are very kind. But—"

"There are no buts. (*So he did not like that word, either!*) And now that Cynthia is restored to you—"

"Mommy, you are going to ask him to stay to supper, aren't you?" Cynthia burst out.

Jacques de Briare shook his head. "I am sure that is exactly what your mother is going to do, Cynthia, and I appreciate it. But, unfortunately, this evening I have another engagement. Besides, my pleasure in remaining here would be greatly lessened by the fact that you would not be at the table with me. I heard correctly, didn't I? Your mother has told you to go to your room. Of course, you are hesitating because it might look rude if you pushed past her on the stairs. However, I understand the situation. You have only to say you are sorry, both for involuntary rudeness now and for any anxiety you might have caused your dear mother by running away if she had looked for you and failed to find you. Good night, Cynthia. Suppose the next time you come to see Victor and me you do it honestly."

There was a moment of complete silence. Cynthia and Jacques de Briare were facing each other and the man was still smiling, this time with no trace of satire in his smile. Margaret waited, in miserable anticipation, for Cynthia to break into rebellious and impudent speech. Instead, her eyes were brimming and, presently, two large tears rolled slowly down her cheeks. She brushed them away and started up the stairs. Then she spoke.

"I'm sorry, Mommy," she said in a low strained voice and went steadily on without glancing back. The others heard the door of her room closing behind her, softly, before they again looked at each other.

46 ❦

Margaret had never been intrigued by grocery shopping. When there had been no one else to do it, she had gone faithfully into Alexandria two or three times a week to get the necessary supplies. Since Rufus had been in her employ, she had sent him with a list. If she had been sufficiently interested in finding unexpected delicacies on the market, she might have made more of an effort. But what woman, she asked herself, cared about ferreting out unexpected delicacies when she had a good old-fashioned cook and only herself and two little girls to cater for? Of course, when her mother was alive, it had been different; it was essential to find something, anything, that would tempt an invalid's fickle appetite and, in those days, there had been so little money for delicacies! Now that there was plenty, it did not matter, unless Margaret were giving a party. And she seemed to have lost interest in giving parties. To make these worth while, in her opinion, you needed a host as well as a hostess. And, of course, if there were a man to cater for—a man who appreciated exotic food—a gourmet. . . . Well, was there ever a Frenchman who was not a gourmet?

She caught herself up short. Jacques de Briare, to be sure, had become a fairly frequent guest, but certainly not to the point where she needed to think of providing for him more than she would think good enough for any other visitor. As a matter of fact, he had praised Cassie's cooking, not just politely, but enthusiastically, and this had led to a discussion of cuisine which had left Margaret almost speechless with astonishment. She had not given any thought to de Briare's household arrangements, but had taken it for granted that in the neighborhood he would have found someone to "do" for Victor and himself. Not at all. He prided himself on doing it all without assistance. *Three meals a day,* Margaret exclaimed, when this phenomenon was revealed to her! *Voyons!* What were three meals a day for two persons? Two meals a day, really—*café au lait* and *brioches,* the latter bought in Alexandria, did not count. A simple lunch—an egg dish, cold meat or a casserole, green salad, carefully chosen cheese, fresh fruit. *Gouter,* of course, for Victor was always hungry by midafternoon. Then a proper dinner. *Pot-au-feu* as a matter of course—a soup kettle was always simmering on the stove. An *entrecote à point,* or a tender little chicken roasted until it was *doré,* French fried potatoes, green vegetables and, on Fridays, the excellent *fruits de la mer,* so abundant in Virginia. It was when he came to the *entremet* that he did not do so well. Baking was a branch of the culinary art that was kept by itself in France, a special department. He could do anything else—the jellies and creams—yes, those he could manage. But when it came to those succulent pies, those mouth-watering cakes, not to mention all those endless varieties of hot breads taken as a matter of course in Virginia, he did not do so well.

"But," Margaret objected, "you must be very tired by night. The light breakfast and luncheon—yes, I can see how you could manage those. Even the *gouter,* too, if you left the dishes for someone else to wash and had that someone else prepare the evening meal. I'm sure Cassie could find just the right person for you. She still has a large family to draw on."

De Briare shook his head. "It's very thoughtful of you. But we're managing finely, Victor and I. *He* helps with the dishes. Afterward, I help him with his lessons. And we get in a little music. We're more independent as to hours than if we had a servant. And expense happens to be a consideration, too. Of course, I'm very well paid here. But I like to send something home every month to my parents."

He had never yet said anything about his family and, naturally, Margaret had not questioned him, though she had wondered about it and the beautiful portrait she had glimpsed so briefly had roused her curiosity. "At least you could come and have supper with us a little more frequently!" she exclaimed impulsively.

"Voyons, Madame," De Briare said again. "Almost every time we all go riding together, Victor and I stay for supper. Almost every Sunday Victor and I come to dinner. If we came any oftener, we should begin to feel we were pensioners on your bounty—unless, of course, we could persuade you that this should be a case of turn and turn about, that occasionally you would come to share our *pot-au-feu,* our *fruits de la mer,* and so on. Would you? Or would you feel, if you did that, you would be overstepping the bonds of propriety within which, so far, you have so scrupulously remained?"

For a moment, Margaret was angry. She was conscious of the satirical note, which came and went in De Briare's voice, just as the note of hardness came and went in Nicolas', and she did not feel he was justified in speaking to her that way. Then, with the sense of fairness which seldom failed her, she decided that he was. She *had* been careful to keep within the bounds of propriety, she had remembered that she was a married woman whose husband was not at home and, though she had been hospitable to a lonely man and his little son who were her neighbors, she had kept that hospitality impersonal, she had never seen the lonely man except when the children were present. That is, only once—no, twice: the first time that he had come to the house and the time he had identified the dueling pistols. And both these times, the meeting had been brief, almost accidental, the intimate quality of a tête-à-tête entirely lacking. Nevertheless, she knew, and thought De Briare knew, that the impersonal element was disappearing from her hospitality, that she was slowly but nonetheless accepting him as her friend. Not that there was anything wrong about that; it was vulgar, it was cheap, to assume that sex must play a major part in every association between a man and a woman. Nicolas was the only man she had ever loved, the only man she ever would love; and Nicolas was the only man who had ever loved her. And that had not lasted long, she told herself bitterly. If she were really as greatly beloved by him as he had claimed, in that wonderful letter to which she still turned for comfort from time to time, he never would have left her for so long. And, even if he had really loved her once, he no longer did so. Therefore, she could not be really desirable or she could have held him. . . .

"You have not answered my question, *Madame*," Jacques de Briare was saying. Startled, she emerged from her reverie.

"I'd like very much to come some time," she said.

She still had not done so. The indefinite invitation had not been followed by one more precise and she was relieved by the delay. She should not have been. Jacques de Briare did not rush his fences, as Nicolas Hale had done. He was too skilled a horseman for that.

Margaret had been thinking this over, in its various aspects, when she finally decided to go into Alexandria and do the grocery shopping. Her errands ended in much the same way they always did: she saw so many things which she would never have thought of if she had stayed at home that she spent twice as much as if she had sent Rufus, as usual. She bought smoked salmon and anchovies and caviar and pâté de foie gras; and she was emerging from Chauncey's, with her arms full of packages, when she came face to face with Jacques de Briare and Victor.

The little boy had become much attached to her, as she had to him. With a shout of joy at this unexpected encounter, he rushed toward her and flung his arms around her neck, jeopardizing the security of her parcels. Somehow, she managed to keep hold of them as she returned his kiss; but she could feel them already slipping when De Briare stepped quickly forward and relieved her of them.

"You should not try to carry such a load," he said reproachfully.

"Where have you parked your car? I will take these bundles to it. And, of course, Victor should not have made things harder for you by giving vent to his feelings as he did on a public street. Not that I find it in my heart to blame him."

She had surrendered the bundles, but she was still standing face to face with Jacques de Briare. They were very close together and, as she looked into his eyes, she knew he wished they were not on a public street, that he might embrace her with the same spontaneous abandon as his son. In the same breathless instant, she knew that this wish was only an echo of her own.

47 ❧

She knew, of course, that he would seek her out as quickly as possible, but she did not realize how soon this would be. She felt certain he would try to choose a time when there would be no danger of interruption and, as far as she was concerned, almost any part of the evening, after Cynthia and Audrey had gone to bed and the servants were normally off duty, would suit his purpose admirably, now that she so seldom entertained or went out any more. But this was the time that he and Victor spent together, over books and music, after their dishes were done. She knew he would hesitate to do anything which would make it appear to his son that he did not feel their intimate companionship during this period was more important than anything else in his life, even if he had been willing to leave the little boy alone in The Lodge. She was, therefore, totally unprepared when, only a few hours after the encounter in Alexandria, which had been so startling and disturbing, she heard footsteps, which she recognized, crossing the porch and stopping at the half-open door from which she was plainly visible as she sat in the library.

"It's Jacques de Briare," he called out pleasantly. "Am I disturbing you? Or are you expecting other visitors? If not, may I come in for a few minutes? Victor has again gone to spend the night with one of his new found school friends and it is rather lonely at The Lodge without him."

"Come in, by all means."

She had risen and gone to meet him, but now that they stood in the hall, facing each other, she did not hold out her hand in welcome nor suggest that he should join her in the library. She was both bewildered and ashamed that her agitation should have so overwhelmed her that she did not know how to make the next move. Jacques de Briare, without the slightest sign of embarrassment, made it for her.

"Could we go into the drawing room? I've always been astonished that you so seldom seem to use it. Is it possible you do not appreciate all that charming and authentic French furniture you are fortunate enough to possess? I have been longing to see it to better advantage. Perhaps this is just the moment for it."

"Perhaps it is."

"You do not sound thoroughly convinced, *Madame*. Suppose we try to find out?"

He stood back, smiling, for her to precede him and then invitingly drew out an armchair for her before selecting for himself the loveseat which Nicolas so despised and settling down in it with every appearance of ease. The distance between the two was sufficient to suggest a slight but unstrained formality in his call and, when he leaned forward a little, as he began to speak, his attitude bespoke great earnestness.

"Will you forgive me if I am very candid in what I say to you?"

"Of course."

"Do you always say 'of course' when you do not say 'but'?" he asked, shaking his head a little, though still smiling. "I am afraid 'of course' may not be the most ap-propriate words for this occasion, which is a rather special one, I think. And I hope that 'but' is not going to figure too largely in our conversation, either."

"What makes you think this is a rather special occasion?" Margaret asked faintly.

"Don't you think so, too? Besides permitting me to be candid, won't you be candid yourself?"

"What do you want me to say candidly?"

"I want you to say you knew, when we met this afternoon, that I would have given anything to greet you as Victor did, even though we were on a public street. I want you to say that you would have been glad to have me do so. I want you to say that you have recognized at last that we are in love with each other—not merely that we love each other, which must have been evident to you almost from the beginning, as it has to me. Of course, I have known for some time that I was in love with you. But I was not sure until today that my feeling was reciprocated."

"M. de Briare, I am afraid you are forgetting—"

"I am not forgetting anything. Certainly not that you are married. The first time I came here, I annoyed you by referring to my occupation, as if it might be a drawback to friendly relations. You were quite indignant at my suggestion of such a possibility. And we did become friends, in spite of my occupation. Now, still in spite of it, we have fallen in love. So it would appear that we should review the situation from another angle."

"You say you haven't forgotten anything. If you haven't forgotten that I am married, how can you talk about 'reviewing the situation' as if I were—free?"

"But aren't you? Or couldn't you be, very easily? Naturally, there is nothing less reliable than rumor. But there is certainly a very widespread impression that your marriage took place under rather unusual circumstances. That's one of the penalties for fame—it's almost impossible for a celebrated man, like your husband, to have any well-kept secrets. And whether you admit it or not, you're quite a prominent person yourself. Forgive me if I say anything indiscreet or anything that wounds you—nothing could be further from my wishes. But wasn't there an arrangement—or at least an understanding—that, even though the usual vows were exchanged, in a church, they weren't to be binding for a lifetime, but only as long as either husband or wife desired to have the union last?"

"I don't know how you happened to hear this. But it's true. At least, it was true in the beginning. The idea of marriage didn't appeal to Nicolas Hale. I believe many men feel the same way he did about it. But he wanted a son. He asked me to marry him because he thought I could give him one. And I accepted him. I hoped and believed that I could. But that wasn't the only reason I married him. I married him because he'd been my idol for years. I'd have married him under any conditions he made."

Her voice broke a little and she turned her head away, fearful that her face betrayed her feelings far more than she was willing it should. De Briare spoke very gently.

"Dear Margaret—I may call you Margaret, mayn't I, whatever the solution for this situation proves to be?—please don't go on if it pains you to do so. I wasn't trying to force your confidence, only to make sure that everything was clear to me, because that might mean there was some hope for me."

"I know. I realize you weren't trying to force anything. But now that I've started, I have to go on. It has never entered my head to divorce my husband. And he wrote me, very soon after we were married, that the original—understanding wasn't to hold good any more. He hadn't pretended to love me in the beginning, but when he found out that he did, he didn't pretend about that, either, any more than he concealed from me that exploring was his great passion. He said most emphatically that he wouldn't consider a divorce."

"And he still feels the same way? There's never been any change in his feeling about it?"

"He's never said there was. He couldn't conceal his disappointment because we didn't have a son, especially after our *second* daughter was born. And certain things came up that led to—estrangement. But I've accepted the fact, from the beginning, that he and I would be separated a great deal. If it hadn't been for one reason, it would have been for another."

"Separation for years at a time? Aren't you rather young, Margaret, to live indefinitely like a widow? Even if Nicolas Hale is still your idol, don't you feel, once in a while, that you'd be happier if you were living —well, a normal married life?"

"Of course I do. But since I know it's impossible—"

"It isn't impossible. I'm sure, if you really had been a widow, you'd have married again by now. You wouldn't have been able to help it. Some importunate suitor would have succeeded in persuading you that you were making a mistake. I'm very much surprised that no such suitor has persuaded you that you should not go on leading a lonely life, even though you're not really a widow. I don't even think he'd have had to try very hard. The mere fact that you're attracted to me proves you're not immune to natural feeling and you ought to be glad of it, not ashamed of it. If there ever was a wife in name only, you're one."

"But I wasn't always!"

"No, you weren't always. You had a baby nine months after you were married and another one ten months after that. With that record, the very fact that you haven't had a third one leads me to conclude you're not living a normal life for a woman your age."

"Aren't you rather inconsistent? I mean, after all—"

"You mean, after all, your husband is living like a widower, even though he isn't one and that I really am a widower and haven't remarried? Well, let us say, if only for the sake of argument, that your husband has been as faithful to you as you have to him. If exploring is not only his great passion, but his only lasting one, perhaps he has. And, as far as I'm concerned, I had a very happy marriage, a normal marriage in every way and I wasn't left a widower until shortly before I came to Virginia. My bereavement left me emotionally numb, except for my relation to my little boy. We'd always been devoted to each other and that mutual devotion was intensified when he lost his mother and I lost my wife. For a long time that devotion has been a compensation, it has sufficed us both. It doesn't any more. Victor wants a mother and he wants you for his mother. He's shown it very plainly. I want a wife and I want you for my wife. I haven't shown it plainly before, but I am doing it now—or at least I'm trying to."

Jacques de Briare paused and then went on, still speaking gently but earnestly, "In case you think the religious angle is one of the things I've forgotten, it isn't. I'm not a Catholic. I'm a Huguenot—my family's been Huguenot for generations. The reason Victor and I go into Alexandria to church is because the Presbyterian Church there is more like the one we go to at home than Pohick. As a matter of fact, the Catholic Church often shows a good deal more understanding and discernment in these matters than the Episcopal Church. There were elements in your prenuptial agreement that might very well render it susceptible to annulment with a different religious setup. As it is, you might be the one who'd have to compromise with either your own conscience or the rules of your church." He waited a minute, giving her time to break in if she wished to do so and, as she remained silent, he went on, "Another thing I haven't forgotten is that I'm classified as a sort of superior hired help on the place next to the one that's yours, that's been in your family for generations. I know that would take some living down, some adjustment. But you've already proved to me that you wouldn't have any false shame about a thing like that. And we could always go back to France, if you decided you couldn't face it out here. We wouldn't have to live at the family *haras,* though my parents would be delighted to welcome you. I've got a charming little house of my own, what used to be called a *vide bouteille* or a *maison de bouteille,* and provided for the enjoyment of young bachelors in much the same way that the loggias did in Italy, built apart from the great houses, or the *garconnières* in Louisiana. We could live very reasonably, but very comfortably, even though very simply, but you've done that before. Of course, I wouldn't be willing for you to accept anything—anything at all—from Dr. Hale, even for the children."

"There hasn't been any question of that for a long time," Margaret spoke impulsively and, though she almost immediately regretted the impulse, it again seemed inevitable that she should go on, having begun. "My uncle Virginius, who was a bachelor, died four years ago and willed almost everything he had to me and my children. He was a good deal richer than any of us had supposed and, shortly before he died, he told me he hadn't had any idea my mother and I had such hard work making both ends meet. He wanted to atone for not contributing more when she was alive. There are trust funds for both little girls—enough to educate them well. And the income from the rest of his principal and the sale of his real estate is large enough to meet all the running expenses at Hills' End. I've done it ever since—"

"Ever since the estrangement of which you spoke took place?"

"Yes, I felt under the circumstances I would rather, since I could. Besides, I knew my husband needed all his money to carry on his work. His salary as Director of the Special Cartographical and Geodetic Commission in Peru isn't large and neither are his independent means."

"But the work's very congenial to him, isn't it?"

"Yes, very. He never would have been satisfied to settle down here. I didn't realize that in the beginning, but I do now. He enjoys coming here for a little while, as if it were for a vacation and seeing his official friends and scientific associates in Washington. But the quiet uneventful life on a Virginia plantation doesn't appeal to him the way—the way it does to some people."

There, she had almost said, "The way it does to you," and though she had bitten the words back, just in time, she realized that Jacques de Briare knew what they were as well as if she had uttered them. He went on quite calmly.

"Well, we might live in Virginia and we might live in France or it might turn out to be half and half. But, wherever we were, we'd be together—you and I and our children. We might have more children and, if we did, though that might mean more of a financial strain, they'd be welcome, too. But they wouldn't enter into our calculations for marriage. We'd be marrying because we love each other, because we know we'd fit into each other's lives and be happy."

As he spoke the last words he rose, not hastily but as if there were nothing else that needed saying, at least for the moment. "Think it over," he said. "Good night, my dear love, and God bless you."

It was not until after he had left her, so deeply stirred that she had not moved from the chair he had drawn out for her, that she realized he had not once touched her. But every word he had said had been like a caress.

48 ❧

*L'Ambassadeur de France
et Madame André de Josselyn
prient Madame Hale
de leur faire l'honneur
de venir dîner
le seize Octobre à huit heures*

Ordres et décorations
R.S.V.P.   2535 Belmont Road, N.W.

The invitation had been delivered by hand. Most official invitations were mailed now, except within Washington city limits, but the French Embassy was still run on the lines that had been *de rigueur* at the turn of the century and Annabelle, also mindful of formalities, had brought the invitation to Margaret on a silver tray. She opened the thick cream colored envelope, engraved in gold with the words *Ambassade de France* in one corner, and regarded its enclosure with some surprise. There were a few embassies to which she still went fairly regularly, because their Chiefs of Mission were old friends; but she hardly knew the De Josselyns, who were fairly recent arrivals. In fact, she did not think she had left cards. The rift between Nicolas and herself had never been generally made known, so, on the rare occasions when she still paid formal visits, she continued to leave his card with hers; and she would certainly have remembered if she had taken one of his from the back of the drawer where they had long lain undisturbed. Now she noticed that the invitation, both inside and out, was addressed only to her, so the De Josselyns must have known her husband was away from home and that his absence, if not actually indefinite, was at least prolonged.

She felt no real desire to accept the invitation; at the same time, she was intrigued by it. She felt there must be some special reason why she had received it and she could not imagine what this was. Involuntarily, she began to review her wardrobe. It was some time since she had bought a new evening dress; the ones she had were all perfectly good, there had been no radical changes in style and, after all, she seldom needed one any more. So-called cocktail dresses took care of practically all her social requirements. But somehow she began to visualize the sort of dress she would like to wear if she were going to the French Embassy: almost Grecian in cut, ivory in tint. The rose-colored cameos, set with pearls and diamonds, which she had inherited from her grandmother, would give it just the touch of color it needed. She never wore the jewelry that Nicolas had given her any more.

Idly, she began to sketch the dress she visualized, when the sound of hoofs in the driveway attracted her attention and, looking up, she saw through the open window near her desk that Jacques de Briare was approaching on horseback at an easy pace. It was now three days since he had declared his love for her and he had made no effort to get in touch with her since. Cynthia had been complaining that she never saw him any more and begging her mother to make a point of asking him to supper, since he had not dropped by of his own accord. Now he waved and called to Margaret in his usual friendly fashion.

"It's a beautiful day, St. Martin's summer at its best. I thought perhaps I could persuade you and Cynthia to go riding with me."

"You wouldn't have to use much persuasion. Cynthia has been pestering the life out of me because she hasn't seen you lately. I'll tell her you're here and in a minute she'll be hurling herself out of the house. You and she can go down to the stable for Felix and Cavalier and I'll join you as soon as I can get into riding breeches and boots."

"Good! Cynthia doesn't realize how much fortitude it has required for me to absent myself. This morning it deserted me, so here I am again, ready to begin where I last left off."

"On horseback? With Cynthia along?"

"Why not? After all, my method of approach is still wholly verbal, though I don't guarantee how long it will remain so. And I don't believe Cynthia will grasp its finer points, precocious as she is."

He had ridden close to the window and was smiling down at Margaret from the saddle. Again she felt his words were like a caress and certainly this was also true of his look. Probably she would be much wiser to decline his invitation. But Cynthia had already somehow discovered his presence, without a word from her mother, and had, indeed, hurled herself out to meet him.

"Please give me a ride to the stable, Jack." And, as he bent over and swept her up behind him, she threw her arms around him and hugged him ecstatically. "Why haven't you been to see us? We've missed you dreadfully! Haven't we, Mommy?"

"Well, M. de Briare's here now, Cynthia. But since when have you been calling him Jack?"

"Oh, I forgot to tell you! We talked it over and he said it was all right. I asked him why he always called me Cherry and he said it wasn't Cherry, it was *chérie,* which is French for honey. So I thought if he could call me something nice in French, I could call him something nice in English and we decided on Jack. It's my favorite name, just as he's my favorite person. Come on, Jack, let's go and get Felix."

They were off without further explanations and Margaret watched them out of sight before she restored the invitation from the French Embassy to its envelope and went upstairs to change into riding clothes, still with some misgivings. On the face of things, it did not seem as if Jacques de Briare could make much headway on horseback; but since even his words and his glances had such an uncanny effect upon her, she did not feel too sure. Of course, she still had no idea of divorcing Nicolas, but she did not see very clearly what she was going to do instead. Unquestionably, she was attracted to the Frenchman in a way she had never been to any man before. Nicolas had first been her idol, worshiped from afar; then her lord and master, with whom she had fallen so passionately in love that she could not do enough to show how she rejoiced in his domination; and later, alas! an absent idol, then a fallen idol, but still the husband who was the father of her children and to whom she was in honor bound to be faithful. The feeling for Jacques de Briare had nothing in it of idolatry, nothing of an impulse for self-abandonment, nothing of tragic disillusionment coupled with a sense of duty. There was a certain freshness and spontaneity about it that belonged, or so she had always believed, only to first love between the very young. And yet this was not first love, either for him or for her and they were both past their early youth. Moreover, it was love that could have no fulfillment in the present and boded no good for the future. She could not understand why it made her so happy.

Nevertheless, the happiness was undeniable and, as she and Cynthia and Jacques found their way to the woodland roads that she loved and rode along under the trees that branched over them, she felt it welling up inside of her, so that she forgot both the passionate past and the ominous future. Cynthia was not satisfied with the leisurely pace her mother enjoyed; she kept galloping ahead and then wheeling about suddenly and galloping back. During the intervals of her absence, her elders rode on, for the most part in companionable silence; anything but small talk would have been subject to frequent and violent interruption, and small talk seemed not only inadequate but superfluous. When they returned to Hills' End, Jacques came in for a glass of sherry, but declined to remain for luncheon on the ground that he had already broken in on the chatelaine so early that she had not had time to organize her household for the day; he should not impose on her further.

"My household really doesn't take much organizing," Margaret said truthfully, after they had gone into the drawing room. "I wasn't facing a number of urgent duties when you arrived. In fact, I wasn't doing anything in the least important—just making a sketch of the sort of dress I'd like to wear if I accepted an invitation which I had almost automatically decided to regret."

"What a charmingly inconsistent and feminine procedure! And why should you automatically decide to regret an invitation? Were you so sure you wouldn't enjoy the occasion in question, whatever it was?"

"I suppose I might have enjoyed it in a way. It was an invitation to dinner at the French Embassy. I don't know the De Josselyns and haven't even left cards on them. I can't imagine why I was invited. But the French parties used to be very pleasant. It's just that I don't go much to that kind any more. I feel rather out of things."

"There's no reason why you should. As a matter of fact, I'm sure the De Josselyns would be very much disappointed if you didn't accept."

"Why, what makes you think that?"

"They told me so."

"*They told you so!* How did they happen to do that?"

"Well, Elise de Josselyn is my aunt—my mother's sister. I've already been to see her and Uncle André several times during the day when Victor was in school, so we've had opportunities for conversation. They know that you are I are neighbors. I'm invited to the same dinner that you are and I'm planning to go. Victor has plenty of friendly classmates now with whom he can spend the night. I thought perhaps you and I could go together."

Margaret set down her sherry glass and stared at him. Then, involuntarily, she burst out laughing.

"So it was actually as simple as that! The French Ambassadress is your aunt and you asked her to invite me to dinner!"

"No, it wasn't quite like that. I was pleased that Aunt Elise wanted to invite you, after I told her a little about you, but I didn't suggest it. It was her idea."

"As Cynthia has still not come in from the stable, where she's probably feeding Felix more sugar than is good for him, perhaps before she gets here, you'll have time to tell me what you told your aunt about me."

"What would you expect me to tell her? That you are a very lovely lady, separated from your husband, and that I'm trying to persuade you to marry me."

"But, Jacques, I'm not separated from my husband! Not—not officially! Your aunt will find that out in no time and she'll be terribly shocked."

"She has found it out. In fact, I told her so myself and she isn't shocked at all. She thinks you ought to be, under the circumstances. You're not dealing with a Spaniard or an Italian, Margaret; you're dealing with a Frenchwoman. Her parents were divorced. She doesn't give that aspect of the case a second thought. She's only wondering if it might not be awkward in some other ways. Actually, though she didn't say this in so many words, I gather she thought it might be simpler all around if we had an affair. As, of course, it would be."

He still spoke with the calmness that, so far, had not deserted him. Margaret, blushing furiously, half rose and tried, quite futilely, to find words adequate to express her indignation at the mere suggestion.

"Please sit down again, Margaret, and listen quietly," Jacques went on, as if there had been no attempted interruption. "There's nothing to be alarmed about. I carefully explained to Aunt Elise that, in this case, an affair would be undesirable, because of the children. I mean, because Victor loves you so much and Cynthia loves me so much. A secret, illicit relationship would cheat him of the mother he wants and Cynthia of the father she not only wants, but needs. Therefore, marriage, with everything open and aboveboard, is our only solution. Otherwise, I should certainly have considered asking you to take me for a lover instead of a husband; and please believe me, the suggestion would not have been an insult. It would have been a tribute. A Frenchman's mistress is very often the being in all the world most dear and most important in his life. You have only to read a little history to know that.

You would have been the most dear and the most important in mine. Can't you see that?"

There was a long silence, broken by the slamming of a door. Cynthia was returning to the house. In another minute, she would burst in on them.

"Yes, I see that," Margaret said very faintly.

"I'm going to ask you one more question and then I'm going to leave you to think over your answer. Can't you see that, if you decline to marry me, the time might come when we wouldn't have any choice? We'd become lovers because we couldn't help ourselves."

She rose with him and held out her hand. "I don't need to think it over," she said less faintly. "I do see. But please leave me, just the same."

49 ❧

She did see, but in the end, she did not have enough will power to decline the dinner invitation from the French Embassy or to veto Jacques' suggestion that he should take her to it.

The fact that she found exactly the dress of which she had dreamed perhaps contributed to her vacillation. It was made of softly pleated crepe, cream colored with just a hint of rose where it fell into folds. The surplice waist was cut in a deep V, both front and back, and it was sleeveless. After Margaret had tried it on, the saleswoman, who had assisted at the fitting, asked her to wait a minute, as she left the cubicle, and returned carrying a wrap of rose colored velvet, lined with ivory brocade and trimmed with summer ermine. When she had draped this casually over her customer's shoulders, Margaret knew she would buy both the dress and the wrap, even though this would use up, for an entire year, the clothing allowance to which she limited herself.

She had never seen Jacques in evening clothes before, and he seldom wore the tiny ribbons and buttons which were the insignia of imposing medals, displayed only on great occasions. Now there was a row of such medals across his chest, besides still another, suspended from a red ribbon that went around his neck and made a wide vivid stripe against his white shirt front. She did not even know what most of these medals stood for, but then, she really knew very little about his life anyway. Evidently, his experiences had been more varied and his achievements more distinguished than she had realized. She wished she could ask him to tell her about these; but since he had never done so of his own accord, she did not feel she would have a right to ask him, unless her life were to be interwoven with his. And that was still unthinkable.

"How lovely you look! And how nice of you to be ready!" he said as he came in. "I expected to wait for you at least half an hour—long enough to say good night to the little girls. Perhaps I might take time to do that anyway."

Margaret nodded her approval and, presently, she heard squeals of delight from the nursery, now located in the erstwhile second floor guest room; and when Jacques returned, he was straightening his tie and pulling down his waistcoat. "Audrey is gentle as a dove, like her mother," he said. "But Cynthia is rather violent in her embraces." Instead of voicing a second comparison which, no doubt, he had in mind, he merely said, "Well, shall we be on our way?" and held out the rose colored velvet wrap for Margaret to put on. "Most appropriate," he added, "everything about you is *couleur de rose*. Let's make that the tone of the evening. No problems—no plans—no self-reproaches—no importunities. Just enjoyment of the moment as it is. Agreed?"

"Since I consented to accept you as my escort, I could hardly do otherwise."

"How right you are! I have a new car, thanks to the Huntingtons. I hope you'll like it."

The new car was a gleaming Jaguar and, like most Frenchmen, Jacques drove with complete disregard for speed limits, mingled with uncanny adroitness at avoiding anything approaching an accident. Their arrival at the embassy was well timed, neither so early as to involve prolonged stress on Jacques' relationship to the host and hostess, nor so late as to make their entry together conspicuous. The guest of honor was a French Cabinet Minister, briefly visiting Washington on official business, and, as Margaret had suspected might be the case, Senator Powers and the LaGuardes were their fellow guests. Most of the others, except for a few relatively recent additions to the French Embassy staff, were already among her acquaintances; but none of them moved in the closer Latin-American and scientific circles that she did or, rather, that she had before her voluntary semi-seclusion. She was illogically relieved that Senator Powers and the LaGuardes had arrived after Jacques and herself. After all, there was no reason why they should have taken the drive in from Virginia separately, since they were neighbors—except that they were also potential lovers and that, of course, the senator and his daughter and son-in-law would have no way of suspecting. Or would they? There was something electric about these things that made themselves felt in a gathering, even when the two persons vitally concerned hardly looked at each other; and she caught the senator's gaze resting on her attentively, more than once, even in the intervals when he was not beside her, which he managed to make surprisingly brief. But she was seated nowhere near him at dinner; the period allotted to cocktails and canapés was much shorter than it would have been in an American house; and after dinner the men withdrew for cigars and brandy, as well as coffee and cigarettes, while the ladies remained in the drawing room. Mme. de Josselyn did not noticeably single Margaret out, but managed to include her in almost every group over which she temporarily presided; and Margaret was aware that this urbane, supremely gracious and elegant woman was also observing her attentively. When the time came for farewells, the ambassadress detained her for a minute.

"You must come again very soon, my dear, just *en famille*. I want to become better acquainted with you. Meanwhile, may I say how much pleasure you have given my husband and myself by coming tonight?"

Senator Powers was at Margaret's elbow again. "Couldn't we persuade you to come out to Georgetown for a nightcap? We never see you these days."

"It's very kind of you. But, as you know, it's quite a long drive to Hills' End."

"No longer than it ever was."

"But I'm getting to be such a confirmed old stay-at-home. I can't keep the late hours I used to. And Audrey has a slight cold. I don't like to leave her too long."

"Oh well then, I won't insist."

It was, of course, inevitable that Jacques should come up to the entrance in the new Jaguar just in front of the senator's chauffeur-driven Cadillac, and that Powers should see De Briare hand her into his car. The older man leaned forward, smiling a little.

"Don't permit the moonlight to let you forget Audrey's cold," he said. "It must be very beautiful tonight, shining on the Potomac, where that's visible from the Memorial Drive to Mount Vernon and, after all, such a short detour from Hills' End! . . . Good night, my dear. We must manage to see each other again very soon. I'm eager for the latest news from Nick."

"Doesn't he know you're out of touch with Dr. Hale? And what's this about Audrey's cold?" Jacques inquired, as soon as they were out of hearing.

"Yes, he does know. I'm afraid he said that with some malice. I'm also afraid I told a lavender lie. I didn't want to go out to Georgetown and I didn't believe you did, either. So I mentioned a slight cold. It's entirely a figment of my imagination."

"Oh—a very commendable fancy on your part! But does this privileged old gentleman call you my dear? I hadn't ventured to do that before, but if he can, certainly I may. And I'm very resentful because he mentioned the Memorial Drive before I had a chance to do so myself. I was, of course, going to suggest we should take that route home."

"At the rate you drive, Jacques, we wouldn't have much chance to look at the moonlight on the water. One brief glimpse and we'd be past it."

"I wasn't planning to drive quite so fast on the way back. After all, we had to arrive at the dinner on time. But, as far as I know, there's no particular hurry about returning to Hills' End—that is, if you're sure Audrey doesn't have a cold."

"Yes, I'm sure."

"Then it's all right to take the longest way around?"

"I'm afraid it isn't. But, after all, you're at the wheel."

"Very true. And I won't really need to give driving my entire attention once we're out of the Alexandria traffic, unless you insist that I should."

Of course, that was what she ought to do, what she would do, she told herself. It would be madness, total madness, to do anything else. She had plenty of time to repeat this, silently, because Jacques did not seem to expect her to talk to him after they had exchanged a few remarks about the dinner: now that Margaret had sampled the cuisine at the French Embassy, didn't she think the De Josselyns' chef was just as good, if not better than the Románs', despite the contention that the Peruvians had the best one in Washington? The French Cabinet Minister was a rather rough and ready looking customer, wasn't he? But he was really a very cultured man and scrupulously honest, too, which was more than you could say for all of them. Did Margaret like Aunt Elise's dress? He understood Balenciaga made everything she wore down to the last wisp of lingerie, but that was doubtless an exaggeration. He drove, if anything, faster than before, until they had left the southern outskirts of Alexandria behind them and were on the final stretches of the Memorial Drive, where there was almost no traffic. Then he gradually slackened his speed and, at the same time, slid one arm around Margaret's shoulders. She knew that if she drew away, even a little, the next instant Jacques would have both hands back on the wheel. But, somehow, she could not draw away. And, presently, the car had come to a standstill, in a sheltered place near the moonlit river, and his arm was no longer around her shoulders, but around her waist. Then both his arms were around her and both hers were around his neck and they were kissing each other. . . .

It was a long time before Jacques raised his head. When he finally did so, it was to say something for which Margaret was wholly unprepared.

"*Mon coeur*, I want you to come home with me tonight."

Mon coeur! My heart! The tenderest term of endearment in the French language! That she knew, that she understood. It was the English words which baffled her.

"Come home with you? But we are on our way home. At least, we ought to be. We mustn't stay here any longer."

"No, we mustn't stay here any longer. And we were on our way home —to our separate homes. But I'm asking you to come with me to mine instead—that is, to all the home I have here."

"You want me to come with you to The Lodge?"

"Yes, dearest. Victor's spending the night with a friend, as you know. And at your house are the servants and the children. It wouldn't do, even if they weren't. Other associations would come to your mind, which would make my presence painful for you. But there aren't any children or any servants or any associations at The Lodge. We'd be starting alone, just you and I—starting a new life together."

"You mean—you want me to stay all night?"

"I want you to stay forever. But of course I realize it's impossible for you to stay even until daybreak. I'll have to take you back to Hills' End before then. But that's still hours off and no one will ever know how long the party lasted. No one will think it strange if you don't get in until very, very late, even if you're heard coming in, which is doubtful."

"Perdita will hear me. She'll bark."

"Well, what if she does? As I've said, no one will know how long the party lasted—certainly not Perdita."

The moonlight was so bright that she could see his smile. She did not understand how he could smile at such a tense moment, and yet she was thankful that he could, thankful, and yet a little frightened. The smile made what he wanted seem so simple, so sinless, so normal. Yet, what he was suggesting was that she should break her marriage vows, that she should be unfaithful to her husband. . . .

"Jacques, I—I can't."

"Why can't you?"

"You know. You know I'm married."

"I know you have been married. I also know you haven't lived with your husband for a long, long while, that you never expect to again. I know you love me—not as much as I love you perhaps, but still a great deal. If you'll come home with me now, you'll find that, by morning, all your scruples and fears will be gone. It'll be as I've told you—we'll have started a new life together. After that, it will seem natural to put your old life behind you. You won't dread getting a divorce—you'll want it. And then, as soon as possible, we'll be married. We'll go to France, to my little house, my *vide bouteille*. We'll take the children with us and leave them with my parents at the *haras* while we have our honeymoon. But, meanwhile, why should we wait any longer to become lovers? I know I said we couldn't make do with an illicit affair, because we had no right to deprive Victor of the mother he wants and Cynthia of the father she wants and that Audrey would be glad to accept. But this way we wouldn't. The affair would be only a prelude to marriage, not a substitute for it. And it would be our secret, yours and mine. Sometimes there's nothing like a shared secret for binding people close together."

"Jacques, if I did what you're suggesting, Nicolas could divorce me."

"On the contrary. If you do what I'm suggesting, you'll divorce him for desertion. You should have done it long ago."

"I might—I just might consider divorcing him for desertion. I never thought I could, but I might—after tonight. I mean," she added hastily, "after what's happened so far. Because I'm afraid I do love you and I know you love me and I know that our marriage would make our children happy. And I don't think Nicolas would be hurt—except possibly his pride. But I've got to be sure. Though you don't realize it, Jacques, I owe a great deal to Nicolas. When he asked me to marry him, I was just a spinsterish recluse and he transformed me into a real woman. If it hadn't been for him, I never would have been a wife and mother. I hadn't had a proposal, even when I was a young girl, and I'd formed such a habit of seclusion that I wouldn't have been able to break away from it. It was Nicolas who discovered that I had possibilities of attraction, it was he who taught me to fulfill them. He gave me a sense of triumph and he made me gloriously happy—for a time. Besides, he saved my heritage for me. Hills' End was going to wrack and ruin when he came here. He rescued it, he made it productive and beautiful again. Even though he isn't contributing anything to its support now, I'm still tremendously his debtor for its restoration—for its preservation."

"Don't you think you've paid your debts to him, Margaret? In a material sense, you've certainly done so by making him the co-owner of a place like Hills' End. Have you any idea what the Huntingtons paid for East Lawn? Well, never mind, that was going to wrack and ruin, too, and they've spent millions without getting the result you've got here with thousands, completely leaving aside the question of prestige. As to the other, I'm not so sure someone else might not have discovered you. It was Hale's good fortune you went to that New York wedding. Sooner or later, you'd have gone to something else. Sooner or later, some man who's not blind in both eyes would have seen how beautiful you are, someone else would have persuaded you to marry him, someone who would have really loved and cherished you, as I want to do."

"But I *wasn't* beautiful until I married Nicolas! And I knew from the beginning my marriage wasn't going to be the usual kind. I shan't feel my debt to him is paid until—"

"Until you've given him a son? *Mon Dieu,* how can you give him a son if he spends all his time in the Andes and you spend all yours in Virginia?"

"I can't. But I've got to be absolutely sure that's the way it's going to continue to be—that exploring *is* his only real passion, that he's reconciled to my failure to give him a son, that he doesn't care about me any more. I'm fairly sure as it is."

"Well, how much longer do you think it will take for you to be absolutely sure?"

"I don't know. I've never considered the situation from that angle. But, Jacques, if things went any further between you and me now, I couldn't ever divorce Nicolas. I couldn't pretend—don't you see? That he was to blame when I was really the guilty party?"

"But you're not. You wouldn't be. You never would have even thought of me, or of any other man, as a lover, if Nicolas Hale hadn't deserted you."

"That's true. But neither you nor any other man would have wanted to be my lover, if Nicolas Hale hadn't done just what I've said—made me desirable. And I'd still be acting a lie, living a lie, if I did what you suggest. You said it would be our secret. But would it—for long? Cassie would guess. She has a sixth sense about such things, like many of her race. And, even if she didn't, even if no one else did, wouldn't we be different persons, you and I, if I were a disloyal wife and you were responsible for my disloyalty?"

"We'd certainly be different persons in that we'd be happier if we stopped talking about an unnatural situation and did something to normalize it. Which is what I've been begging you to do, what I'm still begging you to do. At least give me this one night and let me prove I'm right. I promise I won't ask for another until you're willing to give it to me. But I don't think that will be long. And I don't think you'll ever be sorry, Margaret."

She turned her head away and he could see that she was hesitating, that he might, at last, have prevailed. But when she looked back at him, she shook her head.

"It can't be tonight, Jacques," she said softly. "And that isn't because I don't wish it might be. It's hard for me to say no, harder than I believe you realize. But if I'm going to get a divorce, I've got to do so with a clear conscience. And I promise you I'll think about it— about the divorce, I mean. I won't say any longer that it's out of the question. I'll talk with you about it again, in a few days. Truly, I will. But now I must ask you to take me home—to my home. And not to kiss me again. I don't feel as if I could stand it."

Lights were shining in the big house at Hills' End, both upstairs and down, and Margaret wondered, momentarily, how she had happened to leave so many on and then, with sudden anxiety, if she had spoken the truth, after all, when she told what she thought was a lavender lie, if Audrey might be ill. As predicted, Perdita heard the car and began to bark as it approached the porte-cochere. Then she started scratching at the door on the inside, impatient because it was closed. Suddenly it opened and Perdita, barking still more joyously, rushed out and then rushed back again, making circles of delight around the tall man who was standing on the threshold and who now came quickly forward with outstretched arms.

"Margaret!" he said huskily. "Margaret, it's so late I was beginning to be afraid something had happened! Come quickly and welcome me home!"

50 ༖

Nicolas had reached the bottom of the steps, opened the door of the car and, bending over, drawn her to him before Jacques, springing out from the other side, could come and stand beside him. Therefore, he was only vaguely conscious of an alien presence until Margaret managed to free herself; at first, she had been too stunned, both mentally and physically, either to move or speak. But presently, by making a great effort, she managed to do both.

"Nicolas, where on earth have you come from—and when? Why didn't you let me know?"

"I've come straight from Peru. My plane was late, I arrived only a couple of hours ago. I didn't let you know because I wanted to give you a surprise."

"You've certainly succeeded. Of course, if I'd dreamed. . . . But you needn't have worried. . . . Oh, Jacques, do excuse me! Nicolas, this is our neighbor, Jacques de Briare, whom you haven't met."

As Nicolas briefly acknowledged this rather belated introduction, Jacques, who had been awaiting it without the least visible embarrassment, now bowed rather formally before accepting the proffered hand.

"Your wife and I were both invited to dinner with some relatives of mine," he said evenly. "As you were absent, she was kind enough to let me take her. But now that you have returned, I mustn't intrude on your homecoming. I'll hope to see you again in a day or two. Good night, Dr. Hale. *Soyez le bienvenu!* Good night, Margaret."

He kissed her hand, with the quick gesture natural to a Frenchman, taking courteous but impersonal leave of a married woman, bowed again to Nicolas and stepped into his car, calling back pleasantly, "I'll wait to hear from you," as he drove away. Nicolas continued to gaze after the Jaguar until its taillights disappeared through the gates and Margaret was the first to speak.

"Shall we go in? I hope Cassie gave you some supper?"

"A very good one, thank you. I couldn't possibly eat any more. But I could do with a drink while we catch up a little. What about you?"

"All right, to keep you company."

"Bourbon and soda with lots of ice? Are the necessary ingredients still kept in the same place?"

"Yes. Shall I help you?"

"No, just wait for me in the library. I have a fire going and it's all as pleasant and homelike as ever. One of the best things about an old Virginia house is that, essentially, it doesn't change."

Perhaps the house doesn't, but everything else has, Margaret said to herself, as she took her old seat beside the hearth, not because she wanted to, but because she could think of no logical excuse for not doing so. *How long can I keep up the pretense that it hasn't? What can I say to Nicolas while we're "catching up a little"? I can't very well begin by telling him I want a divorce, but if I don't, what is he going to expect me to do next? What is he going to tell me to explain this sudden unannounced return?* It was so warm in the library that she could not keep on the velvet wrap and, suddenly, she felt overdressed and ill at ease in the formal elegance of attire so unsuited to the intimacy of a tête-à-tête with the husband from whom she had so long been separated. If he had only sent her some word of warning—or, without this, if she had only been at home and alone when he arrived—the situation would not have been so awkward. Somehow she would have known how to meet it, somehow she would have collected herself. But as it was—

Nicolas came back into the room carrying a well-supplied tray and set it down before putting ice in the glasses and pouring the drinks. As he did so, she noticed the great change in his hands. He had always been meticulous in his care of these and they had been as shapely as they were strong. Now they were rough and grimed with blackened nails and coarsened skin. He had changed in other ways, too. He had always been lean, but there had been an easy grace and suppleness to this leanness; now it was too marked, too taut. There were lines in his face and white threads in his black hair which had not been there before. Moreover, his suit was unpressed and she knew it was an old one, because she happened to remember it had been one of her favorites years earlier; his shirt was clean, but it lacked the fine fit on which he had always insisted. When had Nicolas begun to be indifferent to his clothes? She wondered if he would find her as much changed as she found him and, almost regretfully, realized, if he did, this would be for the better and not for the worse in her case. She had gained a little weight, so there were more attractive curves to her figure than when she was too slender. Her color was better and there were no dark circles of fatigue under her eyes. She had no white hairs yet, but when she did they would not show much in the fair waves that Nicolas had loved so. As for her elegant attire, she was becoming more uncomfortably conscious of it every minute. She wondered if Nicolas would notice all this, but if he did he made no comment on it. When he began to talk, he did so in a way which was not quite natural, but at least in a way that showed he was trying to make it so.

"I'm rather intrigued by your escort of the evening. You say he's a neighbor of ours. Which place has he taken over?" Nicolas asked, handing her the drink he had mixed.

"He hasn't taken over any of them. He's the studmaster at East Lawn."

"The studmaster at East Lawn!" Nicolas exclaimed, setting down his own glass without even tasting its contents. "Wearing every medal that his own and various other grateful governments could possibly bestow on him! How come?"

"I haven't the least idea. I really know very little about his life before he came to East Lawn," Margaret replied, hoping she did not sound as nervous as she felt. "He came over here, the first time, because Felix was suddenly taken sick on a Sunday afternoon and I appealed to M. de Briare for help when I couldn't get anyone else. He was very kind—very efficient. Cynthia was naturally extremely grateful to him and she's become deeply attached to him . . . By the way, have you seen the children?"

"Yes, I've seen them, but they were both asleep and there seemed to be no point in waking them up. As a matter of fact, Cassie was quite insistent that I shouldn't. As far as I could tell, in the dim light which was all she'd allow, Cynthia hasn't changed much except that she's ever so much bigger, but Audrey's a lot prettier than she used to be." Nicolas picked up his glass and began to sip the bourbon slowly. "Well, so M. de Briare cured Felix and that established some sort of an *entente cordiale,* but not enough for you to find out much about him. Somehow, his name rings a bell. Who are these relatives of his that invited you to dinner?"

"The French Ambassador and Mme. de Josselyn. She's his aunt."

"Margaret, are you making this up as you go along or are you telling me the truth?"

"I'm telling you the truth. Why shouldn't I?"

"I don't know, but somehow it all sounds fantastic."

"Perhaps it isn't really as fantastic as it sounds at first. I know De Briare is an old Norman name, that Jacques' parents own a famous *haras* somewhere in Calvados and that he has a small house of his own, the type that he calls a *maison de bouteille*. Did you ever hear the term?"

"Certainly I have. . . . I take it he's a bachelor?"

"No, he's a widower. He has a charming little nine year old boy, Victor, to whom he's devoted. They're both very musical, they sing together and play duets. Jacques has done wonders with The Lodge at East Lawn. He's filled it with beautiful old books and pictures."

"Oh—you're on a visiting basis at The Lodge?"

"I've never been to The Lodge but once, the day I went to get help for Felix. But I couldn't help seeing how charming it was. Cynthia's been there one extra time—she ran away. Jacques brought her back and made her promise never to go again without permission. He comes here, off and on, and brings Victor to play with Cynthia and Audrey."

"Apparently often enough so that you and he call each other by your first names."

"That's really Cynthia's doing, too. Jacques called her *chérie* and she thought he was saying Cherry, for a nickname, and loved it. So then she insisted she must call him Jack. And he was so pleased, it seemed silly to protest. After that, he and I stopped being formal, too. . . . Nicolas, couldn't we stop talking about Jacques de Briare for a while and talk about you instead? Did you come alone or is Lester with you?"

"I came alone. Lester can't be spared from camp just now. Whenever he can be, he spends his time courting a girl named Carmen something or other. I'm afraid my hopes of having him for a brother-in-law have been defeated. You probably know that Clarissa turned him down and why."

"I think so. And you really believe he's going to marry this little *Limeña*?"

"It looks that way. They're even talking about the possibilities of living in Quince Mil, which gave me food for thought—especially as a nice girl named Doris Ibarra, who lives there already, had started my thinking along the same lines."

Nicolas poured a little more bourbon in his glass and sipped it slowly. Apparently he felt that particular subject was exhausted, unless Margaret asked questions about it. She decided against this and tried another approach.

"I always liked Lester and I'm interested in hearing about him. But when I asked if we couldn't stop talking about Jacques de Briare for a while and talk about you instead, I meant you personally. After all, there must be something exciting connected with this sudden decision of yours to come back to Hills' End. Won't you tell me what it was?"

"It wasn't a sudden decision. It was something I'd been thinking over for a long while. The only thing that was sudden about it was the timing of my departure. That was something I didn't foresee until just before it happened."

"Well then, tell me what you've been thinking over for a long while and then what precipitated the sudden departure."

He glanced at the clock. "It's a rather long story to begin at two o'clock in the morning. Dinners in Washington must be later than when you and I last went to them. We always used to be able to count on getting home before midnight."

"It was you who suggested having a nightcap while we caught up," Margaret reminded him, without commenting on his indirect question about dinner hours.

"I know. But I didn't realize the time. Nor did I expect to get so thoroughly sidetracked by M. de Briare."

He rose, smiling, and again held out his arms. Margaret hesitated, but there seemed to be no logical way in which she could refuse to rise also and to accept a second embrace. To her immense relief, though Nicolas encircled her waist lightly with one arm, he made no effort to draw her close to him and he did not kiss her again before he asked his next question.

"You said you were telling me the truth and I believe you have—as far as you went. But I can't help feeling it isn't the whole truth. If I'm right, is there any reason why you shouldn't?"

"Only that we've been separated for so long that it doesn't seem natural to talk to you," she said desperately. "I didn't even feel sure you were ever coming back, that you even wanted to come back."

"I know we've been separated for a long while, much too long. But I am back, I did want to come back. When you tell me the whole truth, you're not going to say that I've come too late, are you?"

He put one hand under her chin and tilted her head so that their eyes met. It was the same gesture he had made on their wedding night and again she knew that though he did this gently, he intended to hold her fast and to have her face him until the crucial moment between them had passed. "I'm not certain myself what the whole truth is," she said, still more desperately. "So it's hard for me to know how to answer you, Nicolas. All I can say is I haven't felt, for a long while, as if I were still married to you. How could I? It's two years since we parted in anger and, in all that time, I haven't heard from you, except indirectly."

"We did part in anger. I haven't kept in direct touch with you. I

couldn't blame you if you didn't feel you were still married to me. But
the fact remains that you are. And I've come back hoping that, despite
all my sins of omission and commission, you won't be sorry, that you'll
actually be glad."

"I'm afraid I can't say that tonight, Nicolas. I'm afraid you'll have
to give me time to think everything over before I can be sure how I feel
now. You said it was too late to tell a long story. I think you're right.
But I also think it will be easier for me to answer you after I've heard
it."

"In other words, you're receiving me as a guest to whom you can't
refuse hospitality, but not as an errant husband returning to his own?"

"I'm sorry, Nicolas."

She did not try to avert her gaze or free herself, but continued to look
at him as steadily as he was looking at her.

"I never thought it would come to that, Margaret."

"Neither did I."

He held her with her face uptilted for a minute longer. Then he
slowly released her and picked up the tray. "Very well. I'll take this to
the kitchen and then I'll fix the fire and put out the lights before I
come upstairs. Afterward, I'll bring you your wrap. If you tell me, when
I give it to you, that you don't want me to stay with you, I'll know you
mean it."

"I mean it now, Nicolas."

She was fighting panic as she left him, but she was determined not to
show it. She really did not believe that he would insist on staying with
her against her will and still she had a sense of danger. She could hear
him moving about, putting out the lights. Presumably, the tray was
now back in the kitchen, the fire properly banked. Just as she reached
the top of the stairs, she heard his step at the bottom. At the same moment, she heard the nursery door open and saw Cynthia stumbling
sleepily over the threshold. The little girl cried out and threw herself
into Margaret's arms.

"I had a bad dream, Mommy. I tried to wake Bernice up and I
couldn't. So I came to look for you."

"Of course you did, darling. And you see I'm right here. I'll take you
into my bed and you'll forget all about the bad dream. We'll go to
sleep together."

She realized, while she was speaking, that Nicolas had reached the
top of the stairs, that he had seen Cynthia leave the nursery and heard
what she and her mother had said to each other. Cynthia would be her
deliverance from danger. Whatever had been in Nicolas' mind,
Cynthia would have changed it. But Margaret did not guess how much:
as soon as the child was comforted, she wriggled out of Margaret's
embrace, rubbed her eyes and looked around her. When she caught

sight of Nicolas, she regarded him not with fright, but with animosity.

"Who are you?" she demanded. "What are you doing in our house?"

He came forward quickly and, leaning over, tried to kiss her. She hung back and turned her head away.

"Go away!" she said angrily. "Go away and don't bother me and my mother. You don't belong here."

"Cynthia dear, I'm your father. This is my house, too. I do belong here."

Cynthia stamped her foot.

"My father's way off somewhere," she said. "He never comes home any more. I'm glad of it. I know I wouldn't like him anyway. I want someone I love for a new father. I want Jack."

51 ❧

For a moment, Nicolas stared at the angry child in stupefied silence. Then his gaze shifted to her mother and held.

"So that's the score," he said in a voice of cold rage.

"Oh, Nicolas, please try to understand! She doesn't realize what she's saying. She hasn't seen you in a long time, you're a stranger to her. Jacques has been very kind to her and—"

"And she sees him all the time?"

"No, of course not. Please, please don't look at me like that! Don't speak to me in that tone of voice! Let me take Cynthia to bed and quiet her down. Then I'll come back and talk to you. But I can't do it here in the hall with Cynthia raging between us."

"When you speak of taking Cynthia to bed, I assume you mean our bed."

"Nicolas, she doesn't think of it as *ours!* She doesn't remember ever seeing you in it! She thinks of it as mine. And she's used to taking refuge there when she's had a bad dream. Please, Nicolas, please!"

"Very well. You needn't bother to come back and talk to me tonight. I think I have the situation pretty well sized up without any more conversation. I'll see you in the morning."

He turned and strode rapidly to the boudoir, slamming the door behind him. As he went, he heard Margaret calling after him, but he could not distinguish the words, because Cynthia was wailing, "Oh, Mommy, don't cry!" so loudly that her voice blurred all other sounds; when the door was shut, he did not hear her, either. Probably Margaret had already drawn her into the bed which was her refuge and had silenced her as she comforted her.

He was still stupefied, not because he no longer grasped the significance of Cynthia's outburst, but because it seemed unmistakably to disclose the one situation that he had never regarded as even a remote possibility: that Margaret had not only ceased to love him, but that she had fallen in love with someone else, that she might actually have been unfaithful to her husband. He knew her rigid views on chastity, her uncompromising condemnation of the sins of the flesh, her intolerance of anything approaching laxity. She was not easily moved by male admiration even when this was temperate and conventional in character, and in the cases where there seemed to be danger that this might get out of bounds and become tinged with ardor, she had dealt with it tactfully but firmly. She had never tolerated, much less encouraged, an *amitié amoureuse*, she had never wanted or consented to play the part of a married belle. Though she had been slow to realize how greatly attracted Gordon Holmes had been to her, she had succeeded in convincing him, very quietly, that he must go farther afield than Fairfax County in his prolonged search for butterflies, which seemed so frequently to bring him to a halt at Hills' End. Even more adroitly—because it called for more adroitness—she had succeeded in stressing the fact that her friendship with Miriam Powers LaGuarde included Miriam's father just as it did her husband, but that there were to be no tête-à-tête luncheons with the senator, no dinners at his house or on his yacht, unless Miriam or some redoubtable elderly matron were acting as his hostess. Nicolas knew Margaret had declined a box at the National Convention, at which Powers had again been offered—and again refused—the nomination for the Vice Presidency; that invitations to the Opening of Congress, the Army and Navy games, the races and the theater all met with the same courteous but inflexible rejection. And he knew—or thought he knew—that her attitude was based not only on her unfailing conformity with the standards of her code, but on devotion to her husband so single-hearted that there was not room in her life for the attentions of any other man. The discovery that she was accepting such attentions, that she was obviously enjoying them, was in itself a considerable shock. The implication that these attentions might exceed the rigid bounds of propriety, if they had not already done so, was at first unbelievable and then horrifying. Nicolas' first fury had been short-lived, because it had been so permeated by amazement and revulsion; now it returned in full force.

When he had closed the door, he flung himself into a chair and, exhausted as he was by his long journey, it did not occur to him, for a long while, to undress and get into bed; his fatigue was submerged in appalling thoughts. At last, as daylight began to steal into the room, such reason as he seemed to retain warned him that, if he did not get some sleep, he would be in no position to face the morning's unavoidable encounter with Margaret and he wearily rose, unpacked a pair of pajamas and took off his clothes. The bed had not been turned down and, as he pushed back the counterpane and climbed into it, the linen sheets felt not only cold, but alien. It was a long time since he had slept in such a bed or expected to do so.

His exhaustion proved his salvation. Drowsiness overcame him, just as a few hours before horror and unbelief had overcome him, and he was soon sound asleep. He woke to broad daylight and the vague feeling that he was not alone in the room. Turning over to look about him, still more or less in a state of daze, he saw that a small golden-haired child was standing beside his bed, staring at him with wide but friendly blue eyes.

"Hello!" she said pleasantly. "I heard you had come home, so I thought it would be nice to come and say good morning to you. I'm Audrey."

"Why hello, Audrey!" he managed to say, stifling his surprise. "That was very kind of you."

"Besides," she went on. "It's so long since I've seen you that I couldn't remember what you looked like."

"I'm afraid I haven't made a very good impression on you. I need a shave pretty badly."

She nodded. "I know. When Grandpa comes here, he has to shave. Sometimes he lets me watch him. I think maybe you will look better when you have shaved, too. But I like the way you look anyway. You have nice hair and a nice nose and now that your eyes are open, I can see that you have nice eyes, too."

"Thank you. May I return the compliment?"

"I'm not sure I know just what you mean."

"I mean I think you're a very nice looking little girl."

He spoke with complete sincerity. As he had told Margaret the night before, his first impression of the children, who were already asleep when he saw them, was that Cynthia had not changed very much, but that Audrey was much prettier than she used to be. This impression was now fully confirmed. Audrey had been a thin pale baby, who looked even thinner and paler than she really was, because of the contrast to Cynthia, who was so sturdy and blooming. Now Audrey was plump and rosy, her hair fell in soft fair ringlets around her dimpled face and her eyes were a heavenly blue. It occurred to Nicolas that she must look very much as Margaret had looked at the same age, just as a telltale photograph had betrayed Cynthia's resemblance to him when he was very small.

Audrey smoothed her dress and smiled more engagingly than ever, as if in gratification at his praise. Then she came closer. "You are my daddy, aren't you?" she asked.

"I certainly am."

"Then may I kiss you?"

"Of course. I should like very much to have you."

He stretched out his arms and drew her toward him. There was a petal softness about her kiss that filled him with wonder. He had not known that a little girl's lips would feel like that.

"Would you like me to bring my toys and show them to you? Or do you want to get up and have your breakfast?" Audrey next inquired.

"Well, what about your breakfast?"

"Oh, I've had mine—Mommy and Cynthia and I. We've *all* had breakfast except you. Cassie is going to make you a special one. But Mommy said you were very tired and we mustn't disturb you. I didn't, did I? I wanted to look at you, but I tried very hard to be quiet. Mommy wouldn't like it if she thought I waked you up. I didn't tell her I was coming here."

"You didn't wake me up. I waked myself up. And I was very glad to see you. I *am* very glad to see you. But I think now perhaps I ought to get up and have that shave and a shower and put on my clothes. Maybe you'll wait for me in your room. When I'm dressed I'll come and find you and you can show me some of your toys. Afterward, we'll go downstairs together and you can keep me company while I eat my breakfast. Later, we'll come back and look at the rest of the toys or I'll read you a story. That is, if you'd like me to."

"I'd like to very, very much! Oh Daddy, I'm so glad you've come home at last!"

She flung her arms around his neck and kissed him again and again he drew her to him. This time he was conscious not only of the petal softness of her lips, but of the warmth and vigor of her plump little arms and body, the trustfulness and tenderness of her embrace. He held her to him and she clung to him as if *she* had found a happy haven. When he finally released her, smoothing back her fair curls and stroking her forehead, she looked up at him anxiously.

"You're not going away again, right off, are you, Daddy?" she asked.

"Well, we'll have to talk to Mommy about that," he told her. "But perhaps, if I do, you'd like to come with me."

When he entered the gun room hand in hand with Audrey, he found Margaret waiting for him there and he could sense her feeling of reprieve in the little girl's presence. Margaret was very pale and there were dark circles under her eyes, much darker than those about which he had teased her during their brief engagement. He was sure she had not slept at all and that she had dreaded their meeting this morning more than she had ever dreaded anything in her life, except the "menacing mysteries" of marriage. And, this time, he would not be able to release her from dread by revelation. She would have to release herself by a very different type of revelation, which could bring no joy and no fulfillment to either of them; she had brought herself to this terrible pass. He still would not admit to himself that he might be partially responsible for bringing her there. But the expressions of controlled anger with which he had planned to confront her went unspoken; he could not allow himself to push her past the point of misery she had already reached.

Annabelle brought him a bountiful breakfast and he managed to do it a reasonable amount of justice, largely because Audrey stood watchfully by his chair, ready, he felt sure, to ask him whether he did not think it was good. Margaret and he talked of inconsequential things. Cynthia, it appeared, had recently started kindergarten and would not be home for several hours. This was good news, as far as it went, but it did not seem to offer a solution for dismissing Audrey, who showed every sign of intending to stick to him like a burr. He remembered hearing that she was a docile as Cynthia was refractory and decided to put this information to the test.

"You know, you're going to show me the rest of your toys," he reminded her, "the ones I didn't take time to look at before I came down to breakfast, because I was so hungry. Wouldn't you like to go back to your room and get the others ready for me to see? I mean, I suppose some of them are broken and some of them are out of order. Why don't you separate them and put all the broken ones together, so we could see whether or not I could mend them for you, and arrange the others the way you think they'd look best, so as to give me a chance to make suggestions? Perhaps I could think of other ways you'd like even better."

"Or perhaps you'd read me a story?"

"Yes, perhaps I'd read you a story."

As Audrey, with apparent contentment, smiled and nodded and started toward the hall, he added, "And wait upstairs for me to come back, won't you? I want to talk to Mommy for a little while first." Then, as she trotted out of sight, he turned to Margaret. "She actually came to my room to welcome me. She said you didn't know about it."

"No, it was her own idea. She did tell me afterward. If I had known, I wouldn't have tried to stop her, but I didn't suggest it, either."

"I'm very glad—glad you didn't stop her and glad it was spontaneous. Will she really wait for me upstairs?"

"I'm sure she will."

"Good. Because it looks, doesn't it, as if you and I needed to have a talk?"

"Yes, I'm afraid it does."

"Any ideas as to where we'd be freest from interruption?"

"It's a nice sunny day. What about the arbor? Unfortunately, if we stay in the house, there's always the telephone—not that I'd have to answer it, but we couldn't help hearing it and that's always a distraction."

"I think the arbor's a wonderful idea. The traveller's joy must be at its best now. . . . May I get you a coat?"

"Thanks, but I don't think I need one. As I said, it's a nice sunny day."

It was fantastic, this talk about the telephone and the weather, when they were facing a crisis which could very well affect the course of their lives. Did everyone, they both wondered, without sharing their thoughts, feel as they did, that somehow they should be able to come straight to the point, without all these banalities, without being so studiously polite; but they also failed to see how the banalities could be avoided, how they could be comfortably discourteous to each other. The garden was looking unusually well. . . . Yes, wasn't it? . . . Was the orchard coming along all right, too? . . . Yes, it looked like there would be a fine crop of Winesaps. . . . Had Margaret thought of painting the house again? . . . It had been four years since that was done and Nicolas seemed to remember his mother saying that you shouldn't let a house go more than three years. . . . Then at last they were seated in the arbor, facing each other but not touching each other, and Nicolas was saying, more quietly than he would have believed possible the night before, "Please tell me about it, Margaret."

52

He realized she had lain awake all night knowing he would ask her to do this and that she still did not see how. She would be thankful when the revelation was over, when there was nothing more to tell. But she had no idea how to begin.

"I've remembered why De Briare's name rang a bell," he said at last, breaking the intolerable silence. "He was one of the cadets at the Cavalry School in Saumur who held the Loire from Montsoreau on the east to Gennes on the west, after the Commandant had decided to defend it, despite the Field Marshal's appeal for an Armistice. Every cadet supported the decision and comparatively few survived. Some people think that defense was a futile gesture, that it simply marked the end of the shameful defeat by the Germans. That's never been my opinion or the opinion of most of the military men I know. More correctly, it can be called the beginning of the resistance. The Free French got their inspiration from those boys and most of those who weren't slaughtered went on to victory. De Briare was in the Armored Division when it entered Paris, and he'd taken part in the entire African show, all the way from Lake Chad to Tripoli. He was cited for bravery over and over again, then and afterward. It's surprising that you didn't read about him yourself."

"Yes, it is rather," Margaret agreed in an expressionless voice. There was another pause before she added, "But I never did. As I told you last night, I know almost nothing about his life."

"That seems rather strange, doesn't it, if he wants you to share it? Or, perhaps I should say, if you want to share it. I haven't forgotten how eager you were to have me tell you all the details I could about my methods of exploration."

"I know. And isn't that rather significant? If I'd been planning to share my life with Jacques, wouldn't I have asked him questions, just as I asked you?"

"Asking questions isn't the way to answer them, Margaret. And I think I have a right to ask questions. Don't you?"

"Yes, of course you have. I'm trying to think of how to answer them, truly I am. But it's very hard."

"I'd be glad to make it easier for you if I could. I don't know how to do that. I thought perhaps if I talked to you a little about De Briare, it might help, if I showed you I knew he was really a very distinguished man, that I don't underestimate him because of his present position. I remember that the slogan of those cadets was *soyez élégant*—be elegant! It's a far cry from the Cavalry School at Saumur to the stables at East Lawn and I can't help admiring De Briare for the gallantry with which he still carries on. But it doesn't become such a distinguished man to make love to another man's wife in her husband's absence."

"I don't know much history, but it seems to me I've heard it's happened a good many times, all the way from King David to King Edward."

"You're right, but we're not getting anywhere this way. If you weren't planning to share De Briare's life, that is, in a general sense, what were you planning to do? Accept him for a lover, secretly?"

"Oh, Nicolas, I wasn't planning anything! Something just happened."

"Well, what did happen?"

"He was very kind and helpful. He saved Felix' life. Cynthia grew very much attached to him and his little boy, Victor, liked to come and play with the girls and they liked to have him. So Jacques came, too."

"Yes, you told me all that last night. Now suppose you go on from there."

"The thing that happened was very strange. We met, quite by accident, in the street, when we'd both been grocery shopping. Victor, who was with his father, rushed forward and put his arms around me. He's a very affectionate child and he misses his mother."

"And would be glad to have you for a stepmother, I presume, just as Cynthia would be glad to have De Briare for a stepfather?"

"I'm afraid so. But I didn't know that then. Such an idea hadn't entered my head. I keep telling you, nothing was planned. But I looked at Jacques over Victor's head and, right there in the street, I realized that he wanted to kiss me, too, and that I wouldn't be sorry if he did."

"So then he took advantage of this dual realization? I don't mean right there in the street, I mean as soon as was conveniently possible thereafter?"

"No, he did nothing of the sort. He came to see me that evening and told me he was in love with me, which of course I knew by that time, and that he knew I was—attracted to him. He—made suggestions as to what he thought we ought to do about it. But he didn't kiss me. He didn't try to. He didn't even mention wanting to."

"You mean to tell me he's never kissed you?"

"No, but I do mean to tell you what's absolutely true: he never kissed me until last night, when we were coming back from dinner at the French Embassy. Then he did. But it was the first time he'd ever touched me."

Her voice ended in a sob, which, as far as Nicolas could tell, might either have been relief because the story was finished or regret because it was not more of a story. His own feelings at the moment were certainly those of relief, not unmingled with astonishment. That a man of De Briare's unquestionable virility should have embarked on an illicit courtship, without even getting as far as a kiss, was almost unbelievable to one of his, Nicolas', more direct methods. He had not been able to help taking it for granted that the courtship must have been much further advanced than that. And with the relief and the astonishment had come such overwhelming happiness that he was tempted to sweep Margaret into his arms then and there and tell her that he was through with questions, that now *he* would kiss her and, presently, they would both forget about De Briare because they were so glad to be together again. He had already stretched out his hand to take hers when a warning voice, coming from his inner consciousness, told him that the time for that had not yet come.

418   The Explorer

"I'm greatly impressed by such admirable self-control," he said
rather drily. "At the same time, I'd be very much interested in hearing
more about those suggestions you mentioned a few minutes ago."

"Jacques asked me to marry him."

"Really? Had it escaped his attention that you're married already?"

"Of course not. But neither has it escaped his attention, and that of a
good many other people, that it's a very strange kind of a marriage."

"It's the kind of a marriage to which you consented."

"With the proviso that, if either of us wanted a divorce, we could
have it. Jacques thought I might very reasonably want a divorce. After
all, you've never once been home since he's been at East Lawn. That's
nearly two years now. You've left me alone here while you've gone
on with your work in remote parts of Peru. It's a long time since you've
even mentioned the possibility of coming home. You haven't shown
the slightest desire to be with your wife and children. You had a lot to
say, before we were married, about having me let you act like a
husband, but what you really meant by that was letting you take me as
often as you wanted to. And when I was so ill and so exhausted that I
couldn't respond, your idea of showing me that you still found me
desirable was to get me down on the library sofa and keep me there all
night. You didn't love me enough to cherish me, too. You wanted a
son, but when I had a daughter instead, you wouldn't share me with
her and when I had a second one, you practically ignored us both.
You've always been jealous of Cynthia, you've scarcely bothered to
notice the existence of Audrey. Your work means so much more to you
than we do that you can't even spare the time to visit us briefly once in
a while. When a husband behaves like that, do you think it's strange
that some other man might think his wife would want a divorce, that
she'd prefer to live like the kind of married woman whose husband is
devoted to her and to their children?"

Margaret had stopped speaking as if she were miserably answering
painful questions under compulsion and instead was speaking in vehement and confident defense of a normal man's logical and by no means
dishonorable attitude. Something in Nicolas' expression told her she
had scored and she pressed her advantage while he was still trying to
frame an adequate rebuttal.

"Jacques said that if I would marry him, he would let me decide
where we should live. It was then that he told me about his *maison de
bouteille* in France. He said he wouldn't be willing to accept anything
from you, not even for the children, but that we could manage. He said
this before he knew that I had any money of my own. He could see that
there might be disturbing memories—I mean, because of its association
with my marriage to you—if we tried to stay here, but, on the other
hand, he knew how much I love Hills' End, how hard it would be for

me to leave it. He thought perhaps the best plan would be to live part of the time here and part of the time in France. But all the time it would be quietly in the country and all the time it would be *together*."

"And it never occurred to either of you that a secret love affair might be just as satisfactory and much less upsetting to the general scheme of things?"

"It *wouldn't* have been just as satisfactory. Victor wouldn't have had his mother and Cynthia and Audrey wouldn't have had their father."

"You seem to be forgetting that Cynthia and Audrey have a father."

"I mean someone who would act like a father, someone who would cherish them. You've never done that, you never will. You care more for poor Pete's little redheaded bastard than you do for either of our children. You can't deny it. And Jacques loves my children as much as they love him. We could have a very happy family life."

"It sounds to me as if you had done some planning, after all."

"I've listened to some of Jacques' suggestions—the ones he's made in the last few days. I've been thinking them over. All except one—one he made last night. He'd begun to think, since it would be a long time before we could get married, that perhaps we could be lovers while we were waiting. Of course, he had no idea you were coming back, then or ever—any more than I did. Last night he asked me to go home with him, I mean to The Lodge, and I told him I couldn't. I told him that if I asked you for a divorce, I'd got to do it with a clear conscience. I couldn't have done that if I'd been the guilty party, instead of you. Jacques understood how I felt. He didn't urge me. From the way you spoke about planning, I thought you meant something that had been developing for a long while, perhaps something that had gone pretty far. I don't think you felt at all sure, until I told you Jacques hadn't even kissed me until last night, that I wasn't already his mistress. It was hard for you to give me the benefit of the doubt. You ought to have known me better than that."

Again her voice ended in a sob, but this time it did not suggest either relief or regret and Nicolas had no difficulty in identifying what it did suggest: it was righteous indignation and she was correct; he should have known her better than that. His own reflections, before forgivable surprise had given way to unforgivable anger, had led to straighter thinking than any he had had since. Now he obeyed the delayed—and interrupted—impulse to take her hand and, when she tried to draw it away, he held on to it.

"You're right, I should have known you better than that," he said quietly. "I apologize. Just the same, I'm going to ask you two or three more questions and when you've answered those, I think I'll know how to go on from there. Do you really feel I'm the guilty party?"

"Perhaps guilty isn't the right word. But yes, I do think you'd be partly to blame, if I decided I couldn't go on—the way we have been doing. If I were still an old maid—if I hadn't known what it was like to have a husband make love to me—I wouldn't miss it so much. But I have missed it a good deal. I miss it more and more all the time. I'm a perfectly healthy young woman. I need to be loved. I mean—"

"I know what you mean. So you wanted to go home with Jacques de Briare last night? It was only because you couldn't do it with a clear conscience that you didn't?"

"I'm afraid so."

"And if I went away today, after telling you I wasn't coming back in a long while or left you in doubt as to whether or not I was ever coming back, you'd ask me for a divorce on the grounds of desertion and marry him?"

"I'm not sure. I've told you that this has all happened very quickly. I'm not going to let myself be hurried this time. But yes, I think I would."

"Well, I'm not going to tell you anything of the sort. I'm going to tell you why I came home so suddenly, without letting you know beforehand."

Her startled look met his steadier one. "I know I haven't given you much of a chance to ask questions," he went on. "In fact, I've discouraged you when you tried to. But until you gave me such an unwelcome surprise that it drove everything else out of my head, I was planning—yes, really planning—to give you one that I hoped would be pleasing. You and Jacques de Briare and these other persons to whom you've referred, without telling me just who they were, aren't the only ones who feel you and I have been separated too long, that I haven't been much of a father to my children. I've been growing more and more conscious of it myself, for a long while. But I didn't know just what to do about it. I recognized, as I'm sure you have, that I couldn't fit into the pattern of a Virginia country gentleman, even if I didn't have a full time job, a very interesting and important one, in Peru. But I've told you so many times that I'd never take you there until I made my discovery that I had to overcome a lot of false pride about eating my words. That in itself took time. And then, of course, I didn't know whether or not you'd be willing to pull up stakes and come with me at this late day. If I'd asked you right away, when we were first married, why yes, then you'd have come like a shot. I know that. You'd have had your babies in Quillabamba, if there wasn't time for you to get to Cuzco or Lima, and in Quince Mil if there wasn't time for you to get to Quillabamba and, somehow, you'd have managed. Of course, that's what I ought to have let you do. It's taken me several years to acknowledge that you were right and I was wrong. But I'm doing it now. I only hope it isn't too late. Is it?"

"I—I don't know, Nicolas. I'll have to think that over, too."

"All right. Think that over, too. I'm ready to agree that you shouldn't make a hasty decision this time. And I'll keep my distance. I won't try to act like a husband. I suppose it's all right for me to stay at Hills' End though, isn't it, if I promise not to do that? Audrey and I seem to have arrived at the beginning of a beautiful friendship. I'd like to pursue it."

Margaret had made no further effort to draw her hand away, but it was easy for him to see that she was deeply troubled. "You know I can always go and stay at the Cosmos Club, if that would make you feel any better," he said easily. "But I'm afraid that would give rise to exactly the sort of speculation we'd both like to avoid at this juncture. So far, no one knows I've come home; I traveled under an assumed name. And the taxi driver who brought me here from the airport didn't know me from Adam. Unless De Briare says something—and that's so unlikely that I think we can rule it out—no one needs to know I'm here. At least for several days. If you haven't thought things out by then, I'll go back to Peru without you and leave him a clear field."

"Of course, you mustn't go to the Cosmos Club," she said quickly. "Of course, you must stay at Hills' End. And I believe you when you say you won't harass me, that you'll give me time to think things over. I want to be fair to—to everyone. But there's still something I don't understand. You said *you'd* been thinking things over for a long while. But, in spite of that, your departure for home was a very sudden one. Why didn't you let me know you were coming? Why did you travel under an assumed name? Why don't you want anyone to know where you are for the next few days?"

"That's what I was coming to. I got the feeling that, if there were some special reason for asking you to join me, after all this time, you'd be more likely to say yes. And I don't want the reason to be public property until I've had your answer. The last time I came home, the level of the morass which had once been a lake had been greatly reduced, but we'd nowhere nearly reached rock bottom. Now we have. The American and Peruvian flags and the flag of the Explorers Club are all flying over it."

She caught her breath. "And that means you've found—"

"Everything I've hoped for and a great deal more. I knew about the palace and the causeway already. But I didn't know about the garden."

"The garden?" she repeated in a dazed voice.

"Yes. Of course, the palace and the causeway were obscured by algae, after centuries of submersion. I didn't even try to clear it away when I first went down—that is, not to any extent. But, in pushing it aside enough to get in through a window cavity, I thought I saw something glittering underneath the marine growth and I stopped long enough to break off a bit. I took it with me when I surfaced, at the same time that I took the stone hatchet. But I didn't say anything about it to Harry and Lester. I wanted to look at it carefully by myself first. I wanted to clean it up. That's what I was doing in my tent the afternoon before the earthquake struck us. I've carried it around with me ever since. Would you like to see it?"

She nodded, not trusting herself to speak. He thrust his hand into a pocket of his shabby old coat and took from it a small box. Something in the gesture reminded her of the way he had revealed the box which held her engagement ring and now he asked her the same question he had then.

"Do you want me to open this or will you do it yourself?"

"I—I reckon I want you to do it."

"All right. But this time don't shut your eyes. And hold out your *right* hand."

So he was remembering, too! The battered cardboard box from which he lifted the lid bore no resemblance to the one covered with blue velvet which had held her ring and, instead of a glistening satin lining, shreds of soiled paper were all she could see at first. But as Nicolas parted these, it was to disclose a delicate spray of tiny flowers, complete with stem and leaves, made of shining gold.

"I read a story once, I've forgotten now where or when, about one of the *conquistadores* who was responsible for sending tons of Inca treasure to Spain," Nicolas was saying, with that studied nonchalance which so often veiled his deep emotion and which Margaret had so tardily learned to interpret. "It nearly broke his heart to melt all the beautiful little figures that had been turned over to him. But that was what he had to do, because treasure was sent to Spain in bars. So, many irreplaceable treasures were shattered. But, fortunately, there were some the Spaniards never found, in both silver and gold. This is one of them. And, in the garden that surrounds the palace *I* have found, there are thousands more. We've already got enough of the area cleared, here and there, to know that. But I didn't want to go any further until I could share the secret with you. I want you with me when I tell the world. And, of course, it'll be hard to keep such a secret for any length of time. The news is bound to leak out presently. That's why I didn't send you any advance notice of my coming and flew under an assumed name."

"You mean there's a whole garden filled with gold and silver images?"

"That's exactly what I mean—a garden with all sorts of golden plants and animals and birds and butterflies 'each thing put in the place that was most appropriate to imitate what was most useful,' just as Garcilaso de la Vega described them in his *Comentarios*."

"Who was Garcilaso de la Vega?"

"A sixteenth-century Peruvian author. He described a lot more than that, in reference to one special garden and various other gardens. Even the shovels that were used in such gardens were made of silver and gold and so were the table services and the pitchers and the great rainwater jars used in the palaces themselves. This palace wasn't the only one where the Incas built so lavishly of gold and silver. But, as far as I know, it's the only one that's been discovered since colonial days."

"And it's a very great discovery, isn't it, Nicolas?"

"Yes, I guess so."

Suddenly, he sounded as tired as he looked. He sat fingering the battered box from which he had taken the golden spray, his head bent, his shoulders stooped.

"Why do you say you guess so?" Margaret asked quickly. "Isn't this one of the greatest discoveries of modern times? Don't you know that it is?"

"I know that more than six years have gone into making it," he said wearily. "Six years out of my life—and yours. I've reached the goal I set for myself and I've sacrificed everyone else and everything else to do it. After being lost for centuries, the 'House of the Sun of Gold' is found. It'll be freed from its mire for all the world to see, as soon as I give the final word. I thought, when I could do that, it would be the greatest moment of my life. Now I'm not so sure. It'll depend on you."

53 ༒

It was Audrey who did the most to relieve the tension of the next few days.

When Nicolas went back to the nursery she had gone to sleep, curled up on the floor in a tight little ball, her head pillowed on a life-sized woolly panda, her hands clutching a very dilapidated doll with a torn dress and a missing leg. But her other toys had been divided, as he suggested, so that the hopelessly broken ones were in one stack and those which were not beyond redemption in another, while several battered picture books were arranged in a neat pile. She had finished the stint he had set for her and by then she was so tired that she had lain down to rest; but she had not come after him, though he had been gone much longer than she expected; she had waited for him, as she had promised to do. She had been confident that he would come to her as soon as he could. He was infinitely touched by her trustful obedience.

Cynthia came home from her morning school in time for lunch and, though her expression was stormy and her mood obviously belligerent, she was effectively silenced by Audrey's cheerful chatter. Ordinarily, both little girls took naps after lunch, but Audrey could scarcely be expected to take another, when she had waked just in time to come to the table. So Nicolas suggested that she should make a tour of the grounds and outbuildings with him, an invitation which she accepted with alacrity.

"If you're going to see Felix, I want to come, too," Cynthia announced aggressively.

"All right. We won't go to the stables until you wake up. There are plenty of other things we can do in the meanwhile. Why don't you and your mother take a nap together? I'm afraid that, while she was comforting you because you had a bad dream, she missed some of the sleep she should have had last night."

He spoke pleasantly, and somehow neither Margaret nor Cynthia felt inclined to argue with him; the result was highly satisfactorily to all concerned. He and Audrey went through the gardens and orchard and skirted the fields and woodland before pausing in the arbor, so that he could show her how far up he could send her in the old swing made of grapevines, and she shouted with delight as she went higher and higher. He had thought possibly she might prove to be a rather timid child and one who would tire easily, because she was such a dainty looking little thing. He was entirely mistaken. She trotted along beside him with no sign of fatigue, she watched a small snake slither across their path with interest rather than fear, and she kept urging him to swing her higher than was possible. Since they had agreed to wait for Cynthia before going to the stables, the only buildings, except the old barn, which they were free to visit without her, were the garage and the model hennery, both of which merited Nicolas' inspection in order to make sure they were not in need of repair and that they were well kept otherwise, but both of which were without sightseeing interest as far as Audrey was concerned. The barn, on the other hand, had a strong attraction for her.

"Why don't we go in there, Daddy, and jump on the hay until Cynthia comes?"

"All right. I ought to be good at jumping. I've had lots of practice in Peru, though not with hay. Let's see which of us can jump the farthest."

By tacit agreement, Nicolas and Margaret had never been to the old barn a second time. No matter how deeply in love they continued to be

—and they had been deeply in love for a long while—both had known they could never recapture the supreme ecstasy of the hours they had spent there. But now he felt he could not refuse to go there with Audrey. The barn had been properly repaired, in accordance with his first careful notes, though it had never been used for anything but storage, as the stock was kept in the modernized stables; and though, theoretically, it should have been locked, Nicolas believed that probably it was not, and he was right. He rolled back the great door and he and Audrey went in.

The repair work had been skillfully and unobtrusively done. In appearance and atmosphere, the place was still the same as when he had taken Margaret there. The same silence, the same spaciousness, the same feeling of inviolable secrecy prevailed. Almost immediately Nicolas told himself he had made a mistake in going back, even now. He did not want to leap from the high beams with Audrey; he wanted to go back to the house and find Margaret. He had changed his mind about never wanting to bring her there again—in fact, that was one of the things he had meant to do when he left Peru. He had thought then that she would not refuse to go with him and that, though they would not find there all the rapture they had found before, they would at least find something akin to what she had recognized as such a vital element in their relationship and that it would help to bridge the gap between them. They would soon be forgetful of separation and think only of reunion. There would be no reproaches on one side, no excuses on the other. They would be mindful only of the glorious present moment.

Now this was only an unfulfilled dream. Nicolas did his best to play up to Audrey, but he was thankful when he heard Cynthia calling them and knew that they must go and join her. He brushed the hay from his clothes and Audrey's, put on the coat he had taken off during their jumping contest, and closed the great door after them, latching it carefully and making a note that it should have a padlock. Cynthia was standing just outside.

"Have you been jumping in the hay?" she inquired. "I wanted to do that, too."

"Then you should have told us so," Nicolas replied, with the same even tones he had used in speaking to her before. "We could have waited for you inside. All you told us was that you didn't want us to go to the stables without you, so we haven't even been to see the cows and the new calves, much as I wanted to. Come on, we'll go now."

The livestock was in excellent condition. Mingo and Tam, who now shared the responsibility for this, under the direction of Rufus, with Tam in charge of the cattle and Mingo in charge of the horses, beamed at the unstinted praise of their care by the bossman; like all the rest of the staff, they were delighted to see him back. Miss Margaret was a lovely lady; but a big place like Hills' End, now that it was all in running order, needed a bossman, too.

Nicolas stopped at the empty stalls beside Cavalier's and Felix' and shook his head. "It's almost time there was another pony here, isn't it?" he inquired.

"Oh, Daddy, I hoped you'd say that! Cynthia got Felix when she was three."

"Well, we'll have to see what we can do," he said. "Not right away. I've got too much else on my mind just now. But perhaps in a few days —" And, seeing the disappointment in Audrey's face, he added, "Neither of you has seen the presents I brought you yet. You were both asleep when I got home last night and Cynthia had gone to school before I woke up this morning. Then there was that nap. Why don't we go back to the house now and have a look? I'll race you."

The big box he had brought was in the drawing room, where he had shut the doors after putting it there. Now he told the little girls to run and ask Annabelle for a sheet to lay down on the Aubusson carpet, so they would not get shavings all over it, and then they could help him with the opening.

"Don't you want Mommy to come, too?" Audrey asked. "You brought her something, too, didn't you?"

"Yes, I did, but it isn't in this box. I've already given Mommy the present I brought her. However, I'd be delighted if she'd come and watch while you get yours. Ask her if she'd like to."

Mommy would like to, Audrey reported, racing out and then racing back; and presently Margaret came into the drawing room, apparently refreshed by her nap and with some, if not all, of the tenseness gone from her manner. She sat down in one of the big chairs and looked on, with a pleased expression, while the two little girls eagerly tore away the wrappings. From these emerged two large dolls, one dressed like an Indian boy and the other like an Indian girl, in the festive garments suitable for great celebrations at Cuzco. And after the dolls were unwrapped, Nicolas told them about the celebrations. It seemed there were two of these every year, one on the Monday before Easter, which was strictly Cuzquenian and very solemn, and one on Corpus Christi, the first Thursday after Trinity, which was very joyous. Nicolas could not help having a special feeling about the first, the veneration of the *Señor de los Temblores* (the Lord of the Earthquakes), because of his own experience, and the Indians had been observing this festival for more than three hundred years. They gathered from miles around, thirty or forty thousand of them. The statue of the *Señor* was taken from the cathedral and carried in procession on the shoulders of thirty men, while a great crowd of other Indians, carrying lighted candles and throwing *muccho,* the special flower for the occasion, followed the image. They believed it represented the Saviour Who could protect them from death and destruction when there was an earthquake and Nicolas would be the last to say they were mistaken. The Corpus Christi celebration lasted much longer. There were a great many processions and a great many statues, all gorgeously robed. There were women walking alongside carrying food and drink in their shawls and musicians playing on flutes and conch shells and, by and by, there were fireworks. In the great square of Cuzco, the *Plaza de Armas,* the balconies were draped with shawls and fine carpets and the square itself was swarming with Indians in the native dress of their various regions.

"Dresses like our dolls?" Audrey wanted to know, jumping up and down.

"That's only one of the costumes. But your dolls are dressed like the Indians from the altiplano—the highlands—around Quince Mil."

"Oh, Daddy, I wish we could see those processions. Won't you take us to Cuzco some time?"

"Well, Cynthia, we'll have to see what Mommy thinks, but maybe, if you and Audrey are very good girls."

When the stories were finished and the questions that resulted from them were answered, it was time for the children's supper and then presently it was time for baths and bed. But Audrey begged for one more story, the one she had not heard that morning because she went to sleep. And Nicolas said all right, he would come and read it to her after she was in bed. Cynthia did not ask for another story, but when Nicolas had finished Audrey's, he crossed over to Cynthia's bed and inquired if she would not also like one and, after a pause, in which it was evident she was trying to prove her independence, she reluctantly admitted that she would. So Nicolas asked her to choose one and read that, too. He had rather expected that by the time he had finished this Audrey would be asleep, but instead she suddenly sat bolt upright in bed and asked an astonishing question.

"Aren't you going to hear our prayers?"

"Why, am I supposed to?"

"Mommy always does when she comes to see us after we're in bed. But tonight you're here, because you've been reading us stories and she isn't. Don't you want to be sure we say our prayers?"

The idea was a novel one to Nicolas, but it seemed to make sense. Both little girls scrambled out of bed and came and knelt beside him; both, he noticed, were lovingly clutching their new dolls.

" 'Now I lay me down to sleep
I pray the Lord my soul to keep—'

There is some more," Cynthia raised her head to explain, speaking to him of her own accord for the first time. "But it's about dying, and we don't like that part. Besides, we're sure we're not going to die before we wake. So we go right on to the Blesseds. Bless Daddy and Mommy and Grandpa and Grandma and Clarissa and Narcissa and Cassie and all her family and Jacques and Victor and make us good girls. . . . So we can go to Cuzco," Cynthia added. "Amen."

They rose and scampered back to their beds, still lovingly clutching their new dolls. "And now you kiss us both good night and say sweet dreams, which is very important for Cynthia," Audrey informed him. "You have lots to learn, haven't you?"

Margaret was nowhere to be seen when he went downstairs. Evidently, she had gone to her room, which was no longer their room, while he was with the children. He was greatly disappointed. He had meant to tell her how poignant an experience it had been for him to go back to the old barn. Above all, there were two things he meant to say: that he was beginning to realize how much he had missed by not seeing more of the children; and that he had been right in telling her, years before, she had set a standard for him to which no other woman could possibly live up. Did she remember? Well, he had neglected her, he was blameworthy, he was ready to take the blame and he hoped he could atone for that neglect. But no one had ever taken the place that belonged to her; no one could. Even when he had been tempted, he had known that.

Despite his disappointment, he realized it probably was just as well he had not tried to say any of this that night. He had promised not to hurry her or harry her and, perhaps, by the time she had had a really good night's sleep, on top of her nap, and undisturbed by either Cynthia or himself, she would feel still more like herself than she had when the children were opening their presents, and she would listen more willingly and confidently to anything he had to say. His chief worry was that he might not be able to keep his great news from breaking much longer. But, after all, that was a minor consideration, compared to the all-important one of whether he had kept Margaret or lost her.

His patience was rewarded. After Cynthia had gone to school the next morning and Audrey had settled down with the toys he had mended for her, Margaret came to the gun room, where he was back at his old desk, going through the accumulation of second and third class mail which had piled up and throwing it away. He sprang up to greet her and draw a chair out for her, but she shook her head.

"I'm only going to stay a minute," she said. "I just wanted to ask you two questions. I've been doing a lot of thinking, as I promised you

I would. I don't know that there's anything more I need to say to you
—about Jacques and myself. But there are some things I'd like to say to
him, about you and me. Would you mind very much if I went to see
him? Perhaps this afternoon, if he's at home and free?"

"Not at all. I think it would be a very sensible thing for you to do."
He spoke more calmly than he felt. Nevertheless, he spoke with sincerity.

"Then I think you'll feel the same way about my second suggestion,
which is a minor one. I've discovered that those old dueling pistols on
the upper shelf belonged to his great-grandfather. Evidently, they were
sold to some rich American family because the De Briare family needed
money then, just as it does now. There's some kind of a story connected
with them. I don't know what it is, though Jacques promised to tell me
some time. I don't know whether he'd feel like doing that now, but,
whether he does or not, I'd like to give them back to him."

"I think you should, by all means."

When she telephoned Jacques, he answered immediately and it was
not hard to guess that he had been waiting hopefully for her call. Yes,
Victor was at school and was not expected home for two hours at least,
even if he did not decide to spend the night with one of his classmates,
as was now so often the case. Jacques was quite alone, no one would
interrupt them. It had turned chilly, had she noticed? But he had a fine
fire burning, just as he had when she came there before. They could sit
beside it and talk.

But not about the weather, she said to herself desperately. *We're not
going to stave off a vital discussion with a lot of platitudes, the way
Nicolas and I tried to. I couldn't stand going through that again. It's
bad enough without.* She need not have worried on this score. She was
hardly seated in the room which Jacques had made so livable and so
beautiful, with the unopened box containing the dueling pistols on the
sofa beside her, when he said understandingly, "I can't tell you how
sorry I am that you should have had to face such a dreadful ordeal as I
know these two days must have been for you. And I feel it's largely my
fault. If I hadn't insisted you should go to that dinner with me, you'd
have been alone and at home when your husband came."

"Yes, it would have made things easier—in the beginning. But I still
would have had to tell him that you and I love each other."

"Would you?"

"Why, Jacques, you know I would have! After I'd told you I'd consider divorcing my husband and marrying you, I couldn't welcome him
home as if none of that had happened. It wouldn't have been honest. It
wouldn't even have been decent."

"You're right, it wouldn't have been. But I'm afraid it's the way out a good many women would have taken."

"Would you have chosen me to be your wife and Victor's mother if you'd thought I was that kind of a woman?"

"No. Not if I'd thought so beforehand. But you might have disillusioned me. I'll always be thankful that you didn't."

Something in the way he spoke made her look at him more attentively. He had not moved, his manner was still quiet and relaxed. Yet there was a difference in it.

"You say that as if the thankfulness were going to be part of a memory."

"Well, isn't it? Haven't you come to say you've told your husband everything there's been between us—so much and yet so little? Haven't you told him you'd need to think over what you'd do next? Hasn't he done what any husband of tact and delicacy would have done under those circumstances—left you unmolested while you were doing that very serious thinking? And now haven't you come to tell me that you've decided in his favor?"

"Most of that is true. You've seen very clearly what's been happening. But it isn't quite true to say I've decided in his favor—if by that you mean I've decided I'd *rather* stay with him. I wouldn't."

"My dear—"

For the first time, there was a break in his voice and he made a movement toward her. She shook her head and, at the same time, tried to shake the tears from her eyes.

"I know you'd make me very happy, Jacques—that we'd be very happy together. You and I are close together in many ways. Even in the beginning, Nicolas and I weren't, and we married in such haste that we didn't have time to find that out. I've already told you that he'd been my idol—my distant idol—for years and that he wanted a son and felt I would make the right kind of a mother, but that he didn't intend to give up exploring or let me join his expeditions. That wasn't a very sound basis for a successful marriage on either side, but it's all we had to begin with and, somehow, neither of us hesitated. Then, fortunately, we fell deeply in love. But we didn't become friends or companions, sharing each other's troubles and occupations and pastimes. I doubt if we ever could have, even without our long separations, because our tastes aren't compatible, our standards aren't the same. I also told you I didn't realize, in the beginning, that life at Hills' End would never appeal to Nicolas except briefly, as a vacation interlude to exploring, and, as you know, it's the place I love best in all the world. Nicolas restored it to its former beauty and productiveness, he made every effort to adapt himself to it, he went regularly to church with me, mingled with my friends, spent long quiet evenings reading aloud to me. But all the time he was secretly counting the days until he could get back to the jungle and I knew it, though he thought I didn't."

She paused and it was evident to Jacques that she was trying very hard to be fair, that while it was an effort for her to tell him all this, she did not want to leave anything out that would show him a complete picture, as favorable as possible to her husband. "I don't mean that he began to do that immediately," she went on. "Just after we were married, we went for a long drive after church one Sunday and told each other a great many things that had been locked up in our hearts, troubling us. I was so surprised we could do this that I said, 'Do you know something, Nicolas? We're friends, as well as lovers!' and he said, 'I thought maybe we'd find that out.' I know he believed that. But we never had another afternoon like that. We never unburdened our hearts to each other again. There never seemed to be time. The only part of our life together that really meant anything to Nicolas was our love-making."

She paused again and shook her head and the tears from her eyes. "Don't misunderstand me," she went on after a minute. "I know that, unless two people are irresistibly drawn to each other physically, unless the act of love that unites them is joyous and spontaneous and forceful, their marriage can't be a success. But I don't believe it can be a complete and lasting success unless there are other ties, too. There haven't been enough other ties between Nicolas and me. I don't know that there ever can be now. And though I'm sure he still wants a son and I want him to have one, I don't know whether that special tie can ever be strong and beautiful again. It's very late to begin trying to find out."

"And still you think you ought to try?"

"Yes, I still think I ought to try. Nicolas came home on purpose to ask me to. He realizes at last that we've been separated too long, that he and I are almost strangers, that he's completely a stranger to his children—that is, he was two days ago, though it's astonishing how Audrey took to him at once, how Cynthia's gradually being won over. He wants me to go back to Peru with him, he admits he ought to have taken me there in the first place and now that he's made the great discovery which will crown his career, he wants me to share in his triumph."

"And that pleases you, naturally."

"Not as much as I wish it might. It would have—immensely—a few years ago, but I'd become resigned to the idea that I was never going to Peru. I don't want to go there any more. If I were going to leave Hills' End, I'd much rather go with you to Normandy. But when

Nicolas has conceded as much as he has, when he's pocketed his pride and confessed his mistakes and revealed his yearning, how can I send him away empty-handed? It wouldn't be fair, it wouldn't be merciful."

"I grant there is a great deal in what you say. But—"

"But there's something else. Something I promised. I took two very solemn oaths. I answered, 'I will,' when I was asked if, forsaking all others, I would keep myself only unto Nicolas and this was to be from that day forward, for better or for worse, for richer, for poorer, in sickness and in health, to love and to cherish till death did us part. And if I'd been married a few years earlier, 'obey' would have been part of that oath. I was glad it wasn't there any more, but if it had been, when I was married, I wouldn't have hesitated to swear that I'd do that, too. I'm still not sure it isn't at least implicit. Anyway, I did swear that nothing should part me and my husband except death, and he isn't dead. I did swear I would forsake all others and keep me only to one man. If I married you, I would be forsaking him, I wouldn't be keeping myself to one man. Besides, it isn't just those words you speak then, solemn and binding as they are. It's something that happens inside you afterward. I think the Bible puts it better than the Prayer Book. In a true marriage, a woman's desire is to her husband and he rules over her and they become one flesh. It's impossible to separate them without destroying both. I found this out almost as soon as Nicolas and I came together and I've never been able to forget it or deny it in all these years he and I've been away from each other. I told him, when he came home this time, that I didn't feel married to him any more. It wasn't true. We're still one flesh; we always will be."

She and Jacques both rose and he held out his hands. Again she shook her head.

"Please don't touch me," she said. "If you did—"

"I won't. I understand."

"What about Victor? Can you make him understand, too, why I'm not going to be his mother? Why he doesn't see me any more?"

"I shall try. And just as you said about you and me, Victor and I are very close, in companionship and friendship. So, sooner or later, I'll succeed."

"You'll take him back to France?"

"I think that would be best, don't you? Because, if he and I stayed here, it might be hard for him to understand why you and I were not friends any more. Because I assume that, even if you do go to Peru, you'll come back to Hills' End now and then, whenever you can, it'll still be your real home."

"And we couldn't be—just friends?"

"We've found that out, haven't we, the hard way?"

He went to the door and held it open. Dusk was falling and the blast of air that swept through the warm room was very cold. As Margaret reached the threshold, Jacques spoke to her once more.

"I love you more this minute than I ever have before. I shall keep on loving you more and more all my life."

It was not until long afterward that she realized she had left the dueling pistols behind her without ever hearing their story. But it did not matter any more.

Begun at the Oxbow, Newbury, Vermont—June, 1962.

Finished at Beauregard House, New Orleans, Louisiana—May, 1964.

Intermediate work done in both these places and also in Rome, Italy; Avila, Sanlucar and Madrid, Spain; Lima, Peru; Boston, Massachusetts and Washington, D. C.; and on board the S.S. *Santa Cecilia, Santa Mariana* and *Conte Verdi*.

ABOUT THE AUTHOR

Frances Parkinson Keyes was born at the University of Virginia, where her father was head of the Greek Department; lived for twenty-five years in Washington and nearby Virginia while her husband was in the Senate and for a time after his death; and still spends part of every year there. Several of her most successful novels have been placed in this locality. She has been five times to Peru, has previously used it as a setting for a book of nonfiction and numerous articles and spent the entire winter of 1963–64 there in the interests of *The Explorer.*

Mrs. Keyes has written almost fifty books; her first was published in 1918. She is perhaps most widely known for her best-selling novels that have delighted millions—among them *Joy Street, Came a Cavalier, Dinner at Antoine's,* and *Steamboat Gothic.* She is also justly famous for her distinguished works of nonfiction in the Catholic field.

The latest of her many decorations is the Mother Gerard Phelan Medal awarded her by Marymount College in Arlington, Virginia.